RANDOM
HOUSE
LARGE
PRINT

THE COLLECTED
SHORT STORIES OF
LOUIS L'AMOUR

THE
COLLECTED
SHORT STORIES
OF
LOUIS L'AMOUR

THE FRONTIER STORIES:

Volume Five

Louis L'Amour

RANDOM HOUSE
LARGE PRINT

**The Library of Congress has established
a Cataloging-in-Publication record for
this title.**

ISBN: 978-0-7393-2734-0

www.randomhouse.com/largeprint

FIRST LARGE PRINT EDITION

10 9 8 7 6 5 4 3 2 1

This Large Print edition published in accord
with the standards of the N.A.V.H.

CONTENTS

No Man's Man   1

The Nester and the Piute   34

Desert Death Song   47

Heritage of Hate   71

Hattan's Castle   113

Big Man   129

Showdown on the Tumbling T   151

Waltz Him Around Again, Shadow   211

Rowdy Rides to Glory   238

The Ghost Maker   304

Down the Pogonip Trail   330

The Romance of Piute Bill   358

That Triggernometry Tenderfoot   374

The Sixth Shotgun   397

Barney Takes a Hand   421

Rain on the Halfmoon   450

When a Texan Takes Over   468

Big Medicine   490

Gila Crossing   509

The Marshal of Painted Rock   538

Ride, You Tonto Raiders!   564

No Trouble for the Cactus Kid 630

Medicine Ground 649

Love and the Cactus Kid 676

The Cactus Kid Pays a Debt 708

Battle at Burnt Camp 728

The Cactus Kid 751

THE COLLECTED
SHORT STORIES OF
LOUIS L'AMOUR

No Man's Man

CHAPTER I

He came to a dirty cantina on a fading afternoon. He stood, looking around with a curious eye. And he saw me there in the corner, my back to the wall and a gun on the table, and my left hand pouring tequila into a glass.

He crossed the room to my table, a man with a scholar's face and a quiet eye, but with lines of slender strength.

"When I told them I wanted a man big enough and tough enough to tackle a grizzly," he said, "they sent me to you."

"How much?" I said. "And where's the grizzly?"

"His name is Henry Wetterling, and he's the boss of Battle Basin. And I'll give you a thousand dollars."

"What do I do?"

"There's a girl up there, and her name is Nana Maduro. She owns a ranch on Cherry Creek. Wetterling wants the girl, and he wants the ranch. I don't want him to have either."

"You want him dead?"

"I want him out of there. Use your own judgment. When I hire a man for a job, I don't tell him how to do it." This man with the scholar's face was more than a quiet man; he could be a hard man.

"All right," I said.

"One thing more"—he smiled a little, quietly, as though enjoying what he was about to say—"Wetterling is top dog and he walks a wide path, but he has two men to back him." He smiled again. "Their names are Clevenger and Mack."

The bartender brought a lemon and salt, and I drank my tequila.

"The answer is still the same," I told him, then, "but the price is higher. I want five thousand dollars."

His expression did not change, but he reached in his pocket and drew out a wallet and counted green bills on the dirty table. He counted two thousand dollars.

"I like a man who puts the proper estimate on a job," he said. "The rest when you're finished."

He pushed back his chair and got up, and I looked at the green bills and thought of the long months of punching cows I'd have to put in to earn that much—if anybody, anywhere, would give me a job.

"Where do you fit in?" I asked. "Do you want the girl or the ranch or Wetterling's hide?"

"You're paid," he said pointedly, "for a job. Not for questions. . . ."

* * *

THERE WAS SUNLIGHT on the trail, and cloud shadows on the hills, and there was a time of riding, and a time of resting, and an afternoon, hot and still like cyclone weather when I walked my big red horse down the dusty street of the town of Battle Basin.

They looked at me, the men along the street, and well they could look. I weighed two hundred and forty pounds, but looked twenty-five pounds lighter. I was three inches over six feet, with black hair curling around my ears under a black flat-brimmed, flat-crowned hat, and the brim was dusty and the crown was torn. The shirt I wore was dark red, under a black horsehide vest, and there was a scar on my left cheek where a knife blade had bit to the bone. The man who had owned that knife left his bones in a pack rat's nest down Sonora way.

My boots were run-down at the heels and my jeans were worn under the chaps stained almost black. And when I swung down, men gathered around to look at my horse. Big Red is seventeen hands high and weighs thirteen hundred pounds—a blood bay with black mane, tail, and forelock.

"That's a lot of horse," a man in a white apron said. "It takes a man to ride a stallion."

"I ride him," I said, and walked past them into the bar. The man in the white apron followed me. "I drink tequila," I said.

He brought out a bottle and opened it, then found lemon and salt. So I had a drink there, and another, and looked around the room, and it all looked familiar. For there had been a time—

"I'm looking for a ranch," I said, "on Cherry Creek. It's owned by Nana Maduro."

The bartender's face changed before my eyes and he mopped the bar. "See Wetterling," he said. "He hires for them."

"I'll see the owner," I said, and put down my glass.

A girl was coming up the street, walking fast. She had flame-red hair and brown eyes. When she saw Big Red she stopped dead still. And I stood under the awning and rolled a cigarette and watched her, and knew what she was feeling.

She looked around at the men. "I want to buy that horse," she said. "Who owns him?"

A man jerked a thumb at me, and she looked at me and took a step closer. I saw her lips part a little and her eyes widen.

She was all woman, that one, and she had it where it showed. And she wore her sex like a badge, a flaunting and a challenge—the way I liked it.

"You own this horse?"

One step took me out of the shade and into the sun, a cigarette in my lips. I'm a swarthy man, and her skin was golden and smooth, despite the desert sun.

"Hello, Lou," she said. "Hello, Lou Morgan."

"This is a long way from Mazatlán," I said. "You were lovely then, too."

"You were on the island," she said, "a prisoner. I thought you were still there."

"I was remembering you, and no walls could hold me," I said, smiling a little, "so I found a way out and away. The prison will recover in time."

"How did you know I was here?"

"I didn't," I said. "Remember? I killed a man for you and you left me, with never a word or a line. You left me like dirt in the street."

And when that was said I walked by her and stepped into the saddle. I looked down at her and said, "You haven't changed. Under that fine-lady manner you're still a tramp."

A big young man who stood on the walk, filled with the pride of his youth, thought he should speak. So I jumped the stallion toward him, and when we swept abreast I grabbed him by his shirtfront.

I swung him from his feet and muscled him up, half strangling, and held him there at eye level, my arm bent to hold him, my knuckles under his chin.

"That was a private conversation," I said. "The lady and I understand each other."

Then I slapped him, booming slaps that left his face white and the mark of my hand there, and I let him drop. My horse walked away and took a trail out of town.

But those slaps had been good for my soul, venting some of the fury I was feeling for her! Not the fury of anger, although there was that, too, but the fury of man-feeling rising within me, the great physical need I had for that woman that stirred me and gripped me and made my jaws clench and my teeth grind.

Nana Maduro! And that thin-faced man in the cantina hiring me to come and get you away from this—what was his name?—Wetterling!

Nana Maduro, who was Irish and Spanish and whom I had loved and wanted when I was seventeen, and for whom I had killed a man and been sentenced to hang. Only the man I killed had been a dangerous man, a powerful man in Mexico, and feared, and not all were sorry that he had died. These had helped me, had got my sentence commuted to life imprisonment, and after two years I broke out and fled to the hills, and after two more years word had come that the records had been lost and that I was a free man.

At fifteen Nana Maduro had been a woman in body and feeling, but untried yet and restless because of it.

And at seventeen I had been raw and powerful, a seasoned Indian fighter knowing mining, hunting, and riding, but a boy in emotion and temper.

It was different now that seven years had passed. Nana now was full-flowered and gorgeous. But they had been seven hard, lean years for me, a man who rode with a gun and rode alone, a man who fought for pay, with a gun for hire.

Three days I rode the hills and saw no man, but

looked upon the country through eyes and field glasses. And I saw much, and understood much.

Cherry Creek range was dream range, knee-deep to a tall steer with waving grass and flowers of the prairie. Even on the more barren stretches there were miles of antelope bush and sheep fat, the dry-looking desert plants rich in food for cattle. There was water there, so the cattle need walk but little and could keep their flesh, and there was shade from the mid-day sun.

And this belonged to Nana Maduro, to Nana, whom I'd loved as a boy, and desired as a man. And did I love as a man? Who could say?

She had cattle by the thousand on her rolling hills, and a ranch house like none I had ever seen, low and lovely and shaded, a place for a man to live. And a brand, N M, and a neighbor named Wetterling.

The Wetterling ranch was north and west of hers, but fenced by a range of hills, high-ridged and not to be crossed by cattle, and beyond the ridge the grass was sparse and there were few trees. A good ranch as such ranches go, but not the rolling, grass-waving beauty of Cherry Creek.

Then I saw them together. He was a huge man, bigger than I was, blond and mighty. At least two inches taller than I, and heavier, but solid. He moved light on his feet and quickly, and he could handle a horse.

Other things I saw. Nana was without friends. She

was hemmed in by this man, surrounded by him. People avoided her through fear of him, until she was trapped, isolated. It could be a plan to win her finally, or to take her ranch if the winning failed.

But they laughed together and raced together, and they rode upon the hills together. And on the night of the dance in Battle Basin, they came to it together.

For that night I was shaved clean and dusted, my boots were polished, and though I went to the dance and looked at the girls, there was only one woman in that room for me.

She stood there with her big man, and I started toward her across the floor, my big California spurs jingling. I saw her face go white to the lips and saw her start to speak, and then I walked by her and asked the daughter of a rancher named Greenway for a dance.

As the Greenway girl and I turned away in the waltz I saw Nana's face again, flaming red, then white, her fine eyes blazing. So I danced with Ann Greenway, and I danced with Rosa McQueen, and I danced with the girls of the village and from the ranches, but I did not dance with Nana Maduro.

CHAPTER II

Nana watched me. That I saw. She was angry, too, and that I had expected, for when does the hunter like for the deer to escape? Especially the wounded deer?

Two men came in when the evening was half gone, one of them a thin man with a sickly face and a head from which half the hair was gone, and in its place a scar. This was Clevenger. His partner, Mack, was stocky and bowlegged and red of face.

Both wore their guns tied down, and both were dangerous. They were known along the border for the men they had killed. They were feared men who had not acquired their reputations without reason.

They were there when I stopped not far away from where Wetterling was talking to Nana. I saw Wetterling move toward her as if to take her for a dance, and I moved quickly, saying, "Will you dance?" and wheeled her away as I spoke.

Wetterling's face was dark and ugly, and I saw the eyes of his two killers upon me, but I held Nana close, and good she felt in my arms. And she looked up at me, her lips red and soft and wet, and her eyes blazing.

"Let me go, you fool! They'll kill you for this!"

"Will they now?" I smiled at her, but my heart was pounding and my lips were dry, and my being was filled with the need of her. "You'll remember that was tried once, long ago."

Then I held her closer, her breasts tight against me, my arm about her slim waist, our bodies moving in the dance.

"To die for this," I said, "would not be to die in vain."

It was my mother's family that spoke, I think, for poetic as the Welsh may be, and my father was Welsh, it is the Spanish who speak of dying for love, though they are never so impractical. My mother's name was Ibañez.

When the dance was finished, Nana pulled away from me. "Leave me here," she said, and then when I took her arm to return her to Wetterling, she begged, "Please, Lou!"

My ears were deaf. So I took her to him and stopped before him, and, with his two trained dogs close by, I said, "She dances beautifully, my friend, and better with me than with you—and what are you trying to do with that fresh-cut trail through the woods? Get your cattle onto her grass?"

Then I turned my back and walked away and the devil within me feeling the glory of having stirred the man to fury, wanting that, yet desolate to be leaving her. For now I knew I loved Nana Maduro. Not prison nor time nor years nor her coldness had killed it. I still loved her.

At the door as I left, a red-faced man with bowed legs who stood there said, "You've a fine horse and it's a nice night to ride. Cross the Territory line before you stop."

"See you tomorrow," I said.

"Have a gun in your hand, if you do," he said to me, and went back inside. Mack, a brave man.

In the morning I rode the hills again, doing a sight of thinking. Wetterling wanted both the ranch and the girl, and no doubt one as much as the other. Another man wanted the place, too, and maybe the girl. But why that particular ranch?

Lovely, yes. Rich with grass, yes. But considering the obstacles and the expense—why? Hatred? It could be. A man can hate enough. But my employer was not a hating man, to my thinking. He just knew what he wanted, and how to get it.

Small ranchers and riders with whom I talked could give me no clue. I did not ask outright if they knew my employer, but I could tell they must know the man.

The trail I had found through the woods was guarded now. Two men loafed near the N M side of it, both with rifles across their knees. Through my glasses I studied that trail. It was wide, and it was well cut. When I got into my saddle I saw something else—a gleam of sunlight reflecting on a distant mountainside. Distant, but still on Maduro range.

Big Red took to the trail and I rode for so long that it was after dark before I returned to Battle Basin. I left Big Red stabled in a small, outlying two-horse barn, and, with my guns on, I walked down into town. I moved quietly among the buildings until I reached the street. Merging with the shadows I looked to right and left.

A drunk cowhand staggered along the boardwalk across the street. He lurched against a building, then went on. Starting to step out into the light I froze, for it suddenly had come to me that the drunken cowhand had not been talking to himself, but had spoken to someone in the shadows!

Moving back into the darkness I worked my way along in the shadows toward the corral. There were horses there, saddled, bridled, and tied—an even dozen of them, all wearing the Wetterling brand. I traced it with my finger.

In another hour I knew the Wetterling crew would be all over the town, in ambush, waiting for me. No matter where I showed up, they would have me in a cross fire. There had been some good planning done! They were figuring I'd spoil their beautiful plan and were out to stop me, but they'd forgotten the life I'd lived, and how I'd lived the years I had only through caution. I was an Indian on my feet, quiet and easy.

From the cover of the darkness, I studied the saloon, the roofs of the town. And then I walked up to the back door of the saloon and went in.

Mack was there, at the bar with another man, not Clevenger. One man could be deadly, two were poison, but as I entered I said, "All right, Mack. You looking for me?"

It startled him. I saw his shoulders bunch, then he turned. I was standing half in the shadows, and it was not right for him. His partner was more foolish. The instant he saw me he grabbed for a gun.

Two guns were on my hips, but I had another in

a shoulder holster, a Wes Hardin rig. When both moved for their guns, I shucked it.

Strange how at times like that minutes seem hours, and the seconds are expanded unbelievably. Mack's gun was coming up fast, faster by far than that of the other man. In the background the bartender was transfixed, his mouth gaping, eyes bulging. Another man who had started through the door and was directly in the line of fire stood there, frozen, and in that instant the room was deathly still.

My shoulder gun slid true and easy. My hand rolled outward as I brought my elbow down, and the gun jumped in my hand. The flash from Mack's gun came a breath later. I saw him bunch his shoulders forward as if he'd been struck in the stomach, then my gun muzzle had moved left and the gun bucked again.

Mack's companion pulled his feet together, went up to tiptoes and fell. Mack caught himself on the table corner and stared at me, aware that I'd killed him. With that awful realization in his eyes, his gun fell.

Then I was out the back door, going up the outside stairs, running lightly and through the door, ducking into the first room, luckily empty. I climbed out the window, stood up on the sill and, catching the roof edge, pulled myself up and over.

Men rushed by between the buildings, footsteps pounded in the hallways below. The chase was in full cry. Lying there, stone still, I waited.

Movement in the room below alerted me. Then voices spoke, near the window, and I could hear every word plainly.

"You knew him before?" That would be Wetterling.

"In Mexico," Nana's voice answered. "He rode for my father, and when Sanchez killed my father and took me away with him, Lou Morgan followed. He killed Sanchez in the street, then took me home. He was tried for it and sent to prison."

"You love him?"

"Love him?" Her voice was careless. "How could I? I was a child, and he was a boy, and we scarcely knew each other. And I don't know him now."

"You've been different since he came."

"And you've been insistent." Nana's voice was edged. "I'm not sure which it is you really want—my ranch or me."

He evidently started toward her, for I heard her move back. "No!"

"But you told me you'd marry me."

"I said I might." She was right at the window now. "Now go away and find some more gunmen. You'll need them."

He started to protest, but she insisted. I heard the door close then, and I heard Nana humming. She came to the window and said distinctly:

"Next time you use my window for a ladder, please clean your boots."

Swinging down by the edge of the roof, I went through the window and away from it.

She was wearing a blue riding outfit, her hair beautifully done. I've never seen a girl look more desirable. She saw it in my eyes, for I was making no effort to conceal what I felt.

"What are you, Lou?" she demanded. "An animal?"

"Sometimes."

My blood was heavy in my pulse. I could feel it throb, and I stood there, feet apart, knowing myself for what I was—a big, dark man hunted in the night, looking at a woman for whom a man would give his soul.

"When I'm close to you I am," I added.

"Is that a nice thing to say?"

"Maybe not. But you like it."

"You presume too much."

I sat down, watching her. I knew that the amusement which must be in my eyes bothered her. She knew how to handle men and she was used to doing that. She had been able to handle me, once. That was long ago. I'd left tracks over a lot of country since then.

"You're not safe here," she said. "Twenty men are hunting you. You should go—ride on out of here."

"Know a man with thin hair, nice-looking, like a college professor?"

The question startled her, but the sharpening

of her attention told me she did. "Why do you ask?" she said.

"He hired me to come here. To stop Wetterling."

"You **lie**!"

It flashed at me, a stabbing, bitter word.

An angry word.

"It's true."

She studied me.

"Then you didn't come because I was in trouble?"

"How could I? How could I know?" I smiled. "But the idea of a job to keep a man away from you was attractive. I liked the idea."

Despite her wish not to show it, she was disappointed. She had been seeing me as a knight-errant, come to her rescue. As if she needed it! Most men were toys for her. Yet she did need rescue, more than she guessed.

It was not Wetterling who made me jealous now, but the unknown man, my employer.

"He would not do such a thing," she insisted. "Besides, he doesn't even know about—about Henry."

"He knows. That isn't all he knows. He's after your ranch, too, you know."

She was wicked now. "Oh, you liar! You contemptible liar! He's not even interested in ranching! He's never been on a ranch! He wouldn't think of hiring a—a **killer**!"

The name had been applied before. To an extent, it was true. I shoved my battered hat back on my head and began to build a smoke, taking my time.

"Wetterling doesn't care about the ranch, either," I said slowly. "He's interested in only part of it."

It went against the grain for her to believe that any man was interested in anything but her. Yet she accepted the accusation against Wetterling, but against the other man, no.

That was why the other man bothered me most.

"I don't know what you mean," she said.

"Nana Maduro," I said thoughtfully. "It's a lovely name. An old name. So old there was a Maduro among the first to come to New Spain. He had a brother who was a Jesuit."

"There were Jesuits in your family, too."

"How'd you come to buy that ranch? Because of your grandfather, wasn't it? He left you the money and told you to buy it? That if you did you'd never want?"

She was genuinely puzzled.

"And so?"

Sitting with my big forearms on the back of the chair I straddled, I could see somebody down below, between the buildings. I lit my cigarette and inhaled, tensing slightly.

"Have you forgotten the old stories?" I asked. "Of the **conducta**?"

She paled a little. "But that was just a story!"

"Was it? Your grandfather insisted on this place. Why? When it was so far from all you knew?"

"You mean—it's on **this** place? **My** place?"

"Why do you think they want it?" I shrugged. I

heard a boot grate on gravel and got up, keeping back from the window. "Wetterling, and your scholarly friend?"

"That's ridiculous! How would they know? How could **he** know?"

I moved toward the door, but stopped suddenly. "So beautiful!" I said softly. "Little peasant."

Her face flamed. "You—**you** call **me**, a Maduro, a peasant! Why, you—"

My smile was wide. "A Maduro was a mule driver in the expedition. My ancestor was its **capitán**!"

CHAPTER III

Ducking out the door before Nana could throw something, I glanced quickly up and down the hall, then swiftly stepped back through. Before she realized what was happening I had an arm about her. I drew her quickly to me. She started to fight, but what are blows? I kissed her and, liking it, kissed her again. Was I mistaken or was there a return of the kiss?

Then I let her go and stepped quickly out and shut the door. "Coward!" I heard her say, as I ran lightly down the hall.

Then they were coming. I heard them coming up the back stairs, coming up the front stairs. I dodged into the nearest room, put down my cigarette and dropped two more cigarette papers upon the glowing end; then, ripping a blanket from a bed, I touched the end to it. Instantly, it flared up.

Quickly I crossed the room. The fire would give me only a moment of time before they put it out. I was at the window when I heard a yell as somebody smelled smoke.

"Fire!"

Running steps in the hall outside, then stamping feet. Glancing out the window, I saw only one man below. He had turned his head slightly. Swinging from the window, I dropped the eighteen feet to the ground.

He wheeled, swinging up his rifle, and I grabbed the barrel end and jerked it toward me. Off balance, he fell forward. On one knee I grasped his shirt and crotch and heaved him over my head and into the wall. Then I was up and running.

A shot slammed at me. I grabbed the top pole of the corral and dropped over it. Horses scattered. Running to the gate I ripped it open and, swinging into a saddle, lay far down on the other side of the horse I had grabbed as we came out together. All the horses in a mad rush, and me among them.

Shots rang out, curses, yells. The horses charged down the alley. A guard tried to leap aside, almost made it, then we were racing on. Swinging the horse I rode from the crush, I headed for the stable where Big Red was waiting.

Dropping from the horse, I had started forward when, too late, I saw them waiting there—three men with guns. I felt a violent blow, my leg went from under me, thunder broke around in a wave, and then—pure instinct did it—my guns were shooting, shooting again.

Then somehow the men were gone and I was in the saddle on Big Red, and we were off and running and there was—odd, so close to town—the smell of pines. . . .

Only it was not close to town when the pine smell came to me. The pines were on a far mountain, and I was on the ground. Not far from me Big Red was feeding. Rolling over, I sat up, and the movement started me bleeding again. My head throbbed and a wave of pain went through me. I lay back on the grass and stared up at the sky where clouds gathered.

After a while I tried again, and got up to the stream which had attracted Big Red. I drank, and drank again. Under the low clouds I ripped my jeans and examined my wounds. Then I bathed and dressed them as best I could, thankful that I knew the ways of the Indians and the plants they used in cases like this.

Back in my saddle I rode deeper into the hills. Far behind and below me was the ranch, but I kept riding, looking for a rock shaped like the back of a head. Twice I stopped to look back. Riders were spread across the country below, searching for me.

A spatter of rain came. It felt cool against my face.

Lightning darted, thunder crashed. Feebly I struggled into my slicker. Humped against the pound of the rain, I went on.

The rain would wash out my tracks. I would be safe. Big Red plodded on, and thunder rolled and tumbled among the great peaks, and once an avalanche of rocks roared down ahead of us, but we kept on. And then in a sharp streak of lightning, I saw the head!

Rounding it, I rode right into the tumbled boulders, weaving my way among them. Twice I ran into blind alleys. And then, after retracing my steps, I found the right one and a way opened before me.

Trees, their blank trunks like bars of iron through the steel net of the rain. My body loose in the saddle, somehow guiding the red horse. A dip downward, a mountain valley, a steep trail. Then grass, water, trees—and the arched door of an ancient Spanish mission!

In an adobe house we took shelter, Big Red and I. From **amolillo** and maize I made a poultice for my wounds and rested there, eating only a little at a time from the jerked beef and bread in my saddlebags.

Here I slept, awakened, changed the poultice on my wounds, then slept again.

I would be safe here. No one had found this place in two hundred years, and no one was likely to find it now. And then night came and the wind howled and there was a long time when the rain beat upon the ancient roof, leaking in at places and running along the ancient floor.

There was a long time when there was only lightning, thunder, and the wind. Then came a time when hands seemed to touch me and caress me, and I dreamed that I was not dead and that the lips of my loved one were on mine again.

Morning came and I was awake. Sunlight fell through the ancient door. Outside, I could hear Big Red cropping grass, and his saddle and bridle were in the corner. I could not even remember taking them off.

My head was on a pillow of grass, and a blanket covered me. My wound would need care and I rolled over and sat up. But I saw then that the dressing was fresh and of white cloth that I had never seen before. There were ghosts in this place.

And then I heard someone singing, and a shadow was in the door, and then Nana came through it, bearing an armful of flowers.

She stopped when she saw I was awake.

"So," I said, "you came."

"Who else would come? Who else could find you?"

"You told no one?"

"Not anyone at all."

She came over to me, remaining a respectful distance away because despite my illness there was a hunger in my eyes when I looked at her.

"I'm going back now," she said. "You must rest. I

brought food, so there is plenty. Rest, recuperate, then ride away."

"Away?"

"Wetterling has hunted you like a wild animal. He will not listen. You killed Mack. You killed two other men and wounded several. He is determined to hunt you down."

Then I told her quietly and honestly that I would not ride away, that I would stay there, that her kisses were so rich they had spoiled me for other kisses. I must remain.

She was furious. She told me I was a fool. That she had never kissed me, would never let me kiss her again, that I must go away. She did not want me dead.

"You love me?"

"No!" she spat at me. "Love you? A killer? A hired gunfighter? A no-good? Go away! I just don't want you dead after what you did for me long ago."

Sadly I shook my head. "But if I am gone I will not be able to make love to you. That is bad."

She got up, holding her chin high. It was lovely to see her like that, but she went away and left me. . . .

Days passed into a week, and a week into another. I walked, I snared game. I ate what food was left. I searched the old mine, looked about. I found a place under the floor where—

I heard them coming too late. My guns were across the room.

It was my employer, and he was not alone. With him were two Yaqui Indians. Two of the wild ones. They all had guns and they were definite with them.

"I did not know," he said, "that you are an Ibañez."

"How did you get here?"

"Watched Nana. It was simple. You vanished. You had to be somewhere. What more likely place than here? So I watched her, for if anyone knew, she would. And now I have you."

He sat down. The Yaquis did not. "You failed in your job. Now tell me where the silver was buried, and the mission vessels."

"Who knows?"

His smile was not nice. "You have heard of pinning needles of pitch pine through the skin and lighting them? The Yaquis understand that sort of thing. That is the way we will start unless you talk."

It was a bad way to die. And I was not ready for it. Yet how strong was I? How much recovered?

"We might make a bargain."

"Only one. I'll give you your life if you tell me."

Of course, he lied. The cold ones are the dangerous ones. He would kill me when he had picked the meat from the shell of my story. It was better to die. "All right," I said. "I'm not anxious to die."

He would be difficult to fool, this one. Wetterling would have been easier. I looked at my hand upon my knee. How much of my strength had I lost? How much of my agility? During the snaring of game, the walking, the searching, my strength had seemed to come back, but two weeks was not much, and I had lost blood.

"It is late," I told him, "for we need the morning sun."

He frowned. "Why? This is the place."

My shrug was tolerant. "Here? Such an obvious place? How could they know it would not be found? The trail was good then. No, the silver is not here, nor are the vessels."

Reluctantly, he listened. More reluctantly, they began to bring in blankets and food for the night. They allowed me to help with the fire, and I remembered Nana saying that Wetterling was searching for me feverishly. His men were scouring the country. I thought of that, and of the fire.

It was late afternoon, an hour before darkness. The air was still. Moving slowly, to make them think my strength had not yet returned, I helped gather wood.

So you know the **ocotillo**? Candlewood, it is called. A rare and wonderful plant. Not a cactus, although it is thorny, its stems are straight like canes, and it blossoms with brilliant flowers of scarlet.

We of the desert know it also as strong with resin, gum, and wax, that it burns brightly, fiercely, and has still another quality also.

Rarely does one find a dead **ocotillo**. This plant knows the secret of life. Yet sometimes single canes die, or sometimes one is broken off, or blown down by winds. There was a dead one near, uprooted in a slide. Gathering fuel, I gathered it. Helping to build the fire, I added the **ocotillo**. The Yaquis were not watching, and Borneman, for that was my employer's name, did not know the **ocotillo**. And we were inside the building.

On the fire it crackled, fierce tongues of flame ran along the canes, the fire burned high, and up the fireplace went billows of intensely black smoke!

CHAPTER IV

We ate well that night, for Borneman traveled well. He had plenty of blankets, for he was a man who liked comfort. As who does not? But there are times and times.

They bound me well. He did not trust the Yaquis to do that. Not Borneman. He bound me himself and the Yaquis could have done it better. A blanket was thrown over me, and soon I heard them breathing regularly in sleep. Borneman and I slept near the fireplace. The Yaquis were near the door.

Large as I am, I am nimble, and my insides are resilient. And there was a trick I knew. My wrists were bound behind my back, but by spreading my arms as wide as possible, I backed my hips through them. Like most riding men, my hips are narrow, but it still was a struggle. I got through, though; then drawing my knees high under my chin, I brought my bound hands under my feet so they were in front of me. My teeth worried the knots until they were loose. Two hours it took me, and careful work.

Then I was free. The breathing of my captors was still even, regular. In my blanket I got to my feet and, like a cat, moved to the door. As I moved to the open space a Yaqui's breathing broke. I heard a muffled gasp, and he started to rise. But my right fingers quickly had his throat and my left sank into his wind. He was slippery, like a snake, but I had him off the floor.

He struggled desperately, silently, but my hand remained at his throat and the struggles grew weaker. I took him outside, dropping his body like carrion where they would find it. A killer he was, one who would have tortured me. I felt no regret.

And then I fled—into the trees and to the grassy park where Big Red was concealed. With a hackamore made of the ropes they had used to bind me, I bridled him. My saddle was back there, but I had ridden bareback many a time. I crawled upon him, and rode into the darkness of the night.

After a while, I heard riders and held myself from the path with a hand at my horse's nostrils until they were by. One was a huge man. Wetterling. They had seen the smoke then.

A gun! I must have a gun.

Big Red ran like the wind, and I loved his easy movements. He ran and ran, and when day was not yet gray in the eastern sky, I was riding into the trees near the ranch house of Nana Maduro. Was she here, or in the hotel room above the saloon?

In the last of the darkness I found her window, heard her breathing inside, and put a leg through, then another. I touched her arms, and her eyes opened. Her head turned.

She did not cry out, but she sat up quickly. It was enough to take a man's breath.

"Lou Morgan!" she exclaimed in a startled whisper. "What are you doing here?"

"I'll need a gun," I said, "or better, a pair of guns. Your lovers are snarling at each other at the mission where you left me."

Then I told her of the pitch slivers and the Yaqui. At first her eyes were hot with disbelief, but gradually changed to doubt. Then I told her of the **ocotillo** smoke that had brought Wetterling, and I laughed at my enemies.

She dressed swiftly while I watched out the window and saw dawn throw crimson arrows into the sky. Out in the cool halls of her house she took me and got a pair of pistols, ornamented, beautiful—two Russian .44s, a pistol made by Smith & Wesson. A masterpiece!

With these belted on, plus a Winchester .76 and a belt of ammunition, I was ready.

With her own hands she quickly made breakfast. I drank black coffee, and ate eggs and ham, and looked upon her grace and beauty, and forgot. Until too late.

We heard them come. From the window we saw them. A half-dozen horsemen, one with a bandaged head, one with an arm in a sling, and three horses with empty saddles. But Wetterling and Borneman were riding together, side by side. My enemies had joined hands.

What to do?

It had to be quickly, and it had to be now. These men were conscienceless. They would kill Nana Maduro as soon as they would kill me, and if they forced from us the secret of the mission gold and silver, then we would die.

Into the gray of morning I stepped, and saw the blood of dawn on their faces. My rifle stood by the door, my two guns lay against my thighs.

"Good morning," I said. "The thieves ride together."

Wetterling's eyes were ugly, but those of Borneman were only cold. I made up my mind then—Borneman must die. He was too cool, with his scholar's face and his quiet voice, and his thin, cruel lips.

"Let's be reasonable," he said quietly. "You and Nana are alone here, except for two riders who are old men, and even they have gone to a line camp. Your Indian woman cook is as helpless as you. Tell us where the gold is and we'll leave."

"We'll tell you nothing!" I said.

"He speaks for me," Nana said. "I hope he always speaks for me. And to think I had always believed

you—a famous scientist my grandfather called you—
were his friend!"

Wetterling's hatred was obvious. He still wanted
Nana. "I'll change you!" he said. "I'll break you!"

"With the gold," Borneman said, "you can buy
fifty women."

There was a silence then, while a quail called. Silence while dawn made a glory of the sky; and the
dark pines fringed against the hills; and the air was
cool and good.

Six men, and one of them Clevenger, whose partner I had killed. One of them a Yaqui, hating me.
And a girl behind me whom they would not spare
even if I died, and whom I knew would suffer the
tortures of hell before she'd die, for she had courage,
and would not tell.

That decided me. Numbers give courage, but they
give it to the enemy, too. They gave it to me. Six
men, and growing in me a terrible rage and a terrible
fear. A rage against them, and a fear for her, for Nana
Maduro whom I had loved since she was a child on
her father's ranch.

"You want gold and you've come prepared to buy
it," I said, "with your blood." I took a step forward.
"The price will be high, my friends, and Borneman,
you will owe me, in a few minutes, the five thousand
you offered me to kill Wetterling."

Wetterling's big blond head snapped around.
"What?" he barked. "You paid him to kill me?
Why, you—"

He struck at Borneman and my guns came up shooting. As he struck, his horse swung broadside, cutting off a rider whose gun came up fast. That gave me an instant I desperately needed. Three men were out of the picture, but I saw Clevenger's eyes blazing and shot into them. His scarred head seemed to blast apart as he slid from his horse. Behind me the Winchester barked and another rider was knocked from the saddle, not dead, but hurt.

The Yaqui slammed his heels into his mount and charged me, and I stepped aside, grabbed his arm, and like a cat was in the saddle behind him with a left forearm like a bar of iron across his throat. The plunging horse swung wide and, with the Yaqui's body for a shield, I shot again and again.

Wetterling's horse went down and he was thrown free. Borneman hit the ground and rolled. I threw a quick shot at him and sand splashed his face and into his eyes. He screamed and clawed at his face, then the Yaqui twisted and I felt a knife blade rip my hide. With a great effort I tore him free of me and threw him to the ground. He started up, but the plunging, bucking horse was over him and his scream was drowned in the sound of the Winchester.

I hit the ground, guns empty. Borneman still pawed at his eyes. Clevenger was down and dead. Wetterling was getting to his feet. Another rider was sprawled dead or injured, and still another clutched a broken arm and swore.

Wetterling looked at me and shook himself, then

started for me. Suddenly I felt the fires of hell in my blood and I swung for his chin.

It missed. He came in low and hard, grappling me about the hips, so instead of resisting, I went back quickly and the force of his tackle and my lack of resistance carried him past and over me.

On our feet, we walked toward each other. I feinted, he stepped in, and I hit him with a right that jarred him to his heels. He swung, and then we walked in, punching with both hands.

It was a shindig! A glorious shindig! He swung low and missed me, and I brought my knee into his face. His nose crushed to pulp and I hit him with both hands as he straightened back. He fell, and I walked close. As he started to get up I slugged him again.

My wounded leg was burning like fire, my breath was coming in gasps, my head felt dizzy. Somehow he got up. He hit me again and again, but then I got him by the throat and crotch and threw him to the ground. He started up and I hit him. Blood splashed from his broken nose and he screamed. I hit him again, and he blubbered.

Then I walked back to Nana. "If he moves," I said, "shoot him. I'm going to sit down. . . ."

IF YOU SHOULD, in the passing of years, come to the ranch on Cherry Creek, look for the N M brand. You'll find us there. I've tequila in the cupboard and brandy on the shelf, but if you want women, you'll have to bring your own, for Nana's mine, and we're watching the years together.

The gold we gave to the church, the silver to charity, and the jewels we kept for ourselves.

My hair is grizzled now, gray, and I'm heavier by the years, but Nana Maduro Morgan says I'm as good a man as I ever was.

And Nana should know.

The Nester and the Piute

He was ridin' loose in the saddle when we first saw him, and he was wearin' a gun, which was some unusual for the Springs these days. Out on the range where a man might have a run-in with a locoed steer or maybe a rattler, most of the boys carried guns, but around town Sheriff Todd had sort of set up a rulin' against it.

It was the second time I'd seen him, but he looked some different this mornin', and it took me a minute or two to decide what it was made the difference, and then I decided it was partly the gun and partly that look in his eyes.

He reined in that yellow horse in front of Green's and hooked one long leg around the saddle horn.

"Howdy."

"Howdy." Hatcher was the only one who answered, only the rest of us sort of looked up at him. He dug in his shirt pocket for the makin's and started to build a smoke.

Nobody said anything, just sort of waitin' to see what was on his mind. He had an old carbine in a saddle scabbard, and the scabbard wasn't under his leg, but with the muzzle pointed down and the stock close to his hand. A man ridin' thataway ain't rightly figurin' on usin' a rope on no stock. That rifle would be in the way, but if he was figurin' on needin' a rifle right quick, it would be a plumb handy way to carry it.

When he had his smoke built he lit it with his left hand, and I got a good glimpse of his eyes, kind of cold and gray, and them lookin' us over.

Nobody here was friendly to him, yet nobody was unfriendly, neither. All of us had been around the Springs for years, all but him. He was the nester from Squaw Rock, an' nesters aren't right popular around cow range. However, the times was a changin' an' we all knowed it, so it wasn't like it might have been a few years before, when the country was new.

"Seen a tall-like hombre on a black horse?"

He asked the question like maybe it was a formality that he wanted to get over with, and not like he expected an answer.

"What sort of man?"

It was Hatcher who had started the talkin', as if he was ridin' point for the rest of us.

"Maybe two hundred pounds, sort of limp in his right leg, maybe. Rides him a black horse, long-gaited crittur, and he wears two guns, hangin' low."

"Where'd you see him?"

"Ain't never seed him. I seen his sign."

Yanell, who lived over nigh to Squaw Rock himself, looked up from under his hat brim and spat into the dust. What he was thinkin' we was all thinkin'. If this nester read sign that well and trailed the Piute clean from Squaw Rock, he was no pilgrim.

That description fitted the Piute like a glove, and nobody amongst us had any love for the Piute. He'd been livin' in the hills over toward White Hills for the last six years, ever since he come back to the country after his trouble. The Piute had done a bit of horse stealin' and rustlin' from time to time and we all knowed it, but none of us were right anxious to trail him down.

Not that we were afraid. Only, none of us had ever caught him in the act, so we just left it up to Sheriff Todd, who wanted it that way. This here nester seemed to have some ideas of his own.

"No," Hatcher said, "I ain't seen nobody like that. Not lately."

The nester—his name was Bin Morley—nodded like he'd expected nothin' else. "Reckon I'll ride along," he said. "Be seein' you!"

He swung his leg back over the saddle and kicked his toe into a stirrup. The yellow horse started to walk like it was a signal for something, and we sat there watchin' him fade out down toward the cotton-woods at the end of the town.

Hatcher bit off a hunk of chewing and rolled it in his jaws. "If he meets up with the Piute," he said, "he's askin' for trouble."

Yanell spat into the dust. "Reckon he'll handle it," he said dryly. "Somethin' tells me the Piute rustled cows off the wrong hombre."

"Wonder what Sheriff Todd'll say?" Hatcher wanted to know.

"This here Morley, now," Yanell said, "he sort of looks like a man who could do his own lawin'. He's one of them hombres what ain't felt the civilizin' influences of Sheriff Todd's star, nor he ain't likely to!"

The nester's yellow horse ambled casually out over the trail toward White Hills. From time to time Bin Morley paused to study the trail, but from here it was much easier. He knew the look of the big black's track now, and from what was said later, I reckon the Piute wasn't really expectin' no trouble. Me, I was plumb curious. My pappy always did tell me my bump of curiosity was too big for my britches, but after a few minutes I got up off the porch and walked around to where my steeldust was standin' three legged in the dust. I throwed a leg over him and trailed out after the nester.

Maybe I'd been listenin' too much to the old-timers around tellin' of cattle drives and Injun fightin'. You listen to the stories a mite and you get to honin' to see some of them fracases yourself.

Now I knowed the Piute. Actually, he was only part Piute, and the rest was some brand of white, but whatever it was, the combination had resulted in pure-D poison. That was one reason everybody was plenty willin' to accept Sheriff Todd's orders to leave law enforcement to him. I will say, he done a good job. He done a good job until it come to the Piute.

It was understandable about the Piute. That Injun left no more trail than a snake goin' over a flat rock, and no matter how much we suspected, nobody could ever get any evidence on him. Sheriff Todd had been on his trail a dozen times, but each time he lost it. I knew what Yanell was thinkin' just as well as if it was me. Anybody who could trail the Piute plumb from Squaw Creek wasn't likely to holler calf rope for any Injun rustler without smokin' things up a mite.

ME, I WAS JUST CURIOUS enough and ornery enough to want to see what would happen when this nester cornered the Piute.

He was a big, sullen brute, the Piute was. Rumor had it he'd killed a half-dozen men, and certainly there was several that started out huntin' him that never showed up until somebody found 'em dead, but there'd never been evidence to prove a thing. He could sling a gun, and when we had the turkey shoot around about Thanksgiving, he used to fetch his guns down, and nine times out of ten, he got himself a turkey—and he used a six-gun. You take a man that moves around over the hills like a ghost, Injun footin' it over the rocks an' through the brush, and who shoots like that, and you get an idea why nobody was just too worried about gettin' him in a corner.

Six miles out I got a glimpse of the nester. The yellow horse was amblin' along, takin' it easy in a sort of loose-jointed trot that didn't look like much but seemed to eat up the country right fast.

The day wore on and I kept to the brush, not knowing how Morley would take it if he knew I was trailin' him. Then all of a sudden I saw him swing the yellow horse off the trail and drop to the ground. He was there for a minute, and ridin' closer, I could see he was bendin' over the body of a man. Then he swung back into the saddle and moseyed off down the trail.

When he went over the next rise I turned my horse down the hill. Even before I rode up, I knew who the dead man was. I could see his horse lying in the cactus off to one side, and only one man in that country rode a bay with a white splash on the shoulder. It was Sheriff Todd.

There was a sign around, but I didn't need more than a glance at it to tell me what had happened. Sheriff Todd had run into the Piute unexpected-like and caught him flat-footed with stolen stock, the first time he had ever had that chance. Only from the look of it, Todd had been caught flat-footed himself. His gun was out, but unfired, and he had been shot twice in the stomach.

Lookin' down at that body, I felt something change inside me. I knowed right then, no matter how the nester come out, I was goin' to foller on my own hook. For Sheriff Todd was still alive when he hit the ground, and that Piute had bent over him, put a pistol to the side of his head, and blowed half his head off! There were powder burns around that hole in his temple where the bullet went in. It had been cold-blooded murder.

Swinging a leg over that gelding, I was startin' off when I happened to think of a gun, and turned back and recovered the one Sheriff Todd had worn. I also got his saddle gun out of the scabbard and started off, trailin' the nester.

From now on the sign was bad. The Piute knowed he was up against it now. He was takin' time to blot his tracks, and if it hadn't been for Morley, I'd never have trailed him half as far as I did.

We hadn't gone more than a few miles farther before I saw something that turned me plumb cold inside. The Piute had turned off at the Big Joshua and was headin' down the trail toward Rice Flats!

That scared me, because Rice Flats was where my girl lived down there in a cabin with her kid brother and her ma, and they had lived there alone ever since her dad fell asleep and tumbled off his spring wagon into the canyon. The Piute had been nosin' around the flats long enough to scare Julie some, but I reckon it was the sheriff who had kept him away.

Now Sheriff Todd was gone, and the Piute knowed he was on the dodge from here on. He would know that killin' Sheriff Todd was the last straw, and he'd have to get clean out of the country. Knowin' that, he'd know he might's well get hung for one thing as another.

* * *

As MY GELDING WAS a right fast horse, I started him movin' then. I jacked a shell into the chamber of the sheriff's carbine and I wasn't thinkin' much about the nester. Yet by the time I got to the cabin on the flats, I knowed I was too late.

My steeldust came into the yard at a dead run and I hit the dust and went for that house like a saddle tramp for a chuck wagon. I busted inside and took a quick look around. Ma Frank was lyin' on the bed with a big gash in her scalp, but she was conscious.

"Don't mind me!" she said. "Go after that Injun! He has taken out with Julie on her black!"

"What about you?" I asked, although goodness knows I was wantin' nothin' more than to be out and after Julie.

" 'Brose'll be back right soon. He rid over to Elmer's after some side meat."

'Brose was short for Ambrose, her fourteen-year-old boy, so knowin' he'd be back, I swung a leg over that saddle and headed out for the hills. My steeldust knowed somethin' was in the wind and he hustled his hocks for those hills like he was headin' home from a trail drive.

The Piute had Julie and he was a killin' man, a killin' man who knowed he was up the crick without a paddle now, and if he was got alive he'd be rope meat for sure. No man ever bothered a woman or killed a man as well liked in that country as Sheriff Todd without ridin' under a cottonwood limb. Me,

I'm a plumb peaceable sort of hand, but when I seen the sheriff back there I got my dander up. Now that Piute had stole my girl, I was a wild man.

Ever see that country out toward the White Hills? God must have been cleanin' up the last details of the job when He made that country, and just dumped a lot of the slag and wastin's down in a lot of careless heaps. Ninety percent of that country stands on end, and what doesn't stand on end is dryer than a salt desert and hotter than a bronc on a hot rock.

The Piute knowed every inch of it, and he was showin' us all he knowed. We went down across a sunbaked flat where weird dust devils danced like crazy in a world where there was nothin' but heat and dust and misery for man and beast. No cactus there, not even salt grass or yeso. Nothin' growed there, and the little winds that stirred along the dusty levels made you think of snakes glidin' along the ground.

My gelding slowed to a walk an' we plodded on, and somewhere miles ahead, beyond the wall of sun dancin' heat waves, there was a column of dust, a thin, smoky trail where the nester rode ahead of me. Right then, I began to have a sight of respect for that long-legged yellow horse he was ridin' because he kept on goin' an even gained ground on my steeldust.

Finally we got out of that hell's valley and took a trail along the rusty edge of some broken rock, windin' higher toward some sawtooth ridges that gnawed at the sky like starvin' coyotes in a dry season. That trail hung like an eyebrow to the face of the cliff we skirted, an' twice, away up ahead, I heard shots. I knowed they was shots from the Piute, because I'd seen that carbine the nester carried. It was a Spencer .56.

Never seen one? Mister, all they lack is wheels! A caliber .56 with a bore like a cannon, and them shootin' soft-nosed lead bullets. What they do to a man ain't pretty, like you'll know. I knowed well enough it wasn't the nester shootin' because when you unlimber a Spencer .56 she has a bellow like a mad bull in a rock canyon.

Sundown came and then the night, an' little breezes picked up and blew cool and pleasant down from the hills. Stop? There was no time for stoppin'. I knew my gelding would stand anything the Piute's horse would, and I knowed by the shootin' that the Piute knowed the nester was on his trail. He wasn't goin' to get nary a chance to cool his heels with that nester tailin' him down them draws and across the bunch-grass levels.

The Piute? I wasn't worried so much about Julie now. He might kill her, but that I doubted as long as he had a prayer of gettin' away with her. He was goin' to have to keep movin' or shoot it out.

THE LONGER I RODE, the more respect I got for Bin Morley. He stuck to that Piute's trail like a cocklebur to a sheep, and that yellow horse of his just kept his head down and kept moseyin' along those trails like he was born to 'em, and he probably was.

The stars come out and then the moon lifted, and they kept on goin'. My steeldust was beginnin' to drag his heels, and so I knowed the end was comin'. At that, it was most mornin' before it did come.

How far we'd come or where we were I had no idea. All I knew was that up ahead of me was the Piute with my girl, and I wanted a shot at him. Nobody needed to tell me I was no hand to tie in a gun battle with the Piute with him holdin' a six-gun. He was too slick a hand for me.

Then all of a sudden as the sky was turnin' gray and the hills were losin' their shadows, I rounded a clump of cottonwoods and there was that yellow horse, standin' three-footed, croppin' absently at the first green grass in miles.

The nester was nowhere in sight, but I swung down and with the carbine in hand, started down through the trees, catfootin' it along with no idea what I might see or where they could have gone. Then all of a sudden I come out on the edge of a cliff and looked down at a cabin in a grassy basin, maybe a hundred feet below and a good four hundred yards away.

Standin' in front of that cabin were two horses. My face was pretty pale, an' my stomach felt sick, but I headed for the trail down, when I heard a scream. It was Julie!

Then, in front of the cabin, I heard a yell, and that durned nester stepped right out in plain sight and started walking up to the cabin, and he wasn't more than thirty yards away from it.

That fool nester knowed he was askin' for it. The Piute might have shot from behind the doorjamb or from a window, but maybe the nester figured I was behind him and he might draw him out for my fire. Or maybe he figured his comin' out in the open would make him leave the girl alone. Whatever his reason, it worked. The Piute stepped outside the door.

Me? I was standin' up there like a fool, just a-gawkin', while there, right in front of my eyes, the Piute was goin' to kill a man. Or was he?

He was playin' big Injun right then. Maybe he figured Julie was watchin' or maybe he thought the nester would scare. Mister, that nester wouldn't scare a copper cent.

The Piute swaggered about a dozen steps out from the cabin and stood there, his thumbs in his belt, sneerin'. The nester, he just moseyed along kind of lazylike, carryin' his old Spencer in his right hand like he'd plumb forgot about his handgun.

Then, like it was on a stage, I seen it happen. That Piute went for his guns and the nester swung up his Spencer. There was two shots—then a third.

It's a wonder I didn't break my neck gettin' down that trail, but when I run up, the Piute was lyin' there on his back with his eyes glazin' over. I took one look an' then turned away, and you can call me a pie-eatin' tenderfoot, but I was sick as I could be. Mister, did you ever see a man who'd been hit by two soft-nosed .56-caliber bullets? In the stummick?

Bin Morley come out with Julie, and I straight-

ened up an' she run over to me and began askin' how
Ma was. She wasn't hurt none, as the nester got there
just in time.

We took the horses back, and then I fell behind with the nester. I jerked my head toward the
Piute's body.

"You goin' to bury him?" I asked.

He looked at me like he thought I was soft in
the head.

"What fur? He picked the place hisself, didn't he?"

We mounted up.

"Besides," he said, "I've done lost two whole days
as it is, and gettin' behind on my work ain't goin' to
help none." He was stuffin' something in his slicker
on the back of his horse.

"What's that?" I asked.

"A ham," he said grimly, "a whole ham. I brung it
clean from Tucson, an' that durned Piute stole it off
me. Right out of my cabin. Ma, she was out pickin'
berries when it happend."

"You mean," I said, "you trailed the Piute clean
over here just for a ham?"

"Mister," the nester spat, "you durned right I did!
Why Ma and me ain't et no hawg meat since we left
Missoury, comin' three year ago!"

The steeldust started to catch up with Julie's pony,
but I heard the nester sayin', "Never was no hand to
eat beef, nohow. Too durned stringy. Gets in my
teeth!"

Desert Death Song

When Jim Morton rode up to the fire, three unshaven men huddled there warming themselves and drinking hot coffee. Morton recognized Chuck Benson from the Slash Five. The other men were strangers.

"Howdy, Chuck!" Morton said. "He still in there?"

"Sure is!" Benson told him. "An' it don't look like he's figurin' on comin' out."

"I don't reckon to blame him. Must be a hundred men scattered about."

"Nigher two hundred, but you know Nat Bodine. Shakin' him out of these hills is going to be tougher'n shaking a possum out of a tree."

The man with the black beard stubble looked up sourly. "He wouldn't last long if they'd let us go in after him! I'd sure roust him out of there fast enough!"

Morton eyed the man with distaste. "You think so. That means you don't know Bodine. Goin' in after him is like sendin' a houn' dog down a hole after a badger. That man knows these hills, every crack an' crevice. He can hide places an Apache would pass up."

The black-bearded man stared sullenly. He had thick lips and small, heavy-lidded eyes. "Sounds like maybe you're a friend of his'n. Maybe when we get him, you should hang alongside of him."

Somehow the long rifle over Morton's saddlebows shifted to stare warningly at the man, although Morton made no perceptible movement. "That ain't a handy way to talk, stranger," Morton said casually. "Ever'body in these hills knows Nat, an' most of us been right friendly with him one time or another. I ain't takin' up with him, but I reckon there's worse men in this posse than he is."

"Meanin'?" The big man's hand lay on his thigh.

"Meanin' anything you like." Morton was a Tennessee mountain man before he came west, and gun talk was not strange to him. "You call it your own-self." The long rifle was pointed between the big man's eyes, and Morton was building a cigarette with his hands only inches away from the trigger.

"Forget it!" Benson interrupted. "What you two got to fight about? Blackie, this here's Jim Morton. He's lion hunter for the Lazy S."

Blackie's mind underwent a rapid readjustment. This tall, lazy stranger wasn't the soft-headed drink of water he had thought him, for everybody knew about Morton. A dead shot with rifle and pistol, he was known to favor the former, even in fairly close combat. He had been known to go up trees after mountain lions, and once, when three hardcase rustlers had tried to steal his horses, the three had ended up in Boot Hill.

"How about it, Jim?" Chuck asked. "You know Nat. Where'd you think he'd be?"

Morton squinted and drew on his cigarette. "Ain't no figurin' him. I know him, an' I've hunted along of him. He's almighty knowin' when it comes to wild country. Moves like a cat an' got eyes like a turkey buzzard." He glanced at Chuck. "What's he done? I heard some talk down to the Slash Five, but nobody seemed to have it clear."

"Stage robbed yestiddy. Pete Daley of the Diamond D was ridin' it, an' he swore the robber was Nat. When they went to arrest him, Nat shot the sheriff."

"Kill him?"

"No. But he's bad off, an' like to die. Nat only fired once, an' the bullet took Larrabee too high."

"Don't sound reasonable," Morton said slowly. "Nat ain't one to miss somethin' he aims to kill. You say Pete Daley was there?"

"Yeah. He's the on'y one saw it."

"How about this robber? Was he masked?"

"Uh-huh, an' packin' a Winchester .44 an' two tied-down guns. Big black-haired man, the driver said. He didn't know Bodine, but Pete identified him."

Morton eyed Benson. "I shouldn't wonder," he said, and Chuck flushed.

Each knew what the other was thinking. Pete Daley had never liked Bodine. Nat married the girl Pete wanted, even though it was generally figured Pete never had a look-in with her, anyway, but Daley had worn his hatred like a badge ever since. Mary Callahan had been a pretty girl, but a quiet one, and Daley had been sure he'd win her.

But Bodine had come down from the hills and changed all that. He was a tall man with broad shoulders, dark hair, and a quiet face. He was a good-looking man, even a handsome man, some said. Men liked him, and women, too, but the men liked him best because he left their women alone. That was more than could be said for Daley, who lacked Bodine's good looks but made up for it with money.

Bodine had bought a place near town and drilled a good well. He seemed to have money, and that puzzled people, so hints began to get around that he had been rustling as well as robbing stages. There were those, like Jim Morton, who believed most of the stories were started by Daley, but no matter where they originated, they got around.

Hanging Bodine for killing the sheriff—the fact that he was still alive was overlooked and considered merely a technical question, anyway—was the problem before the posse. It was a self-elected posse, inspired to some extent by Daley and given a semi-official status by the presence of Burt Stoval, Larrabee's jailer.

Yet, to hang a man, he must first be caught, and Bodine had lost himself in that broken, rugged country known as Powder Basin. It was a region of some ten square miles backed against an even rougher and uglier patch of waterless desert, but the basin was bad enough itself.

Fractured with gorges and humped with fir-clad hogbacks, it was a maze where the juniper region merged into the fir and spruce and where the canyons were liberally overgrown with manzanita. There were at least two cliff dwellings in the area and a ghost mining town of some dozen ramshackle structures, tumbled in and wind worried.

"All I can say," Morton said finally, "is that I don't envy those who corner him—when they do and if they do."

Blackie wanted no issue with Morton, yet he was still sore. He looked up. "What do you mean, **if** we do? We'll get him!"

Morton took his cigarette from his lips. "Want a suggestion, friend? When he's cornered, don't you be the one to go in after him."

FOUR HOURS LATER, when the sun was moving toward noon, the net had been drawn tighter, and Nat Bodine lay on his stomach in the sparse grass on the crest of a hogback and studied the terrain below.

There were many hiding places, but the last thing he wanted was to be cornered and forced to fight it out. Until the last moment, he wanted freedom of movement.

Among the searchers were friends of his, men

with whom he rode and hunted, men he had admired and liked. Now they believed him wrong; they believed him a killer, and they were hunting him down.

They were searching the canyons with care, so he had chosen the last spot they would examine, a bald hill with only the foot-high grass for cover. His vantage point was excellent, and he had watched with appreciation the care with which they searched the canyon below him.

Bodine scooped another handful of dust and rubbed it along his rifle barrel. He knew how far a glint of sunlight from a Winchester can be seen, and men in that posse were Indian fighters and hunters.

No matter how he considered it, his chances were slim. He was a better woodsman than any of them, unless it was Jim Morton. Yet that was not enough. He was going to need food and water. Sooner or later, they would get the bright idea of watching the water holes, and after that . . .

It was almost twenty-four hours since he had eaten, and he would soon have to refill his canteen.

Pete Daley was behind this, of course. Trust Pete not to tell the true story of what happened. Pete had accused him of the holdup right to his face when they had met him on the street. The accusation had been sudden, and Nat's reply had been prompt. He'd called Daley a liar, and Daley moved a hand for his gun. The sheriff sprang to stop them and took Nat's bullet. The people who rushed to the scene saw only the sheriff on the ground, Daley with no gun drawn and Nat gripping his six-shooter. Yet it was not that of which he thought now. He thought of Mary.

What would she be thinking now? They had been married so short a time and had been happy despite the fact that he was still learning how to live in civilization and with a woman. It was a mighty different thing, living with a girl like Mary.

Did she doubt him now? Would she, too, believe he had held up the stage and then killed the sheriff? As he lay in the grass, he could find nothing on which to build hope.

Hemmed in on three sides, with the waterless mountains and desert behind him, the end seemed inevitable. Thoughtfully, he shook his canteen. It was nearly empty. Only a little water sloshed weakly in the bottom. Yet he must last the afternoon through, and by night he could try the water hole at Mesquite Springs, no more than a half mile away.

The sun was hot, and he lay very still, knowing that only the faint breeze should stir the grass where he lay if he were not to be seen.

Below him, he heard men's voices and from time to time could distinguish a word or even a sentence. They were cursing the heat, but their search was not relaxed. Twice men mounted the hill and passed near him. One man stopped for several minutes, not more than a dozen yards away, but Nat held himself still and waited. Finally, the man moved on, mopping sweat from his face. When the sun was gone, he wormed his way off the crest and into the manzanita. It took him over an hour to get within striking distance of Mesquite Springs. He stopped just in time. His nostrils caught the faint fragrance of tobacco smoke.

Lying in the darkness, he listened, and after a moment heard a stone rattle, then the faint **chink** of metal on stone.

When he was far enough away, he got to his feet and worked his way through the night toward Stone Cup, a spring two miles beyond. He moved more warily now, knowing they were watching the water holes.

The stars were out, sharp and clear, when he snaked his way through the reeds toward the cup. Deliberately, he chose the route where the overflow from the Stone Cup kept the earth soggy and high-grown with reeds and dank grass. There would be no chance of a watcher waiting there on the wet ground, nor would the wet grass rustle. He moved close, but there, too, men waited.

He lay still in the darkness, listening. Soon he picked out three men, two back in the shadows of the rock shelf, one over under the brush but not more than four feet from the small pool's edge.

There was no chance to get a canteen filled there, for the watchers were too wide-awake. Yet he might manage a drink.

He slid his knife from his pocket and opened it

carefully. He cut several reeds, allowing no sound. When he had them cut, he joined them and reached them toward the water. Lying on his stomach within only a few feet of the pool and no farther from the nearest watcher, he sucked on the reeds until the water started flowing. He drank for a long time, then drank again, the trickle doing little, at first, to assuage his thirst. After a while, he felt better.

He started to withdraw the reeds, then grinned and let them lay. With care, he worked his way back from the cup and got to his feet. His shirt was muddy and wet, and with the wind against his body, he felt almost cold. With the water holes watched, there would be no chance to fill his canteen, and the day would be blazing hot. There might be an unwatched hole, but the chance of that was slight, and if he spent the night in fruitless search of water, he would exhaust his strength and lose the sleep he needed. Returning like a deer to a resting place near a ridge, he bedded down in a clump of manzanita. His rifle cradled in his arm, he was almost instantly asleep.

Dawn was breaking when he awakened, and his nostrils caught a whiff of wood smoke. His pursuers were at their breakfasts. By now they would have found his reeds, and he grinned at the thought of their anger at having had him so near without knowing. Morton, he reflected, would appreciate that. Yet they would all know he was short of water.

Worming his way through the brush, he found a

trail that followed just below the crest and moved steadily along in the partial shade, angling toward a towering hogback.

Later, from well up on the hogback, he saw three horsemen walking their animals down the ridge where he had rested the previous day. Two more were working up a canyon, and wherever he looked, they seemed to be closing in. He abandoned the canteen, for it banged against brush and could be heard too easily. He moved back, going from one cluster of boulders to another, then pausing short of the ridge itself.

The only route that lay open was behind him, into the desert, and that way they were sure he would not go. The hogback on which he lay was the highest ground in miles, and before him the jagged scars of three canyons running off the hogback stretched their ugly length into the rocky, brush-blanketed terrain. Up those three canyons, groups of searchers were working. Another group had cut down from the north and come between him and the desert ghost town.

The far-flung skirmishing line was well disposed, and Nat could find it in himself to admire their skill. These were his brand of men, and they understood their task. Knowing them as he did, he knew how relentless they could be. The country behind him was open. It would not be open long. They were sure he would fight it out rather than risk dying of thirst in the desert. They were wrong.

Nat Bodine learned that himself, suddenly. Had he been asked, he would have accepted their solution, yet now he saw that he could not give up.

The desert was the true Powder Basin. The Indians had called it the Place of No Water, and he had explored deep into it in past years and found nothing. While the distance across was less than twenty miles, a man must travel twice that or more, up and down and around, if he would cross it, and his sense of direction must be perfect. Yet, with water and time, a man might cross it.

But Nat Bodine had neither. Moreover, if he went into the desert, they would soon send word and have men waiting on the other side. He was fairly trapped, and yet he knew that he would die in that waste alone before he surrendered to be lynched. Nor could he hope to fight off this posse for long. Carefully, he got to his feet and worked his way to the crest. Behind him lay the vast red maw of the desert. He nestled among the boulders and watched the men below. They were coming carefully, still several yards away. Cradling his Winchester against his cheek, he drew a bead on a rock ahead of the nearest man and fired.

Instantly, the searchers vanished. Where a dozen men had been in sight, there was nobody now. He chuckled. "That made 'em eat dirt!" he said. "Now they won't be so anxious."

The crossing of the crest was dangerous, but he made it and hesitated there, surveying the scene before him. Far away to the horizon stretched the desert. Before him, the mountain broke sharply away in a series of sheer precipices and ragged chasms, and he scowled as he stared down at them, for it seemed no descent could be possible from there.

CHUCK BENSON AND JIM MORTON crouched in the lee of a stone wall and stared up at the ridge from which the shot had come. "He didn't shoot to kill," Morton said, "or he'd have had one of us. He's that good."

"What's on his mind?" Benson demanded. "He's stuck now. I know that ridge, an' the only way down is the way he went up."

"Let's move in," Blackie protested. "There's cover enough."

"You don't know Nat. He's never caught until you see him down. I know the man. He'll climb cliffs that would stop a hossfly."

Pete Daley and Burt Stoval moved up to join them, peering at the ridge before them through the concealing leaves. The ridge was a gigantic hogback almost a thousand feet higher than the plateau on which they waited. On the far side, it fell away to the desert, dropping almost two thousand feet in no more than two hundred yards, and most of the drop in broken cliffs.

Daley's eyes were hard with satisfaction. "We got him now!" he said triumphantly. "He'll never get off that ridge! We've only to wait a little, then move in on him. He's out of water, too!"

Morton looked with distaste at Daley. "You seem powerful anxious to get him, Pete. Maybe the sheriff ain't dead yet. Maybe he won't die. Maybe his story of the shootin' will be different."

Daley turned on Morton, his dislike evident. "Your opinion's of no account, Morton. I was there, and I saw it. As for Larrabee, if he ain't dead, he soon will be. If you don't like this job, why don't you leave?"

Jim Morton stroked his chin calmly. "Because I aim to be here if you get Bodine," he said, "an' I personally figure to see he gets a fair shake. Furthermore, Daley, I'm not beholdin' to you, no way, an' I ain't scared of you. Howsoever, I figure you've got a long way to go before you get Bodine."

HIGH ON THE RIDGE, flat on his stomach among the rocks, Bodine was not so sure. He mopped sweat from his brow and studied again the broken cliff beneath him. There seemed to be a vaguely possible route, but at the thought of it, his mouth turned dry and his stomach, empty.

A certain bulge in the rock looked as though it might afford handholds, although some of the rock was loose, and he couldn't see below the bulge where it might become smooth. Once over that projection, getting back would be difficult if not impossible. Nevertheless, he determined to try.

Using his belt for a rifle strap, he slung the Winchester over his back, then turned his face to the rock and slid feetfirst over the bulge, feeling with his toes for a hold. If he fell from here, he could not drop less than two hundred feet, although close in there was a narrow ledge only sixty feet down.

Using simple pull holds and working down with his feet, Bodine got well out over the bulge. Taking a good grip, he turned his head and searched the rock below him. On his left, the rock was cracked deeply, with the portion of the face to which he clung projecting several inches farther into space than the other side of the crack. Shifting his left foot carefully, he stepped into the crack, which afforded a good jam hold. Shifting his left hand, he took a pull grip, pulling away from himself with the left fingers until he could swing his body to the left and get a grip on the edge of the crack with his right fingers. Then, lying back, his feet braced against the projecting far edge of the crack and pulling toward himself with his hands, he worked his way down, step by step and grip by grip, for all of twenty feet. There the crack widened into a chimney, far too wide to be climbed with a lie back, its inner sides slick and smooth from the scouring action of wind and water.

Working his way into the chimney, he braced his feet against one wall and his back against the other, and by pushing against the two walls and shifting his feet carefully, he worked his way down until he was well past the sixty-foot ledge. The chimney ended in a small cavernlike hollow in the rock, and he sat there, catching his breath.

Nat ran his fingers through his hair and mopped sweat from his brow. Anyway—he grinned at the thought—they wouldn't follow him down here!

Carefully, he studied the cliff below him, then to the right and left. To escape his present position, he must make a traverse of the rock face, working his way gradually down. For all of forty feet of climb, he would be exposed to a dangerous fall or to a shot from above if they had dared the ridge. Yet there were precarious handholds and some inch-wide ledges for his feet.

When he had his breath, he moved out, clinging to the rock face and carefully working across it and down. Sliding down a steep slab, he crawled out on a knife-edge ridge of rock and, straddling it, worked his way along until he could climb down a farther face, hand over hand. Landing on a wide ledge, he stood there, his chest heaving, staring back up at the ridge. No one was yet in sight, and there was a chance that he was making good his escape. At the same time, his mouth was dry, and the effort expended in descending had increased his thirst. Unslinging his rifle, he completed the descent without trouble, emerging at last upon the desert below.

Heat lifted against his face in a stifling wave. Loosening the buttons of his shirt, he pushed back his hat and stared up at the towering height of the mountain, and even as he looked up, he saw men appear on the ridge. Lifting his hat, he waved to them.

BENSON WAS THE FIRST MAN on that ridge, and involuntarily he drew back from the edge of the cliff, catching his breath at the awful depth below. Pete Daley, Burt Stoval, and Jim Morton moved up beside him, and then the others. It was Morton who spotted Bodine first.

"What did I tell you?" he snapped. "He's down there on the desert!"

Daley's face hardened. "Why, the dirty—"

Benson stared. "You got to hand it to him!" he said. "I'd sooner chance a shoot-out with all of us than try that alone."

A bearded man on their left spat and swore softly. "Well, boys, this does it! I'm quittin'! No man that game deserves to hang! I'd say, let him go!"

Pete Daley turned angrily but changed his mind when he saw the big man and the way he wore his gun. Pete was no fool. Some men could be bullied, and it was a wise man who knew which and when. "I'm not quitting," he said flatly. "Let's get the boys, Chuck. We'll get our horses and be around there in a couple of hours. He won't get far on foot."

NAT BODINE TURNED and started off into the desert with a long swinging stride. His skin felt hot, and the air was close and stifling, yet his only chance was to get across this stretch and work into the hills at a point where they could not find him.

All this time, Mary was in the back of his mind, her presence always near, always alive. Where was she now? And what was she doing? Had she been told?

Nat Bodine had emerged upon the desert at the mouth of a boulder-strewn canyon slashed deep into the rocky flank of the mountain itself. From the mouth of the canyon there extended a wide fan of rock, coarse gravel, sand and silt flushed down from the mountain by torrential rains. On his right, the edge of the fan of sand was broken by the deep scar of another wash, cut at some later date when the water had found some crevice in the rock to give it an unexpected hold. It was toward this wash that Bodine walked.

Clambering down the slide, he walked along the bottom. Working his way among the boulders, he made his way toward the shimmering basin that marked the extreme low level of the desert. Here, dancing with heat waves and seeming from a distance to be a vast blue lake, was one of those dry lakes that collect the muddy runoff from the mountains. Yet as he drew closer, he discovered he had been mistaken in his hope that it was a **playa** of the dry type. Wells sunk in the dry type of **playa** often produce fresh cool water, and occasionally at shallow depths. This, however, was a pasty, water-surfaced **salinas,** and water found there would be salty and worse than none at all. Moreover, there was danger that he might break through the crust beneath the dry, powdery dust and into the slime below.

The **playa** was such that it demanded a wide detour from his path, and the heat there was even more intense than on the mountain. Walking steadily, dust rising at each footfall, Bodine turned left along the desert, skirting the **playa.** Beyond it, he could see the edge of a rocky escarpment, and this rocky ledge stretched for miles toward the far mountain range bordering the desert.

Yet the escarpment must be attained as soon as possible, for knowing as he was in desert ways and lore, Nat understood in such terrain there was always a possibility of stumbling on one of those desert tanks, or **tinajas,** which contain the purest water any wanderer of the dry lands could hope to find. Yet he knew how difficult these were to find, for hollowed by some sudden cascade or scooped by wind, they are often filled to the brim with gravel or sand and must be scooped out to obtain the water in the bottom.

Nat Bodine paused, shading his eyes toward the end of the **playa.** It was not much farther. His mouth was powder dry now, and he could swallow only with an effort.

He was no longer perspiring. He walked as in a daze, concerned only with escaping the basin of the **playa,** and it was with relief that he stumbled over a stone and fell headlong. Clumsily, he got to his feet, blinking away the dust and pushing on through the rocks. He crawled to the top of the escarpment through a deep crack in the rock and then walked on over the dark surface.

It was some ancient flow of lava, crumbling to ruin now, with here and there a broken blister of it. In each of them, he searched for water, but they were dry. At this hour, he would see no coyote, but he watched for tracks, knowing the wary and wily desert wolves knew where water could be found.

The horizon seemed no nearer, nor had the peaks begun to show their lines of age or the shapes into which the wind had carved them. Yet the sun was lower now, its rays level and blasting as the searing flames of a furnace. Bodine plodded on, walking toward the night, hoping for it, praying for it. Once he paused abruptly at a thin whine of sound across the sun-blasted air.

Waiting, he listened, searching the air about him with eyes suddenly alert, but he did not hear the sound again for several minutes, and when he did hear it, there was no mistaking it. His eyes caught the dark movement, striking straight away from him on a course diagonal with his own.

A bee!

Nat changed his course abruptly, choosing a landmark on a line with the course of the bee, and then followed on. Minutes later, he saw a second bee, and altered his course to conform with it. The direction was almost the same, and he knew that water could be found by watching converging lines of bees. He could afford to miss no chance, and he noted the bees were flying deeper **into** the desert, not away from it.

Darkness found him suddenly. At the moment, the horizon range had grown darker, its crest tinted with old rose and gold, slashed with the deep fire of crimson, and then it was night, and a coyote was yapping myriad calls at the stars.

In the coolness, he might make many miles by pushing on, and he might also miss his only chance at water. He hesitated; then his weariness conformed with his judgment, and he slumped down against a boulder and dropped his chin on his chest. The coyote voiced a shrill complaint, then satisfied with the echo against the rocks, ceased his yapping and began to hunt. He scented the man smell and skirted wide around, going about his business.

THERE WERE SIX MEN in the little cavalcade at the base of the cliff, searching for tracks. The rider found them there. Jim Morton calmly sitting his horse and watching with interested eyes but lending no aid to the men who tracked his friend, and there were Pete Daley, Blackie, Chuck Benson, and Burt Stoval. Farther along were other groups of riders.

The man worked a hard-ridden horse, and he was yelling before he reached them. He raced up and slid his horse to a stop, gasping, "Call it off! It wasn't him!"

"What?" Daley burst out. "What did you say?"

"I said . . . it wa'n't Bodine! We got our outlaw

this mornin' out east of town! Mary Bodine spotted a man hidin' in the brush below Wenzel's place, an' she come down to town. It was him, all right. He had the loot on him, an' the stage driver identified him!"

Pete Daley stared, his little eyes tightening. "What about the sheriff?" he demanded.

"He's pullin' through." The rider stared at Daley. "He said it was his fault he got shot. His an' your'n. He said if you'd kept your fool mouth shut, nothin' would have happened, an' that he was another fool for not lettin' you get leaded down like you deserved!"

Daley's face flushed, and he looked around angrily like a man badly treated. "All right, Benson. We'll go home."

"Wait a minute." Jim Morton crossed his hands on the saddle horn. "What about Nat? He's out there in the desert, an' he thinks he's still a hunted man. He's got no water. Far's we know, he may be dead by now."

Daley's face was hard. "He'll make out. My time's too valuable to chase around in the desert after a no-account hunter."

"It wasn't too valuable when you had an excuse to kill him," Morton said flatly.

"I'll ride with you, Morton," Benson offered.

Daley turned on him, his face dark. "You do an' you'll hunt you a job!"

Benson spat. "I quit workin' for you ten minutes ago. I never did like coyotes."

He sat his horse, staring hard at Daley, waiting to see if he would draw, but the rancher merely stared back until his eyes fell. He turned his horse.

"If I were you," Morton suggested, "I'd sell out an' get out. This country don't cotton to your type, Pete."

Morton started his horse. "Who's comin'?"

"We all are." It was Blackie who spoke. "But we better fly some white. I don't want that salty Injun shootin' at me!"

It was near sundown of the second day of their search and the fourth since the holdup, when they found him. Benson had a shirt tied to his rifle barrel, and they took turns carrying it.

They had given up hope the day before, knowing he was out of water and knowing the country he was in.

The cavalcade of riders was almost abreast of a shoulder of sandstone outcropping when a voice spoke out of the rocks. "You huntin' me?"

Jim Morton felt relief flood through him. "Huntin' you peaceful," he said. "They got their outlaw, an' Larrabee owes you no grudge."

His face burned red from the desert sun, his eyes squinting at them, Nat Bodine swung his long body down over the rocks. "Glad to hear that," he said. "I was some worried about Mary."

"She's all right." Morton stared at him. "What did you do for water?"

"Found some. Neatest **tinaja** in all this desert."

The men swung down, and Benson almost stepped on a small, red-spotted toad.

"Watch that, Chuck. That's the boy who saved my life."

"That toad?" Blackie was incredulous. "How d' you mean?"

"That kind of toad never gets far from water. You only find them near some permanent seepage or spring. I was all in, down on my hands and knees, when I heard him cheeping.

"It's a noise like a cricket, and I'd been hearing it some time before I remembered that a Yaqui had told me about these frogs. I hunted and found him, so I knew there had to be water close by. I'd followed the bees for a day and a half, always this way, and then I lost them. While I was studyin' the lay of the land, I saw another bee, an' then another. All headin' for this bunch of sand rock. But it was the toad that stopped me."

They had a horse for him, and he mounted up. Blackie stared at him. "You better thank that Morton," he said dryly. "He was the only one was sure you were in the clear."

"No, there was another," Morton said. "Mary was sure. She said you were no outlaw and that you'd live. She said you'd live through anything." Morton bit off a chew, then glanced again at Nat. "They were wonderin' where you make your money, Nat."

"Me?" Bodine looked up, grinning. "Minin' turquoise. I found me a place where the Indians worked.

I been cuttin' it out an' shippin' it East." He stooped and picked up the toad, and put him carefully in the saddlebag.

"That toad," he said emphatically, "goes home to Mary an' me. Our place is green an' mighty pretty, an' right on the edge of the desert, but with plenty of water. This toad has got him a good home from here on, and I mean a good home!"

Heritage of Hate

BUSHWHACKED MAN

Con Fargo hunched his buffalo coat about his ears and stared at the blood spot. It must have fallen only a minute or two before, or snow would have covered it. And the rapidly filling tracks beside the blood spot were those of a man.

Brushing the snow from his saddle he remounted, turning the grulla mustang down the arroyo. The man, whoever he might be, was wounded and afoot, and the worst storm in years was piling the ravines with drifts.

The direction of the tracks proved the man a stranger. No Black Rock man would head in that direction if badly hurt. In that direction lay thirty miles of desert, and at the end of those miles only the ramshackle ruins of a ghost town.

Con started the mustang off at a rapid trot, his eyes searching the snow. Suddenly, he glimpsed the wounded man. Yet even as his eyes found the stumbling figure, a shot rang out.

Fargo hit the trail beside his horse, six-gun in hand. He could see nothing, only the blur of softly falling snow, hissing slightly. There was no sound, no movement. Then, just as he was about to avert his eyes, a clump of snow toppled from the lip of the arroyo.

He hesitated an instant, watching. Then he clambered up the steep wall of the arroyo and stood looking down at the tracks. Here a man had come to the edge, and here he had waited, kneeling in the snow. He was gone now, and within a quarter of a mile his tracks would be wiped out.

Con Fargo slid back into the arroyo and walked over to the fallen man. The fellow wore no heavy coat, and he was bleeding badly. Yet his heart was beating.

"This moving may cash your chips, old-timer, but you'd die out here, anyway," Con said.

He lifted the man and carried him back to his horse. It took some doing to get the wounded man into the saddle and mount behind him. The mustang didn't like the smell of blood and didn't like to carry double. When Fargo was in the saddle he let the grulla have his head, and the horse headed off through the storm, intent on the stable and an end to this foolishness.

An hour later, with the wounded man stripped of his clothes, Con went to work on him. He had the rough skill of the frontier fighter who was accustomed to working with wounds. The man had been shot twice. The first bullet had been high, just under his left collarbone, but it had spilled a lot of blood. The second shot had gone in right over the heart.

FOR THREE BITTER DAYS he fought for the man's life, three days of blizzard. Then the wounded man began to fail, and at daylight on the fourth morning, he died.

Getting out for a doctor would have been impossible. It was twelve miles to Black Rock, and with snow deep in the passes he dared not make the attempt. And the one doctor in town wouldn't cross the street to help Fargo or anyone like him.

Thoughtfully, Con studied the dead man. To somebody, somewhere, this man meant much. For whatever reason the man came west, it had been important enough to warrant his murder.

For this was no casual robbery and murder. Every effort had been made to prevent identification of the dead man. The labels had been torn from his store-bought clothes. There were no letters, no papers, no wallet and no money. All had been removed.

"Somebody went to a powerful lot of trouble to see nobody ever guessed who this hombre was," Con told himself. "I wonder why?"

The man was young, not over thirty. He was good-looking and had the face of a man with courage. Yet he was unburned by sun or wind, and his hands were soft.

Obviously, the killer thought the first shot had

finished him. He had robbed the man and stripped the identification from his body, and then must have left him. The wounded man recovered consciousness and made an effort to get away. The killer had returned, had guessed the wounded man would keep to the partial shelter of the arroyo, and had headed him off and then shot him down.

"Pardner, I reckon I'm goin' to find out why," Con said softly. "You and me, they didn't want either of us here. You didn't have as much luck as I did. Or maybe you were slower on the draw."

Turning to a drawer in the table he got out a tape measure. Then, while frost thickened on the windows and the snow sifted down into drifts, he measured the body. The height, waist, chest, biceps. There was a small white scar on the dead man's chin; he noted it. On his right shoulder there was a birthmark, so Con put it down in the book.

"Somebody didn't want anybody to know who you was, so that must be important. Me, I aim to find out."

The next day, after he had buried the man in an old mine tunnel, he examined the clothing. One by one, in broad daylight, he went over the articles of clothing. There was red clay against the heels of both shoes, a stain of red clay around the edge of the sole.

On the seat of the trousers and the back of the coat were long gray hairs. "Either this hombre had him a fur-lined coat or he sat on a skin-covered seat.

If a seat, that would most likely be a buckboard or wagon."

More red clay was found on the knees of the trousers. "Reckon this hombre fell onto his knees when shot," Con muttered. "Else a feller as neat as him would have brushed them off."

Red clay. There was a good bit of red clay near Massacre Rocks on the stage trail from Sulphur Springs.

"That mud was soft enough to stick," he said. "And that means he was shot when it wasn't froze none. Now that norther struck about noon the day I found him, so he must've been shot that morning."

An idea struck him suddenly. Bundling the clothes, he put them in a sack and then in a box, which he hid in a hole under the floor. Then he slung his guns around his lean hips, donned his buffalo coat, slipped an extra gun into its spacious pocket, and picking up his rifle, went out to the stable.

The storm had broken about daybreak, so when the mustang was saddled he rode out taking the ridge trail, where the wind had kept the snow thin.

Two months earlier Con Fargo had ridden into Black Rock a total stranger. He came as heir to Tex Kilgore's range and property—and found he had inherited a bitter hatred from many, open dislike from others, and friendship nowhere.

Knowing Tex Kilgore he could understand some of it. Black Rock was a country of clans. It was close-knit, lawless, and suspicious and resentful of outsiders. Tex was bluff, outspoken, and what he believed he believed with everything in him. He was a broad-jawed, broad-shouldered man, and when he came into Black Rock he took up land nobody else had liked. Yet no sooner did he have it than others perceived its value. They tried to drive him out, and he fought back.

BEING A FIGHTING MAN, he fought well, and several men died. Then, aware that his time was running out, and that alone he could not win, he had written to Con Fargo:

> If you got the sand to fight for what's yourn, come a-runnin'.

Tex Kilgore knew his man, and half the money in the venture had been Con's money. Together they had punched cows for John Chisum. Together they had gone north to Dodge and Hay City with trail herds, and together they had been Texas Rangers.

Kilgore, older by ten years, had left to begin the ranch. Con Fargo stayed behind to become marshal of a tough trail town. He went from that to hunting down some border bandits.

Tex, his riders hired away or driven off, had sent the message south by the last rider who left him. Con Fargo had started north within the hour the message arrived. Yet he had reached Black Rock to learn that Tex Kilgore was dead.

It required no detailed study to understand what had happened. The Texan's enemies besieged him and he fought it out with them. Three had been killed and two wounded, and the attackers had had enough. They pulled out and abandoned the fight. What they didn't know was that one of the last bullets had left Kilgore dying on the cabin floor. A few days later they found out when a chuck line rider showed up with the news.

Only, Con Fargo, lean and frosty-eyed, heard it at the same time. He noted the satisfaction on some faces, the indifference on others, and the harsh laughter of a few.

Putney, a huge mountain of a man, had turned to a lean Mexican.

"Mount up, Gomez!" he said. "We'll ride out and take over!"

"Sit still." Con, the stranger, lifted his voice just enough to bring stillness to the room. "I'm Kilgore's partner. I'm takin' over!"

"Another of 'em, huh?" Putney sneered. "You takin' over his fightin', too?"

"He was my friend," Con said simply. "If you were his enemy, you have two choices: get out of the country by sundown, or fill your hand!"

Putney was said to be a fast man. Black Rock changed its ratings on speed that day. Putney's six-gun never cleared leather. Con Fargo, one elbow on the bar, let Putney have the first one in the stomach, the second in the throat.

Gomez was a cunning man, but the sound of gunfire confused him. He went for his gun as the first shot sounded. He was against the wall on Fargo's right, while Putney was straight ahead of the former Ranger. Yet somehow the left hand, the elbow still on the bar, held a gun, too. Fargo's head swung just for an instant, the second gun spouted fire, and Gomez hit the floor, clawing with both hands at the burning in his chest.

Con waited for a moment, letting his eyes survey the room. Then calmly holstering one gun, he thumbed cartridges into the other. He looked up then.

"My name's Con Fargo," he said pleasantly. "I'm goin' to be around here a long time. If," he continued, "any of you had a hand in killin' my pardner, you can join your friends on the floor, or start ridin'. Soon or late, I'll find out who you were."

He rode out to the Kilgore spread and took over. Twice, during the following week, he was shot at from ambush. The second sharpshooter failed to shoot sharp enough, or to move fast enough, having fired. Friends found him lying behind a rock with a bullet between his eyes.

Con Fargo rode alone. He had no friends, no intimates. In town they sold him what he needed, and once they tried to charge him twice what the supplies were worth. He paid the usual price, picked up his goods and left. Yet that very day he mailed a letter to some friends in Texas.

Then he found the dying man. Riding toward Massacre Rocks, he grinned wryly. After all, he had been a lawman, a badge toter. It was only natural that he try to find the killer of this man. Then, in a sense, it was his fight. Both had come into a country full of enemies.

Twice, after he reached the stage trail, Con slipped from the saddle to brush the snow from the road. Each time he found tracks of the buckboard, frozen solid. They headed right across the plain toward the black wall of Massacre Rocks.

AMBUSH WAS EASY HERE. For twenty miles in any direction, there was only one way a man could get through the rock wall with a team: the gate at Massacre Rocks.

Fargo scouted it carefully and, finding no one, he rode on through. Here again he found wheel tracks. Then, fifty yards farther, there were none. Backtracking, he noticed two strange circles under the thin snow. He walked over and kicked the snow from them. They were the iron tires from the buckboard. No doubt somewhere near would be the other two.

Soon he found a charred and partly burned wheel hub, and then he kicked the snow from a piece of what had been a seat. The cushion was covered with an old, mostly burned wolf hide. Carrying the hub and the seat to the rocks he concealed them in a place where there was no snow to leave a mark.

It had been muddy and the murdered man had fallen. There should be marks in the red clay. Studying the situation, Con chose the most likely spot for the dry-gulcher to hide, and from that and the remnants of the burned buckboard, he found the end of the tracks. Nearby, after sweeping several square yards of snow, he found where the wounded man had leaped from the buckboard, then the spot where he had gone to his knees. It was all there, frozen into the earth by the fierce norther.

And there, where the ambushed man had fallen, were boot tracks! Con Fargo knelt quickly. This was what he had been looking for. With his hunting knife he dug carefully around each track, then lifted the circles of frozen earth from the ground. He concealed them in another hollow in the rocks.

He mounted again and, taking a cutoff through the mountains, rode into Sulphur Springs. From there he sent two messages, then strolled over to the livery stable. While he watered the mustang, he talked idly with the graybeard who worked around. "Got ary a buckboard for hire?" he asked.

"Yep! Only one, though. Young feller come in here few days ago and borrowed one. Hired her for a week. Pair of grays. Had some business over to Black Rock, I reckon. Somethin' about a ranch."

"Didn't say who he was, did he?"

"Nope. Wasn't very talkin'. Yank, by the sound of

him. But he could handle them horses! Had him an old-time gun. One of them Patersons like the Rangers used years ago."

CHAPTER II

SALOON BRAWL

A raw, cold wind blew over the desert when he rode down off the mountains and skirted the wastelands, heading home. There was a light in his windows when he neared the cabin. Slipping from his horse, he crept across to the nearest window. What he saw inside brought a slow grin to his lips.

When his mustang was stabled he went up and pushed the door open.

"Howdy!" he said, grinning. "How's Texas?"

Two men sprang to their feet; then, seeing his face, they began to grin.

"Con! By all that's holy! Glad to see you, boss!"

Bernie Quill, a slim youngster with a reckless face and blue eyes, shoved the plate of ham and eggs at Fargo.

"Set, and give us the lowdown. We come up here for a fight. Now don't tell us you've wound it all up!"

Briefly, he explained. José Morales rolled a cigarette and listened carefully.

"Then, señor," he said at last, "we do not know **who** we fight?"

"That's about it," Fargo agreed. "Tex cashed in before I got to him. Who killed him, I don't know. Putney and Gomez were probably in the gang, but they are dead. Still, I got some ideas.

"This place is in a notch of mountain, and Kilgore had control of twenty thousand acres of good grazing land north of the mountains. The Bar M and Lazy S control almost everything south of the mountains except the townsite of Black Rock.

"Tex come in here and found the pass that leads through the mountains from Black Rock. Those mountains look like a wall that a goat couldn't cross, but there's this one pass. So he moved in and took all the land north of the mountains over to the Springer Hills. The joke on the Lazy S and Bar M was that most of the rain falls north of the mountains.

"The Bar M is owned by an eastern syndicate, but all they ask is returns. The Lazy S is owned by Springer Bob Wakeman, old-timer, who made his and went back East to live. The Bar M is managed by Art Brenner, the Lazy S by Butch Mogelo."

"Butch Mogelo?" Quill's eyes narrowed. "Is he the hombre that killed Bill Priest down in Uvalde?"

"Same one," Fargo agreed. "Art Brenner is a big, handsome fellow, and from all I can figure out, a pretty smooth operator. I couldn't tie Putney or Gomez to either of them."

Yet the mention of Bob Wakeman's name started some pulse of memory throbbing. Something that wouldn't quite boil up into his consciousness was working in his mind. Springer Bob had been a friend of Fargo's back in the old trail-herding days. Once they had fought Comanches together down in the Nation. Con had been a boy of seventeen then, but doing a man's work. And had been for nearly four years.

Con got up when his supper was finished. "Morales, you come along with me." He glanced at Quill, grinning. "You stick around. And don't look so durned sour! You got as good a chance of having trouble as we do! I'm expectin' somebody to show up here. So keep your eyes open."

Two hours later Con Fargo walked up on the porch of the hotel and glanced around. The town was quiet enough. José Morales, per instructions, was tying his horse to the hitching rail down the street. They had come to town as strangers to each other.

Fargo stepped inside, just in time to hear laughter and then a polite, smooth voice.

"Yes, of course, Miss Wakeman," the voice said. "Tomorrow would be a good day to see the ranch—if it clears up a little. With all this snow, you know—" the words trailed off as he saw Con.

It was Art Brenner, but Con Fargo was not looking at him. He was looking past the tall foreman of the Bar M at the girl. And she was looking at him.

She was tall, with a graceful figure and a pretty mouth, a mouth losing its laughter now under his intent gaze. There was something hauntingly familiar in that face. Something he could not place—

Of course! It was the resemblance to her father!

"Howdy, Brenner," he said, ignoring the big man's coldness. "Did I hear you address the lady as Miss Wakeman?"

"That's right." Brenner's voice was crisp and sharp. "Now that you've learned that, you can move along. Miss Wakeman has no desire to meet killers and gunmen!"

"Oh, but I do!" she protested suddenly. "I want to meet everyone out here! And haven't you already said it was necessary to have gunmen working for you and for us?"

Brenner's face reddened and Con stifled a chuckle as he stepped forward.

"Since Mr. Brenner doesn't want to introduce me, Miss Wakeman," he said gently, his eyes smiling, "my name is Con Fargo."

HER EYES WIDENED. "Why, of course! I remember. You're in the big picture Daddy had over his desk! The picture of one of his cattle drives. Your name was on it. But I'd never have recognized you now."

"I've changed some. Maybe it's getting older that matters." He could see the cool, quick appraisal in the girl's eyes, and something told him this girl was no fainting or helpless miss. She was, something told him, a daughter of her father.

"It will be nice having an old friend of Dad's near us," she said sincerely.

"Fargo's scarcely a friend," Brenner interrupted. His eyes were cold. "He's the one who settled on that land I told you we'd need. The land your father wanted so badly!"

"Oh, he is? But Mr. Brenner, I don't remember him ever saying anything about it!"

Brenner smiled easily. "Well, he probably didn't talk business with a young girl. He told us."

Con sensed instantly that Brenner had said the wrong thing. Audrey Wakeman, he recalled her name now, was not the kind of a girl who liked being considered helpless.

"The land we settled on was considered inaccessible until we settled there," Fargo said quietly. "Your father would have had no trouble with us."

"You said 'we'?" Audrey said quickly. "Your wife?"

"My partner, Tex Kilgore. I'm not married." Then he said quietly, "Nor do I have a partner now. He was besieged in his cabin and murdered."

"Murdered?"

"Kilgore took land he had no right to!" Brenner protested sharply. "He was no better than an outlaw!"

"He took land as it has always been taken in the West," Fargo said bluntly. "Tex Kilgore has a record that will stand beside any man's. Beside yours, Brenner! He was an honest man and fought the cause of the law wherever it went."

Was it his imagination? Or had Brenner's face tightened when he made the reference to a record?

"Who killed him?" Audrey asked quickly.

"I don't know." Con Fargo shrugged. "Yet."

"Howdy, Brenner. Hello, Miss Wakeman!" The deep voice filled the room. Fargo turned, knowing what he would see, knowing that ever since he had come north he had known this moment would come.

Butch Mogelo, boss of the Lazy S, was not quite as tall as Con, but he was broad and thick. His square, brutal jaw rested solidly on a bull neck, his nose had been broken, and there was a scar over an eyebrow. He gave an impression of brutal power such as Fargo had never seen in any other man.

His small eyes fastened on Con Fargo, and instant recognition came to them. "So?" He stared at Brenner, then at Fargo again.

"You'll be Fargo, then? I never knowed your name."

"You two know each other?" Brenner's voice was sharp.

"Yeah," Mogelo snapped, "he used to be a Ranger. I knowed him in Texas."

"A **Ranger**?" This time there was no doubt. There was genuine shock in Brenner's voice. "Con Fargo— a Ranger?"

"So was Kilgore," Con said quietly. His eyes shifted from Brenner to Mogelo. Audrey Wakeman, he observed, was taking it all in, her eyes alert.

"The last time I saw you, Butch," he said, "you got out of Uvalde in time to keep from being asked some questions about a murder."

Mogelo's eyes were ugly. "You accusin' me?" he snarled. "I'll kill you, if you do!"

Fargo laughed carelessly. "When I accuse you of murder, Butch," he said sharply, "there won't be any doubt about what I'm saying!"

He turned on his heel, nodding to Audrey Wakeman, and walked from the room. Down the street was the Silver Bar. He pushed through the swinging doors and went in.

Morales was at the end of the bar with a drink in front of him. Nearer, four men were bellied against the bar, and all of them were Lazy S riders. Keller, Looby, Cabaniss, and Ross. He had taken care to know who rode for both big ranches, and something about them.

KELLER WAS the troublemaker here. Cabaniss the most dangerous. All of the men were gunslingers.

Art Keller looked up as he stepped to the bar, and said something in a low tone to Mace Looby, who stood near him.

Morales lifted his glass and looked over it at Fargo and lifted an eyebrow. Morales was deadly with a six-gun, and with the knife he carried he was lightning itself.

Con wasn't thinking of the four Lazy S riders, he was thinking of Audrey Wakeman. What was she doing in Black Rock? Why had she come here? He knew how much money Springer Bob had lavished on his daughter, knew he had planned for her to marry eastern wealth. He knew she had had the best of educations and every advantage.

Obviously, she had come in on the stage that afternoon, for it was the first stage in several days. The thought of her going to the ranch with Mogelo chilled him. He knew the man. Butch Mogelo had been the suspect in a brutal murder of a husband, wife, and sister near Uvalde. There had been insufficient evidence to hold him, and he left the country ahead of the lynching party.

Art Keller edged closer to him along the bar.

"When you leavin' the country?" he demanded bluntly.

Con Fargo looked up. "I'm not leaving, Keller. Neither are you."

"You're blasted right I'm . . ." he broke off in midsentence, staring at Fargo. "What do you mean?" he demanded, puzzled.

"If you don't keep your hand away from that gun when you talk to me, you'll never leave this country. You'll be planted right here.

"And another thing," he continued before Keller could speak, "stay away from my range, do you hear? I've seen the tracks of that crowbait of yours, and if I catch you ridin' on my range, I'll set you afoot without your boots!"

Keller was stumped. He had started out to provoke a quarrel, and suddenly it was staring him in the face and he didn't like the look of it at all. Backed by three tough men, he had thought to run a blazer on Fargo. The play was suddenly taken away from him, and he suddenly realized that if shooting did start, he was going to be in an awfully hot spot.

Unable to see a way out, he started to bluster. "You'll do nothin'," he sneered. "Why, I'd—"

Con Fargo stepped close to him, and stared into Keller's eyes. Con's were suddenly icy, and Keller felt his mouth go dry.

"Why wait, Keller? Why not try it now?"

Keller took a step back, wetting his lips.

"Go ahead, Keller," Ross said. "Give him a whippin'!"

Others were staring at him. A dozen of the townspeople were in the saloon, and Chance, the saloon owner, was leaning over the bar, watching.

Keller swung. What happened to the punch he never knew. Hard knuckles drove into his teeth, and something struck him a wicked blow in the wind, then an iron-hard fist smashed him on the angle of the jaw, and he folded into darkness.

It had happened so suddenly that Cabaniss and the others were caught flat-footed. They had expected trouble, had been ready for it. They had waited here hoping to get Fargo in a killing spot. Now they had him, but so suddenly they were unprepared.

Con Fargo, his feet spread, hands held high, was staring at Cabaniss.

"All right, Steve," Con said quietly. "This is it. If you want to buy chips, here's your chance."

Mace Looby moved out from Steve, his eyes watchful. Ross moved away from Looby. The three men spread fanwise, faced him. Con smiled without otherwise changing expression.

"Which one do you want, José?" he said. "You can only have one."

Steve Cabaniss, his hands poised, suddenly froze. Consternation swept over his face, and Mace Looby, almost on tiptoes, settled back on his heels.

"Give to me this Steve, if you please," Morales said smoothly. "I like to shoot him full of holes."

Lucky Chance, the saloon owner, was smiling coldly and with appreciation. He started to speak, but before the words could leave his mouth, Con Fargo moved. His movement was so sudden, and came so closely on the heels of their shocked surprise, that the three men were again caught unprepared.

Con took one leap forward and smashed Looby over the head with the barrel of his six-gun. Looby crashed to the floor, and Fargo lashed left and right. Ross went down as if struck by lightning, and Cabaniss, struck a glancing blow, tottered back against the bar, blood streaming into his eyes.

FARGO WAS on him even as Steve's hand dropped for a gun. Slapping the hand away, Con hooked a short right to the chin, and Cabaniss hit the floor in a heap.

"Nice work, Fargo," Chance said quietly. "I've been hoping to see that happen for a long time."

Con Fargo grinned at him, then turned to go. Butch Mogelo was standing just inside the door.

Astonishment blanked his face, then fury.

"What's goin' on here?" he snarled.

"Your boys got a little troublesome," Con said evenly. "I almost thought they were tryin' to trap me into a three-cornered fight and button me up."

"You slugged my boys?" Mogelo's face was dark with fury. "Why!" Suddenly, he straightened a little, and the fury left his face. "Huh," he said gruffly, "maybe they was askin' for it."

Striding past Fargo he grabbed Ross and jerked him to his feet. Then Looby and Cabaniss. Staggering, the three stumbled out the door ahead of him.

"Well, I'll be hanged!" Chance said. "You bluffed him!"

"No," Fargo replied slowly, "I didn't." Thoughtfully, he stared after Mogelo. What had made the man change so suddenly? Butch Mogelo was not yellow. Brute that he might be, he had the courage of his brutality. There was something more behind this.

José Morales moved up beside Con as the tall gunfighter stepped out the door.

"Something is wrong, no?" Morales suggested.

Fargo nodded. "Mogelo and Brenner are thick as thieves. They got something planned."

He scowled as they took the trail back to the ranch. Who was the stranger who had been murdered? What was Audrey Wakeman doing in Black Rock?

How did it happen that Brenner and Mogelo were so close?

Somehow, some way, he must talk to Audrey. He had a hunch that a talk with her might prove the solution to the puzzle. He was no longer so sure that it was jealousy or range rivalry that had brought about the death of Tex Kilgore. There was something deeper, something stirring beneath the obvious, beneath the surface showings.

What, after all, did he know? Tex Kilgore had been killed, apparently by a number of men who had besieged the cabin. Yet they were obviously acting at someone's command. And was it only because he held a desirable bit of range?

Who was the stranger? Why had he not come into Black Rock on the stage? Why had he left the stage at Sulphur Springs and hired a buckboard to drive in? Who had killed him?

Fargo had the murdered man's clothing with what evidence it offered. He had concealed the charred hub, the partly burned cushion, the frozen tracks. Yet, aside from the tracks, which might or might not prove anything, he had only evidence to show the man was murdered, the buckboard destroyed, and all evidence of identity wiped out. He had nothing that pointed to the killer.

Butch Mogelo was a killer, but Butch was not the man to rip the labels from a man's clothing and destroy evidence so carefully. Mogelo had been an outlaw and a rustler. How did that tie in here?

CHAPTER III
JAILBREAK

The following night, after the two hands had headed off for town, Con opened the hole in the floor and got out the clothes once more. Carefully, he went over them, but they offered no new clue. He stowed them away, as puzzled as ever.

When Bernie Quill and Morales rode in, he met them at the door. "Some news," Quill said. "There's a U.S. marshal in town and a Pinkerton detective. Art Brenner was eatin' dinner with 'em."

Early the next morning Con Fargo mounted up and headed for town. When he was still several miles out, he saw Audrey Wakeman riding toward him from down a hillside. He reined in, waiting.

"Howdy!" he said cheerfully.

She nodded, but her manner was cool.

"Miss Wakeman," he asked, "I wonder if you'd mind tellin' me why you came west?"

Audrey glanced at him, surprise and some suspicion in her eyes.

"Why do you ask?" she demanded.

"Maybe it might help to straighten out some difficulties," he said.

"All right," she said crisply, "I'll tell you: I came because we've been losing cattle. Ever since my father died the income from the ranch has been falling off, and Mr. Mogelo tells me our cattle are being rustled."

Fargo nodded. "I figured maybe it was somethin' like that. Did he have any ideas who was rustlin' them?"

She hesitated, then her eyes flashed. "He said the rustling started when Tex Kilgore moved in here. It hasn't let up any since you came!"

Con's eyes hardened. "Did he tell you he had made rustlin' a profession in Texas? That he did time in prison for it?"

"I trust my foreman, Mr. Fargo." Her manner was crisp. "You, having ridden with my father, should be a friend of his, and of mine."

"What makes you think I'm not?" he asked gently. "There's two sides to every story."

Her chin lifted stubbornly, and she kept her eyes looking ahead. "All right, what's yours?"

He shrugged. "That I never rustled a cow in my life, ma'am. That no more honest man ever lived than Tex Kilgore. That he knew your pappy afore I did, and worked for him for years. That somehow you got a thief and an outlaw for a foreman, and personally, I don't think Brenner's any better."

Her face flushed. "You've evidence to back that, I expect?"

"No," he said frankly, "I haven't."

"Then you'd better keep your accusations to yourself! I don't think Mr. Brenner would like them!" She touched spurs to her horse.

He watched the cloud of dust and stared ruefully after her.

"Well," he muttered, "you sure didn't do yourself no good that time!"

Art Brenner was a smooth-talking man, and he had a way with women. It was making itself felt. Obviously, whatever doubts she may have had were lulled to sleep now. Art Brenner and Butch Mogelo were riding high.

Yet, he did know something. He knew that he had rustled no stock. He knew that Tex Kilgore was a man who would never have dreamed of rustling stock. He knew that Butch Mogelo had been a rustler by profession. Therefore, the chances were that Butch had rustled the stock himself.

But where had it gone?

The town was quiet when he rode in. He dismounted and walked into the saloon. Chance was standing at the end of the bar, and he nodded. Then as Con ordered a drink, he glanced up.

"Better watch, friend. They are brewing big medicine. I think it's for you."

"Could be." He glanced obliquely at Chance. "Know anything about Brenner?"

Chance's lips tightened. "No. And I'm not a talkin' man." He took a swallow of whiskey. "However, he was ridin' a big horse when he came into town. And it had done some fast travelin'."

He walked away and went into his office. Fargo scowled over the idea. A big horse? What did he mean by that? Then a thought struck him. In the north, where there was lots of snow, they used bigger horses than in the south. This wasn't really snow country. The present storm was unusual, and probably the snow wouldn't last long.

So? Art Brenner came from the north, and he was traveling fast. He looked up to see Bernie Quill.

The boyish cowhand lined up beside him at the bar.

"Boss, better light out. I hear they got a warrant for you. For murder!"

"Bernie," Fargo said quietly. "Get over to Sulphur Springs and see if there's any messages for me. Also, send messages to these five towns." Quickly he noted down the message to send and the towns. "Then you and José take turns hunting the hills, I think our place is the best bet, for some rustled cattle."

QUILL TURNED, and just then the door opened. Art Brenner stood there, and beside him were two strange men. Behind them were Mace Looby, his face dark and ugly, and the thin, saturnine face of Steve Cabaniss.

"I'm Spilman," the first man said. He was lean, elderly, cold-eyed. "Deputy United States marshal for this territory. You're under arrest for murder."

"Murder?" he asked. "Who am I supposed to have killed?" Suddenly, he saw Mogelo come in, and beside him was Audrey Wakeman. Her face was pale and tight with scorn.

"Billy Wakeman," Spilman said coldly. "Bob Wakeman's son!"

"That's nonsense!" he said. "I never killed him. I never saw the hombre."

"Esslinger," Spilman said, jerking his thumb at the detective. "Tell him!"

"We found his body buried in an abandoned drift on your place, and we found his clothes hidden under your floor!"

Con Fargo felt dry and empty inside. He'd never thought of that. They had him clinched.

"I didn't kill him!" he protested. "I'd no idea who he was!"

"You didn't know?" Esslinger asked skeptically. "You deny burying him?"

"No," he said, "I buried him. I found him in the snow. He'd been dry-gulched by someone. I took him home and worked over him all durin' the storm. He died without recoverin' consciousness."

Brenner laughed coldly. "Likely story! What did you hide his clothes for? Why didn't you report him being dead?"

"Because I wanted to find the killer," Con said slowly, knowing they wouldn't believe. "I figured," he studied Brenner as he spoke, "he was a man with something to hide. Somethin' more than stolen cattle."

Audrey kept her face averted as he was led from the room. He saw Bernie Quill mounting his horse, and then they took him away to jail. They started to turn away then.

"Wait a minute," he said. Spilman and Esslinger turned.

"Marshal, I wish you'd get in touch with Ransom, in El Paso," he said. "Ask him about Tex Kilgore, and about me."

"The Ranger captain?" Spilman studied him coldly. "Why?"

"Both of us were Rangers. There's something more here than meets the eye, Spilman. Why didn't Wakeman come right to Black Rock, instead of getting off the stage at Sulphur Springs? Ask yourself that. Then tell me who tipped you off that I had the clothes?"

"Mogelo. He went to your cabin, glanced in the window and saw you hidin' them. Then we hunted for the body today while you were gone." Esslinger studied him. "Why do you think Wakeman got off at the Springs?" Then he added, "And how do you know he did?"

"I think it was because he didn't want his own ranch foreman to know he was comin'. I think he wanted a little private look around. I know he got off there because he hired a rig in the Springs. He was dry-gulched at Massacre Rocks, the rig burned, the horses taken away."

Esslinger looked at Spilman. "Well, he's tellin' us how it was done."

Fargo kept his eyes on Spilman. "Something else you might think over. The hombre at the livery stable told me the kid had a Paterson thirty-four caliber. It wasn't on his body. Maybe the killer threw it away. And then again, maybe he kept it."

Carefully, he explained the finding of the body, the final shot. "Figure it for yourselves," he said. "Why, if I had the clothes, would I tear out the labels? Wouldn't I have burned them? Anyway you look at it, just tearing the labels out doesn't make sense. The man who killed Billy Wakeman expected the body to be found when the snow went off—without any identification."

Con slid a hand in his shirt pocket and brought out the notes he had taken from the dead man.

"See? I took these because I figured to find out who was killed, and why."

Spilman cleared his throat. "You make it sound good," he said, and turned on his heel. Esslinger followed him out.

Fargo gripped the bars, staring after them. His words seemed to have had no effect. Knowing the summary way of most western courts, and how all newcomers were disliked here, he realized he had small chance. Most of all, he was hurt by Audrey Wakeman's willingness to believe him guilty. Art Brenner had done his work well.

HE HAD AN IDEA what was behind it all, but without proof his idea amounted to nothing.

No matter how much he believed Brenner to be the motivating force behind the trouble and the killings, without proof it meant nothing. The fact that Mogelo had been an outlaw and killer also meant nothing, for many men in the West had outlived tough reputations to become respected citizens.

Much would depend on what Quill and Morales could find. And such a search might require months, for the hills east and west of his own place were probably unknown to anyone.

For two days he paced the floor, growing more and more anxious. Spilman came in occasionally, bringing his food. He saw no one else. Then José came in, followed by Spilman. The marshal watched them a moment and then went back inside the office.

"This Esslinger? He go up the hills. I see him. Two day he no come back. Bernie Quill he go, he no come back."

Fargo scowled. Now what? If Esslinger had gone into the mountains, it could mean the Pinkerton man had believed him. But still, why to the hills? He had not even suggested his own theory to the man. He shook his head.

"José," he said, "get me two blocks of wood about six inches long, two inches thick. Bring them back here. Then go back to the ranch and keep a sharp eye out."

"Two blocks of wood?" José shrugged, his eyes puzzled. "It makes no sense." He turned and went out.

Con Fargo yelled for the marshal, and when the lean old man came up to the bars, he grinned at him.

"Listen," he said, "I'm goin' nuts. How about something to do? How about a file, or a saw."

"Nothin' doin'!" Spilman said. He spat. "You're not gettin' out of this calaboose, son, I promise you!"

"Well, I can whittle, can't I? At least let me have a couple of sticks and a knife."

Spilman shrugged. "All right, all right! I'll tell that Mex cowhand of yourn."

A few minutes later, the door opened and José, with Spilman at his elbow, brought in the blocks of wood.

"This marshal say bring sticks," José said, smiling.

Twice, later in the evening, Spilman walked to the bars. Con was busy, carving a wooden horse. He grinned at Spilman.

"Marshal," he said, "when I get this horse finished I'm goin' to ride him right out of here!"

Spilman grinned, his frosty eyes softening a little.

"If you can ride out of here on a wooden horse, you can go!" he said cheerfully. "Not a bad horse, at that!" he added, grudgingly.

When the marshal had gone, Fargo slipped the other block of wood from under the blanket and went to work. Three hours later, an hour after Spilman went out, closing the office door after him, Con was ready.

"Now, let's pray that lock is well oiled!" he said.

In his hand he held a six-inch wooden key, neatly carved from the second block of wood.

"Lucky you noticed that key when he opened the door for chow," he said to himself. "Now if this'll only work!"

Carefully he inserted the key in the massive lock. Slowly he turned it. As naturally as though it was the original key, the lock turned and the door opened. Softly, he closed it after him.

Grinning, Fargo picked up the wooden horse and stepped out into the office. His guns hung from a nail on the wall. Belting them on, he shouldered into the buffalo coat, feeling the other gun as he did so. Pocketing the wooden key, he placed the wooden horse in the middle of the marshal's desk. Then picking up his rifle, he slid out through a crack of the door.

It was snowing again. He crept around the wall of the jail and started for the trees. Yet he had scarcely reached them when he heard a low voice.

"Here, señor!"

"José!" he said. "You here?"

"With two horses, señor boss. José he think, mebbe so this boss have one idea, no? Perhaps she work."

Mounting, they turned up through the timber, skirted around and headed for the hills. As they rode, Morales talked. Bernie Quill was still missing on his search into the hills. Nor had Esslinger returned. Did he know the way taken by Quill?

"**Sí, señor**. Each day we mark on map how we go, how much we search. Bit by bit we cross off the map. Now is left only a little bit."

THE SNOW WAS FALLING fast, but winds had blown earlier snow from the trail, or what remained had be-

come hard-packed. They made fast time. Con Fargo
was laboring under no delusion. Spilman would be
after them. When he returned to the jail, he would
look in on his prisoner before turning in, and when
he found him gone he would not wait for daybreak.
Yet, if Fargo could get into the hills, there was a
chance he could trail Bernie Quill. He could not believe the young puncher was dead.

It would be deathly cold in the mountains, no
weather for any man to be out at night. Esslinger,
too, was gone.

They rounded the last turn of the trail, and
Morales grasped his arm.

"Señor, a light!"

The cabin windows were aglow. Bernie, perhaps?
He slid from the saddle at the door.

"José, saddle two fresh horses—the buckskin and
the grulla!" He swung the door open and stepped
inside.

Audrey Wakeman stood, her face white, in the
center of the floor.

"You? . . . **Here?**" He walked toward her, shed-
ding the buffalo coat and dropping it on the bed.

"Yes." She stepped toward him. "How can you
ever forgive me? I thought you'd killed my brother,
and then I found this." She held out the Paterson
.34, her brother's gun.

"Where'd you find it?" he demanded.

The voice that cut across his words was sharp
and even.

"Hold right still, Fargo! And don't get any ideas. If you haven't guessed, I'm Bent Ryler!"

"Sure," Con said, "I guessed, Brenner! You were too durned scary about Rangers. Then I got a tip you'd come from the north. That made me guess who you was. Bent Ryler was wanted for murder in Butte."

Ryler sneered. "Doesn't do you much good, does it? The great Con Fargo, under my guns!" He smiled quizzically. "Might have been quite a show at that, Fargo. Ryler and Fargo! They say we're two of the fastest men in the West."

"Do they?" Con shrugged. "Ryler, you're a tin-horn and you know it. You never saw the day you could draw with me. You got the drop, so you can talk, but with an even break . . . man, you wouldn't have a chance."

"No?" Bent Ryler's face hardened. "Well, if it's an even break you're fishing for, you won't get it. Nobody knows I'm Bent Ryler but you and the girl here. They still call me Brenner. In a few minutes I'm going to drop you, and then when I'm through with her, she won't want to talk."

The door opened and Keller came in with Ross. They grinned at Fargo and covered him with their guns.

Keller's mean little eyes gleamed with triumph. "Got you, huh?" he said.

That Ryler would kill him, Fargo had no doubt. The man was cold-blooded and had always been. If only Audrey were not here! Without her, he could take a chance. Still, death might be a break for her. Bent Ryler was no break for any girl.

Where was José? Had they got him?

"I'm going to kill you, Fargo," Ryler said. He slipped his guns back into their holsters. His lips thinned. The fingers on his hands spread, hovering over his guns. "When I do, I'm goin' to let you see what a fast draw is!"

Suddenly, there was a crash of broken glass, and José's smooth voice said:

"If you please to lift the hands?" The rifle barrel was wavering between Keller and Ross.

Ryler swore, and his hands dropped. Fargo glimpsed their blurring speed; then a gun thundered and Ryler, his gun clear of the holster, stopped with his hand half lifted. He teetered on his feet, an expression of blank astonishment on his face.

Almost unconsciously, Con Fargo had drawn and fired. Now, he fired again. Bent Ryler's gun boomed at the floor, and then he crumpled to the boards.

"You beat me!" he gasped, amazement frozen into his features.

Con Fargo faced the others. Keller was back against the wall, blood dripping from his right hand. Ross was down on the floor. Con had never even heard the shots that stopped them.

CHAPTER IV

BULLETS FOR PAYMENT

Quickly the door swung open and Morales came in. Behind him were Marshal Spilman and Lucky Chance with three other men, all armed.

Spilman glanced at the men on the floor, then at Fargo.

"What happened here?" he demanded sternly.

Quickly, Fargo explained. When he had finished, Audrey Wakeman nodded.

"What he said is true, Mr. Spilman. I reached here just a few minutes before Brenner—Ryler, I mean.

"He was riding to the Bar M with me, and we stopped in passing his place. I waited in the house while he gave some orders, and saw a heavy coat hanging on a hook. The butt of a gun was visible from the pocket, so I took it out—I guess there was something familiar about it. Then I saw it was Billy's Paterson. I knew it from a scratch on the butt.

"I ran outside and got on my horse and rode here as quickly as I could. I wanted help, and then I was," she hesitated, glancing at Con, "awfully sorry for accusing him when I had known Mr. Fargo was my father's friend."

Spilman stared at the bodies thoughtfully; then he looked up at Fargo.

"I never was sure," he said. "Your story sounded good. Esslinger, he figured you was guilty. But then he says to me that while he's sure, he's goin' to check up. I ain't seen him since."

A faint yell sounded from outside, and Fargo lunged to the door. They scrambled out of the way, and he threw the door open. A weary horse was struggling through the snow. One man was on his back, another over the saddle in front of him. The rider was Bernie Quill.

"Hurry!" he said faintly. "I guess I'm—all in!"

Morales grabbed him as he fell. The second man was Esslinger. The detective had been shot twice. Quill had a hole in his leg and one trouser leg was soaked with blood.

One of the possemen swung into the saddle and started for town and a doctor. Fargo went swiftly to work on Esslinger while Audrey Wakeman cut away Quill's trouser leg and began to bathe the leg wound.

Quill's eyes fluttered open. "Never reckoned you'd be workin' on no wound for me, ma'am," he said, grinning faintly. He looked up at Spilman. "Esslinger found the rustled cattle, same time I did. Then Cabaniss and Looby rode up on him. They shot him down. Me, I was under cover, so I opened up and drove 'em off.

"I got Esslinger into the woods, and we holed up in a cave. He was in durned bad shape, and they kept me so busy I couldn't help much. He's game, though, plenty game! He told me what happened."

Bernie's face twisted with pain. "He got busy after Con talked to him at the jail. Didn't figure it was true, but he checked at Sulphur Springs, then checked Massacre Rocks. Then he found out about the messages Con sent, askin' about recent shipments of cattle. That gave him a lead, and he puts it all together, like Con done, and figured there must be rustled cows in the mountains."

Spilman looked around as Con got up. "Lost blood, mostly. The doc can tell you more'n I can. I reckon he may get through, all right. Somebody'd better find a way to get more blood into a wounded man, shot like that."

"What happened, Fargo?" Spilman asked. "What was goin' on?"

"The way I figure it, Mogelo and Ryler worked out a deal between 'em. Kilgore figured he was the first to find that pass, but Mogelo and Ryler were usin' that pass to get rustled cattle out. They had a place back there somewheres, where they was holdin' cattle, then shippin' 'em out.

"When Tex moved in, he camped right across their trail. They couldn't get in to the cattle without being seen, and they couldn't smuggle no more through the pass. By accident he sure choused up the layout for 'em.

"If they was goin' on with the rustlin' and they maybe figured to bust up both ranches and buy 'em cheap—they had to get Kilgore out of there."

Quill's eyes opened again. "Indian Valley," he said. "They got about six hundred head of cows and two mighty fine gray horses up in that valley."

"Two gray horses?" Fargo turned to the marshal. "There it is, Spilman. Those were the horses Wakeman hired from the livery stable at the Springs. I've got the footprints of the killer stuck in a hole in the rocks down there, and a piece of the wheel hub, too."

SPILMAN TURNED. "Well, Chance, you and the boys come along and we'll pick up Butch Mogelo and his pals!"

When they had gone, Audrey walked over to Con. She put her hand on his sleeve.

"I'm sorry, Con. I don't think I ever really believed it, but when they found Billy's body here and his clothes. . . . Well, it was so much evidence, and then, Ryler was so smooth about it. He made it seem obvious that you should be the one."

She looked up at Con. "Daddy always liked you, Con. You were his favorite. Time and again he used to wonder what ever became of you. He used to say he hoped Billy would be half the man you were."

Quill opened his eyes. "Didn't Daddy say nothin' 'bout me? Shucks, now. That ain't fair!"

"Shut up!" Fargo said, grinning. "You're a wounded man!"

Horses' hoofs beat on the hard-packed snow. Glancing around, Con's face went pale.

"Audrey," he said quickly. "Stay out of sight! It's Butch Mogelo."

Quickly, he checked his guns, then stepped to the door. He opened it and stepped out on the snow.

It was a gray day; flat, expressionless clouds lay across the sky, and a chill wind whispered through the pines. Butch Mogelo had dropped from the saddle. Steve Cabaniss and Mace Looby still sat their horses.

"Looks like the showdown," Butch said, grinning through his broken teeth. "You busted up a good deal, Fargo. Now we bust one up for you!

"Waited back there," he jerked his head at the trees, "until the marshal rode off. Reckoned to have you here alone. Then, when we get through with you, we can finish off that detective and that kid cowhand of yourn."

"Con," Quill's voice sounded from the door. "If you'll shift a little when the shootin' starts I'll be durned pleased to show Mogelo this kid cowhand can handle a six-gun."

Propped against the doorjamb, Bernie Quill stared at the three, smiling pleasantly.

Snow crunched at the stable door, and Con's quick eye caught the lazy figure of José Morales. **"Sí, señor,"** he said. "You have send for Quill and I for the fight. Now here it is!"

Butch Mogelo's face twisted. "Evened it up, huh? Well, let it go this way, then." His big hands swept down.

Con stepped aside and started blasting with his right-hand gun. His first bullet turned Mogelo half around, and then the big man steadied down and opened up. The bullet knocked Con's hat into the snow, and Fargo fired his gun twice more, holding it low.

He could hear the pounding of other guns, saw Cabaniss topple into the snow, struggle to get up, and then be smashed back as though struck by a mighty fist. He walked toward Mogelo, snapping another shot. The big man's face was twisted with hate.

The big gun in his hand came up, and he was sneering. He went to his knees, then got up. Chill wind blew across Con's face, drying the sweat. He spread his legs and using the border shift, swapped hands with his guns. He turned his left side away, and fired fast, two quick shots. Mogelo's face was struck blank, and then across the sudden whiteness came a thin trickle of blood. He took one slow, questioning step forward, and fell on his face.

The sudden stillness after the sound of guns was like death. Con, unhurt, glanced across at José Morales. The Mexican was leaning against the doorjamb of the stable.

"One small scratch!" he said. "It is good shooting, no?"

"Quill?" Fargo turned.

"All right," Bernie said. "Threw splinters in my face a couple of times. Those boys weren't smart. They should have hit the snow sooner."

Con walked over to Butch Mogelo. The big outlaw was dead. Three shots had gone through his body, one through the muscles where his neck joined his shoulder, and the last one between the eyes.

Cabaniss had been hit three times. At least two of the wounds, one inflicted by Morales and one by Quill, would have been fatal.

Mace Looby was still alive, sitting in the snow.

He looked up at Fargo.

"My luck run out," he said, and died.

Morales walked toward the house, wiping blood from his cheekbone.

"You inherit much trouble, **sí**?"

Con Fargo turned and looked up at the pines clothing the long razor-backed ridge.

"Yeah," he said. "A lot of trouble, but a wonderful country—a man's country!"

"No room for a woman?" Audrey said from the door.

He looked at her, smiling slowly. "A western woman," he said.

Audrey said quickly, "My mother rocked me to sleep in a prairie schooner with a rifle across her knees."

"That's western!" Fargo said, and slipping an arm around her waist they walked through the door together.

Hattan's Castle

Hattan's Castle, a towering pinnacle of rock that points an arresting finger at the sky, looks down on a solitary frame building with a sagging roof, a ruined adobe, and several weed-covered foundations, all that is left of a town that once aspired to be a city.

On a low mound a quarter of a mile away are three marked graves and seventy-two unmarked, although before their wooden crosses rotted away a dozen others had carried the names and dates of pioneers.

East of the ruined adobe lies a long and wide stone foundation. Around it there is a litter of broken bottles and a scattered few that the sun has turned into collector's items. Twenty feet behind the foundation, lying among the concealing debris of a pack-rat's nest, is a whitened skull. In the exact center of that skull are two round holes less than a half inch apart.

Several years ago the scattered bones of the skeleton could still be seen, but time, rain, and coyotes being what they are, only the skull remains.

Among the scattered foundations are occasional charred timbers, half-burned planks, and other evidences of an ancient fire. Of the once booming town of Hattan's Castle nothing more remains.

In 1874, a prospector known as Shorty Becker drank a stolen bottle of whiskey on the spot. Drunk, he staggered to the edge of the nearby wash and fell over. Grabbing for a handhold he pulled loose a clump of manzanita and the town of Hattan's Castle was born.

Under the roots and clinging to the roots were flecks and bits of gold, and Shorty Becker, suddenly sober, filed on one of the richest claims in the state's history.

Nineteen other lucky gentlemen followed, and then a number who were only fairly lucky. Hattan's Castle went from nothing to a population of four thousand people in seven days, and three thousand of the four came to lie, cheat, steal, and kill each other and the remaining one thousand-odd citizens, if such they might be called.

Spawned from an explosive sink of sin and evil, the town lived in anarchy before the coming of John Daniel. When he arrived the town had found its master. With him were the hulking Bernie Lee and a vicious little murderer who called himself Russ Chito.

Marshal Dave Allen went out in a burst of gunfire when he had words with John Daniel. Daniel faced him but fired only one shot, the others were fired by

Russ Chito and Bernie Lee, in ambush on opposite sides of the street and taking the marshal in a deadly cross fire.

Shorty Becker was found dead two days later, a gun in his hand and a bullet in his brain. John Daniel, a self-appointed coroner, pronounced it suicide. Becker was found to be carrying a will naming Daniel as his only friend and heir.

Daniel turned the working of the mine over to others, and opened the Palace Saloon & Gambling Hall. From the Barbary Coast he imported some women and a pair of bartenders skilled in the application of mickeys, knockout drops, or whatever most suited the occasion.

Four years passed and Hattan's Castle boomed in lust, sin, and murder. The mines continued to prosper, but the miners and owners remained to spend, to drink, and to die. The few who hoarded their gold and attempted to leave were usually found dead along the trails. Buzzards marked their going and if a body was found it was buried with the usual sanctimonious comments and some hurry, depending on the condition of the remains. John Daniel, aloof, cold, and supercilious, ruled the town with a rod of iron.

Chito and Lee were at his right hand but there were fifty others ready to do his bidding. Immaculate always, coldly handsome and deadly as a rattler, John Daniel had an air of authority which was questioned by none. Of the seventy-five graves on Boot Hill at least twenty had been put there by him or his hench-men. That number is conservative, and of those found along the trail at least half could be credited to John Daniel's cohorts. Then Bon Caddo came to town.

He was Welsh by ancestry, but what more he was or where he had come from nobody ever knew. He arrived on a Sunday, a huge man with broad, thick shoulders and big hands. His jaw was wide and hard as iron, his eyes a chill gray and calm, his head topped with a wiry mass of rust-colored hair. The claim he staked four miles from the Castle was gold from the grass roots down.

Within two hours after the strike Russ Chito dropped in at the Palace. John Daniel stood at the end of the bar with a glass of sherry.

"Boss," Chito said, "that new feller in town struck it rich up Lonetree."

"How rich?"

"They say twenty thousand to the ton. The richest ever!"

John Daniel mentally discounted it by half, possibly even less. Even so it made it extremely rich. He felt his pulses jump with the realization that this could be what he was waiting for, to have enough to be free of all this, to buy a home on Nob Hill and live the life of a gentleman, with no more Russ Chitos to deal with.

"Invite him in. Tell him I want to see him."

"I did tell him, and he told me where I could go."

Russ Chito's eyes flickered with anger. "I'd like to kill the dirty son!"

"Wait. I want to talk to him."

Bon Caddo did not come to Hattan's Castle and his gold did not leave the country. Every stage, every wagon, and every rider was checked with care. Nothing left the country but Bon Caddo continued to work steadily and hard, minding his own affairs, uninterested in the fleshpots of the Castle. He was cold to all offers from John Daniel, and merely attended to business. Efforts to approach him were equally unsuccessful, and riders always found themselves warned away by an unseen voice and a rifle that offered no alternative.

At the beginning of the third month, John Daniel called Cherry Creslin to his office. She came at once, slim, beautifully curved and seductive in her strictly professional way.

"You like to ride," Daniel said, "so put on that gray habit and ride my black. How you do it is your own affair, but get acquainted with Bon Caddo. Make him like you."

She protested. "Sorry, John. Get one of the other girls. I want no part of these drunken, dirty miners."

"You'll do as I tell you, Cherry, and you'll do it now. This man is neither drunken nor dirty. He is big, and tough, and, I think, dangerous. Also, he cares nothing for gambling or whiskey."

She got up. "All right, I'll go. But you'll wish you'd never sent me. I'm sick of these jobs, John! Why don't we cash in our chips and pull out? Let's go to New York, or San Francisco."

"Get started. I'll tell you when to go, and where."

The canyon of the Lonetree was warm in the spring sunshine. The cottonwoods whispered secrets to each other above the stream that chuckled humorously to the stones. There was no other sound but the trilling of birds, and on the bank above the stream the sound of Caddo working.

He wore a six-shooter, and a rifle stood nearby, and just out of sight in the tunnel mouth was a shotgun, a revolving weapon made by Colt.

Standing with his feet wide apart in their heavy miner's boots, he made a colossal figure. He was freshly shaved, and his shock of rusty hair was combed. His red flannel shirt was open at the neck, and his huge forearms, bulging with raw power, showed below his rolled-up sleeves. Cherry Creslin, impressed by few things, was awed.

At the sound of hoofs splashing in the water, he looked around. Then he saw the rider was a woman, and a beautiful woman, at that. He smiled.

Long before he had come to Hattan's Castle he had heard of John Daniel, and knew his every trick. Moreover, he knew this woman by name and knew she was reputed to be John Daniel's own woman. He could see, as she drew nearer, that she was genuinely beautiful and despite the hard lines that showed through her lovely skin, there was warmth there, but a restrained, carefully controlled warmth.

"Good morning, Bon Caddo." Her voice was low and lovely, and deep within him something stirred, and he tried to bring up defenses against it. She was all woman, this one, no matter what else she might be.

"Hello, Cherry."

"You know me? I don't remember you." She looked at him again. "I don't think I could forget."

"You've never seen me, Cherry, and I've never seen you, but I've been expecting you."

He gestured to a seat under a tree. "Won't you get down and stay for a while? It's quite pleasant here."

"You—you've been expecting me?" She was irritated. She was accustomed to handling men, to controlling situations. This man, she realized, was different. Not only was he a physical giant but he was intelligent, and . . . she admitted it reluctantly . . . he was exciting.

"Of course." He smiled pleasantly. He had, she thought, a truly beautiful smile. "John Daniel has tried everything else, hasn't he? Everything but you . . . and murder."

Her features stiffened and her eyes went hard, but she did not pretend to misunderstand. "So you think he sent me? You think I am the kind of woman a man can send on some dirty business?"

He leaned on his shovel. "Yes," he said, and she struck him across the face with her quirt.

He did not move nor change expression although the red line of the blow lay vividly across his cheek and lips. "Yes," he repeated, "but you shouldn't be. You've got heart and you have courage. You've just been riding with the tide."

"You're very clever, aren't you?"

"No. But this situation isn't very hard to understand. Nor are you, Cherry Creslin. It's a pity," he continued, "that you're tied up with such a murdering lot. There's a lot of woman in you, and you'd make some man a woman worth keeping."

She stared at him. The situation was out of hand. It would be difficult now to get him back in the right vein. Or was this the right one?

"You may be right," she said, "maybe I've been waiting for you."

He laughed and stuck his shovel down hard into the pile of muck. Then he walked over to her, and the black horse nuzzled his arm. "Not that way, Cherry. Be honest. I'm not so easy, you know. Actually the only way is to be honest."

She measured him, searching herself. "Honest? I don't know whether I could be. It's been so long."

"Ah, now you are being honest! I like that, Cherry." He leaned his big shoulder against the horse's shoulder. "In fact, Cherry, I like you."

"Like me?" A strange emotion was rising within her, and she tried to fight it down. "And you know what I am?"

"What are you? A woman. Perhaps no worse and no better than any other. One cannot always measure by what a person seems to be or even has been. Anyway, it is always the future that counts."

"You believe that? But what of a woman's past?"

Bon Caddo shrugged. "If a woman loved me I'd start counting the days of her life from the time she told me she loved me. I would judge by what happened after that, although I'd be a hard judge for the after years."

She was irritated with herself. This was not what she had come for. "How did we start talking like this? I did not intend to get into anything like this."

"Of course. You came to get me to fall in love with you or at least to lure me down to that sinkhole at Hattan's Castle. You might manage the first, but not the last."

"If you were in love with me and I asked you to come, would you?"

"Certainly not. Doing what a woman asks is not proof of love. If a man isn't his own man he isn't worthy of love. No, I'd use my own judgment, and my judgment tells me to stay away from Hattan's Castle and the Palace."

His eyes seemed to darken with seriousness. "We of Welsh or Irish blood, Cherry, sometimes have a power of prophecy or intuition, call it what you will, and mine tells me that when I come to Hattan's Castle it will mean blazing hell and death. For me, the town, or both of us."

Something cold and frightening touched her and

suddenly she put her hand on his. "Then, then don't come, Bon Caddo. Don't come at all. Stay here, or better still, take your gold and go."

"You advise me that way? What would John Daniel say?"

"He wouldn't like it," she replied simply. "He would not like it at all. But it is my best advice to you."

"I shall stay until my claim is worked out. I'll not be driven off."

"May I come back again?"

"Come soon. Come often."

Caddo watched her go and then returned to his work. There would be trouble, of course. He doubted that Cherry would tell John Daniel of her failure. Not yet, at least. She would come back, and perhaps again. If she continued to fail, John Daniel would try something else.

Three times she came in the days that followed and each time they talked longer. Inevitably the day came when she returned to Hattan's Castle to find John Daniel awaiting her. When their eyes met she knew she was in trouble.

"Well?" His question was a challenge. "When is he coming in?"

"He is not coming at all." There was no use evading the issue. She had probably been spied upon. "He is not coming, but I am leaving. We're to be married."

"**What?**" Of all things, this was the least expected.

"Do you think you can trick me that way? Marry him and get it all for yourself?"

"You'd not understand, John, but I love him. He's a real man and a fine man, so don't try to stop me."

"Try? I'll not just try, I'll do it!" His eyes were ugly. "Hereafter you will stay in town. I shall find other means of handling it."

"Sorry." She got to her feet. "I am going back to him."

He struck her across the mouth with the back of his hand and she fell to the floor, a trickle of blood running from her mashed lip. She looked up at him. "You shouldn't have done that, John. I am sorry for you, or I would be if there was a decent bone in your body."

Furious, he strode from the room and returned to the Palace. The first person he saw was Chito. "All right. You want to kill Caddo. Go do it."

Without another word, Russ Chito left the room. From her window Cherry saw him go and divined his purpose. Filled with terror she rushed to the door but hulking Bernie Lee stood there. "You ain't goin' no place. Get back inside."

She stepped back. There would be no chance to warn Caddo. Chito would be halfway there by now, and he would kill without warning, and from ambush.

At the Palace John Daniel stared from the window, thinking. The boom was over here, anyway. He would sell out and go away. Within the past few months the population had fallen by a third. It was time to move. With the gold from Caddo's claim he could leave all this behind. He would go to San Francisco as they had planned, and he would take Cherry with him. Once away from all this the foolish notions would leave her head. She would be his woman again.

During the months they had been associated he had never won her love, and it galled him to think that Bon Caddo had, or so it seemed.

John Daniel hated all that resisted him, anything he did not or could not possess and control.

The afternoon wore on, and he paced the floor. Chito had not returned. Of course, he was a careful man. He was taking his time. Still—

In her own cabin, Cherry packed her belongings and waited. She feared, she doubted, yet inside there was a kind of stillness. Terror there was, and fear for the man she now loved, but through it all there was something else, a kind of confidence, a belief that somehow, some way, Bon Caddo would triumph.

At the Palace Saloon John Daniel was no longer patient. He lit a black cigar and muttered under his breath. He walked to the door and looked down the street. There was no sign of Chito.

Darkness came and he went to his office. The saloon business began but in a desultory fashion. The whole town seemed to be waiting, watching, wondering. Seven o'clock passed, then eight. John Daniel walked into the saloon and looked quickly around.

Many of the familiar faces were missing. Nine came and went and suddenly there was a crash of glass. Men sprang to their feet, staring.

Where the alley window had been was a gaping hole, and sprawled on the floor inside was Russ Chito. He had taken a shotgun blast through the chest.

Men rushed to him, and only John Daniel remained where he was, white-faced, his cigar clamped in his teeth.

Then the swinging doors parted and Bernie Lee tottered into the room and fell sprawling on the floor. He was alive, but brutally beaten.

John Daniel reached behind the bar and took up a spare pistol. Methodically, he checked it, then tucked it behind his belt. His own gun in his hand, he strode down the street.

Cherry was gone.

Her house was lighted, the door stood open, but Cherry was gone.

John Daniel swore, shifted the cigar in his teeth. "Pete! Dave! Ed! Cherry's gone and I want her back, and I want Bon Caddo dead!"

Suddenly, from down the street a voice shouted **"Fire!"** John Daniel rushed to the door. One glimpse was enough, down the street, in a direct line with his saloon, a deserted shack was ablaze.

A glance told him that with the wind there was no chance. That whole side of the street must go, and he owned every building there.

Suddenly he became aware that nobody was moving to fight the blaze. They were watching, and a few were throwing water on buildings across the street, buildings he did not own. He yelled at them, but there was no response.

Cursing, he turned on his heel and went into the Palace. Rage filled him, a bitter, futile rage. He was whipped . . . whipped. But he still had the money.

He went to his secret drawer and took out the gold. He went to his safe for more, carefully changed into bills for easier carrying. There was more gold under the foundation but that could wait. Now, while the others watched the fire, he would go.

From his room he brought a pair of saddlebags, kept handy for the purpose, and into them he stuffed bills and gold. Straightening up he turned swiftly and started for the back door. A few steps beyond was the stable and his black horse.

He stopped abruptly. Bon Caddo stood in the door. "Going someplace, John?" he asked mildly.

John Daniel stood stock-still, caught in midstride. For the first time he knew fear.

He was alone. Russ Chito was dead. Bernie Lee was beaten within an inch of his life. The others were scattered, hunting for Caddo. And Caddo was here.

John Daniel had always accounted himself a brave man. He was not afraid, but there was something indomitable about Caddo.

"All your life, John Daniel, you've lived by murder and robbery, and you've gotten away with it. Now your town is burning, Daniel, and you're going with it."

John Daniel's hand reached for a bottle at the end of the bar and threw it. The bottle missed, shattering against the wall. Bon Caddo started for him.

John Daniel moved to meet him, since there was no escape. He struck out viciously, and Caddo took the blow coming in without so much as a wince. Then Caddo struck in return, and the blow made Daniel's knees buckle.

Caddo moved after him, coolly, relentlessly. "Like hitting women, John? How does it feel to be hit? Do you like killing, John? How does it feel to die?"

In a wild burst of panic-born strength, John Daniel struck out. The blow caught Caddo coming in again but the power of it staggered him and he tripped over a fallen chair, falling to the floor.

John Daniel lunged for the back door and made it. With Caddo coming after him he reached the stable.

His horse was gone!

Trapped, he turned swiftly, reaching for his gun. In front of Bon Caddo a red eye winked, then winked again. Thunder roared in John Daniel's ears and a terrible flame seemed to rush through him. He did not see the red eye wink again for he was falling, falling, already dead, into the broken branches of a manzanita.

There is a place in the Tonto Basin where a long, low ranch house looks out upon a valley. Cottonwood leaves whisper their secrets around the house and on the veranda a woman watches her husband walking up from the barn with his two tall sons. Inside the house a daughter sings songs more haunting than those her mother sang in the Palace, long ago. The big man, whose hair is no longer rust red, pauses by her side.

Before them, the peace of the meadows, and the tall sons washing for supper in the doorside basins. Inside, the song continues.

"It's been a good life, Mother, a good life," he says quietly.

Far to the north there is an adobe wall with a bullet buried in it, a bullet nobody ever saw. A smashed elbow bone, covered now by the sand of the wash, lies among the debris of a pack-rat's nest, and where the manzanita grew there is a whitened skull. In the exact center of that skull are two round bullet holes, less than a half inch apart.

Big Man

Cherry Noble rode into Wagonstop on a black mule. He was six feet seven in his socks, and he habitually wore boots. He weighed three hundred and thirty pounds. He swung down from the mule and led it and his three pack animals to water. As he stood by the trough with his mules, the bystanders stared in unadulterated amazement.

Noble looked up, smiling in a friendly fashion. "What's off there?" He indicated the country to the west with a bob of his head.

From where he stood nothing was visible to the west but the sun setting over a weird collection of red spires and tabletopped mountains.

Lay Benton replied. "Nothin' but wilderness, some of the wildest, roughest country on earth and some bloodthirsty Indians."

"No people?"

"None."

"Water? And grass maybe?"

"Could be a little. Who knows?"

"Then that's where I'll go. I'll go there so when folks do come there'll be a place waiting for them.

Sooner or later people come to most every place, and mostly when they get there they are hot and tired. I'll have grass, water, and beef a-waiting."

"You'd be crazy to try," Benton said. "No white man could live in that country even if the Indians would let him."

Cherry Noble's laugh boomed, his face wrinkling with the memories of old smiles. "They'll let me stay, and I guess there's no place a man can't live if he sets his mind to it." He slapped a bulging saddlebag. "Know what I've got here? Cherry pits, that's what! When I stop I plan to plant cherries! Ain't no better fruit, anywhere, and that's why people call me as they do. Noble's my name and folks call me Cherry. You could trail me across the country by the trees I've planted."

Lay Benton was a trouble-hunter, and he did not like Cherry Noble. Lay had been the biggest man around until Noble arrived, and he still considered himself the toughest. The big man's easy good humor irritated him. "If you go into that country," he said contemptuously, "you're a fool!"

" 'Better to be a fool than a knave,' " quoted Noble. He was smiling, but his eyes were measuring Benton with sudden attention and knowledge.

Benton came to his feet ready for trouble. "What was that you called me?"

Cherry Noble walked to the foot of the steps where Benton stood. "Friend," he spoke gently, still smiling, "I didn't call you, but if you heard your name just keep a-coming."

Benton was irresolute. Something in the easy movement and confidence of the big man disturbed him. "You don't make sense!" he said irritably. "What's the matter? Are you crazy?"

Noble chuckled, his big hands on his hips. "Now as to that," he said judiciously, "there's a division of opinion. Some say yes, some say no. Me, I've not rightly decided, but at any rate I'm not a very wise man.

"Feller back in Missouri when I was about hip-high to a short burro, he give me five books, he did. He said, 'Son, you take these books and you read them. Then you read them through again and then you ponder on 'em. After that you give them to somebody else, but there'll be something that will stay with you all the days of your life. I'm giving you the greatest gift any man can give to another.' "

Cherry Noble put one huge booted foot on the step. "Now I read them there books, and more times than twice. One was the Bible, mighty good reading whether a man is of a religious turn or not. Another was a bunch of poetry like by a man named Shakespeare. That one only made occasional sense to me until the third time around and then everything began to fall into place, and it's stayed in my mind ever since. Then there was a book on law, or that's what I was told, by Blackstone. Seemed to me that book made a lot of sense, and mostly it was rules and ideas on how folks can get along together. There was another by a man named Plato that seemed to me conversations with some other folks, but one that worried me some was an account of the death of this Socrates.

"Seems they had something against him, and the powers that were said he should take poison hemlock. Well, from the account of what happened afterward it seemed to me the man was writing about something he never actually saw because we have a sight of poison hemlock in parts of the country where I've lived and it's a very agonizing death, no way so calm and easy as this man seemed to have it.

"Man told me later, a man who was up on such things, that Plato wasn't even there when it happened. I don't think a man should write things unless he can write the truth about it, or as near as he can come to it. The other book was some sayings by Jefferson, Franklin, and the like, the sort of conclusions any reasonable man comes to in a lifetime.

"Now I read those books up one side and down the other and nothing in those books told me I was crazy and nothing in them told me I was a wise man, either. So"—he smiled cheerfully—"I just let 'er rest, an' that's a good way to do with arguments."

Noble mounted the steps and went into the store and Benton stared after him. He spat into the dust. Now what kind of a man was that?

Hack, another of the bysitters, glanced slyly at Benton. "He sure is big," he commented.

"Size doesn't make the man!" Benton said contemptuously.

The older man chuckled, looking Benton up and down. "Now that's what I've always said!" Hack agreed. "That's what I'll always say!"

The door opened and Noble stepped out. He had two one-hundred-pound sacks of flour under one arm and held another by the top. He walked to his pack mules and began strapping on the sacks. Then he went around to the corral and returned with three horses. Bringing out more supplies, he strapped them on the pack saddles he had brought along with the horses.

Benton had the feeling he had come out on the short end of the exchange and did not like it. Nor was he sure just how it had happened. He watched Noble loading up with growing displeasure. "Some Mormons tried to settle over there one time and the Injuns run 'em out. The Green boys went in there with cattle, and the Greens were killed. You ain't got a chance back in there alone. There was six or seven of the Greens.

"Besides," he argued, "how would you make a living? Suppose your cherries grew? Where would you sell 'em?"

Cherry Noble's chuckle was rich and deep. "Why, friend, I don't worry about that. The Lord will provide, says I, and when folks come they will find the earth flowering like the gardens of paradise, with fat black cherries growing, and if by chance the Injuns get me my trees will still be growing. For I say he who plants a tree is a servant of God, which I heard somewhere long ago. Even if there's no fruit on the limbs there'll be shade for the weary and a coolness in summer."

"You talk like a damned sky pilot," Benton scoffed.

"Well, I'm not one. Nor am I really what you'd call a religious man, nor a learned one. That feller who gave me the books said, 'Son, it isn't how many books you read, it's what you get from those you do read. You read those books I gave you and neither life, nor death, nor man will hold any fears for you.' That's what the man said, and he seems to have been right."

"You'll need a lot more than talk if those Piutes jump you!" Benton replied.

Noble chuckled again. "If they don't understand that kind of talk I can always use this!" He picked an empty whiskey bottle from the dust and flipped it into the air. As the bottle reached its high point he palmed his six-shooter and fired.

The shot smashed the bottle, his second and third shots broke fragments of the bottle into still smaller fragments.

Lay Benton sat down on the top step, shocked and a little sick to the stomach. To think he had been hunting trouble with a man who could shoot like that!

Noble swung into the saddle on the big mule, a huge and handsome creature who only swished his tail at the great weight. "Come visit me," he invited, "where you find me there will be green grass and trees, and if you give me time there will be black cherries ripening in the sun!"

"He'll get himself killed," Benton said sourly.

"Maybe," Hack agreed, "but Injuns take to his kind."

They watched him ride down the dusty street toward the trail west, and he only stopped once, to let Ruth McGann cross in front of him. She was going over to the Border house to borrow a cup of sugar . . . at least that was what she said.

They saw that he spoke to her, and they might as well have overheard it because old man Border repeated the words.

Noble drew up and gallantly swept the hat from his head. "Beauty before industry, ma'am. You may pass before I raise a dust that might dim those lovely eyes."

She looked up at him suspiciously. "My name is Noble," he said, "and I hope that sometimes I am. They call me Cherry because it's cherries I plant wherever I've time to stop. And your name?"

"Ruth," she replied, her eyes taking in the great expanse of chest and shoulder, "and where might you be going, riding out that way?"

"Like the Hebrew children," he said, "I go into the wilderness, but I shall return. I shall come back for you, Ruth, and then you shall say to me as did Ruth of the Bible, 'Wither thou goest, I will go; and where thou lodgest, I will lodge; thy people shall be my people, and thy God, my God.' "

Ruth looked him over coolly. Seventeen and pert, she had hair like fire seen through smoke, and eyes of hazel. The prettiest girl in all that country it was said, but with eyes for no man. "Oh, I will, will I? You've a smooth tongue, big man. What else do you have?"

"Two hands and a heart. What else will I need?"

"You'll need a head," she replied calmly. "Now be off with you. I have work to do."

"Well spoken!" He replaced his hat on his head and as Ruth passed on across the street, he added, " 'Fare you well, hereafter in a better world than this, I shall desire more love and knowledge of you.' "

Ruth McGann turned on the steps of the Border house and watched him disappear down the trail. It was only a dim trail, for not many went that way and fewer returned. "Who was that?" she asked. "I haven't seen him before."

"Some stranger," Border said, "but a mighty big man. About the biggest I ever did see."

Ruth crossed the porch and went into the house for her cup of sugar, a strange thing, as old man Border commented, for her ma had bought a barrel of sugar only a few weeks before, looking to a season's canning. The story was told around the sewing and the knitting circles for days after, and around the horse corrals and in the blacksmith shop as well. She was chided about her big man, but Ruth offered no reply.

A month passed, and then six months, and then Port Giddings came in with three riders. They had crossed the rough country to the west and stopped by the McGanns. "Wild country yonder," Port said, "but right in the midst of it we found Noble. He asked to be remembered to you, Ruth. He said to tell you when his place was in better shape he'd be coming for you."

Her eyes flashed, but she said nothing at all. Only when they talked she listened and went on with her sewing.

"The way that valley has changed you wouldn't believe," Giddings said. "He's broken sod on more than a hundred acres and has it planted to corn and oats. He's got two hundred cherry trees planted and sprouting. Then he rounded up those cattle the Green boys lost, and he's holding them on meadows thick with grass. He's using water from those old Mormon irrigation ditches, and he's cut a lot of hay.

"Best of all, he's built a stone house that's the best I've seen in this country. That man sure does work hard."

"What about the Indians?" McGann asked.

"That's the peculiar part. He seems to have no trouble at all. He located their camp when he first rode into the country, and he went in and had a long talk with the chief and some of the old men. He's never been bothered."

Cherry Noble could not have taken oath to that comment. The Indians living nearby had caused no trouble, nor had he made trouble for them. The same could not be said for passing war parties. A raiding band of Piutes had come into the country, stealing horses from the other Indians and at that very moment Noble was hunkered down behind some rocks at a water hole.

Luckily, he had glimpsed the Indians at the same time they saw him. He had reached the rocks around the water hole just in time. He shot the nearest Indian from the saddle and the rest of them went to the ground. Noble got the mule down on its side and out of rifle range. He readied his Winchester and reloaded his six-gun.

It was a long, slow, hot afternoon. There was no water nearer than fifteen miles except what lay in the water hole behind him. He knew that and so did the Piutes, only he had the water and they did not.

Sweat trickled down the big man's neck. He took a pull at his canteen and put a reassuring hand on the mule. The animal had been trained from birth for just this eventuality and lay quiet now.

They came suddenly and with a rush and Noble took his time. He dropped one, then switched his rifle and missed a shot as they disappeared.

There were at least five Indians still out there. A buzzard soared expectantly overhead. He moved suddenly, farther into the rocks and only in time. A warrior, knife in hand, dove at him from a rock and Noble threw up a hand, grasping the Indian's knife wrist and literally throwing the man to the ground near the pool.

Noble put a gun on him and the Indian looked up at him, judging his chances. "No good," Noble said. "You," he gestured, "drink!"

The Indian hesitated. "Drink, damn you!" And the Indian did, then again.

"Now get up and get out. Tell them to leave me alone. I want no trouble, do you hear? No trouble.

"You steal even one head from me and I'll hunt you down and kill you all." How much the Indian understood he had no idea. "Now go!"

They went, wanting no more of this big man who lived alone.

Noble returned to his work. There were more trees to plant, a vegetable garden to fence, traps to be set for rabbits that were playing havoc with his crops.

Four days later, as if testing him, he found several steers driven off and tracked them to their camp. They had eaten heavily and were sleeping, doubting one lone man would attempt to pursue them.

He went into their camp on cat feet. He gathered their rifles and was taking a pistol from one of them when the man awakened. His eyes riveted on Noble's face and he started a yell, but the pistol barrel across his head stopped it.

Walking out of their camp he gathered their

horses and led them to where his horse waited. Surprisingly, they were still asleep. Perhaps somewhere in their raiding they had found some whiskey, for they slept too soundly.

Picking up an armful of brush he tossed it on the fire and at the first crackle of flame they came awake. He was waiting for them with a gun in his hand.

They started to rise and he shouted, "No! You stay!"

They waited, watching him. They were tough men, and thank God, one of them was old enough to have judgment. "No trouble!" he reiterated. "I want no trouble!"

"My cow," he gestured, "all mine! You go now. Don't come back!"

The oldest of the warriors looked up at him. "You say we come again, you kill all."

"I don't want to kill. White Stone Calf is my friend. You can be friend also."

"You say you kill. Can you kill me?"

"I can kill you. I do not wish to. I am a man who plants trees. I grow corn. If an Indian is hungry, I will feed him. If he is sick, I will try to make him well, but if he harms my crops, if he attacks me or steals my cows or horses, I will kill him. Some have already died, how many must die before you understand me?"

"We will go," the Indian said. "You will give us our horses?"

"I will not. You have taken my time. I take your

horses. Next time I shall take more horses. You go. If you come again, come in peace or I will follow to your village and many will die."

The following year there were two raids into the area, but they rode around the big man's land; and when the next winter was hard and the snows were heavy and icy winds prowled the canyons he rode into their village, and they watched him come.

He brought sides of beef and a sack of flour. He rode to the Indian to whom he had talked and dropped them into the snow before him. "No trouble," he said, "I am friend."

He turned and rode away, and they watched him go.

GIDDINGS STOPPED AGAIN at the McGann home. "Dropped by to buy some stock from that Noble feller. Got fifty head of good beef from him. I reckon he's got at least three hundred head of young stuff, and he's kept a few cows fresh for milking."

"Did you say milking?" McGann was incredulous. "I never heard of a man milkin' a cow west of the Rockies."

"He's doing it." Giddings glanced slyly at Ruth. "He says womenfolks set store by milk cows. Gives 'em real butter and cream. For a woman who bakes, he says, that's a big help."

Ruth seemed not to hear, continuing with her sewing.

"His cherry trees are growing, and they look

mighty nice. Long rows of them. He's put in a kitchen garden, too. Seems he came prepared with all kinds of seed. He eats mighty good, that feller. Corn on the cob, cabbage, peas, carrots, onions, lots of other stuff. He's found a little gold, too."

It was this last item that reached the attention of Lay Benton. It was just like that crazy man, he thought, to find gold where nobody else had even looked for it. His grudge against Noble had grown as stories of his improving ranch continued to spread. He took that success as a personal affront.

Late on a night after another of Giddings's visits, Lay met with Gene Nevers and Ab Slade. "He's got gold, horses, cattle, and some cash money Giddings paid him. Must run to seven or eight hundred dollars."

"How do you figure to do it?" Slade asked.

"Take no chances. We lay for him and shoot him down. There's nobody there but him and everybody will think Injuns done it."

At daylight they rode out of town, and Giddings saw them go. He stopped by the McGann house. "I shouldn't have mentioned that gold," he said. "Benton, Slade, and Nevers rode out of town, then circled and headed west."

"You think they're going after Noble?" McGann asked.

"Where else? Benton never liked him, and we all know what Benton is."

Ruth sat quietly sewing and did not look up. Giddings glanced at her. "You don't look worried," he commented.

She looked up at him. "Why should I be? If a man can't look after himself of what account is he?"

"By the way," Giddings smiled at her. "He said for you to get to work on that trousseau."

Her eyes flashed. "Does he think me a fool?"

Three days went by and there was no change in Ruth, or if there was it went unnoticed by old man Border, who missed nothing. Except, he added, that lately Ruth had been watering her flowers nine or ten times a day, and each time she took a long time shading her eyes down the trail toward the west. The trail was always empty, and the purple hills of evening told her nothing.

Benton might have been loudmouthed and Ab Slade a coward, but Gene Nevers was neither. He was an experienced outlaw and stock thief, and he had killed several men.

Benton wanted to slip up on Noble and shoot him down from ambush, but Nevers was practical. "He'll have that gold hid, and we'll never find it."

"Maybe we should catch him and burn him a little. Make him talk."

Nevers was impatient. "Don't be a fool! His kind never talk."

At the last they decided that was the way to do it. They slipped down near the house and were waiting when Noble went to the spring for water. As he straightened up his eye caught the glint of light on a rifle barrel, and he was unarmed.

He made a very big target, and he was no fool. These men had come to rob him first and then kill him. Had it been only the latter he would already be dead. He thought swiftly and coolly. The only reason he was alive was because they needed him to locate the gold.

As the three stepped into the open his eyes went from one to the other. Nevers was at once the most dangerous and the most reasonable. Slade hung back, either overly cautious or a coward. That Benton disliked him he knew.

"Howdy, gents! Why all the guns? You been hunting?"

"We were hunting you," Benton said.

"A long way to come and a big risk for what there is in it," he said.

"Where's the gold, Noble?" Nevers asked. "It will save trouble if you tell us."

"Most likely, but I never paid much mind to trouble. Kind of liked it now and again. Keeps the edge on a man." If he could just get within reach—

He moved toward the door and instantly the guns lifted. "Hold it now!" Benton was eager to shoot.

"Just aimin' to set my bucket inside. No use to talk out here in the sun. I was just fixin' to have breakfast, so if you boys don't mind, we'll just have breakfast first and then talk. I'm hungry."

"So am I." Slade moved toward the door.

"Ab," Nevers said, "you go inside and pick up his guns. Move them into the farthest corner, behind where we will sit. We will let this man fix our breakfast, like he says. I'm hungry, too."

Ab Slade went inside and Noble knew what he was doing, he could follow his every move. He came to the door. "All right, just a Winchester and a couple of forty-fours."

They went inside. Putting down his bucket Noble went to work. He had no plan, no idea. He would fix breakfast as promised. Besides, he was hungry himself.

They stayed across the room from him, but Nevers was very alert. Several times he might have surprised the others but not Nevers.

"I found gold, all right"—he talked as he worked—"but not much of it yet. You boys came too soon. You should have waited another month or two when I'd cleaned up the sluice after some long runs. I'd just finished the sluice and now it's a loss. Too bad."

"Why too bad?" Benton asked.

"The claim will be lost. Nobody could find it but me, and after you boys kill me you'll have to skip the country. You'll never dare show face around Wagonstop again, so the gold won't do you any good."

"We ain't leavin'," Slade said. "We'll say it was Injuns."

"That won't work." Noble slapped some beef in

the frying pan. "I'm friends with all the Indians. In fact, they're due over here now. I promised them some beef and some tobacco."

Nevers glanced uneasily out the door. Giddings had said that Noble was friendly with the Indians. Suppose they appeared now, and suspected something was wrong?

Noble knew what was in his mind. "You boys may have to kill your horses getting out of here because those Injuns will be right after you. I've been helping them through some hard times." He forked beef from the pan. "How you figuring on getting out? Unless you know the country you're in a trap."

"Southwest," Benton said, "to Arizona."

"See? You don't know this country. The Colorado Canyon, looks like it's a mile deep, lies right in the way."

Gene Nevers swore mentally, remembering that canyon only then. He had never been south from here, only east and north. Wagonstop was east and the Indians were north. For the first time he was worried.

"You'd better get outside, Ab, and watch for those Indians."

"They're touchy," Noble said, "shoot one of them, and they'll really come after you."

He dished up the food, placing plates before Nevers and Benton. Both men had drawn their guns and placed them on the table beside their plates. Cherry

Noble noted the fact and turned back to the fireplace.

Beside the woodpile was the old burlap sack in which he had the guns he had taken from the Piutes. An old blanket was partly thrown over it. In that sack there were weapons . . . but were they loaded? Could he, he asked himself, be sure of getting a loaded weapon if he dropped to one knee and grabbed? There was no certainty, and there would be no second chance.

Carefully he placed two cups on the table and picked up the coffeepot. Nevers watched him with hawk eyes as he filled the cups. Then they took their cups in their left hands and as Noble filled his own cup inspiration came. He reached for a spoon and accidentally knocked it to the floor. Stooping to retrieve it, he hurled himself against the legs of the table.

His three hundred and thirty pounds hit the table like an avalanche, smashing it back into the two outlaws. Nevers grabbed wildly at his gun and it exploded, sending a bullet into the wall as the table hit him waist-high. He was smashed backward and with Benton slammed against the wall, the boiling coffee cascading over them.

Leaping up, Noble sent a huge fist that smashed into Benton's face. His head hit the wall with a thud. Nevers pulled free of the table, gasping for breath, and lunged at Noble sending them both crashing to the floor. Nevers swung wildly, and the blow caught Noble on the chin. He might as well have hit a stone wall.

Jerking free, Nevers grabbed for his gun, which lay on the floor. Nevers got a hand on the gun and Noble grabbed for Benton's gun. Nevers fired wildly and missed, then fired again and didn't. Noble felt the bullet hit him and fired in return.

He saw Nevers fall and heard running feet as Ab Slade rushed the door. He turned, swaying, and fired as Slade framed himself in the door.

Slade fell. Fully conscious, slumped against the doorjamb, he said, "You got Gene?"

"Yes."

"And Benton?"

"He's out cold."

Slade stared at him, almost pleading. "I tried, didn't I? They can't say I was yella, can they?"

"You tried, Ab. You really tried. You could have run."

"Tell them that. Tell them I—" He rolled over, out of the doorway to the hard-packed earth outside.

He died like that and Cherry Noble went back inside.

On the sixth day after Benton, Slade, and Nevers rode out of town, Ruth McGann walked up the street to the store. She lingered over her shopping, listening for the news. There was none.

Then somebody in the street let out a yell. The store emptied into the street.

There was no mistaking the rider on the black mule. Behind him there were three horses. Two with empty saddles, the third with a rider tied to his horse. That rider's face was battered and swollen. Cherry Noble drew up before the store.

"They came hunting me. Two are buried back yonder. If anybody wants to collect them, they can. I caught one but not bad. Not enough to worry about. This one"—he indicated Benton—"put them up to it and as he sort of figured himself a fighter, I turned him loose and let him have at it. He didn't cut much ice as a fighter."

Ruth stepped off the porch and walked away in the dust. Cherry Noble glanced after her, threw one longing look at the saloon and the beer he had wanted for the last thirty miles, and followed.

He caught her in three long strides. She had shortened hers, just a little. He was at a loss for words but finally he said, "I've come back."

"So you have," she replied coolly.

"We can be married by the preacher, and start for home in the morning. It's a long ride."

"Do you think I'm such a fool?" she burst out. "You told Giddings I should start a trousseau!"

"Was that foolish of me? Ruth, I loved you the moment I saw you and knew that for me there could be no other. Ruth, will you marry me?"

"You told him to tell me to start my trousseau!" she repeated. "Did you think me such a fool?"

"Why, I just thought—"

"You're the fool," she said, "I started it the morning after meeting you in the street."

" 'Women,' " Cherry started to quote, " 'are—' "

"For you," Ruth said sweetly, "the word has now become singular . . . so do not say 'women'!"

Showdown on the Tumbling T

CHAPTER I

DEATH TRAP

Under the slate-gray sky the distant mountains were like a heap of rusty scrap iron thrown helter-skelter along the far horizon. Nearby, the desert was the color of pink salmon and scattered with the gray of sagebrush and a few huddles of disconsolate greasewood. The only spot of green anywhere in sight was the sharp, strong green of tall pines in a notch of the rust-red mountains.

That was the place I'd come from Texas to find, the place where I was to hole up until Hugh Taylor could send word for me. It was something to have a friend like Hugh, someone to give you a hand up when the going was rough. When I had returned from Mexico to find myself a fugitive from justice, he had been the only one to offer help.

A few scattered drops of rain pounded dust from the desert. I dug into my pack for my slicker. By the time I had it on the rain was coming down in a steady downpour that looked fair to last the night through as well as the afternoon.

Rowdy, my big black, was beginning to feel the hard going of the past weeks. It was the only time I had ever seen the big horse even close to weariness, and it was no wonder. We had come out of Dimmit County, Texas, to the Apache country of central Arizona, and the trails had been rough.

The red rocks of the mountains began to take on form and line, and I could see the raw cancers of washes that ate into the face of the plain, and the deep scars of canyons. Here and there lines of gray or green climbed the creases in the rock, evidence of underlying water or frequent rains among the high peaks.

The trail curved north, skirting the mountains toward the sentinel pines. "Ride right to the Tin Cup ranch," Hugh Taylor had said, "and when you get there, ask for Bill Keys. He'll be in charge, and he'll fix you up until this blows over. I'm sure I can get you cleared in a short time."

The mountains cracked wide open on my left and the trail turned up a slope between the pines. Blue gentians carpeted both sides of the road and crept back under the trees in a solid mass of almost sky-blue. The trail was faint, and apparently used very little, but there were tracks made by two riders and I watched them curiously. The tracks were fresh and they were headed into the Tin Cup canyon.

You can bet I had my eyes open, for even so far

away from anyone that knew me there might be danger, and a man on the dodge learns to be careful.

Then I heard a shot.

It rapped out sharp and clear and final, bringing my head up with a jerk and my hand down to the stock of my Winchester. My rifle rode in a scabbard that canted back so that the stock almost touched my right thigh, and I could draw that rifle almost as fast as a man could draw a six-gun.

Rowdy heard that shot, too, and Rowdy knew what shooting could mean. He skirted the rocks that partially barred the way into the Tin Cup, and I looked down into a little valley with a stone barn and stone house, two corrals, and two riderless horses.

Then I saw the men. The air was sharp and clear, and they were only a couple of hundred yards off. There were three of them, and one was lying on the ground. The man who stood over the body looked up and yelled at the other one near the corner of the house. "No, it ain't him!" And then they both saw me.

Panic must have hit them both, but one of them made a break for his horse while the other swung his hand down for his gun. Honest men don't start shooting when a stranger rides up; so as his six-gun lifted, my rifle cleared the boot. He fired, but I wasn't worried. He was much too far away.

He made a dive for his horse and I held my fire. As he settled in the saddle I squeezed off my shot. He jerked like he was hit and I saw the gun fall from his hand into the rocks, and then they were taking out of there, but fast. They wanted no part of my shooting.

Rowdy wasn't gun-shy. With me in the saddle he had no cause to be, after all we had been through down Mexico way. That was a part of my life I never talked about much, and even Hugh, who was my best friend, knew nothing about it. To him I was still the quiet kid he had seen grow up on our uncle's ranch, the XY.

Rowdy was in no shape for a chase, so I let the riders go and swung down beside the old man and felt of his pulse. That was mostly a matter of form. No man with that last bullet hole where he had it was going to be alive. The first shot was a bit high, and I could see there had been some interval, for the blood around the first wound was coagulated.

A horse's hoof clicked on stone and I turned with my hands spread. You don't pull anything fancy when four men are looking down rifles at you.

"What did you kill him for?" The speaker was a squat, broad-chested man with a square red face and gimlet eyes. He looked tough as a winter in the mountains, and at least two of the riders with him looked fit to side with the devil on a ride through hell.

"Don't jump your fences, pardner," I told him, pretty chilly. "I didn't shoot this gent. When I rode into the Cup two hombres were standing here, one right over him. They took a shot at me, then lit out, ridin' up the valley as I came in."

"We heard shootin'," the square-faced man replied. "He's dead an' you're here."

My eyes went over them, sizing them up. Nobody needed to burn any brands on this hide for me. Here I was on the dodge from one killing of which I wasn't guilty, and now I'd run smack-dab into another. Nobody had seen those other riders but me, so what happened now depended a whole lot on just who and what these men were.

At first glance I could see there was only one man of the four who would give anybody a break. He was a young fellow with brown eyes and dark hair, and a careful look in his eyes. He looked smart and he looked honest, although a man can be fooled on both counts.

The square-built man who had done the talking seemed to be the big gee. "Who are you, anyway?" he demanded. "What brings you here?"

Something in the way he asked that question let me get downwind of an idea. I decided to tell this hombre nothing, least of all that I was Wat Bell. "Why, they call me the Papago Kid, and I'm from down Sonora way.

"As for what brings me here, it was this black horse brought me, and the trail through the pines. A lot of trails have brought me a lot of places, and"—I added this with some meaning—"when I wanted to ride out, nobody stopped me."

His eyes sharpened down and his lips thinned out.

I could see the old devil coming up in his eyes. This man was not one you could push far. He figured he was some salty, and he had no liking for being called up to the mark by any casual drifter. However, there was a funny little frown came into his eyes when I mentioned my name; and somehow the idea was there, full-size and ready for branding, that he had expected another name. That feeling was so strong in me that it started me thinking about a lot of things.

Sometimes a man rides trails and reads sign so long that he develops an instinct for things. There was the strong smell of trouble in my nostrils now, and for some reason I knew that I'd made a good bet when I told him I was the Papago Kid. The funny part of it was that if he could find a way to check back down the Sonora trail, he'd find out I hadn't lied. A man sometimes can have two names that take separate trails, and if I was young Wat Bell in Dimmit County, Texas, I was also the Papago Kid down in Sonora.

"Lynch," the young fellow interrupted, "let's get in out of this rain, and get the body in, too. I liked old Tom Ludlow, and I don't like his body lying around like this." Then he added, "We can talk just as well over some coffee, anyway."

Lynch hesitated, still not liking me, and itching for gunplay. "All right," he agreed, and turning to the other riders, a fat-faced man and a tall, stoop-shouldered rider, he added, "you two pick Ludlow's body up and cart it out to the stable. Cover it with a blanket and then come on in. Better put the horses in, too." He looked at the tall man. "Don't leave anything undone, Bill," he added.

When I heard the tall man called Bill a faint suspicion stirred in me, but I didn't look up. When I did, the fat man answered my question for me without any talking from me. "You take his feet, Keys. I'll get his shoulders."

Lynch turned abruptly toward the door of the stone house and I followed with the young fellow behind me. Inside, Lynch got out of his slicker and I got a shock. He was wearing a sheriff's badge on his vest.

"The coffee was your idea, Dolliver," Lynch suggested. "Want to start it?"

Dolliver nodded, and I knew he had seen my reaction to that badge and was curious about it. He turned toward the shelves and began taking things down as if he knew the place. In the meantime I was trying to scout my trail and read the sign of this situation I'd run into.

Hugh Taylor had told me to ride to the Tin Cup and ask for Bill Keys. Yet when I arrived here, there was a dead man on the ground who isn't Bill Keys but is apparently the owner of the place. Meanwhile, Keys appears to be riding for the sheriff and with what reason I had no idea.

It was a neat little house, tidy as an old maid's boudoir, and the smell of coffee that soon filled the room gave it a cozy, homelike feel. The fireplace was big enough, and all the cooking utensils were bright and clean. A blanket over a door curtained off an inner room.

Lynch dropped astride a chair and began to build a smoke. He had a bullet head covered with tight ringlets and a mustache that drooped in contrast. Slinging my hat on a hook, I hung up my own slicker and dropped into another chair. Lynch saw my two guns and his face chilled a little. Something about me disturbed him, and I decided it was partly the guns—the fact that I was wearing them, not that he feared them.

"You call yourself the Papago Kid?" Lynch's question was sharp.

My eyes held his and I knew Sheriff Lynch and I were not going to be friends. He was distinctly on the prod, but he was digging for something, too. I was beginning to wonder if I didn't know what it was he wanted. "I've been called that," I said, "and I like the name. You can use it."

"Did you get a good look at those two riders who lit out of here? The two you said you saw?"

"I did see them. No, the look I got wasn't too good. One of them legged it for his bronc and the other grabbed iron. Naturally, with a man drawing a gun on me, even at that distance, I wasn't wasting any time looking him over."

"How many shots did you hear?"

"One."

Dolliver turned around from the coffee. "I heard three."

"That's right," I agreed. "One shot apparently killed the old man. Then I rounded into sight and one of these hombres took a shot at me. I shot back." I hitched my chair back a little. "However, as you no doubt saw, the old man was shot twice. I figure he was wounded someplace away from the ranch, then trailed down by the killers, who finished the job."

"What gives you that idea?" Lynch demanded.

"If you noticed, Sheriff," I said, "the rain hadn't washed out the old man's tracks. Those tracks came from toward the corrals, and even from where I stood I could see the old man had fallen down twice on that little slope, and there were blood spots on his clothes."

It was obvious enough that the sheriff had seen nothing of the kind, and he studied me carefully. I was doing some thinking on my own hook. The reason the sheriff hadn't seen those tracks was because all his attention had been centered on me.

Dolliver, whose attitude I liked, brought the coffee up to the table and filled our cups. He was a clean-cut youngster and no fool.

The door opened then and Bill Keys came in with his fat friend. They knocked the rain from their hats and shed their slickers, both of them looking me over while they were doing it. Dolliver filled cups for them and they found chairs and sat down.

It struck me as faintly curious that Sheriff Lynch was making no effort to trail the men I had mentioned, nor to see if there were tracks to back up my story. I wondered what Dolliver thought of that, and was glad that he was with us. This was new country for me, and I was definitely in a bad spot, and unless the breaks came my way I'd soon have the choice of shooting my way out or I'd find myself looking into my past through the leaves of a cottonwood with the loop end of a rope around my neck.

"You ever been in this country before?" Lynch demanded.

"Never. When I left my home in California, I crossed Arizona down close to Yuma and went into Mexico."

"How'd you happen to find this place? It ain't the easiest valley to find." He stared at me suspiciously, his eyes trying to pry behind my guileless eyes. I was wearing my most innocent face, carefully saved for just such emergencies.

"Did you ever cross that desert behind here?" I asked. "The only spot of green a man can see is right here. Naturally, I headed for the pines. Figured there might be people where there was water."

That was simple enough even for him, and he mulled over it a little. "You said you came from California? You sound like a Texan to me."

"Hell," I grinned cheerfully, "it's no wonder! On the last spread I rode for down Mexico way there were eight Texans. My folks spoke Spanish around home," I lied, "so when I talked English with that Texas outfit, naturally I picked up their lingo."

The story was plausible enough, but Lynch didn't like it. He didn't get a chance to ask any more questions for a minute, as I beat him to it. "What's up, Sheriff?" I asked. "Is this a posse? And if it is, why ⸻ ⸻ ⸻ ⸻?"

Lynch didn't like that, and he didn't like me. "Huntin' a Texas outlaw supposed to be headed this way," he said, grudgingly, "a murderer named Wat Bell. We got word he was headed west so we're cuttin' all the trails."

"Bad weather to be riding," I sympathized, "unless you're on a red-hot trail. Is this Bell a bad hombre? Will it take four of you?"

Dolliver's eyes were shrewd and smiling. "I'm not one of them," he told me. "I have a little ranch just over the mountain from here, and joined these boys back in the pines when they headed this way. My ranch is the Tumbling T."

CHAPTER II
PUZZLE ON THE TUMBLING T

Lynch ended his questions and devoted himself to his coffee. From the desultory conversation that followed while Lynch mulled things over, I learned that the dead man, old Tom Ludlow, had owned the Tin

Cup, and had no enemies that anybody knew. Win Dolliver was his nearest neighbor, and liked the old man very much, as had his sister, Maggie Dolliver.

The nearest town was Latigo, where Sheriff Ross Lynch had his office. The fat rider was Gene Bates, but nothing more was said about Wat Bell or what made the sheriff so sure he could find him that he started out on a rainy day. Knowing the uncertainties of travel in the West, and the liking of sheriffs for swivel chairs, I had a hunch that somebody had tipped the sheriff. It was less than reasonable to suppose he would start out with two men in bad weather merely on the chance that the man he sought was coming to Arizona.

Lynch looked up suddenly. "We'll be ridin' on into Latigo," he said, "and I reckon you'd better come along."

"Are you arresting me?"

His blue eyes turned mean again. He didn't like me even a little bit. "Not necessarily," he said, "but we'll be wantin' to ask you questions, an' we'll be gettin' answers."

"Look, my friend." I leaned forward just a little, and having my hands on my hips as I did, the move put my gun butts practically in my palms. "I'm not planning to get stuck for something somebody else did. You rode down here and for some reason assumed I was the guilty man. Anyway, you're all set on taking me in.

"You made no effort, and I'll leave it to Dolliver

here, to check my story. You've sat here while the rain washed or partly washed those tracks away. You made no effort to get after those killers.

"You claim you're hunting some killer named Wat Bell, yet when you got here all the ambition seemed to leave you. Mr. Sheriff, I'm not your man. I didn't kill Tom Ludlow. I never saw him before. I have all the money I need, and a better horse than any of you ride. Ludlow had nothing at all that I could want. The only shot I've fired was from my rifle, and Ludlow was shot with a pistol, and that last one was fairly close up."

Lynch looked ugly. "I know what I'm doin'!" he stated flatly. "I've got my reasons!"

This looked like a good time to let them in on something. How anxious they were for gunplay, I didn't know. I did know that I stood a much better chance right here than on the trail. I'd a sudden hunch that might be haywire as could be, but it might be correct. I'd a hunch Lynch had been told Wat Bell was coming right to the Tin Cup. I'd a further hunch that Wat Bell was not supposed to leave this ranch alive, and also that while Lynch now had doubts that I was Wat Bell, he was very apt to gun me down once I was on the road with the three of them.

"All right!" I said, "you've got your reasons! Well, I have mine for not going into Latigo with you! I don't wear two guns just for fun, and if those two shots had been fired at Ludlow by me he'd never have come back to this ranch. If you want to call my bluff and see whether I savvy guns or not, just buy chips in my game and you'll see!"

He was madder right then than a wildcat in a swarm of bees, but he wasn't very happy about the spot he was in. Ross Lynch was not yellow, not by a jugful, but I knew there were several things about this setup he didn't like. The presence of Win Dolliver, who I now knew had joined him by accident, was one of them. Another was the fact that I said I was the Papago Kid. That name meant nothing to him. But if, as I now believed, he had been tipped off that Wat Bell was coming to this ranch, then I had confused the issue enough so that he wasn't sure who I was.

Also, he was no fool. He had seen those two guns, and the guns had seen use. If we cut our dogs loose in this cabin, somebody was going to get hurt besides me. Nobody knew that better than Lynch.

Dolliver smoothed things over. He was a smart hombre, that one. "There's something to what he says, Ross. After all, why should we suspect him? It could just as easily have been me who found Ludlow. I was headed this way when I met you boys.

"We should have looked for those tracks, too. I'm honest to say that I never thought of it." He turned to me. "Did you hit the man you shot at?"

"Burned him, I think. His horse was moving. I held my fire, but it was the best chance I had." Right then I decided to say nothing about the gun the rider had dropped, but to have a look the first chance I got. That gun might be a clue that would help me ferret out the answer to this deal.

Lynch was getting ready to say something, and I was sure I wouldn't like it. Dolliver interrupted. "Look, Ross," he said quietly, "don't blame the Kid here for being on the prod. You can't blame him, riding into a deal like this. He certainly could have no reason to shoot Ludlow. Let him come on over to my place with me. I can use a hand for a few days, and when you want to see him, ride over. That will clear this situation up, and I think Papago will agree to work for me. I'll pay him top hand's wages."

"That's good for me," I agreed. "I'm not hunting trouble. I'll do all I can to find that killer, and if you want, I'll try to trail those men for you. I've ridden trails before," I added, and I pointed this one right at Lynch, "and found out right where they ended."

Lynch didn't like it, but no more than any other man did he have a stomach for gunplay in that close quarters. The presence of Win Dolliver was a big help, and allowed him a chance to back out and save face.

The same questions kept coming into my mind. How had they learned Wat Bell was headed this way? Why had Hugh Taylor told me to ask for Bill Keys on the Tin Cup when it was owned by Ludlow? Who had killed the old man, and why?

Bill Keys was another puzzle. Taylor had said the man could be trusted, but he didn't size up right to me. How good a description did he have of me? Or did he have one at all? Hugh might not have known him so well, and could have been mistaken in trusting him. For one, I was doing no talking until I understood the lay of the land.

Something else had come into my mind that somehow I'd never thought of before. When Hugh Taylor had met me that night and told me of my uncle's murder, and that I was wanted for it, I had thought of little else. True, I had left town rather suddenly after a quarrel with old Tom Bell, but that he had been murdered on the night I left for Mexico, I'd had no idea until then. Hugh had showed me the reward poster, but had assured me that he didn't believe me guilty. He had investigators working on the crime, and advised me to go away and stay in hiding until he sent for me.

My mind was full of questions. Had my uncle left a will? And to whom had he left two hundred thousand acres of his ranch? And who **had** killed him?

Bill Keys got up and turned toward the door and my eyes dropped to his gun, absently noting that a chip had been broken from the bone handle, and the break looked recent. Sheriff Ross Lynch and Bates followed him out, and then Dolliver and I. When he rode around the corner of the house, Keys was saddling a horse with which to carry the body into town.

Once around the house, I slid from the saddle and scrambled into the rocks. A hasty look showed me only one thing. The gun was gone!

Win Dolliver looked at me curiously, but said nothing until we were well along the trail to the Tumbling T. It was just six miles, and Dolliver talked pleasantly and easily of the country, the cattle, and the rain. Ludlow had been running only about six hundred head, while he had four times that many. Keys and Bates, holding a ranch in partnership, ran a few head over west.

When we were in sight of his own ranch, Win turned. "Did you get a good look at those riders? Enough to know them again?"

"No," I admitted, realizing this was the first pointed question he had asked, and wondering what was behind it, "but one of them lost a gun back there. When I looked it was gone."

"Maybe you just didn't find it?"

"No, I saw where it had been. There was a boot track near it."

We didn't say anything more right then because the door opened and a girl stepped out on the porch and I forgot everything I had been thinking and all that had happened.

There is no description for a girl like that. It was simply that this was the girl I had been looking for all my life. It wasn't a matter of eyes nor hair, although hers were beautiful; it was simply that here she was, the girl that was meant for me. She was trimly shaped and neat, and there was quick laughter in her eyes, and there was interest and appraisal, too.

"Mag," Dolliver said, swinging down, "meet the

Papago Kid. He's riding through the country and has had a little trouble with Ross Lynch."

"That's nothing against him on the T!" Maggie Dolliver replied with spirit. "You know what I think of Ross!"

Win chuckled. "Everybody should, after the way you told him off at the last Latigo dance! But what about Howie Taber?"

She flushed, and I didn't miss that. The name struck me, too. "Who did you say?" I asked.

"Taber. He is a partner of Lynch's in a ranch they have out here. At least Taber owns the ranch and Lynch runs the cows when he's not working at being sheriff. Pretty well off, Taber is. And he made quite a play for Maggie when he was out here last."

Maggie made better coffee than Win, I found, and her cookies were wonderful. I listened mostly, and answered a few random questions about Mexico. Then I started in, and asked my first question. "What about Keys? Who is he?"

"Keys?" The question puzzled Dolliver. "Frankly, I don't like the man. He ranches some with Bates, as I said, and he and Lynch are thicker than thieves. There's a story around that he ran with that horse-stealing outfit down in the Bradshaws, but I wouldn't know how true it is. He's also supposed to be something of a gun hawk. He has killed one man I know of—a drifter in Latigo."

Maggie looked at me curiously; then a thought

seemed to occur to her and she turned to Win. "What I can't understand is why anyone would want to kill a nice old man like Uncle Tom Ludlow!"

"It was a mistake," I said, repeating what I had overheard when I rode up on the killers. "I think they were looking for someone else."

"But who?" Win puzzled. "And why?"

"I think," I said deliberately, "they were looking for me. I think they saw a rider at the expected place and shot him, then finished him off to prevent him talking when they found their mistake."

"But who was it they were after?" Maggie demanded.

"Me," I repeated dryly. "I think they wanted me."

Moreover, I told myself, if they had wished to kill me and had failed, they would surely try again. Had they been sure that I was Wat Bell rather than the Papago Kid, they would have insisted I go to town with them, and shot me, "trying to escape" on the way in. As it was, probably Win Dolliver's presence had saved me at first sight.

"Don't take what I said about working too seriously," Win volunteered, after a moment. "My main idea was to get you away from Lynch without a fight. He's tough, and he didn't like you. I could see that. Dangerous as he is, I think you've more to fear from Bill Keys."

Neither of them asked me any questions, nor why I believed it had been me the killers wanted. Whatever their reason for inviting me here, and I was convinced there was a reason, they asked no questions and offered no information.

CHAPTER III
PAPAGO MAKES A HAND

Nevertheless, I was up at daybreak with the hands, ate breakfast with them and with Win, and rode out to work with them. Later in the morning when Maggie came out to join us, I overheard him tell her, "Whatever else he may be, Mag, he's a hand. He's done more work than any two of the regular boys."

Maybe it was because these cedar brakes were a pipe after brush-popping down in the Big Bend, where I had worked two years, but I did get a lot done. And maybe because it was good to have a rope in my hands and a cow by the tail instead of only a gun. Yet all the time I worked, my mind was busy, and it didn't like what seemed to be truth.

A lot of loose ends were beginning to find their way to a common point, and I had begun to see that in skipping out of Texas I had made a big mistake. Hugh Taylor, aside from being my cousin, was also my friend, or so I had believed. From anyone but him I would never have taken the advice he had given.

Hugh Taylor had run off from the ranch where we

were growing up when he was sixteen, and returned again after four years. After being around a year, he took off again, and returned some months later with money and a silver-mounted saddle. He was bigger than I, and rugged. He was also two years older. A top hand at anything he did, he stood high in my uncle's esteem.

Yet I'd worked on at the ranch, never leaving, punching cows, mending fence, riding herd. I had taken two herds north over the trail, and I'd had a gunfight in Abilene, and killed my man. I wasn't proud of that, and as only a few of the trail hands returned, and they promised not to talk, nobody around the XY knew. Later, when I was down in the Big Bend with a bunch of cattle, we had trouble with Mexican bandits, and I went into their camp, brought back some stolen horses, and did it without firing a shot.

Finally, when I was twenty-four, Uncle Tom and I had a big argument, and I got mad and lit out for Mexico. Crossing the border, I didn't want to be known as Uncle Tom Bell's nephew, so I called myself the Papago Kid. Riding through Coahuila to Durango, I had several fights, and then, moving up into Sonora, I tied up with old Valverdes and protected his ranch against bandits. While there I had two more gunfights, one with a Mexican gunman, the other with an American.

Then, after being away two years, I had returned

across the border and the first person I'd met was Hugh. At the time it seemed a stroke of luck, and I remember how startled he was to see me.

"You here, Wat?" he had exclaimed. "Don't you know you're wanted for murder?"

That got me, and in reply to my heated questions, he told me that the night of our quarrel Uncle Tom had been shot and killed, that I was sought as the killer, but a story had returned to the XY that I had been killed by bandits in Mexico.

"Your best bet is to get out of here," he told me. "Ride west to Arizona. I've some friends out there, and in the meantime I'll do what I can to straighten this up."

So my uncle was dead, and they believed I had killed him. I hadn't, but somebody else had, and who was that somebody? Also, what kind of a deal had Hugh sent me into at the Tin Cup? I arrive to find a man murdered, and the sheriff hunting a "Texas outlaw" known as Wat Bell—and knowing exactly where to find him and when.

That last didn't make sense until I began to remember my last stop before getting there. It had been in Lincoln, New Mexico, and I had stopped there with a friend of Hugh Taylor's. Now if that friend had wired Sheriff Lynch, and Lynch had done a little figuring as to miles a day, it would not be too hard to arrive at the day of my arrival at the Tin Cup—a sufficiently secluded spot for murder.

Uncle Tom Bell had no relatives anyone knew of

but Hugh and myself, so he would naturally leave his two hundred thousand acres to us, and if one of us died, then the other would inherit everything. I didn't like to think that of Hugh, but he had been a little greedy, I remembered, even as a youngster.

A few discreet inquiries around proved that nobody had ever heard of Hugh Taylor, yet Taylor knew people here, and they knew him. I was still studying about that when Mag loped her pony over to where I sat my horse, watching the herd we'd bunched.

"Win tells me you're a hand!" she said, smiling at me. "I hope you decide to stay. He likes you, and it will be lonesome for him after I leave."

That hit me hard. I turned in my saddle. "After you leave? Then you're going away?"

She must have seen something in my face because hers suddenly changed and the smile went out of it. "I . . . I'm going to be married," she said quietly.

That was all. Neither of us had another thing to say right then. For me, she had said it all. If in all the world there was a girl for me, this was the one. I wanted her as I never had wanted anything. But I was just the Papago Kid, and a fugitive from the law.

What she was thinking I have no idea, but she didn't look happy. We just sat there watching the herd until it started to move. There were enough men to handle it and I made no move to follow.

"You're quiet," she said finally. "You don't say any-thing."

"What can I say?" I asked her honestly enough. "You've just said it all."

She didn't act mystified and want an explanation, for she knew as well as I what I meant and how I felt. She did finally say something, and it was so much what a lot of girls would have said that it enabled me to get my feet on the ground again. She said, "You've only known me a few hours."

"How long does it take? Is there a special time, or something? A special set of rules that says flatly a man has to know a girl three weeks, seventeen hours and nine minutes before he can fall in love with her? And another set that says she must know him six months, four hours and five minutes before she can admit she likes him?

"There isn't any time limit and there never has been," I told her. "To some people it comes quick, to others slow. With me it was the minute you walked out on the porch back there, and I rode into the yard. That's exactly when it was. The rest doesn't matter."

My voice wasn't a lover's voice. It was pretty sharp and hard because I felt just that way. Then it hit me all of a sudden and I could see it plain as day. "Well, at least he didn't steal you!"

She looked up quickly, her eyes going wide with surprise. "Steal me? Who?"

"Hugh Taylor," I said.

"Who?" She looked puzzled and a little frightened. "What do you mean?"

"I mean Howie Taber—the one who was a friend

of Lynch's, only his name is Hugh Taylor, and he's my cousin."

"Your cousin?" She was staring at me now, but there was not so much surprise in her eyes as I had expected. "What are you talking about?"

"I'm talking about a big blond and handsome man with broad shoulders and deep-set blue eyes, a man with a small scar on the point of his chin, who rides good horses and wears flashy clothes and handles a gun well. That's who I mean. A man who is my cousin but who could easily have called himself Howie Taber."

Her face was white now, but she was staring right through me. "And what is your name?" she demanded.

"I'm Wat Bell," I told her. "I am the man Lynch was looking for at the Tin Cup, and how did he know I'd be there? Only one man in all the world knew it, and that man was Hugh—who I thought was my best friend."

"I don't believe that," she said. "I don't believe any of it. You may know him, but you're an outlaw, masquerading under a false name. You've made all this up."

"All right," I said, "I made it up!" With that I reined my horse around and started back for the T. If I had been riding Rowdy I'd never have gone back at all, but this was a cowhorse I'd borrowed, wanting to save the big black after his long trek across country.

There was only one thing in my mind then, to get

Rowdy and hit the trail out of there, but fast. And where to? Back to Texas! To prove that I hadn't killed my uncle. To prove that I was no outlaw.

The cowhorse I was on was a good horse and he took me over the hill to the T at a fast lope, and I came up from behind the corrals and hit the dirt, and then stopped. Right there across the yard from me was Ross Lynch, and beside him was Gene Bates. Win Dolliver was on the step, and his face looked dark as death and just as solemn. Lynch stepped out toward me and stopped. "Wat Bell!" he said. "I arrest you for murder!"

"Whose murder?" I demanded.

"The murder of Tom Ludlow!" he said. Then he smiled. "There is a charge against you in Texas, but we'll hang you for this one!"

I was mad all the way through. My hands swinging at my sides, I looked at him. "Ross Lynch, I did not murder Ludlow, and you damn' well know it. You know it because you know who did! And I know! It was—!"

Gene Bates's hand swept down for a gun and so did Lynch's. My own guns were coming up and I took a quick step forward and right and fired quickly—too quickly. My first bullet knocked the gun from the sheriff's hand, and I hadn't intended it that way. I wanted to kill him. The second one took Gene Bates right over the belt buckle.

Win Dolliver hadn't moved. He stood there on the steps, his eyes wide. But what he thought he wasn't saying. I don't know where Maggie was. On the bunkhouse steps were two of the boys and another one stood at the corral. He turned to his saddle pockets and dug out a box of .44s. "Catch!" he said simply, and tossed it.

"Thanks!" I caught the box in my left hand and backed toward the corral. Lynch was holding his numbed hand and staring at me.

"I'll kill you for this!" he said. "I'll kill you if it's the last thing I do!"

"If you do, it will be!" I told him. Astride the cowpony, I looked at Win. "Thanks, Dolliver. You've been mighty square. Tom Ludlow was killed by Gene Bates and Bill Keys. That chip on the bone-handle of Keys's gun was broken off when it fell into the rocks, you know where!"

Then I reined my horse around and hit the trail at a fast run.

THAT PONY HAD WORKED HARD, but he was game. He stayed with that run until he hit timber, and then I slowed him down to a canter, and then to a walk. After that I began to Injun my trail. I took so many twists and turns I was dizzy, and I rode up and down several streams, across several shelves of rock and through some sand. And then I doubled back and headed for the Tin Cup.

My horse wouldn't go far and he needed rest. I needed food. There was food in the cabin, and every chance they wouldn't think of it right away. Also, it was within striking distance of the T, and I had no idea of leaving Rowdy. That big black horse meant a lot to me, and ever since old Valverdes gave him to me, I'd treated him like a child.

Now I was an outlaw, having resisted arrest, the first crime I'd committed. But if I could prove that Bates and Keys had killed Ludlow, and with the sheriff's knowledge, I'd be in the clear even on that. And it was something I intended to prove.

From the expression on Lynch's face I knew that shooting of mine had been a distinct shock. Hugh hadn't warned them about that simply because he didn't know. Hugh had always beaten me in shooting matches. That was before I went to Mexico. He had probably told Lynch I was only a fair shot. Well, the shooting that knocked the gun from his hand and drilled Bates had been good shooting, the kind he wouldn't be too anxious to tackle again.

By sundown I was bedded down in the pines watching the Tin Cup ranch house. All through the final hours of daylight I watched it and studied the trails. I wanted no traps laid for me, although I doubted if they would think of the Tin Cup right away.

It was well after midnight before I started down the trail to the ranch, and I took my horse only a short distance, then left him tied in the brush and cat-footed it down by myself, leaving my spurs on the horn of my saddle.

Nothing looked very good right then. I had killed

Gene Bates and resisted arrest. Hugh Taylor, whom I'd considered my best friend, had tried to trap me into an ambush, and Maggie Dolliver, the girl I wanted more than anything in life, was in love with Hugh. Right then I'd about as little to live for as any man, but I'd a lot of resentment—nor was I one to bow my head before the storm and ride off letting well enough alone.

When I did ride off it would be with my name clear, and also I would know and the world would know who had killed Uncle Tom Bell. Until then I had a job to do.

The warm sun of the late afternoon had baked the ground hard after the rain, and I moved carefully. The stone house was dark and still when I tried the door, and it eased open without a sound. Once inside I wasted no time, for while Win had been making coffee on the day of the killing, I had seen where the food was kept. Hastily, I reached for the coffee sack. It was almost empty!

Puzzled, for it had been nearly full when I last saw it, I reached for the beans, and they were gone. And then there was a whisper of movement behind me and I turned, palming my gun as I moved.

"Don't shoot!" The voice was low, but the very sound of it thrilled me so that I couldn't have squeezed a trigger if I'd wished. "The food is on the table, all packed."

"Mag! You did this . . . for me?" I couldn't believe that, and moved around the table toward her. She had been in that inner room, waiting behind the blanket-covered door.

"Yes." The word was simple and honest. "I did it for you, and I've no idea whether I'm doing right or not. Maybe all they say about you is true. Maybe you did kill your uncle and maybe you did kill Tom Ludlow."

"You don't believe that?"

"No." She hesitated. "No, I don't believe I do. I know Ross Lynch, Wat—that is your name, isn't it? He has been mixed up in so many wrong things. It was the only fault I could find with Howie—that he trailed with Lynch and that devil, Bill Keys."

In the darkness I could not see her eyes, but suddenly my hands lifted to her shoulders. "Mag," I said softly, "I've got to ride out of here. Whatever else I do, I've got to clear myself, and I'm going to do it, an' if the trouble strays over on somebody else's range, I'm going to follow it there.

"I could go away now, taking the blame for Old Man Ludlow like they've already hung the blame on me for Uncle Tom, but I won't do it. I won't have you doubting me, even if I never see you again. Nor do I want folks to think I've killed Uncle Tom, after he did so much for me."

She didn't say anything for a moment, and with her arms all warm under my hands it was all I could do to keep from drawing her close. Finally, she spoke. "Do what you have to do, Wat. I know how you feel."

"But, Mag, suppose that somebody you— Well, I mean, suppose that when I find who did this killing, I find it was somebody close to you. What then?"

She looked up at me again. "Why, then, Wat, it would have to be that way. I guess I knew you felt like this, I knew who you believed was guilty, but I came here and got this food ready for you, sure that you'd come. I brought your horse, too, Wat. He's in the shadow by the stable."

"Rowdy?" My voice lifted, then lowered. "You did that? Oh, you darlin'! Now I'll feel like a man again! This pony, he tries hard and he's got a great heart, but he's not Rowdy."

"I knew how you felt about him." She drew back. "Now you'd better go. Ride out of here, and good luck, whatever you do, or whatever comes!"

CHAPTER IV

HORSETHIEF VALLEY

That was just the way I left, with that pack over my shoulder, slipping out to find Rowdy, who nudged me with his nose and stamped contentedly. But I waited there until she was on her horse and gone, and then I slid into the saddle and headed for the hills. When I got to where I'd left the pony, I tied the bridle reins up and turned him loose, knowing he'd find his way back to the T.

Already I'd had an idea. Bill Keys had come from

the Bradshaws, and that was where I was heading, right for Horsethief Valley. There had to be a tie-up there. Nor was I waiting until morning. Rowdy was rested and ready for the trail, and I took it, riding west across the mountains, skirting Latigo, and heading on west. On the third night I camped at Badger Spring, up a creek from the canyon of the Agua Fria, and after a quick breakfast in the morning, crossed the Bumblebee and Black Canyon and headed up the Dead Cow. Skirting the peak on a bench I cut down the mountainside into Horsethief Canyon.

Western men knew the West, and it was no wonder that even as far east as Dimmit County, Texas, we knew about the horsethief trails that cut through the country from Robber's Roost and the Hole in the Wall to Mexico. This place was only a way station, but from all I'd heard I knew some of the crowd that trailed stolen horses, and they were a hard bunch of men.

Rowdy had a feeling for trouble. The big black pricked his ears toward the ramshackle cluster of cabins and corrals that lay on the flat among the mountains. Nobody needed to tell me that we were not watched all the way down that trail, and when Rowdy drew up in front of the combination saloon and store that was the headquarters at Horsethief, a half-dozen men idled on the steps.

Across at the big barn a man sat on a bench with a Henry rifle across his knees, and another man whittled idly in front of a cabin even farther along.

When I swung down I tied Rowdy to the rail and stepped up on the porch and dug out the makings. "Howdy," I offered.

A lean, hatchet-faced man, who looked the type to murder his mother-in-law, looked up. "Howdy."

Nobody said anything and when I'd built a smoke I offered the tobacco around, but nobody made a move to accept. A short, stocky rider with run-down heels on his boots squatted against the wall. He looked up at me, then nodded at Rowdy. "Quite a hoss. Looks like he could make miles."

"He made 'em to here." I looked at Shorty again. "Want a drink? I'll buy."

He got up with alacrity. "Never refused a drink!" he warned me. We pushed through the doors and bellied up to the bar. There was a smell of cured bacon, dry goods, and spices curiously intermingled. I glanced around the store, and sized up the fat man in the dirty shirt who bounced around to the bar side and made a casual swipe at the bar top with a rag.

"What'll it be, gents?"

Shorty chuckled. "He says 'what'll it be' ever'time, an' he ain't had nothing but Injun whiskey over this bar in a year!"

Fatty was indignant. "Injun whiskey, my eye!" he exploded. "This here's my own make, an' mighty good rye likker if I do say so! Injun whiskey!" he snorted. "You've been drinkin' out of horse tracks an' buffalo wallers so long you don't know a good drink when you get one!"

He placed two glasses on the bar and a bottle. Shorty poured for them both, but Fatty reached for the bottle as he put it down. "Leave the bottle," I told him, "we'll want another." I placed a gold piece on the bar, and Fatty picked it up so fast it looked like a wink of light.

"Better not flash that coin around if you've got more of it," Shorty warned. "Especially when Wolf Kettle is around. He's the hombre you talked to out yonder, an' while Davis is away, he's ramroddin' the outfit."

"Things look kind of slow," I suggested.

"They sure are!" Shorty's disgust was evident. "Nothing doing at all! From what we hear there's to be something big movin' soon, but you can't tell. Where you from?"

"Down Sonora way. They call me the Papago Kid."

"Shorty Carver's my handle." He looked up at me. "Sonora, is it? Well, I sure figured I knew you." He spoke softly all of a sudden. "I'd of sworn you were an hombre I saw sling a gun up to Dodge, one time. An hombre name of Wat Bell, from a Texas outfit."

"If you think I look like him," I suggested, "forget it. He might not like the resemblance!"

Shorty laughed. "Sure thing! You can be anybody you want with me. What's on your mind? You wantin' to join up?"

"Not exactly. I'm huntin' a couple of friends of mine. Bill Keys and an hombre named Taber."

Shorty Carver's face hardened. "You won't find

'em here, an' if they are friends of yours, sure you'd better hunt another sidekick than me. That Taber an' I didn't get along."

I took a sidelong look at Shorty. "He's been here then?"

"Been here?" Shorty looked around at me. "He was here yesterday!"

"What?"

My question was so sharp that a half-dozen heads turned our way, and I lowered my voice. "Did you say—**yesterday**?"

"Sure did! He rode in here about sunup, an' him an' Davis had a long confab. Then Davis takes off for Skull Valley, and where Taber went, I don't know. He rode out of here, headin' east."

For several minutes I didn't say a word. If Hugh was out here, that meant the time for a showdown had come. Yet what had I found? Nothing to date that would help. That Hugh Taylor had been known to the outlaws of Horsethief Canyon was something, but not much.

Right then I began to wonder for the first time about those absences from the ranch when Hugh was growing up. And that time he had returned with that silver-mounted saddle and a good bit of money. It was becoming more apparent where that money had come from. Had Uncle Tom Bell guessed? He was a sharp old man, and had not ridden the trails and plains for nothing. He could read sign wherever it was . . . and here was another thought: perhaps he had read the truth and guessed at what lay behind those absences and jumped Hugh about it.

Had Hugh killed his uncle?

There was enough of the old feeling for Hugh left to make me revolt at the idea, and yet it began to seem more and more possible. Uncle Tom and I had a violent quarrel and I left. What would be easier than to kill him and let me take the blame? Hugh's surprise at my sudden return could have come from his consternation at what it might mean to him, and also he might have believed those rumors that I had been killed in Mexico.

Certainly, he managed to get me out of the country without seeing anyone else.

The swinging doors shoved wide and Kettle came in. He took a sidelong glance at me and walked up to the bar at my side and ordered a drink. I could smell trouble coming and could see there was something in Kettle's craw.

He got his drink and turned to me. "We don't welcome strangers here!" he said. "State your business, an' ride on out!"

That turned me around, but I took my time. The man irritated me, and I didn't feel like side-stepping trouble. I was tired of running and ready for a showdown, and ready to back it with lead. "Kettle," I said clearly, "I didn't come in here to see you. I never heard of you. You may run a big herd where you come from, but where I ride that herd looks like mighty small gathering!"

His face darkened a little, and the yellow lights in his eyes were plainer. He half-turned before I spoke, but I gave it to him fast. "Don't try to run any blazers on me, Kettle, because they won't stick. If you make rough talk with me, it's gun talk, and if you draw on me, I'll kill you!"

Shorty Carver had stepped wide of me and was standing there facing the room. What his play would be, I couldn't know. He was a friend of only a few minutes, yet there had been some spark of comradeship there such as one often finds with men of the same ilk and the same background. He spoke before either of us could make a move. "He came to see Taber and Keys," Shorty warned, "they sent for him!"

"What?" Carver's statement obviously stopped Kettle. "How do you know that?"

"Because I told him," I said simply.

He glared at me suspiciously. Something was gnawing at the man, and it might be something about me, but I had the feeling that he was naturally mean, a trouble hunter, a man with a burr under his saddle. "Where'd you know Taber?" he demanded.

"In Texas," I said calmly, "and I knew Bill Keys in Sonora." That last was sheer hope, for whether Keys had ever been below the border, I didn't know.

"He's the Papago Kid," Carver said.

"Never heard of him!" Kettle returned sharply.

Another man spoke up, a lean-faced man with a drooping black mustache. "I have," he said. "He's the hombre that killed Albie Dick."

Kettle's eyes sharpened, and I knew that meant something to this man. Albie Dick had been a dangerous man, and a killer with fifteen dead men on his trail when we tangled in Sonora.

"That's neither here nor there," I said calmly. "I want to talk to Howie Taber!"

"You'll have to wait," Kettle said grudgingly. "He ain't here."

Somehow, the men relaxed. Shorty returned to the bar and took another drink. Under his breath, he warned, "You'd better watch yourself. Wolf was never braced like that before. He'll be careful to make his play at the right time, but you've got trouble. The man's mean as a rattler."

He downed his drink. "Also," he added, "I'm beginning to remember things. That Wat Bell who downed that man in Abilene was ramrodding an XY herd . . . and that's the ranch we're going to use in Texas!"

"What do you mean? Going to use?"

He looked at me quickly, sharply. "So? You don't know the inside on this, do you?" He was silent, tracing circles on the bar with the bottom of his glass. "Just what is between you and Taber, Kid?"

That was a sticker, and I hesitated. Shorty had said earlier that he had no use for Taber. Right then I knew my time here was short, and a friend would be a help. Another enemy would be little worse. "Taber's my cousin," I said frankly, speaking low. "I think he killed my uncle and framed me with the murder while I was in Mexico. Furthermore, I think he sent me out here to lay low and planned to have me murdered when I arrived."

Quietly, I explained in as few words as possible and from time to time he nodded. "Glad you told me," he said. "Also there's no posters on Wat Bell out here, so you must be right on figuring that Lynch was out to get you."

"No posters on me? How do you know that?"

He grinned, and he said softly, "Because I'm a Cattle Association detective, pardner, an' I'm studyin' into the biggest steal of horses an' cattle ever organized!"

Together we walked outside, and the story he told me answered a lot of questions. For several years a steady stream of stolen stock had been sent south over the old horsethief trail from the Hole in the Wall and Robber's Roost to Mexico, and this valley was one of the important way stations. Lately, it had become apparent that even larger things were in the wind, for a man lately associated with the gang had suddenly become owner of a Panhandle ranch in Texas. There was a reported tie-up with the XY in central southern Texas, and large quantities of stock had begun to disappear and move south toward the border. It had begun to look as if mass stealings of stock had begun, moving south under cover and with large ranches as way stations.

"Who's behind it?" I asked him. "Any guesses on that?"

"Uh-huh. There is." Shorty Carver lit a smoke. "Howie Taber's behind it. That cousin of yours has turned out to be the brains of the biggest stock-stealing ring in the country."

From the time he was sixteen until he was twenty, Hugh Taylor had been absent from the XY. He had gone again shortly after, and obviously, he had been gone at least once during the time I was in Mexico. It was then, no doubt, that he had begun to round up old cronies of his earlier days and build the ring that Carver now told me about.

"Shorty," I said, "can you slip out of here?"

"Uh-huh."

"Then wire the sheriff in Dimmit County. See if I'm really wanted there for murder. Also, check on Tom Bell's will, see who that XY spread was left to when he died. I'm having a talk with that cousin of mine!" I hesitated, thinking. "See you at the Tin Cup!"

"Watch your step!" Shorty warned. "Hugh isn't so bad, but you watch Bill Keys and Kettle!"

CHAPTER V

POWER OF THE PAPAGO KID

After he was gone, I idled around, getting the lay of the land and thinking things over. It was well along in the afternoon, and night soon to come. By this time Hugh would know that I was still alive, that the plot to get me at the Tin Cup had failed. Evidently, the Tin Cup had been chosen because of its secluded position, and Lynch and Keys had been informed by the friend where I had stopped last that I was coming. Accordingly, they had evidently waited. It might be that I had been spotted and reported at several places since then, and they had come out to meet me, either at the Tin Cup or on the trail near there.

Probably they had managed to get Ludlow away from his ranch, or had reason to believe he would be away. Then they had either killed him by mistake, or had killed him because he returned too soon. No doubt they had plans for the Tin Cup, anyway, as the ranch was ideal for such a venture as they planned.

The jumpiness was in me now that presaged danger. I could sense it all around me, and I was restless. Every man here would be an enemy once it was realized who I was, and at any moment Bill Keys, Hugh Taylor, or Ross Lynch might ride in, and then the lid would blow off. I was surrounded by unfriendly guns, and to blast my way out would be a forlorn hope.

Mingled with the realization of my danger was an acute longing to be back with Maggie Dolliver. No woman had ever affected me as she had, and despite the fact that there was an understanding between herself and Hugh, I had the feeling that she had felt for me as I had for her. That she had brought Rowdy to me and packed the food was enough to show that she believed in me.

Time and again I walked down to the corral to talk to Rowdy. Time and again I noted exactly where my saddle was, and calculated every move it would take to resaddle him. That was something I wanted to do, but not until it was dark. To saddle him now would serve only as a warning of impending departure. I wanted them to believe that I was content to await the return of the man they knew as Howie Taber.

Yet I could feel the suspicion, and my own restlessness contributed to it. Wolf watched me sharply, his yellowish eyes rarely leaving me. Other men seemed always around, but apparently Shorty Carver had managed to slip away. Since he was accepted here, his going and coming would occasion little remark.

My thoughts kept reverting to Maggie and Win. At least Win was my friend, and it was something to have even one friend now. Once more I returned to the saloon and seated myself in a chair against the wall, careful to keep my guns clear. Evening was coming, and the sun had slipped down behind Wasson Peak and the ridges around it. All the bright glare of the Arizona sun was gone, and the desert and mountains had turned to soft pastel shades. A blue quail called out in the brush, and somewhere a burro yawned his lonely call into the cool air of twilight. A door slammed, and then I heard water splashing as someone dipped a bucket into the spring. There was a subdued murmur of voices, and the rattle of dishes. There was no hunger in me, only that poised alertness that kept my eyes moving and my every muscle and nerve aware and ready.

Casually I arose to my feet and stretched. Then, as I had a dozen times before, I sauntered carelessly down to the corral. Wolf Kettle watched me, but I ignored him, stopping near the corrals to look around. Then I stepped over and put my hand on Rowdy's neck and spoke to him. After a minute I crawled through the poles and was out of sight of Wolf or any of the others.

My movements were swift and sure. Rowdy was never bridled or saddled faster in his life, and in what seemed scarcely no time, I was sauntering back into sight, crawling once more through the corral bar. I slowly rolled a smoke, struck a match, and then ambled placidly and nonchalantly back toward the store. "Brother," I told myself, "if you get out of here with a whole skin, you're lucky."

Back in my chair I listened to the casual talk, scarcely paying attention until suddenly two horses rounded into sight. They were walking, and they came so suddenly that it was a surprise to all of us. They came from the other side of the saloon and stopped at the end of the porch opposite me.

Two men swung down. "Wolf? You got some grub ready?"

It was Hugh Taylor!

My heart pounding, I slowly lowered my hands to my knees, my eyes riveted on him.

"You'd better have!" The second man was speaking, and it was Bill Keys. "I'm hungry as a grizzly!"

It was late dusk, and no faces could be distinguished. Hugh came up on the porch, looking tall, strong, and familiar. Suddenly it was hard to think of him as being an outlaw, an enemy. I could only recall the times we went swimming together, the horses we swapped, and the times we played hooky from school and went hunting.

He happened to turn his head then, and he looked right at me. He could have seen no more than a black figure of a man, seated there, but there must have been something familiar about it. "Who's that?" His voice rang sharply.

"It's me, Hugh!" I said softly, "I figured it was about time we had a little talk."

At my voice Keys jerked like he'd been struck, and he turned. Wolf was facing me, too. The three of them ringed around me, from my extreme left to full front. On the right side, the edge of the porch, there was no one.

"You . . . ? Wat?" There was an edge of something in his voice, doubt, uncertainty or something. Maybe he was remembering, too. "We've nothing to talk about, nothing at all."

"What about Uncle Tom, Hugh? I didn't kill him. . . . Did you?"

His breath drew sharply. "We won't talk about that, Wat. Not right now. You shouldn't have come here, you know that."

"Do I, Hugh? You sent me to the Tin Cup, didn't you? Was I supposed to be killed there? Did you figure to send your own cousin, who grew up with you, to get killed?"

I knew Western men. Even the outlaws were rarely cruel men. Many of them were punchers who had rustled the wrong stock once too often, some of them were men who had been too handy with a gun, but few of them were really bad men. Rather they were often reckless and careless in a land where many men were reckless and where property rights were uncertain. Among them were, of course, killers and men of criminal instincts, yet I was playing for those others.

He didn't answer me, so I went on talking, not raising my voice, just an easy conversational tone, yet all the time every nerve was on edge.

"They killed the wrong man, Hugh, and now I'm looking into things. I've been asking questions— about Uncle Tom's will, and whether I'm really wanted for murder or not, and now I'm getting mighty curious about you."

"You're too curious." His mind seemed to be made up, and I sensed an almost regretful note. "You should never have come back from Mexico, Wat. You messed up everything when you did that. You should have stayed down there. Now you're into something that's too big for you. You're playing with company that's too fast."

"Am I?" I laughed, although there was no humor in it. "No, I'm not, Hugh. You've just continued to think of me as your kid cousin. I've covered a lot of country since then, and traveled in faster company than you'll ever know."

"That's right, boss." It was the man with the black mustache again. "This hombre is the Papago Kid. He rubbed out Albie Dick an' led the roundup of his outfit. Nobody got away."

"So the kid's grown up!" There was an edge of sarcasm in Hugh's voice. "That makes it a little better. I'd not like to be responsible for anybody taking advantage of you."

"You've still got a chance, Hugh," I said quietly. "You can break this up right now. Turn the killers of Ludlow over to the law, confess your part in this plot, and leave the country."

"Are you crazy?" He was genuinely angry now. "**You**! Giving **me** a chance!"

"Then your answer is no?" I could see that Bill Keys and Kettle were growing restive. For their taste we had talked too long, and neither of them liked the tone of it.

"You fool!" Contempt was thick in his voice. "You should never have come back from Mexico! Worse, you should have never come here! You should have hightailed it out of the country! I don't want to kill you, but there's no choice!"

There was one more thing. Nor could I resist it. "How could I leave, Hugh? I fell in love with Maggie!"

"What?" He wheeled so quickly to face toward me again that he gave me the one big break I'd needed. I went off that porch in one jump and ducked around the corner of the house. I'd never have dared chance it with Keys and Kettle having their eyes on me, but when Hugh turned he partially blocked them off. I hit the ground running and skidded into the shadow of a clump of mesquite. Then I gave out with a piercing whistle.

One shot cut the brush in reply to my whistle, but that whistle stopped them. They didn't know what it meant. It seemed like a signal and they were immediately afraid I had help nearby. It was a signal, but not for help. It was for Rowdy.

He knew what to do. On that signal he would untie himself if tied with a slip knot, or nose down corral bars. It was a trick I'd taught him, along with a dozen others.

The rattle of hoofs sounded, and I heard somebody yell, "The corral's open! Somebody's there!"

I whistled again, and the big black horse wheeled between the buildings. Somebody cracked down on me again, and that time I had enough of being the target in a shooting gallery. I glimpsed a dark form and let fly, and heard a grunt, and the sound of something falling, and then I was in the saddle and taking out across the valley.

My route was in my mind. I'd gotten it from Shorty, who knew the area. Rowdy took off down Horsethief Canyon at a dead run, then slowed and turned sharply left up a trail to the bench. We had the mountain for a background and were lost in the blackness there, and Rowdy could walk like a cat when the chips were down. We crossed the shoulder of the mountain south of the ranch and hit the head of Sycamore, and down Sycamore to the trail that ran south, running parallel to Black Canyon. Then I crossed the table to the Agua Fria again, and took off up Squaw Creek.

The advantage of darkness and the best horse was mine, and I used it. Danger would come with morning, but I was hoping that Shorty would meet me at the Tumbling T with news that was good. Whatever else happened, I would see Maggie once more, and it was worth the ride and worth the danger.

MORNING LIFTED the darkness away and brought back the sun-bright hills to view. I liked the feel of the country and the air on my face, and the feel of a good horse between my knees. Behind me was the end of something, the end of all the old days when I was a kid on the XY, of Uncle Tom Bell, crabby and lovable, but honest as the day—and Hugh, older than I, and skillful in all things. We'd never been close, and yet we'd done a lot together, as boys will, and we had grown older together. It is a sad thing to leave a friend behind, to find one you've admired changed.

When the sun was high I turned into a deep arroyo and found a wide shadow where I could swing down and strip the saddle from Rowdy. After I'd cared for him, I picketed him on a little grass, then slept for an hour. After I'd eaten, I saddled up again. The sun had bridged the space that divides morning from afternoon and, still blazing hot, had turned just a little toward the west when I started on. Altogether I'd spent nearly three hours in the arroyo.

The sun reflected from a distant flat rock, and the clouds left shadows on the desert floor. I studied the far reach of the valley and then kept to the low ground, moving in shadows of clouds and up washes and where the ground was broken, yet I saw no one. We were headed for a showdown, Rowdy and I, but it would be at the T, or maybe the Tin Cup. It would not be here.

THE TIN CUP LAY chill and quiet in the moonlight when Rowdy walked down the trail. We drew up, looking the place over, and it was still as death. The comparison came into my mind and made me shiver a little. That was striking too close to the truth.

Skirting the place warily, I seemed to detect a darker spot among the pines, and circled toward it.

Then I drew up and listened. I heard a horse stamp and blow, then stillness. Speaking to Rowdy so he would not whinny, I moved in.

A lone man was camped in the pines near a stream. Watching, I heard a light footfall, then turned. Shorty Carver was standing there on the edge of the brush. "Rolled my bed up an' laid out in the brush, myself," he said. "Figured it some safer. They might get wary of me."

He held out two wires, and shielding the flame with my hat, I struck a match and read them.

DISCHARGED MEXICAN HAND CONFESSED SLAY-
ING OF BELL. NO ONE WANTED HERE.

A distinct feeling of relief hit me, just as much for Hugh as for myself. If he had taken advantage of my absence to claim the ranch all for himself, I could not have blamed him, but if he had killed Uncle Tom . . . I ripped open the other message.

TOM BELL'S WILL LEAVES XY TO WAT BELL WHEN
HE RETURNS. BELL'S REASON WAS "HE STAYED
WITH ME AND HELPED TO BUILD IT." IN EVENT
OF BELL'S NOT RETURNING, RANCH TO GO TO
HUGH TAYLOR.

So, then I was not a fugitive, but owner of two hundred thousand acres of rangeland and a huge herd of cattle. Somehow, I couldn't find it in me to blame

Hugh too much. Probably he had believed me killed in Mexico, and that he was the owner of the XY.

This crooked business was another thing. Uncle Tom would turn over in his grave if he thought the old XY was being used as a clearing ground or holding ground for rustled stock.

"We're heading for the T," I told Carver, "you've seen these messages?"

"Read 'em when they came in," he said. "Taylor tried to have you ambushed here. That isn't a theory anymore. We've got Ross Lynch."

"Got him? Arrested?"

"Yeah, last night. There was hell to pay in Latigo. We found Ross in the hills with some rustled stock, an' he ran for it. We got him in Latigo. He confessed on his deathbed."

CHAPTER VI
THE HARD WAY OUT

Right then I knew we were in the wrong place. If Ross Lynch had been shot down and confessed, by this time Hugh would know it. So would Keys and Kettle!

In that event they would know their game was up, and that within a matter of hours they would have posses closing down on them from all sides. Which meant that Hugh Taylor would be riding to the Tumbling T!

Or would he?

"Let's ride!" I said sharply. "He'll head for the T to see Mag, or I'm off my head! Or maybe to see me for a showdown. In any event, Keys and Kettle will want to see me, an' from what I told them at Horsethief Canyon, they'll know where to come! Let's go!"

Not waiting for Shorty to saddle, I threw a leg over Rowdy and lit out over the trail to the Tumbling T. That ride was one of the fastest I ever made on a horse, and Rowdy felt like running. We took off down the trail and skirted the cliffs until I could see the moonlight on the roofs at the T. The whole place was ablaze with lights, so I slowed down. Leaving Rowdy in the shadow of the stone stable, I moved up toward the house.

It was almost daylight, and the sky was growing gray. In the ranch yard were several horses, and I could see a dark group of them standing beyond the house, and several men were loitering about. Whoever was here was on the ground in force. On cat feet, I Injuned up to the house and slid in close to a window. Inside were several people. I could see Win Dolliver, his face dark and angry, and with him was Maggie. She was as pale as he was dark, and her eyes were wide.

"He's not here and he hasn't been here in days!" Maggie was saying. "Now take your men and get out!"

"He'll come here!" That was Keys speaking. "He's gone soft on you. He told Hugh he was in love with you!"

Her eyes went to Hugh. "He said that?" Her chin lifted. "Well, all right, then! I'm in love with him!"

My heart jumped and I gripped the windowsill hard. Yet Hugh was speaking now, and I listened. "So? You sold me out, did you? You dropped me for another man?"

She turned to him. "I'm sorry, Hugh. I was intending to tell you. I was never in love with you, and you know it. I liked you, yes. You persuaded me and I listened, but I never felt sure about you, never liked the company you kept." Bill Keys laughed harshly at that. "And I hoped you'd change. You didn't.

"Then he came along, and from then on I knew there could never be anyone else."

"He beats me out of my ranch and out of my girl!" Hugh said bitterly. "That's a pretty thing!"

"I think you tried to rob him, Hugh," Maggie said, "and you tried to have him murdered!"

"I wish I had!" he complained bitterly.

"Boss," Keys interrupted, "let's get outside an' get the boys set. If he's comin', he'll be here soon."

"Hugh," Maggie warned, "if you don't take your men and leave here at once, I'll hate you!"

"Wouldn't that be awful!" Keys sneered.

Hugh Taylor turned on him. "Be still!" he said sharply. "I'll make the comments here!"

Keys's eyes narrowed angrily. "You'd better make 'em, then!" he snapped. "You've sure played hell with all your fancy figurin'! Mixin' this fancy doll into this has messed it up for sure! Take the boys an' light out of here! I'll take care of Mister Wat Bell when he comes!"

"You'd better get outside and wait until I come!" Hugh said sharply. "I don't want any comments made about Miss Dolliver!"

Bill Keys stared at Hugh, his eyes ugly with hatred. "Don't get high an' mighty, Taber, or whatever your name is! We follered you because you figured things right and we made money. This deal looked good until you got to mixin' women with it, but don't think we can't get shut of you just as quick if we decide we want to!"

Hugh Taylor turned on Keys. "Are you huntin' a showdown?" he demanded.

That was my cue to get away from that window. In three long, silent jumps I made it to the back door and eased inside. I took it easy, and no more than a word or two could have passed before I was just inside the kitchen and could hear them in the next room. Keys was on the prod, I could see that.

"Showdown?" Keys was saying. "I reckon there wouldn't be no showdown betwixt you an' me, Taber. If we're goin' to kill Wat Bell we'd better get outside. We can settle this later, but I'm tellin' you, don't go to givin' me orders! Not in that voice!"

Hugh's voice was icy. "All right, Keys! Let's go outside!"

I knew that tone! I'd heard it before, and this was a showdown whether Keys wanted it or not. He had ridden some rough trails since I'd known him, Hugh had, but I doubted that he was gun-slick enough to stack up right in a gun scrap with either Keys or Kettle.

Keys and Kettle went outside, and Hugh followed them. In a quick step I was into the room. Win wheeled at the sound of my movement, and Mag stood riveted where she was. "Wat! Oh, you mustn't be found here! Go away!"

"Win, you take care of her!" She had come right to my arms, and I was holding her close, looking over my shoulder at Dolliver. "Get a shotgun—you've got one, I know. Get all your shells. If the worst comes to the worst, stand them off with that. I'm going out there!"

"You're a fool to do that, Wat!" Win said seriously. "You won't have a chance, man!"

"No, I've got to side Hugh. They are going to kill him. He can't see it, either. He can't see that Keys wants a showdown. They've got the idea from him, most of the work and planning is done, so now Keys an' Kettle figure it's all over. They want to get rid of him."

"You'd side the man who tried to have you killed?" Win was incredulous.

I shrugged, knowing I was probably a fool. "He's my cousin. We grew up like brothers, and Uncle Tom would have liked it that way. Anyway, those men out there are my enemies as well as his."

From the door I took a quick, careful look at the yard. This was it, all right. Keys had walked a dozen feet away from Hugh and turned to face him. Wolf Kettle had strolled off to the right, at least fifty feet from Keys. They made two corners with Hugh Taylor as the point of the triangle.

Keys spoke first. "Taber, we don't like this setup. We don't like you lordin' it over us an' comin' the high an' mighty around. We don't like you takin' most of the money, either. We've decided to cut you out of the deal."

Maybe I'm cold-blooded, but I was curious. I wanted to see how much of the Bell blood there was in Hugh. For the first time in his life, so far as I knew, Hugh was called face to face, and if ever a man was called by a pair of curly wolves from the way back and rough, it was these two. What would he do? That was what I wondered.

For almost a half minute he didn't say anything, but he must have been thinking plenty, and when he spoke, I could have cheered. The hombre may have tried to frame me, he may have hit the wrong trails, but he was my cousin. "Why, sure, Bill!" he said. "You do want a showdown, don't you? And you, Kettle? Sure there's more of the coyote in you than the wolf. This is what they called giving a man the Black Spot in a story I read once. Funny thing, it was a pirate story, and I read it with Wat—a better man than either of you!"

He took a step farther toward them, his eyes shifting from one to the other. "Spread wide, aren't you? Well, I'll take one of you to hell with me, anyway!"

Their hands were poised when I stepped out of the door. As I stepped out, I spoke. "Which one do you want, Hugh? I'll take the other! I'm siding you!"

Keys's eyes lifted to me, then Kettle's. They weren't happy about this change in the situation, not even a little bit! Hugh did not turn a hair. "Take Kettle," he said, "Keys has been begging for it!"

"There's a good bit of skunk in both of them," I said calmly. "Trot out your coyote, Kettle! You asked for it!" I hit the ground with a jump, digging in both heels and drawing as I landed.

Kettle flashed a fast gun, I'll say that for him, and he dropped into a crouch snarling like the Wolf he was named for. I saw his gun wink red, and then I was walking into him, triggering my right-hand Colt.

Kettle fired and fired again, and then my second shot hit him just below the shirt pocket and he lifted up on his tiptoes and I slammed another one in for good measure. He went down, clawing at the dirt with both hands, and then I turned on my heel to see Hugh was down on his face, but struggling to get up, and Keys was cursing viciously and trying to get a gun up for one more shot.

"Drop it, Bill!" I yelled. "Drop it or take it!"

The face he turned on me was a mask of viciousness. Down he might be, and badly wounded, but he was a cornered cougar at that moment, boiling with all his innate viciousness. His gun came up, and I felt the shock of the bullet, then the report. I got my balance and lifted my gun, then fired. The shot turned him around on his knees and dropped him, but he wouldn't die.

With a lunge, he got to his feet. His shirt was soaked with blood and he stood there tottering and opened up on me with both guns. They turned into coughing, spitting flame, and I took another step straight forward and fired again, then shifted guns and slammed two more into him.

Still snarling, he took a step back, so full of lead he was top-heavy, but he stood there, cursing wickedly and glaring at me. Then his eyes seemed to glaze over, and mouthing curses, he went to the ground. I turned and took a look back at Kettle, but he was done for.

Looking up at the dark line of men near the horses, I told them, "This is it, boys! Drop your guns!"

They must have thought me completely crazy. I was hit once and maybe more, and my guns were almost empty, yet I was calling twelve hardcase riders, all of them gun handlers.

"That's right!" It was Shorty Carver from the barn. "Let go your belts easy! We've got you covered!"

"I'm holding a shotgun, and there's plenty of shells!" Win chimed in from the house.

They hesitated, and I didn't blame them. There were a dozen of them, but they could see the rifle from the barn, and the shotgun from the house. The rifle was a Spencer, firing a .56-caliber bullet of 360 grains. It took no great imagination to realize that while some of them might, and probably would, get away, the Spencer would account for several, and a man hit with a .56-caliber bullet doesn't travel far. As for the shotgun, it had twin barrels, and that meant two dead men without reloading. As for me, I was tottering on my feet, but I'd missed only one shot of all I'd fired, and nobody wanted to gamble I'd miss more. It was a cinch anywhere from four to seven of them would hit dirt before the rest got away. And nobody was sure he wouldn't be one of the seven.

"To hell with it!" The black-mustached man who had recalled me from Sonora let go his belts, and it was a signal. They all did likewise.

At that moment a half-dozen riders swept down the hill and into the yard. Two of them wore badges. I turned and walked slowly toward Hugh as Win and Maggie rushed from the house toward me.

Dropping on one knee, I turned Hugh over gently. His eyes flickered open, and he looked at me. There was nothing anybody could do for him. Bill Keys hadn't been missing any shots, and the only wonder was that Hugh was still alive.

"Thanks, kid!" he whispered. "You were right on time! You an' Mag . . . I'm glad! Real glad!" His breath sobbed in his lungs for three deep, agonized gasps, and then he spoke again. "Unc . . . le Tom . . . he told me why . . . left ranch . . . you. Knew I was . . . crook. . . . I was a fool."

We got him inside then, and along about three that morning, he hung up his spurs.

In another room, I was having my own trouble, for I'd taken two slugs instead of one, and the Doc had to dig one of them out. It came hard, but I had a bullet to bite on while he probed for it. Mag was with me, with me all the time, although twice I sent her to see how Hugh was coming.

He came out of it, Hugh did, just before the end, and when he did, I got out of bed and went in. Doc told me I was crazy, but I went.

He looked up at me from the bed. "It's all square, Hugh," I said, "Tell Uncle Tom hello."

"You think I'll see him?" he asked me, and his voice was mighty hoarse.

"Sure you will!" I said. "Any cowhand might take a wrong trail once, or put the wrong brand on a cow! I think the Inspector up there can read your brand right!"

"Thanks, kid," he said. "When you grew up, you sure grew tall!"

I took his hand then, and he was looking up at me when his eyes blinked and his grip tightened, then loosened. "He's all yours, boy," I said softly. "Let him have his head!"

You know, I'll swear he smiled. . . . It was really something, after all, to have a friend like Hugh.

Waltz Him Around Again, Shadow

Deke Murphy, wrangler for the Stockman's Rodeo in Bluff Springs, drew back against the corral, his keen gray eyes on the girl who was passing with Bill Bly, the rodeo star. In the three days he had been in town, Deke had seen the girl several times—and had fallen completely in love with her. As for Bly, Deke would not have liked him even if he had not been with Carol Bell.

The boots with their run-down heels, faded Levi's and his patched wool shirt made Murphy a distinct contrast to the immaculate gray of Bly's rodeo costume, but the contrast did not end there.

Bill Bly was a splendidly built man, two hundred and ten pounds of muscle, and easily over six feet. He was cock of the walk, looked it, acted it, and wanted it known. Bill Bly was the hero of the rodeo world and Deke Murphy was an unknown, a hard-faced youngster who had dropped off a freight train and rustled a job handling stock for the rodeo.

Bly and the girl halted by the corral and peered through the horizontal bars to watch the milling horses. "I'd like to ride that Highbinder horse," Bly told the girl. "He's the worst horse in this show an' a man could make a good ride up on him. The judges always watch the men who come out on bad horses. The Highbinder's never been rode."

He glanced tolerantly at Deke, who leaned against the corral, eyes for nothing and nobody but Carol Bell, "That Highbinder's plenty bad, ain't he, boy?"

Deke Murphy bristled. He disliked being called "boy." He was all of twenty-two, and they had been rough years, even by the standards of the West. "Not really," he said.

A shadow of dislike appeared in Bly's eyes. He was used to being yessed by the wranglers. "I suppose you could ride him?" he suggested sarcastically.

"I reckon," Deke said calmly. "Anyway, he's easy compared to that Shadow horse." He nodded toward the lean, narrow-headed grulla that idled alone near the far wall of the corral. "Shadow will pitch circles around him!"

Bly looked for the first time at the sleepy, mouse-colored horse. "Him? He couldn't buck four sour apples!" Bly glanced again at Murphy. "If you think you can ride the Highbinder," he said, with amusement, "you should be in the show! You'd be better than half the riders we've got! Maybe better than all of them!"

"Maybe," Deke said shortly, starting to turn away. But Bly's voice stopped him, and he turned back.

"Just for fun," Bly said, "an' since you're such a good rider, I'll bet you twenty bucks you can't stay up ten seconds on Sonora, there."

Sonora, a mean-eyed buckskin with a splash of white on one hip, stared thoughtfully at them. Deke glanced at him.

"I can ride him," he said.

"Then put up your money! Talk is cheap!" Bly taunted.

Deke flushed. "I can ride him!" he said stubbornly, but he glanced left and right, looking for an escape.

"Come on!" Bly insisted, his eyes sneering at Deke under the guise of affability. "You said you could ride him! Let's see you do it! Put up your money!"

Several people had gathered around, and among them was a man of sixty-odd years, a white-haired man with keen blue eyes and a worn Stetson.

"Don't insist, Bill!" Carol said gently. "Maybe he doesn't feel like riding!"

"All right, honey." Bly looked back at Murphy. "Don't let me hear any more of that big talk! You got to put up or shut up," he said sharply.

Slowly the crowd drifted away and Deke Murphy turned miserably toward the corral, leaning against it, his head down. He had been made to look like a four-flusher. Anyway you take it, she would think he was a piker, a loudmouth. But how could he admit he didn't have twenty dollars? Or ten, or even five? How could he admit in front of Carol that he was broke?

She didn't know him, and she probably never would. She would not care, but he did. He cared desperately. From the first moment he had seen her, he knew she was the girl for him, and yet the gulf that separated them was bottomless.

"You think that Shadow horse can buck?" The voice was friendly.

Murphy looked up. "You just bet he can buck!" he said sharply. "Highbinder won't come near him!"

"You seen him?" the man persisted. It was the old-ish man with the blue eyes and white hair, his brown face seamed and wind worn.

"Me? Why, uh, not exactly." Deke's words stumbled and he hesitated. "A friend of mine told me about him."

"I see." The old man nodded. "I'm Tim Carson. Been around long?"

"Just pulled in," Deke admitted. "I don't know nobody here. Saw this rodeo, an' braced 'em for a job feedin' an' waterin' stock."

"Got any money?"

Deke's head came up sharply, his eyes cold and bitter. "That just ain't none of your business!" he said.

Carson shrugged. "If you had money you wouldn't get so het up about it," he said. "Figured you might need a few bucks for grub an' such."

Murphy studied him suspiciously.

"What do I have to do?" he demanded. "I won't do nothing crooked an' I won't take money for nothin'."

"I figured on a loan, but if you want to earn it—"

Carson waved a hand at the buckskin. "Throw a saddle on that horse an' I'll pay off if you ride him."

"How much?" Deke demanded.

"Oh, say twenty bucks!" Carson suggested.

"What you want to see me ride him for?" Deke asked cautiously.

"See if I'm right or not," Carson said. "I figure I know folks. I figure the only reason you wouldn't get up on that horse was because you didn't have the money to bet an' wouldn't admit it in front of that girl."

"Old man," Deke said, "you figure too darn close. Now put up your money."

"It's in my pocket," Carson said. "You get a saddle an' we'll ride this horse."

Without another word Deke went off to get a saddle, and as he walked away Carol Bell came from between the buildings, slapping her boots with a quirt. "Uncle Tim," she demanded, "what are you up to now? Why do you want that boy to ride that horse?"

DEKE MURPHY CAME BACK trailing a saddle which he grasped by the horn, and with a bridle over his shoulder. With the help of Carson he saddled and bridled the buckskin. The arena was empty at this early hour and Deke climbed the bars of the chute to mount the horse. Carol had drawn back to one side, and he had not seen her. He dropped into the saddle and Carson turned the horse loose.

The buckskin made a run for the center of the arena, skidded to halt with his head down, and when his rider stayed in the saddle, scratching with both heels, the buckskin swapped ends three times as fast as he could move and then buck-jumped all over the arena, ending his spurt and the ten seconds by sunfishing wildly for three full seconds. Carson yelled, and Deke unloaded hurriedly.

Together they caught up the buckskin and led him back to the corral. "They'll raise Old Nick when they find out I rode this horse!" Deke said worriedly.

"Forget it. I know them." He dug into his pocket— "An' here's your twenty bucks, son. Good luck!"

"Thanks," Deke said, gripping the twenty and staring at it with unbelieving eyes. "Man, that's the fastest money I ever made!"

Carson studied him. "You ride mighty well, son. Ever do any ridin' in a rodeo?"

Deke looked up, hesitated, then shook his head. "Not exactly," he replied. "I'd better beat it. I've got a lot of work to do an' I want to go up to town for a little bit!"

Tim Carson watched him go, glanced toward the place where his niece had been watching, and seeing she was gone, he turned toward the office with purposeful strides. "It's him!" he said grimly. "I'd bet money it's the same kid!"

DEKE MURPHY WALKED DOWN the town's dusty, banner-hung street and turned into a general store. "I want to buy a new pair of Levi's," he said, "an' a shirt, a good shirt!"

A half an hour later, with the new clothes on and a good meal under his belt, he walked back to the corrals. It would soon be time for the parade down the main street that would end at the rodeo grounds, and then the Grand Entry Parade that would open the show. He would have much to do.

In his pocket were three dollars and some change, but he felt better. Still a far cry from the glamorous clothes of the rodeo stars, his were at least neat, and he looked much better than in the shabby clothes he had been wearing, too redolent of the stable, and slept in too many times.

There was a job to do here, and he had to get on with it. He shook his head over his dislike of Bill Bly. It would never do to have trouble with him. All he knew was horses and cattle, and if he made an enemy of Bly he would be blackballed around every rodeo in the country. And he wanted very much to stick close to rodeos. The man he was looking for was somewhere around them, and if he looked long enough, somehow he would find him. Wherever the man was, he still wore the brand Deke Murphy had given him.

TIM CARSON WATCHED him return to his job in the new clothes and studied him through careful eyes. The build was similar. The kid was lean and rugged, muscular, but not big. He carried himself well and moved well. It could be the same one.

Bill Bly watched his horse being saddled for him and then turned to greet Carol as she walked up. "Hello, Bill." She smiled up at him. "Say, it's lucky that kid didn't take you up on your bet this morning. Uncle Tim offered him twenty dollars to ride the buckskin, and the kid rode him—scratched him high, wide, and handsome!"

Bly's brows tightened a little. "He did? Well, good for him!" His words were affable, but there was none of that in his mood. Deke had irritated him, and he did not like being irritated. Moreover, he had decided that Deke was a loudmouth and he disliked being proved wrong.

Another idea struck him. "Why did your uncle do that?"

"Oh, there's no accounting for Uncle Tim! He's liable to do anything! But it isn't that this time: he's interested in this fellow, I can see it. He was watching him like a cat all the time."

"I wonder why?" Bly remarked absently. He was thinking of how he would look in the parade with this girl beside him. Old Curly Bell's only child—not a bad idea, marrying her.

"I don't know," Carol said, "but Uncle Tim's funny. He used to be a United States marshal, you know. Over in Nevada."

Bly turned abruptly. "In Nevada, you say?" He caught himself. "You'd never suspect it. He seems so quiet."

"I know, but he's that way. He's still angry, and has

been for the past three years over that gold shipment robbery."

"Oh, yes! I recall something about it, I think. The bandits held up a train and got away with two hundred thousand dollars in freshly minted gold, wasn't that it?"

"I guess so. Uncle Tim believes that gold is still intact and has never been used, that it is cached somewhere."

"But he's not even an officer anymore, is he?"

"No, but that doesn't matter to Uncle Tim. In fact, I've heard him say more than once that he believed the thieves would come back, that the gold was hidden someplace not too far from here, in the mountains."

"You think that's why he's interested in this Murphy kid? One of the bandits was supposed to be no more than a boy. He was the one who killed the messenger."

"Oh, no!" The protest was sharp, dismayed. For some reason the idea frightened and disturbed Carol. It had not occurred to her before that such might be the reason for her uncle's interest in Deke Murphy.

Carol Bell would not have admitted her interest in Deke Murphy even to herself. In fact, she was scarcely aware of that interest, yet she remembered what he had practically told her uncle, that Deke had not wanted to be shown up as being broke in front of her.

She was a thoroughly aware young lady, and had

seen his eyes follow her from place to place, and his interest pleased her. Moreover, he **could** ride. She had seen him ride, and she was enough of a rider herself to know that he would compare favorably with many of the contest hands.

IN THE OFFICE, after calling his wire through to the telegraph office, Tim Carson turned to Tack Hobson. "Hobby," he said, "you know that Shadow horse? How many shows has he been in and where were they?"

"Funny you should ask that," Hobson remarked, "but he's never been ridden by anybody, an' he's shown in just four rodeos . . . all of them in prisons."

"I see. Was the Highbinder in any of these shows?"

"One of them. He was ridden once by a convict." Hobson stoked his pipe. "Reason I said it was funny you should ask is that you're the second man who asked that question. Bill Bly was in here, just a few minutes ago. He wanted to know the same thing."

DEKE MURPHY HAD NO IDEA just how he was to find his man, or exactly what he would do when he found him. From the moment he had been released from prison that had been his one idea. He had been framed and framed badly, and had done two years for a crime in which he had no part.

It had been a dark night when he had ridden up from his last camp near Singing Mountain, a tough and lonely kid, eager only to escape from his home in the Robber's Roost country and to find an honest job. Riding since he could first remember, he had lived a lonely life back in the brakes with his mother and his stepfather.

His stepfather had been a kindly man around home, and despite the fact that he was a rustler, had been a good father and a good husband, yet Deke's mother had reared him to be an honest man, and had made him promise that when he was old enough he would leave the Roost behind and start out on his own. His mother had died of pneumonia, alone and unattended except by himself, and his stepfather had been killed in a gunfight shortly after. Deke, true to his promise, had left the Roost behind.

He rode for a ranch in Utah, then one in Nevada, and started down the country looking to get himself as far from the Roost as possible. Leaving Singing Mountain, broke and without food, he had come upon an outlaw camp on the site of Sand Springs.

Three men had loafed by the fire. Deke knew all three, and about only one of them could he say anything good. Frank Wales had been a friend of his father's, an outlaw, but a man of some decency. Jerry Haskell and Cass Kubela he knew mostly by reputation but their reputation wasn't anything his mother would have approved of.

"Hey," Kubela had said, sitting up, "how about the kid? When we take the next shipment he could be the fifth man."

Wales glanced at him. "The kid's no outlaw," he said. "Leave him out of this!"

Jerry Haskell was a lean, dry whip of a man with a saturnine expression in his black eyes. He had killed two men that Deke knew about. "He's in now," he said, "he knows us an' he's seen us. Whether he likes it or not, he's in."

"I'm in nothing!" Deke had said hotly. "I'm ridin' through. Figured I might get me a bait of grub, then ride on. I ain't seen nothin', don't know nothin'!"

At Wales's invitation, he ate, eager only to finish and get away. That the three were waiting for their leader to get back, he knew. That they had just committed a robbery and were planning the holdup of a shipment from the mines, he soon learned. He knew Wales was his only friend here, but the older man would not dare go against the two seasoned outlaws. Cass Kubela had killed more than one man. A short, tough fellow with narrow eyes and big hands, he was even more dangerous than Haskell. Of the three here, Wales was without doubt the weakest link.

When he had eaten he rose to go, but Kubela motioned to him to sit down. "Stick around, kid," he advised, and the suggestion had been an order. Deke Murphy, his heart pounding, had sat down. The shotgun lying across Kubela's knees added emphasis to the command.

Later, when he had dozed off, he opened his eyes enough to know the fourth man had returned. He overheard a few words. "His old man was a weak sister," someone was saying, "the kid's ma preached to him. I say we can't trust him."

Wales's protest was overruled, but then the fourth man spoke. "Keep him for now, we can use him. Get some sleep and we'll move out early. . . . They may still be on my trail."

Although he waited and listened, Deke heard no more, and somewhere along the trail of his waiting, he fell asleep again. He awakened to a confusion of shots, and for one startled instant, he stared around wildly, then grabbed his boots and, tugging them on, made a break for his horse.

Another man, a big man, came charging up, and he too grabbed at Deke's horse. "That's my horse!" Deke protested.

The man turned half around, but in the darkness Deke Murphy could not see his face. "Shut up, you fool!" he snapped, and he slashed viciously at Deke with the barrel of his gun.

It caught the boy a glancing blow across the skull and lights exploded in his brain. As he started to go down, he grabbed out and got a hand in the edge of the big man's pocket. He jerked and the pocket ripped, and the man toppled back to the ground. He sprang up and aimed a vicious kick at the boy's head, but Deke lunged to his feet and struck out hard. The blow landed, and Deke followed it in. His unknown antagonist smashed up with his right, and then the gun bellowed, fired by their struggles. With a curse of panic the man flung him off and sprang into the saddle. There was a rattle of hoofs and he was gone!

An instant later a half-dozen men charged down on Deke. He was surrounded, searched, and taken away. Later, tried and convicted, he was sentenced to five years in the penitentiary for a holdup that had been committed the previous day. His stepfather's record was known. He admitted his acquaintance with all the robbers but one, and his denials that he had any part in the holdup were laughed out of consideration.

The man he sought was the leader of the band, the man who had stolen his horse and left him to be captured and sentenced to prison. His sole clue was a comment made by Kubela on that memorable night when half awake he heard them talking. Kubela had said, "The boss can ride, all right! He's a top contest hand!" And it was that boss who had left him for the law, and while the posse was making him a prisoner, the actual outlaws escaped.

Frank Wales, the only man who could have testified to his actual connection with the robbers, was now dead. He had escaped only to be killed near the ghost town of Hamilton two years before, resisting arrest.

TIM CARSON SAUNTERED DOWN to the chutes and stopped near chute three where Deke Murphy was working. "You should be riding in this show, kid. There's some good prizes!"

"You know I'm broke," Deke said sullenly. "How could I enter?"

"Suppose I paid your entry fees?" Carson persisted. "Would you ride?"

"You're darn tootin' I would!" Deke said. His eyes followed the leaders of the Grand Parade, looking enviously at Bill Bly riding beside Carol Bell. The girl's eyes happened to turn his way, and she smiled. Deke felt his heart leap. "You loan me that money, mister! I'll pay you back out of my winnin's!"

Carson watched the parade thoughtfully, and for a minute or two he did not speak. Then he said, "You're entered, Murphy. I already paid your fees. You're entered in every event, take what you want of them!"

Deke stared, his eyes incredulous. "You mean, you—" He hesitated, uncertain what to say.

"I like to see a kid get his chance," Carson said, "an' that in particular when he's had bad breaks. You get on out there, let's see you bust 'em wide open!"

An hour later, hurrying up to Tim Carson's place by the chute, Carol caught his arm. "Uncle Tim! Did you enter that boy in the rodeo? Did you?"

Carson smiled gravely. "I sure did, honey, an' if you want to gamble I'll bet you he puts Bly in the shade!"

Carol said nothing, her eyes following the young

rider who was saddling the roping horse Carson had provided for him. "Uncle Tim, do you think he is one of those men who robbed that two hundred thousand dollars?"

Carson took the pipe from his mouth. "Now where'd you get that idea? An' whoever told you it was two hundred thousand?"

"Bill did, but I got the idea from you. You've never let that old crime rest. I know it still bothers you."

"It does at that." Carson returned his pipe to his teeth. "Carol, I hate crooks. I also hate like poison anyone who'll let an innocent man do his time. You asked me if I thought Deke was one of them, an' I'll tell you: I **know** he wasn't. But he's been in prison for it, an' I've a hunch he's huntin' the man who led that holdup—a man we know as Jud Kynell, one of the old bunch that hung out at the Roost."

"He was in prison?" Carol watched the young rider, her eyes serious. "Do you suppose—I mean, do you think he's honest now? I—I know some men become thieves or worse while in jail."

"Honey, I think the boy's honest. He wouldn't take money from me without working for it."

Deke walked toward them, leading his horse. He grinned shyly at the girl. On impulse, Carol removed her handkerchief and handed it to him, then took it back and knotted it about his neck herself.

"You need something that shows you're riding for us now," she said. "Good luck." For a breathtaking instant they were very close, and as she pulled the knot into place, she looked up at him. His face was pale and he looked almost frightened.

"Ma'am," he said sincerely, "you watch me! I'll kick the frost out of anything they've got—for you!"

BEFORE THE CONTEST was more than a few minutes old the entire arena had awakened to the fact that out there on the tanbark a fierce duel was beginning, a duel between tall, powerful Bill Bly, and the unknown newcomer.

"Ladies and gents! Billy Bly, star of rodeo and stock corral, makes his tie in eleven and six-tenths seconds!" Hobson, the announcer, drew a breath and then continued to bellow into the small end of his speaking trumpet. "That's the fastest time so far today, and ties the record for this here arena!"

He turned and waved a hand. "Now out of the chutes—Deke Murphy!"

Carson's horse was a sorrel streak, and Deke's rope shot out like a thrown lance, the loop opening just as the calf dodged, and dropped over its head! Murphy stepped down as his horse put on the brakes, dropped to one knee alongside the calf, and made his tie. As he sprang back, dust rising from the bound calf, a gasp went over the arena.

Hobson's voice boomed out. "Well, folks! Now there's a **record**! Deke Murphy at eleven and four-tenths seconds, to win the first go-around!"

Amid cheers, Murphy swung into the saddle and cantered across to where Carol stood waiting with her uncle Tim and Bly. Bly looked up, the same cold expression in his eyes, his lips forcing a smile. "Nice going," he commented, but his voice was flat.

"Oh, Deke! You were **wonderful**!" Carol exclaimed.

BLY WON THE STEER WRESTLING, with Deke a close second, and Red Roller, a big cowhand from Cheyenne, a tight third. In the Brahma riding, Deke came out on No. 66, an ugly mass of bull meat weighing all of two thousand pounds and a fighter as well as a rodeo veteran.

He knew what he was out there for and he went at it with a will, buck-jumping and twisting his tail. Deke was hanging on for dear life and the bull was out to ditch him or die. Somehow, Deke stayed up until the whistle blew.

He threw a leg over the bull's back, hit the ground, and the bull swapped ends and came for him. The clowns rushed in with flapping cloaks and slapping hats to draw the animal's attention. It sprang this way and that, trying desperately to get at its enemies, not so much in torment as in sheer enjoyment of battle and lust for conquest.

Deke limped back to the chute, grinning at Carol, his face dusty and a trickle of blood coming from his nose. "Rough!" he said, shaking his head.

"You made a good ride," Carson admitted. "Bly's drawn Highbinder for the bronc riding."

"Who did I get?" Deke demanded, looking up quickly. Then he grinned wryly. "As if I didn't know!"

"Shadow," Carson confessed, "you'll be up on Shadow!"

"Highbinder's the worst horse," Bly said casually. "Whoever heard of Shadow?"

"I did." Murphy clipped the words. "I've seen him buck. Highbinder won't touch him."

"As if you knew," sneered Bly, his eyes cold.

"I do." Deke snapped the words. "I rode him!"

"What?" Bill Bly put an open hand to Deke's chest and pushed, backing him up. "Why, you little liar! You—"

Deke's balled fist smashed him in the mouth and the big man staggered. Then Bly straightened, his eyes utterly vicious. "Now you've done the wrong thing!" he said. "I'll beat your head in!"

Bly rushed, swinging. His right was a long arc that encountered nothing but air. Deke Murphy rose inside of Bly's arms and landed a series of short, wicked punches to the stomach and ribs. Bly clinched and hurled Deke back into the corral fence with sheer strength, then charged.

Again Deke, working coolly, went under the blow, and again he smashed away at Bly's ribs with those strength-sapping short punches. This time he ducked away before Bly could clinch, and when Bly swung a left, Deke caught it on his right forearm, and chopped down with a wicked punch to the big man's chin.

Bly blinked, he was bleeding from his split lips, and stared confusedly through the sweat and his hanging hair at the much shorter man.

"You want some more?" Deke asked calmly. "Or have you had enough?"

Deke looked him over coolly, then turned and walked away. As he drew near to Carol he paused. "Sorry," he said, "I didn't want trouble!"

Bly shook his head to clear it and stared after him. "Jailbird!" he sneered. "Highbinder was never rode but once! In prison!"

Deke's face was white and still. He turned, and his voice was low but clear. "That's right," he said, "that was where I rode him!"

As HE HEADED for the stable, staring grimly ahead, Deke passed close by two men whom he did not see. Jerry Haskell and Cass Kubela watched him go. "It's him, all right," Cass said. "The boss was right. It's the kid!"

"He knows us," Haskell said.

Kubela's eyes were cold. He took the cigarette from his lips and dropped it into the dust. "Not for long!"

CARSON STOOD BY, watching Deke bathe his face and hands, smoking quietly. When Deke had dried himself he looked at Carson.

"Now you know, I was in prison."

"Knew it all the time. I even knew your step-father."

"You what?"

"Sure. Knew your ma, too. He wasn't a bad man . . . just didn't stop rustling when it went out of style."

Tim Carson smoked thoughtfully. "Son, at the trial you said you knew the men who robbed that train, but you wasn't with them. You named Cass Kubela an' Jerry Haskell."

"Right." Deke waited, curiously.

"Now I've never seen those hombres. Until that job they always worked east of the mountains. Would you know them again?"

"I reckon I would."

"How about their boss? You said at the trial you didn't know him but that he was Jud Kynell. Folks thought you were coverin' up. Were you?"

"No. Robber's Roost covered miles, an' outlaws used to work back an' forth from the Hole in the Wall to the Roost an' clean down over the old horse-thief trail to the border. We heard about a lot of men we never saw. Jud Kynell was around when I was a kid. He's some ten years older than me, as I figure it."

"Know anything about him?"

"That's about all, except that he did this; rodeoin' I mean. That and he wears my brand." Deke explained about what he had overheard, and his belief that the outlaw wore a deep scar on his chest. "There was an awful lot of blood for a scratch," he finished. "I figure it ripped pretty deep."

"That's an item." Carson was thoughtful. "Son, I got a tip that Kubela was headed this way, ridin' with another man."

"Haskell, most likely." Deke looked at Carson. "You better watch it. Those two are killers."

"I know," Carson replied. "Kid, can you sling that gun you're wearin'?"

Deke smiled. "Some . . . what have you got in mind?"

"I'm goin' to swear you in as a deputy. Everybody figures I'm no longer an officer . . . you see this?"

The older man held forth a wallet containing a badge and some papers. "Deputy U.S. Marshal. It's my theory those two were comin' here, an' comin' to meet their boss, get that gold an' hightail it out of the country. I trailed those boys to the vicinity of Forlorn Hope Spring in the foothills of the Opal Mountains, an' I'd bet that gold ain't cached more than a few miles from there."

BILL BLY'S RIDE on Highbinder was something to see, for the big red horse was a fighter, and Bly, say what one would of the man, was a rider. They went out of the chute like a miniature explosion and the red horse leaped for the sun. He landed and swapping ends he let go with both hind feet, almost standing on his head.

Then he settled down to a wild, unrestrained and wholly murder-minded job of bucking. Eyes rolling, the beast went to work with a will, but when the whistle blew Bly was still on deck.

Bly walked back to the chute with the crowd's roaring cheers around him. It had been a great ride, a wicked ride. As he passed a small group of men not far from the chute, he saw Jerry Haskell. The lean-faced man nodded toward the opposite end of the arena, and tapped his pistol butt.

Bly walked on to where Shadow, an evil-eyed grulla, was being saddled for Deke Murphy, who perched on the side of the chute. Deke dropped into the saddle as Bly glared up at him. "Nice ride!" Deke said. "Too bad Highbinder was feelin' sort of poorly!"

"Shut up, you fool!" Bly snapped.

Deke's head came up with a jerk and his mouth opened in astonishment. Those words!

"You ready?" Red Roller glared at him. "Better get your mind on your business, boy! This one's a fighter!"

"I'm ready!" Murphy was suddenly grim and cold. "Give 'im air!"

Shadow was a horse with a mission. He hated men, all men, but he reserved a special and bitterly vindictive brand of hate for those who tried to ride him. He came out of that chute like a rattlesnake with the DTs and went to sunfishing.

He jumped straight up, all four legs hanging and

his back bowed like an angry cat. Hitting the ground he went straight up again as if lifted by a charge of powder.

Deke hung on as the horse twisted his whipcord body sharply to the left. Switching and humping, that bronc went to work to give the crowd a show and to beat his rider into submission. He bucked straightaway, seesawing wickedly as he jumped, and contorted his back and writhed his spine.

He headed north with a wicked forward jump, then sprang straight back and swapped ends three times. Deke felt air under him and for one frantic instant thought he was a goner, but then he slapped the saddle with the seat of his Levi's and the world around him was a crazy quilt of tossing color and blurred shadows where nothing seemed to exist but that writhing, twisting, fighting explosion beneath him.

Somewhere far off he heard a whistle blowing and suddenly the horsemen were tearing toward him.

But Shadow was not through. Shadow had his own ideas about quitting and this was not the time or the place. He swapped ends and headed for the stands on a dead run, with the horsemen swinging to follow.

At the wall of the stands, he swung broadside and hurled himself at the board. Deke, in a long leap, grabbed at the front rail of the stands and left the saddle with a bound, leaving the frustrated, screaming horse behind him to be gathered up by the riders.

Dazedly, he stared around at the cheering crowd,

then he managed a grin. He pulled his hat from his head and lifted it, and then as his hand came down, his face went blank with astonishment. There was a bullet hole through the crown!

Instantly, he remembered.

Shut up, you fool!

Wheeling, he vaulted over the rail and dropped to the ground. His hand felt for his gun, and it was still with him. He started across the arena, walking fast. Bill Bly stood alone, staring at him. Behind Bly, back by the barns, Carson held a pistol on Haskell. Haskell slowly lowered a rifle to the ground. Deke stood there looking at Bly.

SUDDENLY, THE NOISE of the crowd seemed gone, and he stood alone in the sun-washed stillness, his legs spread, staring at the man who faced him. Out of the tail of his eye he saw a man step slightly away from the crowd, partly under cover of the stands. It was Cass Kubela.

"I know you now," Deke said.

"You're crazy!"

"Open your shirt then, an' if you've no scar on the left side of your chest, I'll apologize."

"Go to the devil!" Bly said viciously.

Between them a cigarette lay in the dust, lifting a thin column of hazy smoke upward. A horse stomped in a chute, and somewhere a child cried in petulant irritation. And then out of the corner of his eye, Deke saw Kubela's gun coming up.

Kubela's gun came up, and Deke pivoted on the ball of his left foot and fired from hip level. He felt Kubela's bullet hit him, and he fired again. The outlaw took a staggering step forward and fell headlong, the gun dribbling from his fingers.

Bly, with a snarl of fury, had grabbed for his gun. As it swung up, Deke came around and fired!

Bly took it standing, a little puff of dust leaping from his gray shirt. Bly stepped forward, seemed to hesitate, then his knees wilted under him and he folded up like a punctured accordion.

Dazed, Deke turned, thumbing shells automatically into his gun. The crowd was pouring from the stands, moving desperately to get out of the way of any more shooting.

Deke's leg felt numb, and he turned and stared down at it. There was no blood or sign of injury, and then he saw the smashed silver ornament on his belt over his right hip where the bullet had struck and glanced off.

Tim Carson rushed up to him. "You hurt, boy? Did he get you?"

"No." Deke limped over to Jud Kynell's body. Bending over, he pulled back the shirt. There on the man's chest was a ragged white scar made by the muzzle blast of his gun on that night long ago when he and Deke had struggled over it. "Funny, I never figured Bly was my man," he said. "Not until I heard his voice just before I came out on Shadow."

"I knew," Carson said, "in fact we've been pretty

sure for over a year, but just lacked the right dope on him. Then he talked to Carol today about the holdup, an' he mentioned it was two hundred thousand. That was kept secret, an' nobody ever knew but the outlaws an' the government. Just one man at the mines actually knew an' he kept his mouth shut. Tyin' that in with what else we knew, it had to be him."

CAROL'S HAND WAS on his arm, and he looked down. "You know," he said, "wearin' your colors brought me luck, I think."

"Then why not keep wearing them?" she asked.

"Well, ma'am," he said, smiling, "that's not a bad idea . . . and it's probably safer to ride when there's no one shootin' at you!"

Rowdy Rides to Glory

FOR WANT OF A HORSE

Rowdy Horn stared gloomily at Cub's right hind leg and shook his head with regret.

"No use even thinkin' about it, Jenny," he admitted ruefully to the girl he wanted to marry. "Cub won't work at the Stockman's Show this year. Not with that leg!"

Jenny Welman nodded, faintly irritated. Something was always going wrong. "No," she agreed, "you can't ride him, and without a good roping horse you wouldn't have a chance at first money, and without five thousand dollars—"

"I know! Without it we can't get married!" Rowdy ran his fingers through his dark, curly hair. "Jenny, does that money make so much difference? Lots of folks I know started with a darned sight less, and if I get a good calf crop this year we would be all set."

"We've talked of this before," Jenny replied quietly. "If you want to marry me, you've got to provide a home for me. I won't start like my mother did."

"She was pretty happy," Horn insisted stubbornly, "and your mother was a mighty fine woman."

"True, but just the same, I want to be comfortable! I don't want to slave my youth away trying to get ahead like she did." Suddenly, and excitedly, Jenny caught his arm. "Rowdy! I just happened to think. Why don't you see Bart Luby?"

"Luby?" Horn's mouth tightened. "What would I see him for?"

"Maybe he would let you borrow Tanglefoot to ride! He's going to ride Royboy, I know, so why don't you ride over and ask him?"

"Ask a favor of Bart Luby?" Rowdy's eyes smoldered. "I will not! I'll let the rodeo go to kingdom come, and the ranch, too, before I'll go to him for help! Anyway, he'd turn me down flat. He knows well enough that with Cub and me out of the running he is a cinch to win."

"Will it do any harm to ask?" Jenny insisted impatiently. "Why you imagine he holds anything against you, I can't guess. He's the wealthiest man in the whole South Rim country, and has the biggest ranch, so why he should worry about you, I wouldn't know."

THERE WAS AN UNDERCURRENT in Jenny's voice that stirred Rowdy's resentment. He glanced up, studying her carefully. He had been in love with Jenny Welman for a long time, and had been going around with her for almost a year, yet somehow of late he had been experiencing vague doubts. Nothing he could put his finger on, but little things led him to believe that she placed more emphasis upon whether a man had money than how he got it.

"If you'd like," she suggested, her eyes brightening, "I could see him for you."

"No." Horn shook his head stubbornly. "I won't ask him, and I don't want you asking him. He knows exactly how I feel about him, and he knows I think there was something wrong about that Bar O deal."

"But Rowdy!" she protested, almost angry. "How can you be so foolish? After three years I was hoping you'd forgotten that silly resentment you had because you didn't get that ranch."

"Well, I haven't!" Rowdy told her firmly. "If there was one man I knew, it was old Tom Slater, and I know what he thought of Bart. There was a time when he thought of leaving that ranch to both of us together, but after Bart Luby left and went to cattle buying, Slater never felt the same about him. Something happened then that old Tom didn't like. Why, three times he told me he didn't even want Luby on the place, and that he was leaving it to me. It doesn't make sense that he would change his mind at the last minute!"

"It was not at the last minute!" Jenny protested. "He had given Bart a deed to the ranch—over a year before his death. Why, with that deed he didn't even need the will, but all the same, the will left everything to him. You heard it read yourself."

Jenny's chin lifted, and in her eyes Rowdy Horn could see the storm signals flying. This old argument always irritated Jenny. She was just like nearly everybody in the South Rim: admired Luby's cash and show as well as his business ability. And of course, the man **had** made money.

It was easy to admire Bart Luby if you accepted him from the surface appearance. He had a dashing way, and he was a powerful man physically, handsome and smooth-talking. He was the one who had the Stockman's Show organized, and for three years now had been featured in it for his fine riding, roping, and bulldogging. He was the local champion, because for those three years he had won all the major events.

But that will—that was something else.

Rowdy Horn was usually reasonable, but on the subject of that will he ceased being reasonable. It was flatly contradictory to everything he knew of Tom Slater, who had been almost a father to him.

Besides that, nobody could work with a man as Rowdy had worked with Bart Luby without knowing something of him, and Bart had always been unscrupulous in little things. He had left the Bar O to become a rodeo contest rider and a cattle buyer, and there had been vague rumors, never substantiated and never investigated, that his success as a buyer was due to his association—suspected only—with Jack Rollick.

Rollick was a known rustler who haunted the broken canyon country beyond the Rim, and did his rustling carefully and with skill among the brakes south of the Rim. It was hard to get proof of his depredations—nobody had, as yet—for he never drove off large numbers of cattle and never rustled any stock with unusual markings. He weeded cattle from the herds, or the lone steers that haunted the thick brush, and it was generally believed he gathered them in some interior valley to hold until he had enough to drive to market. Such shortages as his rustling caused would not show up until the roundup.

"Well, I'm riding back into Aragon, then, if you won't listen to a thing I say," Jenny said, swinging into her saddle. "But I do wish you'd change your mind and let me see Bart for you."

Rowdy shook his head, grinning up at her. Looking at him, Jenny thought for the thousandth time that he was easily the handsomest cowboy, the best-looking man afoot or in the saddle in the whole South Rim country. It was too bad he was so stubborn and such a poor manager.

"Don't worry," he said, smiling. "One way or another I'll be in that rodeo, and I'll win first money. Then we can be married."

She gave him her hand. "I know you will, dear. Luck."

With a wave of her hand, she wheeled the paint and rode off at a snappy trot. He watched her go, uncertain again. Cub nickered plaintively, as if unaware of the disaster his misfortune had brought upon them.

Rowdy ran his hand under Cub's mane and scratched the horse's neck.

"Too bad, old boy. We worked mighty hard, trainin' you for that rodeo, and all for nothing. That hole you stepped into was sure in the wrong place."

Gravely, he studied the situation, but could see no way out, no escape. His Slash Bar was a small ranch, the place upon which Tom Slater had made his start. Rowdy had bought the ranch from the bank, making the down payment with his savings and the reward for the capture of Beenk Danek, a bank robber.

There had been a few good months after the ranch was his, then the roundup—and he had been missing more than two hundred head of cattle, more than any other one rancher, even those with much larger herds. His was small.

Then there had been fence trouble with Luby's men, although never with Luby himself, and more than once it had almost led to shooting. Despite Luby's smooth excuses, he was sure the cattleman was deliberately instigating trouble. To top it all, water shortages had developed, and he had fallen behind in his payments to the bank. So it had been the Stockman's Show and Rodeo that had offered him the best chance to make a substantial payment on the ranch as well as to provide the things on which Jenny insisted. Until Cub's injury, he had been certain he had at least an even chance with Bart Luby, and Bart had been aware of it, too.

Now still another worry had developed. One of his two hands, Mike McNulty, had ridden in a couple of days before to tell him the water hole at Point of Rocks was shrinking—the only water supply for miles of range. It had been considered inexhaustible. That was a matter which Rowdy must look into himself—and now.

Mounting a steeldust he used for rough riding, he started off for the dim and lonely land under the gigantic wall of the Rim. There, at the end of a trailing point of rocks, lay the water hole.

It was an hour's ride from the home ranch, and when he drew rein near the water hole the sun was still almost an hour high. His fears were realized the instant his eyes fell upon what always had been a wide, clear pool, for around it lay a rim, at least six feet wide, of gray mud, indicating the shrinkage. This was the last straw.

A hoof struck stone, and surprised, he glanced up. Lonely as this place was, other riders than the two men who worked for him hardly ever came to this water hole. But here was one—and a girl.

She was tall, slender, yet beautifully built. He wondered instantly who she was. He had never seen her before. Her dark hair was drawn to a loose knot at the nape of her neck, and her eyes were big and dark. She was riding a splendid palomino mare, with an old-fashioned Spanish-type saddle.

He swept off his hat and she flashed a quick smile at him.

"You are Rowdy Horn?" she inquired.

"That's right, ma'am, but you've sure got the best of me. I thought I knew every girl in this country, and especially all of the pretty ones, but I see I don't."

She laughed. "You wouldn't know me," she said sharply. "I'm Vaho Rainey."

His interest quickened. The whole South Rim country knew about this girl, but she had never been seen around Aragon. The daughter of French and Irish parents, she had been left an orphan when little more than a baby, and brought up by old Cleetus, a wealthy Navaho chieftain. When she was fourteen she had been sent to a convent in New Orleans, and after that had spent some time in New York and Boston before returning to the great old stone house where Cleetus lived.

"Welcome to the Slash Bar," Rowdy said, smiling. "I met old Cleetus once. He's quite a character." He grinned ruefully. "He sure made a fool out of me, one time."

HE TOLD HER how the old Indian had come to his cabin one miserable wintry night, half frozen and with a broken wrist. His horse had fallen on the ice. Rowdy had not known who he was—just any old buck, he had thought—but he had put Cleetus to bed, set the broken bone, and nursed the old man through the blizzard. Returning to the cabin one day after the storm, he had found the old man gone, and with him a buckskin horse. While the old man was still sick, Rowdy had offered him a blanket and food when he left. These Cleetus had taken.

Over a year later, Rowdy Horn had discovered, quite by accident, the identity of the old man he had befriended. And he had learned that Cleetus was one of the wealthiest sheepmen among the Navahos, and one of the first to introduce Angora goats into the lonely desert land where he lived.

Vaho laughed merrily when she heard the story.

"That's like him. So like him. Did he ever return the horse?"

"No," Rowdy said dryly, "he didn't. That was a good horse, too."

"He's a strange man, Rowdy," she said. He was glad, somehow, that Vaho did not stand on ceremony. He liked hearing her call him by his first name.

"Maybe he could use a good man with his flocks," Rowdy suggested, a little bitterly. "I'm sure going to be hunting a job soon."

She looked at him quickly. "But you have this ranch? Is that not enough?"

Rowdy did not know just why he had an impulse to tell this girl, a stranger, his trouble—but he did.

CHAPTER II

JILTED—AND GLAD OF IT

Shrugging, Rowdy explained, and Vaho Rainey listened attentively, watching him with her wide dark eyes. She frowned thoughtfully at the receding water.

"There must be a reason for this," she said. "There has always been water here. Never in the memory of the Navaho has this water hole been so low."

"Sure, there's a reason," Rowdy said glumly, "but what is it? Maybe there's somebody takin' water before it gets to this pool, but who and where? I always figured this water came off the Rim, somewhere."

"Or from under it," Vaho said thoughtfully.

That remark made no impression on Rowdy at the moment, although he did recall it later, and wondered what she had meant. Right now, his interest in this tall, dark girl was quickening. There was warmth in her, understanding, and sympathy for his problems—all the things that he had missed in Jenny.

He glanced up suddenly. The sun had slid behind the mountains, and it was growing dark.

"You'd better be getting home!" he warned Vaho. "Riding in the mountains at night is no good."

"Not when you know them as I do," she said, smiling. "Anyway, I've not far to go. Some of our people are camped only a few miles from here. I shall go to them."

When he had watched her ride away into the dusk

that lay thick among the dark pines, he swung into the saddle and turned the steeldust down the road home. But he was conscious of a strange excitement, and the memory of that tall, dark girl was like a bright fire in his thoughts. He was remembering the curves of her lips and the way she had moved, how her laughter had sounded an echo in his heart. With a quick start of guilt he realized that in his mind he was being a little disloyal to Jenny. Despite his guilty feeling, though, he would not forget that girl from the canyons, or the strange warmth she had left with him.

He had ridden home and had stripped the saddle from the steeldust, when he heard a man's voice inside the stable. For an instant he hesitated. It was dark inside and he could see nothing. Then he saw a subdued glow, and stepped quickly to the door. "Who's there?" he demanded.

A man who had been kneeling to examine Cub's leg got to his feet. As he stepped out of the door Rowdy Horn could see him plainly—a tall, thin man in a battered hat not of western vintage, and a shabby suit of store clothes.

"How are you?" he said. "I hope you won't think I'm butting in. I stopped to ask for something to eat and a place to sleep, but finding nobody at home, I walked around a little. Then I found your horse with the bad leg. What happened to him?"

"Stepped into a gopher hole. My roping horse. I'd figured on riding him in the rodeo."

"Too bad." The man hesitated. "How about that grub?"

"Sure. Come on up to the house. I haven't eaten myself. You passin' through?"

"Uh-huh. I'm a tramp printer, Neil Rice by name. My doctor told me if I expected to live I'd better get west. I'm not really sick, but he told me that any more of that city air and I would be, so I packed up and started west."

"Broke?"

"I am now. I ran into a poker game back in Dodge, and I'd played a lot of poker with other printers. Those Dodge people played too fast a game for me."

Rowdy chuckled. "All right, Rice. I know how that is. I'm Rowdy Horn. You hunting a job?"

"Any kind of a job. I know a little about horses, but not much about cattle. And I can cook."

"There's what you need," Rowdy said cheerfully. "Let's see what you can do. I am probably the worst cook who ever died of slow poisoning from his own cookin'. I'd hesitate to ask a stranger to eat it."

Two HOURS LATER, with a good dinner behind their belts and pipes lighted, they sat back and stared thoughtfully at the fire. Rowdy by that time knew most of Rice's troubles, and the printer was aware of the precarious situation on the Slash Bar.

"This fellow Luby," Rice said thoughtfully. "Has he always lived around this country?"

"Here, Texas, New Mexico, and California, as far as I know. He seems to know a good bit, though."

"I wouldn't be surprised." Rice hesitated. "Is there any way in which I could get my hands on that deed? And the will? I know a little about such things."

Horn shrugged. "Not that I know of. Maybe I can figure out a way. Why? Are you a lawyer?"

Rice chuckled. "Just a printer, but I know a little about documents. I wouldn't promise anything, but it might be that if the deed was faked and if the will was forged, I could tell. How, I don't know, and I couldn't promise anything. I'd have to examine them, and preferably have them for a while."

"That's tough. Luby wouldn't turn loose of them. We'll see, though, for it's sure an idea." He scowled. "You can't forge a deed, can you? This one's got a big seal on it. I gave up when I saw that."

"Well," Rice said, "that might be the very reason it's on there. Did you have a good lawyer look at it?"

"Lawyer?" Horn exclaimed. "Man, there's no lawyer in Aragon but old Hemingway, and he's drunk most of the time. I don't think he knows much law, anyway."

The following day, Rowdy worked hard, roping and tying calves, roping horses, and attempting to improve his own speed and skill, though the steeldust wasn't nearly the horse Cub was. Neil Rice had taken right hold, had cleaned out the house and organized the cooking situation. Then he had handed Horn a list of supplies. Rowdy had grinned at it.

"All right, Rice," he had said, "I reckon we might as well eat and leave this place on full stomachs anyway. I'll head into Aragon and pick up this stuff."

With a packhorse Rowdy Horn headed for Aragon. All the way to town he was studying ways and means of getting the documents into his hands once more. There must be some way. During their talk at breakfast Rice had told him that it was often possible to move a seal from one document to another, that such a thing had been done in more than one place.

Aragon was crowded when Rowdy rode down the main one of the town's three streets. Banners were hanging across the street, and the town was bright with posters heralding the coming Stockman's Show and Rodeo. News had got around about the injury to Cub's leg, however, and everywhere he went he found the odds of his winning first money had dropped. He was no longer given an even chance to win, for everyone had known how much trust he placed in Cub, and all had seen the horse perform at one time or another.

He called at the house for Jenny, but she was out. Her mother smiled at him, but her eyes looked as if she were disturbed.

"I'm sorry, Rowdy," Mrs. Welman told him, "Jenny's gone out. You may see her downtown."

He walked back down the street, telling himself that he was foolish to feel irritated. Jenny had had no idea he would be coming in, and there was no reason why she should be at home. He laughed at himself, then strode back downtown and went to the Emporium, where he began buying groceries. He was packing them on his lead horse when he heard a familiar voice and, glancing up, saw Bart Luby. Clinging to his arm was Jenny Welman!

Rowdy's face flushed, and he looked away, but not before Luby had seen him.

"How are you, Horn?" Bart said, making no effort to conceal his triumph. "Sorry to hear about Cub! I was looking forward to the chance of beating him."

JENNY LOOKED AT ROWDY, paling slightly. His eyes met hers for an instant and then he looked away.

"Think nothing of it, Luby," he said, "but don't count me out. I'll be there yet."

"A man can't do much good on just a fair horse," Luby said, "but come along in. Be glad to have you."

Jenny hesitated. "I didn't know you were coming to town," she said.

"I see you didn't," he said, a little wryly.

Her chin lifted and her eyes blazed. "Well, what do you expect me to do? Stay home all the time? Anyway," she added suddenly, "I'd been planning to ride out and see you. I don't think—well, we'd better call this off. Our engagement, I mean."

He had a queer sinking feeling, but when he lifted his eyes, they revealed nothing. "All right," was all he said, calmly.

Her blue eyes hardened slightly. "You certainly don't seem much upset!" she flared.

"Should I be?" he asked. "When a girl tosses a man over the first time he gets in a tight spot, she's small loss."

"Well!" she flared. "I—!"

"Come on, Jenny," Bart said. "You told me you were comin' out to my place to look at the sorrel mare." He grinned at Horn. "Out to the Bar O."

Stung, Rowdy glared at Luby.

"Better enjoy the Bar O while you can, Bart," he said.

Bart Luby froze in midstride and for a second stood stock-still. Then slowly he turned, his face livid. "What do you mean by that?" he barked.

"Nothing"—Rowdy grinned—"nothing at all! Only—" He hesitated, then shrugged. "You'll know all about it soon."

"Oh"—Jenny tugged at Bart's arm—"don't pay any attention to him. He's always fussing about that ranch."

The remark was intended to appease Bart and get him away. It had the effect of adding fuel to the man's uncertainty after Rowdy's veiled comment. Bart Luby stared down at Rowdy as he stood in the street, and watched him finish his diamond hitch.

"If you're smart, you'll leave well enough alone!" Bart said then, carefully and coldly.

Rowdy smiled, but he felt warm with triumph.

Luby was worried, and if that deal had been straight, why should he worry? His sudden remark had brought a greater reaction than he had expected, yet suddenly he was aware of something else. That had been a dangerous thing for him to say, for now Luby knew that the loss of the ranch was not a closed matter to Rowdy Horn.

In the saddle on the way back to the Slash Bar, Horn began to feel the letdown. Despite his immediate reaction to Jenny's sudden breaking off of their engagement, and despite the fact that he realized she was small loss, he felt sick and empty inside. He felt so low that he took no notice of the ride he had always loved. The great wall of the Rim did not draw his eyes, nor did the towering mass of cumulus that lifted above it, nor the darkening fringe of the pines against the distant sky.

When he got back home none of his problems were any nearer a solution either. Cub's leg was but little better, and there was absolutely no chance of his recovering before the rodeo date. And more than ever now, Rowdy wanted to win that first place.

Again and again he studied the situation, comparing his own ability with that of Luby, who would be the main competitor. Each time, it all came down to the roping event. A lot would depend, of course, on the kind of mounts each of them drew in the bucking events, but there was little to choose between the two men. To give the devil his due, Bart Luby was a hand.

CHAPTER III
GIRL OF THE WILDS

At daylight Rowdy Horn was out looking at Cub's leg. When he had done that, he saddled a powerful black for a ride out to the Point of Rocks. Today he must try to find out what was wrong with his water supply. He could delay no longer. He was just cinching the saddle tight when he heard a rattle of hoofs and looked up to see Vaho Rainey sweep into the yard.

His face broke into a smile. This morning the girl was riding a blood bay, a splendid horse. She reined in, swung down, and walked over to him with a free-swinging stride that he liked.

"Rowdy," she asked excitedly, "did you ever hear of Silverside?"

"Silverside?" He looked at her curiously. "Who hasn't? The greatest roping horse this country ever saw, I reckon. Buck Gordon rode him and trained him, and Buck was a roper. There will never be a greater horse."

"Could you win that rodeo on him?"

He laughed. "Could I? On **that** horse? Vaho, I could win anything on that horse. He had the speed of a deer and was smarter than most men. I saw him once, several years ago, before he was killed. He was the finest roping horse I ever saw, and Buck the greatest hand."

"He's not dead, Rowdy. He's alive, and I know where he is."

Rowdy Horn's heart missed a beat. "You aren't foolin'? This isn't a joke?" He shook his head. "It couldn't be Silverside," he protested, "and if you've heard it is, somebody is mistaken. Buck Gordon was riding Silverside when the Apaches got him down near Animas—in one of their last raids over the border. They killed Silverside at the same time. A long time after that somebody found his skeleton, some of the hide, and Buck's saddle."

"He's alive, Rowdy!" Vaho repeated earnestly. "I know where he is, I tell you! Some Mexican picked up Buck's saddle, and when he was killed later, riding a paint, it was that horse that was found, or it must have been. Silverside was taken by the Apaches and they have him now."

Horn shook his head. "It couldn't be, Vaho. The Apaches are at least pretendin' to be friendly now, and have been for a long time. If they had that horse, somebody would have seen him." His eyes sparkled. "Man, I wish they had! With that horse I could sure make Luby back up! There never was a great roper without a great horse, and don't you forget it!"

"You said the Apaches were friendly," said Vaho. "All of them are not."

"Oh? You mean old Cochino? No, he sure isn't. But if that horse was alive and old Cochino had him, I'd still be out of luck. In the first place, nobody knows where he and his renegades hang out, and in the second place, it would be like committing suicide to look for him—if you found him."

"You wouldn't try it?" she persisted. "Not even for Silverside?"

"You bet I would!" Rowdy stated emphatically. "I'd ride through perdition in a celluloid collar for that horse!"

Vaho laughed, and her eyes were bright. "All right, put on your celluloid collar! I know where Cochino is, and I **know** he has Silverside!"

"If you mean that—"

Rowdy hesitated, thinking rapidly. She was positive, and after all, there had long been rumors of a friendship between old Cochino and Cleetus. The Navahos and the Apaches had never been too friendly, but the two old chiefs had found something in common. In fact, it had long been rumored that if Cleetus wanted to, he could tell where Cochino was at any time. But that was just cow-country gossip, and nobody was really looking for the tough and wily old Apache any longer.

"Yes," Rowdy said finally, "if you're positive, Vaho, I'll take a chance. Tell me where he is."

"I can't," Vaho said quietly, "but I'll take you there. But let me warn you—it's an awful ride."

"**You'll** take me there?" He was incredulous. "Nothing doing! I'd take a chance on Cochino myself, but not you!"

"Without me you wouldn't have a chance, Rowdy. With me, you may have. It's a big gamble, for old Cochino is peculiar and uncertain. He still believes the soldiers are after him, and he and the twenty or so renegade Apaches he has with him are dangerous. But he knows me, and he likes old Cleetus. Will you chance it?"

"You're sure you'll be safe?" he protested.

She grew suddenly serious. "I think so, Rowdy. Nobody knows about Cochino. He's like a tiger out of the jungle, one that has been partly trained. He may be all right, and he might turn ugly. But I'm willing to chance it. I want to see you win this rodeo, and I want to see you keep your ranch!"

He looked at her strangely, and as he looked into the soft depths of those lovely dark eyes, he remembered the momentary hardness of Jenny's blue eyes. Suddenly he knew that Jenny would never have ridden with him in that weird, sun-stricken desert where the Apache lived. Aside from the danger, she would have shied at the discomfort.

SCARCELY WERE ROWDY and Vaho on the trail when doubts began to assail him. The horse Cochino had simply couldn't be Silverside—and it had probably been years since he had been used for roping. Besides, the horse would be ten or eleven years old! Perhaps older. He scowled and mopped his brow, then glanced at the girl riding at his side, her eyes on the horizon.

The devil with it! If he found no horse, if he lost the ranch, if he couldn't beat Luby, the ride with this girl would be worth any chance he took. . . .

* * *

BACK ON THE RANCH, alone in the cabin, Neil Rice finished cleaning up and put away the dishes. There was work to do outside, but he felt in no mood for it. Idly, he began to rummage around the house, hunting for something to read. The few books failed to strike his interest, but when he was about to give up he remembered having seen several books in an old desk and bookcase in the inner room.

He found them and studied them thoughtfully, one by one. He was about to replace the last one, when he noticed what appeared to be a thin crack in the walnut of the old desk. Curious, he ran his hand back into the space from which he had taken the book. It was then that he noticed, on closer inspection, that there seemed to be some waste space in the desk, or some unaccounted-for space.

Remembering that many such old secretaries or cabinets had secret compartments, he felt around with his fingers, finally dug his nails into the crack, and pulled. The wood moved under his hand, and a small panel slid back!

In the small space beyond, he felt several pieces of paper. One had the feel of parchment. Slowly, he got his fingers on them and drew them out, then took them to the window for better light.

The first was an old legal paper, a corporate charter of some long-defunct mining company. What caught his eye at once was the missing seal. His eyes narrowed thoughtfully. Then he opened the next paper. Glancing at the heading, he read:

LAST WILL AND TESTAMENT OF
THOMAS B. SLATER

His eyes sharpening, he read on:

I, Thomas B. Slater, being of sound mind, make this my last will and testament. After payment of my just debts and funeral expenses, I devise and bequeath all my worldly goods and properties to Rowell D. Horn, who has been as a son to me through many months and whose friendship and interest in the future and well-being of the Bar O have shown him a fit person to possess this property.

There was more, and it was followed by the signature of the old rancher and that of two witnesses. Rice had never heard of either of them. He studied the document for a long time, then closed the compartment and replaced the book. He retained the charter with the missing seal and the will.

"Now wouldn't Bart Luby like to know about **this**!" he muttered thoughtfully.

He scowled. Possibly Luby **did** know about it. Hadn't Rowdy said that this place had been for a long time a line cabin for the Bar O? And after that for a while it had been headquarters for Bart Luby's cattle buying. No doubt Luby had taken the seal from this document, and then had concealed it and the will, believing that he might have some further use for it, at least for the signature; so he had hidden the will until he could make up his mind. He might have expected the place to be in his possession longer than it had been, but when Rowdy Horn had made his down payment without Luby's knowledge and had appeared suddenly and unexpectedly to take over, it may have left no chance for Luby to get into the old cabinet—until he could slip back secretly. And he had probably believed it safely hidden.

That the will was in existence at all was a serious oversight on Luby's part. Once in his hands, he should have destroyed it. Here, Rice thought, was the key to the whole situation in the South Rim. With this, Rowdy could get the Bar O and prove that Luby was the crook Rowdy believed him to be. But suppose Luby got it? There might be a lot of money in these papers if handled discreetly.

Neil Rice was painfully conscious of the emptiness of his own pockets. He came to a decision suddenly. He would ride into Aragon. . . .

OUT ON THE RANGE with Rowdy Horn, Vaho Rainey led the way, and the route she took led across the wide sagebrush flats toward the vague purple of distant mountains. Before they had ridden a mile they seemed lost in a limitless sea of distance where they moved at the hub of an enormous wheel of mountains. They talked but little, riding steadily onward into the morning sunlight, but Rowdy Horn kept his mind on the slim, erect girl who rode sometimes before him and sometimes behind.

As they drew nearer the mountains beyond the wide disk of the desert, Rowdy could see that what had appeared to be a wall of purple was actually broken into weird figures and towers, strange, grotesque monsters sculptured from the sandstone by sun, wind, and rain. The trail led along the valley floor between these rows of columns or battlemented walls, the sagebrush fell behind, and there was mesquite, a sure sign of undersurface water.

The afternoon was spent among the columns of sandstone and granite, then Vaho guided Rowdy into what was scarcely more than a crease between rolling hills. A mile of this and it widened, and they went down through a forest of saguaro. Then the trail wound steeply up among towering crags, and the saguaro was left behind, traded by the trail for borders of piñon and juniper. Some of their squat, gnarled trunks seemed gray with age and wind, but the bright green of their foliage was a vivid, living streak across the reds and pinks of the Kaibab sandstone.

Yellow tamarisks, smoke trees, and orange-hued rabbit brush brightened the way, but the mountains became more lonely. As dusk drew on they rounded into a small basin, grass-floored and cool, and here Vaho swung down. For all the heat and the length of the ride, she appeared fresh. "We'll camp here," she said, indicating the water hole.

"All night?" he asked.

She looked at him and smiled lightly. "Of course. The devil himself couldn't travel by night where we're going."

"You aren't afraid?" he asked curiously. "I mean, well—you don't know me very well, do you?"

"No, I'm not afraid. Should I be?"

He shrugged, not knowing whether to be pleased or deflated.

"No, of course not," he said.

There was plenty of dry wood, bone-dry and dusty, most of it. In a few minutes he had wood gathered and a fire going. He picketed the horses while Vaho began to prepare food. He watched her thoughtfully.

"You're quite a girl, you know," he said suddenly.

She laughed. "Why did you think I started this if it wasn't to show you that?" she asked. "I'm not a town girl, Rowdy. I could never be. Not all the time I was away at school, nor in all my traveling to New Orleans or New York or Boston did I ever forget the desert."

"I'm glad," he said, although he knew as he spoke that he was not quite sure why he should be glad. So he added lamely, "Some man is going to get a fine girl. He'll be lucky!"

She looked at him thoughtfully, then lifted the coffee from the fire.

"He will be if he likes the desert and mountains," was her only comment.

When they had finished eating he threw more wood on the fire and stretched out on the sand where he could look across the flames into Vaho's eyes. He felt vastly comfortable and relaxed, with myriad stars littered across the sky. The black loom of the cliffs, the ranch, the rodeo, and even Jenny seemed far behind.

They talked for a long time, while in the distance a coyote yapped at the stars. The grass rustled softly with the movements of the horses as they cropped quietly of the rich green grass.

CHAPTER IV

SILVERSIDE

Daybreak found Rowdy and Vaho moving again, and dipping down into the wide white bowl of another arm of the desert. Sweat broke out on Rowdy's forehead as the heat waves banked higher around them. There was no air, no movement save their own, and always and forever the heat.

Suddenly, Vaho Rainey turned her bay at right angles and dipped steeply down a narrow path to the bottom of a great sink. It was at least a thousand yards across, and all of two hundred feet from bottom to rim. Against the far wall, walled in by a huddle of stones, was a pool of clear cold water, and the dozen or so wickiups of Cochino, the Apache chief.

Rowdy Horn's pulse leaped as he saw the horses scattered nearby, feeding quietly, for among them was the tall black horse with the single great splash of white upon his left side—Silverside, the greatest roping horse he had ever seen!

His eyes turned again to the village. Nobody was in sight, neither squaws nor children, but he was conscious of watching eyes. For years the old renegade Apache had refused to live on a reservation, instead retreating steadily into the farthest vastnesses of the desert and mountains. At times he had fought savagely, but in the last years he had merely held to his loneliness, fiercely resenting any attempt to come near him or lure him out. It was reported that his braves were insane, that he was mad, that they had eaten of the fruit of a desert plant that rendered them all as deadly as marijuana addicts.

Vaho drew rein. "Be very careful, Rowdy," she said, low-voiced. "Make no quick moves, and let me do the talking."

From behind the wickiups and out of the rocks the Indians began to appear. Attired only in the skimpiest of breechclouts, their dusky bodies were dark as some of the burned red rocks of the desert, and looked as rough as old lava. Their black eyes looked hard as flint, as one by one they came down from the rocks and slowly gathered in a circle about the two riders.

Rowdy could feel his heart pounding, and was conscious of the weight of the six-shooter against his leg. It would be nip and tuck if anything started here. He might get a few of them, but they would get him in the end. Suddenly he cursed himself for a fool for having come here or letting Vaho come.

An old man emerged from the group and stared at them with hard, unblinking eyes. Vaho suddenly started to speak. Knowing a few words of Apache, Rowdy could follow her conversation. She was explaining that she was the adopted daughter of Cleetus, that he sent his best wishes to Cochino, the greatest of all Apache war chiefs.

The old man stared at her, then at Rowdy. His reply Horn could not interpret, but Vaho said to Rowdy suddenly, "He says for us to get down. He will talk."

That was no proof of their safety, yet it was something. Rowdy swung down and allowed an Indian to take their horses, then he followed Cochino to the fire, and all seated themselves. After a few minutes the girl took some of the presents they had brought from the bag she had prepared with Rowdy's help. A fine steel hunting knife, a package of tobacco, a bolt of red calico, other presents.

Cochino looked at them, but his expression was

bleak. He lifted his eyes to Vaho, and there was a question in them. Slowly, she began to explain. This friend—she gestured to Rowdy—was the friend of Cleetus also. She told how he had taken the old Indian in, treated his broken wrist, fed him and cared for him until he was able to move. She explained how Rowdy was a great warrior, but that in the games of his people he could not compete because his horse was injured, that he was an unhappy man. Then she had told him that her friend Cochino, the friend also of Cleetus, had a magnificent horse that he might lend or sell—the great Silverside.

For an hour the talk went on. Following it with difficulty, Rowdy Horn could be sure of nothing. Cochino should have been a poker player, he reflected. His expression was unreadable. Little by little, however, he seemed to be showing approval of Rowdy, and of Vaho. Suddenly he asked a question, looking from Rowdy to the girl, and she flushed.

Rowdy glanced at her quickly. "What did he want to know?" he said.

SHE WOULD NOT MEET his eyes, but continued to talk. He listened, straining his ears to get every syllable, doing his best to interpret what she was saying. The old Apache suddenly chuckled. It was a grim, hard sound, but there was a glint of ironic humor in his eyes as he looked from the girl to Rowdy. Finally, he nodded.

"Yes," he said, speaking plainly in English.

Her face flushed with happiness, Vaho turned to Rowdy, putting her hand impulsively on his arm.

"He says you can have the horse! He gives him to you, and he wishes you luck."

The old Indian got to his feet, and they did also.

"Tell him," Rowdy said impulsively, "that when he wishes, if there is anything a friend can do for him or his people, to come to me, or to send a messenger. There is only peace and brotherhood between the people of Cochino and Rowdy Horn."

She explained briefly, and the old Indian nodded gravely.

"Invite him to the rodeo if he wishes to come," Rowdy added.

Vaho spoke swiftly, and the old Indian stared at them, his eyes bleak. Then he shook his head.

"He says," Vaho explained, "he is too old to give up now. As he has lived, so will he die."

A long time after that, riding away through the great broken hills, Rowdy glanced back again and again at the splendid horse he was leading. And that night when they camped again beside the pool, he talked with the tall horse, curried him carefully. The horse nuzzled him, eager for affection.

Vaho walked out to them from the fire, and he looked around at her. "This horse is almost human," he said. "Somehow he gives a man the feeling of standing near something superb, something beyond just horseflesh."

She nodded. "I know. He likes you, too, Rowdy. Already that is plain." She hesitated for a moment. "But Rowdy, it has been a long time since he has worked with cattle. Do you think he will be as good?"

"I've no idea," he admitted, "but he's my only chance, and somehow I think we'll make it. Anyway, it will be a treat to ride this horse."

Yet he was scarcely thinking of that. He was thinking of the girl by his side—tall, clean-limbed, and lovely—and he was remembering the long ride through the desert beside her, the calm way she had talked to Cochino, the strange feeling of ease and happiness he had when riding with her, when knowing she was close to him. She was in his thoughts even as he slept—and dreamed. . . .

"Rowdy," Vaho said suddenly the following morning, "there's another trail, a way through the Rim to the back of your place. Old Cleetus showed it to me when I was just a little girl. Let's go that way. I think it's shorter."

Turning their horses they cut off through the pines toward the blue haze that hung in the distance, and abruptly they drew up on the very edge of an amazing canyon whose sides dropped sheer away to the sandy bottom where a small stream slid over a bottom now of rocks, now of sand. Skirting the cliff, they came to a steep path and wound their way down. When they and their horses had rested and had drunk long of the clear, cold water, they mounted again and turned downstream.

It was cool in the shadow of the cliffs. When they had followed the canyon for several hours, Rowdy called softly to Vaho, who had ridden on ahead.

"Look here." He drew up, pointing.

In the sand of the canyon bottom were the tracks of several shod horses.

"No Indian ponies," he said grimly, "and no white man that I know of knows this country. Except one."

"You think it's Rollick?" she asked.

"Who else? Times have changed since the old days, but there's still a market for rustled beef, and Jack Rollick is supposed to be back in here somewhere."

"The tracks go the same way we're going," she said, "but there's no way out of here now except downstream."

"Let's go," he said grimly.

He reached back and slipped the thong from the butt of his six-gun. His rifle he always carried in a scabbard that pointed forward and down just ahead of his right knee so that the stock of the rifle was within easy grasp of his right hand. He was glad now that it was so handy.

Riding cautiously downstream they had gone no more than two miles when suddenly the canyon widened out and the rock walls fell back. They drew up sharply in the screen of aspen and willow beside the trail. Before them was a wide green meadow through which coursed the stream. The meadow was all of fifty acres in extent. A branch canyon seemed to lead off an immeasurable distance to the right. Within view were at least one hundred head of cattle, fattening on the grass.

Beyond, and close to the sheer wall at the far end of the little meadow, was a stone cabin, and a corral. There were several horses in the corral. No saddled horses were in sight.

Skirting the cliff wall, they circled to the right, trusting to the sparse trees and the brush, as well as to the wide shadow of the encircling cliffs, to hide them. As they neared the cabin, Rowdy saw that the stream had been dammed and there was a large pool, all of an acre in extent.

Vaho touched his arm, indicating the pool. "That may be your trouble," she said, low-voiced. "This stream is probably the source of your water supply."

He had been thinking the same thing, and he nodded. When they had a better view, he could see that no more than a trickle seemed to be escaping from the pool, and the waters of the stream had been diverted to irrigate another small meadow.

More cattle were in view in the branch canyon. Rowdy Horn estimated that three hundred head were held here. From the brands he saw, nearly every ranch in the South Rim country was represented except the Bar O. That was, in itself, evidence of a kind. He stored the fact grimly away in his mind.

"Nobody around," he said thoughtfully. "I'm going to have a look in that cabin."

"I'll wait here," Vaho said. "Be careful."

He left her with Silverside and rode forward slowly. When near the cabin he dismounted and walked nearer on cat feet. A glance through the window showed the cabin to be empty. Stepping inside, he took a hasty look around. Six or seven men were bunking here, and they had supplies and ammunition enough to last a long time. Also, the house gave every evidence of long occupancy.

Under one of the bunks he saw a square black box and drew it out. It was padlocked, but picking up a hatchet, he smashed the lock with a few well-directed blows. Inside the box were a couple of engraved six-shooters, some odds and ends of letters addressed to Jack Rollick, and a small black tally book. He had picked it up and opened it, when he heard a scream.

With a lunge he was on his feet, racing to the door. He sprang outside, his eyes swinging to the woods where he had left Vaho. The bushes were thrashing, and he heard another low cry. Instantly he vaulted into saddle and the black horse lunged into a dead run for the woods. Rowdy hit the ground running, and dived through the bushes.

Vaho, her blouse torn, was fighting desperately with a tall, powerful man in a sweat-stained red shirt. When Rowdy plunged through the brush, the man's head turned. With an oath he hurled the girl from him and grabbed for his gun.

His draw was like a flash of light, and in an instant of desperation as the big man's hand darted, Rowdy Horn knew he could never match that draw, yet he palmed his own gun. The rustler's six-shooter roared, then Rowdy fired.

The big man lifted on his tiptoes, raised his eyebrows, and opened his mouth slowly, then plunged over on his face.

CHAPTER V
FRAMED INTO JAIL

Carefully, gun ready, Rowdy walked forward. He had never killed a man before, and he was frightened. The rustler's shot had been hasty and had missed. Evidently, the big fellow had stumbled when he tried to move, for Rowdy's bullet had gone into his back, just behind his left arm, and had come out under the heart.

"Oh, Rowdy!" Vaho cried, her eyes wide. "You killed him!"

"I reckon I did!" he said. "And I reckon we'd better make tracks out of here before they get back! There's at least five or six more of them around somewhere."

Swiftly they rode away, and in his hip pocket was the black tally book, forgotten.

They were skirting the Slash Bar range when Vaho spoke up suddenly. "Rowdy, hadn't you better ride on into Aragon and report this to the sheriff? Wouldn't it be best?"

"That's a good idea," he said worriedly. "What about you?"

"I'll wait at the Point of Rocks with Silverside. You can cut across to town; then come back here and we'll go on to your place."

Despite the fact that the killing had been in self-defense, and to protect Vaho, Rowdy was worried. It was no small thing to kill a man, even a thief and rustler. He rode swiftly, hurrying by every shortcut he knew, for Aragon. Yet when he arrived, the sheriff's office was deserted. He walked down the street, but could find him nowhere.

Eager to be back with Vaho, and worried about her—for he realized that the dead rustler's friends might trail them—Rowdy finally abandoned his quest for the sheriff and returned to the Point of Rocks. Together they rode on to the Slash Bar.

Riding into the yard, he called out, but there was no reply. Neil Rice was evidently away. Rowdy swung down, and wearily the girl dismounted. He stripped the saddles and bridles from the sweat-stained horses and turned all three of them into the corral. He and Vaho walked toward the house, but Vaho halted suddenly.

"Rowdy," she said, "I'm as tired as can be, but I should be going back to the Indians. Cleetus was to come today, and he'll be worried about me."

"All right." He turned back and saddled a paint

horse for her to ride. As she sat in the saddle, he took her hand. "Vaho," he said, "you've been swell. I didn't know they made them like you."

"It's all right. I liked doing it."

"Look," he said. "After the rodeo there's a big dance. Will you go with me?"

Her eyes brightened. "Oh, Rowdy! I'd love to! A dance! Why, I haven't danced since I left Boston! Of course I'll go!"

When she was out of sight in the gathering dusk, he turned back again toward the cabin. Opening the door, he walked in. The place was hot and stuffy, so he left the door open. Striking a match, he lit the coal-oil lamp, then turned around to replace it in the bracket. With the lamp in his hand, he stopped, riveted to the spot.

There on the floor of his cabin lay the body of a dead man. The red-shirted man he had killed at the hideout!

But how on earth had he come here? Rowdy did not even hear the approaching horses until a voice spoke abruptly behind him: "Here! What's this?"

Turning, he found Sheriff Ben Wells staring from him to the body.

"What's happened here?" demanded the lawman. "Who is this hombre?"

Behind Wells were Bart Luby and Mike McNulty. "That's cold-blooded killing, Ben!" Luby said triumphantly. "This man was shot in the back."

"He was not!" Horn declared hotly. "He was left

side toward me, and he fired, then started to move. My bullet went in where you see it, back of his arm."

"It's still in his back!" Luby said. "And," he added grimly, "we have only your story for it. You say he fired a shot. Why, his gun's still in its holster!"

"He wasn't killed here!" Horn said angrily. "This hombre grabbed Vaho Rainey when we were riding back of the Rim. I rushed up to help and he drew and fired. He missed and I shot and killed him!"

Sheriff Wells knelt beside the body. Drawing the gun, he checked it, then looked up, his face grave.

"This gun is fully loaded," he said, "and hasn't been fired!"

"What?" Rowdy was dumbfounded. "Why, that couldn't be. He—" He shrugged. "Well, I reckon the man or men who brought him here changed guns with him."

Wells gnawed at his gray mustache. Secretly, he had always liked Rowdy Horn as much as he disliked Bart Luby, but this story was out of all reason.

"You mean to say," he demanded, "that you killed this man back of the Rim? And that somebody packed his carcass down here and dumped him on you?"

"That's exactly what happened!" Rowdy Horn said flatly. "It's the only way it could have happened."

Luby laughed. "Give him credit for being original, Ben. But he certainly hasn't much respect for your intelligence, to try a story like that."

"You'll have to come into town, son," Wells said, his voice hardening. "This will have to be explained."

"But you can't put me in jail!" Rowdy pleaded. "Think, man! The rodeo's tomorrow."

"You should have thought of that," Luby suggested, "before you killed this man. Anyway, that's no excuse. Your ropin' horse is laid up, so you can't compete!"

On the verge of bursting out with an explanation about Silverside, he caught himself just in time. If he had to go to jail, and there was nobody to watch the horse, it might easily be stolen.

"I knew this hombre," McNulty said suddenly. "He was Jake Leener, one of the Rollick outfit."

"No matter," Wells said positively. "He was shot in the back. We had nothing against him, even if he did ride with Rollick. The law can't call a man a crook until he's known to be one. This here hombre hadn't no record I know of, and he sure ain't wanted now."

"But listen!" Rowdy protested. "I've a witness! Vaho Rainey saw all this! She knows what happened!"

"Vaho Rainey?" Wells stared at him. "Rowdy, what you giving us? If that girl was with you, where is she now? You know as well as I do that if there is any such girl nobody has seen her around. You're just pullin' rabbits out of your hat. Tell us what happened, and I'll see you get a break if you've got one comin'."

"I told you what happened!" Horn said stubbornly. "Take it or leave it!"

"We'll take you," Wells said. "Mike, rustle this gent's horse, and be quick!"

Bart Luby glanced thoughtfully across the room toward the door of the bedroom. He was thinking of that old cabinet. Now that he was arrested, Horn would be away from the house. In the dozen or so times he had tried to enter, he had failed to find him away even once. But with a killer charge hanging over him he would not return, and he was out of the rodeo. . . .

IT WAS A SOLEMN and silent group that rode over the trail to Aragon. Grimly, Rowdy thought that this was the last straw. He was through now. The rodeo had been his last hope. With that money, even though he had lost Jenny, he could pay off the mortgage on his ranch.

His thought of Jenny brought it home to him that he had scarcely thought of her for days. Ever since he had first seen her, several years before, he had dreamed of her. She had been an ideal girl, the prettiest one around, and all his attentions had been centered upon her. When they had become engaged, it was almost more than he could believe.

Yet after he had begun to see more of her and know her better, his first doubts of her had arisen. After all, there were other things than beauty, and although he told himself he was being unjust, Jenny seemed to be lacking in too many of them. Despite this, his loyalty made him refuse to accept the evidence of his senses until the day she had broken their engagement. For in spite of the shock and pain of that moment, he had felt a queer sense of escape and relief.

In town Rowdy was safely lodged in jail, and the morning sun was making a latticework of bars on the wall opposite the cell window when he awakened with a start. For an instant he lay still, then it hit him, and his heart went sick. After all his planning, he was stuck in jail on the day of the rodeo!

HE GOT UP SLOWLY, dressed, and splashed his face in the bucket of cold water that had been left for him. Gloomily he stared out of the barred window at the crowded streets. Already the hitching rails were lined with horses, and there were many buckboards and spring wagons in town. In another hour the streets would be jammed. It began to look as if the boosters of Aragon and the annual Stockman's Show and Rodeo would be right: that between two and three thousand spectators would be on hand for the show.

Yet as he paced the floor, cursing his luck and alternately staring out the window and going to the barred door, hours passed. He heard the band playing, and the confusion that heralded the big parade that opened the rodeo. And then suddenly Sheriff Ben Wells was at the bars.

"Rowdy, if I turn you loose to compete in this

show, will you promise not to leave town?" Wells gnawed at his mustache. "I know you, son, and I never figured you'd shoot a man in the back, but that story of yours is plumb far-fetched. But just now I got a lead that may help. Maybe we jumped to conclusions, so I'm goin' to turn you loose for the duration of the rodeo."

With a whoop of joy, Horn jumped to the opening door. Grabbing the sheriff's hand, he tried to thank him, but Wells shook his head.

"Don't thank me. Thank this young lady here."

Rowdy turned quickly to face Vaho Rainey.

"You? You got here?"

"You invited me for the dance. Have you forgotten?" She laughed. "When I heard you were in jail, naturally I had to get you out! A girl can't go to a dance with a man who's in jail, can she, Sheriff?"

Ben Wells shook his head, his eyes twinkling. "Son," he said seriously, "I don't know where you found her or how you rate it, but you've got a wonderful girl there, and I'd sure latch onto her if I was you."

Vaho reddened, but her eyes were bright. She was still wearing her denims and blue shirt, but she was sparkling this morning. Rowdy took her arm and squeezed it.

"How in the world did you do it?" he exclaimed.

"I'll tell you later. Only it wasn't just what I did. Now we have to get down to the rodeo grounds. Silverside is down there, waiting for you. We've covered him with a blanket so nobody will know who he is."

Vaho had thought of everything, Rowdy found. Mike McNulty had rousted out the outfit Rowdy had purchased to wear in the rodeo, and in a short time Rowdy had bathed and changed. He came out, immaculate in dove-gray shirt and trousers, with a white hat and a black neckerchief. Black braid outlined his pockets. He wore his guns, but in new holsters, black and shining. His boots, which he had been breaking in around the ranch, felt good.

Vaho's eyes widened. "Why, Rowdy!" she exclaimed. "You're handsome!"

He blushed. "Me?" he choked. And as Mike McNulty and Pete Chamberlain went into roars of laughter, he flushed even deeper.

Hurriedly, he rushed over to Silverside and stripped the blanket from the horse. After a brief workout with the animal, he brought him back to the stall they had procured for him.

"Don't let anybody near him," he warned. "All I'll have to do on that horse is throw the rope! He's so smart he scares me!"

CHAPTER VI
DEVIL MAY CARE

With Vaho at his side, Rowdy turned toward the arena. The stands were jammed. Going through the gate toward the chutes, almost the first person Rowdy saw was Bart Luby. And with him was Jenny Welman!

Bart started and scowled. "What are you doin' out?" he demanded.

Jenny's eyes had gone immediately to the girl, taking in Vaho's shabby outdoor clothes with a quick contemptuous smile.

"I'm ridin' in the show, Bart," Rowdy drawled. "Reckon you'll have me to beat, ropin' and everything."

"Where'd you get a horse?" Luby demanded suspiciously.

"I've got one." Rowdy's eyes shifted to Jenny. Suddenly he was no longer angry or even irritated with her. "Jenny," he said pleasantly, "I want you to know Vaho Rainey. Miss Rainey, Miss Welman and Bart Luby."

"Oh!" Jenny exclaimed. "You're that Indian girl, aren't you? Or a white girl who lives down in the wickiups? I've forgotten which."

"Yes, that's who I am," Vaho said easily, and Rowdy grinned at the quick smile on her lips. It wouldn't be necessary to protect Vaho, he could see. The contempt in Jenny's voice had been evident, as was the malice, but Vaho was equal to it. "And it's nice to be here today," Vaho added.

"It must be," Jenny fired back. "I hear it's very dirty down there, and it would be a relief to get away for a while."

"Any change is a relief," Vaho replied gently. "You should try it sometime, or"—her voice was suddenly level—"would you rather continue to be a girl of the town?"

Before Jenny, whose face went white with fury, could reply, Vaho took Rowdy's arm.

"Shall we go, dear?" she said sweetly.

As they strolled away, Jenny got her voice back. "Girl of the town!" she cried furiously. "Why, that no-account Indian! I could—"

"Forget it!" Bart said, shrugging. "She just meant you were a city girl."

"I know what she meant!" Jenny flared.

But Luby was not listening. He was staring at his toes, thinking, and his thoughts were not pleasant. In spite of all his plans, Rowdy Horn would ride in the rodeo today, and if Wells had released him, it could only be on sufficient evidence to clear him.

Could it have been the testimony of this girl, Vaho, alone? He weighed that thoughtfully. Doubt arose, for there had been triumph in Rowdy Horn's eyes. Well, no matter. Rowdy had no roping horse, and that was one event he could not hope to win. Nor would he win the bronc riding. For all that, however, Luby's mind was not at ease. There was something wrong, something very wrong, where he was concerned.

As soon as Vaho Rainey and Rowdy reached the chutes, she had excused herself and disappeared. The parade was lining up for the ride around the arena, and McNulty led Silverside, saddled, but still under a blanket, up to where Rowdy Horn was waiting. Beside him was the palomino for Vaho.

The band began to play, and there were excited shouts from the crowd. Silverside's head lifted, and the splendid-appearing horse tossed his head, eyes bright and nostrils distended, as old memories of parades and triumph flooded back. Rowdy stepped to his side.

"Yes, this is it, boy! Show them for me, just like you did for Buck!" The big horse bobbed his head, as if in assent.

Suddenly, Mike let out an awed exclamation. "Boss!" he whispered hoarsely. "Look!"

Startled by McNulty's voice, Rowdy turned, and his mouth dropped open. Before him, resplendent in formfitting forest green and silver, was Vaho Rainey!

Never more beautiful in her life, the tall, dark girl looked proudly into his eyes—proudly, yet hesitantly—looking for the evidence that he found her lovely. And it was there. It was in the eyes of every man who had turned at Mike's astonished exclamation.

Never in all her days had Jenny Welman been as lovely as this. Her pale blond beauty was a poor shadow beside this vivid loveliness, dark, flashing, proud.

"Am I all right?" Vaho asked, her eyes bright with fun. "I had the suit made, and saved it. I knew, somehow, you'd ride. And I wanted you to be proud of me!"

"**Proud** of you?" he shouted. "Honey, I feel like some fairy princess had waved a wand over a little woods girl and turned her into something better than the Queen of Sheba and Helen of Troy rolled into one! Wait till the crowd sees you!"

"Don't you want, just a little," she said gently, "to have Jenny Welman see me?" Her eyes sparkled as she asked the question primly.

He grinned. "I sure do!" he said.

Mike McNulty jerked the blanket from Silverside, and after helping Vaho into the saddle on the palomino, Rowdy Horn swung up himself.

Sheriff Ben Wells walked up with Dick Weaver, the rodeo boss. Weaver froze in midstride.

"Hey!" he shouted. "Ain't that Silverside?"

At the magical name of the greatest rodeo horse of the southwest, men wheeled about. There were shouts, and others came running. They gathered around, staring.

"He's Silverside, all right," Horn said quietly.

Then the band struck up once more, and the parade began to move.

As if by magic that name had flown across the arena, so that by the time the contestants rode into the arena all eyes were turned to find the great horse, so miraculously back from the dead. And the eyes of the crowd went from the great horse to the rider, tall in the saddle, and to the girl in green and silver who rode beside him. Jenny Welman, hearing all the excited talk, turned in her saddle—she was riding beside Luby—and the smile on her face froze. The laughter went out of her. Beside that girl with Rowdy she herself looked shabby and small, and she knew it.

Bart Luby heard the name of Silverside, but would not turn. His heart pounded, and his lips tightened. This rodeo meant more to him than anything in the world, and he was going to win! He was going to win, no matter how!

There was scarcely a person in the crowd but understood what drama and excitement lay before them. Gossip in a small town flies quickly, and the fact that Jenny Welman had returned Rowdy Horn's ring was known to them all, as was the trouble and rivalry between Bart Luby and the young rancher who would ride against him today.

The mysterious girl from the mountains, whom all had heard of but never seen, was before them now, riding proudly beside Rowdy. And to top it all, Rowdy Horn—out of the running when his horse, Cub, had gone lame—had come in at the last minute, freed from jail, to ride. And he was mounted on the greatest horse of the generation—Silverside!

Rowdy Horn watched carefully as he waited beside the chute. There were some good hands riding in this show. Still, he knew, the man he had to beat was Bart Luby.

Never before had he appeared before a crowd of this size. He had been riding all his life, and had appeared in various small-town rodeos, and had spent two summers breaking wild broncs for the rough string. For the sheer sport of it and a little mount money, he had ridden in tryouts when big showmen were testing contest stock for the big shows. But he was in no sense the professional that Luby was.

Roping was his specialty; it was part of his day's work and had been for a long time, but he had never competed in such a show as this, even if it did not rank anywhere near tops in size.

Bart Luby, on the other hand, had been appearing in all the big shows and winning consistently, and he had been competing against the greatest performers in the business. Today, in the first event, the preliminaries in the calf roping, Rowdy would be riding a horse which for all its greatness was unfamiliar to him. Bitterly, he stared out at the dusty arena, soon to be the scene of battle and danger, and for the first time realized what this attempt really meant.

He was no stranger to the flying hoofs and tigerish bucking of outlaw horses or Brahma bulls. He had seen men die in the arena, had seen others crippled or broken under the lashing hoofs of some maddened bronc. But for Rowdy more than life was at stake out there today, and remembering Luby from the old days on the Bar O, he knew the man was fast and skillful. Undoubtedly, he had grown more so.

"I'm a fool," Horn told himself. "I'm bucking a stacked deck. I'm not good enough for these hombres."

After the parade was over, gloomily, Rowdy watched the first leppy dart from the chute and leg it across the arena, with a cowboy on a flying paint horse behind it. That was Gus Petro, a Greek rider from Cheyenne. Doubts lost in sudden interest, Rowdy watched the dust clear, and heard the time called. He smiled. He could beat that. He knew he could beat it.

Yet when the official announcer announced his own name, and he heard that voice rolling out over the arena, something leaped inside him.

"Folks, here comes Rowdy Horn, of the Slash Bar, ridin' that greatest ropin' horse of all time—**Silverside**!"

The calf darted like a creamy streak, and Silverside took off with a bound. Instantly, Rowdy knew that all he had heard of the horse he bestrode was only half the truth. With flashing speed, the black horse with the splash of white on his side was after the fleeing calf. Horn's rope shot out like an arrow, and in almost the same breath, Rowdy was off the horse, grounding the bawling, struggling calf and making a quick tie. He sprang away from the calf.

"There it is, folks!" Weaver's voice boomed out

over the arena. "Eleven seconds even, for Rowdy Horn on Silverside!"

Bart Luby's eyes narrowed. It was a tough mark, yet he had tied it twice. He was off like a streak when his calf darted away from the chute. He roped, flopped the calf, and made his tie.

"Eleven and one-fifth seconds!" Weaver bawled.

Luby swore softly, his eyes bitter. With a jerk he whipped his horse's head around and rode off to the stands. These were only preliminaries, and the final test was yet to be made. But he had never believed that Rowdy Horn would beat him, even by a fifth of a second in a tryout, and he didn't like being beaten.

While the band played and the clowns ripped and tore around the tanbark, mimicking the performances of the preceding event, the contestants headed for the shack to draw horses for the saddle bronc riding contest.

Vaho was waiting for Rowdy near chute 5, from which he would ride. He found that he had drawn Devil May Care, a wicked bucker that had been ridden only twice the preceding year in twenty-two attempts, and not at all in the current season. Bart Luby had drawn an equally bad horse, Firefly.

"You were wonderful!" Vaho said, as Rowdy walked up. "I never saw anyone move so fast!"

He grinned a little. "It's got to be better, honey," he said honestly. "Bart Luby has done that well, and he'll be really trying next time."

"You can do it!" she insisted. "I know you can!"

"Maybe," he said. "But if I do, it will be that horse. I'll know him better next time. Let's just hope I draw a calf that's fast."

"How about this event?" she asked, worriedly. "You drew a bad horse."

"Just what I wanted. You can't win in these rodeos on the easy ones. The worse they buck, the better the ride—if you stay up there."

Bart Luby was first out of the chute on Firefly, and the horse was a demon. It left the chute with a rush and broke into a charge, then swapped ends three times with lightning speed and went into an insane orgy of sunfishing. Luby, riding like the splendid performer he was, raked the big horse fore and aft, writing his name all over its sides with both spurs. At the finish he was still in the saddle and making a magnificent ride. He hopped off and lifted a hand to the cheers of the crowd.

ROWDY STARED OUT through the dust and touched his tongue to dry lips. He mounted the side of the chute and looked down at the trembling body of the sorrel, Devil May Care. Sheriff Ben Wells stood nearby, and he looked up at Horn.

"Watch yourself, boy. This horse is a mean one. When you leave him, don't turn your back or you're a goner."

Rowdy nodded and, tight-lipped, lowered himself into the saddle and eased his feet into the stirrups.

His fingers took a tighter hold on the reins, and he heard Weaver's voice booming again.

"Here it comes, folks! Right out of chute five! Rowdy Horn on that bundle of pure poison and dynamite, Devil May Care!"

Rowdy removed his hat and yelled, "Let 'er go, boys!"

The gate tripped open and Devil May Care exploded into the arena in a blur of speed and pounding hoofs. His lithe body twisting in unison with the movements of the horse, Rowdy Horn got one frenzied view of the whirling faces of the crowd, then the horse under him went mad in a series of gyrations and sunfishing that made anything Rowdy had ever encountered before seem a pale shadow.

The sorrel outlaw was a fighter from way back, and he knew just exactly why he was out here. He was going to have this clinging burr out of the saddle or know the reason why. Devil May Care swallowed his head and lashed at the clouds with his heels and went into another hurricane of sunfishing, all four feet spurning the dust, his whipcord body jackknifing with every jump. He swapped ends as Rowdy piled up points, scratching the sorrel with both spurs.

Suddenly, with less than a second to go, the sorrel raced for the north wall and swung broadside in a wicked attempt to scrape his rider off. In one grasping breath, Rowdy saw that the horse was going to miss the wall by inches. He kept his foot in the stirrup, fighting the big horse's head around. Devil May Care came around like the devil he was and, as the whistle sounded, went into a wicked burst of bucking that made anything in the past seem mild by comparison.

CHAPTER VII
UNLISTED EVENT

Riders rushed from near the judges' stand, and Rowdy kicked loose both feet and left the horse just as all four feet of the sorrel hit ground. Wheeling, teeth bared, Devil May Care sprang for his rider, but the horsemen wheeled alongside and snared the maddened bronc. With cheers ringing in his ears, Rowdy Horn walked slowly back across the arena. The crowd was still cheering when he walked up to chute 5.

Wells grinned at him. "That horse must be on your side, son," he said. "Goin' for you like that sure impressed the crowd, and the judges, too! Showed he had plenty of fight!"

"If he's friendly"—Rowdy grinned—"deliver me from my friends!"

Wells spat. "You've got a couple of mighty good friends, son. And neither of them are horses."

Luby was standing nearby. He turned, his elbows on the crossbar of the gate.

"You were lucky," he said. "Plain lucky."

Rowdy's eyes darkened. "Maybe. If so, I hope my luck holds all day. And tomorrow."

"It won't," Luby said flatly. "Your luck's played out! I've protested to the judges. I told them that allowin' a killer to ride would ruin the name of the show."

"Killer?" Rowdy wheeled. "Why, you—"

Bart Luby had been set for him, and too late Rowdy saw the punch coming. It was a smashing right that caught him on the side of the jaw. His feet flew up and he hit the dust flat on his back. Bart lunged for him. Rowdy rolled over and came up fast, butting Luby in the chest and staggering the bigger man. Bart set himself and rushed, smashing Horn back against the gate with a left and right, then following it up with a wicked hook to the head that made Rowdy's knees wobble.

Ducking a left, Horn tried to spring close, but Luby grabbed him and threw him into the dust. His face smeared with blood and dust, Rowdy came up, and through a fog of punch-drunkenness, he saw the big rancher coming in, on his face a sneer of triumph.

The man's reach was too long. Rowdy tried to go under a left and caught a smashing right uppercut on the mouth. Bart, his face livid with hatred, closed in, punching with both hands. Then Rowdy saw his chance. Luby drew his left back for a wide hook and

Horn let go with a right. It beat the hook and caught Luby on the chin with the smash of a riveting hammer.

The big man staggered, his face a study in astonishment, and then Rowdy closed in, brushed away a left, and smashed both hands to the body, whipping them in with wicked sidearm punches, left and right to the wind. Luby threw a smashing right, but Rowdy was watching that left. It cocked again, and he pulled the trigger on his right.

Bart hit the dust on his shoulders. He rolled over, and Rowdy stood back, hands ready, waiting for him to get up. Blood dribbled from Rowdy's mouth and there was a red welt on his cheekbone, but he felt fine.

Luby was up with a lunge and caught Rowdy with two long swings, but Horn was inside of them, smashing a left to the body and a right to the head. Luby backed off, and suddenly, sensing victory, Rowdy Horn closed in. He chopped a left to the head, then a right, then another left. He smashed Luby with a straight left, and as Luby cocked a right, knocked him down.

Bart Luby lay there in the dust, thoroughly whipped. Reaching down, Rowdy jerked him to his feet and shoved him back against the corral bars. He cocked his right hand to smash the bigger man in the face, then hesitated.

Coolly, he stepped back.

"Nothing doing, Bart," he said calmly. "You started

this, and you've had a beating comin' for a long time, but I'm givin' you no alibis. I want your eyes open because I'm goin' to beat your socks off out there in the arena. When I win, I'll win on the tanbark!"

Deliberately, he turned his back and walked toward the stables.

Bending over a bucket he bathed the dust and blood from his face and combed his hair. He scowled suddenly, remembering Neil Rice. What had become of the printer? In the hurry and confusion of being arrested, and then the rodeo, there had scarcely been time to think. Still, Rice might be back at the ranch by now.

What did Ben Wells have up his sleeve? Who were the friends he had mentioned, and had they effected his release to compete in the rodeo? He was puzzled and doubtful, and recalling the finding of the body in his cabin, he realized how desperate his situation truly was. Aside from Vaho, he had no evidence of any kind. To the sheriff, as well as to people generally, his story of killing a man in a remote canyon and then finding his body in his own cabin would seem too utterly fantastic.

Deliberately, he forced his thoughts away from that. First there were the contests. Each thing in its own time.

· The next event was bareback bronc riding, then came steer wrestling and bull riding. After that, the finals in calf roping. Four men would compete in the finals: Cass Webster from Prescott and Tony Sandoval from Buffalo, Wyoming, besides Bart Luby and himself.

Bareback bronc riding was a specialty of Rowdy's, and he took a fighting first, riding Catamount, a wicked devil of a horse. Luby took second, with Webster a close third. Luby won the steer wrestling, beating Rowdy by two-fifths of a second. Sandoval, the Wyoming rider, won the bull riding, and again Rowdy took a second, with Luby a third.

Sweating and weary, he walked slowly back to the corrals at the day's end. Tomorrow would decide it, but he was ahead of Luby so far. . . .

MORNING CAME, and the air was electric with expectancy. Even the other contestants eyed Rowdy thoughtfully as he strolled quietly down to the stables. Silverside nickered softly as he came up, and Rowdy Horn stopped to talk to the horse as it nuzzled him under his arm with a delicate nose.

Cass Webster stopped nearby.

"This killin' stuff don't go with me, boy," he said quietly. "I don't savvy this fuss, but you stack up A-one where I stand." He ground his cigarette into the dust. "Luby washed himself out with me down to White Rock last year. He's dirty, Horn. You keep your eyes open."

"Thanks," said Rowdy.

His attention had turned from the cowboy and was centered on Vaho Rainey, who was walking toward him, followed by the admiring glances of everyone.

"We've visitors," she said, "so be careful what you say."

His frown was puzzled. "I don't get it," he protested.

"You will. . . . Look!"

As she spoke, he turned his head. A small group of Indians was approaching. The first was old Cleetus, and the others were all men of his tribe, except one. That one, carefully concealed by a blanket, was Cochino!

"Glad to see you here," Rowdy told the Indians sincerely. "Very glad. If there's anything I can do, tell me."

They looked at Silverside and talked in low tones.

"They were here yesterday, too," Vaho whispered. "They watched you ride."

Suddenly, Cochino spoke to the girl, swiftly, with gestures. Her eyes brightened and she turned quickly.

"Oh, Rowdy! He says you can keep the horse! He is a present to you!"

"Good glory!" Beside himself with excitement and delight, he could scarcely find words. "But what'll I say? What can I give him?"

"Nothing. That is—well, he asks only one thing." Vaho was blushing furiously.

"What is it? Whatever it is, I'll do it!"

"I—can't tell you now. Later."

She quickly hurried away, and the old Indian chuckled. Cleetus smiled, showing broken teeth, but his eyes were grimly humorous.

An even bigger crowd swelled the arena to over-flowing, and men crowded every available space. Pete Drago and his Demon Riders did their trick riding, their efforts augmented by the clowns, some of them rivaling Drago's amazing riders for sheer ability and thrills. The chuck wagon race followed, and an exhibition with bullwhips.

By the time the finals in the calf roping came around, Rowdy Horn was up on Silverside and ready. This time he was following Bart Luby. The piggin' strings he kept in Silverside's stall were checked, and he brought them out ready for the tie. Momentarily, he draped them around the saddle horn, and at a call from Wells, walked over to him.

"Soon's this event is over," the sheriff said, "I want to see you."

Rowdy nodded grimly. "Sure," he said, "I'll look you up. It was mighty fine of you to give me this chance, Ben, and I'll be ready to go back to jail."

DESPITE THAT, his heart was heavy as he walked back to his horse and swung into the saddle. Thoughtfully, he stared out at the arena. Eleven seconds, the time he had made yesterday, was fast time. It was fast enough to win in many shows, but could he equal it today?

He picked up the piggin' strings and kept one in his right hand. The other he put in his teeth. Suddenly his consciousness, directed at the arena where Bart Luby had just charged out after his calf, was jerked back to himself. His lips felt something strange with the rawhide piggin' string. Jerking it from his teeth, he stared at it. Both strings had been carefully frayed with a file or some rough object. When drawn taut, to bind the calf's legs, they would snap like thread!

"Time!" Weaver's voice boomed out over the arena. "Bart Luby ties his calf in the record-breaking time for this show of ten and nine-tenths seconds!"

Cheers swept the arena, and Rowdy Horn felt something go sick inside of him. He heard his name called, and he twisted in the saddle.

"Cass!" he yelled. "Piggin' strings! Quick!"

Webster sprang as if stuck with a pin and thrust some piggin' strings in Rowdy's fingers. At the same instant, Rowdy tossed the frayed strings to the other contestant.

"Look!" he yelped.

He saw his calf leave the chute with a bound and take off down the arena like a bolt. Silverside saw it go and was in a dead run, heading down the arena. Rowdy's rope whirled and shot out, and he left the saddle with a leap, swept the calf from its feet and down deftly, swiftly. His heart pounding and the dust swirling in his nostrils, he made his tie and sprang free, arm uplifted!

Dead silence held the arena, and then, his voice wild with excitement, Weaver announced:

"Folks! Rowdy Horn, ridin' the great Silverside, wins the calf ropin' with the record time of ten and eight-tenths seconds!"

Cheers boomed across the arena, and Rowdy swung into the saddle and trotted his horse across to the judges' stand. His great horse reared high, and Rowdy's hat swung wide, acknowledging the cheers. Then, to the martial music of the band, Silverside dance-stepped across the arena to accompanying cheers. Then Rowdy turned the horse and rode him back to the chutes.

The memory of those frayed piggin' strings was in his mind. There was only one time it could have been done, hastily but deftly, and obviously planned for, and that had been while he was exchanging his few words with the sheriff.

Bart Luby had been sitting his horse, awaiting his signal, right beside Silverside!

Swift work, but it could have been done, for several minutes must have elapsed before Rowdy had returned to his horse. Only the sudden feel of the frayed place by his lips had saved him, for a snapped piggin' string would have meant too much loss of time.

He swung down and approached the tight little circle of men—Sheriff Ben Wells, Cass Webster, Tony Sandoval, Neil Rice, and others. And in the center of them, pale and defiant, his eyes hard with hatred, was Bart Luby.

Rowdy shoved through the crowd. "All right, blast you!" he flared. "Now you can have that beatin'!"

"Hold it, Horn!" Wells said sternly. "Step back now! This is in my hands!"

"All this talk is foolishness!" Luby declared harshly. "Why would I do a thing like that? I don't care what Webster says, I never touched those piggin' strings!"

"Same thing you done at White Rock!" Webster said flatly. "And you say I'm a liar, Bart Luby, and you've me to whip!"

Wells turned on him, scowling.

"Will you shut up!" he said testily. "That piggin' string deal was bad enough, but I'm arrestin' Luby for fraud, and for rustlin'."

"What?" Luby's face paled. "What are you talkin' about?"

"What I said," Ben Wells replied calmly. "This here hombre"—he gestured to Rice—"found Tom Slater's true will hid in a cabinet in the old Slash Bar ranch house. He also found a document there that had its seal removed. Meantime, I'd sent a couple of deputies with a posse back to hunt for that valley Rowdy told us about. They hit the jackpot and rounded up Jack Rollick and two of his boys. Rollick confessed that he helped you tote that body over to the Slash Bar, Luby, to dump it on Horn. Besides that, when I jugged Horn, I searched him, and found what he had plumb forgot—Rollick's tally book showin' he rustled cows he'd sold through you and to you, even tellin' about the percentage he took off whenever you tipped him to good steals."

"It's all a pack of lies," Luby said, but his protest lacked emphasis.

"A search warrant got us into your house while you was down here," Wells went on remorselessly, "and we scared up that fake deed. Rice, here, he showed me how that seal was removed from one paper and used on the other. He also showed how the will you had was actually an old letter to you from Slater, but changed so to make it a will. You can tell by the creases where words were changed and added on."

Rowdy Horn looked up and saw Jenny Welman standing on the edge of the crowd, her lips parted. She stared at Luby, horrified, then at Rowdy. Abruptly, she turned and fled.

Horn had no wish to hear more. He was cleared now. Rice caught his eye.

"Boss," he said, "I did what I thought was right. You were gone, so I acted on my own."

"Fine," Rowdy said, "I'm glad you did." His eyes were straying, searching for the face he wanted. "You've got your job with me as long as you want it."

Vaho Rainey walked out from the stables, leading her palomino. Rowdy walked past Rice and stopped her. For an instant, their eyes held.

"Honey," he said then, "how many sheep would I have to swap Cleetus for you?"

She laughed. "He'd probably give you sheep to be rid of me. He loves me, I know, but now that I'm a young lady, I think I worry him."

"Maybe you wouldn't want to marry a cowman, even one with a ranch," he suggested.

"Why, Rowdy!" She laughed suddenly, her eyes dancing. "We've been engaged, or practically engaged, ever since we got Silverside!"

"What?" He stared at her. "What do you mean?"

She blushed, but her eyes were happy. "Why, I told Cochino that it was the custom of your people for the bride to bring a pony to her husband, and only the finest pony would do. That was what he was saying by the stables this morning. He said all he wanted in return for the horse, which he had actually given me to give you, anyway, was for you to take good care of your squaw!"

He chuckled. "Why, I reckon that's a good deal," he said whimsically. "The cheapest durned horse I ever got!"

The Ghost Maker

Marty Mahan, tall in the saddle of his black gelding, rode in the Grand Entry Parade of the Wind River Annual Rodeo, but beside him rode fear. Tall and splendidly built, clad in silver and white, Mahan was a fine-looking rider, and the crowd, which looked down to applaud, and to whose applause he responded with a wave of his Stetson, knew he was one of the greatest riders the West had seen.

For two years he had won top honors in the Wind River show. At a dozen other rodeos he was considered, by performers as well as spectators, one of the finest all-around cowboys riding the tanbark. Yet today fear rode with him, and hatred and contempt rode beside him. The fear was in the memory of a day and a horse; the hatred was in the person of big Yannell Stoper, the hard-faced roughneck of the contests, who rode beside him in the parade.

"How does it feel, Pretty Boy?" Yannell sneered. "How does it feel to know you're through? You know what they'll say when they find out? You're yellow! Yellow, Mahan! Just as yellow as they come! That

Ghost Maker will show 'em today! You mark my words!"

Mahan said nothing, his face stiff and white. There was too much truth in what Stoper was saying. He was afraid—he had always been afraid of Ghost Maker.

YANNELL STOPER HAD REASON to know. Three times hand running, three years before, Marty Mahan had beaten Yannell out for top money, and Stoper was not a man who took losing lightly. His animosity for Mahan developed, but he had detected no flaw in the other rider until that day at Twin Forks.

It was a small rodeo, just a fill-in for riders of the stamp of Stoper and Mahan, and neither of them had figured on much trouble. Marty had won the calf roping without even extending himself, and Stoper had taken the steer wrestling easily. Both riders had allowed the lesser names to come in for money in other events, pointing themselves at the bronc riding.

Marty Mahan had been his usual devil-may-care self until the names of the riders and their mounts were posted. Marty Mahan was posted as riding Ghost Maker.

"What a name!" he said, grinning. "I wonder who thinks them up?"

Red Blade shrugged. "This one deserves his name!" he said wryly. "You should do top money if you top off that horse! He earned his name up in Calgary!"

"Calgary?" Yannell noticed a subtle change in Mahan's voice, and had turned to watch him. "This Ghost Maker from up there?"

"Sure is!" Blade spat. "Killed a man up there two seasons ago. Mighty fine rider, too. Man by the name of Cy Drannan. Throwed him an' then tromped him to death! Caught him in his teeth, flung him down, then lit in with all four feet! He's a reg'lar devil!"

"A big zebra dun?" Marty asked. Stoper recalled afterward that it had seemed less a question than a statement.

"That's right! An' pure poison!"

Marty Mahan was taken suddenly ill and could not ride. Yannell Stoper thought that one over, and curiously he watched both Marty and the dun horse. Mahan had come out to see the bronc riding, but he seemed pale and hollow-eyed. Yannell studied him shrewdly and decided that Mahan was sick all right, sick with fear. He was afraid, deathly afraid of the big dun!

And Ghost Maker did his best to live up to his name. Bud Cameron asked for the horse when Marty could not ride. Bud was thrown, lasting scarcely two seconds on the hurricane deck of the squealing, sunfishing devil of a dun. He hit the ground in a heap and staggered to his feet. Amid the roar of the crowd, Mahan leaped up, screaming!

His voice was lost in the thunder of shouting, lost to all but Stoper, who was watching the man he hated. He saw that scream was a scream of fear, but of warning, too! For the zebra dun, neck stretched and teeth bared, knocked the puncher sprawling and lit into him with both feet. They got the maddened animal away from the fallen man, but before night-fall the word was around. Bud Cameron would never ride again. He would never walk again. He was crippled for life.

Big, tawny, lion-headed Yannell Stoper had no thought of Bud Cameron. The breaks of the game. What he did think about was Marty Mahan, for Marty was afraid. He was afraid of Ghost Maker. It was something to remember.

At Prescott and Salinas, Mahan beat Stoper out for top money, but Ghost Maker was not around. He was piling riders down in Texas and killing his second man. Stoper made sure that Marty knew about that. After Marty won at Salinas, Yannell congratulated him.

"Lucky for you it wasn't the Ghost Maker," Yannell said. Mahan's head came up, his face gone pale. "I see he killed another man down in Texas!"

Mahan, his face white, had walked away without speaking. Behind him, Yannell had smiled grimly. This was something to know.

Yannell Stoper had his own ideas about men. A man who was afraid of anything was a man who was yellow. It was just in him, that was all. He did not know that a man who can face fists is often deathly afraid of a gun, and that a gunman may shrink from the cold steel of a knife. Or a man of utmost cowardice before some kinds of danger may face another kind with high courage. To Yannell Stoper a man who was yellow was yellow, and that was final. And to his satisfaction, Marty Mahan was yellow. It was a fact to be remembered and to be used.

Yannell Stoper was big, rugged, and rough. In a lifetime of battling with hard broncs and harder men he had rarely known defeat, and never known fear. He had nothing but contempt for men who were afraid of anything, or who admitted doubt of themselves in any situation that demanded physical courage.

Now, on this day at the Wind River Rodeo, Yannell Stoper was ready for his triumph. It was a triumph that would mean much to him, one he had carefully engineered. For it was at Stoper's suggestion that the contest officials had secured the string of rough buckers of which the Ghost Maker was one.

Here in Wind River, before the world of the rodeo and the eyes of Peg Graham he would expose the cowardice of Marty Mahan for all the world to see.

"He's here!" Yannell taunted. "Right here in Wind River, an' if you duck ridin' him here they'll all know you're yellow!"

THEY WOULD, TOO! Even Marty had heard, or rather, overheard, the stories. He knew Stoper had started them himself, planting the seeds for the exposure, removing at once his rival for top rodeo honors and for Peg Graham.

"They say Mahan will drop out rather than ride Ghost Maker," a big rancher had said the evening before. "He's scared of the hoss! Dropped out of a show down in Texas rather than tackle him!"

"He's a bad horse," Red Carver admitted, "but you never make a good ride on an easy one!"

Marty had turned away and walked back toward the hotel, sick and ashamed. For he was afraid. He had been afraid of Ghost Maker from the day he had first seen him on that lonely Nevada range where he had run wild. He had been afraid of him ever since he had seen the dun lift his head, nostrils flared, and then come mincing toward him, walking so quietly away from the herd.

A wild horse that did not run. That should have warned him, and if it had not, the reaction of his own mount would have, for his horse began to quiver and edge away, blowing with fright. An old rancher had told Marty once, "Kill him the second he shows he's a killer, or he'll get you sure!"

Real man-killers were rare, but there was in them something of a fiend, of a destroying demon that came on so gently, then charged with wide jaws and flaring eyes. And Ghost Maker was such a horse, a horse marked from birth with a vicious hatred of man or even of other horses, of anything that moved and was not of his own herd.

Mahan had been seventeen at the time he first

glimpsed the Ghost Maker. He had felt his horse shy, felt the quivering fright in the animal. Marty was younger then and he was curious. Above all, this wild horse seemed so tame, so friendly.

Suddenly the dun had darted at them, frenzied with killing fury. In a flash he had struck down Mahan's saddle horse. Marty had fallen free and the dun had rushed at him, but the effort of his gray to get off the ground distracted the maddened horse, and the stallion had wheeled and struck wickedly at the gray. Fighting like a very fiend incarnate, the zebra dun had attacked the gray horse and struck and slashed until the saddle horse was a bloody heap of dead flesh, hammered, chopped, and pounded until all life was gone and even the saddle was a ruined and useless thing.

Marty, crouching weaponless between two boulders, watched that holocaust of butchery with horror-stricken eyes, unable to do anything to protect the old saddle horse he had ridden. And then, his killing fury unabated, the dun had come for him, lunging with slashing hoofs at the rocks, but unable because of the position in which he lay, to get at the boy.

For three fear-haunted hours the killer dun had circled those rocks. Time and again he struggled to get at the boy lying in the crevice. In those hours had been born an overwhelming horror of the horse. A horror that was never forgotten. Long after the horses had gone, led away by the dun on some whim of the wild, Marty had lain there, cramped and still, fearing to move, fearing to show himself in the open where the stallion might again come upon him.

Never again had he gone up on the range without a pistol, but never again had he gone to that section of the range. He had seen no more of the horse until that day in Calgary when the dun had shown itself under the saddle of Cy Drannan, Marty's best friend. Marty had hurried to the rider and told him the horse was a killer.

"So what?" Drannan shrugged. "I've heard of killers but never seen one! I always figured I'd like to top one off!"

Cy Drannan, happy, friendly, a good companion and rider, died on the bloody tanbark that day under the lashing hoofs of a horse that was a cunning, hate-ridden devil.

Now that horse was here, in this show, and **he** was to ride him. He, Marty Mahan.

PEG GRAHAM WAS WAITING for him when the parade ended. Her eyes were bright.

"Oh, Marty! Dad's said that after the rodeo if you will buy that Willow Creek range he will give his consent!"

Marty nodded soberly. "Does it have to be right away, honey?" he asked. "I mean, I . . . well, I may not make enough money in this show. Added to what I have, it will have to be a good fifteen hundred to swing that deal. I'd have to win four events to make it."

"Not if you win the bronc riding, Marty! They've upped the prize money and have offered a flat thousand dollars for top money! You can win it! You've already beaten both Red Carver and Yannell Stoper before!"

He hesitated, his face flushing. "I'm not riding broncs in this show, Peg," he said slowly. "I'm going to go in for calf roping, bull riding, steer wrestling, and some other stuff, but not bronc riding."

Peg Graham's face had turned a shade whiter, and her eyes widened. "Then . . . then it's true what they say! You are afraid!"

He looked at her, then glanced away, his heart miserable within him. "Yeah, I guess I am," he said, "I guess I am afraid of that horse!"

Peg Graham stared at him, "Marty, I'll never marry a coward! I'll never have it said that my man was afraid to ride a horse that other men would ride! Red Carver has asked for that horse! Yannell says—"

"Yannell?" Marty looked at the girl. "You've been talking to him?"

"Yes, I have!" she flashed. "At least, he's not afraid of a horse!" She turned on her heel and walked swiftly away, every inch of her quivering with indignation.

Mahan started to turn, then stopped. An old man

with a drooping yellowed mustache leaned against the corral.

"Tough, kid!" he said. "I didn't aim to overhear, but couldn't help it. You up to ride the Ghost Maker?"

Marty nodded. "I'm not ridin' him, though!" he said. "That horse is a devil! He shouldn't be allowed in shows like this! That isn't sport or skill. . . . It's plain, unadulterated murder!"

"Reckon I agree with you," the old-timer said seriously. "It ain't a bit smart to tackle a horse like that! I've seen him in action, an' he's a killer all through!"

Marty nodded unhappily. "He's from my home range in the Black Rock Desert country. He killed my ridin' horse once, about five years ago."

"You Marty Mahan?" the old man inquired. "I'm Old John. Heard a lot about you. You don't look like no coward."

Marty's eyes flashed. "I'm not! But I am afraid of that horse! I'm not aimin' to fool anybody about that!"

"Takes a good man to admit he's scared," Old John commented thoughtfully. "Who rides him if you don't?"

"Carver an' Stoper both want him. I wish they'd leave him out of this. He's a killer and a devil. There's something in that horse that ain't right."

"Like some men I know," John agreed. "There's killers in all sorts of critters. Just got a streak of meanness an' devil in 'em." He hitched up his pants. "Well, luck to you, son. I'll be amblin'."

Marty Mahan stared after the old man, his brow furrowed. He had never seen **him** around before.

The memory of Peg's face cut him like a knife. She believed him a coward. . . . Well, maybe he was! He walked over to Jeff Allen, chairman of the rodeo committee.

"Jeff, I'm withdrawin' from the bronc ridin'. I won't ride that Ghost Maker."

Allen shifted his cigar in his jaws. "Heard you didn't aim to. You say he's a killer?"

"He sure is." Briefly, Marty related his own experiences with the horse. "Personally, I think you should take him out of the lists."

Jeff Allen shook his head. His cold blue eyes showed disdain. "Not a chance! Just because you're afraid to tackle him don't mean others won't! Stoper has been around here, beggin' for him!"

MARTY SAW NOTHING of Peg Graham, nor of her father. Alone, he waited by the chutes for the calf roping, which was the first event in which he was entered. None of the rodeo hands stopped near him, nor did the contestants. Bitterly, his heart heavy in his chest, he watched them and watched the crowd. Once, over beyond the corral he saw Peg Graham. She was with Yannell Stoper.

Stoper opened in the calf roping and made a

quick chase, a clean catch, and a fast tie. It was good time. Red Carver and Bent Wells fell a little short. Marty Mahan's black was a darting flash when the calf left the pens. He swept down his rope streaking like a thrown lance. The catch was perfect and he hit the ground almost as the rope tightened. He dropped his calf, made his tie, and straightened to his feet, his hands in the air.

"Folks!" Roberts boomed. "That's mighty fast time! Marty Mahan, internationally famous rodeo star, makes his tie in eleven and two-tenths seconds!"

Three-tenths of a second better than Stoper: Marty turned, amid cheers, toward his black horse, and then somebody—and away down within him Marty was sure it was Stoper—yelled:

"Where's the Ghost Maker? Get Ghost Maker!"

The crowd took it up, and as Marty cantered from the arena his ears rang with the taunting word.

"Get Ghost Maker! Let him ride Ghost Maker! **Yellow!**"

White-faced, he dropped to the ground. Old John looked up at him.

"Hard to take, ain't it, boy?"

Mahan did not reply, but his face was pale and set. Yannell Stoper came around the corral, several riders with him.

"There's the hero! Wants milk-wagon horses!"

Marty turned sharply. "That will be enough of that!" he snapped.

Yannell halted, astonished. Then his eyes narrowed. "Why, you yeller-bellied, white-livered son—!"

They started for each other, fists clenched. The loudspeaker boomed out.

"Stoper! Ready for steer wrestling! Stoper! On your horse!"

With a curse the big tawny-headed man turned. "Saved you from a beatin'!" he sneered. "You get the breaks!"

"See me later, then!" Marty flashed back at him. "Anywhere! Any time!"

Grimly, he walked away. Behind him he heard the roar of the crowd as Yannell went after his steer. For a minute Marty Mahan stood still, listening to that roar behind him. Soon he would be going out there, facing that crowd again, and they would taunt and boo again. It was no use. . . . Why bother? He might as well quit now!

Then another thought came and he stopped in midstride. Run? Like the devil he would! He'd go back there and make them eat their taunts. Every word! He wheeled and walked back. When the time came for him to go out he went like a demon, flashing with speed. He took his steer down faster than ever before in his life, and as the loudspeaker boomed out his time, he swung into the saddle.

Taunts and jeers burst from the stands, but this time instead of riding out, he rode over before the stands and sat there, his hat lifted in salute. As the yells, boos, and hisses swept the arena, he sat perfectly still, his face dead-white, his eyes bright, waiting for stillness. It came at last. Then he waved his hat once more and, turning his horse, walked him quietly from the arena, leaving dead silence behind him.

Old John stood beside Peg Graham, who watched, her eyes wide. "That," Old John commented dryly, "took sand!"

She turned quickly to look at him. Then her eyes went back to the man riding from the arena. "I . . . guess it did," she agreed hesitantly. Her brows puckered. "I don't know you, do I?"

Old John rolled his quid in his jaws. "No, ma'am, you don't. Nor a real man when you see him!" He turned abruptly and walked off, leaving the girl's face flushing with embarrassment and shame.

As she turned away, she wondered. Had she wronged Marty Mahan? Was he a coward because he refused to ride that horse? If a man went into contest riding, he was not expected to be afraid of bad horses. He was expected to ride anything given him. Mostly the riders wanted bad horses because it gave them the best chance to make a good ride. Even if this horse was as bad as Mahan claimed, was it reason for refusing?

In the last analysis, she guessed it was simply that she could not bear to have him called a coward, or to love a man who was yellow.

Yannell Stoper won the bareback bronc riding in both the first and second go-rounds. Then he appeared in his usual exhibition of trick riding, and the first day of the rodeo ended with Stoper as the hero of the show despite his loss to Marty in the calf roping. His insistence on riding the horse that Mahan refused caught the crowd's interest.

Mahan was disconsolate. He walked the streets, feeling singularly out of place in his expensive trappings, and wishing he were miles away. Only the knowledge that if he left the show he would be branded a quitter, and through in the arena, kept him in town. That and the fascination exerted over him by the dun horse.

As the evening drew on he heard more and more talk of the dun. Despite their willingness to call him a coward for refusing the horse, people were beginning to wonder if the animal were not a killer after all. At all these rumors Yannell scoffed.

Marty Mahan was at supper when the café door slammed open and big, tawny-haired Stoper came in with Red Carver and Peg Graham. When the girl saw Marty sitting at the table alone she would have turned to leave, but Yannell would have none of it. They trooped in and, with several hangers-on, seated themselves at tables near Mahan's. At the counter not far away sat Old John, calmly eating doughnuts and drinking coffee.

"Sure I'll ride him!" Stoper boomed loudly. "I'm not yellow! I'll ride anything that wears hair!"

Mahan looked up. Inside he was strangely still and at ease. It was only his mind that seemed suddenly white-hot, yet his eyes were clear and hard. He looked across at Yannell Stoper and their eyes met.

"Finally got showed up, didn't you?" Stoper sneered. "You was always a four-flusher!"

"And you were always a loudmouth," Marty said quietly.

Stoper's face flushed red. Then his blue-white eyes narrowed down and he began to smile. He pushed back from the table.

"I always wanted to get my hands on you and in just about a minute I'll slap all the coward to the surface!"

He got up and started around the table. Carver called to him, and Peg Graham got up, her hand going to her mouth, eyes wide and frightened.

"And in just about a half minute," Marty said, sliding out of his chair, "you'll wish you'd never opened your mouth!"

Stoper walked in smiling and when he got to arm's length, he swung. It was a powerful, wide-armed punch, but Mahan's left shot straight from the shoulder to Stoper's mouth, setting the big rider back on his heels. Then Marty crossed with a smashing right that dropped Yannell to his haunches.

Mahan stepped back, his face calm. "If you want to ride that horse tomorrow," he said, "you'd better save it!"

Stoper came up with a lunge and dove for Marty, who stepped into a chair and tripped. Before he could regain his balance, Stoper was on him with a smashing volley of punches. Mahan staggered and Yannell was all over him, his face set in a mask of fury, his punches smashing and driving. Yet somehow Mahan weathered the storm, covered and got in close. Grabbing Yannell by the belt with one hand and a knee with the other, he upended the furious puncher and dropped him to the floor.

Stoper came up with a growl of rage and Mahan smashed a left and right to the face. The left went to the mouth, to Stoper's already bleeding lips, and showered him with blood. Marty stepped to the side and avoided a right, then countered with a wicked right to the wind. Yannell gasped and Mahan stabbed a left, then hooked hard to the face. Stoper bulled in close and the two men stood toe to toe amid the wreckage of smashed crockery and threw punches with both hands.

Both men were big and both were powerful. Stoper weighed well over two hundred and Mahan scaled close to the one-ninety mark. Both were in excellent shape. Stoper roared in close and grabbed Marty. They went to the floor. Stabbing at Mahan's eyes with his thumbs, Stoper missed and fell forward just as Marty smashed upward with his head. Blinded by pain, Stoper was thrown off, and then Marty lunged to his feet. Stoper got up, blinking away the tears the smash had brought to his eyes. Mahan measured him with a left, then hooked right and left to the body. Yannell shook his mane of tawny hair and swung a powerful, freckled fist. It missed, and Marty hit him again in the middle. The big rider stooped and Mahan slugged him twice more and the big man wilted and went to the floor.

"Who's yellow, Yannell?" Marty said then. He mopped the sweat from his brow with a quick motion of his hand and stepped back. "Get up if you want more. You can have it."

"I'll get up!" Stoper gasped, and heaved himself erect.

Mahan stared at the swaying, punch-drunk rider. Stoper's eyes were glazed; blood dripped from his smashed lips and from a long cut over his eye. A blue mouse was rising under the other eye. His ear was bleeding. Marty stepped back and dropped his hands.

"You're no fighter," he said dryly, "an' too good a rider to beat to death!" He turned abruptly and walked out of the café.

Yannell Stoper brushed a hand dazedly across his eyes and stared after him in drunken concentration, trying to make sense of a man who would walk away from a helpless enemy. He shook his big head and, turning, staggered blindly to a chair at a vacant table. He slumped into it and rested his head on his arms.

THE SECOND DAY of the rodeo was a study in delay. Despite his beating of the night before, Yannell Stoper looked good. His face was raw and battered, but physically he seemed in good shape and he was fast and smooth. Marty Mahan, working to absolute silence from the crowd, won the finals in the calf tying by bettering his previous time by a tenth of a second. Stoper was second.

Stoper won the steer wrestling, and took the finals in the bareback bucking contest.

Marty came out on Old Seven-Seventy-Seven, a big and vicious Brahma bull who knew all the tricks. The bull weighed a shade more than a ton and had never had a stiff battle. He came out full of fight, bucking like a demon, swiveling his hips, hooking left and right with his short, blunted horns, fighting like mad to unseat the rider who clung to the rigging behind his hump. Marty was going and he was writing over both flanks, giving the big Brahma all the metal he could stand.

Old Seven went into a wicked spin, then suddenly reversed. The crowd gasped, expecting the speed of it to unseat Mahan, but when the dust cleared, Marty was still up there, giving the bull a spur-whipping he would never forget. The whistle blew and Mahan unloaded with a dive. But Old Seven wasn't through by a whole lot. He wheeled like a cat on a hot stove and came for Marty full tilt. Mahan swung around, and then the clowns dove in and one of them flicked the big bull across the nose and the maddened animal came around and went for the clown. Marty walked off the tanbark to the scattered cheers of the crowd.

"Quiet today, Marty," Carver said, hesitantly.

Mahan looked up, a queer half-smile on his face.

"They are waiting, Red. They want to see the Ghost Maker."

"Stoper's riding him. I lost out."

"You're lucky," Mahan said dryly. "That's no ordinary bad horse, Red. Take it from me."

Suddenly he saw Jeff Allen before him and he turned abruptly and walked toward him.

"Jeff," he said abruptly, "I want to be in the arena when Stoper rides Ghost Maker."

The older man hesitated, looking coldly at Mahan. "You had your chance to ride him," he said briefly. "Now let Stoper do it."

"I aim to," Mahan replied. "However, I don't want to see him killed!"

Allen jerked his head impatiently. "You leave that to Stoper. He ain't yellow!"

"Am I?" Marty asked quietly.

For a moment the eyes of the two men held. The hard-bitten oldster was suddenly conscious that he was wearing a gun. It was only part of the rodeo trappings, but it was loaded, and so was the gun on Mahan's hip. The days of gunfighting were past, and yet . . . Marty's eyes met his, cold and bleak.

"Why, I don't reckon you are," Jeff said suddenly. "It just seemed sort of funny, you backin' out on that horse, that's all!"

Mahan looked at him with hard eyes. "The next time something seems funny to you, Jeff, you just laugh! Hear me? Don't insinuate a man is yellow. Just laugh!" He turned on his heel and walked away.

Dick Graham looked after him thoughtfully, then said, "Jeff, I thought for a minute you were goin' to fill that long-time vacant space up in Boot Hill!"

Allen swallowed and mopped the sweat from his face. "Darned if I didn't myself!" he said, relieved. "That hombre would have drawed iron!"

"You're not just a-woofin'!" Graham said dryly. "That boy may be a lot of things, but he isn't yellow! Look what he did to Yannell last night!"

YANNELL STOPER WALKED DOWN to chute 5. The Ghost Maker, a strapping big zebra dun, stood quietly waiting in the chute. He was saddled and bridled, and he made no fuss awaiting the saddle, having taken the bit calmly. Now he knew what was coming, and he waited, knowing his time was soon. Deep within his equine heart and mind something was twisted and hot, something with a slow fuse that was burning down, close to the dynamite within him.

At one side of the arena, white-faced and ready, astride his black roping horse, sat Marty Mahan. Time and again eyes strayed to him wonderingly, and one pair of those eyes belonged to Peg Graham. Yannell, despite himself, was nervous. He climbed up on the chute, waved a gloved hand, and settled in the saddle. He felt the horse bunch his muscles, then relax.

"All right," Stoper said. Then he yelled, "Cut her loose!" And then the lid blew off.

Ghost Maker left the chute with a lunge, sandwiched his head between his forelegs, and went to bucking like a horse gone mad. He was leaving the ground thirty inches at each jump and exploding with such force that blood gushed from Yannell's mouth with his third jump.

He buck-jumped wickedly in a tight circle, and then, when Yannell's head was spinning like a top, the maddened horse began to swap ends with such speed that he was almost a blur. Caught up in the insane rhythm of the pounding hoofs, Yannell was betrayed by a sudden change as the horse sprang sideways. He left the saddle and hit the ground, jarred in every vertebra.

Drunken with the pounding he had taken, he lunged to his feet, to see the horse charging him, eyes white and glaring, teeth bared. The crowd came off its seats in one long scream of horror as the maddened horse charged down on the dazed and helpless rider.

In some blind half-awareness of danger, Yannell stumbled aside. At the instant, Mahan's black horse swept down upon the maddened beast and Mahan's rope darted for the killer's head. Distracted, Ghost Maker jerked and the throw missed. Like an avenging demon he hurled himself at Marty's black, ripping a gash in the black horse's neck. The black wheeled, and the crowd screamed in horror as they saw him stumble and go down.

Out of the welter of dust and confusion somebody yelled, "Marty's up! Marty's on him!"

In the nightmare of confusion as the black fell, Marty, cold with fear of the maddened horse, grabbed out wildly and got one hand on the saddle horn of Ghost Maker. With every ounce of strength he had, he scrambled for the saddle and made it!

Out of the dust the screaming, raging horse lunged, bucking like mad, a new rider in the saddle. In some wild break of fortune, Mahan had landed with his feet in the stirrups, and now as Yannell crawled away, blood streaming from his nose, and the black threshed on the ground, Marty was up in the middle of the one horse on earth that he feared and hated.

Ghost Maker, with a bag full of tricks born in his own hate-filled brain, began to circle-buck in the same vicious tight circle that had taken Stoper from the saddle. At the height of his gyrations he suddenly began to swap ends in a blur of speed. Mahan, frightened and angry, suddenly exploded into his own private fury and began to pour steel to the horse. Across the arena they went while riders stood riveted in amazement, with Marty Mahan writing hieroglyphics all over the killer's flanks with both spurs.

Pitching like a fiend, Ghost Maker switched to straightaway bucking mingled with snakelike contortions of his spine, tightening and uncoiling like a steel spring.

Riders started cutting in from both sides, but Marty was furious now.

"Stay away!" he roared. "I'll ride him to a finish or kill him!"

And then began such a duel between horse and man as the rodeo arena at Wind River had never seen. The horse was a bundle of hate-filled energy, but the rider atop him was remembering all those long years down from his lost riding horse on the desert, and he was determined to stay with the job he had shunned. Riders circled warily out of reach, but now long after any ten-second whistle would have blown, Marty was up on the hurricane deck of the killer and whipping him to a frazzle. The horse dropped from his bucking and began to trot placidly across the arena, and then suddenly he lunged like a shot from a cannon, straight for the wall of the stands.

People screamed and sprang away as if afraid the horse might actually bound into the stands, but he wheeled and hurled his side against the board wall with force that would have crushed Marty's leg instantly. Mahan, cool and alert now, kicked his foot free and jerked the leg out of the way the instant before the horse hit.

As the animal bounded away, injured by its own mad dive, Mahan kicked his toe back into the stirrup and again began to feed steel to the tiring killer. But now the horse had had enough. Broken in spirit, he humped his back and refused to budge. For an instant Marty sat there, and then he dropped from the beaten horse to the ground and his legs almost gave way under him.

He straightened, and the killer, in one last burst of spirit, lunged at him, jaws agape. Standing his ground, Marty smashed the horse three times across the nose with his hat, and the animal backed up, thoroughly cowed.

Taking the bridle, Marty started back toward the chute, leading the beaten horse and trembling in every limb. Behind him, docile at last, walked Ghost Maker.

The emotion-wracked crowd stared at this new spectacle, and then suddenly someone started to cheer, and they were still cheering and cheering when Marty Mahan stopped by the corral and passed the bridle of the horse to a rider. He turned and leaned against the corral, still trembling. For the first time he realized that his nose was bleeding and that the front of his white rodeo costume was red with spattered blood.

Yannell Stoper, his own clothing bloody, walked up to him, hand out.

"Marty," he said sincerely, "I want to apologize. You sure ain't yella, an' you sure saved my bacon! An' that was the greatest ride a man ever made!"

"You sure weren't afraid of that horse!" Dick Graham said. "Why, man . . . !"

"Afraid of him?" Marty looked up grimly. "You're durned right I was afraid of him! I was never so scared in my life! I didn't get on that horse because I

wanted to! It was the safest place there was! An' once up there, I sure enough had to stay on or be killed! Scared? Mister, I was never so scared in my life!"

Old John was standing nearby grinning at him. "Nice goin', boy. An' by the way, I heard you an' the lady here"—he indicated Peg Graham—"were interested in my Willow Creek ranch outfit. If you still are, I would sell it mighty cheap, to the right couple!"

Peg was looking at him, wide-eyed and pale. "I . . . I don't know if . . . ?" Her voice was doubtful.

Marty straightened and slid an arm around her. "Sure thing, John! Looks like it would be a nice place to raise horses an' . . ."

"Cattle?" Red Carver asked, grinning.

"Kids!" Marty said. "Lots of kids! All rodeo riders!" He looked at Peg, grinning. "Okay?"

"Okay," she agreed.

Down the Pogonip Trail

It was cold, bitter, bitter cold, and the wind from off the mountains cut through even the warmest clothes. Jeff Kurland's clothes were not warm, for the long, dry summer had brought only disaster, and the few cattle he had been able to sell paid only for his groceries, leaving no margin for clothes.

Now he seemed to be facing another winter without snow, and it was melting snow which watered the grasslands far below, the grasslands where his cattle grazed. He bowed his head into the wind and headed his horse for the timber. Broke as a drunken miner after ten days in town, he would have no chance now of marrying Jill Bates.

The scarf tied around his head under his hat kept slipping down, but it did help to keep his forehead and the back of his neck warm. Without it, his brow would be cold as chilled iron, riding in this wind.

The mustang broke into a canter for the last few yards to the trees. They would be shelter from the wind, at least.

Now if he could just catch Ross Stiber! Five thousand dollars was a lot of money. Then he could fix up the cabin, get married, and maybe buy a few head of cattle to increase his small herd.

Only a few hours ago Sheriff Tilson had told him Stiber was believed to be hiding out somewhere in the icy peaks and ridges that loomed above Kurland's cabin. Tilson had warned him. The man was a killer.

If Tilson was smart, he would not go up into those peaks after Stiber. Jeff knew those peaks from harsh experience, and nothing could last a winter up there. All Tilson had to do was wait and watch. Stiber would have to come out.

The earth beneath his horse's hoofs was iron-hard, the sky above a dull, forbidding gray. Where the small creeks flowed, the rocks were sheathed with ice. On the trail that wound through the spruce he was at least out of the wind, and it was a mere three miles to his cabin.

Home! Four walls and a dirt floor, but a good fireplace and plenty of fuel. If a man was handy with an axe there was plenty of wood just from deadfalls, but food was scarce. What he would do if there were a heavy snowfall he could only guess.

Even his visit to Jill had turned out badly. Not that she was anything but adorable, or lacked affection, but the house was so warm and pleasant that he shuddered to think of her comments if she were to see his own harsh cabin.

He felt shy in the Bates's house. His clothes were shabby, and his big hands were blue with cold. He could hardly tear himself away from the fire for the warm meal, and when Kurt Saveth had started to banter him about his rugged life he had frozen up inside, unable to find words with which to reply. He was cold, resentful, and unhappy. It was no wonder Jill's parents preferred Saveth to him.

The worst of it was it was Saveth, from whom he bought supplies. It went against the grain to ask his rival for credit. Kurt knew how little he bought, how badly off he must be, and how things must be up there on his ranch.

The mustang's pace quickened. Cold as the barn might be, the horse was ready for it after the forty miles it had traveled this day. Jeff rode the gray into the yard and stepped down from the saddle. Leading the animal inside, he stripped off the gear, put a halter on him, and tied him to the manger. Then he forked down hay; at least he had plenty of that! He got out a blanket and covered the horse, buckling it in place. It was a light blanket, but at least it was some help against the cold. Fortunately, the barn was snug and secure from the raw wind. When Jeff Kurland built, he built well.

His steps were loud on the hard ground as he crossed the frozen yard. Lifting the latch, he stepped inside and, dropping his sack of supplies, he started for the fireplace to light a fire.

He stopped short. Neatly piled atop the ashes was a small cone of twigs and shreds of bark.

"Don't make no sudden moves." The tone was

harsh. "You just go ahead and light that fire. I was aimin' to do just that when you came into sight."

Without turning, Jeff struck a match and lighted the prepared fire. As it blazed up he added heavier sticks.

Of course, it would be Ross Stiber, and the man was a killer. Jeff half turned his head. "All right to get up now? I'm not armed."

"Get up an' start fixin' some grub. Hope you brought somethin' with you. You surely ain't fixed for winter."

Jeff Kurland got up and glanced across the room at the man sitting on the bunk. He was a big, raw-boned man, unshaved, and with a heavy jaw. His bleak gray eyes were taking in Jeff Kurland, his worn clothes and thin face.

"I'm Stiber," he said, "but it ain't goin' to do you one particle of good."

He came up behind Jeff and ran a hand over his pockets. He sounded surprised when he stepped back. "No gun, huh? I already looked the cabin over, so where is it?"

"Ain't got one." Kurland was embarrassed.

"Don't get any ideas about that there **ree**ward. I'm wide awake all the time, and I can shoot the buttons off your coat."

"I know that. I just haven't got a gun."

Kurland went to work preparing the meal. He was hungry after his long ride, and wanted to eat. He also wanted time to think his way out of the situation he was in. How much of a situation, he was not sure. The outlaw settled himself back against the wall, watching his every move. Stiber seemed to want to talk.

"You sure aren't fixed well, friend. I looked your place over. Isn't enough grub here to feed a rat. How could you expect to last out a storm, no more grub than you've got?" He glanced at the sack Jeff had brought in. "An' you surely didn't pack much, considerin' you had a forty-mile ride."

Jeff was irritated, but he made no comment. What business was it of Stiber's to come nosing around, butting into his business? If he was going without now and again, it was his business and nobody else's. He got coffee on and mixed biscuits.

"Shoulder of venison on the chair yonder," Stiber suggested. "Better fix it. I killed me a deer night before last. Not much game around. Must be the drouth." He glanced at Kurland. "Got your cattle, too, I'll bet."

He eased forward to the edge of the bunk again. "Hey? You got any smokin' in that bag? I run out of it up yonder in the peaks. I might have stuck it out if it hadn't been for that."

Jeff reached into the sack and tossed Stiber a package of tobacco. "Keep it," he said. "I've got another."

Stiber caught the sack and lowered it between his knees and got out some papers. "Thanks, amigo. Don't you just figure I'd have taken it, anyway? I could have. I probably would have, too. I wouldn't take both of them, though. A man can do without his grub, but his smokin'? No way.

"Up yonder in the peaks I smoked dried leaves; ain't done that since I was a youngster, shredded barl, just anything." He lit up and smoked in silence for several minutes. Then he said, "Who's the girl?"

Kurland's head came up sharply. He was as big as Stiber, but the hard months had made him lean. His eyes were bleak and dangerous. Stiber noticed it, and there was a flicker of humor in his eyes.

"Where's that picture? Did you take it?"

"What would I want with your picture? No, I didn't take it, an' I'm meanin' no disrespect. She's a right pretty girl, though."

"She's a fine girl and a decent girl."

"Did I say she wasn't?" Stiber protested. "Sure, she's a fine girl. I know her."

"**You** know her?" Jeff was startled.

"Jill Bates? I should smile, I know her. Don't look at me that way. Was a time when I wasn't no outlaw, havin' to hide out in the hills. I knew her when she was a youngster. Nine, ten years ago. I was a young cowpuncher then, drifted into this country after shootin' a man down at Santa Rita. That was my first shootin' and I was some upset. I wasn't fixin' to kill anybody. Then I met a girl up here. Blonde, she was. Cute as a bug's ear. Name of Clara Dawson."

Jeff grinned. "You should see her now."

"I don't aim to. Rather remember her as she was.

Comes to that, I don't look so fine my own self. It was different then. About that time I was cuttin' a wide swath among the womenfolks.

"You should have seen me then! Had me a silver-mounted saddle and bridle. Had a fine black horse, best one I ever owned. Comanches got him. I was lucky to get away with my hair."

"Come an' get it," Jeff put plates on the table. "You can put up that six-shooter, too. I don't plan on bustin' your skull until we've had something to eat."

Stiber chuckled. "Don't try it, boy. That's a right pretty little girl, and I'd hate to put tears in her eyes. Pour me some of that coffee, will you? Been two weeks since I've drunk coffee."

Stiber waited until the coffee was poured. He tucked the pistol in his waistband. "How come you haven't got a gun? I seen the holster."

Jeff flushed. "I borrowed money on it. From Kurt Saveth."

"Tough." Stiber was eating with obvious enjoyment. "You cook a mighty fine meal. You sure do." He looked up. "You fixin' to marry that Bates girl? If you are, you better go out and rob yourself a bank. You can't bring the likes of her to a place like this."

Jeff slammed down his fork. "Listen! You bust in here an' take a meal at gunpoint an' you can do it. I'd begrudge no man a meal! But you keep your nose out of my private business or I'll bust it all over your face!"

Stiber chuckled, lifting a protesting hand. "No offense! I was just talkin', that's all. As for bustin' my nose, even if I didn't have a gun you couldn't whip one side of me. Not that I'm aimin' to give you the chance.

"You fix a good meal, friend, but you make a wrong move and it will be the last one you ever fix. I've got five thousand in blood money restin' on my head, and that's a lot of money to a man in your fix."

Jeff ate in silence while the outlaw continued to talk. From time to time Jeff's thoughts returned to the subject of that reward. Five thousand dollars was a lot of money, and the man **was** wanted for a killing.

What was in Stiber's mind now? He scarcely dared try to leave the country, yet it was impossible to live among the peaks in this weather. It would be worse before it got better. Of course, if he had a good hideout—?

It was then Jeff Kurland remembered the cave on Copper Mountain.

Could that be where Stiber was hiding? Sheriff Tilson had said that Stiber did not know this country, yet if Stiber had been around here ten years ago, something Tilson obviously did not know, he might know of the cave on Copper Mountain.

Where else could a man live in those mountains in such cold? But had Stiber ever come through a **pogonip** fog in this country? Did he know what it was like when the fog turned to ice and settled in a chill blanket over everything?

If a man was caught in a cave, he'd better have

plenty of food and be prepared to wait it out, because escape would be impossible. And unless Jeff Kurland was mistaken, the weather was shaping up for something like that now. Within the past few minutes he seemed to feel warmer, and not only because the room was heating up.

The outlaw's droning voice penetrated Jeff's thoughts.

"That Jill Bates, she's growed into a mighty handsome woman! Used to fetch her candy, I did, and maple sugar. That was when I was courtin' Clara. Thought the world of that kid. Even let her ride my black horse one time."

He pushed back his chair and got to his feet. "Got to be goin'. You split that grub in half, and leave me the sack. Ain't likely you'll have callers but I can't chance it."

"Listen," Jeff protested, "that's all the grub I've got! And I've no money!"

Ross Stiber chuckled. "You ain't sold your saddle yet, and I'll just bet that Kurt Saveth would like to buy it off you!"

"Sell my **saddle**? I'm not that broke! You know damned well that when a cowpuncher sells his saddle he's through . . . finished!"

"Then maybe you ain't quite finished. Why don't you go slaughter one of Cal Harter's Pole Angus steers? I hear theirs is the best beef you can find."

When he was gone Jeff dropped into a chair, thoroughly discouraged. With the little grub he had brought in he **might** have made it. As it was, he didn't have a chance.

Half the little food he had was gone, and he had no money nor any chance to get any. Nor would anybody be hiring hands in this kind of weather. They had let go what extra hands they had for the winter season, keeping on just a few trusted standbys. It looked like the end of everything. His chance to have his own ranch, his chance to marry Jill, all gone down the drain.

He had started his own outfit three years before, with three hundred head of cattle. It was a herd carefully built from strays or injured cattle. Here and there he bought a few head, mostly calves from cattle drives, where the calves were an impediment. He had driven his herd into these high green valleys and built his cabin.

In the months that followed he had labored to build a small dam for a reservoir against the hot, dry months. Grass grew well along the bottoms, and he had worked from daylight until dark mowing hay with a scythe and stacking it against the long winter ahead. He had built shelters of poles and brush, knowing the snow would bank against it and add to the warmth. Nobody had held cattle up this high, but he believed he could do it. A few years back he had come upon some wild cattle that had survived a winter in the high country.

His first year had gone well. Although he lost a few head, the calves more than made up for it, and during the summer they increased and grew fat. Then had come a bitter winter that shut down early, locking the land in an icy grip that broke only in the late spring.

When he took stock he found he had lost over a hundred head, and the others were gaunt and unfit for sale.

The summer had been hot and dry, and as it grew hotter and dryer he had fought with all he had to keep his cattle in shape and get them through until fall. Late rains, on which he had depended, changed to snow, and now he was into the second of the awful winters. Bigger cattlemen than he were hard hit, but they had large herds and could stand some loss. Every one he lost hurt severely. With all his money gone, he had sold off his gear until all he had left was his Winchester .44 and his riding gear.

Wearily, he got to his feet, banked the fire, and crawled into his bunk, too exhausted to even worry.

He awakened to utter blackness and cold. Huddling in his blankets, he dreaded the thought of the icy floor and the shivering moments before he got the fire going.

The instant his feet hit the floor he felt an icy chill, and knew at once what it was.

The **pogonip**! The dreaded fog that even the Indians feared, an icy fog that put a blanket of death over every shrub, every tree, even every blade of grass. Bitterly cold, and the ground so slick it was inviting broken legs to even move, the air did strange things with sound so that voices far away could be distinctly heard.

Kicking back the blanket, he pulled on his socks and raced across the floor to stir up the fire. Uncovering some coals, he threw kindling into the fireplace and then raced back to the warmth of his bed to wait until some of the chill had left the cabin.

The kindling caught fire and the flames leaped up. After a while he got out of bed, added more fuel, and put coffee water on the fireplace stones. Then he dressed, and as he tugged on his boots he saw the cigarette ashes spilled on the floor from Stiber's cigarette.

Where was he now? Had he reached the cave on Copper Mountain? Or had he realized what a trap it might be? The cave was deep, and held a certain amount of warmth, but to have reached it Stiber would have had to travel half the night over rough and dangerous trails. Yet he might have done just that.

On the third day of the **pogonip** snow fell, covering the ice with a few scant inches of snow. Taking his rifle and slipping on his snowshoes, he started his hunt. From now on life would be a grim struggle to stay alive. He cruised through the woods, seeking out likely places for deer. He had been out for more than two hours and was slowly working his way back toward his cabin when he saw a mule deer floundering in the deep snow. It was not until he killed it that he discovered its leg was already broken, evidently from a fall on the deadly ice.

The following day it snowed again, snowed slowly, steadily. Cold closed its icy fist upon the mountains, and his thermometer dropped to ten below, then to twenty below zero. On the morning of the tenth day it was nearly fifty below; his fuel supply was more than adequate, but it kept him adding fuel every fifteen to twenty minutes.

Long since, knowing the cold at this altitude, he had prepared for what was to come, stopping up all the chinks in the log walls, few though they were. He had squared off the logs with an adze when building the cabin, and they fit snugly. Only at the corners, carefully joined though they were, did some cold air get in. With newspapers he had papered the inside of the cabin, adding several layers of insulation.

With careful rationing of his venison, he figured he could get through the cold spell if it did not last too long.

Despite himself, he worried about the fugitive on Copper Mountain, if that was indeed where he was. Unless Stiber had been able to kill some game, he would by this time be in an even worse situation than himself. And in this kind of weather there would be no game in the high country.

Awakening a few days later, Jeff Kurland lay in bed, hands clasped behind his head. The thought of Stiber alone on Copper Mountain would not leave him. Outlaw and killer he might be, but it was not Jeff's way to let even an animal suffer. If Ross Stiber had been in the cave on Copper Mountain he would surely have come out by now, and there was no other way out except right by this cabin.

He made his decision suddenly, yet when he thought of it he knew the idea had been in his mind for days. He was going to scale Copper Mountain and find out just what had happened to Stiber. The man might have broken a leg and be starving in his cave.

The air was crisp and still, colder than it seemed at first. Buckling on his snowshoes and slinging his rifle over his shoulder, Jeff Kurland hit the trail. Knowing the danger of perspiring in this cold, he kept his pace down, despite his anxiety. Sweat-soaked undergarments could quickly turn to a sheath of ice in such intense cold. After that, freezing to death was only a matter of time.

The trail wound upward through a beautiful forest of lodge-pole pine which slowly gave way to scattered spruce as he climbed higher on the mountain. Despite the slow pace he made good time, and would reach the most difficult stretch shortly before noon. Deliberately, he refused to think about the return trip.

Pausing once, on a flat stretch of trail, he looked up at the mountain. "Kurland," he told himself, "you're a fool."

What he was doing made no kind of good sense. Ross Stiber had chosen the outlaw trail, and if it ended in a cave on Copper Mountain instead of a noose it was only what he might have expected. It might even be what Stiber would prefer.

Jeff knew the route, although he had visited the cave but twice before. After reaching the shelf there would be no good trail, and his snowshoes offered the only way of getting there at all.

The air was death still, and the cold bit viciously at any exposed flesh. He plodded on, taking his time. Fortunately, on this day there was no wind. His breath crackled, freezing as he breathed. He walked with extreme care, knowing that beneath the snow there was ice, smooth, slick ice.

When he reached the stretch of trail along the face of Red Cliff, he hesitated. The snow was very thin along that trail where the wind had blown, and beneath it was the slick ice of the **pogonip**. The slightest misstep and he would go shooting off into space, to fall on the ice-covered boulders four hundred feet below.

On this day he was wearing knee-high moccasins with thick woollen socks inside. They were better for climbing, and worked better with the snowshoes.

Removing the snowshoes, he slung them over his back and, keeping his eyes on the trail a few feet ahead, he began to work his way along the face of the cliff.

Once fairly on his way there was no turning back, for turning around on the slick trail, while it could be done, was infinitely more dangerous than continuing on. It took an hour of painstaking effort to traverse the half mile of trail, but at last, panting and scared, he made it. Ahead of him towered the snow-covered bulk of what was locally called Copper Mountain.

He scanned the snow before him. No tracks. Not even a rabbit had passed this way. If Ross Stiber was actually living on the mountain, he had not tried to come this way.

Carefully, he worked his way up along the side of the mountain, keeping an eye out for Stiber. The man might see him, shoot, and ask questions later. If there were anything left alive to question.

White and silent, the mountain towered above the trees, and Jeff paused from time to time to study it, warily, for fear of avalanches. Under much of that white beauty there was **pogonip** ice, huge masses of snow poised on a surface slicker than glass, ready to go at any instant. He put his snowshoes on once more and started, very carefully, along a shoulder of the mountain.

Only a little way farther now. He paused, sniffing the air for smoke. There was none. Nor was there any sound.

The mouth of the cave yawned suddenly, almost unexpectedly, for with snow covering the usual landmarks he had no longer been sure of its position. The snow outside the cave was unbroken. There were no tracks, no evidence of occupation.

Had he come all this way for nothing?

He ducked his head and stepped into the cave. Unfastening his snowshoes, he left them at the entrance and tiptoed back into the cave. Lighting a branch of fir for a torch, he held it high to get the most from its momentary light. It was then he saw Stiber.

The outlaw lay upon a bed of boughs covered with some blankets and his coat. Nearby were the ashes of a fire, long grown cold. Here, away from the mouth, the cold was not severe, but, taking one glance at Stiber's thin, emaciated face, Jeff Kurland dropped to his knees and began to kindle a fire.

He got the fire lighted using half-burned twigs and bits of bark, then he hurried outside the cave for more fuel. All that in the cave had evidently been burned long since.

As the flames leaped up and the cave lightened, Stiber's eyes opened and he looked at Kurland. "You, is it? How did you get here?"

"The same way you did. Over the trail from my place. I was worried."

"You're a fool, if you worried about me. I ain't worth it, and you've no call to worry."

"I was afraid you'd busted a leg."

"You guessed right," Stiber said, bitterly. "My leg is busted. Right outside the cave, on the first morning of that ice fog. I dragged myself back in here and got some splints on it."

"How's your grub?"

"Grub? I run out seven days ago."

Jeff opened his pack and got out some black tea. He was a coffee man, himself, but he carried the tea for emergencies, and now he brewed it hot and strong.

"Try this," he said when it was ready, "and take it easy. The cup's hot."

With water from his canteen and some dried venison he made a broth, thickening it a little with corn flour.

Stiber put his cup down and eased himself to a sitting position. "Figured tea was a tenderfoot drink," he said, "but it surely hits the spot."

"Best thing in the world if you're in shock or rundown. Wait until you get some of this broth."

Later, a flush on his cheeks and warmed by the hot drinks and the fire, Ross Stiber looked over at Kurland with cold gray eyes. "Well, this is your show. You're here, and the grub you brought won't last more than two days. What d' you figure to do?"

Kurland had been thinking of that. In fact, he had been thinking of it all the way up, and there was only one possible answer.

"Come daybreak I'm packing you out of here."

"You've got to be crazy. You couldn't pack a baby over that icy trail! And I'm a full-grown man."

"Get some sleep," Kurland said, "and shut up before I change my mind and leave you here."

At daybreak he was up. Deliberately, he kept his thoughts away from the ordeal before him. It was something he had to do, no matter how much he feared it, no matter how much he disliked the injured man.

He helped Stiber into all the clothes he had, then wrapped him in a heavy blanket. "You will be heavy, but you'll not be moving, and I don't want you frozen. You will be just that much harder to carry."

With a stick, Stiber hobbled to the cave mouth. The morning was utterly still and bitterly cold. "You'll never make it. Go down alone and send them after me."

"They wouldn't come. Nobody but a damn fool would tackle that trail before spring, and I'm the damn fool."

He studied the trail for a moment, calculating. It did no good to look. He already knew how tough it was, and what he had to do.

"Once I get you on my back," he said, "don't move. Don't talk, don't even wiggle a toe."

When he had his snowshoes adjusted, he took the injured man on his back and started over the snow. The man was heavy, and there was no easy way to carry him. "You'll have to hang on," he said. "I'll need my hands."

Step by careful step, he worked his way over the snow toward the head of the eyebrow trail along the cliff face. At the near end of that trail he lowered the injured man to the snow.

Leaving Stiber on the snow he slung his snowshoes over his back and went out on the narrow thread of trail. The very thought of attempting to carry a man over that trail on his back sent cold prickles of fear along his spine. Yet there was no other way.

Now, scouting the trail with care, he tried to envision every step, just how he would put his feet down, where there was the greatest danger of slipping, where he could reach for a handhold.

Reaching the end of the trail, he left the snowshoes and rifle, then returned for Stiber. Resolutely, he refused to accept the obvious impossibility of what he intended to do. The man would die if he did not get him out. That he might die in the attempt was not only possible, it was likely. Yet he had spent years in the mountains, and he knew his strength and his skill. He had to depend on that. Was he good enough? That was the question.

When he returned he sat down beside Stiber. The outlaw looked at him quizzically. "I wasn't really expectin' you back."

"You're a liar. You knew damned well I'd be back. I'm just that kind of a damned fool."

"What happens now?"

"I'm packing you, piggyback, over that trail."

"Can't be done. There's no way it can be done. Man, I weigh two hundred and twenty pounds."

"Maybe two weeks ago you weighed that. I'd lay fifty bucks that you don't weigh over two hundred right now."

Using a nearby tree Stiber pulled himself erect and Kurland backed up to him. Careful not to injure the broken leg Kurland took the man on his back. "Now, whatever you do, don't even wiggle. You can throw me off balance on that trail. If you do, we're both gone."

He avoided looking at the trail now. He knew very well what faced him and that he must take the trip one step at a time. The slightest misstep and both would go over the brink. Under the snow was the ice of the **pogonip**.

Carefully, he put a foot out, testing for a solid foothold. Wearing moccasins, he could feel the unevenness, even grip a little with his toes. Little by little, he edged out on the trail. Icy wind plucked at his garments and took his breath. He did not look ahead, feeling for each new foothold before he put his weight down.

Sweat broke out on his face, trickled down beside his nose. Desperately, he wanted to wipe it away but there was no chance, for his arms were locked under Stiber's knees.

How long a trail was it? A half mile? He could not remember. His muscles ached. Dearly, he wanted to let go just a little, to rest even for a moment. Once, just past the middle, his foot slipped on the icy trail, and for an instant their lives hung in the balance. Jeff felt himself going, but Stiber's knees gripped him tighter.

"Get your feet under you, lad." Stiber's voice was calm. "I've got hold of a root."

Darkness was falling when at last they came to the cabin. Over the last miles Kurland had dragged Stiber on a crude travois made of branches, holding the ends of two limbs in his hands while dragging Stiber over the snow, lying on his makeshift litter. When they reached the cabin, he picked the big man up and carried him inside, and dumped him on the bunk.

The cabin was icy inside, and hurriedly Jeff Kurland built his fire. Soon there was a good blaze going, and warmth began to fill the room. An hour later, Stiber looked at him over a bowl of hot soup.

"Now you can turn me in for that **ree**ward," he said, almost cheerfully.

Kurland's head snapped up. He felt as though he had been slapped.

"Go to blazes! I didn't risk my neck getting you down off that mountain just to see you hung. When you can walk, you get out of here, and stay out!"

"No need to get your back up. I wouldn't blame you. I et up half your grub, and caused you no end of grief."

Jeff Kurland did not reply. He knew only too well the long, difficult months that lay ahead, and that when spring came there would be hardly enough cattle left to pay off his debts, if there were any at all. He would have nothing with which to start over.

Moreover, if he did not report Ross Stiber, and if he was caught with the man in his cabin, he could be accused of harboring a criminal. The fact that the man had a broken leg would help him none at all.

At the same time, he knew he could not turn him in. One cannot save a man's life without having a certain liking for him thereafter, nor can a man share food with another without developing a feeling of kinship, for better or worse.

He did not want Stiber in his cabin. He resented the man. His food was all too limited, and game was scarce. Nor did he like Stiber's company, for the man talked too much. Yet he could not turn him in. He would wait until the leg was mended, when Stiber would have a running chance, at least.

The cold held the land in a relentless grip. More and more snow fell. Finally, desperate for food, he killed one of his steers. The fuel supply burned low, and Kurland fought his way through the snow to the edge of the timber, where he felled several trees and bucked them up for fuel. Stiber watched, with small gray eyes holding a flicker of ironic humor.

"You live through this winter an' you'll have a story to tell your grandchildren."

Kurland glared. "What grandchildren? What chance would I have to marry Jill with a setup like this?" He waved a hand at the earthen floor and the shabby bunk. "I was hoping for some good years. I was planning to build a cabin up yonder, where there's a view, close to the spring. It would have been a place for any woman."

"You should have kept your gun. You could have stuck up the Charleston stage. She carries a sight of money sometimes."

"I'm no thief! You tried it, and where did you wind up? Half frozen in a cave on Copper Mountain!"

"That's no more than plain truth," he admitted. "Well, each to his own way. I took mine because I killed a man. He wasn't much account, either. I end up starvin' in a cave, and you starve in this miserable cabin. Neither of us gets much of a break."

"I'll make my own breaks," Kurland replied. "Just wait until spring. I'll get me a riding job and save some money."

Stiber's tone was mocking. "At forty a month how much are you goin' to save? You think that girl will wait? Maybe somebody else is shinin' up to her? Somebody who doesn't freeze and starve on hopes? You think she'll wait? A time comes for marriage, and a woman marries, doin' the best she can. You're dreamin', boy."

Maybe he was. Jeff Kurland stared into the fire. He had been taking too much for granted. What made him think she loved him? Because he loved her? Because he wanted her love so much?

He had never so much as spoken of his dreams to her, just the simple facts of the case, yet how many times must she have heard that? Every cattleman, sheepman, and mining man had the same dream.

And all the while there was Kurt Saveth, who had a small but charming home in town which he had inherited from his folks; he also had a successful store, and people around all the while, not a lonely cabin in the far-up mountains.

Footsteps crunching in the snow caused his head to lift. Ross Stiber's grab for his pistol was just an instant slower than Jeff's. "Not today, Stiber! We will have no shooting here!"

There was a loud knock, and at his "Come in!" the door opened and Sheriff Tilson entered, followed by Kurt Saveth, looking handsome in a new mackinaw, and following him, Doc Bates, and, of all people, Jill!

His face flushed with shame. He had not wanted her to see how he lived until he had something better, something fit to show her. He saw her glance quickly around, but as her eyes came to him he looked quickly away.

"All right, Stiber, you're under arrest." He turned to Jeff. "What's this mean, Kurland? You harborin' this outlaw?"

"He has a broken leg," Jeff spoke with dignity. "What could I do, carry him down on my back?"

"You could report it," Tilson replied. "You're in trouble, young man."

"He found me dyin' in the cave on Copper Mountain, Sheriff. He packed me over Red Cliff trail on his back."

"You expect me to believe that? After that **pogonip** a rabbit couldn't come down that trail, to say nothing of a man packin' another man on his back."

"He done it," Stiber insisted. "I'd come down and taken grub away from him, but when he figured I was starving he came up and got me. I'm his prisoner. If there is any reward he should get it."

Tilson laughed with humor. He glanced around at Saveth. "Hear that? They'd probably split it. Your guess that Stiber was hidin' here was a good one, Kurt. He had to be here, because there's no other place on the mountain where he could keep warm."

Doc Bates looked around from examining Stiber's leg. "This man does have a broken leg, Tilson."

"That doesn't make Kurland's story true. No man in his right mind would risk that trail. Kurland will be lucky if we don't prosecute him."

Jeff Kurland felt nothing but disgust and despair. He did not care about the reward. He had never thought seriously of that, anyway, but he sensed that Saveth disliked him and wanted him out of the way. Well, this ended it. When the cold broke he'd sell whatever he had left and head south.

Then he felt a hand slip into his. Startled, he looked down to see Jill had moved close beside him.

She was looking at Ross Stiber. "I remember you. You're Jack Ross, the rider from Cheyenne."

"You've a good memory, ma'am. Look, don't you believe what they're saying. All they want is that reward money. You've got your hand on the best and squarest man I know. If you take your hand off his arm you'll have lost the best of the breed."

"We'll fix a travois and haul him down to jail," Tilson said, and he glanced at Jeff. "You'll have a tough time provin' you didn't harbor a criminal."

"Sheriff," Doc Bates interrupted, "I know this man Stiber. He may be wanted as an outlaw, but I can put fifty men on the stand that will testify he's no liar. Before he got into trouble Jack Ross, that's how we knew him, was a respected man and a top hand. If he says Kurland brought him over the Red Cliff trail, I'll believe him. So will those others."

"And I'll swear to it on the stand," Stiber added. "He had me. I was his prisoner."

"We'll see about that," Saveth said.

Tilson was irritated. "Let's get out of here," he said. "Doc? You comin' with us?"

"I guess we all are," Bates said. "We wouldn't want anything to happen to our prisoner now, would we?"

Tilson went outside to put together a travois, and Stiber turned quickly to Jill. "Ma'am? You won't be tellin' Clara that I'm Jack Ross now, will you? I wouldn't want her to see me in jail. Not that she meant much to me. Fact is, I was glad to get away. She struck me as one of those who'd get mean and cantankerous as she grew older."

"You were right about that," Jeff assured him. "She has a disposition like a sore-backed mule. Just ask Tilson."

"Does he know her?"

"**Know** her? He married her!"

All the way to town Sheriff Tilson wondered if Ross Stiber wasn't a little crazy. He kept chuckling and laughing, and what did a man with a broken leg, maybe headed for a hanging, what did he have to laugh about?

The Romance of Piute Bill

Tom Galway rode the sorrel out of the juniper and down the hillside toward the rock house on the creek. He was still two hundred yards off and cutting across a field bright with larkspur, paintbrush, and sego lily when he saw Piute Bill come to the door, a Winchester in his hands.

Galway rode up to the door and hooking one leg around the saddle horn he reached for the makings. "You're going to need that rifle, Bill. That is, if you're up to chasing some horse thieves."

"What's happened?" Piute Bill pushed his hat back on his head, then put the Winchester down beside the door. He accepted the tobacco sack Galway handed him. "You losin' stock?"

"Those boys over yonder in the Rubies ran off twenty head of horses last night. I figure to go get 'em."

"All right." Bill touched his tongue to the paper. "Must be eight or nine of them up there. Who do you figure to take along?"

"You and me. No use to clutter things up. All I want is somebody to keep them off my back."

"Sure enough. Wait until I saddle up."

He came back from the corral leading a paint horse with one blue eye and one brown eye. Tom Galway was sitting on the porch waiting for him, with a gourd dipper in his hand.

"There's a jug inside," Piute Bill said. "My own make."

Piute Bill threw his saddle on the paint. "Ain't bad whiskey, at that. I'm beginning to think that alkali adds a little bite to her."

"Could be." Galway hefted the jug, then threw it over his bent arm and drank. "Could be," he repeated. "You know, Bill, I'm beginning to think that what you need is a woman. Somebody to sort of cook things up and keep things revved up a mite. Then you could give more time to making whiskey and herding cattle."

Piute Bill glanced at him sourly. "I'm doin' all right. You ready?"

Galway put the jug down inside the door and pulled the door shut. Then he swung into the saddle, and they started off at a walk across the flower-blanketed meadow.

"Cassidy will be there," Piute Bill said, "and Gorman, too." He glanced sidewise at Galway. "You better watch Cassidy. He's a fair hand."

"No man's goin' to run off my stock. I rounded up those horses out on the range. Wild stock. I broke 'em myself and gentled them down. Cassidy's got his business and I have mine. As long as he stays on the other side of the creek, I won't bother him but when he runs off my stock he'd better hunt himself a hole."

The trail led up a shallow gulch bordered by juniper and brush. "You know, Bill," Galway said, "the more I think of you having a woman around, the better I like the idea." He squinted against the sun as they topped out on the rise and looked the country over with care. "Be a sort of a civilizing influence. You ain't getting no younger, and you've been living alone in that shack for some time now. I figure a woman could sort of rev things up around and keep you washed behind the ears."

"You mean," Piute commented sourly, "you figure to drop over time to time for homecooked meals. I know you. I ain't been ridin' the range with you these past four or five years without cuttin' your sign."

"I'm only thinking of you," Galway said, keeping his face straight. "You just think of that schoolmarm over to Summit," Galway continued, ignoring the interruption. "That's a right solid bit of woman, and I hear she's a good cook."

"You'd better be thinkin' of Digger Cassidy. He's no soft touch, and if he stole your horses he wanted them bad. He put lead into Dean Russell over to Battle Mountain, two or three months ago. If you recall, he was one of the roughest of that Charleston outfit."

"Gorman's just as good with a gun."

"There's a slick-ear kid, too. Named Robbins. He shot up a saloon over to Ten Mile last week."

"Heard about him. He files notches on his gun."

"One of them, huh? I never knowed of any real bad man who done that. He's a tinhorn."

The gulch down which they had been riding opened upon a wide, white salt flat and they cut across on an angle, walking their horses to raise no more of the white, smothering dust than necessary. The sky was clear and hot. Their lips became parched and white, their eyes smarted from sweat. Heat waves danced over the flats. They rode in silence, each busy with his own thoughts. The lurking devil in the paint's blue eye went dull with the heat and the slogging pace.

It was two hours before they topped a small rise and left the desert behind them. The sagebrush smelled good after the parched stillness of the salt flats.

Cottonwoods showed some distance off and they pointed their horses, ignoring the trail of the stolen stock, knowing the men they pursued would also need water, and the tracks would begin again when they found it. The horses, smelling water, quickened their pace.

It was a small but cold stream. Men and horses drank. Tom Galway sat down on a rotting tree trunk and scanned the area. Horses had been held here only a few hours before. Their tracks were in the mud and in the grass.

"About two miles, isn't it? The cabin sets out in the open."

"You got any ideas?"

"I want to talk to Cassidy."

"You want to **talk** to him? Do you reckon he will set around and talk when he knows you're huntin' him?"

Tom Galway was running this show and Piute Bill figured he knew what he was about, but talking to Cassidy at such a time? It didn't make much sense. There had been a good deal of talk about Tom Galway since he had ridden into the Ruby Creek country, and a lot of wondering about him.

"He'll talk," Galway said.

Cassidy and Gorman were known men, both of them had been involved in shootings. With them would be at least six others, all used to fighting for whatever they got. Until now they had confined their raids to the big outfits where weeks might go by before a tally showed that stock was missing. Apparently Tom Galway's stock had been too much of a temptation, and Galway was new in the Ruby Creek country. In the three or four years he had lived there he had kept out of trouble. He had been a hard worker, and obviously a top hand with horses.

Walking to his horse Galway took two strips of rawhide from his saddlebags and tied his gun down to his thigh. Then he took out another gun belt and holster and, after strapping it on, tied it down also. It was the first time Piute had ever seen a man wear two guns, although he had heard of such things.

Piute studied Galway. He was a lean, brown man, tanned by sun and wind. There was a scar over one eye and another along the jawbone. Piute turned his horse and started upstream. Galway cantered until beside him.

"There's timber along the stream," he said, "fifty yards from the cabin. If they open fire we'll take cover there."

Piute couldn't quite make up his mind about Galway. He glanced at the younger man but saw no signs of nervousness or excitement. No more than if he was going after a bunch of cows.

His mind turned to other things. Maybe Galway was right. Maybe he did need a woman. It was lonely there in the cabin in the creek. He was a healthy man, forty years old now, and he had a nice bunch of cattle and a few head of horses. The ranch was doing well, if they didn't start rustling this side of the creek. He figured he could make a wife comfortable, and he wasn't a cantankerous sort.

The creek turned west and they entered the canyon. There was a narrow opening lined with aspen and a few spruce. The trees fell back and the two men cantered over the meadow toward the cabin. It was a squat, stone cabin with a corral almost directly behind it in which Galway could see his horses. Near the stone cabin were three other horses, ground-hitched.

Pulling up about a dozen yards from the door, two men came out, followed by a third and a fourth. The first was Gorman, the second Robbins. The other two Galway did not know. The squat, bull-like figure of Digger Cassidy was nowhere to be seen.

"Howdy," Galway said casually. His eyes scanned their faces and settled on Gorman. "Where's Digger?"

"What d' you want with him?" Robbins demanded belligerently.

"Shut up, Robbins!" Gorman spoke sharply. "I'll do the talking."

He looked at Galway, then at Piute Bill, whose paint had been stopped about ten feet behind and well to the right of Galway. "What do you want?"

"I think Digger made a mistake." Galway spoke gently. "He drove off twenty head of horses for me. Nice meadow here, but I'd rather have them close to home. Thought I'd just ride over and drive them back."

"You thought what?" Robbins's face flushed red. "Just who—!"

"Shut up!" Gorman said impatiently.

There was something here he did not like, and Gorman had pursued a long outlaw career by being cautious. Only two men, and they looked like fighters. Piute Bill he knew about, and he was no man to trifle with.

The other man, a stranger, seemed to be taking the lead, and his quiet, confident manner disturbed Gorman.

"You'll have to talk to Cassidy," Gorman suggested. "He's the boss."

"I know," Galway replied, "but I can't wait. You tell Cassidy that Tom Galway came for his horses. He'll understand."

"You **know** Cassidy?"

"I do. What's more, Digger knows me. You tell him I came for my horses. If he wants me for anything, I'll be at my cabin. Tell him to come whenever he's ready . . . day or night."

He did not turn his head but spoke to Piute. "Kick those corral bars down, Bill. We can't stay long."

Robbins had enough. He stepped forward. "You keep your hands off that corral," he said, "and you, Galway! You get goin' while you're able!"

Gorman was in a quandary. They were four to two. Still, this man said he knew Cassidy, and—

Piute Bill had ignored Robbins. He rode to the corral and leaned toward the bars. Robbins, his face flushed with anger, turned back to Galway. "Stop him! Or I'll kill you!"

Tom Galway's lips smiled, but his eyes did not. "Gorman, this kid's askin' for it."

Robbins's hand streaked for his gun and Galway's sorrel sidestepped suddenly at a touch of the spur. Galway fired . . . then again.

Robbins, his gun half-drawn, stopped dead still, staring at Galway, his eyes blank and unseeing.

Swearing viciously, Gorman went for his gun, trapped into a gun battle he had not wanted. Galway fired, knocking one man into the cabin wall where he fell, knocking the man beside him off balance.

Piute Bill, half behind them, turned at the first shot and fired at Gorman, who went down, his fingers digging into the earth.

The last man dropped his six-shooter as if it were red-hot and flattened against the wall. Galway looked at him over his gun.

The horses were out of the corral and starting toward the bottleneck opening.

Piute Bill's Winchester was ready, and Galway looked at the last man. "You tell Digger Cassidy to stay on his own side of the creek. Tell him Galway said that, Galway of Tombstone!"

He turned his horse away, watching the man. "And you tell Digger I didn't start the shooting. It was that fool kid, Robbins."

The horses would head for their own corral, now that they were free, but they could always hurry them along a bit.

They were almost out of the bottleneck when a sharp, feminine voice came from the aspens. "All right! Hold up there!"

A buxom, determined-looking young woman of perhaps thirty stepped from the trees. She held a double-barreled shotgun as if she knew how to use it.

Galway and Piute Bill drew up warily. A man with a shotgun was bad enough, but a woman—

"What's the trouble, ma'am?" Galway asked politely. "Can we do something for you?"

"You killed my man back there, and if you think you're gettin' off scot-free, think again!"

Piute Bill started to speak, then swallowed and looked helplessly at Galway.

Lifting his hand slowly, Tom Galway removed his

hat. "Now, I'm sorry to hear that, ma'am, but those men stole my horses and when I came after them they made the mistake of trying to shoot it out."

He noted no sign of tears. "Ma'am? Which one was it, Robbins?"

"That puppy?" Contempt was in her tone. "He killed a few tenderfeet and figured he was a tough man. My man was Ned Wavers."

"We're almighty sorry, ma'am," Galway said gently. "We came after our horses. We'd no intention of killing anybody."

"But you did!" There was no grief in her tone, just a hard matter-of-factness. "Ned wasn't much," she said, "but he made me a home, and when he wasn't drunk he took care of me. Now I'll be left here for Cassidy and that bullyin' Tinto Bill."

Tom Galway smiled. "Why, ma'am, if you would rather not stay here, and if it is a home you're looking for, we've got one for you!"

She was, Tom decided, quite a pretty woman. Moreover, she looked neat, and clean. "Of course," he added, "you'd have to be able to cook."

"There isn't a better cook west of the Pecos," she said flatly, "and I can make pies—"

"Of course," Galway said, smiling, "and we've got just the place for you! It's a pretty little stone house by a creek, and a good, thoughtful man to go with it."

"Hey!" There was sheer panic in Piute's eyes. "Look, you can't—!"

"A good, thoughtful man, ma'am, and a good provider. He's one of the finest hunters around, always has meat for the table."

The shotgun lowered. "What's going on here?" The woman was puzzled. "Somehow, I don't under—"

"Ma'am"—Tom Galway rested his palms, one atop the other, on the saddle horn—"ma'am, this gent with me is Piute Bill. He's a known and respected man. Now he's a mite on the shady side of forty, but steady. He can fork a bronc with any man, one of the best hunters around and he's got him that stone cabin I spoke of.

"It needs a woman's touch, that's all. The right woman. Needs a woman like you, a pretty woman who's neat about the house and who will cook his chuck and keep the place revved up. I know he'd be speakin' for himself, but he's a shy man, not given to talking much."

"Tom! Listen! For God's sake!" His voice trailed off helplessly as Galway continued.

"He makes a little 'shine now and again, but I've never seen him drunk. Don't drink no more than to be sociable. He owns seven hundred head of steers and a milk cow."

"Did you say a milk cow?" The woman looked thoughtful. "If he's got a milk cow he's a sight more of a plannin' man than most. Mister, I reckon you've talked me into it!"

"Mount up then!" Galway said cheerfully. "Mount up right there behind Piute and put your arms around him and hang on tight. By the time you get to his place on the creek I think he'll be convinced!"

Piute Bill, his eyes vicious and his face red, helped the young woman up behind him. She flashed a smile at Galway which suddenly faded.

"Now see here! Ned wasn't much and he beat me when he was drunk. I wasn't sorry to lose him, him bein' what he was, but we were all married up, fittin' and proper!"

"Of course, ma'am!" Galway looked shocked. "I'll ride into Ten Mile as soon as I get you to the house. We will have a preacher out here before sundown. The barkeep was tellin' me there was a preacher there now. I'll get him. Meanwhile," he added, "you better just bake a wedding cake. Somehow without a cake a wedding doesn't seem real, does it now?"

"Maybe the preacher won't come?" Bill suggested hopefully.

"He'll come!" Galway said. "I'll see to that!"

"I just bet you will!" Piute said savagely.

Whistling, Tom Galway turned his sorrel toward Ten Mile. "Horse," he said, "I'd make a poor Cupid but sometimes there's things a man just has to do. And besides, she had a scatter-gun."

When Galway rode into Ten Mile the only sign of life was around the Gold Camp Saloon. Galway tied his horse and pushed through the batwing doors.

There were six men in the place. One sat alone at a table. He was a red-haired man, short and stocky, with a pious look.

Galway stepped to the bar, noticing one of the men was Digger Cassidy, another was Tinto Bill.

"Rye," Galway ordered, and jerking a thumb toward the redhead he asked, "Is that the preacher?"

"It is." The bartender looked up curiously.

"If you've got a horse," he said to the preacher, "better get him saddled. I've got a wedding for you."

"A wedding? Of course, but——?"

"Everything is going to be all legal and proper, this woman wants to marry this man, and by this time," he chuckled, "he'll be wanting to marry her. If she doesn't have him convinced by now she doesn't have the taking ways I think she has. She looked to me like a woman with a mind of her own."

"Who's gettin' married?" the bartender asked.

"Piute Bill. He's been looking for a wife for a long time."

"Who's marryin' him? There ain't more'n three or four single women in the county!"

"Piute Bill," Galway replied carefully, "is marrying Mrs. Ned Wavers."

Tinto Bill choked on his drink. Digger Cassidy turned for the first time and looked right at Tom Galway. "Who?" he demanded, unbelievingly.

"Mrs. Ned Wavers and Piute Bill," Galway repeated. "They are getting married this evening. Soon as I can get the parson up there."

"But she's married!" Tinto Bill said. "She's got a husband, and any time she hasn't, I guess I'd be first in line."

"There must be some mistake," Cassidy said. The light was not good and Galway's hat shaded his face somewhat. "Ned Wavers is—"

"Dead," Galway replied. "Mrs. Ned Wavers has been a widow for almost four hours."

Digger Cassidy spoke softly. "You say Ned Wavers is dead."

"That's right, Digger. Seems some of your boys drove off some horses of mine last night, so I rode over to drive them back. Robbins made a fool play and Gorman and Wavers tried to back him up."

Silence filled the room. The preacher swallowed, and the sound was loud in the room.

"Mrs. Wavers didn't want to be left behind and as she kind of hit it off with Bill they decided to get married."

He was watching Cassidy, and a few feet to one side, Tinto Bill. "By the way, Cassidy, I told that other fellow, the one who's alive, to suggest you keep to your side of the creek and I'd keep to mine. I went to a good deal of trouble to catch and train those horses, and I don't want to lose them."

Neither Cassidy nor Tinto Bill had moved. Without turning his attention from them, Galway said, "Rev'rend, get your horse. I'll be with you in a minute."

The preacher vanished through the door.

Cassidy spoke suddenly. "You can't get away with this! I don't care if you are Galway of Tombstone!"

"Take it easy. If we shoot it out now, I'll kill you. Maybe you'd get me, but that wouldn't help you any. You'd be just as dead, and I never missed nobody at this range.

"Why should you get killed over horses you didn't have no business stealin' and a woman who's obviously been living a dog's life?"

"I didn't steal your damn horses!" Cassidy said. "It was that fool Robbins!"

"I can believe that," Galway agreed. "In fact, I'd of bet money on it. So why should we shoot it out? It makes no sense. Now I'm going to leave. I've got to get that preacher back up on the mountain because that's a decent woman yonder."

"Damn it, Galway!" Cassidy protested. "Why couldn't you have come when I was to home? Once I knew those were your horses I'd have driven them back!"

"All right," Galway said, "I'll take your word for it." Deliberately he started to turn his back and when he did, Tinto Bill went for his gun.

Galway palmed his gun and shot across the flat of his stomach. Tinto, his gun up, fired into the ceiling, took two slow steps and fell on his face, his gun skidding along the floor.

Digger Cassidy stood very carefully near the bar, his hands in plain sight.

"Looks to me, Digger," Galway said, "like you're fresh out of men. Why don't you try Montana?"

He turned abruptly and walked out.

Digger Cassidy moved to the bar and took up the drink the bartender poured for him. "Damn him!" he said. "Damn him to hell, but he can sure handle a gun!"

He downed his drink. "Bartender," he said, "if you ever go on the road, steer clear of hotheaded kids who think they are tough!"

Tom Galway rode up to the stone cabin with a saddle-sore preacher just after sundown. Piute Bill, in a clean shirt and a fresh shave, was seated by the fireplace with a newspaper; from the stove came a rattle of pans.

The future Mrs. Piute Bill turned from the stove. "You boys light an' set. It surely isn't right to have a wedding without a cake!"

"I couldn't agree with you more, ma'am!" Galway said. "Nobody likes good cooking more than me."

Piute Bill stared at Galway, the venom in his eyes fading under a glint of humor. "You durned catamount! You durned connivin' Irish son of a . . ."

"Ssh!" Tom Galway whispered. "There's a preacher present!"

That Triggernometry Tenderfoot

It was shortly after daybreak when the stage from Cottonwood rolled to a stop before the wide veranda of the Ewing Ranch house. Jim Carey hauled back on the lines to stop the dusty, champing horses. Taking a turn around the brake handle, he climbed down from the seat.

A grin twisted his lips under the brushy mustache as he went up the steps. He pulled open the door and thrust his head inside. "Hey, Frank!" he yelled. "Yuh t' home?"

"Sure thing!" A deep voice boomed in the hallway. "Come on back here, Jim!"

Jim Carey hitched his six-shooter to a more comfortable position and strode back to the long room where Frank Ewing sat at the breakfast table.

"I brung the new schoolma'am out," he said slowly, his eyes gleaming with ironic humor as the heads of the cowhands came up, and their eyes brightened with interest.

"Good thing!" Ewing bellowed. His softest tone could be heard over twenty acres. "The boys are rarin' t' see her! So's Claire! I reckon we can bed her down with Claire so's they can talk all they're a mind to!"

Jim Carey picked up the coffee cup Ma Ewing placed for him. "Don't reckon yuh will, Frank," he said. "Wouldn't be quite fittin'."

"What?" Ewing rared back in his chair. "Yuh mean this here Boston female is so high an' mighty she figgers she's too good for my daughter? Why . . . !"

"It ain't thet," Jim's grin spread all over his red face, "on'y the new schoolma'am ain't a she, she's a he!"

"What?"

Frank Ewing's bellow caused deer to lift their startled heads in the brakes of the Rampart, ten miles away. The cowhands stiffened, their faces stricken with disappointment and horror, a horror that stemmed from the realization that anything wearing pants could actually teach school.

"Sure thing!" Jim was chuckling now. "She's a he! He's waitin' outside now!"

"Well!" Ma Ewing put her hands on her wide hips, "yuh took long enough t' tell us! Fetch the pore critter in! Don't leave him standin' out there by hisself!"

Carey got up, still chuckling at the stupefied expressions on the faces of the cowhands and walked to the door. "Hey, you! Come on in an' set for chuck! Reckon," he added, glancing around, "I'll be rollin'. No time t' dally."

He hesitated, grinning. "Reckon yuh boys'll be right gentle with him. He's plumb new t' the West! Wanted t' git off and pet one o' them ornery long-horns up the pass!"

Stretch Magoon's long, homely face was bland with innocence. "Wal, now! I calls that right touchin'! I reckon we'll have t' give him a chance t' pat ol' Humpy!"

The cowhands broke into a chuckle and even Claire found herself smiling at the idea. Then, at the approaching footsteps in the hall they all looked up expectantly.

The new schoolma'am stepped shyly into the door carrying a carpetbag in one hand, a hard black hat in the other.

He wore a black suit, stiff with newness, and a high white collar. His hair was dark and wavy, his eyes blue and without guile. His face was pink and white with a scattering of freckles over the nose.

He was smiling now, and there was something boyish and friendly about him. Claire sat up a little straighter, stirred by a new and perplexing curiosity.

"Come in an' set," Ma Ewing declared heartily. "You're jest in time for breakfast!"

"My name's Vance Brady," he suggested. "They call me Van."

"Mine's Ewing," the big cattleman replied. "This here's my wife, an' thet's my daughter, Claire. She's been teachin' the young uns, but they's a passel o' big uns, too big for her t' handle."

He glanced at Brady. "An' some o' them's purty durned big, an' plenty ornery!"

"That's fine!" Brady said seriously. "There is nothing like the bright energy of youth."

Stretch Magoon's long, melancholy face lifted. "Thet sure touches me," he said solemnly, "thet bright energy of youth. I'm Stretch Magoon," he added, "an' we'll do all we kin t' make yor stay onforgettable!"

Ma Ewing frowned at Magoon, and he averted his eyes and looked sadly down at his plate.

"Reckon yuh come a fur piece," Ewing suggested, chewing on a broom straw. "From Boston, ain't yuh?"

"Near Boston," Brady replied, smiling. "Is the school close by?"

"Down the road about ten mile," Ewing replied, "jest beyond the old Shanahan place."

Brady glanced up. "The Shanahan place? Is that a farm? I mean . . . a ranch? Maybe I could live there, a little closer to my work?"

Ewing shook his leonine head and tugged at his yellow mustache. "Nobody lives there. Old Mike Shanahan was killed nigh on a year back. If none of his relatives come t' live on the place afore thet year is up, then it's open t' anybody who will claim it an' hold it."

"It was a damn' fool idea!" Curly Ward said. He was a big, blond puncher, handsome in a strong, masculine way. "Old Mike should of knowed it was jest an invitation for Pete Ritter t' move in! With his gunfightin' cowhands an' the money he's ready t' spend, nobody around here can buck him. He's got more'n he needs now."

"Wal," Stretch said positively, "he's sure goin' t' have thet place! The will done said if'n any of his relatives showed up they'd have t' live on the place thirty days o' this year t' claim it!"

"It would appear," Van Brady said, "that my staying there would be impractical. From what you say I doubt if Mr. Ritter would allow it."

Ward grinned, faint humor in his eyes. "He sure wouldn't! Not even a **he** schoolma'am!" The contempt in his voice was undisguised.

Claire's face flushed with embarrassment for the teacher, and Brady looked up. "I take it you are unaccustomed to male teachers," he said politely. "There are many in the East. I believe this would be a good country for some of them."

He looked over at Ewing. "Have you a conveyance? A horse or something that would get me down to my school? I'd like to look it over."

"Now ain't thet pecoolyar!" Magoon looked up, a warm smile illuminating his face. "I was jest thinkin' yuh'd be wantin' a hoss! We got a yaller hoss out here I'm sure would be jest the thing for yuh!"

Claire sat bolt upright and she started to speak, but before she could utter her protest, Van Brady smiled. "Why, how nice, Mr. Magoon! Thank you very much!"

When Brady followed Magoon from the room

Claire started to her feet. "Father!" she protested. "Are you going to let them put that boy on that buckskin devil?"

"Now, Claire, don't fret yourself!" Ewing said, grinning. "He won't do no such thing! Buck will toss him afore he gits settled in the saddle! The fall won't hurt him none. Let the boys git it out of their system. Besides," he added glumly, "I ain't so sure I like no he schoolma'am m'self!"

Claire Ewing got to her feet and started for the door, the others trooping expectantly behind.

Magoon already had a saddle on the lazy-looking buckskin, and was cinching it tight, plenty tight, and talking to Brady. Curly Ward was standing nearby, lighting a smoke and grinning with anticipation. Web Fancher and the other hands gathered around, striving to look innocent.

"He's a right nice hoss," Stretch said sorrowfully, "a gentle hoss. I reckon the boss might let yuh ride him all the time."

"Better put on these spurs," he added. "He's kind o' lazy an' won't really git goin' less yuh nudge him right sharp."

Van Brady sat down and fumbled with the spurs until Stretch knelt beside him and helped put them on. Then Van got up. The yellow horse looked around, speculative curiosity on his face, a face almost as sad and woebegone as Magoon's.

Brady put a tentative foot in the stirrup, then swung his leg over the buckskin. Stretch Magoon stepped back warily, putting distance between himself and the horse. "Yuh'll have t' gouge him purty stiff," he called. "He's sho nuff lazy!"

Van Brady touched the yellow horse with the spurs, then at no movement, he jerked his heels out and jammed both spurs into the buckskin's flanks.

The buckskin exploded like a ton of dynamite. With one catlike leap, he sprang forward and dug in his forefeet. The he schoolma'am shot forward, but somehow barely missed losing his seat, then the yellow horse swapped ends three times so fast he was merely a blur of movement, and then he began to buck like a fiend out of hell.

Brady lost a stirrup, and swung clear around until he was facing the buckskin's rear, clawing madly for the saddle horn. But when the horse swapped ends again, he miraculously flopped back into the saddle. Three times the buckskin sunfished madly, and then went across the ranch yard swapping ends and buck jumping until every bone in Brady's body was wracked. Yet somehow the he schoolma'am held on.

Then the equine cyclone went completely berserk. He leaped wildly toward the morning clouds, then charged for the corral fence, but just as he swung broadside to it the schoolma'am lost a stirrup! His hard hat was gone, his coattails flying in the wind, but he was still aboard.

As suddenly as it had begun, the yellow horse stopped bucking and trotted toward the ranch house,

Brady pulled him to a halt, and the buckskin stood, trembling in every limb.

Stretch Magoon's face was a blank study, and Curly Ward was staring, half angry.

Van Brady smiled and wiped the perspiration from his brow with a white handkerchief. "He **is** spirited, isn't he?" he said innocently. Then he glanced at Stretch Magoon. "Would you hand me my hat? I'm afraid he bucked it off!"

Walking as if in a trance, his solemn eyes even more owllike than before, Magoon went over and picked up the hard hat. Almost subconsciously, he brushed off the dust, then handed it to Brady.

The he schoolma'am smiled. "You've been very kind," he said. "I don't know what I'd have done if I got one of those really excitable horses you cowmen ride!" He looked at Ewing. "Which way do I go to the school?"

"That road right ahead," Ewing said. "Foller past them cottonwoods an' cross the crick when you come t' the willows. That's where you'll see the old Shanahan place. The schoolhouse is a might farther on."

Curly Ward stared after him. "Did you see that?" he demanded. "Talk about a fool for luck! That pilgrim was almost off four, five times, an' then bucked right back into the saddle! If I hadn't seen it I wouldn't believe it! He was all over that hoss like a cork in a mill stream! How he stuck with him is more'n I can guess!"

Claire's eyes were narrow as she stared after the teacher. The light in them was faintly curious. "I'm not so sure!" she said softly. "I'm not so sure!"

Van Brady rode straight, sitting stiffly erect in the saddle until he was over the crest of the hill. Then he glanced around, safely out of sight of the ranch house, and out of hearing he exploded into laughter. He roared and laughed and finally settled into chuckling. "That Magoon!" he said to the yellow horse. "I won't forget that long horse face of his if I live to be a hundred! He stood there with his mouth open like the end of a tunnel!"

He patted the yellow horse on the shoulder. "You sure can buck, you yellow hunk of misery!" he said, grinning. "I was afraid I was overplaying my hand!"

" 'You'll have t' gouge him pretty stiff,' Magoon says," Van repeated, chuckling. "Why, that long-faced baboon probably never saw the day he could ride this sinful old coyote bait!"

The old Shanahan place was a cluster of buildings gathered in a hollow of the hills not far from Willow Creek. Van Brady glanced at them curiously, but did not stop. When he had skirted the hill he rode down the slight grade to the log school, built on a pleasant little flat not far from the creek.

For an hour he scouted around, getting the lay of the land. Twice, back in the willow grove, he dismounted and dug in the soil. Each time he carefully covered the spot with sod and then with dry grass.

Not over two miles away Web Fancher was sitting

among the junipers on the hillside, talking to burly Neil Pratt, foreman for Pete Ritter. "He ain't nobody," Web said, disgustedly, "jest a he schoolma'am from back Boston way. He's the on'y stranger that's been around.

"Hell!" he exploded. "Why don't Pete move in an' take over the place instead o' all this pussyfootin' around? Ever'body 'lows he kin do it!"

Pratt shrugged. "He's pretty shrewd. Knows what he's doin' most always. If'n anybody makes a pass at movin' in over here, you get word t' me right fast!"

In her room at the ranch, Claire was writing a letter to Spanish John Roderigo, a rodeo and circus hand who had once worked for the ranch. She ended the brief note with a concise paragraph.

What I want is the name, and description if possible, of the man who did the clown riding act with the Carson Shows two years ago. You will remember, you took me to that show when I was attending school.

"We'll just see, Mr. Schoolteacher Brady!" she said to herself. "I've a few ideas of my own!"

Sunday morning was the time Magoon rode in for the mail. He saddled his horse, then went up to the kitchen. When he returned, he swung into the saddle.

Instantly, the paint exploded into a squealing fury of bucking. Caught entirely by surprise, for the paint hadn't humped his back in weeks, Magoon hit the ground and rolled over in a cloud of dust while the paint went buck jumping away across the ranch yard.

Nearly everyone had been outside, and Stretch heaved his six feet five from the dust with a pained expression on his face. The eight or nine cowhands were roaring with laughter.

The schoolma'am shook his head sadly. He walked over and picked up Magoon's sombrero, dusted it carefully, and handed it to him. "He **is** spirited, isn't he?"

"Now what do you s'pose got into that mangy crow bait?" Magoon demanded. "He ain't bucked in a long time . . . hey?" He stopped, glaring at Curly. "You ain't been up t' no monkey business?"

"Me?" Curly was honestly startled. "Not a bit of it!"

Stretch limped after the paint and led it up to the corral once more. Then, feeling under the loosened saddle, he found the cockleburr. He glared at Curly Ward. "Why, you ornery, cow rastlin' horny toad, I got a notion t'—"

"Better get that mail," Claire said. "You can settle it later."

Still growling, Magoon started for town. Claire turned and looked at Van Brady. He wiped the grin from his face. "Ever hear of that little cowboy prank, Mr. Brady?" she asked sweetly. "Putting a burr under a man's saddle?"

"Is that what happened?" he asked innocently. "I thought his horse was just a little excited."

When he turned away, she looked after him. Her father walked up and put his hand on her shoulder. "What's the matter, Claire? You look like you had somethin' on your mind. Ain't fallin' for that he schoolma'am are you?"

"No," she said sharply, "I'm not! And between us, I'm not so sure he's a teacher!"

The next day she kept her ears tuned to what was happening in the other room of the two-room school. Not only was Van Brady teaching, but he had even the bigger boys interested. He was making the fight at Lexington and Concord so interesting that Claire overheard the boys discussing it when they rode toward home.

"You know," he said to her as they started toward the ranch. "I am going to miss these rides, but I believe I could do some things around the school that need doing if I stayed right here at the school. Anyway, I always wanted to camp out a little."

"You mean, you're going to move up here? Camp out?" she was incredulous.

"Yes, I am. Right over there in the willows by the stream. I think I'd like it."

The following day he moved his gear into the willows and set up camp. Van Brady scratched his head thoughtfully. "This is going to be tough," he told the buckskin. "How am I going to make that camp comfortable without letting them know I'm no greenhorn?"

Web Fancher rode over to the Circle R. "That

new schoolteacher's done moved over t' the school," he said. "Didn't know if it mattered none."

"The school?" Pratt shook his head. "Just so's he don't take no fool notion t' move over to the Shanahan place."

THE FIRST CLASS WAS in session the following morning when there was a clatter of horse's hoofs outside and the door was suddenly flung open. Neil Pratt strode into the room, slapping his thigh with a quirt. "You!" he pointed with the quirt at Tom Mawson, the nester's son. "Ain't I told you t' stay off'n the Circle R? You come here! I'm goin' t' learn you a thing or two!"

He grabbed Tom's shoulder and jerked him from the seat. The next instant, a hand seized him by the belt, and he was jerked bodily from the floor and slammed back into the wall. Before he could realize what had happened, Van Brady was standing in front of him.

"Listen, you!" Brady snapped. "You keep your hands off these kids! And don't come barging into one of my classes when it's in session. Understand?"

Pratt heaved himself erect, his face suffused with rage. "Why, you . . . !" His fist started, but almost as soon as it started, something smashed his lips back into his teeth and he hit the door, tumbling to the ground outside.

He scrambled to his feet with an inarticulate

growl of fury. Claire, her face white, saw Neil Pratt hurl himself at Brady.

The Circle R foreman was a notorious brawler, a huge man weighing over two hundred. Brady could never have weighed more than one hundred and fifty. Slim, wiry, but with broad shoulders, Brady looked much smaller than the Circle R foreman.

Neil Pratt, blood trickling from his smashed lips, stared at Brady. "Why, you white-livered baby!" he sneered. "I'll beat you t' a pulp!"

Four Circle R riders sat their horses, watching with interest. Pratt walked in, his face ugly. Coolly, Van Brady waited for him. A cowhand from boyhood, he had been places and learned other things. Pratt lunged, but his right missed, and Brady stepped inside, smashing two wicked blows to the body, then whipping a right hook to Pratt's cheek that cut to the bone.

Furious, Pratt tried to grab him. Van Brady was smooth, easy on his feet, his lips set, he glided in and out, boxing coolly, battering Pratt with punch after punch. Claire, astonished, suddenly realized what an incredible thing was happening. The schoolteacher was whipping Pratt!

Pratt caught Brady with a right swing and knocked him against the 'dobe wall of the school; when he lunged after him, Brady's foot caught him in the chest and shoved him back. Then, before he could get set, Van Brady moved in, smashed a left jab into his teeth, and crossed a chopping right to the chin. Pratt ducked his head and charged, but Brady was out of the way, and a snapping left bit into Pratt's ear, making his head ring.

He whirled, glaring wildly, and Brady moved in, feinted Pratt into a right swing, and then smashed a right to the body. Pratt tried again and took a left and a right. Brady wasn't moving away now, he was weaving inside of Pratt's vicious punches and nailing the big foreman with blow after blow in the stomach.

Pratt's breath was coming heavily now. The cut on his cheekbone was staining his shirt with blood, his lips were pulpy, his ear swollen. He ducked his head and started in, but two fast left jabs cut his eyebrow, and a right smashed his nose.

With an oath, Lefty Brooks, one of the Circle R hands, dropped from his horse and started forward. "Hold it!" Stretch Magoon stepped around the corner of the school. "Jest set still an' watch this," he said grimly. "You all reckoned Pratt was some shakes of a fighter. Wal, watch a man fifty pounds lighter beat his thick head in!"

Neil Pratt wiped the blood from his face with the back of his hand; he was swaying on his feet. Somehow, something was wrong. In all his fights his huge fists or his great strength had won quickly. Here was a man who didn't run away, who was always in there close, cutting, stabbing, slicing him with knifing punches, yet he couldn't hit him!

Pratt spread his hands, trying to get close. Suddenly Brady's shoulder was invitingly close. He lunged to grab it, but somehow Brady caught his wrist, bent suddenly, and Pratt found himself flying through the air to land heavily on the turf a half-dozen feet away.

Van Brady was breathing easily, and he was smiling now. "Get up, Big Boy!" he said softly. "I want to show you what happens to men who bust into my classes!"

Pratt heaved himself heavily to his feet. Brady did not wait. He walked up to him, and hooked both hands hard to the head. Pratt started to fall, and Brady caught him by the hair and smashed him in the face with three wicked uppercuts. Then he let go and shoved, and Pratt toppled over on the ground.

"Take him," Brady said to the Ritter hands, "take him home. He'll need a good rest!"

Sullenly, the Ritter hands helped Pratt to a horse and started off. Van Brady turned, wiping the sweat from his face. His clothes were not mussed, not even his wavy hair. The children stood staring admiringly as he walked to the pump to wash his bloody fists.

"You did a job," Magoon said solemnly. "I never seen a man fight like that. He couldn't hit you."

"They call it boxing," Van said, straightening up. "Fighting is just like punching cows or trapping fur. It has to be learned. It isn't anything fancy, it is just a lot of tricks learned over many years by a lot of different men, each one a good fighter. When you know a lot of them you become a skillful boxer."

He looked up at Stretch. "Thanks," he said, "for keeping that monkey off my back."

"It won't be enough, though," Magoon said. "You got t' get a gun. They'll be back. That Pratt is mean!"

The Circle R was standing around staring as Neil Pratt was helped from his horse. Both eyes were swollen tight shut. His face was a scarred and bloody mass.

"What happened?" Ritter demanded.

He was a tight-faced, hard-mouthed man with mean eyes. Some said he was a killer. That he had twenty killings behind him. He always wore two guns.

"That schoolteacher," Brooks said, "the one that's livin' at the schoolhouse."

Pete Ritter stepped down from the porch, his face livid. "Livin' at the schoolhouse?" he snapped. "Don't you know that's on the Shanahan place? Jest loaned for a school? You pack o' flea-brained dolts, that hombre may be a Shanahan!"

In her own room, Claire Ewing was reading a letter from Spanish John.

That hombre wot done the clown trik ridin ack was Shanahan Brady. He cum from Montana somewheres, but his pappy cum from Arizony, like us. He was a plumb salty hombre. For moren a year he was a prizefighter in Noo Yawk, an he done trick shootin in the show, too. If'n he's out thar, yuh tell the boys to lay off. He ain't no pilgrum.

The table was crowded when she walked in with the letter in her hands. Coolly, she read it.

"Why, that ornery coyote!" Magoon declared. "He done that ridin' ack afore! I got a good notion t' beat his . . ." The memory of Neil Pratt's face came back to him. "No," he finished, "I guess I better not."

"How'd you guess?" Ewing asked her.

"That riding. I saw him do it on a circus, back East, when I was in school. He was supposed to be a clown, nearly got bucked off all the time, but always stayed on."

"Ritter'll guess," Magoon said. "He'll run him off."

Web Fancher shoved back from the table. He got up. "I ain't hongry," he said, and disappeared through the door. A moment later there was a clatter of a horse's hoofs.

"Goin' t' warn Ritter. I wondered what that coyote was up to!" Ward said. He got up. "Well, ain't speakin' for nobody but myself, but I'm sidin' the teacher!"

IN THE CAMP among the willows, Shan Brady was digging into his war bag. He had little time, he knew. Ritter would hear of this, and from all he had learned the Circle R boss would be smart enough to put two and two together. Besides, he might know that Old Mike had allowed the school to be built on his place.

They would come for him, and he wanted to be ready. He had never killed a man, and he didn't want to now. There were four, no, that Mexican in Sonora made five, who had tried to kill him. Each of them had lived through it, but each time they had collected a bullet in the hand or arm.

Digging deeper in the war bag he drew out twin cartridge belts and two heavy Colt .45s in black, silver-mounted holsters. The belt and holsters were rodeo showman's gear. The guns were strictly business, and looked it.

With those guns he had shot cigarettes from men's mouths, shot buttons from their coats.

Rolling up a fresh smoke, he studied the situation. His position had not been chosen only for camping facilities, and not only because it was on the Shanahan place. It had been chosen for defense, as well.

Logs had rolled downstream during flood seasons, and he had found several of them in an excellent position. He had dragged more down close, and under the pretext of gathering wood, he had built several traps at strategic places. Now, working fast, he dragged up more logs and rolled them into place. The stream provided him with water, and he had plenty of grub. He had seen to that.

They had laughed at him for that, behind his back. "That teacher must think he's goin' t' feed an army!" they had said. But he was planning, laying in a supply of food.

His position was nicely chosen. From three sides he could see anyone who approached. The willows and the log wall gave him some concealment as well as cover.

It was an hour after daylight when he saw them coming, Pete Ritter himself in the lead. Behind him were six men, riding in a tight knot. When they were thirty yards away, he lifted his rifle and spoke, "Keep back, Ritter! I don't want any trouble from you!"

"You got trouble!" Ritter shouted angrily. "You get off that place, an' get out of the country!"

"I'm Shanahan Brady!" Shan yelled, "an' I'm stayin'! Come any closer, an' somebody gets hurt!"

"Let's go!" Ritter snarled angrily. "We'll run the durned fool clear over the border!"

He started forward. Shan threw down on him and fired four fast shots. They were timed, quick and accurate. The first shot dropped a horse, the second picked the hat from Ritter's head, taking a lock of hair with it, the third burned Lefty Brooks's gun hand, and he dropped his six-shooter and grabbed the hand to him with a curse of rage. The fourth shot took the lobe from a man's ear.

The attack broke and the riders turned and raced for shelter. Shan fired two more shots after them, dusting their heels.

Calmly, he reloaded. "That was the beginning," he said. "Now we'll get the real thing."

Chewing on a biscuit, he waited. Suddenly, he glanced at the biscuit. "That Claire girl," he said, "can cook, too! Who'd a thought it?"

The morning wore on. Several times, he sized up the rocky slope behind him. That was the danger point. Yet he had built his log wall higher there, and he had a plan.

Suddenly, rifles began to pop and shots were dusting the logs around him. He waited. Then he glimpsed, four hundred yards away, what seemed to be a man's leg. He fired, and heard a yell of pain.

Suddenly, a shot rang out from behind him and a bullet thudded into the log within an inch of his head. Hurriedly, he rolled over into the shelter of the log wall. No sooner there than getting to his knees he crawled into the willows away from camp, then slid into the streambed.

Rising behind the shelter of the banks, he ran swiftly upstream. Rounding a bend, he crawled up behind some boulders, then drifted along the slope. Panting, he dropped into place behind a granite boulder and peered around the edge.

A man he recognized as one of those who had come to the school with Pratt was lying thirty yards away, rifle in hand. Shan fired instantly, burning the sniper's ribs with a bullet. The man let out a yell of alarm and scrambled to his feet and started to run.

Lying still, Shan hazed the fellow downhill, cutting his clothes to ribbons, twice knocking him down with shots at his heels.

"All right!" The voice was cold, triumphant. "The fun's over! Git up!"

Turning, he saw Pete Ritter standing behind him, gun in hand. With him were Lefty Brooks and a man Brady recognized as Web Fancher from the Ewing ranch. "I figgered you might use that crickbed!" Pete sneered. "Figgered I might use it my ownself. Now we got you. Fust, you go back t' the ranch an' we let Neil get his evens with you. Then you start for the state line. . . . You never get there!"

It was now or never. Shan Brady knew that instantly. Once they got their hands on him he was through. Ritter had him covered, but . . . his hands were a blur as they swept down for the guns.

Somebody yelled, and he saw Pete's eyes blazing behind a red-mouthed gun. Something hit him in the shoulder, and he shot, and even as he triggered his first six-gun, he realized that what he had always feared was not happening . . . he was not losing his head!

Coolly as though on exhibition, he was shooting. Ritter wavered in front of him, and suddenly he saw other Circle R riders appearing, and there seemed to be a roaring of guns behind him. Gunsmoke filled the air.

Fancher was down on his hands and knees, a pool of blood forming under him; Ritter was gone; and Lefty Brooks was backing up, his shirt turning dark, his face pale.

Then, suddenly as it began, it was over. He

stepped back, and then a hand dropped on his shoulder. He turned. It was Magoon.

"Some shootin'!" Magoon said, grinning. Curly Ward and big Frank Ewing were also closing in, all with ready guns. "You took Ritter an' Brooks out of there! I got Fancher! That yeller belly of a traitor! Eatin' our grub an' working for Ritter!"

Claire rode up the slope, her hair blowing in the wind. She carried a rifle. He looked up at her. "You, too? I didn't know women ever fought in this man's country?"

"They do when their men—!" Her face flushed. "I mean they do when their schools are in danger! After all, you're our best teacher in years!"

He turned and started down the slope with her. "Reckon that old Shanahan place could be fixed up?" he asked. "I think it'd be a good place t' have the teachers live, don't you? It could be mighty livable."

"Why, yes, but . . . ," she stopped.

"Oh, we'd get a preacher down from Hurston!" he said, grinning. "That would make it all sort of legal, and everything. Of course," he added, remembering the biscuits, "you'd have to find time to cook, too!"

She flushed. Then laughed. "For you, I think I could!"

Shan Brady looked down at the house Old Mike had built. It was a nice house. It was a very nice house. With some curtains in the window, and the smell of cooking . . .

The Sixth Shotgun

They were hanging Leo Carver on Tuesday afternoon, and the loafers were watching the gallows go up. This was the first official hanging in the history of Canyon Gap, and the first gallows ever built in the Territory. But then, the citizens at the Gap were always the kind to go in for style.

The boys from the ranches were coming in, and the hard-booted men from the mines, and the nine saloons were closing up, but only for the hour of the hanging. On the street behind the Palace where the cottonwoods lined the creek, Fat Marie had given three hours off to the girls. One for the hanging and one for mourning and the third for drinking their tears away.

For Leo had been a spending man who would be missed along the street, and Leo had been a singing man with a voice as clear as a mountain echo and fresh as a long wind through the sage. And Leo was a handsome man, with a gun too quick to his hand. So they were hanging Leo Carver on the gallows in Canyon Gap, and the folks were coming in from the forks of every creek.

From behind the barred window Leo watched them working. "Build it high!" he yelled at them. "And build it strong, for you're hanging the best man in Canyon Gap when tomorrow comes!"

Old Pap, who had prospected in the Broken Hills before the first foundation was laid at the Gap, took his pipe from his mouth and spat into the dust. "He's right, at that," he said, "and no lie. If the 'Paches were coming over that hill right now, it's Leo Carver I'd rather have beside me than any man jack in this town."

Editor Chafee nodded his head. "Nobody will deny that he's a fighting man," he agreed. "Leo was all right until civilization caught up with him."

And there it was said, a fit epitaph for him, if epitaph he'd have, and in their hearts not a man who heard it but agreed that what Chafee said was right.

"There'll be some," Old Pap added, "who'll feel a sigh of relief when they spring that trap. When Leo's neck is stretched and the sawbones says the dead word over him, many a man will stop sweating, you can bet on that."

"Better be careful what you say." Jase Ford shifted uneasily. "It ain't healthy to be hintin'."

"Not since they put Leo away, it ain't," Old Pap agreed, "but truth's a luxury the old can afford. There's nothing they can take from me but my life, and that's no use to me. And to do that they'd have to shoot me down from behind, and that's the sort of thing they'd do unless they could hang me legal, like Leo Carver's to be hung."

Nobody said anything, but Chafee looked gloomy as he stared at the gallows. There was no living doubt that Leo Carver was an outlaw. No doubt that he had rustled a few head here and there, no doubt that he had offended the nice people of the town by carousing at the Palace and down the street of the cottonwoods. There was no doubt, either, that he'd stuck up the stage that night on Rousensock—but from there on there was doubt a-plenty.

Mitch Williams was dead, buried out there on Boot Hill with the others gone before him—Mitch Williams, the shotgun messenger who never lost a payload until that night on Rousensock, the night that Leo Carver stuck up the stage.

IT WAS A STRANGE STORY no matter how you looked at it, but Leo was a strange man, a strange man of dark moods and happy ones, but a man with a queer streak of gallantry in him and something of a manner all his own.

Mitch had been up on the box that night when Leo Carver stepped from the brush. Oh, he was wearing a mask, all right, wearing a mask that covered his face. But who did not know it was Leo?

He stepped from the brush with a brace of six-guns in his hands and said, "Hold those horses, Pete! You can—" He broke off sharp there, for he saw Mitch.

Now Mitch Williams was a hand. He had that shotgun over his knees but the muzzle was away from Leo. Mitch could never have swung that shotgun around under Leo's gun, and he knew it. So did Doc Spender, who was stage driver. Leo Carver had that stage dead to rights and he had Mitch Williams helpless.

"Sorry, Mitch!" He said it loud and clear, so they all heard him. "I thought this was your night off. I'd never rob a stage you were on, and I'd never shoot you or force you to shoot me." He swung his horse. "So long!" And he was gone.

That was Leo for you. That was why they liked him along the Gila, and why as far away as the Nueces they told stories about him. But what happened after that was different.

The stage went on south. It went over the range through Six-Shooter Gap and there was another holdup. There was a sudden blast of fire from the rocks and Mitch Williams toppled dead from the box, and then another blast—it was a shotgun—and Doc took a header into the brush and coughed out his life there in the mesquite.

Inside they were sitting still and frightened. They heard somebody crawl up to the box and throw it down. They heard it hit, and then they heard somebody riding off. One horse, one rider.

The next morning they arrested Leo.

He was washing up at the time, and they'd waited for just that. He had his guns off and they took him without a fight. Not that he tried to make one. He didn't. He just looked surprised.

"Aw, fellers," he protested. "I never done nothing! What's the matter?"

"You call that nothing? You robbed the stage last night."

"Oh, that?" He just grinned. "Put down those guns, boys. I'll come along. Sure, you know by this time I didn't rob it. I just stuck it up for a lark, and when I seen Mitch, I knowed it was no lark. That hombre would have sat still while I robbed it and drilled me when I left. He was a trusty man, that one."

"You said 'was,' so I guess you know you killed him."

Leo's face changed then. "Killed who? Say, what is this?"

And then they told him, and his face turned gray and sick. He looked around at their faces and none of them were friendly. Mitch had been a family man, and so had Doc. Both of them well liked.

"I didn't do it," Leo said. "That was somebody else. I left 'em be."

"Until you could get a shotgun!" That was Mort Lewand, who shipped the money for the bank. "Like you said, Mitch would shoot. You knew that, and he had the gun on you, so you backed out. Then you came back later with a shotgun and shot him from ambush."

"That's not true." Leo was dead serious. "And he didn't have me covered. Mitch had that shotgun pointed the other way. I had the drop and if I'd been planning to kill him, I'd've shot him then."

OH, THEY HAD A TRIAL! Judge come over from Tucson to hold court. They had a trial and a big one. Folks come from all over, and they made a big thing of it. Not that there was much anybody could say for Leo.

Funny thing, that is. Most of us, right down inside, we knowed the kind of man Leo Carver was, but most of what we knew wasn't evidence. Ever stop to think how hard it is to know a man isn't a murderer and yet know that your feeling he isn't ain't evidence?

They made it sound bad. Leo admitted he had killed seven men. Fair, stand-up fights, but still the men were dead by his gun. He admitted to rustling a few cows. Leo could have denied it, and maybe they couldn't have proved it in a court of law, but Leo wasn't used to the ways of courts and he knowed darn well we all knew he had rustled them cows. Fact is, I don't think he ever thought of denying it.

He had stuck up a few stages, too. He even admitted to that. But he denied killing Mitch Williams and he denied getting that box.

Twenty thousand, it held. Twenty thousand in gold.

Everybody thought Webb Pascal would defend Leo, but he refused, said he wanted no part of it. Webb had played poker with Leo and they'd been friends, but Webb refused him. Leo took that mighty hard. Lane Moore refused him, too, so all he could do was get that drunken old Bob Keyes to handle his case.

Convicted? You know he was. That's why they are hanging him. Keyes couldn't defend a sick cat from a bath. When they got through asking questions of Leo Carver, he was a dead Injun, believe me.

He had tried to stick up the stage once. He was a known killer. He had rustled cows. He traveled with a bad element in Canyon Gap. He had no alibi. All he had, really, was his own statement that he hadn't done it—that and the thing we knew in our hearts that isn't admissible as evidence.

"Shame for you fellers to go to all that trouble," Leo said now. That was Leo. There's no stopping him. "Why don't we just call the whole thing off?"

Mort Lewand stood in his doorway chewing his cigar and watching that gallows go up, and it made me sore, seeing it like that, for if ever one man had hated another, Mort Lewand had hated Leo.

Why? No particular reason. Personality, I'd guess you'd say. It was simply that they never tied up right. Mort, he pinched every dime he made. Leo spent his or gave it away. Mort went to church regular and was a rising young businessman. He was the town's banker and he owned the express company, and he had just bought one of the finest ranches in the country.

Leo never kept any money. He was a cattleman when he wanted to be, and as steady a hand as you'd find when he worked. One time he saved the CY herd almost single-handed when they got caught in a norther. He took on the job of ramrodding the Widow Ferguson's ranch after her old man was killed, and he tinkered and slaved and worked, doing the job of a half-dozen hands until she had something she could see for money enough to keep her.

Leo never kept a dime. He ate it up, drank it up, gave it away. The rest of the time he sat under the cottonwoods and played that old guitar of his and sang songs, old songs like my mother used to sing, old Scotch, Irish, and English songs, and some he made up as he went along.

He got into fights, too. He whipped the three Taylor boys single-handed one day. I remember that most particular because I was there. That was the day he got the blood on Ruth Hadlin's handkerchief.

THE HADLINS WERE the town's society. Every town's got some society, and Judge Emory Hadlin was the big man of this town. He had money, all right, but he had name, too. Even in the West some folks set store by a name, and whenever the judge said his name it was like ringing a big gong. It had a sound. Maybe that was all some names had, but this one had more.

Honor, reputation, square dealing, and no breath of scandal ever to touch any of them. Fine folks, and everybody knew it. Mort Lewand, he set his cap for Ruth but she never seemed to see him. That made him some angered, but tickled most of us. Mort figured he was mighty high-toned and it pleased us when Ruth turned him down flat.

Don't get the idea she was uppity. There was that time Old Pap come down with pneumonia. He was in a bad way and nobody to look after him but little Mary Ryan from down on the Street. Mary cared for him night and day almost until Ruth Hadlin heard about it.

She came down there and knocked on the door, and when Mary opened it and saw Ruth she turned seven colors. There she was, a mighty pert little girl, but she was from the Street, and here was Ruth Hadlin—well, they don't come any farther apart.

Mary flushed and stammered and she didn't know what to say, but Ruth came right on in. She turned around and said, "How is he, Mary? I didn't even know he was ill."

Ill, that's what she said. We folks mostly said sick instead of ill. Mary was shocked, too, never guessing that anybody like Ruth would know her name, or speak to her like that.

"He's bad off, Miss Ruth, but you shouldn't be here. This is the—it's the Street."

Ruth just looked at her and smiled, and she said, "I know it is, Mary, but Old Pap is ill and he can be just as ill on the Street as anywhere. I just heard about it, Mary, and how you've been caring for him. Now you go get some rest. I'll stay with him."

Mary hesitated, looking at that beautiful blue

gown Ruth was wearing and at the shabby little cabin. "There ain't—isn't much to do," she protested.

"I know." Ruth was already bending over Old Pap and she just looked around and said, "By the way, Mary, tell somebody to go tell Doctor Luther to come down here."

"We tried, miss. He won't come. He said all his business was the other side of town, that he'd no time for down here."

Ruth straightened up then. "You go tell him that Ruth Hadlin wants him down here!" Her voice was crisp. "He'll come."

He did, too.

But that was Miss Ruth. She was a thoroughbred, that one. And that was where she first met Leo Carver.

It was the third day she had been sharing the nursing with Mary Ryan, and she was in the shack alone when she heard that horse. He was coming hell-bent for election and she heard him pull up in front of the house and then the door opened and in stepped Leo Carver.

She knew him right off. How could you miss him? He was two inches over six feet, with shoulders wider than two of most men, and he was dark and clean-built with a fine line to his jaw and he had cold gray eyes. He wore two guns and his range clothes, and right then he had a two-day growth of beard. It must have startled her. Here was a man known as an outlaw, a rustler, and a killer, and she was there alone with a sick man.

He burst in that door and then drew up short, looking from Ruth to the sick old man. If he was surprised to find her there, he didn't let on. He just swept off his hat and asked, "How is he, Miss Hadlin?"

For some reason she was excited. Frightened, maybe. "He's better," she said. "Miss Ryan and I have been nursing him."

Mary had come into the room behind him, and now she stepped around quickly. "He's a lot better, Leo," she said.

"Maybe I can help nurse him, then," Carver said. He was looking at Ruth and she was white-faced and large-eyed.

Old Pap opened one eye. "Like hell," he said expressively. "You think I want a relapse? You get on out of here. Seems like," he protested plaintively, "every time I git to talk to a good-lookin' gal, somebody comes hornin' in!"

Leo grinned then and looked from Ruth to Mary. "He's in his right mind, anyway," he said, and left.

Mary stood there looking at Ruth, and Ruth looked after Leo and then at Mary.

"He's—he's an outlaw," Ruth said.

Mary Ryan turned very sharp toward Ruth, and I reckon it was the only time she ever spoke up to Ruth. "He's the finest man I ever knew!"

And the two of them just stood there looking at each other and then they went to fussing over Old Pap. That was the longest convalescence on record.

But there was that matter of the blood on her handkerchief. Ruth Hadlin was coming down the street and she was wearing a beautiful gray dress and a hat with a veil—very uptown and big city.

She was coming down the boardwalk and everybody was turning to look—she was a fine figure of a woman and she carried herself well—and just then the doors of the Palace burst open and out comes a brawling mass of men swinging with all their fists. They spilled past Ruth Hadlin into the street and it turns out to be the three Taylors and Leo Carver.

They hit dirt and came up swinging. Leo smashed a big fist into the face of Scott Taylor and he went over into the street. Bob rushed him and Leo ducked and took him around the knees, dumping him so hard the ground shook.

Bully Taylor was the tough one, and he and Leo stood there a full half-minute slugging it out with both hands, and then Leo stepped inside and whipped one to Bully's chin and the pride of the Taylors hit dirt, out so cold he's probably sleeping yet.

Ruth Hadlin had stopped in her tracks, and now Leo stepped back and wiped the blood from his face with a jerk and some of it spattered on Ruth's handkerchief. She cried out. He turned around and then he turned colors.

"Miss Hadlin," he said with a grin on his face,

"I'm right sorry. I'd no intention getting blood on you, but"—and he grinned—"it's good red blood, even if it isn't blue."

She looked at him without turning a hair, and then she said coolly, "Don't stand there with your face all bloody. Go wash it." And then she added just as coolly, "And next time don't lead with your right. If he hadn't been so all in, he'd have knocked you out." With that she walks off up the street and we all stood there staring.

Leo, he stared most of all. "Well, I'm a skinned skunk!" he said. "Where do you reckon she ever heard about leading with a right?"

Mary Ryan, she heard about it, but she said nothing, just nothing at all, and that wasn't Mary's way. Of course, we all knew about Mary. She was plumb crazy about Leo but he paid no particular attention to any one of the girls. Or all of them, for that matter.

There was talk around town, but there always is. Some folks said this was as good a time as any to get shut of Leo Carver and his like. That it was time Canyon Gap changed its ways and spruced up a bit. Mort Lewand was always for changing things. He even wanted to change the name of Canyon Gap to Hadlin. It was the judge himself who stopped that.

So WE SAT AROUND NOW and listened to the hammers and thought of how big an occasion it was to be. Some of the folks from the creek were already in town, camped out ready for the big doings to-morrow.

Ruth Hadlin was not around and none of us gave it much thought. All of this was so far away from the Hadlin folks. Ruth bought a horse, I remember, about that time. It was a fine big black. The Breed done sold it to her.

Funny thing, come to think of it, because I'd heard him turn down five hundred for that horse—and that in a country where you get a good horse for twenty dollars—but Ruth had ways and nobody refused her very much. What she wanted with a horse that big I never could see.

Editor Chafee, he hoisted his britches and was starting back toward the shop when Ruth Hadlin came down the street. She stopped nearby and she looked at that gallows. Maybe her face was a little pale, but the fact that all those roughnecks were around never seemed to bother her.

"Tom," she said right off, "what do you believe Leo Carver did with that money?"

Chafee rubbed his jaw. "You know," he scowled, "I've studied about that. I can't rightly say."

"What has he always done with it before?"

"Why, he spent it. Just as fast as he could."

"I wonder why he didn't use it to hire a better lawyer? He could have had a man from El Paso for that. Or for much less! A good lawyer might have freed him."

"I wondered about that." Chafee looked a little

anxiously at Mort Lewand. Mort was a power in town and he disliked Carver and made no secret of it. Lewand was looking that way, and now he started over. "It doesn't really matter now, does it?" Chafee added.

Lewand came up and looked from one to the other. Then he smiled at Ruth. "Rather noisy, isn't it, Ruth? Would you like me to escort you home?"

"Why, thank you," she said sweetly, "but I think I'll stay. I've never seen a gallows before. Have you, Mr. Lewand?"

"Me?" He looked startled. "Oh, yes. In several places."

She stood there a few minutes watching the carpenters work. "Well," Ruth said slowly, "it's too bad, but I'm glad no local people lost anything in that holdup."

We all looked at her, but she was watching the gallows, an innocent smile on her lips.

Editor Chafee cleared his throat. "I guess you weren't told, Miss Hadlin. The fact is, that money belonged to Mort here."

She smiled brightly. Women are strange folk. "Oh, no, Tom. You've been misinformed! As a matter of fact, that money was a payment on Mr. Lewand's ranch, and when he consigned it for carriage it became the property of the former owner of the ranch. That was the agreement, wasn't it, Mr. Lewand?"

For some reason it made Mort mad, but he nodded. "That's right."

Ruth nodded, too. "Yes, Mr. Lewand was telling me about it. He's very farsighted, I think. Isn't that wonderful, Tom? Just think how awful it would have been if he had paid that whole twenty thousand dollars and then lost it and had to pay it over! My, it would take a wealthy man to do that, wouldn't it now?"

Editor Chafee was looking thoughtful all of a sudden, and Old Pap had taken the pipe from his lips and was staring at Ruth.. Mort, he looked mad as a horny toad, though for the life of me, I couldn't see why. After all, it had been a smart stunt.

"Those awful shotguns!" From the way she was talking you wouldn't have believed that girl had a brain in her head. "I don't believe people should be allowed to own them. I wonder where Leo got the one he used?"

"Claimed he never owned one," Chafee commented slowly.

"He probably borrowed one from a friend," Mort said carelessly. "I suppose they are easy to find."

"That's just it!" Ruth exclaimed. "The man who loaned him that shotgun is just as guilty as he is. I think something should be done about it."

"I doubt if anybody loaned him one," Mort said, offhand. "He probably stole it."

"Oh, no! Because," she added hastily, "if he did, he returned it. Everybody in town who owns a shotgun still has it. There are only six of them in Canyon Gap. Daddy has two, Editor Chafee has one,

Pap here has an old broken one, and Mitch always carried one."

"That's only five," Old Pap said softly.

"Oh!" Ruth put her fingers to her mouth. "How silly of me. I'd forgotten yours, Mr. Lewand."

There was the stillest silence I ever did hear, with nobody looking at anybody else. Suddenly Ruth looked at a little watch she had, gasped something about being late, and started off.

Editor Chafee began to fill his pipe, and Old Pap scratched his knee, and all of us just sat there looking a lot dumber than we were. Mort Lewand didn't seem to know what to say, and what he finally said didn't help much. "If a man wanted to find a shotgun," he said, "I don't suppose he'd have much trouble." With that he turned and walked off.

You know something? The sound of those hammers wasn't a good sound. Editor Tom Chafee scratched his chin with the stem of his pipe. "Pete," he says to me, "you were supposed to ride shotgun that night. Whose shotgun would you have used?"

"Mitch always lent me his. I was feeling poorly and Mitch took over for me. Leo, he called my name when he first rode up, if you recall."

That shotgun business was bothering all of us. Where **did** Leo get a shotgun? This was rifle and pistol country, and shotguns just weren't plentiful. Ruth Hadlin could have narrowed it down even more, because everybody knew that Judge Hadlin wouldn't let anybody touch one of his guns but himself. They were expensive, engraved guns, and he kept them locked up in a case.

Where had Leo picked up a shotgun? What had he done with the money?

Editor Chafee looked down at Old Pap all of a sudden. "Pap," he said, "let's walk over to my place. You, too, Pete. I want you to look at my shotgun."

We looked at that gun and she was all covered with grease and dust. That shotgun hadn't been fired in six months, anyway. Or for a long time. It certainly hadn't been the gun that killed Mitch and Doc.

"Just for luck," Chafee said seriously, "we'd better go have a look at the judge's guns."

Behind us we could hear those hammers a-pounding, and we could hear O'Brien rehearsing his German band. From where we walked we could see six or seven wagons coming down the road, all headed into Canyon Gap, for the hanging.

CERTAIN THINGS HAPPENED that I didn't hear until later. I didn't hear about Ruth Hadlin, all pretty as ever a picture could be, walking into that jail to see Leo Carver. When she got into the office the sheriff was standing there looking down at a cake on his desk. That cake had been cut and it was some broken up because he had taken two files from it. Mary Ryan was standing by his side.

Sheriff Jones looked mighty serious. "Mary," he was saying, "this here's a criminal offense, helping a man to break jail. Now, where's those other two files? No use you stalling—I know you bought four of 'em."

"You're so smart," she said, "you find 'em!" She tossed her head at him and gave him a flash of those saucy eyes of hers.

Sheriff Jones leaned over the table. "Now look, Mary," he protested, "I don't want to make trouble for you, but we just can't have no prison break. Why, think of all those folks coming for miles to see a hanging! They'd be mad enough to string **me** up."

"Why not?" she said, short-like. "He's no more guilty than you are."

Jones started to protest again and then he looked up and saw Ruth Hadlin standing there in the door. Her face was cool as she could make it, and, mister, that was cold! In one hand she held Leo's guitar.

The sheriff straightened up, mighty flustered. Here he was, talking confidential-like with a girl from the Street! Suppose that got around among the good folks of the town. Be as much as his job was worth, and election coming up, too.

He flushed and stammered. "This here—this young woman," he spluttered, "she was trying to smuggle files to the prisoner. She—"

Ruth Hadlin interrupted, her eyes cold and queenlike on the sheriff. "I can assure you, Sheriff Jones, that I am not at all interested in your relations with this young lady, nor in the subject of your conversation.

"I have brought this guitar to the prisoner," she continued. "I understand he enjoys singing, and we think it cruel and inhuman that he be forced to listen to that banging and hammering while they build a gallows on which to hang him. It is cruel torture."

Jones was embarrassed. "He don't mind, ma'am," he protested. "Leo, he's—"

"May I take this instrument to him, Sheriff Jones?" Her voice was cold. "Or do you want to examine me? Do you think I might be smuggling files, too?"

Sheriff Jones was embarrassed. The very idea of laying a hand on Ruth Hadlin, the daughter of old Judge Emory Hadlin, gave him cold shivers.

"No, no, ma'am! Of course not." He gestured toward the cells. "Just you give it to him, ma'am! I'm sorry. I—"

"Thank you, Sheriff." Ruth swept by him and up to the cell.

"Young man,"—her voice was clear—"I understand that you play a guitar, so I have brought you this one. I hope the music that you get out of it will make your heart free."

Leo looked startled, and he took the guitar through the bars. "Thank you, Miss Hadlin," he said politely. "I wish—" He broke off, his face a little flushed. "I wish you didn't have to see me in here. You see, I didn't—I never killed those men. I'd like you to believe that."

"What I believe," Ruth said sweetly, "is of no importance. The music from the guitar will be pleasant for you, if played in private." She turned abruptly and walked out, and she went by Sheriff Jones like a pay-car past a tramp.

Mary told it afterwards, and Mary said that Leo plunked a string on that guitar and then he looked at it, funnylike. "It sure didn't sound right," Mary said. I shouldn't wonder.

That was late Monday afternoon. By sundown there was maybe two hundred people camped around town waiting for the big hanging next afternoon. Old Pap, he wasn't around, nor was Editor Chafee. Some said that when they left the judge's house, the judge himself was riding with them.

When next I come across Old Pap, he was standing on the corner looking at that gallows. That was near the jail, and from the window Leo could see us.

"Folks would be mighty upset if they missed their hanging, Pap," Leo said.

"They won't!" Pap was mighty short and gruff. "They'll git their hanging, and don't you forget it."

That gallows looked mighty ghostly standing there in the twilight, and it didn't make me feel no better. Leo, well, he always seemed a right nice feller. Of course, he had rustled a few head, but I wouldn't want to take no oath I hadn't, nor Old Pap, nor most of us. Leo, he was just a young hellion, that was all.

Even when he stuck up those stages he just done it for drinking money. Not that I'm saying it's right, because I know it ain't, but them days and times, folks excused a lot of a young man who was full of ginger, long as he didn't hurt nobody and was man enough.

Especially of Leo's sort. If you was in trouble you just let him know. Come prairie fire, flood, stampede, or whatever, Leo was your man. No hour was too late, no job too miserable for him to lend a hand. And never take a dime for it.

So we all went to bed, and the last thing Leo said was, "I never did cotton to no rope necktie. I don't figure it's becoming."

"Wait'll tomorry," Old Pap said.

THE SUN WAS NO MORE than up before the lid blew off the town. Somebody yelled and folks came a-running. I slid into my pants and scrambled outside. The crowd was streaming toward the Plaza and I run down there with 'em. The bars was out of the jail window, filed off clean as you'd wish, then bent back out of the way. Tied to one of them was a sheet of paper. It was a note:

"Sorry I couldn't wait, but I don't think you folks want me hanging around here, anyway."

Mary Ryan was there by the jail. She had tears in her eyes but she looked pleased as a polecat in a henhouse, too. Sheriff Jones, he took on something fierce.

"Figured she was talking poetry," he said angrily. "She told him the music he'd get out of that guitar would make his heart free. No wonder Mary wouldn't tell me what became of the other two files."

One big bearded man with hard eyes stared at the sheriff with a speculative eye. "What about the hanging?" he demanded. "We drove fifty mile to see a hanging."

Editor Tom Chafee, Judge Emory Hadlin, and Old Pap came up around them. They looked across the little circle at Jones.

"Ruth figured it right," the judge said. "Only six shotguns in town. My two shotguns, and by the dust of the cases you can see they'd not been disturbed; Editor Chafee's, which hadn't been cleaned in months; Old Pap's was broke, and Mitch had his with him. That leaves just one more shotgun."

Everybody just stood there, taking it all in and doing some figuring. Suppose that twenty thousand never left the bank? Or suppose it did leave and it was recovered by the man sending it? His debt would be paid and he would still have the money, and a young scamp like Leo Carver'd be blamed for it all.

Of course, Leo was gone. Some folks said he rode that big black Ruth Hadlin bought. What happened to that horse we never did know, because Ruth was gone, too, and her gray mare.

The trail headed west, the trail they left, and somebody living on the edge of town swore he heard two voices singing something about being bound for Californy.

We figured the judge would about burst a gasket, but he was a most surprising man. Something was said about it by somebody and all he did was smile a little.

"Many's a thoroughbred," he said, "was a frisky colt. Once they get the bridle on 'em, they straighten out. As far as that goes," he added, "every blue-blooded family can use a little red blood!"

So everybody was happy. We celebrated mighty big. I reckon the biggest in the history of Canyon Gap. O'Brien's German band played, and everybody had plenty to eat and drink.

The folks that came for the hanging wasn't disappointed, either. They got what they wanted. They got their hanging, all right. Maybe it wasn't a legal hanging, but it was sure satisfactory.

We hung Mort Lewand.

Barney Takes a Hand

Blinding white sun simmered above the thick, flourlike dust of the road, and the ragged mesquite beside the trail was gray with that same dust. Between the ranch and the distant purple hills, there was nothing but endless flats and sagebrush, dusty and dancing with heat waves.

Tess Bayeux stood in the doorway and shaded her eyes against the sun. The road was empty, empty to the horizon beyond which lay the little cow town of Black Mesa.

With a little sigh of hopelessness, she turned away. It was too soon. Even if Rex Tilden had received her note and decided to come, he could never come so quickly.

After an hour, during which she forced herself not to look even once, she returned to the door. The road was still empty, only white dust and heat. Then her eyes turned the other way, and she looked out across the desert, out to where the road dwindled off to a miserable trail into the badlands where nothing lived. For an instant then, she thought the heat played tricks with her eyes, for between her and the distant cliffs was a tiny figure.

Struck by curiosity, she stood in the doorway, watching. She was a slender girl with a pert, impudent little nose above a friendly mouth and lips that laughed when her eyes did.

She was still there, much later, when the figure took shape and became a man. The man wore no hat. His shaggy black hair was white with dust, his heavy woolen shirt was open at the neck, and his hairy chest was also dusty.

The man's face was unshaven, and his jaw was heavy, almost brutal under the beard and dust.

The jeans he wore were strange to the cow country, and his feet wore the ragged remains of what had been sneakers. His jeans were belted with a wide leather belt, curiously carved.

He wore no gun.

Several times the man staggered, and finally, when he turned from the road and stopped at the gate, he grasped the top with his big hands and stared at Tess Bayeux.

For a long time he stared while she tried to find words, and then one of the big hands dropped and he fumbled for the latch. He came through the gate and closed it behind him. It was a small thing, yet in his condition it told her something.

THE MAN CAME ON toward the house, and when she saw his face she caught her breath. Sunburn had cracked the skin until it had bled, and the blood had dried. The face was haggard, a mask of utter weariness from which only the eyes glowed and seemed to be alive.

Brought to herself suddenly, she ran inside for water. She tried to pick up the dipper, but dropped it. Then she carried the bucket to the man, and he seized it in his two big hands and lifted it to his mouth. She put out a hand to stop him, but he had merely taken a mouthful and then held it away, sloshing the water about in his mouth.

He looked at her wisely, and suddenly she had a feeling that this man knew everything, that he was afraid of nothing, that he could do anything with himself. She knew how his whole body must be crying for water, yet he knew the consequences of too much too soon and held the bucket away, his face twisted as though in a sneer at his fervid desire for its cool freshness.

Then he swallowed a little, and for a moment his face twisted again. He straightened it with an effort and picking up the washbasin beside the door, filled it and began to bathe his face and hands, slowly, tenderly. In all this time he said nothing, made no explanation.

A long time ago Tess had ridden with her brother into the badlands beyond the desert. It was a waterless horror, a nightmare of gigantic stones and gnarled cacti, a place where nothing lived.

How far had this man come? How could he have

walked all that distance across the desert? That he had walked was obvious, for his sneakers were in tatters and there was some blood on the ground where he stood.

He shook the water from his eyes and then, without speaking, stepped up on the porch and entered the house. Half frightened, she started to speak, but he merely stretched out upon the floor in the cool interior and almost at once was asleep.

Again she looked at the road. And still it was empty. If Rex Tilden were to come in time, he must come soon. Judge Barker had told her that as long as she had possession, there was a chance.

If she lost possession before he returned from Phoenix, there was little chance that anything could be done.

It was sundown when she saw them coming. It was not Rex Tilden, for he would come alone. It was the others.

It was Harrington and Clyde, the men Tess feared.

They rode into the yard at a canter and reined in at the edge of the veranda.

"Well, Miss Bayeux"—George Clyde's silky voice was underlined with malice—"you are ready to leave?"

"No."

Tess stood very still. She knew there was little Clyde wouldn't stoop to if he could gain an end. Harrington was brutal, rough. Clyde was smooth. It was Clyde she feared most, yet Harrington would do the rough work.

He was a big man and cruel.

"Then I am afraid we will have to move you," said Clyde. "We have given you time. Now we can give you only ten minutes more to get what you want and get out on the road."

"I'm not going." Tess held her head high.

Clyde's mouth tightened. "Yes, you are. Of course"—he crossed his hands on the saddle horn—"if you want to come to my place, I think I could make you comfortable there. If you don't come to my place, there will be nothing in Black Mesa for you."

"I'll stay here."

Tess stood facing them. She couldn't win. She knew that in her heart. Rex was too late now, and the odds were against her. Still, where would she go? She had no money; she had no friends who dared help her. There had been only Tilden.

"All right, Harrington," Clyde said grimly. "You move her. Put her outside the gate."

Harrington swung down from the saddle, his face glistening with evil. He stepped up on the porch.

"Stay where yuh are!" a voice said from behind her.

Tess started. She had forgotten the stranger, and his voice was peculiar. It was low, ugly with some fierceness that was only just covered by an even tone.

"You come a step farther and I'll kill yuh!" he said.

Harrington stood flat-footed. George Clyde was quicker.

"Tess Bayeux, who is this man?"

"Shut up!" The man walked out on the porch,

and his feet were catlike in their movements. "And get movin'."

"Listen, my friend," Clyde said, "you're asking for trouble. You're a stranger here and you don't know what you're saying."

"I know a skunk by the smell." The stranger advanced to the edge of the porch, and his red-rimmed eyes glared at Clyde. "Get goin'!"

"Why, you—"

Harrington reached for him.

He reached, but the stranger's left hand shot out and seized Harrington by the throat and jerked him to his tiptoes. Holding him there, the stranger slapped him twice across the face. Slapped him only, but left him with a trickle of blood at the corner of his mouth. Then, setting him down on his heels, the stranger shoved, and big Deek Harrington sprawled at full length in the dust.

Clyde's face was deadly. He glanced at Harrington and then at the stranger, and then his hand shot for his gun. But the stranger was quicker. He seized the bridle and jerked the horse around and, catching Clyde by his gun arm, whipped him from the saddle to throw him into the dust.

Clyde's gun flew free, and the stranger caught it deftly and thrust it into his own waistband.

"Now," he said, "start walkin'. When yuh're over the horizon, I'll turn yore hosses loose. Until then, walk!"

Harrington staggered to his feet, and Clyde got up more slowly. His black coat was dusty. The stranger looked at Harrington.

"You still wear a gun," he said coolly. "Want to die? If yuh do, why don't yuh try drawin' it."

Harrington wet his lips. Then his eyes fell and he turned away.

"That goes for later," the stranger said. "If yuh want to try a shot from up the road, do it. I haven't killed a snake in a week!"

The two men stumbled from the yard, and the stranger stood there, watching them go. Then he picked up the bucket and drank, for a long time. When the two recent visitors were growing small toward the horizon, he turned the horses loose, hitting each a ringing slap on the haunches.

They would never stop short of town if he knew Western horses.

"I'm going to get supper," Tess told him. "Would you like to eat?"

"You know I would." He looked at her for a moment. "Then yuh can tell me what this is all about."

TESS BAYEUX WORKED SWIFTLY, and when she had the coffee on and the bacon frying, she turned to look at the man who had come to her rescue. He was slumped in a chair at the table. Black hair curled in the V of his shirt, and there was black hair on his forearms.

"You aren't a Western man?" she asked him.

"I was—once," he answered. "but that was a long time ago. I lived in Texas, in Oklahoma, then in Utah. Now I'm back in the West to stay."

"You have a home somewhere?"

"No. Home is where the heart is, they say, and my heart is here"—he touched his chest—"for now. I'm still a dreamer, I reckon. Still thinkin' of the one girl who is somewhere."

"You've had a hard time," she said, looking at him again.

She had never seen so much raw power in a man, never seen so much sleeping strength as in the muscles that rolled beneath his shirt.

"Tell me about you," he said. "Who are them two men that was here?"

"Harrington and Clyde," she told him. "The H and C Cattle Company. They moved in here two years ago, during the drouth. They bought land and cattle. They prospered. They aren't big, but then, nobody else is either.

"The sheriff doesn't want trouble. Clyde outtalks those who dislike him. My father did, very much, and he wasn't outtalked. He died, killed by a fall from a bad horse, about a year ago. It seems he was in debt. He was in debt to Nevers, who runs the general store in Black Mesa. Not much, but more than he could pay. Clyde bought up the notes from Nevers.

"Wantrell, a lawyer in Phoenix who knew my father, is trying to get it arranged so we will have water here. If we do, we could pay off the notes in a short time. If we had water I could borrow money in Prescott. There is water on government land above us, and that's why Clyde wants it. He tried to get me to move away for the notes. Then he offered to pay me five hundred dollars and give me the notes.

"When I refused, he had some of his men dam the stream and shut off what water I had. My cattle died. Some of my horses were run off. Then he came in with some more bills and told me I'd have to leave or pay. He has some sort of a paper on the place. It says that my father promised to give Nevers the place if he didn't pay up or if anything happened to him."

"No friends?" asked the man.

"Yes, a man named Rex Tilden," Tess said. "He rode for Dad once and then started a ranch of his own. He's good with a gun, and when I wrote to him, he said he would come. He's five days late now."

The stranger nodded. "I know." He took a small wallet from his pocket. "That his?"

She caught it up, her face turning pale. She had seen it many times.

"Yes! You know him? You have seen him?"

"He's dead. Dry-gulched. He was killed near Santos three days ago."

"You knew him?" Tess repeated.

"No. I got kicked off a train I was ridin'. I found him dyin'. He told me about you, asked me to help. There was nobody else around, so I came."

"Oh, thank you! But Rex! Rex Tilden dead. And because of me!"

His face didn't change. "Mebbe." He brought out the gun he had taken from Clyde and checked it. "Mebbe I'll need this. Where's that dam?"

"Up there, on the ridge. But they have it guarded."

"Do they?" He didn't look interested.

She put the bacon on his plate and poured coffee. He ate in silence, and when he had finished, it was dark. He got up suddenly.

"You got a gun?" he asked.

"Just a small rifle, for rabbits."

"Use it. If anything moves, shoot."

"But it might be you!" she protested. "When you come back, I mean!"

He smiled, and his whole face seemed to lighten.

"When anything moves, shoot. It won't be me. When I come back yuh won't hear me."

"Who are you?" It was the first time she had asked that.

He hesitated, looking at the ground and then at her, and his eyes glinted with humor.

"My name is Barney Shaw," he said then. "That mean anything to yuh?"

She shook her head.

"Should it?"

"No, I reckon not."

"A few years ago I was punchin' cows. Then I worked in the mines. A man saw me in a fight once and trained me. In two years I was one of the best.

Then I killed a man in a dice game and got two years for it. He was cheatin', I accused him, he struck at me.

"When the two years was up—I'd been sentenced to ten, but they let me out after two—I went to sea. I was at sea for four years. Then I decided to come back and find a place for myself, here in the West. But first, a job."

TESS LOOKED AT HIM understandingly.

"I need a man," she said, "but I haven't the money to pay."

"How about a workin' share?"

"All right. Fifty-fifty." She smiled ruefully. "But it isn't much. I think Clyde will win, after all."

"Not if I can help it. How much do yuh owe?"

"A thousand dollars. It might as well be a million. We don't have more than fifty head of cattle on the place, and only four saddle horses."

He went out the back door and vanished. Or so it seemed. Tess, glancing out a moment later, could see nothing. She should have told him about Silva, the guard at the dam. Silva was a killer and quick as a snake.

She turned again to the house and began putting things in order. First, she barricaded the front door and then opened the window a slit at the bottom. She got out her rifle, checked it, and laid out some ammunition.

Barney Shaw had seen the draw when he approached the house by the road, so when he left the house he hit it fast. It was deep enough by a head, and he started away. Fortunately, it led toward the dam. It was the old streambed.

From the shadow of a gigantic boulder, he looked up at the dam. Largely brush, logs, and earth, it was a hasty job and homemade. He watched for twenty minutes before he saw the guard. Silva, a Mexican, had found a place for himself where he could command all the approaches to the dam.

In the moonlight, a rock cedar made a heavy shadow. Barney Shaw moved, and then as Silva's head moved, he froze. He was out in the open, but he knew the light was indistinct. For a long time he stood still, and then as Silva's head moved again, Shaw glided forward to the shelter of the rock cedar.

He was no more than a dozen feet from the guard now, and through a hole in the bushy top of the cedar he could see Silva's long, lantern jaw, and even the darkness seemed to mark the thin mustache the man wore.

When Silva stood up, Shaw could see that the man was tall, yet feline in his movements. Silva stretched and then turned and came toward the cedar, walking carelessly. He had put his rifle aside and walked with the aimlessness of a man without care. Yet something in that very carelessness struck Shaw as the guard moved closer.

Silva stepped past the tree and then whirled and

dived straight at Shaw, his knife flashing in the moonlight!

Only that sense of warning saved Barney Shaw. He stepped back, just enough, and whipped a left hook for Silva's chin. It landed, a glancing blow, and the Mexican dropped.

But catlike he was on his feet and, teeth bared, he lunged again. Shaw stepped in, warding off the knife, and slashed with the edge of his hand for the Mexican's neck. The blow was high and took the man across the temple and ear.

Silva went to his knees and lost his hold on the knife. Barney stepped in, and as the Mexican came up, he hit him once, twice. The blows cracked like whips in the still air, and the guard dropped to his face.

Dragging him roughly into the open, Shaw hastily bound him hand and foot. Then he walked over and picked up the guard's rifle. It was a Winchester and a good one.

Rustling around, he found an ax and a pick. Without so much as a glance toward the guard, he dropped down the face of the dam and, setting himself, sank the ax into one of the key posts. When he had cut through the posts and the timbers back of them, he was sweating profusely. He was aware, too, that the ax was making a ringing sound that would carry for at least a mile in that still air.

Putting the ax down, he took the pick and began

digging at the dirt and rock that were piled on the water side of the dam. In a few minutes there was a trickle of water coming through, then a fair-sized stream.

Carrying the rifle, he went back to the edge of the draw where the timbers had been fitted into notches cut into the rock with a double jack and drill. It took him more than an hour, but he cut two timbers loose.

Dropping his tools he walked over to look at Silva. The Mexican was conscious, and his eyes blazed when Shaw looked at him, grinning.

"Don't worry," Barney said grimly. "Yuh're safe up here, and when the dam goes out they'll be up here in a hurry."

He turned and started away, keeping to the shadows of the cedars. And before he had walked a hundred yards he heard a whoosh and then the rustle of rushing water.

It was a small stream, and the water wasn't much, but it would more than fill the pools down below where Tess Bayeux's cattle came to drink.

There was no warning, and he was still some distance from the girl's cabin when he saw a rifle flash. Simultaneously something struck him a terrific blow alongside the head and he tumbled, face downward, into the gravel. He felt his body sliding headfirst, and then he lost consciousness.

WHEN BARNEY SHAW OPENED his eyes it was daylight.

He tried to move his head, and pain shot through him like a burning iron. For an instant then he lay still, gathering the will to try again. The side of his head and face that was uppermost was caked with dried blood, and his hair was matted with it. That the morning was well along he knew, for his back was hot with sun, and from the feel, the sun was high.

Shaw moved his head and, despite the pain, forced himself to his knees. His head swimming, he peered about.

He lay on a rocky hillside. Below him, half hidden by a clump of cedar, and almost two miles away, was the house of Tess Bayeux. At his right he could hear water running, and that meant the stream he had released had not yet been stopped.

His rifle and pistol were still with him. Gingerly he felt his head. It was badly swollen, and the scalp was furrowed by a bullet. He had bled profusely, and he decided that if his dry-gulchers had looked at him they had decided the bullet had entered his skull.

What about Tess? Had they thrown her out? Or was she still holding the place? The silence was ominous, and obviously hours had passed.

Whoever had shot him had no doubt left him for dead and had also freed Silva. How many enemies were there? He had no way of knowing, and Tess had told him nothing. Harrington, Silva, and Clyde were three, and of them all, George Clyde was the most dangerous because he was the most intelligent.

From a position behind some boulders and cedar

Shaw studied the small ranch house. There was no evidence of activity, nothing to indicate how the tide of battle had gone.

Then a door banged at the house and he saw a man come out, walking toward the corral. He roped two horses, and in a few minutes two riders started off to town. One of them was Silva.

It took Barney Shaw a half hour of painstaking effort to get to the wall of the house without being seen. He edged along to the corner and then stopped. Cautiously, he peered around. Not ten feet away a man was sitting on the edge of the porch, a rifle on his knees.

He was a short man, but square-jawed and tough. As Barney looked, the man put the rifle against the post, took out a pipe, and began to fill it. Shaw made a quick calculation of his chances and decided against it. With Harrington, perhaps. Not this jasper. This hombre was different.

Suddenly Barney Shaw saw a slim piece of pipe, and it gave him an idea. Picking it up, he glanced to see if it was clear and then looked around for some pebbles. He selected a half dozen. In school, too many years ago, he had been an artist with a beanshooter.

The man on the porch had a beak of a nose that jutted out above his heavy jaw like the prow on a ship. Taking careful aim, Shaw blew the first pebble. It missed.

The man glanced in the direction of the sound

where the pebble hit the ground and then turned back, puffing contentedly at his pipe. Then Barney fired a second pebble.

It was a direct hit. The pebble, fired from the beanshooter with force, hit him right on the nose!

With a cry of pain, the man leaped to his feet, one hand grasping his nose. His pipe had fallen to the ground.

Instantly, Barney was around the corner. The man, holding his nose, his eyes watering, never saw him coming. It was only when Barney, picking up the rifle, knocked it against the porch, that the man whirled about. And Shaw slapped him alongside the head with the butt of the rifle, swinging it free-handed.

The fellow went down, grabbing for his gun, but Shaw stepped in and kicked it from his hand. Then as the fellow started to rise, Shaw slapped him across the temple with a pistol barrel. The man went down and out.

Coolly Barney shouldered the fellow and, walking with him to the barn, tied him securely and dropped him into a feed bin. Then he went outside and roped a horse. When it was saddled he led it to the house, left it ground-hitched, and took a quick look. There was no sign of Tess Bayeux. Hiding the extra rifle, he swung into the saddle and started at a canter for town.

HE WAS A TOUGH-LOOKING figure when he rode into town. His shock of black hair was still thick with dust, and his face was stained with blood. The two pistols were thrust into his waistband, and he carried a rifle in his hands.

He was cantering up the street when he saw Silva. The Mexican had come to the door of the saloon, and when he saw Barney he swore and dropped a hand for a gun. Shaw swung the rifle and fired across the pommel of the saddle.

The first shot knocked the gun from Silva's hand, the second slammed him back into the wall. It was a shoulder shot. Silva stood there, staring stupidly.

Swinging down, Barney tied the horse and walked along the boardwalk. A dozen people had rushed out at the sound of a shot, but he ignored them. He merely walked to Silva and stopped. For a long time he looked at him.

"Next time I'll kill yuh!" he said, and walked inside.

Three men were in the bar besides the bartender. One of them was a powerfully built man with big hands and a flat nose. Behind the bar were some photos of him, posed like a boxer.

"You a fighter?" Shaw demanded. "If yuh are, I can lick yuh!"

The man looked at him, his eyes hard.

"I fight for money," he said.

"So do I," Shaw said. He looked at the bartender. "I'll fight this hombre, winner take all, skintight kid gloves, to a finish!"

The bartender's face whitened and then turned red.

"Yuh know who this is?" he demanded. "This is the Wyoming Slasher!"

"All right. Line up the fight." Shaw hesitated. "One thing—it must be one thousand dollars for the purse."

The bartender laughed.

"Yuh'll get that, easy. If yuh win. The boys like to see the Slasher fight!"

Barney Shaw nodded and walked out.

"Who was that?" Harrington demanded as he burst in from the back room. "Who was that man?"

"Some gent with his face all bloody, dusty as sin, wantin' to fight the Slasher for a thousand dollars!"

"The Slasher? A thousand dollars?" Harrington's eyes hardened. "Why, I'll fix his clock!"

"No you won't." Clyde walked into the room. "Let it ride. The Slasher will kill him. That will settle everything!"

Barney Shaw walked to the hotel, carrying his rifle in the hollow of his arm. He was going up the steps when he saw Tess. Her eyes widened.

"I thought—you were dead or gone!" she exclaimed.

"No." He looked at her. "What happened?"

"They surprised me, just before morning. The sheriff was with them, and he made me leave. They had some papers, and they said I had to leave. If I can pay in ten days I can go back."

"In ten days yuh'll pay," he promised and walked past her to the desk. "I want a room and a telegraph blank," he told the clerk.

The clerk shook his head.

"We don't have any rooms."

Barney Shaw reached over the desk and caught the clerk behind the neck and dragged him half over the desk.

"Yuh heard me," he said harshly. "I want a room and a telegraph blank! Yuh never sold this hotel out since it was built! Now get me that room!"

"Yes, sir!" The clerk swallowed and turned the register. "I just remembered. There is a room left."

He put a blank on the desk, and Barney wrote hastily, "Now is the time for all good men to come to the aid of their party." Then he signed his name. He told the clerk to send the message to the depot and have the agent get it off at once.

TESS CAME OVER and stood beside him.

"What are you going to do?" she asked.

"Fight the Slasher for a thousand dollars," he said. "That will pay off for yuh."

"The Slasher?" Her face paled. "Oh, not him, Barney! He's awful! He killed a man in a fight! And those men with him! That Dirk Hutchins, McCluskey, and the rest. They are awful!"

"Are they?" Barney smiled at her. "I'm goin' to wash up, then sleep." He turned and walked upstairs.

A man got up from across the room and walked over to the desk.

"What do yuh think, Martin?" he asked.

Martin Tolliver, the clerk, looked up and his face was grim.

"This one's different, Joe. I'm goin' to bet on him."

"I think I will, too," Joe said. "But we'll be the only ones."

"Yes," Martin agreed. "But he took hold of me. Joe, that hombre's got a grip like iron! It was like bein' taken in a vise! I was never so scared in my life!"

By NOON the day of the fight, punchers were in from the ranches and miners from the mines. The ring had been pitched in the center of the big corral. Martin Tolliver, the hotel clerk, and Joe Todd were betting. They were getting odds.

A little after noon the train came in. By that time everyone was at the corral waiting for the fight to start, and only Silva saw the men get off the train. There were nine of them who got out of the two passenger coaches. Four were cattlemen, one was a huge, bearded man with blue anchors tatooed on his hands, and the other four were nondescripts in caps and jerseys.

The Wyoming Slasher was first in the ring. He came down, vaulted the ropes, and stood looking around. His hair was cropped short and he wore a black John L. Sullivan mustache. His eyes were blue and hard, and his face looked like stained oak.

Harrington and another man were in his corner. The sheriff had been selected as the referee.

Barney Shaw came from the hotel, walking across the street wearing an old slicker. As he stepped through the ropes a stocky man in a checked suit and a black jersey stepped up behind him and put a professional hand on his shoulder.

They got into the ring and walked to the center. The Slasher was half a head taller than Shaw and heavier. His wide cheekbones and beetling brows made him look fierce. The back of his head slid down into a thick neck.

Shaw's hair had been cut, and it was black and curly. He looked brown, and when he turned and walked to his corner, there was an unexpected lightness in his step.

The Wyoming Slasher dropped his robe, and there was a gasp from the crowd who looked at the rolling muscles of his mighty shoulders and arms. He was built like a wrestler, but his weight was in his gigantic shoulders and deep chest.

He strode to the scratch, skintight gloves pulled on. The sheriff motioned, the slicker slid from Barney's shoulders, and he turned and came to scratch. His broad shoulders were powerful and tapered to narrow hips and slim, powerful legs. The Slasher put up his hands and Barney hit him, a quick left that tapped the blood at his thin lips. The Slasher lunged, and Barney slid away, rapping a quick right to the body.

The Slasher strode in, and Barney tried a left to the head that missed, and the Slasher grabbed him by the waist and hurled him to the ground. Shaw lit in a pile of dust, and the sheriff sprang in. "Round!" he shouted.

Shaw walked to his corner.

"He's strong," he said. He waved away the water bottle.

"Them new Queensbury rules would be better for you," his second said out of the corner of his mouth. "London Prize Ring rules was never no good. Yuh hurt a man and if he goes down the round is over."

They started again at the call of time, and Barney walked out quickly. The Slasher rushed, and Barney lanced the fellow's lips with another left and then stepped around and jabbed with the left again. There was a mix-up. Then Barney stepped away, and the Slasher hit him.

It was a hard right, and it shook Shaw to his heels, but he stepped away. He was skillfully, carefully feeling the bigger man out. Instinctively he knew it would be a hard fight. The other man was like iron, big and very, very strong. It would take time to down him. Barney was trying each punch, trying to find out what the big man would do.

All fighters develop habits. Certain ways of blocking lefts, ducking or countering. By trying each punch a few times Barney Shaw was learning the pattern of the Slasher's fighting, getting a blueprint in his mind.

When the second round had gone four minutes, he took a glancing left to the head and went down, ending the round.

When the minutes were up, he went out with a rush. The Slasher put up his hands and without even stopping his rush, Barney dropped low and thrust out his left. It caught the Slasher in the midriff and set him back on his heels.

Instantly Barney was upon him. Hitting fast, he struck the Slasher five times in the face with a volley of blows before the bigger man was brought up by the ropes. Then setting himself, he whipped a hard right to the Slasher's ribs!

THE CROWD WAS YELLING wildly, and the Slasher came off the ropes and swung. Barney went under it and whipped a right to the heart. Then the Slasher's left took him and he rolled over on the ground!

He was badly shaken. In his corner, "Turkey Tom" Ryan, his second, grinned.

"Watch it," he said. "He can hit, the beggar!"

They had wiped the blood from the Slasher's face, and the big man looked hard. Near the Slasher's corner Barney could see George Clyde.

Barney Shaw went up to scratch and as the Wyoming Slasher rushed he stabbed a left to the mouth, parried a left himself, and hit hard to the body. Inside, he hammered away with both hands. He took a clubbing right to the head that cut his forehead and showered him with blood. But suddenly he knew that his time had come, and instead of backing away, he set himself and began slugging with everything he had.

The Slasher was caught off balance. He tried to get set, but he was too heavy. He struck several ponderous blows, but Barney was knifing his face with those skintight gloves. Jabbing a left, he turned his fist as it struck and ripped the Slasher's face. Then he stepped in and threw a wicked uppercut to the body. Then another and still another.

The Slasher started to fall, but Shaw caught him under the chin with the heel of his glove and shoved him erect against the ropes. Stepping back, he smashed both hands to the chin.

With the crowd roaring, Shaw leaped away and the Wyoming Slasher rolled off the ropes and fell flat on his face!

Instantly his seconds were over the ropes and swarming over him. Harrington rushed across the ring and seized one of Barney Shaw's hands, shouting something about his fists being loaded.

Turkey Tom shoved him away, and Shaw took off the glove and showed him his bare fist. Harrington snarled something, and Shaw slugged him in the ribs. As the big man started to fall, one of his friends stepped up, and instantly the ring was a bedlam of shouting, fighting men.

It was ten minutes before the ring was cleared,

and then the Slasher was able to get to the scratch. He rushed immediately, and Shaw ducked, but as he ducked he slipped and the Slasher hit him and knocked him to his knees. He started to get up, and the Slasher rushed and struck him another ponderous blow. He went down hard. And the round ended.

He was barely on his second's knee when the call of "time" came again and, groggy, he went to scratch. The Wyoming Slasher charged. Shaw ducked, went into a clinch, and threw the Slasher with a rolling hiplock. The Slasher went down with a thud.

Still groggy, he came to scratch again, but as they came together, he feinted suddenly. As the Slasher swung, Shaw threw his right, high and hard. It caught the Slasher coming in and knocked him to the ropes. As he rebounded Shaw hit him with a one-two, so fast that the two blows landed with almost the same sound.

The Slasher hit the ground all in one piece and rolled over. After ten minutes he was still unable to stand.

As he shoved to his feet and held there, Harrington suddenly shouted. As one man, his thugs charged the ring and began tearing down the posts.

But even as they charged, the four cattlemen leaped into the ring, as did the man with the blue anchors on his hands. In a breath there was a cordon of men with guns drawn around Barney, around the two stakeholders, and around the shouting Turkey Tom.

Harrington's thugs broke against the flying wedge formed by the cattlemen and Shaw's friends, and the wedge moved on to the hotel.

Tess met them at the door, her eyes wild with anxiety.

"You're all right? Oh, I was so afraid! I was sure you'd be hurt!"

"You should see the Slasher, ma'am," Turkey Tom said, grinning to show his five gold teeth. "He don't look so good!"

"We've got the money to pay off now," Barney told her, smiling. His lips were puffed and there was a blue welt alongside his ear. "We can pay off and start over."

"Yes, and that ain't all!" One of the cattlemen, a big man wearing a black hat, stepped in. "When yuh wired about the water, I was in Zeb's office. We went to the governor and we got it all fixed up. So I decided it might be a right good idea for me to come up here and get yuh to feed about five hundred whiteface cows for me—on shares!"

"She can't," snarled a voice behind them.

As ONE MAN they turned. George Clyde stood in the doorway, his lips thinned and his face white.

"She can't, because there's mineral on that place, and I've filed a mining claim that takes in the spring and water source!"

His eyes were hard and malicious. Harrington, his face still bloody, loomed behind him. The big man with the anchors on his hands stepped forward and stared hard at Clyde.

"That's him, Sheriff," he said. "The man who killed Rex Tilden!"

George Clyde's face stiffened.

"What do you mean?" he shouted. "I was here that night!"

"You were in Santos that night. You met Rex Tilden on the road outside of town and shot him. I was up on the hill when it happened and I saw you. You shot him with that Krag Jorgenson rifle! I found one of the shells!"

"He's got one of them Krags," the sheriff said abruptly. "I seen it! He won it from some Danish feller last year in a game of faro. I never seen another like it!"

Barney Shaw had pulled on his trousers over his fighting trunks and slipped on his shirt. He felt the sag of the heavy pistol in his coat pocket and put on the coat. Half turning, he slid the pistol into his waistband.

"That means," he said coolly, "that his mineral claim won't be any use to him. I know he hasn't done any assessment work, and without that he can't hold the claim!"

Clyde's eyes narrowed.

"You!" he snarled. "If you'd stayed out of this I'd have made it work. You'll never see me die! And you will never see me arrested!"

Suddenly his hand dropped for his gun, but

even as his hand swept down, Barney Shaw stepped through the crowd, drew, and fired!

Clyde staggered, half turned, and pitched over on his face. Harrington had started to reach, but suddenly he jerked his hand away from his gun as though it were afire.

"I had nothin' to do with no killin'," he said, whining. "I never done nothin'!"

When the sheriff had taken Harrington away, Barney Shaw took Tess by the arm.

"Tess," he asked hesitantly, "does the fifty-fifty deal still go?"

She looked up, her eyes misty and suddenly tender.

"Yes, Barney, for as long as you want it!"

"Then," he said quietly, "it will be for always!"

Rain on the Halfmoon

Jim Thorne came down off the Mules at daybreak with a driving rain at his back. But when he rode out of the pines on the bench above Cienaga Creek he could see the bright leap of flames through the gray veil of the rain.

Too big to be a campfire and too much in the open. The stage bearing Angela should have left twenty minutes ago, but Dry Creek Station was afire.

Leaving the trail, Thorne put his horse down the slope through the scattered pines, risking his neck on the rain-slick needles. He hit the flat running, and crowded the dun off the trail to the more direct route across the prairie.

Flames still licked at the charred timbers with hungry tongues when he came down the grade to Dry Creek, but the station was gone. Among the debris, where the front of the building had been, lay the blackened rims of the stage wheels and the remains of the hubs, still smoldering.

His mouth dry with fear, Jim Thorne drew up and looked around, then swung in a swift circle of the fire. There was but one body in the ruins, that of a belted man. The glimpse was all he needed to know, it was the body of Fred Barlow, station tender at Dry Creek.

Where, then, was Angela? And where was Ed Hunter, who drove the run?

A splatter of footprints in the mud pointed toward the stable, and at their end he found Hunter.

The driver had been shot twice, once in the back while running, the second fired by someone who had stood above him and deliberately murdered the wounded man.

There was, nowhere, any sign of Angela.

Keeping to the saddle, he swung back. With a rake handle he poked at the ruins of the stage, rescuing a burned valise from which spilled the charred remnants of feminine garments. They were Angela's.

She had, then, been here.

He sat his saddle, oblivious to the pounding rain. Angela had reached the stage station, had obviously seen her valise aboard the stage. She must have been either in the stage or about to get in when it happened.

Apaches?

A possibility, but remote. There had been no trouble in almost a year, and the body of Ed Hunter was not mutilated.

The nearest help was in Whitewater, fifteen miles north. And with every minute they would be taking Angela farther and farther away.

Wheeling the dun, he rode again to the stable.

The horses were gone. He swung down and studied the floor. At least one man had been in here since the rain, for there was mud, not yet dry, on the earth floor.

Four stage horses habitually occupied the stalls, but there was ample evidence that eight horses had been stabled there the night before. Knowing Barlow shod the stage horses, and his shoes were distinctive, Thorne studied the tracks.

The four draft horses were easily identified. Three of the other horses were strange, but the fourth had at least one Barlow shoe. The stalls of the four strange horses were not muddy, which meant the riders must have stabled their horses before the rain began.

It was not unusual for Barlow to stable the horses of travelers, but the horse with the Barlow shoe implied at least one of the riders had passed this way before.

Jim Thorne walked to the door and built a smoke. Going off half-cocked would not help Angela. He must think.

Four men had arrived the previous night. Angela must have arrived earlier and probably went to bed at once. Trouble had apparently not begun until after the arrival of the morning stage.

Fred Barlow and Ed Hunter had both known Angela. Both were old friends of his, and solid men. They would have seen no harm come to her. Therein, he decided, lay the crux of the situation.

Angela was not merely pretty. She was steady, loyal,

sincere. But Angela had a body that drew the eyes of men. Suppose one of the strangers made advances? Barlow would allow no woman to be molested, and Hunter was stubborn as well as courageous.

Suddenly, Jim Thorne saw it all. And as suddenly as that, there was no remaining doubt. The Ottens and Frazer.

They were a Tennessee mountain outfit, surly, dangerous men who made no friends. Quarrelsome, cruel, and continually on the prowl after women, they had settled on the Halfmoon six months before.

"Tough outfit," Barlow had commented once. "Wherever they come from they was drove out. An' left some dead behind, I'll gamble."

Jim Thorne had seen them. Lean, rangy men with lantern jaws and swarthy skin. The odd man, who was Frazer, was thickset and sandy. The leader was Ben Otten, a man with thin, cold lips and a scar on his cheekbone.

They raised no cattle, lived on beef and beans, rode a lot at night, and made a little whiskey, which they peddled.

A month after they arrived in the country, they had killed a man down at Santa Rita. Three of them had boxed him and shot him down. There had been some trouble over at Round Mountain, too, but since it was known that trouble with one meant trouble with all, they were left strictly alone.

When Angela left him, she had come here to catch the stage, just as she told him in the note she left on the table. The Ottens and Frazer must have ridden in; they often stayed over at the station when the weather was bad, although they were tolerated rather than welcomed guests. One of them had started some kind of trouble, and Barlow had been killed. They had murdered Hunter, burned the station, then taken Angela and left.

Tearing a sheet from his tally book, Jim wet his stub of pencil and wrote what he surmised and where he had gone. The stable door opened inward so he left the note fastened to the door out of the rain. Then he walked to the corner of the blacksmith shop, and drawing aside an old slicker that hung there, Jim took down Barlow's backup gun.

It was a Roper four-shot revolving shotgun with several inches sawed off the barrel. Checking the loads, he hung it under his slicker and walked back to the dun. It had undoubtedly been this gun Ed Hunter was running for when shot down.

Hesitating, Jim Thorne then walked back to the stable, sacked up some grain, and tied it behind the saddle under his bedroll. Then he led the dun outside and swung into the leather.

It was a twenty-mile ride to Halfmoon the way he would go, but almost thirty miles by the route they would be taking. He was quite sure the Ottens had not been in the country long enough to have scouted the route up Rain Creek and over the saddle to West Fork.

Two of his friends lay dead, a stage station burned,

his wife kidnapped. There was in his heart no place for mercy.

Angela was an eastern girl, lovely, quiet, efficient. She had made him a good wife, only objected to his wearing a gun. She had heard that he had killed a man, a rustler. But that had been in Texas and long ago. There had been no black mark on their marriage until the arrival of Lonnie Mason.

Jim Thorne had recognized him for what he was at first sight. Deceptively shy, good-looking, and not yet twenty, Lonnie Mason had seemed a quiet, inoffensive boy to Angela. Jim Thorne had seen at once that the man was a killer.

Several times he had stopped by the ranch, talked with Angela, and in his eyes a veiled taunt for Jim. He had heard of Jim Thorne, for while Thorne had killed but one man, he had been a Ranger in Texas, and he had won a reputation there. And a reputation was bait for Lonnie.

It had come unexpectedly. Some stage company stock had drifted, and Thorne had gone with Fred Barlow to find it. They had come upon Lonnie and another man with a calf down and an iron hot . . . a Barlow calf.

Lonnie had grabbed for his gun, incredibly fast, but Jim Thorne had not forgotten what he had learned on the Nueces. Lonnie went down, shot through the heart, and one of the stranger's bullets cut Barlow's belt before Thorne's guns saved the rheumatic elder man's life.

Angela was profoundly shocked. Jim would never forget the horror in her eyes when he rode into the ranch yard with the bodies over their saddles, en route to the sheriff.

She would listen to his explanations, but they never seemed to get through to her. It was incredible that Lonnie had been a thief, ridiculous that he might be a killer. Jim Thorne had simply been too quick to shoot. She had known this would happen if he continued to wear a gun. Fred Barlow had tried to explain, but all she could remember was that her husband had killed two men, one of them that soft-voiced boy with the girlish face.

They argued about it several times and Jim had become angry. He said things he should not have said. He declared she was no fit wife for a western man. To go back East if that was how she felt. It was said in anger, and he had been appalled to return one day to find her gone.

Low clouds, heavy with their weight of rain, hung above Haystack when he skirted the mountain and rode into Rain Canyon. Taking the high trail above the roar of runoff water, he cut back into the hills. The dun was mountain-bred and used to this. Thunder rolled down the canyons, crashing from wall to wall like gigantic boulders rolling down a vast marble corridor. Ponderous echoes tumbled among the stern-walled mountains.

The pines were no longer green, but black with rain. The dun plodded on, and squinting his eyes against the slanting rain, he stared ahead, watching for the saddle he must cross to West Fork.

When Jim Thorne reached the saddle, the rain was sweeping across in torrents. On either side loomed the towering peaks of more than ten thousand feet each. The saddle was itself over eight thousand feet, and at this point was almost bare of timber, rain blackening the boulders and falling in an almost solid wall of water.

Pushing on, Jim watched the lightning leaping from peak to peak, and striking the rocky slopes with thunderous crashes. Rain pounded on his shoulders until they were bruised and sore, and several times the dun tried to turn away from the pelting rain, but Jim forced the horse to move on, and soon the saddle was crossed and they began the descent.

From an open place in the timber, Jim Thorne looked over toward Halfmoon. The country between was an amazing spiderweb of broken canyons and towering peaks. It was a geological nightmare, the red rocks streaked with rain and the pines standing in somber lines, their slim barrels like racked guns against the dull slate gray of the sky and the surrounding rock. He pushed on, and the dun had an easier trail now, picking its way surefooted down the mountain.

The Ottens would have slower going of it, for they must go around, and knowing the country less well, they would be picking their way with care. Suddenly he saw a deep crack in the earth on his right.

Swinging the dun, he walked the horse down through the pines and found the narrow trail that led to the canyon bottom.

Below him there was a tumbling mass of roaring white water, along the edge of which the trail skirted like an eyebrow. The dun snorted, edged away, and then, at his gentle but persistent urging, put a tentative hoof on the trail, starting down. A half hour later the trail left the gorge and slanted up across the mountain, and then around through a small park between the hills, and when he drew up again he was in thick pines above Halfmoon.

Finding several pines close together that offered shelter from the downpour, Jim Thorne slid to the ground, and removing the bit, hung on the nose bag with a bait of grain. Leaving the dun munching the grain, he worked his way along through the trees and looked down on the high mountain park.

There was the old cabin as he had remembered it, a long, low building with a stable and corrals some fifty yards away. He squatted on his heels against the bole of a tree and built a smoke. The rain had dwindled away to a fine mist, and he waited in the growing dusk, watching the trail.

It was almost dark when he saw them coming. Six riders and several stolen horses loaded down with packs. They had taken time out to loot the stage station before firing it. With his field glasses he studied their faces, looking first at Angela. She looked white and drawn, but defiant. One of the men pulled her down off of the horse and took her inside. The others stripped the horses of their saddles and turned them into a corral.

There was but one door to the cabin, and no windows. There were portholes for defense, but they offered no view of the interior. There was only one means of entering the cabin, and that was right through the front door.

He sat down on the edge of the hill and studied the scene with cold, careful eyes. He knew what he was going to do. It was what he had to do—go in through that door. And quickly . . .

Angela Thorne rubbed her wrists and stared around the long room.

Along both sides of the opposite end were tiers of bunks, two high, and wide. Several were filled with tumbled, unwashed bedding. A bench was tipped over at the far end, and there were muddy boots, bits of old bridles, a partially braided lariat, and various odds and ends lying about. The air was hot and close, and smelled of stale sweat.

Frazer was bending over the fire, warming up some beans in a greasy pot. Dave Otten, a darkly handsome man with a wave of hair above his brow, had pulled off his boots. He grinned at her from the nearest bunk, his hands clasped behind his head.

It had been Dave who had grabbed her when she refused to reply to his opening remarks, and Barlow had struck his hand away.

One of the others had knocked Barlow down and started kicking him. Dave had left her and walked over and joined the kicking. It had been slow, methodical, utterly brutal. Ed Hunter had come to the door at her scream, and had wheeled and rushed for the stable. . . . Ben Otten had walked to the door, lifted a gun, and deliberately shot him down.

Then he had walked outside, and a moment later there was another shot.

By that time Barlow was lying on the plank floor, his face a bloody wreck, all life gone.

They forced her up on a horse. Through the open door of the station she could see two of them shoveling embers out of the stove, dumping them on the floor and piling them under the curtains. Jude set the stock loose as the roof of the building, despite the rain, went up in a rush of flame. On the way back to his horse he picked up a burning shingle and tossed it into the stagecoach.

Dave Otten laughed as he watched the flames. He was still laughing as they set out on the trail that led into the mountains.

Now Ben Otten slowly rolled a smoke and watched his brother stretch out on the bunk. "Dave," he said slowly, "you get them horses saddled come daybreak. We're takin' out."

Dave rolled up on his elbow. "Ain't no need, Ben," he protested. "Who'd figure it was us? Anyway, what could they prove?"

Jude rolled his tobacco in his jaws and spat expertly at the fire. "Folks won't need to prove nothin'," he said. "They'll know it was us, an' they'll come. Ben's right."

"If you are wise," Angela said suddenly, "you'll give me a horse and let me go right now. My husband will be coming after you."

Dave turned his head and looked at her with lazy eyes. "Never figured you for married."

"You'd better let me go," she repeated quietly.

Ben Otten lighted his cigarette. "We ain't worried by no one man. But folks get riled up when you mess with their womenfolks. It's them in Whitewater that worries me."

She sat very still. Ben Otten was the shrewd one. If only she could make him see. . . . "My husband will know where I am. By now he has found the station burned. He will know what happened."

Dave chuckled, that lazy, frightening chuckle. "Ain't likely. Left him, didn't you? I heard some talk betwixt you an' Barlow. Didn't know what it meant until you said you was married."

"I left him a note."

Ben Otten was watching her. He seemed to be convinced she was not lying. "Better hope he don't foller you."

In desperation she said, "He can take care of himself. He was a Ranger in Texas."

Otten's back stiffened and he turned on her. "What was his name?"

She lifted her chin. "Jim Thorne."

A fork clattered on the hearthstone. Frazer put down the pot and got up. He didn't look well. "Ben, that's him. That's the feller I was tellin' you about. He kilt Lonnie Mason."

Nobody spoke, but somehow they were impressed. Despite her fears she felt a wild hope. If they would only let her go! Let her ride away before Jim could get here . . . for she suddenly realized with a queer sense of guilt that he would come, he would not hesitate.

She saw his face clearly then, cool, quiet, thoughtful. The tiny laugh wrinkles at the corners of his eyes, the little wry smiles, the tenderness in his big, hard hands.

"He done a good job." That was Silent Otten. The oldest one except for Ben, the one who never talked. "Lonnie was a dirty little killer."

"But fast," Frazer said. "He was fast. An' Baker was with him."

He squatted again by the fire.

Ben Otten drew on his cigarette. "Maybe she's right," he said. "Maybe we better let her go."

Dave came off the bunk, his eyes ugly. "You crazy?" His voice was hoarse. "She's mine, not yours! I ain't a-lettin' her go."

Ben turned his black eyes toward Dave and for a long minute he looked at him. "You forgettin' who got us into this mess?" he asked softly. "It was you, Dave. If'n you'd kept your hands off her, we'd still be safe here, an' no trouble. I'm gettin' so I don't like you much, Dave. It was you make us leave Mobettie, too. You an' women."

"She'd tell off on us," Jude Otten said. "Come daybreak we better get shed of her. They'd never prove nothin' then."

Ben Otten frowned irritably. The idea of anybody proving anything angered him. They would not try to prove. They would decide, and there would be a necktie party. He drew on the last of his smoke. No chance for—

The door opened and the lamp guttered, then the door closed and they all saw the tall man standing inside. He had rain-wet leather chaps on, and crossed belts. Under his slicker something bulked large. With his left hand he lifted his hat just a little, and Angela felt a queer little leap in her throat.

"You boys played hob," Jim Thorne said quietly.

"It was you that played hob," Ben said, "comin' here."

"Got the difference." Jim Thorne's voice was quiet. But as he spoke the muzzle of the sawed-off four-shot Roper tilted up. "You boys like buckshot?"

Frazer was on his knees. He came in range of the gun. So did Ben and Jude. Frazer looked sick and Jude sat very quiet, his hands carefully in view.

"So what happens?" Ben asked quietly.

"I'm takin' my wife home," Thorne said quietly. "The rest is between you boys an' the town."

"You're takin' nobody." Dave rolled over and sat up, and his .44 was in his hand. "Drop that shotgun."

Jim Thorne smiled a little. He shook his head.

Ben Otten's eyes seemed to flatten and the lids grew tight. "Dave, put that gun down," he said.

Dave chuckled. "Don't be a fool, Ben. This here's a showdown."

"Three for one," Thorne said quietly. "I'll take that."

"Put down that gun, Dave." Ben's voice was low and strange.

Dave laughed. "You don't like me much, Ben. Remember?"

"Dave!" Frazer's voice was shrill. "Put it down!"

Angela sat very still, yet suddenly, watching Dave, she knew he was not going to put down the gun. He would risk the death of his brothers and of Frazer— he was going to shoot.

Ben knew it, too. It was in his face, the way the skin had drawn tight across his cheekbones.

Jim Thorne spoke calmly. "I've seen a man soak up a lot of forty-four lead, Dave, but I never saw a man take much from a shotgun. I've got four shots without reloadin', and pistols to follow. You want to buy that?"

"I'll buy it." Dave was still smiling, his lips forcing it now.

Angela was behind and to the left of Ben, a little

out of range. She was opposite Dave. And beside her, scarcely an arm's length away, was Silent.

Angela's fingers lifted. That gun . . . if she . . . and then Silent slid the six-gun into his hand. "Put your gun down, Dave," he said. "You'd get us all kilt."

Dave's eyes flickered, and hate blazed suddenly in their depths. He swung toward Angela. "Like h—!" He started to rise and thrust the gun toward her, and Silent Otten shot his brother through the body.

Dave's gun slid from his fingers to the floor and blood trickled down his arm. He looked around, his face stunned and unrealizing, looking as if awakened from a sound sleep.

Jim Thorne did not fire. He stood wide-legged in the door and said quietly, "Better for you boys. Now set tight." He did not shift his eyes, but he spoke quietly. "Angela, get up and come over here. Don't get between me an' them. I ain't aimin' to kill nobody if I can help it."

Angela got shakily to her feet, and nobody else moved. Ben was staring at Jim. "If it wasn't for that shotgun—!" His voice sounded hoarse.

She walked around Ben, fearing he might try to grab her, but he did not. She moved to her husband's side, and Jim said quietly, "Just open the door, Angela, and get out—fast."

The Roper four-shot was out in the open now, and Jim Thorne had both hands on it. "You're through around here," he said. "You'd better scatter and run. There'll be a hangin' posse after you."

"There's time," Ben Otten said thickly. "We'll catch up to you. You hadn't no time to go to Whitewater."

" 'Bout an hour after I left Dry Creek," Jim Thorne replied, "the stage bound for Whitewater came through. I left a note on the stable door. By now there's fifty men headed for here. You ain't goin' to get away, but you can try."

Angela opened the door, the lamp guttered again, and Jim sprang back, jerking the door to and then leaping to catch Angela's hand. Quickly, he sprang around the corner of the house and ran for the woods. Stopping at the corral gate he threw it open, and waving his arms he chased the animals through the gate while trying to keep an eye on the cabin.

Below them a door banged and there was a shout, then running feet. In the stable door a light flared. Whipping his shotgun up, Thorne dropped three quick, scanning shots at the area of the light. The match went out and there was darkness and silence.

Jim Thorne led the way up to the bench where he had left the dun. Riding double and leading the spare horse, they turned up the slope toward the saddle between the peaks. Angela spoke softly in his ear. "Will they follow?"

"No." He took his poncho from the bedroll and put it around her shoulders. "Unless they can catch up those horses."

"Then they'll be caught?"

"Most likely."

They rode in silence for several minutes. Somewhere off over the hills they heard the sudden clatter of the hoofs of many horses. There was a long silence then, and after the silence, a shot, then a rattle of shots . . . silence . . . then a single shot.

The water in the canyon was much lower. Hours later, they reached the flat again. Angela leaned against him, exhausted. "You want to ride into Whitewater?" he said. "You can catch a stage there."

"I want to go home, Jim."

"All right," he said.

In the gray cold light of a rain-filled dawn, they rode across a prairie freckled with somber pools. He reached a hand down to hold her hand where it rested at his waist, and they rode like that, across the prairie and past the blackened ruins of the stage station, and up to the mountain and into the pines.

When a Texan Takes Over

When Matt Ryan saw the cattle tracks on Mocking Bird, he swung his horse over under the trees and studied the terrain with a careful eye. For those cattle tracks meant rustlers were raiding the KY range.

For a generation the big KY spread had been the law in the Slumbering Hill country, but now the old man was dying and the wolves were coming out of the breaks to tear at the body of the ranch.

And there was nobody to stop them, nobody to step into the big tracks old Tom Hitch had made, nobody to keep law in the hills now that old Tom was dying. He had built an empire of land and cattle, but he had also brought law into the outlaw country, brought schools and a post office, and the beginnings of thriving settlement.

But they had never given up, not Indian Kelly nor Lee Dunn. They'd waited back in the hills, bitter with their own poison, waiting for the old man to die.

All the people in the Slumbering Hill country knew it, and they had looked to Fred Hitch, the old man's adopted son, to take up the job when the old man put it down. But Fred was an easygoing young man who liked to drink and gamble. And he spent too much time with Dutch Gerlach, the KY foreman . . . and who had a good word for Dutch?

"This is the turn, Red," Ryan told his horse. "They know the old man will never ride again, so they have started rustling."

It was not just a few head . . . there must have been forty or more in this bunch, and no attempt to cover the trail.

In itself that was strange. It seemed they were not even worried about what Gerlach might do . . . and what would he do? Dutch Gerlach was a tough man. He had shown it more than once. Of course, nobody wanted any part of Lee Dunn, not even Gerlach.

Matt Ryan rode on, but kept a good background behind him. He had no desire to skyline himself with rustlers around.

For three months now he had been working his placer claim in Pima Canyon, just over the ridge from Mocking Bird. He had a good show of color and with persistent work he made better than cowhand's wages. But lately he was doing better. Twice in the past month he had struck pockets that netted him nearly a hundred dollars each. The result was that his last month had brought him in the neighborhood of three hundred in gold.

Matt Ryan knew the hills and the men who rode them. None of them knew him. Matt had a streak of Indian in his nature if not in his blood, and he knew how to leave no trail and travel without being seen. He was around, but not obvious.

They knew somebody was there, but who and why or where they did not know, and he liked it that way. Once a month he came out of the hills for supplies, but he never rode to the same places. Only this time he was coming back to Hanna's Stage Station. He told himself it was because it was close, but down inside he knew it was because of Kitty Hanna.

She was something who stepped out of your dreams, a lovely girl of twenty in a cotton dress and with carefully done hair, large, dark eyes, and a mouth that would set a man to being restless. . . .

Matt Ryan had stopped by two months before to eat a woman-cooked meal and to buy supplies, and he had lingered over his coffee.

He was a tall, wide-shouldered young man with a slim, long-legged body and hands that swung wide of his narrow hips. He had a wedge-shaped face and green eyes, and a way of looking at you with faint humor in his eyes.

He carried a gun, but he carried it tucked into his waistband, and he carried a Winchester that he never left on his saddle.

Nobody knew him around the Slumbering Hills, nobody knew him anywhere this side of Texas . . . they remembered him there. His name was a legend on the Nueces.

Big Red ambled on down the trail and Matt

watched the country and studied the cattle tracks. He would remember those horse tracks, too. Finally the cow tracks turned off into a long valley, and when he sat his horse he could see dust off over there where Thumb Butte lifted against the sky.

Indian Kelly . . . not Dunn this time, although Dunn might have given the word.

Kitty was pouring coffee when he came in and she felt her heart give a tiny leap. It had only been once, but she remembered, for when his eyes touched her that time, it made her feel the woman in her . . . a quick excitement such as she felt now.

Why was that? This man whom she knew nothing about? Why should he make her feel this way?

He put his hat on a hook and sat down, and she saw that his hair was freshly combed and still damp from the water he had used. That meant he had stopped back there by the creek . . . it was unlike a drifting cowhand, or had it been for her?

When he looked up she knew it had, and she liked the smile he had and the way his eyes could not seem to leave her face. "Eggs," he said, "about four of them, and whatever vegetable you have, and a slab of beef. I'm a hungry man."

She filled his cup, standing very close to him, and she saw the red mount under his dark skin, and when she moved away it was slowly, and there was a little something in her walk. Had her father seen it, he would have been angry, but this man would not be angry, and he would know it was for him.

Dutch Gerlach came in, a big, brawny man with bold eyes and careless hands. He had a wide, flat face and a confident, knowing manner that she hated. Fred Hitch was with him.

They looked at Ryan, then looked again. He was that sort of man, and something about him irritated Gerlach. But the big foreman of the KY said nothing. He was watching Kitty.

Gerlach seated himself and shoved his hat back on his head. When his meal was put before him, he began to eat, his eyes following the girl. Fred seemed preoccupied; he kept scowling a little, and he said something under his breath to Dutch.

Gerlach looked over at Matt Ryan. "Ain't seen you around before," he said.

Ryan merely glanced at him, and continued eating. The eggs tasted good, and the coffee was better than his own.

"Hear what I said?" Gerlach demanded.

Ryan looked up, studying the bigger man calmly. "Yes," he said, "and the remark didn't require an answer."

Gerlach started to speak, then devoted himself to his food.

"That bay horse yours?" Fred Hitch asked suddenly.

Ryan nodded . . . they had seen the horse, then? That was one trouble with Big Red, he was a blood bay, and he stood out. It would have been better to have a dun or a buckskin . . . even a black.

"It's mine," he said.

Yet their curiosity and Fred's uneasiness puzzled him. Why should Fred be bothered by him?

"Don't take to strangers around here," Gerlach said suddenly. "You move on."

Ryan said nothing, although he felt something inside of him grow poised and waiting. No trouble, Matt, he warned himself, not here . . .

"Hear me?" Gerlach's voice rose. "We've missed some cows."

Kitty had come to the door, and her father was behind her. Hanna was a peace-loving man, but a stern one.

"I heard you," Ryan replied quietly, "an' if you've missed cows, ride toward Thumb Butte."

Fred Hitch jerked as if he had been slapped, and Gerlach's face went slowly dark. His eyes had been truculent, now they were cautious, studying. "What's that mean?" he asked, his voice low.

"Ain't that where Indian Kelly hangs out?" Ryan asked mildly.

"You seem to know." Gerlach was suddenly cold. "I figure you're a rustler your own self!"

It was fighting talk, gun talk. Matt Ryan made no move. He forked up some more eggs. "One man's opinion," he said. "But what would make you think that? You've never seen me with a rope on my saddle, you've never even seen me before. You don't know where I'm from or where I'm going."

All this was true. . . . Gerlach hesitated, wanting trouble, yet disturbed by the other man's seeming calm. He had no gun in sight, and his rifle leaned against the wall. Still, you couldn't tell.

He snorted and sat down, showing his contempt for a man who would take an insult without fighting, yet he was uneasy.

Matt glanced up to meet Kitty's eyes. She turned her face deliberately, and he flushed. She thought him a coward.

He lingered over his coffee, wanting a word with her, and finally the others left. He looked up when the door closed behind them. "There's a dance at Rock Springs," he said suddenly. "Would you go with me?"

She hesitated, then stiffened a little. "I'd be afraid to," she said. "Somebody might call you a coward in front of people."

Scarcely were the words out than she was sorry she had said them. His face went white and she felt a queer little pang and half turned toward him. He got up slowly, his face very stiff. Then he walked to the door. There he turned. "You find it so easy to see a man die?" he asked, and the words were shocking in their tone and in the something that spoke from his eyes.

HE WENT OUT, and the door closed, and Hanna said to his daughter, "I don't want you speakin' to men like that. Nor do I want you goin' dancin' with strangers. Just the same," he added, "I'd say that man was not afraid."

She thought about it and her father's words remained with her. She held them tenderly, for she wanted to believe in them, yet she had seen the stranger take a deliberate insult without a show of resentment. Men had killed for less. Of course, she had not wanted that. (How he could have shown resentment without its leading to bloodshed she did not ask herself.)

She was at the window when he rode out of town, and was turning away from it when the side door opened and a slender, narrow-faced man stood there. She felt a start of fear. This was not the first time she had seen Lee Dunn, and there was something about him that frightened her.

"Who was that?" he demanded. "That man who walked out?"

"I . . . I don't know," she said, and then was surprised to realize that it was the truth. She knew nothing about him, and she had seen him but twice.

Lee Dunn was a narrow, knifelike man with a bitter mouth that never smiled, but there was a certain arresting quality about him so that even when you knew who and what he was, you respected him. His manner was old-fashioned and courteous, but without graciousness. It was rumored that he had killed a dozen men . . . and he had killed two here at the Springs.

Kitty rode to the party in a buckboard with Fred Hitch. And she was dancing her third dance when she looked up and saw the stranger standing at the floor's edge. He wore a dark red shirt that was freshly laundered and a black string tie. There was a short jacket of buckskin, Mexican style, over the shirt. His black boots were freshly polished.

She saw Dutch Gerlach watching him, and was aware of worry that there would be trouble. Yet two dances passed, one of them with Dutch, whom she hated but could not avoid without one dance, and he did not come near her. Someone mentioned his name. Matt Ryan . . . she liked the sound.

Lee Dunn came into the room and paused near Gerlach. She thought she saw Dutch's lips move, but he did not turn his head. But that was silly . . . why would the foreman of the KY talk to a rustler?

When she looked again Matt Ryan was gone . . . and he had not even asked her for a dance.

Something seemed to have gone from the lights, and her feet lost their quickness. Suddenly, she knew she wanted to go home. . . .

MATT RYAN WAS RIDING FAST. He had seen Dunn come into the room and turned at once and slipped out through the crowd. What was to be done had to be done fast, and he went at it.

The big bay was fast, and he held the pace well. An hour after leaving the dance Ryan swung the big horse into the KY ranch yard and got down. With only a glance at the darkened bunkhouse he crossed to the big house and went in.

He had not stopped to knock, and he startled the big Mexican woman who was dusting a table. "Where's Tom?" he demanded.

"You can't see him." The woman barred his way, her fat face growing hard. "He sick."

"I'll see him. Show me to him."

"I'll not! You stop or I'll—"

"Maria!" The voice was a husky roar. "Who's out there?"

Matt Ryan walked by her to the bedroom doorway. He stopped there, looking in at the old man.

Tom Hitch had been a giant. He was a shell now, bedridden and old, but with a flare of ancient fire in his eyes.

"You don't know me, Hitch," Ryan said, "but it's time you did. You're losin' cattle."

Before the old man could speak, Ryan broke in, talking swiftly. He told about forty head that had left the day before, in broad daylight. He told of other, smaller herds. He told of the rustlers' growing boldness, of Lee Dunn at the dance, of Indian Kelly riding down to Hanna's Stage Station.

"They wouldn't dare!" The old man's voice was heavy with scorn. "I learnt 'em manners!"

"And now you're abed," Matt Ryan said roughly. "And you've a fool and an outlaw for an adopted son, a gunman for a foreman."

Hitch was suddenly quiet. His shrewd old eyes

studied Ryan. "What's in you, man? What d' you want?"

"You're down, Hitch. Maybe you'll get up, maybe not. But what happens to the country? What happens to law an' order when——"

Somebody moved behind him and he turned to see Fred Hitch standing there with Dutch Gerlach. Fred was frightened, but there was ugliness in the foreman's face.

"You invite this gent here?" Dutch asked thickly.

"No." Old Tom sat up a little. "Tell him to get out and stay out."

The old man hunched his pillow behind him. "He forced his way in here with some cock-an'-bull story about rustlin'."

Gerlach looked at Ryan and jerked his head toward the door. "You heard him. Get **out**!"

Matt Ryan walked to the door and went down the steps. Then swiftly he turned the corner and ran for his horse. A rifle shot slammed the darkness and knocked a chip from a tree trunk, but his turn had been sudden and unexpected. He hit the saddle running and the bay bounded like a rabbit and was gone into the darkness under the trees. A second and a third shot wasted themselves in the night.

How had they gotten on his trail so suddenly? They must have left the dance almost as soon as he had. And where was Kitty Hanna?

* * *

MILES FELL BEHIND HIM, and the trail was abandoned for the sidehills and trees, and he worked his way across ridges and saddles, and found himself back at Pima Canyon with the sun coming up.

All was still below, and he watched for half an hour before going down. When he got there he packed his spare horse and rode out of the canyon, leaving his diggings. They were good and getting better, but no place for him now. There were too many marks of his presence.

Why had he gotten into this? It was no business of his. What if the lawless did come from the hills and the good times of the old KY were gone? Could he not ride on? He owned nothing here, he did not belong here. This was a problem for others, not himself. But was it?

Was not the problem of the law and of community peace the problem of all men? Could any safely abandon their right of choice to others? Might not their own shiftlessness rob them of all they valued?

Bedding down in the high pines under the stars, Matt Ryan thought himself to sleep over that. He had taken a foolish step into the troubles of others. He would stay out. Old Tom did not want his help, nor did Kitty want his love.

Two days he rode the hills, for two days shifting camp each night. For two days he was irritable. It was none of his business, he kept telling himself. The old man had sent him packing, Kitty had turned him down. Nevertheless, he could not settle down. He rode back to Pima Canyon and looked around.

Their tracks were everywhere. They had found this place, and had without doubt come looking for him. So he was a hunted man now. It was good to know.

Yet he did not leave. Without reason for remaining, he remained.

And on the third day he rode to Hanna's Station. Kitty was not there, but her father was. Hanna looked at him carefully. "Maria huntin' you. Come in here ridin' a mule. Acted like she didn't aim to be seen. Left word you was to see her."

"All right," he said.

Hanna brought him coffee and a meal. "Ain't Kitty's grub," he said. "She's to town."

The older man sat down. Dutch Gerlach was in with two men, he told Ryan, hunting for him. Or maybe, he added, hunting Fred Hitch.

"Hitch?"

"He's gone. Dropped out of sight. Nobody knows why."

A rattle of horses' hoofs sounded and Matt Ryan came to his feet quickly. Outside were four men. Dutch Gerlach, two hands . . . and Lee Dunn.

Ryan turned sharply. He had left his horse in the trees and there was a chance it had not been seen. Stepping into the kitchen, he moved back to a door on his right. He opened it and stepped through. He was in Kitty's room.

There was a stamp of boots outside and a distant sound of voices, then a rattle of dishes.

What had happened? If Lee Dunn and Gerlach were together, then—

SUDDENLY HE WAS CONSCIOUS of a presence. In the shadowed room he had seen nothing. Now his hand dropped to his gun and he started to turn.

"Don't shoot, Ryan. It's me. Hitch."

In a quick step Ryan was at the bedside. Fred Hitch lay in the bed, his face drawn and pale. His shoulder and arm were bandaged.

"It was them." He indicated the men outside. "Gerlach egged me into sellin' some of the KY cows for gamblin' money, said it would all be mine, anyway. Then he began sellin' some himself, dared me to tell the old man.

"Lee Dunn was in it with him, and I was scared. I went along, but I didn't like it. Then, when you saw the old man, they got worried. They couldn't find you, and they decided to kill the old man, then to take over. I wouldn't stand for it, and made a break. They shot me down, but I got to a horse. Kitty hid me here . . . she went after medicine."

"They'll wonder why she isn't here now," Ryan said half aloud. Then he looked down at the man on the bed. "What about Tom? Did they kill him?"

"Don't think so. They want me for a front . . . or him. Then they can loot the ranch safely. After that, other outfits."

Ryan stepped to the window. With luck he could make the trees without being seen. He put a hand on the window and slid it up.

"Ryan?"

"Yeah."

"I ain't much, but the old man was good to me. I wouldn't see no harm come to him. Tell him that, will you?"

"Sure."

He stepped out the window and walked swiftly into the woods. There he made the saddle and started for the KY. He had no plan, he had not even the right to plan. It was not his fight. He was a stranger and . . . but he kept riding.

It was past midnight when he found the KY. He had been lost for more than an hour, took a wrong trail in the bad light . . . there were no lights down below. He rode the big horse down through the trees and stepped out of the saddle.

There were a dozen saddled horses near the corral. He could see the shine of the starlight on the saddles. He saw some of those horses when he drew closer, and he knew them. They were riders from Thumb Butte . . . so, then, they had the ranch. They had moved in.

And this ranch was the law. There were no other forces to stand against Gerlach and Dunn now. There were ten thousand head of cattle in the hills, all to be sold. It was wealth, and a community taken over.

He stood there in the darkness, his face grim, smelling the night smells, feeling the danger and tension, knowing he was a fool to stay, yet unable to run.

The old man might still be alive. If he could move in, speak to him once more . . . with just the shadow of authority he might draw good men around him and hold the line. He was nobody now, but with the authority of old Tom Hitch, then he could move.

He loosened his gun in his belt, and taking his rifle walked across the clearing to the back door. He saw a man come to the bunkhouse door and throw out a cigarette. The man started to turn, then stopped and looked his way. He kept on walking, his mouth dry, his heart pounding. The fellow watched him for a minute, barely visible in the gloom, and then went back inside.

MATT RYAN REACHED the back of the house and touched the latch. It lifted under his hand and he stepped in. Carefully, he eased across the room, into the hall. When he made the old man's room, he hesitated, then spoke softly. There was no reply.

He struck a match . . . it glowed, flared. Matt looked at the old man, who was slumped back against the headboard of his bed, his flannel nightshirt bloody, the eyes wide and staring. They had murdered Tom Hitch. Killed him without a chance.

Matt drew back, hearing a noise at the bunkhouse. The match died and he dropped it, rubbing it out with his toe.

A faint rustle behind him and he turned, gun in hand.

A big old form loomed in the dark, wide, shapeless. "It me . . . Maria. He say give you this." A paper rattled and he took it. "You go . . . quick now."

He went swiftly, hearing boots grating on the gravel. They were suspicious, and coming to look. He stepped out the back door and a man rounded the corner. "Hey, there!" the fellow started forward. "Wait . . . !"

Matt Ryan shot him. He held the gun low and he shot at the middle of the man's body, and heard the other man's gun blast muffled by his body.

He started by him, and a light flared somewhere and its light caught the man's face. He had killed Indian Kelly.

Rifle in hand, he ran, ducking into the trees. There were shouts behind him, and he saw men scatter out, coming. He could see their darker shapes against the gray of the yard. He fired four fast shots from the hip, scattering them across the yard. A man stumbled and went down, then the others hit the dirt.

He ran for the bay, caught the bridle reins, and stepped into the leather. "Let's get out of here!" he said, and the big red horse was moving . . . fast.

Day was graying when he neared Hanna's Station. He saw no horses around, so he rode boldly from the woods to the back door. In the gray of the light, he swung down and knocked.

Kitty opened the door. He stepped in, grim, un-shaven. "Got some coffee?" he said. "And I want to see Fred."

"You . . . they killed him. Gerlach and Dunn. They found him."

"Your father?"

"He's hurt . . . they knocked him out."

He looked at her hungrily, anxious to feel her need of him. With his fingers he spread the paper Maria had given him.

MATT RYAN: TAKE OVER.
TOM HITCH

The signature was big and sprawled out, but a sig-nature known all over the Slumbering Hills.

So . . . there it was. The problem was his now. Looking back, he could remember the old man's eyes. Hitch had known that if he had shown the slightest willingness to listen to Ryan, they would both have been killed. But now the battle had been tossed to him.

Kitty looked at him, waiting. "There it is, Matt. You're the boss of Slumbering Hills."

The boss . . . and a hunted man. His only sup-porters an old man with an aching head, and a girl.

One man alone . . . with a gun.

THEY WOULD BE COMBING the hills for him. They would come back here. Kitty had been left alone, but then they were in a hurry to find him and Tom Hitch was living. Now it would be different.

"Saddle up," he said. "You and your dad are riding. Ride to the ranches, get the men together."

"What about you?" Her eyes were very large. "Matt, what about you?"

"Me? I'll wait here."

"But they'll come here! They'll be looking for you."

"Uh-huh . . . so I show 'em who's boss." He grinned suddenly, boyishly. "Better rustle some help. They might not believe me."

When they had left, he waited. The stage station was silent, the throbbing heart gone from it. He poured coffee into a cup, remembering that it was up to him now. . . . Suppose . . . suppose he could do it without a gun. . . . A time had come for change, the old order was gone . . . but did Lee Dunn know that? And in his heart, Matt Ryan knew he did not. For Lee Dunn was the old order. He was a relic, a leftover, a memory of the days when Tom Hitch had come here, Hitch already past his prime, Dunn not yet to reach his. . . .

In the silent house the clock ticked loudly. Matt Ryan sipped his coffee and laid his Winchester on the table.

He checked his gun while the clock ticked off the measured seconds.

It was broad day now. . . . Kitty and her father would be well into the valley. Would the ranchers come? His was a new voice, they did not know him.

They had only that slip of paper and the words **Take over**.

He got up and walked to the window. And then he saw them coming.

HE PLACED HIS RIFLE by the door and stepped outside. There were ten of them . . . ten, and one of him. A fleeting smile touched his lips. Old Tom Hitch had stood off forty Apaches once . . . alone.

"Tom," he whispered, "if you can hear me . . . say a word where it matters."

He stepped to the edge of the porch, a tall man, honed down by sparse living and hard years, his wedge-shaped face unshaven, his eyes cool, waiting. It had been like this on the Nueces . . . only different.

They drew up, a line of men on horses. Lee Dunn and Gerlach at the center.

He saw no others, he thought of no others. These were the ones.

"Hello, Dunn."

The knifelike man studied him, his hands on the horn of his saddle.

"Dunn, I'm serving notice. Tom Hitch sent me a note. His orders were for me to take over."

"Think you can?"

"I can."

Lee Dunn waited . . . why he waited he could not have said. He had heard from Gerlach that this man was yellow. Looking at him, seeing him, he knew he was not. He knew another thing—this man was a gunfighter.

"Who are you, Ryan? Should I know you?"

"From the Nueces . . . maybe you heard of the Kenzie outfit."

Lee Dunn's lips thinned down. Of course . . . he should have known. It had been a feud . . . and at the last count there were five Kenzies and one Ryan left. And now there was still one Ryan . . .

"So this is the way it is," Matt said, making his plea. "The old days are over, Lee. You an' me, we're of the past. Old Tom was, too. He was a good man, and his guns kept the peace and made the law. But the old days of living by the gun are gone, Lee. We can admit it, or we can die."

"Where's the girl?" Gerlach demanded.

"Gone with her father. They are in the valley now rounding up all of Old Tom's supporters from the Slumberin' Hills."

His eyes held on them, seeing them both, knowing them both. "What's it to be, Dunn?"

A voice spoke behind him. "I did not go. . . . Dad went. I'm here with a shotgun and I'm saying it's between Matt Ryan and the two, Gerlach and Dunn. I'll kill any man who lifts a gun other than them."

"Fair enough." It was a lean, hatchet-faced hand. "This I wanta see."

Lee Dunn sat very still, but he was smiling. "Why, Matt, I reckon mebbe you're right. But you know, Matt, I've heard a sight about you . . . never figured

to meet you . . . an' I can't help wonderin', Matt—
are you faster than me?"

He spoke and he drew and he died falling. He hit
dust and he rolled over and he was dead, but he was
trying to get up, and then he rolled over again, but
he had his gun out. The gun fired and the bullet
plowed a furrow and that was all.

Gerlach had not moved. His face was gray and
seemed suddenly thinner. As though hypnotized, he
stared at the thin tendril of smoke from the muzzle
of Ryan's .44 Colt.

Slowly, his tongue touched his dry lips, and he
swallowed.

"You boys will be ridin' on," Ryan said quietly.
"That rope you got there should be handy. There's a
tree down the trail . . . unless you want to ride out
with a yella-belly."

"Ain't honin' to," the hatchet-faced man said. He
looked down at Lee. "He made his try, Ryan. Give
him a send-off, will you?"

Matt nodded, and Kitty walked out and stood beside him, watching them ride away, gathered around
Gerlach, who sat his horse as if stunned. Only now
his hands were tied.

Matt Ryan looked down at Kitty, and he took her
arm and said, "You know, you'll do to ride the river
with, Kit. You're a girl to walk beside a man . . .
wherever he goes."

"Come in," she said, but her eyes said more than
that. "I've some coffee on."

Big Medicine

Old Billy Dunbar was down flat on his face in a dry wash swearing into his beard. The best gold-bearing gravel he had found in a year, and then the Apaches would have to show up!

It was like them, the mean, ornery critters. He hugged the ground for dear life and hoped they would not see him, tucked away as he was between some stones where an eddy of the water that once ran through the wash had dug a trench between the stones.

There were nine of them. Not many, but enough to take his scalp if they found him, and it would be just as bad if they saw his burros or any of the prospect holes he had been sinking.

He was sweating like a stuck hog bleeds, lying there with his beard in the sand and the old Sharps .50 ready beside him. He wouldn't have much of a chance if they found him, slithery fighters like they were, but if that old Sharps threw down on them he'd take at least one along to the happy hunting ground with him.

He could hear them now, moving along the desert

above the wash. Where in tarnation were they going? He wouldn't be safe as long as they were in the country, and this was country where not many white men came. Those few who did come were just as miserable to run into as the Apaches.

The Apache leader was a lean-muscled man with a hawk nose. All of them slim and brown without much meat on them, the way Apaches were, and wearing nothing but breechclouts and headbands.

He lay perfectly still. Old Billy was too knowing in Indian ways to start moving until he was sure they were gone. He lay right there for almost a half hour after he had last heard them, and then he came out of it cautious as a bear reaching for a honey tree.

When he got on his feet, he hightailed it for the edge of the wash and took a look. The Apaches had vanished. He turned and went down the wash, taking his time and keeping the old Sharps handy. It was a mile to his burros and to the place where his prospect holes were. Luckily, he had them back in a draw where there wasn't much chance of them being found.

Billy Dunbar pulled his old gray felt hat down a little tighter and hurried on. Jennie and Julie were waiting for him, standing head to tail so they could brush flies off each other's noses.

When he got to them he gathered up his tools and took them back up the draw to the rocks at the end. His canteens were full, and he had plenty of grub and ammunition. He was lucky that he hadn't shot that rabbit when he saw it. The Apaches would have heard the bellow of the old Sharps and come for him, sure. He was going to have to be careful.

If they would just kill a man it wouldn't be so bad, but these Apaches liked to stake a man out on an anthill and let the hot sun and ants do for him, or maybe the buzzards—if they got there soon enough.

This wash looked good, too. Not only because water had run there, but because it was actually cutting into the edge of an old riverbed. If he could sink a couple of holes down to bedrock, he'd bet there'd be gold and gold aplenty.

When he awakened in the morning he took a careful look around his hiding place. One thing, the way he was located, if they caught him in camp they couldn't get at him to do much. The hollow was perhaps sixty feet across, but over half of it was covered by shelving rock from above, the cliff ran straight up from there for an easy fifty feet. There was water in a spring and enough grass to last the burros for quite some time.

After a careful scouting around, he made a fire of dead mesquite, which made almost no smoke, and fixed some coffee. When he had eaten, Dunbar gathered up his pan, pick, shovel, and rifle and moved out. He was loaded more than he liked, but it couldn't be helped.

The place he had selected to work was the inside of the little desert stream. The stream took a bend and left a gravel bank on the inside of the elbow. That gravel looked good. Putting his Sharps down within easy reach, Old Billy got busy.

Before sundown he had moved a lot of dirt and tried several pans, loading them up and going over to the stream. Holding the pan under the water, he began to stir the gravel, breaking up the lumps of clay and stirring until every piece was wet. Then he picked out the larger stones and pebbles and threw them to one side. He put his hands on opposite sides of the pan and began to oscillate it vigorously under water, moving it in a circular motion so the contents were shaken from side to side.

With a quick glance to make sure there were no Apaches in sight, he tipped the pan slightly, to an angle of about thirty degrees so the lighter sands, already buoyed up by the water, could slip out over the side.

He struck the pan several good blows to help settle the gold, if any, and then dipped for more water and continued the process. He worked steadily at the pan, with occasional glances around until all the refuse had washed over the side but the heavier particles. Then with a little clean water, he washed the black sand and gold into another pan, which he took from the brush where it had been concealed the day before.

FOR SOME TIME he worked steadily. Then, as the light was getting bad, he gathered up his tools and, concealing the empty pan, carried the other with him back up the wash to his hideout.

He took his Sharps and crept out of the hideout and up the wall of the canyon. The desert was still and empty on every side.

"Too empty, durn it!" he grumbled. "Them Injuns'll be back. Yuh can't fool an Apache."

Rolling out of his blankets at sunup, he prepared a quick breakfast and then went over his takings of the day with a magnet. This black sand was mostly particles of magnetite, ilmenite, and black magnetic iron oxide. What he couldn't draw off, he next eliminated by using a blow box.

"Too slow, with them Apaches around," he grumbled. "A man workin' down there could mebbe do sixty, seventy pans a day in that sort of gravel, but watchin' for Injuns ain't goin' t' help much!"

Yet he worked steadily, and by nightfall, despite interruptions he had handled more than fifty pans. When the second day was over, he grinned at the gold he had. It was sufficient color to show he was on the right track. Right here, by using a rocker, he could have made it pay, but he wasn't looking for peanuts.

He had cached his tools along with the empty pan in the brush at the edge of the wash. When morning came, he rolled out and was just coming out of the hideout when he saw the Apache. He was squatted in the sand staring at something, and despite his efforts to keep his trail covered, Dunbar had a good idea what that something would be. He drew back into the hideout.

Lying on his middle, he watched the Indian get to his feet and start working downstream. When he got down there a little farther, he was going to see those prospect holes. There would be nothing Dunbar could do then. Nor was there anything he could do now. So far as he could see, only one Apache had found him. If he fired to kill the Indian, the others would be aware of the situation and come running.

Old Billy squinted his eyes and pondered the question. He had a hunch that Indian wasn't going to go for help. He was going to try to get Dunbar by himself, so he could take his weapons and whatever else he had of value.

The Indian went downstream farther and slipped out of sight. Billy instantly ducked out into the open and scooted down the canyon into the mesquite. He dropped flat there and inched along in the direction the Indian had gone.

He was creeping along, getting nearer and nearer to his prospect holes, when suddenly instinct or the subconscious hearing of a sound warned him. Like a flash, he rolled over, just in time to see the Indian leap at him, knife in hand!

Billy Dunbar was no longer a youngster, but he had lived a life in the desert, and he was as hard and tough as whalebone. As the Apache leaped, he caught the knife wrist in his left hand, and stabbed at the Indian's ribs with his own knife. The Apache twisted away, and Billy gave a heave. The Indian lost balance. They rolled over and then fell over the eight-foot bank into the wash!

Luck was with Billy. The Indian hit first, and Billy's knife arm was around him, with the point gouging at the Indian's back. When they landed, the knife went in to the hilt.

Billy rolled off, gasping for breath. Hurriedly, he glanced around. There was no one in sight. Swiftly, he clawed at the bank, causing the loosened gravel to cave down, and in a few minutes of hot, sweating work the Indian was buried.

Turning, Billy lit out for his hideaway, and when he made it, he lay there gasping for breath, his Sharps ready. There would be no work this day. He was going to lie low and watch. The other Indians would come looking, he knew.

After dark he slipped out and covered the Indian better, and then he used a mesquite bush to wipe out as well as possible the signs of their fighting. Then he cat-footed it back to the hollow and tied a rawhide string across the entrance with a can of loose pebbles at the end to warn him if Indians found him. Then he went to sleep.

At dawn he was up. He checked the Sharps and then cleaned his .44 again. He loaded his pockets with cartridges just in case and settled down for a day of it.

*   *   *

LUCKILY, HE HAD SHADE. It was hot out there, plenty hot. You could fry an egg on those rocks by ten in the morning—not that he had any eggs. He hadn't even seen an egg since the last time he was in Fremont, and that had been four months ago.

He bit off a chew of tobacco and rolled it in his jaws. Then he studied the banks of the draw. An Apache could move like a ghost and look like part of the landscape. He had known them to come within fifteen feet of a man in grassy country without being seen, and not tall grass at that.

It wouldn't be so bad if his time hadn't been so short. When he left Fremont, Sally had six months to go to pay off the loan on her ranch, or out she would go. Sally's husband had been killed by a bronc down on the Sandy. She was alone with the kids, and that loan about to take their home away.

When the situation became serious, Old Billy thought of this wash. Once, several years before, he had washed out some color here, and it looked rich. He had left the country about two jumps ahead of the Apaches and swore he'd never come back. Nobody else was coming out of here with gold, either, so he knew it was still like he remembered. Several optimistic prospectors had tried it and were never heard of again. However, Old Billy had decided to take a chance. After all, Sally was all he had, and those two grandchildren of his deserved a better chance than they'd get if she lost the place.

The day moved along, a story told by the shadows on the sides of the wash. You could almost tell the time by those shadows. It wasn't long before Dunbar knew every bush, every clump of greasewood and mesquite along its length, and every rock.

He wiped the sweat from his brow and waited. Sally was a good girl. Pretty, too, too pretty to be a widow at twenty-two. It was almost mid-afternoon when his questing eye halted suddenly on the bank of the wash. He lay perfectly still, eyes studying the bank intently. Yet his eyes had moved past the spot before they detected something amiss. He scowled, trying to remember. Then it came to him.

There had been a torn place there, as though somebody had started to pull up a clump of greasewood and then abandoned it. The earth had been exposed and a handful of roots. Now it was blotted out. Straining his eyes he could see nothing, distinguish no contours that seemed human, only that the spot was no longer visible. The spot was mottled by shadows and sunlight through the leaves of the bush.

Then there was a movement, so slight that his eye scarcely detected it, and suddenly the earth and torn roots were visible again. They had come back. Their stealth told him they knew he was somewhere nearby, and the logical place for him would be right where he was.

Now he was in for it. Luckily, he had food, water,

and ammunition. There should be just eight of them unless more had come. Probably they had found his prospect holes and trailed him back this way.

There was no way they could see into his hollow, no way they could shoot into it except through the narrow entrance, which was rock and brush. There was no concealed approach to it. He dug into the bank a little to get more earth in front of himself.

No one needed to warn him of the gravity of the situation. It was one hundred and fifty miles to Fremont and sixty miles to the nearest white man, young Sid Barton, a cowhand turned rancher who had started running some cattle on the edge of the Apache country.

Nor could he expect help. Nobody ever came into this country, and nobody knew where he was but Sally, and she only knew in a general way. Prospectors did not reveal locations where they had found color.

Well, he wasn't one of these restless young coots who'd have to be out there tangling with the Apaches. He could wait. And he would wait in the shade while they were in the sun. Night didn't worry him much. Apaches had never cared much for night fighting, and he wouldn't have much trouble with them.

One of them showed himself suddenly—only one arm and a rifle. But he fired, the bullet striking the rock overhead. Old Billy chuckled. "Tryin' t' draw fire," he said, "get me located."

* * *

BILLY DUNBAR WAITED, grinning through his beard. There was another shot and then more stillness. He lay absolutely still. A hand showed and then a foot. He rolled his quid in his jaws and spat. An Indian suddenly showed himself and then vanished as though he had never been there. Old Billy watched the banks cynically. An Indian showed again and hesitated briefly this time, but Dunbar waited.

Suddenly, within twenty feet of the spot where Dunbar lay, an Indian slid down the bank and with a shrill whoop, darted for the entrance to the hideaway. It was point-blank, even though a moving target. Billy let him have it!

The old Sharps bellowed like a stricken bull and leaped in his hands. The Apache screamed wildly and toppled over backward, carried off his feet by the sheer force of the heavy-caliber bullet. Yells of rage greeted the shot.

Dunbar could see the Indian's body sprawled under the sun. He picked up an edged pieced of white stone and made a straight mark on the rock wall beside him, then seven more. He drew a diagonal line through the first one. "Seven t' go," he said.

A hail of bullets began kicking sand and dirt up around the opening. One shot hit overhead and showered dirt down almost in his face. "Durn you!" he mumbled. He took his hat off and laid it beside him, his six-shooter atop of it, ready to hand.

No more Indians showed themselves, and the day

might work! It could work! At least, it was a chance, and somehow, some way, he had to be rid of those Apaches!

He knew something of their superstitions and beliefs. It was a gamble, but as suddenly as he conceived the idea, he knew it was a chance he was going to take.

Digging his change of clothes out of the saddlebags, he got into them. Then he took his own clothing and laid it out on the ground in plain sight—the pants, then the coat, the boots, and nearby, the hat.

Taking some sticks he went to the entrance of the wolf den and built a small fire close by. Then he hastily went back and took a quick look around. The draw was empty, but he knew the place was watched. He went back and got out of line of the wolf den, and waited.

The smoke was slight, but it was going into the den. It wouldn't take long. The wolf came out with a rush, ran to the middle of the pocket, took a quick, snarling look around, and then went over the parapet and down the draw!

Working swiftly, he moved the fire and scattered the few sticks and coals in his other fireplace. Then he brushed the ground with a branch. It would be a few minutes before they moved, and perhaps longer.

Crawling into the wolf den he next got some wolf hair, which he took back to his clothing. He put some of the hair in his shirt and some near his pants. A quick look down the draw showed no sign of an

drew on. It was hot out there. In the vast brassy vault of the sky a lone buzzard wheeled.

He tried no more shots, just waiting. They were trying to tire him out. Doggone it—in this place he could outwait all the Apaches in the Southwest—not that he wanted to!

Keeping well below the bank, he got hold of a stone about the size of his head and rolled it into the entrance. Instantly, a shot smacked the dirt below it and kicked dirt into his eyes. He wiped them and swore viciously. Then he got another stone and rolled that in place, pushing dirt up behind them. He scooped his hollow deeper and peered thoughtfully at the banks of the draw.

Jennie and Julie were eating grass, undisturbed and unworried. They had been with Old Billy too long to be disturbed by these—to them meaningless—fusses and fights. The shadow from the west bank reached farther toward the east, and Old Billy waited, watching.

He detected an almost indiscernible movement atop the bank, in the same spot where he had first seen an Indian. Taking careful aim, he drew a bead on the exposed roots and waited.

He saw no movement, nothing, yet suddenly he focused his eyes more sharply and saw the roots were no longer exposed. Nestling the stock against his shoulder, his finger eased back on the trigger. The old Sharps wavered, and he waited. The rifle steadied, and he squeezed again.

The gun jumped suddenly and there was a shrill yell from the Apache, who lunged to full height and rose on his tiptoes, both hands clasping his chest. The stricken redskin then plunged face forward down the bank in a shower of gravel. Billy reloaded and waited. The Apache lay still, lying in the shadow below the bank. After watching him for a few minutes, alternating between the still form and the banks of the draw, Dunbar picked up his white stone and marked another diagonal white mark, across the second straight line.

He stared at the figures with satisfaction. "Six left," he said. He was growing hungry. Jennie and Julie had both decided to lie down and call it a day.

As LUCK WOULD have it, his shovel and pick were concealed in the brush at the point where the draw opened into the wider wash. He scanned the banks suddenly and then drew back. Grasping a bush, he pulled it from the earth under the huge rocks. He then took the brush and some stones and added to his parapet. With some lumps of earth and rock he gradually built it stronger.

Always he returned to the parapet, but the Apaches were cautious and he saw nothing of them. Yet his instinct told him they were there, somewhere. And that, he knew, was the trouble. It was the fact he had been avoiding ever since he had holed up for the fight. They would always be around somewhere now.

Three of their braves were missing—dead. They would never let him leave the country alive.

If he had patience, so had they, and they could afford to wait. He could not. It was not merely a matter of getting home before the six-month period was up—and less than two months remained of that—it was a matter of getting home with enough money to pay off the loan. And with the best of luck it would require weeks upon weeks of hard, uninterrupted work.

And then he saw the wolf.

It was no more than a glimpse, and a fleeting glimpse. Billy Dunbar saw the sharply pointed nose and bright eyes and then the swish of a tail! The wolf vanished somewhere at the base of the shelf of rock that shaded the pocket. It vanished in proximity to the spring.

Old Billy frowned and studied the spot. He wasn't the only one holed up here! The wolf evidently had a hole somewhere in the back of the pocket, and perhaps some young, as the time of year was right. His stillness after he had finished work on the entrance had evidently fooled the wolf into believing the white man was gone.

Obviously, the wolf had been lying there, waiting for him to leave so it could come out and hunt. The cubs would be getting hungry. If there were cubs.

The idea came to him then. An idea utterly fantastic, yet one that suddenly made him chuckle. It

Indian, but that they had seen the wolf, he knew, and he could picture their surprise and puzzlement.

Hurrying to the spring, he dug from the bank near the water a large quantity of mud. This was an added touch, but one that might help. From the mud, he formed two roughly human figures. About the head of each he tied a blade of grass.

Hurrying to the parapet for a stolen look down the draw, he worked until six such figures were made. Then, using thorns and some old porcupine quills he found near a rock, he thrust one or more through each of the mud figures.

They stood in a neat row facing the parapet. Quickly, he hurried for one last look into the draw. An Indian had emerged. He stood there in plain sight, staring toward the place!

They would be cautious, Billy knew, and he chuckled to himself as he thought of what was to follow. Gathering up his rifle, the ammunition, a canteen, and a little food, he hurried to the wolf den and crawled back inside.

On his first trip he had ascertained that there were no cubs. At the end of the den there was room to sit up, topped by the stone of the shelving rock itself. To his right, a lighted match told him there was a smaller hole of some sort.

CAUTIOUSLY, BILLY CRAWLED BACK to the entrance, and careful to avoid the wolf tracks in the dust outside, he brushed out his own tracks and then retreated into the depths of the cave. From where he lay he could see the parapet.

Almost a half hour passed before the first head lifted above the poorly made wall. Black straight hair, a red headband, and the sharp, hard features of their leader.

Then other heads lifted beside him, and one by one the six Apaches stepped over the wall and into the pocket. They did not rush, but looked cautiously about, and their eyes were large, frightened. They looked all around, then at the clothing and then at the images. One of the Indians grunted and pointed.

They drew closer and then stopped in an awed line, staring at the mud figures. They knew too well what they meant. Those figures meant a witch doctor had put a death spell on each one of them.

One of the Indians drew back and looked at the clothing. Suddenly he gave a startled cry and pointed—at the wolf hair!

They gathered around, talking excitedly and then glancing over their shoulders fearfully.

They had trapped what they believed to be a white man, and knowing Apaches, Old Billy would have guessed they knew his height, weight, and approximate age. Those things they could tell from the length of his stride, the way he worked, the pressure of a footprint in softer ground.

They had trapped a white man, and a wolf had escaped! Now they found his clothing lying here, and on the clothing, the hair of a wolf!

All Indians knew of wolf-men, those weird creatures who changed at will from wolf to man and back again, creatures that could tear the throat from a man while he slept and could mark his children with the wolf blood.

The day had waned, and as he lay there, Old Billy Dunbar could see that while he had worked the sun had neared the horizon. The Indians looked around uneasily. This was the den of a wolf-man, a powerful spirit who had put the death spell on each of them, who came as a man and went as a wolf.

Suddenly, out on the desert, a wolf howled!

The Apaches started as if struck, and then as a man they began to draw back. By the time they reached the parapet they were hurrying.

Old Billy stayed the night in the wolf hole, lying at its mouth, waiting for dawn. He saw the wolf come back, stare about uneasily, and then go away. When light came he crawled from the hole.

The burros were cropping grass and they looked at him. He started to pick up a pack saddle and then dropped it. "I'll be durned if I will!" he said.

Taking the old Sharps and the extra pan, he walked down to the wash and went to work. He kept a careful eye out, but saw no Apaches. The gold was panning out even better than he had dreamed would be possible. A few more days—suddenly, he looked up.

Two Indians stood in plain sight, facing him. The nearest one walked forward and placed something on a rock and then drew away. Crouched, waiting, Old Billy watched them go. Then he went to the rock. Wrapped in a piece of tanned buckskin was a haunch of venison!

He chuckled suddenly. He was big medicine now. He was a wolf-man. The venison was a peace offering, and he would take it. He knew now he could come and pan as much gold as he liked in Apache country.

A few days later he killed a wolf, skinned it, and then buried the carcass, but the head he made a cap to fit over the crown of his old felt hat, and wherever he went, he wore it.

A month later, walking into Fremont behind the switching tails of Jennie and Julie, he met Sally at the gate. She was talking with young Sid Barton.

"Hi," Sid said, grinning at him. Then he looked quizzically at the wolfskin cap. "Better not wear that around here! Somebody might take you for a wolf!"

Old Billy chuckled. "I am!" he said. "Yuh're durned right, I am! Ask them Apaches!"

Gila Crossing

CHAPTER I

There was an old wooden trough in front of the livery barn in Gila Crossing and at one end of the trough a rusty pump. When Jim Sartain rode up the dusty street, four men, unshaven and tired, stood in a knot by the pump, their faces somber with dejection.

Two of the men were tall, but in striking contrast otherwise. Ad Loring was a Pennsylvania man, white-haired but with a face rough-hewn and strong. It was a thoughtful face, but resolute as well. The man beside him was equally tall but much heavier, sullen and black-browed, with surly, contemptuous eyes. His jaw was a chunk of granite above the muscular column of his neck. Roy Strider was the kind of man he looked, domineering and quick to use his muscular strength.

Peabody and McNabb were equally contrasting. McNabb, as dry and dour as his name suggested, with narrow gray eyes and the expression of a man hard-driven but far from beaten. Peabody carried a shotgun in the hollow of his arm. He was short, and inclined to stoutness. Like the others, he turned to look at the man on the dusty roan when he dismounted and walked to the pump. The roan moved to the trough and sank his muzzle gratefully into the cool water.

Sartain was conscious of their stares, yet he gave no sign. Taking down the gourd dipper, he shook out the few remaining drops and began to pump the protesting handle.

The men studied his dusty gray shirt as if to read his mission from the breadth of his powerful shoulders. Their eyes fell to the walnut-butted guns, long-hung and tied down, to the polished boots now dust-covered, and the Mexican-type spurs. Jim Sartain drank deep of the cold water, a few drops falling down his chin and shirtfront. He emptied two dippers before he stopped drinking.

Even as he drank, his mind was cataloging these men, their dress, their manner, and their weapons. He was also studying the fat man who sat in the huge chair against the wall of the barn, a man unshaven and untidy, with a huge face, flabby lips, and the big eyes of a hungry hound.

This fat man heaved himself from his chair. "Put up your hoss, stranger? I'm the liveryman." His shirt bulged open in front and the rawhide thong that served as a belt held his stomach in and his pants up. "Name of George Noll." He added, "Folks around here know me."

"Put him in a stall and give him a bait of grain," Sartain said. "I like him well fed. And be careful, he's touchy."

Noll chuckled flatly. "Them hammerheads are all ornery." His eyes, sad, curious, rolled to Sartain. "Goin' fer? Or are you here?"

"I'm here." Sartain's dark eyes were as unreadable as his face. "Seems to have been some fire around. All the range for miles is burned off." The men beside him would have suffered from that fire. They would be from the wagons behind the firebreak in the creek bottom. "Noticed a firebreak back yonder. Somebody did some fast work to get that done in time."

"That was Loring here," Noll offered. "Had most of it done before the fire. He figured it was coming."

Sartain glanced at Loring. "You were warned? Or was it an accident?"

But it was Strider who spoke. "Accident!" The dark-browed man spat the word. Then he stared at Sartain, his eyes sullen with suspicion. "You ask a lot of questions for a stranger."

SARTAIN TURNED HIS BLACK EYES to Strider and looked at him steadily while the seconds passed, a look that brought dark blood to Strider's face and a hard set to the brutal jaw. "That's right," Sartain said at last. "When I want to know something I figure that's the way to find it out." His eyes swung back to Loring, ignoring Strider.

"We assume we were burned out by the big ranchers," Loring replied carefully. "We've been warned to leave, but we shall continue to stay. We are not men to be driven from our homes, and the land is open to settlement.

"Three ranchers control approximately a hundred miles of range. Stephen Bayne, Holston Walker, and Colonel Avery Quarterman. We deliberately chose a location that would interfere as little as possible, moving into the mountainous foothills of Black Mesa, north of the Middle Fork. Despite that, there was trouble."

"With the men you named?"

"Who else? Bayne accused Peabody of butchering a Bar B steer, and at Peabody's denial there would have been shooting except that McNabb and I were both there. Then a few days ago Peabody and I rode to Oren McNabb's place, the brother to this gentleman, and found him dead. He had been shot down while unarmed. His stock had been run off, his buildings burned."

"Then there was a rumpus here at the Crossin'," Peabody said. "Loring, Strider, an' me, we jumped Colonel Quarterman on the street. He was mighty stiff, said he knew of no murder and we could get out or take the consequences. Strider here, he came right out an' accused him of murder, then called him out."

"He didn't fight?"

"He's yeller!" Strider sneered. "Yeller as saffron! With no riders at his back he'd never raise a hand to no man!"

"Sometimes," Sartain replied dryly, "it needs more courage to avoid a fight. If this Quarterman is the one I've heard of, he has proved his courage more than once. He's a salty old Injun fighter."

"So he kills a lone rancher who's unarmed?" Again Strider sneered. The big man's dislike for Jim Sartain was evident.

"Had you thought somebody else might have done it? Did you find him there? Or any evidence of him or his riders?"

"Who else would have done it? Or could have done it?"

"You might have."

"Me?" Strider jerked as if struck and his face went pale, then ugly with fury.

"Hold your hand, Roy." George Noll was speaking from the barn door, and there was unexpected authority in his tone, casual as it sounded. "Draw on this hombre an' you'll die. He's the Ranger, Jim Sartain."

CHAPTER II

Strider's big hand was spread above his gun butt and it froze there, then slowly eased to his side. "Sorry," he said resentfully. "I didn't know you was no Ranger."

It was not respect for the law that stopped Strider. Nor was it fear; blustering he might be, but not afraid.

"I was saying that you might have done it," Sartain repeated, "or Loring, or myself. You have no more evidence against the ranchers than they would have against us."

"That's what I've said, Roy," Loring interposed. "We can't go off half-cocked when it will lead to bloodshed. The odds are all against us, anyway. Before we move we must be sure."

"This Ranger won't help **us** any!" Peabody declared. "Who sent for you . . . Quarterman?"

"That's right, and that should prove something to you. If he were guilty he wouldn't call in a Ranger, he'd wipe you out himself, and they must muster a hundred riders between them. He thinks there is something else behind this."

"He does, does he?" Strider sneered. "All he called you for was to get it done legal."

Noll walked up on the other side of the trough. "Hotel up the street. Clean beds, too, an' down this-away a mite Amy Booth has her eatin' house. Best grub west o' the Pecos. Reckon I'll see you there."

Sartain nodded, then turned back to Loring. "You men take it easy. I'll look into this."

"An' we starve while you do?" McNabb spoke for the first time, bitterness edging his voice. "Man, those wagons you saw belong to us! Those women an' kids are ours! We're nigh out of grub an' our stock's been run off! How can we wait? What can we do? You talk about takin' it easy! Them ain't **your** womenfolks!"

"Will it help if you crowd those cowhands into a gunfight an' get killed? How would your families leave the country then? Who would care for them? Be patient, man!"

They were silent, acknowledgment of the truth of what he had said obvious on their faces. Grim, lonely, frightened men. Not frightened of trouble for themselves, for they had known thirst, dust storms, and flash floods, they had fought Indians and hunger. They were frightened of an uncertain future and what would become of their families. "We'll sit tight," Loring said. "I never heard of you giving a man a raw deal yet!"

AT THAT MOMENT the three ranchers awaited him at the Longhorn Hotel up the street, and Sartain knew their appearance now would have led to shooting. Furthermore, their riders would be in town tonight, so the situation was like a powder keg.

The quiet authority he remembered in Noll's voice made him wonder, it was so unexpected. The man seemed to have judgment and might provide the essential balance wheel the community needed.

Quarterman was a tall man of nearly sixty with a white mustache and goatee. He stood up when Sartain entered, an immaculate man in a black broadcloth coat and white hat. His blue eyes twinkled as he held out his hand. Beside him was a tall girl with dark eyes and hair, her figure lovely. She looked at him, then again. "How are you, Colonel? I'm Sartain."

"Recognized you, sir, from stories I've heard. Mr. Sartain, my daughter, Carol." He turned slightly toward a big young man with red hair and a rugged face. "This is Steve Bayne, and the other gentleman"—he indicated a short, powerful man with a broad-jawed face and keen blue eyes—"is Holston Walker, of the Running W."

Jim Sartain acknowledged the introductions, aware of the possessive air adopted by Bayne toward Carol, and to his wry amusement, he found himself resenting it.

It was Walker who interested him most. Holy Walker was a successful rancher, but stories of his skill with his deadly six-guns were told wherever cowhands congregated, and also of his almost fabulous treatment of his hands.

As their hands gripped, Sartain thought he had never felt such power latent in any man as in the leonine Walker. His rusty hair showed no hint of gray, and his face was smooth, the skin taut over the powerful bones of his face.

"There's been a lot of range burned off," Sartain commented. "Who did that?"

"The nesters," Bayne said irritably. "Who else would do it?"

"They claim some of you did it," Sartain suggested mildly. "Maybe you're both wrong."

Bayne stared at him. "Who did you come here to act for?" he demanded. "Those infernal nesters or us?"

"For neither of you," Sartain replied. "I'm to see

justice done, to find who is breaking the law and see they are punished, whoever they may be. The law," he added, "is not an instrument to protect any certain group against another."

Bayne turned on Quarterman. "I told you it wouldn't do any good to send for Rangers, Colonel! We could handle this better our own way! Let me turn John Pole loose on them! He'll have them out of here, and mighty fast!"

"Let me hear of you starting anything like that," Sartain said coolly, "and you'll be thrown in jail."

Bayne turned on him impatiently. "You fatheaded fool! Who do you think you are? I've fifty riders at my call, and a dozen of them better men than you! We don't need any overrated, blown-up Ranger braggarts to do our fighting!"

Sartain smiled. It was a rare smile and had a warm, friendly quality. He glanced at Quarterman, and then his daughter. "Evidently opinions are divided," he said dryly. He turned back to Bayne. "I'm not here to resent your opinions of the Texas Rangers"—there was no smile in his eyes now—"I'm here to settle your trouble, and I will settle it. However," he added, "if you have any more riders of the quality of John Pole, it's no wonder you've got trouble. He's a known killer, and a suspected rustler. He's been a troublemaker everywhere he's gone. It might go far toward solving the situation if he were fired and packed out of the country."

Bayne snorted his contempt. "Riders like Pole

helped build my ranch," he said. "I want men in my outfit who can handle guns, and as for his being a killer, at least he hasn't been hiding behind the skirts of the law!"

"Here, here, Steve!" Quarterman interrupted. "That's no way to talk! Sartain is here at my request, and we aren't getting any results this way!"

"By the way, Colonel"—Sartain turned toward Quarterman—"I want to get about six head of beef to feed those people in the creek bottom. We can't let them starve."

Stephen Bayne had started to walk away, now he whirled and charged back, eyes bulging. **"What?"** he roared. "You ask us to feed those lousy beggars? Why, you—"

Jim Sartain's face was suddenly hard and cold. "You've said enough, Bayne! I'll let you get away with it because I'm here on business! You finish that statement and I'll slap all your teeth down your throat!"

Devilish eagerness sprang into Bayne's face. "Stinkin' coward, was what I was goin' to call you," he said deliberately.

CHAPTER III

Sartain's hands were chest-high in front of him as he was rubbing the fingers of his right hand against the palm of his left. Now, at Bayne's words, his left leaped like a striking rattler and his hard knuckles smashed Bayne's lips back into his teeth. The blow stopped Bayne in his tracks momentarily, and that was all Sartain wanted. He moved in fast with all his bottled-up anger exploding in smashing punches.

A left and right to the wind that jerked Bayne's mouth wide as he gasped for his lost wind, and then a cracking right to the jaw that felled him to his knees, his face contorted with fury and pain.

Sartain was cool. He glanced quickly at Quarterman, who was obviously astonished, and at Holy Walker, who smiled faintly. "You move fast, friend," he said quietly.

Then his eyes went to Carol, who was staring down at Steve Bayne, a peculiar expression on her face, then she looked up at Jim Sartain. "I'm sorry, Miss Quarterman," he said. "He asked for it. I wasn't looking for trouble."

"You accept your opportunities quickly, though, don't you?" she asked coldly. "No wonder you've killed men."

"Nobody would have been surprised had I drawn. Men have been killed for less," he replied. He turned back to Quarterman. "I want to renew my request, Colonel. I appreciate the situation, but your fight is not with women and children, and these are good, honest people. How about it?"

Quarterman hesitated, gnawing his mustache, resenting the position he was in. Behind Sartain, Walker spoke. "I reckon I can spare a few head, but those are proud folks. Will they take them?"

Sartain turned. "Thanks, Walker. An' let's go see, shall we?"

"May I come along?"

Sartain turned on Carol, surprised and pleased. "Glad to have you, ma'am. We sure are!"

FIRES BLAZED CHEERFULLY among the huddle of wagons. There were ten families there, and seventeen children in all. As the three rode toward the fires a man stepped from the shadows with a shotgun. It was Peabody.

"What you want?" he demanded suspiciously, glancing from Sartain to Holy Walker. Then he detected Carol Quarterman and he jerked his hat off in confusion. "Pardon me, ma'am." His eyes went back to the men. "What is this, Ranger? What you want?"

"A talk with you, Loring, and McNabb. Right here will do."

"I reckon not." McNabb stepped from the shadows near a wagon with a Spencer over his arm. "Anything to be said will be said to all of us, right in the circle!"

DISMOUNTING, THEY FOLLOWED MCNABB into the firelight. Loring got to his feet, and beside him, Strider. A buxom woman with a face crimson from the fire turned and looked up at them, and a young woman holding a very young baby moved closer, her eyes grave and frightened.

Surprisingly, Walker took the initiative. "You folks

know who I am, but I don't think we've been very neighborly. Now I know what it means to lose an outfit because I lost mine a couple of times. If I can help any, I'd be right glad to."

McNabb's voice was brittle. "We ain't askin' nor takin' any help from you! We ain't on charity!"

Strider thrust forward. "This here's a trick!" he exploded. "I don't like the look of it! Why should you give us anythin'? So's you can find the hides in our camp later, after you kill us? Look mighty bad for us, wouldn't it?"

"Don't be a fool, man!" Walker replied impatiently. "We didn't want you people here, but you've come an' stayed. You never bothered me, but you did take water we needed. That's not the question now. You've been burned out, an' we're neighbors."

"So you want to help?" Strider sneered. "Well, we don't need your help!"

"Walker volunteered, Strider," Sartain interposed. "I told Quarterman the situation and Walker offered to help."

"We don't need no help! Why didn't he think of that before he burned us out?"

"I didn't burn you out!" Walker declared irritably. "I—"

"You didn't burn us out?" A wiry little man with a face like a terrier thrust himself forward, his eyes burning. "You're a dir—!"

Loring grabbed the man by the arm and flung him bodily back into the darkness. "Grab that man, somebody!" Loring shouted. "What's the matter? You men gone crazy? Do you want to start a gunfight here among our women and children?"

For once Sartain was stopped. The deep antagonisms here were beyond reason, and Walker, although a generous man, was also an impatient one. He would take little more of this. Then into the gap where anything might have happened stepped Carol Quarterman. She went directly to the woman with the baby in her arms. She was smiling with genuine interest, and holding out her arms to the child. "Oh, look at him! Isn't he a darling? And his hair . . . it's so red!"

The girl flushed with pleasure, and the baby responded simply and stretched out his little arms to Carol. She took him, then looked at the girl, smiling. "What's his name? How old is he?"

"He's ten months," the girl said, wiping her palms on her apron, "his name's Earl . . . after my husband." A tall, shy young man with big hands and a shock of blond, curly hair grinned at Carol.

"He's big for his age," he volunteered. "I reckon he'll be quite a man."

Sartain looked at Carol with genuine respect. In the moment when the situation seemed rapidly slipping out of control she had stepped neatly into the breach and in one instant had established a bond of warmth and sympathy. Strider stared at the girls and the child, and Holy Walker's face relaxed.

"How about the beef?" Sartain asked Loring.

"Not for me!" McNabb was stiff-necked and angry. "I won't take charity!"

The woman bending over the fire straightened up, holding a ladle in her hand which she pointed at the man. "Angus McNabb! I'm surprised at you! Talkin' of charity! These are good folks an' it's right neighborly of them to offer it! Have you forgotten the time Lew Fuller's house burned down back on the Washita? We all got together an' helped them! It ain't charity, just bein' neighborly!"

The blond-headed Earl looked around. "You send one of your hands with me, Mr. Walker," he said, "an' I'll ride for that beef, an' thank you a mighty lot."

"Then it's settled!" Walker said. "Maybe if we folks had got together before we'd not have had this trouble."

CHAPTER IV

Jim Sartain built a smoke and looked thoughtfully at the men. For the moment the issue was sidetracked, yet nothing was settled. Underneath, the problem remained, and the bitter antagonisms. McNabb was bitter, and Roy Strider belligerent, and he knew that Steve Bayne would be likewise. The real sore spot was still to be uncovered.

Back at the livery barn George Noll had watched the three ride by, and there had been no gunfire from the bottom. He bit off a corner of his plug tobacco, and watched Steve Bayne draw nearer. An instant his jaws ceased to move, then began again, a methodical chewing.

"Howdy!" He jerked his head toward the bottom. "Looks like that Ranger an' Holy Walker fixed things up. First thing you know they'll be back in the canyons livin' off beef."

"Not mine, they won't!" Bayne turned his angry eyes on Noll. "Holy may soften up for that Ranger's talk, but not me! The Colonel was a fool to send for him! We can handle our own affairs!"

"That's what I always say," Noll agreed. "Well, that fire was a godsend, anyway. It got them off the range. If they are smart they'll keep movin' . . . fact is," he suggested, rolling his tobacco in his cheeks, "they oughta be kept movin'."

Bayne scowled. Success had made him bigheaded, and he was unable to distinguish between luck and ability. He had had luck, but more than that, he owed much of his success to John Pole's running iron. More of it than to his own handling of cattle.

Colonel Avery Quarterman, he had decided, was an old fool. He said nothing because he wanted to marry Carol. Holy Walker he resented, partly for his reputation, and partly because there was no escaping the fact that Walker's was a tightly managed outfit, and a very profitable one. Bayne had the feeling that Walker despised him.

He was positive now that they were taking the wrong tack. He was confident that the nesters would not fight, but would run at the first show of force. Nothing in his experience fitted him to judge men like McNabb, Peabody, or Loring. Bayne had respect for obvious strength and contempt for all else, a contempt grown from ignorance.

Had anyone suggested that his feelings had been carefully nurtured by George Noll, he would have been furious. Noll had found many men open to suggestion, but the two he handled most easily were Strider and Bayne.

Seated unshaven against the wall of his barn, his sockless feet in broken shoes, his shirt collar always greasy with dirt, his gray hat showing finger marks, he was not a man to inspire respect or confidence, yet the barn was a focal point, and he heard much and was able to drop his own seemingly casual remarks.

He was a cunning man, and he possessed the power to hate beyond that of most men. His hatred had been a rambling and occasional thing until that day in the livery barn when he made advances to Carol Quarterman.

He had mistaken her friendly air for invitation, and one day when stabling her mare, he put his hands on her. She sprang away with such loathing and contempt that it bit much deeper than the lash of her quirt across his face, and something black and ugly burst within him. He sprang for her, and only the arrival of Holy Walker had saved her. Walker had come quickly into the barn, but had seen nothing.

Not wanting her father to kill Noll, Carol said

nothing, but took care to avoid him. Yet George Noll's anger burned deep and brooding, and he began to plot and plan. If Quarterman were destroyed, and the girl in need, he would see her pride humbled. Had it required much effort, the chances were that he would have done nothing, but the situation was sparking, and needed only someone to fan the blaze.

He chewed tobacco in silence while the insult to his pride grew enormously. As all ignorant men, he possessed great vanity, and nothing had prepared him for the loathing on the face of Carol Quarterman. His lewd eyes watched her coming and going, and her bright laughter seemed to be mocking him. He could not believe she had almost forgotten his action, and believed she deliberately tormented him.

CAREFULLY, HE FED the flames of envy and resentment in Roy Strider, and the vanity and contempt of Steve Bayne. It was only a step to outright trouble, which began when Roy Strider gave a beating to a Bar B cowhand in a fistfight. Bayne was furious and would have ridden down on Strider at once but for Quarterman.

Noll, who knew most things, knew that John Pole was rustling, but hinted to Quarterman and Walker that it was the nesters. All he actually said was a remark that they always had beef, but such an idea grows and feeds upon uncertainty and suspicion.

His hints to Bayne had apparently sown the seeds of action, for he saw the young rancher stride purposefully down the street to join in a long conversation with John Pole, Nelson, and Fowler. Pole, a lean, saturnine man, seemed pleased. Noll spat and chuckled to himself.

Sartain walked up the street, his boot heels sounding loud upon the boardwalk, and Carol Quarterman, watching him draw near, felt a curious little throb of excitement.

How tall he was! And the way he walked, it was more the quick, lithe step of a woodsman—speaking of strong, well-trained muscles—than the walk of any rider. Yet she sensed worry in him now. "What's the matter, Ranger?" she asked, smiling. "Troubles? I thought we settled things."

"We've settled nothing." His voice was worried. "You know that. There is a bit of kindly feeling now, but how long will it last? The basic trouble is still there, and what is it? Where is it? Who can gain by trouble?"

She caught something of his mood. "I see what you mean. It is strange how such things start. Father and Holy griped a little when they moved in, but only Steve seemed much impressed by it, and he is always being impressed by something. Then cattle were missed and we warned them off. They wouldn't go."

He nodded. "I've seen these things start before, but always with much more reason. It's almost as if somebody **wanted** trouble. I've seen that, too, but who could profit from it here?"

"Nobody ever seems to win in a fight," Carol

agreed. "Everyone gets hurt. The only way anyone could hope to win would be to stay out of it and pick up the pieces."

Sartain nodded, musing. "There are other motives. Men have been known to do ugly things without any hope of gain, over a woman, or out of envy or jealousy. There seems no way to realize any gain, but unless there is somebody around who hates either the ranchers or the nesters, I can't figure it."

"There's nobody I know of," she said doubtfully. It was odd that right then she remembered George Noll, but it was absurd to think all this could stem from so small a thing.

"Steve is angry enough to kill you," Carol said suddenly. "He'll get over it, but the fact that you knocked him down hurt worse than the blows."

She was realizing then that her feelings toward Steve had undergone a change. For months she had been resigned to the idea of marriage to him. He was handsome, and could be very charming, yet she had never been in love with him, and now in comparison with Sartain he seemed suddenly very juvenile, with his easy angers, his vanity and petulance. "Be careful," she warned Sartain. "Steve might go further than we believe. He's very sure of his rightness."

"In a way," he replied, "I can understand his not liking me. He's in love with you and he can see very well that I like you!"

The suddenness of it took her breath, but before she could make any reply, he stepped from the walk and strode quickly away. Yet as he was walking off, incongruously, a remark of Carol's recurred to him. **The only way to win,** she had said, **would be to stay out of it and pick up the pieces.**

Yet if the cattlemen and nesters fought, who would be left to pick up any pieces? He spent a busy afternoon and evening, visiting the town's banker, the doctor, both of the lawyers, and two keepers of stores. When he left the last one he was very thoughtful. He had learned a little, but it was all very flimsy, too flimsy.

CHAPTER V

Surprisingly, the night passed quietly. When it was well past midnight Sartain returned to the hotel and to bed. He awakened with the sun streaming through his window and the street full of excited shouts. Hurriedly scrambling into his clothes, he rushed for the street.

Men were crowding the street, most of them riders from the ranches, and Steve Bayne was up on the steps of the harness shop shouting at them, his face red and angry. Sartain broke through the crowd and confronted him. "What's going on here?" he demanded.

Bayne wheeled on him, his eyes ugly. "You!" He sneered. "You and your peacemaking! The damn nester killed Parrish!"

"What nester?" he asked patiently. "Who's Parrish?"

"Parrish"—Bayne's face was flushed with temper—"was Holy Walker's cowhand who went after those cattle with Earl Mason. Mason killed him!"

"That doesn't make sense," Sartain replied calmly. "You are telling us Mason killed a man who was getting beef for him?" He spoke loudly so the assembled crowd could hear.

"What you think doesn't matter!" Bayne bellowed. "Parrish was found dead along the trail, **an' we're hangin' Mason right now!**"

A half-dozen rough-handed men were shoving Mason forward, their faces dark with passion. Another man had a rope.

Suddenly someone shouted, "Look out! Here come the nesters!"

They were coming, all right, a tight little band of hardheaded, frightened men. Frightened, but ready to fight for what they believed.

Sartain wheeled. "Quarterman! Walker! Call off your men! Send them hack to the ranches and tell them to stay there! If one shot is fired in this street by those men, I'll hold you accountable!"

"It's too far gone to stop now," Quarterman said. "Mason killed Parrish, all right."

"Call them off!" Sartain warned. "Get them off this street at once or you'll be held accountable! There's going to be blazing hell if you don't!"

Bayne laughed. "Why, you meddling fool! You

can't stop this now! Nothing can stop it! Pole, the second those nesters pass that water trough, cut them down!"

Time for talking was past, and Sartain struck swiftly. Steve Bayne never even got his hands up. Sartain struck left and right so fast the rancher had no chance even to partially block the punches. Both caught him in the wind, yet even as he gasped for breath Jim Sartain grabbed him around the waist, spun him around, and jammed a six-gun into his spine. "Pole!" he yelled. "One shot and I'll kill Bayne! I'll shoot him right here, and you'll be next! Get off the street!"

He shoved Bayne forward. "Tell them!" he snapped. "Order them off the street or I'll blow you apart!"

Bayne gasped the words: "I will not!"

Sartain groaned inwardly. The nesters were almost to the trough, and although outnumbered at least five to one, they kept coming. His pistol barrel came up and he slapped Bayne across the skull with it, one sweeping blow that dropped him to the dust.

Springing over him, his face dark with bitter fury, he faced the mob, both guns drawn now. "All right!" His voice roared in the suddenly silent street. "You wanted a fight! By the Lord Harry, you can have it and now! **With me!**

"Back up! Get off the street or start shootin' an' I'll kill the first man who lifts a gun! I've got twelve shots here and I never miss! Who wants to die?"

His eyes blazing, trembling with fury, he started

for the mob. It was a colossal bluff, and one from which he could not turn back, yet stop that slaughter he would, if he must die to do it.

"Back up!" His fury was mounting now and the mob seemed half hypnotized by it. Not a man in that crowd but knew the reputation of Jim Sartain and the unerring marksmanship of which those guns were capable. They recalled that he had at one time shot it out with five men and come out unscathed. To each the black muzzles of the guns seemed pointed directly at himself, and not a man of them but suddenly believed that he had but to lift a hand to die.

Behind him the nesters were equally appalled. A lone man had sprung between them and almost certain death, and that man was slowly but surely backing the crowd up the street.

Carol Quarterman, her heart pounding, watched from the door of the hotel. At first, one man shifted his feet, but the feeling of movement caught the mob and those in front, eager to be out of reach of those guns, felt their backing easing away from them, and they, too, backed away, almost without conscious thought.

Then Sartain called out. "Quarterman! Walker! You get a last chance! Order these men back to their ranches or I'll see you both jailed for inciting to riot! If a man dies here today I'll see you both hang for murder!"

CHAPTER VI

Quarterman stiffened. "You needn't warn me, Sartain. I know my duty." He lifted his voice. "Mount up, men, and go home. We'll let the law handle this."

Walker added his voice, and the cowhands, aware of a cool breath of relief, were suddenly finding the street too narrow for comfort.

Sartain turned to see the rope on Mason's neck, and John Pole standing beside him, and only a few feet away, Newton and Fowler. "Take off that rope, Pole!" he said sharply.

The gunman's face was cold. "I'll be damned if I do!" he flared.

Sartain was suddenly quiet inside. "Take it off," he repeated, "and with mighty easy hands!"

Carefully, John Pole let go the rope. He stepped a full step to one side, his arms bent at the elbows, hands hovering above his guns. "You throwed a mighty big bluff, Ranger," he said, "but I'm callin' it!"

Carol Quarterman saw Pole's hands move, and as if all feeling and emotion were suddenly arrested, she saw Sartain's hands move at the same instant. And then she saw the lifting muzzle of a rifle from the livery-stable door!

"**Jim!**" Her cry was agonized. "Look out! **The stable!**"

Sartain, his eyes blazing from beneath the brim of his low-crowned hat, palmed his guns and fired. It was that flashing, incredible draw, yet even as his right gun spat flame he heard Carol's cry.

A thundering report blasted on his right and he was knocked sprawling, his right-hand gun flying from him. Throwing his left gun over, he caught it deftly with his right hand and snapped a quick shot at the black interior of the barn, just below the round muzzle of a Spencer.

His head was reeling and the street seemed to be rocking and tipping, yet he got his feet under him.

John Pole was still erect, but his blue shirt was stained with blood and his guns were flowering with dancing blooms of flame. Guns seemed to be thundering everywhere and he started forward, firing again.

Staggering, Sartain lurched toward Pole and saw a shot kick up dust beyond the gunman, and believed he'd missed, having no realization that the shot had kicked dust only after passing through him.

Amazed, he saw Pole was on the ground, clawing at the dirt with bloody hands. A gun bellowed again from the barn door and he turned, falling to his face in the dust. He could taste blood in his mouth and his head felt big as a balloon, but he struggled to his feet, thumbing shells into his gun. Again a shot blasted from the barn, but he kept walking, then caught the side of the door with his left hand and peered into the gloom.

George Noll, his flabby face gray, stared at him

with bulging, horror-filled eyes. He had a rifle in his hands and he stared from it to Sartain with amazement. And then Jim lifted his six-gun level and fired three fast shots.

Noll caught them in his bulging stomach and he went up on his toes, mumbled some words lost in the froth of blood at his lips, then pitched over to grind his face into the hay and dirt of the floor.

Sartain's knees seemed suddenly to vanish and the floor struck him in the mouth, and the last thing he remembered was the taste of dirt and straw in his mouth, and the sound of running feet. . . .

For a long time he was aware of nothing, and then there was sunlight through a window, a pump complaining, and a woman's voice singing. He was lying now in a strange bed, and the hand that lay on the coverlet was much whiter than when he had last seen it.

A door opened and he looked into the eyes of Carol Quarterman. "Well!" she exclaimed. "I didn't think you were ever coming out of it! How do you feel?"

"I . . . don't really know. What house is this?"

"Dr. Hassett's. He's my uncle and your doctor. I'm your nurse, and you had four bullets in you, two rifle, and two pistol. That's what Uncle Ed says, although I don't think he could tell one from the other."

"Noll?"

"He's dead. You grazed him once, hit him three times. John Pole is dead, too. You . . . killed him."

"Wasn't there some other shooting?"

"That was Holy Walker and Dad. They finished off Newton and Fowler when they started to help Pole. Dad got hit in the side, but not badly, but Walker wasn't scratched."

"Mason?"

"He was luckiest of all. He was hit three times by bullets aimed at other people and none of them more than broke the skin. All of them are back in the canyons again, and not even Steve Bayne has a word to say."

"How long have I been here?"

"A week, and you'd better settle down for a long rest. Uncle Ed says you can't be moved and that you'll have to stay in bed, with me to nurse you, for at least two more weeks."

Sartain grinned. "With you as nurse? I'll go for that, but what about Steve Bayne?"

She shrugged. "He's gone back to his ranch with more headaches than the one you gave him. Pole had been rustling, branding some of it with Steve's Bar B and selling the rest. Newton worked with him, and he talked before he died; he also swore he saw George Noll set the fire on the range that burned everybody out.

"Apparently he hated me, but when they went through his office they found figures showing how he had planned to buy up the ranches after the range war killed off most of the men. The questions you asked around town started the investigation of his effects, and proved you'd guessed right. As you knew, he was the only one with money enough to take advantage of the situation the range war would leave."

"Anything on Parrish?"

"Nothing exact. However, he had been back to the ranch and talked with the wrangler after leaving Mason. Probably that was Pole. Parrish must have caught him rustling, but we'll never know."

Jim Sartain stared out of the window at the sunlit street. He could see the water trough and the two lone trees. A man sat on the edge of the walk, whittling in the sun. A child was chasing a ball. Farther along, a gray horse stamped a patient foot and flicked casually at the flies.

It was a quiet street, a peaceful street. Someday all the West would be like Gila Crossing. . . .

The Marshal of Painted Rock

Late as it was, the street of Painted Rock was ablaze with light. Saddled horses lined the hitch rails, and the stage was unloading down at the Empire House. Bearded men hustled by in the streets, some of them with packs, some hurrying to get packs. Word of the strike had gone out, and the town was emptying swiftly.

Matt Sabre stood against the wall of the Empire House and watched it absently. This he had seen many times before, this hurry and bustle. He had seen it over cattle, over land, over silver and gold. Wherever it seemed that money might quickly be had, there men thronged.

Good men, many of them. The strong, the brave, the true. But they were not alone, for here also were the scum. The cheats, the gamblers, the good-for-nothings. The men who robbed, who killed, who lived by deceit or treachery. And here also were those who felt that strength or gun skill made them the law—their own law. And these were often the most dangerous. And it was for these that he was here.

Two days now Matt Sabre had been marshal of

Painted Rock. Yet the job was not new to him, for he had been marshal before in other towns. And this town was no different. Even the faces were the same. It was strange, he thought, how little difference there was in people. When one traveled, got around to many towns, one soon realized there were just so many types, and one found them in every town. Names were different, and expressions, but it was like many casts playing the same roles in a drama. The parts remained the same; only the names of the cast had changed.

Darius Gilbert, who owned the gambling house, for example. And Owen Cobb, the banker. Or tall, immaculate Nat Falley, with mining interests. The three were partners in the general store, and they ran the town. They were the council, and they had hired Matt Sabre as town marshal. A tough man for a tough job.

His eyes veiled as he watched the dismounting stage passengers, considering the three men, and most of all Nat Falley. Gilbert and Cobb were good men, upright men, but not fighters. If he was to get help or hindrance, it would come from Falley. In this town or any other, a man like Falley was a man to consider.

A girl was getting down from the stage, a girl dressed in gray. Her cheekbones were high yet delicate, her mouth too wide for true beauty, yet it added to her perfection. She stepped up to the walk, stared at by all, and then asked a question. A man gestured toward Matt Sabre. At once, her eyes turned to him, and he felt their impact. He took a step forward, removing his hat.

"You were looking for me? I'm the town marshal."

She smiled at him, a quick, woman's smile that told him she found him attractive, and also that she wanted something from him . . . and she could see that he believed her beautiful.

This was a woman to quicken the blood in a man, Sabre thought. As he stepped toward her, he saw Falley come from the Empire House and look down the street toward them. Strange, until then he had not noticed. Falley never seemed to carry a gun.

The girl in gray held out her hand to him. Her eyes were clear and very, very lovely.

"I am Claire Gallatin. I came as quickly as I could, but I've been afraid I'd be too late."

"Too late?"

"To see about your prisoner, about my brother."

Matt Sabre returned his hat to his head, and when his hand returned to his side, his eyes were again quiet. "I see. Your brother is a prisoner of mine? Under another name perhaps?"

"Yes. He was known here as Rafe Berry."

Matt Sabre somehow knew he had expected this. And yet he showed nothing in his face. "I am sorry, Miss Gallatin, sorry for you and your family. It is most unfortunate, but you see, Rafe Berry is to be hanged the day after tomorrow."

"Oh, no!" Her fingers touched his arm. "He

mustn't be! It's all a dreadful mistake! Rafe couldn't have done what they accuse him of doing! I just know it!"

Her face was agonized, showing the shock and pain she must be feeling. He glanced around at the curious gathering about them. None listened obviously, yet all were attentive.

"We'd better go inside. We can talk in the dining room," he said quietly.

When they were seated at a table over coffee, she looked across the table at him; her eyes were very large. She leaned toward him, her hand resting on his sleeve. The touch was light yet intimate, and Matt found that he liked it. "Rafe wasn't a bad boy," she said quickly, "although he was reckless. But he never did hurt anybody, and I am sure he would not. There's been some dreadful mistake."

"The evidence was quite conclusive," Matt said quietly. "And in any event, I am only the marshal. I arrested him, but I did not try him. Nor could I free him."

She ignored this. Her voice was low and persuasive as she talked, telling him of their Louisiana home, of her ailing mother, of how they needed Rafe at home. "I'm sure," she added, "that if he were home again, he would never come back here." And she talked on, her voice low. She was, he decided, just exactly what one would expect a cultured lady of Louisiana to be like.

He shook his head slowly. "Unfortunately, ma'am,"

he said gently, "Rafe has already been sentenced. There's nothing I, or anyone, could do."

She bit her lip. "No," she said, lifting her handkerchief, "I suppose not, but if there is anything—just anything—I could do, no matter how much it costs, would you let me know? After all, what will be gained by his death? If he goes away and is never seen again, wouldn't that be just as good?"

"I'm afraid folks wouldn't think so, ma'am. You see, the jury sentenced Rafe for murder, but it wasn't only that that they had in mind. This is to be an example, ma'am. There have been a lot of murders around here lately. They have to stop."

She left him then and went to her room, and Matt Sabre returned to the street. It was quiet that night, more quiet than usual. It was almost as if the whole town were waiting to see Rafe Berry hanged and if he was hanged on schedule . . . if not, the whole lid might blow off.

The lawless element had been running Painted Rock with complete immunity, and the first blow at this immunity had been struck by the arrest of Rafe Berry and his sentencing. For Sabre had demanded an immediate trial for Berry, and before anybody had time to cool off and before his friends had a chance to frighten the jury, Rafe Berry was tried and convicted and sentenced to hang.

The first attempt to save him had followed the trial when a note was found by Matt Sabre lying on his bed. The note told him to see that Berry escaped or die. He not only ignored the note's warning but took added precautions. He double-locked the cell door and carried one key himself.

On the street, he paused, lighting a cigarette and letting his eyes travel slowly along the loafers who were beginning to gather with the ending of day. His eyes hesitated slightly as they reached the walk before Gilbert's Palace. Burt Breidenhart was standing there leaning against an awning post.

He bulked big standing there, and he bulked big in Painted Rock, too. Sabre watched with cold, knowing eyes as men turned across the street to avoid the man. And some of them were tough men. Breidenhart was cruel, vindictive, and dangerous. A brute with his fists, he was also a gunman of sorts. Yet it was his willingness to fight and kill that worried more peaceful men. And Breidenhart had trailed with Rafe Berry.

Matt Sabre turned from his place and walked slowly down the street, purposely walking close to Breidenhart. The big man turned slowly as he neared, and he smiled, his hard eyes dancing with a reckless light. "Hello, marshal!" He said it softly, yet with a certain lifting challenge in his voice. "Hope you ain't all set for that hangin'."

Sabre paused. "It doesn't really matter whether I am or not, Burt," he said quietly. "The hanging is scheduled and it will go off on schedule."

"Don't bet on it," Breidenhart said, hitching up his jeans. "Just don't you bet on it."

"It would be a safe bet," Sabre said quietly. And then he walked on, feeling Breidenhart's eyes following him. Other eyes followed him, too. And then he felt a queer little start. Across the street were three horses, and he knew those horses and knew their riders. Johnny Call was in town!

Darius Gilbert came out of the Emporium with Cobb and Falley. They stopped when they saw him, and Cobb said worriedly, "Matt, things don't look so good. Maybe we made a bad bet."

His eyes strayed from one to the other of them and rested finally on Nat Falley. "You boys getting the wind up? Nothing to worry about."

"Breidenhart's in town, spoiling for trouble." Gilbert looked over his cigar at Sabre. "You know he doesn't bluff. If he came in, he won't leave without starting something."

"I'll handle it."

"It isn't that easy," Falley said suddenly, irritably. "We've property to consider. Rafe Berry has fifty friends in this town right now, and they are all armed and ready for trouble. People will be killed and property damaged. If we go through with this hanging, they'll tear the town to pieces."

"And if we don't, they've got us whipped, and they'll know it. They'll bleed the town white. Sorry, but you've got to make a stand somewhere. We've got to show our teeth."

Gilbert cleared his throat and then nodded worriedly. "I suppose you're right, but still—"

"The jury found him guilty; the judge sentenced him." Matt Sabre let his eyes wander off up the street. "Sorry, gentlemen, but that's the way it stands."

"That's easy for you to say!" Cobb burst out. "What about us? What about our property?"

"You'll be protected," Sabre replied shortly. "I'm sorry, gentlemen, but there is something more than your property at stake. I refer to the welfare of the community. We are making a decision here today whether this community is to be ruled by justice and by law or by force and crime." Sabre took a step back. "Good evening, gentlemen!"

Yet as he turned away, he was uneasy. He needed support; one man alone could not stand before a mob. And these three were the town's wealth and power. Among them, they owned everything but the homes of the workers in the mines and small claims. Men with wives and families, but with little property and no power.

And Johnny Call was in town. Never forget that, Matt Sabre, he told himself. If you forget that, you die.

Johnny Call was a killer. Scarcely nineteen, utterly vicious, with nine killings behind him. His friends bragged that he was faster than Billy the Kid, that by the time he was twenty-one, he would have more killings chalked up and would still be alive.

Johnny Call had been a friend of Rafe Berry's, too. Not that it mattered. Johnny had been hunting an excuse to tackle him, Matt knew. Yet the Johnny

Calls of the West were an old story to Matt Sabre of Mobeetie. Matt Sabre of the cattle drives, Matt Sabre who had been Major Sabre and Colonel Sabre in more than one army.

He stopped at the corner, glanced both ways, then turned and started back, taking his time. Suddenly, he cut across the street. Long ago, he had practiced these sudden deviations from the way he appeared to be taking, and to it he probably owed his life on more than one occasion.

He was a tall man, lean in the body and wide in the shoulder. He wore a .44 Russian in the holster on his leg and had another, invisible to the casual eye, thrust behind his waistband under the edge of his coat.

He had known Johnny Call before. He had seen him before and watched his climb up the ladder of gunslinging fame. Johnny was not yet nineteen, and he had done most of his killing in two years. Four of the dead men had been town marshals, the last one had been the marshal of Painted Rock, who preceded Matt Sabre.

Lights were out now, and the street that had been crowded was about empty. With a curious sense of loss, he realized the men who had voted to hang Rafe Berry were gone on this gold rush. He considered that . . . Suppose it had been a ruse?

No matter what the reason, they were gone, and what came he must face alone. He walked down to the Empire House and entered. It was the quietest night he had known.

Forcing the jail would not be easy. Jeb Cannon was jailer, and Jeb was a man who knew no compromise with duty. The building was strongly built, carved, in fact, from solid rock. It could be got at only from in front, and Jeb was inside with several rifles, two shotguns, and plenty of ammunition.

Still Breidenhart had seemed very sure of himself. Sabre thought that over and decided he did not like it. The big man would stop at nothing, but the place was invulnerable . . . unless they had a cannon. If a shell exploded against the door . . . Sabre felt a queer sense of premonition go through him, a subtle warning from his subconscious.

Blasting powder!

Quickly, over a cup of coffee, he surveyed the possible places where they might secure it. The store . . . he would have to see Falley and the others and block that. Or one of the claims. That could not be blocked, but there was probably little around. Those on the rush had probably taken their supplies with them.

Mentally, he reviewed the case against Rafe Berry. The man had shot and killed Plato Zappas, a Greek prospector, and had stolen his poke and his equipment. He had been seen on the road before Zappas's death, and he had been caught trying to sell Zappas's horse and pack mules.

It was given in evidence that he had also sold a horse once known to belong to Ryan, an Irish miner recently murdered. He was utterly vicious. He had laughed when they arrested him. He had laughed at the trial. He had said he had friends, that he would be set free. He had seemed very sure.

Breidenhart? Somehow Matt Sabre did not find that logical. Nor Johnny Call. To set him free against the will of the town would not be easy. It meant somebody of influence.

He shook his head. He was imagining things. Suddenly, he looked up to see Claire Gallatin beside him. "May I join you?" She smiled widely, then sat down. "I'm still hoping to persuade you to help us, you know." Her purse had fallen open, facing him. There was a fat sheaf of bills visible. "I must free my brother."

Matt shook his head. "Sorry. The answer is the same as before."

Her eyes searched his. "You're a strange man, Matt. Tell me about yourself."

"Nothing much to tell." His eyes were faintly humorous as he looked across the table. "I'm past thirty, single, and own a ranch south of here. I've covered a lot of countries and places." He smiled as he said this. "And I've known a lot of women, in Paris, in London, in Vienna and Florence. Twice women got things from me that I shouldn't have given them. Both times were before I was eighteen."

Her eyes chilled a little. "You mean you can't be

persuaded now? Is it so wonderful to be hard? To be cold? Do you find it so admirable to be able to refuse a girl who wants to help her only brother to escape death? Is that something of which to be proud?" Her lips trembled. Her chin lifted proudly. "I'll admit, I had little hope, but I'd heard that western men were gallant and that if . . . if they lacked gallantry, they might . . . they might be persuaded by other means." She touched the packet of bills.

"And if that failed?"

"Matt Sabre," she said, her voice low and pleading, "can't you see? I am offering all that I have! Everything! I know it is very little, but—"

He smiled at her, his eyes twinkling faintly. "Very little? I think it is quite a lot. There must be two thousand dollars in that sheaf of bills!"

"Three thousand."

"And you . . . you're very lovely, very exciting, and you play your role even better than you did when I saw you play in **East Lynne**. That was last year, in El Paso."

Her face stiffened with anger. "You've been laughing at me! Why, you—"

Matt Sabre got up quickly and stepped back. "Laughing at you? Of course not! But this performance has been preposterous. Two days ago, I became marshal. My first official act was to arrest Rafe Berry and bring him to trial. He was convicted. Almost at once you appear and claim to be his sister."

"I was close by! I am his sister!" Her face was hard,

and her lips had thinned, yet she was still, he admitted, beautiful.

"His sister? And you haven't even asked to see him?" Matt chuckled. "But don't be angry. I've enjoyed it. Only"—he leaned over the table—"who paid you to come here?"

She rose and walked away from him, walking rapidly toward the steps. He watched her, frowning thoughtfully.

Three thousand dollars was a lot to protect Rafe Berry. Or was it to protect somebody else? Somebody who could afford three thousand dollars to keep him quiet?

Nat Falley had come in, and he watched the girl go up the stairs. "You're lucky," he said dryly. "She's very beautiful."

Sabre nodded. "Yes," he agreed, regretfully, "but maybe too expensive for me. For some things, the price is always too high."

Falley watched him go out the door, frowning thoughtfully. He looked up the steps, hesitated, then shrugged and walked away.

BACK AT THE JAIL, Jeb opened the door for Sabre. "Town's full up," Jeb commented, "with mighty tough hombres. Reckon there'll be trouble?"

"Could be." Matt took a worn ledger from the desk. In this ledger, arrests and dispositions were entered. Jeb eyed him dyspeptically as he opened it.

"Ain't much in there," he said. "What you huntin'?"

"I don't know exactly," Sabre admitted, "but Berry isn't the only man here who deserves hanging. And there's somebody behind this."

Jeb said nothing, watching the big man loitering across the street. Others were coming. They were beginning to close in. "You all right here?" Sabre asked him.

"Yep." Jeb turned his head. "Better'n you'll be out there. You better stay until day comes."

"I've work to do. I'll be able to do more outside, anyway. Keep back from the door. I've an idea they'll use blasting powder."

"They'd have to throw it," Jeb replied. "That won't be easy."

He closed the door behind Matt Sabre, and the marshal strolled forward; men faded back into the shadows, but anxious to avoid precipitating trouble, he seemed unaware of them. Yet he knew he must hurry. There was little time.

Darius Gilbert, one of the owners of the general store, was seated in the big buffalo-hide chair. He looked pale and worried. His usually florid cheeks had lost color, and his brows were drawn in. As Matt entered the Empire House, he got hurriedly to his feet and thrust a note into his hands. Matt glanced at it, the same cheap paper, the penciled words: **Call off your marshal or we'll burn you out.** It was unsigned.

"They won't." Sabre folded the note and put it in his pocket. It was not, he realized, an entire sheet. It had been torn from a larger sheet, as had his own warning note. Each had been written on the bottom of a page. Hence, if he found that tablet and these torn sheets fitted . . . "Where's Owen Cobb?" he asked.

"At the store. He's worried about it. He's sittin' over there with a rifle."

Sabre tapped his pocket. "You sell paper like that note?"

"I don't know. Cobb does the buyin' an' sellin'. I've just got money invested, like Nat Falley."

Matt Sabre sat down and opened the ledger he had brought with him. Time and again, the same names. Most were simple drunk and disorderly charges, yet there were a number of arrests for robbery, most of them released for lack of evidence.

"Did you ever stop to think, Gilbert, that somebody has been protecting the crooks around here?"

Gilbert turned his big head and stared at Sabre. His eyes blinked. "You mean somebody is behind 'em? That I doubt."

"Look at this: Berry bailed out three times. No evidence to bring him to trial at any time. And this man Dickert. His fines paid, witnesses that won't talk, some of them bribed and some frightened."

Sabre tapped the book as Falley joined them. "Checking this book and the one I examined last night, I find Breidenhart bailed some of these men out and paid fines for others. It figures to be more than a thousand dollars in the past three months."

Gilbert rubbed his jaw. "That's a lot of money."

"It is. And did Breidenhart ever impress you as a philanthropist? Where does he get that kind of money? To my notion, he's the middleman, and somebody else is behind all this, taking the major portion of the loot for protection and tipoffs."

Sabre tapped a folded paper. "Here's a list of robbed men. All had money. In the very nature of things, thieves would make an occasional bad guess, but not these fellows. That means they were told who carried money and who did not."

"What do you plan to do?" Falley asked.

Sabre got to his feet. He looked at Nat Falley and shrugged. "The answer is obvious. Get the leader and your crime will drop to nothing at all. He's the man we want. And I may ask you gentlemen for help."

HE MUST SEE OWEN COBB. He walked swiftly along the street, noting the increasing number of men who loitered about. But there was time. He found Cobb in his room, one shoe off. "Yes," Cobb admitted, "I did sell some powder today. Sold it to that man Dickert."

Sabre got to his feet. "Thanks. Just what I wanted to know."

Cobb looked up, rubbing his foot. "Matt, you forget it. This is too big for us. Let Berry go. If we don't let him go, there'll be hell to pay. I been settin' here wonderin' if I dare go to bed."

"You go to bed." Sabre's face was somber in the reflected lamplight. "This is my problem."

At the door he hesitated, considering again the problem before him. He must talk to Nat Falley. It was just a hunch, but Falley would know about the mining claims.

Outside, he paused, listening. There was subdued movement, and he knew his time was growing short. So far, they were still gathering; then they would bunch and talk before moving against the jail. He turned into a dark alleyway and walked swiftly along it.

There was a cabin a block off the main street, and a light was showing. Sabre's step quickened, and he dropped a hand to his gun to make sure it was ready. At the cabin, he did not knock or stop; he lifted the latch and stepped in.

Dickert was sitting at the table cutting a short piece of fuse still shorter. A can of powder was on the floor near him. As he saw Sabre, he started to his feet, clawing for a gun. Matt struck swiftly, and Dickert toppled back, knocking the table over. Yet the miner was a burly man, and rugged. He came up swiftly and swung. Matt, overly eager, stepped in and caught the punch on the cheekbone. Springing after him, Dickert stepped into a wicked, lifting right uppercut to the brisket. He gulped and stepped back and, grabbing his stomach, turned sideways. Sabre struck swiftly and without mercy, smashing the man behind the ear with his fist.

Dickert hit the floor on his face and lay still. Swiftly, Matt Sabre bound him. Then he picked up the powder, and dabbing at the cut on his cheekbone, he left the cabin.

When he again reached the street, he moved quietly up to the gathering of men. One man hung on the edge of the crowd, and Matt tapped him gently on the shoulder, then drew him to one side. In the vague light from a window, he recognized the man as a tough miner he had seen about. "Hello, Jack," he said quietly. "Kind of late for you to be around, isn't it?"

Uneasily, the miner shifted his feet. That he had not expected Sabre was obvious, and also that he had planned to shield his own identity in the anonymous shadow of the crowd. Now he was suddenly recognized and in the open. He had no liking for it. "You know, Jack," Sabre suggested, "I've never found you in trouble so far, but I'm here to stay, Jack, and if there's trouble, I'll know one man to arrest. You want to be the goat?"

"Now, look Matt," Jack protested, "I'm just lookin' on. I ain't done a thing!"

"Then why not go home and keep out of it?" Sabre suggested.

The miner shrugged. "Reckon you're right. See you." He turned and walked quickly away.

Sabre watched him go, searching for Breidenhart. No sign of him yet. Knowing much of the psychology of mobs, Sabre circulated through the crowd, staring long into this face and that, occasionally making a suggestion. Here and there, a man slipped away and vanished into darkness. Mobs, he reflected, must be anonymous. Most men who make up mobs act only under influence of the crowd. Singled out and suddenly alone, they become uncertain and uneasy. Deliberately, he let them know that he knew them. Deliberately, he walked among them, making each man feel known, cut off.

Returning to the shadows, Sabre unlocked a door and picked up a bundle of tied-up man. He cut loose the ropes around his ankles. "Just walk along with me and you'll have no trouble."

"You can't get away with this!" Dickert protested. "I ain't done nothin'!"

"And you aren't going to. You've been arrested and the powder confiscated until things quiet down. I'm keeping you out of trouble."

As they moved into the light beside the jail door, there was a shout from the crowd. Men surged forward. "There's Dickert! What's up? Why's he arrested?"

Sabre glanced at them, then said, "Prisoner, Jeb." He shoved Dickert inside, then turned to the angry crowd. He singled out their angry stares one by one, nodding at each recognition. "I arrested Dickert to keep him out of trouble. There's been some fool talk about blowing the jail, and he had possession of some powder. He'll stay inside until he's safe."

Sabre smiled. "I suppose you boys are down here to be sure the prisoner isn't taken away. Well, he's in safe hands. You'll have your hanging, all right. No need to worry." His eyes settled on the face of one man. "Hello, Bill. I noticed on the jail books that you're out on bond. Don't leave town as I'll pick you up in a day or two. There are eight or ten of you here tonight who are due for trial within the next few weeks. I'm going to clean the books fast. I know you don't want to have to wait for trial.

"Those of you"—he spoke louder—"who deserve hanging will get it. Any attempt at mob violence here tonight will be punished by hanging. I've a man who will talk to save his own skin, so there will be evidence enough."

Inwardly, his stomach was tight, his mouth dry. He stood in the full light, outwardly calm and confident, aware that he must break their shell of mob thinking and force each man to think of his own plight and the consequences to himself. He must make each man sure he was recognized, known. As a mass, thinking with one mind, they were dangerous, but if each began to worry . . . "Glad to see you, Shroyer. I'll be picking you up tomorrow. And you, Swede. No more protection, boys; that's over."

There was a sudden stir in the crowd, and Breidenhart pushed his way through. He grinned at Sabre. "All right, boys! Let's bust this jail open and turn Rafe loose!"

Breidenhart half turned his head to speak to the crowd, and Matt took a swift step forward and grabbed him by the back of the shirt collar, jerking him backward, off balance. As the big man toppled, Sabre took a quick turn on the collar, tightening it to a strangling grip. His other hand held a quickly drawn .44 Russian. "Stand back! Let's have no trouble now!"

Breidenhart struggled furiously, kicking and thrashing while his face turned dark.

"He's stranglin'," Shroyer protested.

"That's too bad," Sabre replied shortly. "A man who hunts trouble usually gets it."

"Take him!" a voice shouted from the rear. "Rush him, you fools! He's only one man! Don't let him get away with this!"

The voice was strangely familiar. Sabre strained his eyes over the heads of the crowd as they surged forward. Shroyer was in the lead, not altogether of his own volition. Sabre dropped Breidenhart and kicked him away with his foot. Then he shot Shroyer through the knee. The man screamed and fell, and that scream stopped the crowd.

"The next shot is to kill," Sabre said loudly. "If that man in the rear wants trouble, send him up. He's mighty anxious to get you killed, but I don't see him up in front!"

Behind him, Jeb Cannon's voice drawled lazily

from the barred window of the jail door. "Let 'em come, Matt," he said. "I got two barrels of buckshot ready and enough shells laid here on a chair to kill an army. Let 'em come."

Breidenhart was tugging at his collar, still gasping. He started to rise, and with scarcely a glance, Sabre slashed down with his gun barrel, and Breidenhart fell like a dropped log and lay flat. Sabre waited, his gun ready, while Shroyer moaned on the ground.

Men at the back of the crowd slipped quietly away into the darkness, and those in front, feeling the space behind them, glanced around to see the crowd scattered and melting.

When the last of them had drawn back and disappeared, Jeb opened the jail door. He collared Breidenhart and dragged him within. Sabre picked up Shroyer and carried him inside. The bone was shattered, and the wound was bleeding badly. Sabre worked over it swiftly, doing what he could. "I'll get the doctor," he said then.

At breakfast, Matt Sabre looked up to see Claire Gallatin come into the room. He got up quickly and invited her to join him. She hesitated, then crossed the room and sat down opposite him. "What happened last night? I'm dying to know!"

After explaining briefly, he added, "I've nothing against you, but tell me. Who paid you to come here?"

"I have no idea." She drew a letter, written on the already-familiar tablet paper, from her purse. It was an offer of five hundred dollars if she would claim to be the sister of the prisoner and use her wiles on the marshal. If that failed, she was to offer a bribe. "I wasn't much good at it," she told him, "or else you aren't very susceptible."

Sabre chuckled. "I'm susceptible, but you're better in the theater. I've seen you in New Orleans as well as El Paso. In fact, you're very good."

Her smile was brilliant. "I feel better already! But"—her face became woeful—"what will we do? The company went broke in El Paso, and now I won't get the rest of my money. I'd planned on the pay to get us back East again."

"You still have the bribe money?"

She nodded.

"Then keep it." He shrugged. "After all, to whom could you return it? You just go back to El Paso and get the show on the road."

The door opened before she could protest, and Nat Falley came in with Gilbert and Cobb. Falley smiled quickly, looking from the girl to Sabre. Gilbert looked worried, and Cobb was frowning. When they were seated, Sabre explained about the bribe money. "You agree?" he asked.

Gilbert hesitated, then shrugged. "S'pose so." Cobb added his agreement, and then Falley.

"You seem to have handled a bad situation very well," Falley said. "Who was hurt by that shot?"

"Shroyer. He's in jail with a broken leg."

"You'll try him for that old killing?" Falley demanded.

Sabre shook his head, looking at the mining man again. "No, I promised him immunity."

"What? You'd let him go?" Cobb protested. "But you know he's one of the worst of them!"

"He talked," Sabre said quietly. "He gave me a sworn statement. Since then, I've been gathering evidence."

"Evidence?"

Falley sat up straight. Only Cobb seemed relaxed now. He was watching Sabre, his eyes suddenly attentive. Nat Falley crossed and uncrossed his legs. He started to speak, then stopped. His eyes were on Sabre. Gilbert hitched his chair nearer.

"What evidence?" Gilbert demanded. "What did you find out?"

"All we need now is a jury. We can hold our trial today. That's one blessing," he said grimly, "about making your own law and having no court calendar to consider."

"But who was it? Who is behind this crime?"

Matt Sabre looked into the tightly drawn face of the man opposite him. "Don't try anything, Falley," he said quietly. "I've had you covered under the table ever since you came in."

To the others, he explained, "There was more behind it than the loot. Falley was trying to grab all the valuable claims by having the owners murdered. Checking over the list, I noticed the apparent coincidence, that the victims not only carried money but in each case owned a valuable claim. The murderers got the money, while Falley moved in and took over the claims. Rafe Berry and Breidenhart were the right-hand men."

With his left hand, he drew a tablet from his coat pocket. "Ever see that before?"

Cobb leaned forward. "Why, it's Falley's! Those are his notations on the pages, I'd know them anywhere!"

"Flip the pages to the back and you'll see the note you found, Gilbert, will fit perfectly in one of the torn sheets. The same thing is true with the note that reached me."

Cobb looked at Falley. "Anything to say, Nat? He's got you cold."

"Only that he'll never get out of town alive." Falley's eyes were ugly. "I made sure of that."

Cobb disarmed Falley, and then at a movement near the door, their heads turned. It was Johnny Call.

Matt Sabre nodded to him. "I was hoping you'd come around, Johnny. I wanted to say good-by."

"Good-by?" Johnny blinked stupidly. "What's the idea?"

"Why, you're leaving town, Johnny. You're leaving inside the hour—and you're not coming back."

"Who says so?" Johnny took a sliding step farther into the room. His hands hovered above his guns. "Who says so?"

"Johnny"—Sabre's voice held a great patience—"you'll do all right with guns as long as you shoot up old men and common cowhands, but stay away from the good ones. Don't start anything with Jeff Milton, Bat Masterson, or Luke Short. Any one of them could tell just when you're going to draw by the way you move your feet."

"My feet?" Johnny looked down. Instantly, his eyes came up, only now he was looking into Sabre's .44 Russian.

"That's it, Johnny." Sabre was low-voiced. "You aren't good with a gun; you've just been trailing with slow company. And you think too slow, Johnny. Now unbuckle your belts."

For a long minute, Johnny Call hesitated. He had bragged that he would kill Matt Sabre. He had told Nat Falley he would kill him. But Matt Sabre was a dead shot, and the range was less than twenty feet. Carefully, he unbuckled his belts and let them drop. "Now get out of town, Johnny. If you're here after one hour, I'll kill you." His eyes held Call's. "Remember, it's better to be a live cowhand than a dead gunman."

Call turned and went out the door, and he did not look back. Matt got to his feet. "Let's go, Falley."

Heavily, the man got to his feet. He glanced at his former friends and started to speak, then walked out ahead of Sabre.

Claire Gallatin looked after Sabre. "He's—he's quite a man, isn't he?" she said, wistfully.

Gilbert nodded slowly. "Any man," he said, "can run a town with killings, if he is fast enough. To clean up a tough town without killing, that takes a **man**!"

Ride, You Tonto Raiders!

THE SEVENTH MAN

The rain, which had been falling steadily for three days, had turned the trail into a sloppy river of mud. Peering through the slanting downpour, Mathurin Sabre cursed himself for the quixotic notion that impelled him to take this special trail to the home of the man that he had gunned down.

Nothing good could come of it, he reflected, yet the thought that the young widow and child might need the money he was carrying had started him upon the long ride from El Paso to the Mogollons. Certainly, neither the bartender nor the hangers-on in the saloon could have been entrusted with that money, and nobody was taking that dangerous ride to the Tonto Basin for fun.

Matt Sabre was no trouble hunter. At various times, he had been many things, most of them associated with violence. By birth and inclination, he was a western man, although much of his adult life had been lived far from his native country. He had been a buffalo hunter, a prospector, and for a short time, a two-gun marshal of a tough cattle town. It was his stubborn refusal either to back up or back down that kept him in constant hot water.

Yet some of his trouble derived from something more than that. It stemmed from a dark and bitter drive toward violence—a drive that lay deep within him. He was aware of this drive and held it in restraint, but at times it welled up, and he went smashing into trouble—a big, rugged, and dangerous man who fought like a Viking gone berserk, except that he fought coldly and shrewdly.

He was a tall man, heavier than he appeared, and his lean, dark face had a slightly patrician look with high cheekbones and green eyes. His eyes were usually quiet and reserved. He had a natural affinity for horses and weapons. He understood them, and they understood him. It had been love of a good horse that brought him to his first act of violence.

He had been buffalo hunting with his uncle and had interfered with another hunter who was beating his horse. At sixteen, a buffalo hunter was a man and expected to stand as one. Matt Sabre stood his ground and shot it out, killing his first man. Had it rested there, all would have been well, but two of the dead man's friends had come hunting Sabre. Failing to find him, they had beaten his ailing uncle and stolen the horses. Matt Sabre trailed them to Mobeetie and killed them both in the street, taking his horses home.

Then he left the country, to prospect in Mexico, fight a revolution in Central America, and join the Foreign Legion in Morocco, from which he deserted after two years. Returning to Texas, he drove a trail herd up to Dodge, then took a job as marshal of a town. Six months later, in El Paso, he became engaged in an altercation with Billy Curtin, and Curtin called him a liar and went for his gun.

With that incredible speed that was so much a part of him, Matt drew his gun and fired. Curtin hit the floor. An hour later, he was summoned to the dying man's hotel room.

Billy Curtin, his dark, tumbled hair against a folded blanket, his face drawn and deathly white, was dying. They told him outside the door that Curtin might live an hour or even two. He could not live longer.

Tall, straight, and quiet, Sabre walked into the room and stood by the dying man's bed. Curtin held a packet wrapped in oilskin. "Five thousand dollars," he whispered. "Take it to my wife—to Jenny, on the Pivotrock, in the Mogollons. She's in—in—trouble."

It was a curious thing that this dying man should place a trust in the hands of the man who had killed him. Sabre stared down at him, frowning a little.

"Why me?" he asked. "You trust me with this? And why should I do it?"

"You—you're a gentleman. I trust—you help her, will you? I—I was a hot—headed fool. Worried—impatient. It wasn't your fault."

The reckless light was gone from the blue eyes, and the light that remained was fading.

"I'll do it, Curtin. You've my word—you've got the word of Matt Sabre."

For an instant, then, the blue eyes blazed wide and sharp with knowledge. "You—Sabre?"

Matt nodded, but the light had faded, and Billy Curtin had bunched his herd.

IT HAD BEEN a rough and bitter trip, but there was little farther to go. West of El Paso there had been a brush with marauding Apaches. In Silver City, two strangely familiar riders had followed him into a saloon and started a brawl. Yet Matt was too wise in the ways of thieves to be caught by so obvious a trick, and he had slipped away in the darkness after shooting out the light.

The roan slipped now on the muddy trail, scrambled up and moved on through the trees. Suddenly, in the rain-darkened dusk, there was one light, then another.

"Yellowjacket," Matt said with a sigh of relief. "That means a good bed for us, boy. A good bed and a good feed."

Yellowjacket was a jumping-off place. It was a stage station and a saloon, a livery stable and a ramshackle hotel. It was a cluster of 'dobe residences and some false-fronted stores. It bunched its buildings in a corner of Copper Creek.

It was Galusha Reed's town, and Reed owned the

Yellowjacket Saloon and the Rincon Mine. Sid Trumbull was town marshal, and he ran the place for Reed. Wherever Reed rode, Tony Sikes was close by, and there were some who said that Reed in turn was owned by Prince McCarran, who owned the big PM brand in the Tonto Basin country.

Matt Sabre stabled his horse and turned to the slope-shouldered liveryman. "Give him a bait of corn. Another in the morning."

"Corn?" Simpson shook his head. "We've no corn."

"You have corn for the freighters' stock and corn for the stage horses. Give my horse corn."

Sabre had a sharp ring of authority in his voice, and before he realized it, Simpson was giving the big roan his corn. He thought about it and stared after Sabre. The tall rider was walking away, a light, long step, easy and free, on the balls of his feet. And he carried two guns, low hung and tied down.

Simpson stared, then shrugged. "A bad one," he muttered. "Wish he'd kill Sid Trumbull!"

Matt Sabre pushed into the door of the Yellow-jacket and dropped his saddlebags to the floor. Then he strode to the bar. "What have you got, man? Anything but rye?"

"What's the matter? Ain't rye good enough for you?" Hobbs was sore himself. No man should work so many hours on feet like his.

"Have you brandy? Or some Irish whiskey?"

Hobbs stared. "Mister, where do you think you are? New York?"

"That's all right, Hobbs. I like a man who knows what he likes. Give him some of my cognac."

Matt Sabre turned and glanced at the speaker. He was a tall man, immaculate in black broadcloth, with blond hair slightly wavy and a rosy complexion. He might have been thirty or older. He wore a pistol on his left side, high up.

"Thanks," Sabre said briefly. "There's nothing better than cognac on a wet night."

"My name is McCarran. I run the PM outfit, east of here. Northeast, to be exact."

Sabre nodded. "My name is Sabre. I run no outfit, but I'm looking for one. Where's the Pivotrock?"

He was a good poker player, men said. His eyes were fast from using guns, and so he saw the sudden glint and the quick caution in Prince McCarran's eyes.

"The Pivotrock? Why, that's a stream over in the Mogollons. There's an outfit over there, all right. A one-horse affair. Why do you ask?"

Sabre cut him off short. "Business with them."

"I see. Well, you'll find it a lonely ride. There's trouble up that way now, some sort of a cattle war."

Matt Sabre tasted his drink. It was good cognac. In fact, it was the best, and he had found none west of New Orleans.

McCarran, his name was. He knew something, too. Curtin had asked him to help his widow. Was the Pivotrock outfit in the war? He decided against asking McCarran, and they talked quietly of the rain and of cattle, then of cognac. "You never acquired a taste for cognac in the West. May I ask where?"

"Paris," Sabre replied, "Marseilles, Fez, and Marrakesh."

"You've been around, then. Well, that's not uncommon." The blond man pointed toward a heavy-shouldered young man who slept with his head on his arms. "See that chap? Calls himself Camp Gordon. He's a Cambridge man, quotes the classics when he's drunk—which is over half the time—and is one of the best cowhands in the country when he's sober.

"Keys over there, playing the piano, studied in Weimar. He knew Strauss, in Vienna, before he wrote 'The Blue Danube.' There's all sorts of men in the West, from belted earls and remittance men to vagabond scum from all corners of the world. They are here a few weeks, and they talk the lingo like veterans. Some of the biggest ranches in the West are owned by Englishmen."

Prince McCarran talked to him a few minutes longer, but he learned nothing. Sabre was not evasive, but somehow he gave out no information about himself or his mission. McCarran walked away very thoughtfully. Later, after Matt Sabre was gone, Sid Trumbull came in.

"Sabre?" Trumbull shook his head. "Never heard of him. Keys might know. He knows about ever'-body. What's he want on the Pivotrock?"

* * *

LYING ON HIS BACK in bed, Matt Sabre stared up into the darkness and listened to the rain on the window and on the roof. It rattled hard, skeleton fingers against the glass, and he turned restlessly in his bed, frowning as he recalled that quick, guarded expression in the eyes of Prince McCarran.

Who was McCarran, and what did he know? Had Curtin's request that he help his wife been merely the natural request of a dying man, or had he felt that there was a definite need of help? Was something wrong here?

He went to sleep vowing to deliver the money and ride away. Yet even as his eyes closed the last time, he knew he would not do it if there was trouble.

It was still raining, but no longer pouring, when he awakened. He dressed swiftly and checked his guns, his mind taking up his problems where they had been left the previous night.

Camp Gordon, his face puffy from too much drinking and too sound a sleep, staggered down the stairs after him. He grinned woefully at Sabre. "I guess I really hung one on last night," he said. "What I need is to get out of town."

They ate breakfast together, and Gordon's eyes sharpened suddenly at Matt's query of directions to the Pivotrock. "You'll not want to go there, man. Since Curtin ran out they've got their backs to the wall. They are through! Leave it to Galusha Reed for that."

"What's the trouble?"

"Reed claims title to the Pivotrock. Bill Curtin's old man bought it from a Mex who had it from a land grant. Then he made a deal with the Apaches, which seemed to cinch his title. Trouble was, Galusha Reed shows up with a prior claim. He says Fernandez had no grant. That his man Sonoma had a prior one. Old Man Curtin was killed when he fell from his buckboard, and young Billy couldn't stand the gaff. He blew town after Tony Sikes buffaloed him."

"What about his wife?"

Gordon shook his head, then shrugged. Doubt and worry struggled on his face. "She's a fine girl, Jenny Curtin is. The salt of the earth. It's too bad Curtin hadn't a tenth of her nerve. She'll stick, and she swears she'll fight."

"Has she any men?"

"Two. An old man who was with her father-in-law and a half-breed Apache they call Rado. It used to be Silerado."

Thinking it over, Sabre decided there was much left to be explained. Where had the five thousand dollars come from? Had Billy really run out, or had he gone away to get money to put up a battle? And how did he get it?

"I'm going out." Sabre got to his feet. "I'll have a talk with her."

"Don't take a job there. She hasn't a chance!" Gordon said grimly. "You'd do well to stay away."

"I like fights when one side doesn't have a chance," Matt replied lightly. "Maybe I will ask for a job. A man's got to die sometime, and what better time than fighting when the odds are against him?"

"I like to win," Gordon said flatly. "I like at least a chance."

Matt Sabre leaned over the table, aware that Prince McCarran had moved up behind Gordon, and that a big man with a star was standing near him. "If I decide to go to work for her"—Sabre's voice was easy, confident—"then you'd better join us. Our side will win."

"Look here, you!" The man wearing the star, Sid Trumbull, stepped forward. "You either stay in town or get down the trail! There's trouble enough in the Mogollons. Stay out of there."

Matt looked up. "You're telling me?" His voice cracked like a whip. "You're town marshal, Trumbull, not a United States marshal or a sheriff, and if you were a sheriff, it wouldn't matter. It is out of this county. Now suppose you back up and don't step into conversations unless you're invited."

Trumbull's head lowered, and his face flushed red. Then he stepped around the table, his eyes narrow and mean. "Listen, you!" His voice was thick with fury. "No two-by-twice cowpoke tells me—!"

"Trumbull"—Sabre spoke evenly—"you're asking for it. You aren't acting in line of duty now. You're picking trouble, and the fact that you're marshal won't protect you."

"Protect me?" His fury exploded. "Protect me? Why, you—!"

Trumbull lunged around the table, but Matt sidestepped swiftly and kicked a chair into the marshal's path. Enraged, Sid Trumbull had no chance to avoid it and fell headlong, bloodying his palms on the slivery floor.

Kicking the chair away, he lunged to his feet, and Matt stood facing him, smiling. Camp Gordon was grinning, and Hobbs was leaning his forearms on the bar, watching with relish.

Trumbull stared at his torn palms, then lifted his eyes to Sabre's. Then he started forward, and suddenly, in midstride, his hand swept for his gun.

Sabre palmed his Colt, and the gun barked even as it lifted. Stunned, Sid Trumbull stared at his numbed hand. His gun had been knocked spinning, and the .44 slug, hitting the trigger guard, had gone by to rip off the end of Sid's little finger. Dumbly, he stared at the slow drip of blood.

Prince McCarran and Gordon were only two of those who stared, not at the marshal, but at Matt Sabre.

"You throw that gun mighty fast, stranger," McCarran said. "Who are you, anyway? There aren't a half-dozen men in the country who can throw a gun that fast. I know most of them by sight."

Sabre's eyes glinted coldly. "No? Well, you know another one now. Call it seven men." He spun on his heel and strode from the room. All eyes followed him.

Coyote Trouble

Matt Sabre's roan headed up Shirt Tail Creek, crossed Bloody Basin and Skeleton Ridge, and made the Verde in the vicinity of the hot springs. He bedded down that night in a corner of a cliff near Hardscrabble Creek. It was late when he turned in, and he had lit no fire.

He had chosen his position well, for behind him the cliff towered, and on his left there was a steep hillside that sloped away toward Hardscrabble Creek. He was almost at the foot of Hardscrabble Mesa, with the rising ground of Deadman Mesa before him. The ground in front sloped away to the creek, and there was plenty of dry wood. The overhang of the cliff protected it from the rain.

Matt Sabre came suddenly awake. For an instant, he lay very still. The sky had cleared, and as he lay on his side, he could see the stars. He judged that it was past midnight. Why he had awakened he could not guess, but he saw that the roan was nearer, and the big gelding had his head up and ears pricked.

"Careful, boy!" Sabre warned.

Sliding out of his bedroll, he drew on his boots and got to his feet. Feeling out in the darkness, he drew his Winchester near.

He was sitting in absolute blackness due to the cliff's overhang. He knew the boulders and the clumps of cedar were added concealment. The roan would be lost against the blackness of the cliff, but from where he sat, he could see some thirty yards of the creek bank and some open ground.

There was subdued movement below and whispering voices. Then silence. Leaving his rifle, Sabre belted on his guns and slid quietly out of the overhang and into the cedars.

After a moment, he heard the sound of movement, and then a low voice: "He can't be far! They said he came this way, and he left the main trail after Fossil Creek."

There were two of them. He waited, standing there among the cedars, his eyes hard and his muscles poised and ready. They were fools. Did they think he was that easy?

He had fought Apaches and Kiowas, and he had fought the Tauregs in the Sahara and the Riffs in the Atlas Mountains. He saw them then, saw their dark figures moving up the hill, outlined against the pale gravel of the slope.

That hard, bitter thing inside him broke loose, and he could not stand still. He could not wait. They would find the roan, and then they would not leave until they had him. It was now or never. He stepped out, quickly, silently.

"Looking for somebody?"

They wheeled, and he saw the starlight on a pistol barrel and heard the flat, husky cough of his own gun. One went down, coughing and gasping. The other staggered, then turned and started off in a stumbling run, moaning half in fright, half in pain.

He stood there, trying to follow the man, but he lost him in the brush.

He turned back to the fellow on the ground but did not go near him. He circled wide instead, returning to his horse. He quieted his roan, then lay down. In a few minutes, he was dozing.

Daybreak found him standing over the body. The roan was already saddled for the trail. It was one of the two he had seen in Silver City, a lean, dark-faced man with deep lines in his cheeks and a few gray hairs at the temples. There was an old scar, deep and red, over his eye.

Sabre knelt and went through his pockets, taking a few letters and some papers. He stuffed them into his own pockets, then mounted. Riding warily, he started up the creek. He rode with his Winchester across his saddle, ready for whatever came. Nothing did.

The morning drew on, the air warm and still after the rain. A fly buzzed around his ears, and he whipped it away with his hat. The roan had a long-striding, space-eating walk. It moved out swiftly and surely toward the far purple ranges, dipping down through grassy meadows lined with pines and aspens, with here and there the whispering leaves of a tall cottonwood.

It was a land to dream about, a land perfect for the grazing of either cattle or sheep, a land for a man to live in. Ahead and on his left he could see the towering Mogollon Rim, and it was beyond this rim, up on the plateau, that he would find the Pivotrock. He skirted a grove of rustling aspen and looked down a long valley.

For the first time, he saw cattle—fat, contented cattle, fat from the rich grass of these bottomlands. Once, far off, he glimpsed a rider, but he made no effort to draw near, wanting only to find the trail to the Pivotrock.

A wide-mouthed canyon opened from the northeast, and he turned the roan and started up the creek that ran down it. Now he was climbing, and from the look of the country, he would climb nearly three thousand feet to reach the rim. Yet he had been told there was a trail ahead, and he pushed on.

The final eight hundred feet to the rim was by a switchback trail that had him climbing steadily, yet the air on the plateau atop the rim was amazingly fresh and clear. He pushed on, seeing a few scattered cattle, and then he saw a crude wooden sign by the narrow trail. It read:

PIVOTROCK . . . 1 MILE

The house was low and sprawling, lying on a flat-topped knoll with the long barns and sheds built on three sides of a square. The open side faced the rim and the trail up which he was riding. There were cottonwood, pine, and fir backing up the buildings. He could see the late afternoon sunlight glistening on the coats of the saddlestock in the corral.

An old man stepped from the stable with a carbine in his hands. "All right, stranger. You stop where you are. What you want here?"

Matt Sabre grinned. Lifting his hand carefully, he pushed back his flat-brimmed hat. "Huntin' Mrs. Jenny Curtin," he said. "I've got news." He hesitated. "Of her husband."

The carbine muzzle lowered. "Of **him**? What news would there be of him?"

"Not good news," Sabre told him. "He's dead."

Surprisingly, the old man seemed relieved. "Light," he said briefly. "I reckon we figured he was dead. How'd it happen?"

Sabre hesitated. "He picked a fight in a saloon in El Paso, then drew too slow."

"He was never fast." The old man studied him. "My name's Tom Judson. Now, you sure didn't come all the way here from El Paso to tell us Billy was dead. What did you come for?"

"I'll tell Mrs. Curtin that. However, they tell me down the road you've been with her a long time, so you might as well know. I brought her some money. Bill Curtin gave it to me on his deathbed; asked me to bring it to her. It's five thousand dollars."

"Five thousand?" Judson stared. "Reckon Bill must have set some store by you to trust you with it. Know him long?"

Sabre shook his head. "Only a few minutes. A dying man hasn't much choice."

A door slammed up at the house, and they both

turned. A slender girl was walking toward them, and the sunlight caught the red in her hair. She wore a simple cotton dress, but her figure was trim and neat. Ahead of her dashed a boy who might have been five or six. He lunged at Sabre, then slid to a stop and stared up at him, then at his guns.

"Howdy, old-timer!" Sabre said, smiling. "Where's your spurs?"

The boy was startled and shy. He drew back, surprised at the question. "I—I've got no spurs!"

"What? A cowhand without spurs? Well have to fix that." He looked up. "How are you, Mrs. Curtin? I'm Mathurin Sabre, Matt for short. I'm afraid I've some bad news for you."

Her face paled a little, but her chin lifted. "Will you come to the house, Mr. Sabre? Tom, put his horse in the corral, will you?"

The living room of the ranch house was spacious and cool. There were Navajo rugs upon the floor, and the chairs and the divan were beautifully tanned cowhide. He glanced around appreciatively, enjoying the coolness after his hot ride in the Arizona sun, like the naturalness of this girl, standing in the home she had created.

She faced him abruptly. "Perhaps you'd better tell me now; there's no use pretending or putting a bold face on it when I have to be told."

As quickly and quietly as possible, he explained. When he was finished, her face was white and still.

"I—I was afraid of this. When he rode away, I knew he would never come back. You see, he thought—he believed he had failed me, failed his father."

Matt drew the oilskin packet from his pocket. "He sent you this. He said it was five thousand dollars. He said to give it to you."

She took it, staring at the package, and tears welled into her eyes. "Yes." Her voice was so low that Matt scarcely heard it. "He would do this. He probably felt it was all he could do for me, for us. You see"—Jenny Curtin's eyes lifted—"we're in a fight, and a bad one. This is war money.

"I—guess Billy thought—well, he was no fighter himself, and this might help, might compensate. You're probably wondering about all this."

"No," he said. "I'm not. And maybe I'd better go out with the boys now. You'll want to be alone."

"Wait!" Her fingers caught his sleeve. "I want you to know, since you were with him when he died, and you have come all this way to help us. There was no trouble with Billy and me. It was—well, he thought he was a coward. He thought he had failed me.

"We've had trouble with Galusha Reed in Yellowjacket. Tony Sikes picked a fight with Billy. He wanted to kill him, and Billy wouldn't fight. He—he backed down. Everybody said he was a coward, and he ran. He went—away."

Matt Sabre frowned thoughtfully, staring at the floor. The boy who picked a fight with him, who dared him, who went for his gun, was no coward. Trying to prove something to himself? Maybe. But no coward.

"Ma'am," he said abruptly, "you're his widow. The mother of his child. There's something you should know. Whatever else he was, I don't know. I never knew him long enough. But that man was no coward. Not even a little bit!

"You see," Matt hesitated, feeling the falseness of his position, not wanting to tell this girl that he had killed her husband, yet not wanting her to think him a coward, "I saw his eyes when he went for his gun. I was there, ma'am, and saw it all. Bill Curtin was no coward."

Hours later, lying in his bunk, he thought of it, and the five thousand was still a mystery. Where had it come from? How had Curtin come by it?

He turned over and after a few minutes went to sleep. The next day, he would be riding.

THE SUNLIGHT WAS BRIGHT the next morning when he finally rolled out of bed. He bathed and shaved, taking his time, enjoying the sun on his back, and feeling glad he was footloose again. He was in the bunkhouse belting on his guns when he heard the horses. He stepped to the door and glanced out.

Neither the dark-faced Rado nor Judson was about, and there were three riders in the yard. One of them he recognized as a man from Yellowjacket, and the tallest of the riders was Galusha Reed. He was a big man, broad and thick in the body without being fat. His jaw was brutal.

Jenny Curtin came out on the steps. "Ma'am," Reed said abruptly, "we're movin' you off this land. We're goin' to give you ten minutes to pack, an' one of my boys'll hitch the buckboard for you. This here trouble's gone on long enough, an' mine's the prior claim to this land. You're gettin' off!"

Jenny's eyes turned quickly toward the stable, but Reed shook his head. "You needn't look for Judson or the breed. We watched until we seen them away from here, an' some of my boys are coverin' the trail. We're tryin' to get you off here without any trouble."

"You can turn around and leave, Mr. Reed. I'm not going!"

"I reckon you are," Reed said patiently. "We know that your man's dead. We just can't put up with you squattin' on our range."

"This happens to be my range, and I'm staying."

Reed chuckled. "Don't make us put you off, ma'am. Don't make us get rough. Up here"—he waved a casual hand—"we can do anything we want, and nobody the wiser. You're leavin', as of now."

Matt Sabre stepped out of the bunkhouse and took three quick steps toward the riders. He was cool and sure of himself, but he could feel the jumping invitation to trouble surging up inside him. He fought it down and held himself still for an instant. Then he spoke.

"Reed, you're a fatheaded fool and a bully. You

ride up here to take advantage of a woman because you think she's helpless. Well, she's not. Now you three turn your horses—turn 'em mighty careful—and start down the trail. And don't you ever set foot on this place again!"

Reed's face went white, then dark with anger. He leaned forward a little. "So you're still here? Well, we'll give you a chance to run. Get goin'!"

Matt Sabre walked forward another step. He could feel the eagerness pushing up inside him, and his eyes held the three men, and he saw the eyes of one widen with apprehension.

"Watch it, boss! Watch it!"

"That's right, Reed. Watch it. You figured to find this girl alone. Well, she's not alone. Furthermore, if she'll take me on as a hand, I'll stay. I'll stay until you're out of the country or dead. You can have it either way you want.

"There's three of you. I like that. That evens us up. If you want to feed buzzards, just edge that hand another half inch toward your gun and you can. That goes for the three of you."

He stepped forward again. He was jumping with it now—that old drive for combat welling up within him. Inside, he was trembling, but his muscles were steady, and his mind was cool and ready. His fingers spread, and he moved forward again.

"Come on, you mangy coyotes! Let's see if you've got the nerve. **Reach!**"

Reed's face was still and cold. His mouth looked

pinched, and his eyes were wide. Some sixth sense warned him that this was different. This was death he was looking at, and Galusha Reed suddenly realized he was no gambler when the stakes were so high.

He could see the dark eagerness that was driving this cool man; he could see beyond the coolness on his surface the fierceness of his readiness; inside, he went sick and cold at the thought.

"Boss!" the man at his side whispered hoarsely. "Let's get out of here. This man's poison!"

Galusha Reed slowly eased his hand forward to the pommel of the saddle. "So, Jenny, you're hiring gunfighters? Is that the way you want it?"

"I think you hired them first," she replied coolly. "Now you'd better go."

"On the way back," Sabre suggested, "you might stop in Hardscrabble Canyon and pick up the body of one of your killers. He guessed wrong that night."

Reed stared at him. "I don't know what you mean," he flared. "I sent out no killer."

Matt Sabre watched the three men ride down the trail and he frowned. There had been honest doubt in Reed's eyes, but if he had not sent the two men after him, who had? Those men had been in Silver City and El Paso, yet they also knew this country and knew someone in Yellowjacket. Maybe they had not come after him but had first followed Bill Curtin.

He turned and smiled at the girl. "Coyotes," he said, shrugging. "Not much heart in them."

She was staring at him strangely. "You—you'd have killed them, wouldn't you? Why?"

He shrugged. "I don't know. Maybe it's because—well, I don't like to see men take advantage of a woman alone. Anyway"—he smiled—"Reed doesn't impress me as a good citizen."

"He's a dangerous enemy." She came down from the steps. "Did you mean what you said, Mr. Sabre? I mean about staying here and working for me? I need men, although I must tell you that you've small chance of winning, and it's rather a lonely fight."

"Yes, I meant it." Did he mean it? Of course. He remembered the old Chinese proverb: If you save a person's life he becomes your responsibility. That wasn't the case here, but he had killed this girl's husband, and the least he could do would be to stay until she was out of trouble.

Was that all he was thinking of? "I'll stay," he said. "I'll see you through this. I've been fighting all my life, and it would be a shame to stop now. And I've fought for lots less reasons."

HOT NIGHT IN YELLOWJACKET

Throughout the morning, he worked around the place. He worked partly because there was much to be done and partly because he wanted to think.

The horses in the remuda were held on the home

place and were in good shape. Also, they were better than the usual ranch horses, for some of them showed a strong Morgan strain. He repaired the latch on the stable door and walked around the place, sizing it up from every angle, studying all the approaches.

With his glasses, he studied the hills and searched the notches and canyons wherever he could see them. Mentally, he formed a map of all that terrain within reach of his glass.

It was midafternoon before Judson and Rado returned, and they had talked with Jenny before he saw them.

"Howdy." Judson was friendly, but his eyes studied Sabre with care. "Miss Jenny tells me you run Reed off. That you're aimin' to stay on here."

"That's right. I'll stay until she's out of trouble, if she'll have me. I don't like being pushed around."

"No, neither do I." Judson was silent for several minutes, and then he turned his eyes on Sabre. "Don't you be gettin' any ideas about Miss Jenny. She's a fine girl."

Matt looked up angrily. "And don't you be getting any ideas," he said coldly. "I'm helping her the same as you are, and we'll work together. As to personal things, leave them alone. I'll only say that when this fight is over, I'm hitting the trail."

"All right," Judson said mildly. "We can use help."

Three days passed smoothly. Matt threw himself into the work of the ranch, and he worked feverishly.

Even he could not have said why he worked so desperately hard. He dug postholes and fenced an area in the long meadow near the seeping springs in the bottom.

Then, working with Rado, he rounded up the cattle nearest the rim and pushed them back behind the fence. The grass was thick and deep there and would stand a lot of grazing, for the meadow wound back up the canyon for some distance. He carried a running iron and branded stock wherever he found it required.

As the ranch had been shorthanded for a year, there was much to do. Evenings, he mended gear and worked around the place, and at night he slept soundly. During all this time, he saw nothing of Jenny Curtin.

He saw nothing of her, but she was constantly in his thoughts. He remembered her as he had seen her that first night, standing in the living room of the house, listening to him, her eyes, wide and dark, upon his face. He remembered her facing Galusha Reed and his riders from the steps.

Was he staying on because he believed he owed her a debt or because of her?

Here and there around the ranch, Sabre found small, intangible hints of the sort of man Curtin must have been. Judson had liked him, and so had the half-breed. He had been gentle with horses. He had been thoughtful. Yet he had hated and avoided violence. Slowly, rightly or wrongly Matt could not tell, a picture was forming in his mind of a fine young man who had been totally out of place.

Western birth, but born for peaceful and quiet ways, he had been thrown into a cattle war and had been aware of his own inadequacy. Matt was thinking of that, and working at a rawhide riata, when Jenny came up.

He had not seen her approach, or he might have avoided her, but she was there beside him before he realized it.

"You're working hard, Mr. Sabre."

"To earn my keep, ma'am. There's a lot to do, I find, and I like to keep busy." He turned the riata and studied it.

"You know, there's something I've been wanting to talk to you about. Maybe it's none of my affair, but young Billy is going to grow up, and he's going to ask questions about his dad. You aren't going to be able to fool him. Maybe you know what this is all about, and maybe I'm mounting on the offside, but it seems to me that Bill Curtin went to El Paso to get that money for you.

"I think he realized he was no fighting man, and that the best thing he could do was to get that money so he could hire gunfighters. It took nerve to do what he did, and I think he deliberately took what Sikes handed him because he knew that if Sikes killed him, you'd never get that money.

"Maybe along the way to El Paso he began to wonder, and maybe he picked that fight down there with the idea of proving to himself that he did have the nerve to face a gun."

She did not reply, but stood there, watching his fingers work swiftly and evenly, plaiting the leather.

"Yes," she said finally, "I thought of that. Only I can't imagine where he got the money. I hesitate to use it without knowing."

"Don't be foolish," he said irritably. "Use it. Nobody would put it to better use, and you need gun hands."

"But who would work for me?" Her voice was low and bitter. "Galusha Reed has seen to it that no one will."

"Maybe if I rode in, I could find some men." He was thinking of Camp Gordon, the Shakespeare-quoting English cowhand. "I believe I know one man."

"There's a lot to be done. Jud tells me you've been doing the work of three men."

Matt Sabre got to his feet. She stepped back a little, suddenly aware of how tall he was. She was tall for a girl, yet she came no farther than his lips. She drew back a little at the thought. Her eyes dropped to his guns. He always wore them, always low and tied down.

"Judson said you were a fast man with a gun. He said you had the mark of the—of the gunfighter."

"Probably." He found no bitterness at the thought. "I've used guns. Guns and horses; they are about all I've known."

"Where were you in the army? I've watched you walk and ride and you show military training."

"Oh, several places. Africa mostly."

"Africa?" She was amazed. "You've been there?"

He nodded. "Desert and mountain country. Morocco and the Sahara, all the way to Timbuktu and Lake Chad, fighting most of the time." It was growing dark in the shed where they were standing. He moved out into the dusk. A few stars had already appeared, and the red glow that was in the west beyond the rim was fading.

"Tomorrow I'll ride in and have a look around. You'd better keep the other men close by."

Dawn found him well along on the trail to Yellowjacket. It was a long ride, and he skirted the trail most of the time, having no trust in well-traveled ways at such a time. The air was warm and bright, and he noticed a few head of Pivotrock steers that had been overlooked in the rounding up of cattle along the rim.

He rode ready for trouble, his Winchester across his saddlebows, his senses alert. Keeping the roan well back under the trees, he had the benefit of the evergreen needles that formed a thick carpet and muffled the sound of his horse's hoofs.

Yet as he rode, he considered the problem of the land grant. If Jenny were to retain her land and be free of trouble he must look into the background of the grant and see which had the prior and best claim, Fernandez or Sonoma.

Next, he must find out, if possible, where Bill Curtin had obtained that five thousand dollars. Some might think that the fact he had it was enough and that now his wife had it, but it was not enough if Bill had sold any rights to water or land on the ranch or if he had obtained the money in some way that would reflect upon Jenny or her son.

When those things were done, he could ride on about his business, for by that time he would have worked out the problem of Galusha Reed.

In the few days he had been on the Pivotrock, he had come to love the place, and while he had avoided Jenny, he had not avoided young Billy. The youngster had adopted him and had stayed with him hour after hour.

To keep him occupied, Matt had begun teaching him how to plait rawhide, and so, as he mended riatas and repaired bridles, the youngster had sat beside him, working his fingers clumsily through the intricacies of the plaiting.

It was with unease that he recalled his few minutes alone with Jenny. He shifted his seat in the saddle and scowled. It would not do for him to think of her as anything but Curtin's widow. The widow, he reflected bitterly, of the man he had killed.

What would he say when she learned of **that**? He avoided the thought, yet it remained in the back of his mind, and he shook his head, wanting to forget it. Sooner or later, she would know. If he did not finally tell her himself, then he was sure that Reed would let her know.

Avoiding the route by way of Hardscrabble, Matt Sabre turned due south, crossing the eastern end of the mesa and following an old trail across Whiterock and Polles Mesa, crossing the East Verde at Rock Creek. Then he cut through Boardinghouse Canyon to Bullspring, crossing the main stream of the Verde near Tangle Peak. It was a longer way around by a few miles, but Sabre rode with care, watching the country as he traveled. It was very late when he walked his roan into the parched street of Yellow-jacket.

He had a hunch and he meant to follow it through. During his nights in the bunkhouse he had talked much with Judson, and from him heard of Pepito Fernandez, a grandson of the man who sold the land to Old Man Curtin.

Swinging down from his horse at the livery stable, he led him inside. Simpson walked over to meet him, his eyes searching Sabre's face. "Man, you've a nerve with you. Reed's wild. He came back to town blazing mad, and Trumbull's telling everybody what you can expect."

Matt smiled at the man. "I expected that. Where do you stand?"

"Well," Simpson said grimly, "I've no liking for Trumbull. He carries himself mighty big around town, and he's not been friendly to me and mine. I reckon, mister, I've rare been so pleased as when you made a fool of him in yonder. It was better than the killing of him, although he's that coming, sure enough."

"Then take care of my horse, will you? And a slip knot to tie him with."

"Sure, and he'll get corn, too. I reckon any horse you ride would need corn."

Matt Sabre walked out on the street. He was wearing dark jeans and a gray wool shirt. His black hat was pulled low, and he merged well with the shadows. He'd see Pepito first and then look around a bit. He wanted Camp Gordon.

Thinking of that, he turned back into the stable. "Saddle Gordon's horse, too. He'll be going back with me."

"Him?" Simpson stared. "Man, he's dead drunk and has been for days!"

"Saddle his horse. He'll be with me when I'm back, and if you know another one or two good hands who would use a gun if need be, let them know I'm hiring and there's money to pay them. Fighting wages if they want."

IN THE BACK OFFICE of the Yellowjacket, three men sat over Galusha Reed's desk. There was Reed himself, Sid Trumbull and Prince McCarran.

"Do you think Tony can take him?" Reed asked. "You've seen the man draw, Prince."

"He'll take him. But it will be close—too close. I

think what we'd better do is have Sid posted somewhere close by."

"Leave me out of it." Sid looked up from under
his thick eyebrows. "I want no more of the man. Let
Tony have him."

"You won't be in sight," McCarran said dryly, "or
in danger. You'll be upstairs over the hotel, with a
Winchester."

Trumbull looked up and touched his thick lips
with his tongue. Killing was not new to him, yet the
way this man accepted it always appalled him a little.

"All right," he agreed. "Like I say, I've no love
for him."

"We'll have him so you'll get a flanking shot.
Make it count and make it the first time. But wait
until the shooting starts."

The door opened softly, and Sikes stepped in. He
was a lithe, dark-skinned man who moved like an animal. He had graceful hands, restless hands. He wore
a white buckskin vest worked with red quills and
beads. "Boss, he's in town. Sabre's here." He had
heard them.

Reed let his chair legs down, leaning forward.
"**Here?** In town?"

"That's right. I just saw him outside the Yellowjacket." Sikes started to build a cigarette. "He's got
nerve. Plenty of it."

The door sounded with a light tap, and at a word,
Keys entered. He was a slight man with gray hair and
a quiet, scholar's face.

"I remember him now, Prince," he said. "Matt Sabre. I'd been trying to place the name. He was marshal of Mobeetie for a while. He's killed eight or nine men."

"That's right!" Trumbull looked up sharply. "Mobeetie! Why didn't I remember that? They say Wes Hardin rode out of town once when Sabre sent him word he wasn't wanted."

Sikes turned his eyes on McCarran. "You want him now?"

McCarran hesitated, studying the polished toe of his boot. Sabre's handling of Trumbull had made friends in town, and also his championing of the cause of Jenny Curtin. Whatever happened must be seemingly aboveboard and in the clear, and he wanted to be where he could be seen at the time, and Reed, also.

"No, not now. We'll wait." He smiled. "One thing about a man of his courage and background, if you send for him, he'll always come to you."

"But how will he come?" Keys asked softly. "That's the question."

McCarran looked around irritably. He had forgotten Keys was in the room and had said far more than he had intended. "Thanks, Keys. That will be all. And remember—nothing will be said about anything you've heard here."

"Certainly not." Keys smiled and walked to the door and out of the room.

Reed stared after him. "I don't like that fellow, Prince. I wouldn't trust him."

"Him? He's interested in nothing but that piano and enough liquor to keep himself mildly embalmed. Don't worry about him."

FUGITIVE

Matt Sabre turned away from the Yellowjacket after a brief survey of the saloon. Obviously, something was doing elsewhere for none of the men were present in the big room. He hesitated, considering the significance of that, and then turned down a dark alleyway and walked briskly along until he came to an old rail fence.

Following this past rustling cottonwoods and down a rutted road, he turned past a barn and cut across another road toward a 'dobe where the windows glowed with a faint light.

The door opened to his knock, and a dark, Indianlike face showed briefly. In rapid Spanish, he asked for Pepito. After a moment's hesitation, the door widened, and he was invited inside.

The room was large, and at one side, a small fire burned in the blackened fireplace. An oilcloth-covered table with a coal oil light stood in the middle of the room, and on a bed at one side, a man snored peacefully.

A couple of dark-eyed children ceased their playing to look up at him. The woman called out, and a blanket pushed aside, and a slender, dark-faced youth entered the room, pulling his belt tight.

"Pepito Fernandez? I am Matt Sabre."

"I have heard of you, señor."

Briefly, he explained why he had come, and Pepito listened, then shook his head. "I do not know, señor. The grant was long ago, and we are no longer rich. My father"—he shrugged—"he liked the spending of money when he was young."

He hesitated, considering that. Then he said carelessly, "I, too, like the spending of money. What else is it for? But no, señor, I do not think there are papers. My father, he told me much of the grant, and I am sure the Sonomas had no strong claim."

"If you remember anything, will you let us know?" Sabre asked. Then a thought occurred to him. "You're a **vaquero**? Do you want a job?"

"A job?" Pepito studied him thoughtfully. "At the Señora Curtin's ranch?"

"Yes. As you know, there may be much trouble. I am working there, and tonight I shall take one other man back with me. If you would like the job, it is yours."

Pepito shrugged. "Why not? Señor Curtin, the old one, he gave me my first horse. He gave me a rifle, too. He was a good one, and the son, also."

"Better meet me outside of town where the trail goes between the buttes. You know the place?"

"**Sí, señor.** I will be there."

Keys was idly playing the piano when Matt Sabre opened the door and stepped into the room. His quick eyes placed Keys, Hobbs at the bar, Camp Gordon fast asleep with his head on a table, and a half-dozen other men. Yet as he walked to the bar, a rear door opened, and Tony Sikes stepped into the room.

Sabre had never before seen the man, yet he knew him from Judson's apt and careful description. Sikes was not as tall as Sabre, yet more slender. He had the wiry, stringy build that is made for speed and quick, smooth-flowing fingers. His muscles were relaxed and easy, but knowing such men, Matt recognized danger when he saw it. Sikes had seen him at once, and he moved to the bar nearby.

All eyes were on the two of them, for the story of Matt's whipping of Trumbull and his defiance of Reed had swept the country. Yet Sikes merely smiled and Matt glanced at him. "Have a drink?"

Tony Sikes nodded. "I don't mind if I do." Then he added, his voice low, and his dark, yellowish eyes on Matt's with a faintly sardonic, faintly amused look, "I never mind drinking with a man I'm going to kill."

Sabre shrugged. "Neither do I." He found himself liking Sikes's direct approach. "Although perhaps I have the advantage. I choose my own time to drink and to kill. You wait for orders."

Tony Sikes felt in his vest pocket for cigarette papers and began to roll a smoke. "You will wait for me, **compadre.** I know you're the type."

They drank, and as they drank, the door opened, and Galusha Reed stepped out. His face darkened angrily when he saw the two standing at the bar together, but he was passing without speaking when a thought struck him. He stopped and turned.

"I wonder," he said loudly enough for all in the room to hear, "what Jenny Curtin will say when she finds out her new hand is the man who killed her husband?"

Every head came up, and Sabre's face whitened. Whereas the faces had been friendly or noncomittal, now they were sharp-eyed and attentive. Moreover, he knew that Jenny was well liked, as Curtin had been. Now they would be his enemies.

"I wonder just why you came here, Sabre? After killing the girl's husband, why would you come to her ranch? Was it to profit from your murder? To steal what little she has left? Or is it for the girl herself?"

Matt struggled to keep his temper. After a minute, he said casually, "Reed, it was you ordered her off her ranch. I'm here for one reason, and one alone. To see that she keeps her ranch and that no yellow-bellied thievin' lot of coyotes ride over and take it away from her!"

Reed stood flat-footed, facing Sabre. He was furious, and Matt could feel the force of his rage. It was almost a physical thing pushing against him. Close beside him was Sikes. If Reed chose to go for a gun, Sikes could grab Matt's left arm and jerk him off balance. Yet Matt was ready even for that, and again that black force was rising within him, that driving urge toward violence.

He spoke again, and his voice was soft and almost purring. "Make up your mind, Reed. If you want to die, you can right here. You make another remark to me and I'll drive every word of it back down that fat throat of yours! Reach and I'll kill you. If Sikes wants in on this, he's welcome!"

Tony Sikes spoke softly, too. "I'm out of it, Sabre. I only fight my own battles. When I come after you, I'll be alone."

Galusha Reed hesitated. For an instant, counting on Sikes, he had been tempted. Now he hesitated, then turned abruptly and left the room.

Ignoring Sikes, Sabre downed his drink and crossed to Camp Gordon. He shook him. "Come on, Camp. I'm puttin' you to bed."

Gordon did not move. Sabre stooped and slipped an arm around the big Englishman's shoulders and, hoisting him to his feet, started for the door. At the door, he turned. "I'll be seeing you, Sikes!"

Tony lifted his glass, his hat pushed back, "Sure," he said. "And I'll be alone."

It was not until after he had said it that he remembered Sid Trumbull and the plans made in the back room. His face darkened a little, and his liquor suddenly tasted bad. He put his glass down carefully on the bar and turned, walking through the back door.

Prince McCarran was alone, idly riffling the cards and smoking. "I won't do it, Prince," Sikes said. "You've got to leave that killing to me and me alone."

Matt Sabre, with Camp Gordon lashed to the saddle of a led horse, met Pepito in the darkness of the space between the buttes. Pepito spoke softly, and Sabre called back to him. As the Mexican rode out, he glanced once at Gordon, and then the three rode on together. It was late the following morning when they reached the Pivotrock. All was quiet—too quiet.

Camp Gordon was sober and swearing, "Shanghaied!" His voice exploded with violence. "You've a nerve, Sabre. Turn me loose so I can start back. I'm having no part of this."

Gordon was tied to his horse so he would not fall off, but Matt only grinned. "Sure, I'll turn you loose. But you said you ought to get out of town awhile, and this was the best way. I've brought you here," he said gravely, but his eyes were twinkling, "for your own good. It's time you had some fresh, mountain air, some cold milk, some—"

"Milk?" Gordon exploded. "Milk, you say? I'll not touch the stuff! Turn me loose and give me a gun and I'll have your hide!"

"And leave this ranch for Reed to take? Reed and McCarran?"

Gordon stared at him from bloodshot eyes, eyes

that were suddenly attentive. "Did you say McCarran? What's he got to do with this?"

"I wish I knew. But I've a hunch he's in up to his ears. I think he has strings on Reed."

Gordon considered that. "He may have." He watched Sabre undoing the knots. "It's a point I hadn't considered. But why?"

"You've known him longer than I have. Somebody had two men follow Curtin out of the country to kill him, and I don't believe Reed did it. Does that make sense?"

"No." Gordon swung stiffly to the ground. He swayed a bit, clinging to the stirrup leather. He glanced sheepishly at Matt. "I guess I'm a mess." A surprised look crossed his face. "Say, I'm hungry! I haven't been hungry in weeks."

With four hands besides himself, work went on swiftly. Yet Matt Sabre's mind would not rest. The five thousand dollars was a problem, and also there was the grant. Night after night, he led Pepito to talk of the memories of his father and grandfather, and little by little, he began to know the men. An idea was shaping in his mind, but as yet there was little on which to build.

In all this time, there was no sign of Reed. On two occasions, riders had been seen, apparently scouting. Cattle had been swept from the rim edge and pushed back, accounting for all or nearly all the strays he had seen on his ride to Yellowjacket.

Matt was restless, sure that when trouble came, it

would come with a rush. It was like Reed to do things that way. By now he was certainly aware that Camp Gordon and Pepito Fernandez had been added to the roster of hands at Pivotrock.

"Spotted a few head over near Baker Butte," Camp said one morning. "How'd it be if I drifted that way and looked them over?"

"We'll go together," Matt replied. "I've been wanting to look around there, and there's been no chance."

The morning was bright, and they rode swiftly, putting miles behind them, alert to all the sights and sounds of the high country above the rim. Careful as they were, they were no more than a hundred yards from the riders when they saw them. There were five men, and in the lead rode Sid Trumbull and a white-mustached stranger.

There was no possibility of escaping unnoticed. They pushed on toward the advancing riders, who drew up and waited. Sid Trumbull's face was sharp with triumph when he saw Sabre.

"Here's your man, marshal!" he said with satisfaction. "The one with the black hat is Sabre."

"What's this all about?" Matt asked quietly. He had already noticed the badge the man wore. But he noticed something else. The man looked to be a competent, upstanding officer.

"You're wanted in El Paso. I'm Rafe Collins, deputy United States marshal. We're making an inquiry into the killing of Bill Curtin."

Camp's lips tightened, and he looked sharply at Sabre. When Reed had brought out this fact in the saloon, Gordon had been dead drunk.

"That was a fair shooting, marshal. Curtin picked the fight and drew on me."

"You expect us to believe that?" Trumbull was contemptuous. "Why, he hadn't the courage of a mouse! He backed down from Sikes only a few days before. He wouldn't draw on any man with two hands!"

"He drew on me." Matt Sabre realized he was fighting two battles here—one to keep from being arrested, the other to keep Gordon's respect and assistance. "My idea is that he only backed out of a fight with Sikes because he had a job to do and knew Sikes would kill him."

"That's a likely yarn!" Trumbull nodded to him. "There's your man. It's your job, marshal."

Collins was obviously irritated. That he entertained no great liking for Trumbull was obvious. Yet he had his duty to do. Before he could speak, Sabre spoke.

"Marshal, I've reason to believe that some influence has been brought to bear to discredit me and to get me out of the country for a while. Can't I give you my word that I'll report to El Paso when things are straightened out? My word is good, and that there are many in El Paso who know that."

"Sorry." Collins was regretful. "I've my duty and my orders."

"I understand that," Sabre replied. "I also have my duty. It is to see that Jenny Curtin is protected from those who are trying to force her off her range. I intend to do exactly that."

"Your duty?" Collins eyed him coldly but curiously. "After killing her husband?"

"That's reason enough, sir!" Sabre replied flatly. "The fight was not my choice. Curtin pushed it, and he was excited, worried, and overwrought. Yet he asked me on his deathbed to deliver a package to his wife and to see that she was protected. That duty, sir"—his eyes met those of Collins—"comes first."

"I'd like to respect that," Collins admitted. "You seem like a gentleman, sir, and it's a quality that's too rare. Unfortunately, I have my orders. However, it should not take long to straighten this out if it was a fair shooting."

"All these rats need," Sabre replied, "is a few days!" He knew there was no use arguing. His horse was fast, and dense pines bordered the road. He needed a minute, and that badly.

As if divining his thought, Camp Gordon suddenly pushed his gray between Matt and the marshal, and almost at once Matt lashed out with his toe and booted Trumbull's horse in the ribs. The bronc went to bucking furiously. Whipping his horse around, Matt slapped the spurs to his ribs, and in two startled jumps he was off and deep into the pines, running like a startled deer.

Behind him a shot rang out, and then another. Both cut the brush over his head, but the horse was running now, and he was mounted well. He had started into the trees at right angles but swung his horse immediately and headed back toward the Pivotrock. Corduroy Wash opened off to his left, and he turned the black and pushed rapidly into the mouth of the wash.

Following it for almost a mile, he came out and paused briefly in the clump of trees that crowned a small ridge. He stared back.

A string of riders stretched out on his back trail, but they were scattered out, hunting for tracks. A lone horseman sat not far from them, obviously watching. Matt grinned; that would be Gordon, and he was all right.

Turning his horse, Matt followed a shelf of rock until it ran out, rode off it into thick sand, and then into the pines with their soft bed of needles that left almost no tracks.

Cinch Hook Butte was off to his left, and nearer, on his right, Twenty-Nine-Mile Butte. Keeping his horse headed between them, but bearing steadily northwest, he headed for the broken country around Horsetank Wash. Descending into the canyon, he rode northwest, then circled back south and entered the even deeper Calfpen Canyon.

Here, in a nest of boulders, he staked out his horse on a patch of grass. Rifle across his knees, he rested.

After an hour, he worked his way to the ledge at the top of the canyon, but nowhere could he see any sign of pursuit. Nor could he hear the sound of hoofs.

There was water in the bottom of Calfpen, not far from where he had left his horse. Food was something else again. He shucked a handful of chia seeds and ate a handful of them, along with the nuts of a piñon.

Obviously, the attempted arrest had been brought about by the influence of either Galusha Reed or Prince McCarran. In either case, he was now a fugitive. If they went on to the ranch, Rafe Collins would have a chance to talk to Jenny Curtin. Matt felt sick when he thought of the marshal telling her that it was he who had killed her husband. That she must find out sooner or later, he knew, but he wanted to tell her himself, in his own good time.

BUSHWHACK BAIT

When dusk had fallen, he mounted the black and worked his way down Calfpen toward Fossil Springs. As he rode, he was considering his best course. Whether taken by Collins or not, he was not now at the ranch and they might choose this time to strike. With some reason, they might believe he had left the country. Indeed, there was every chance that Reed actually believed he had come there with some plan of his own to get the Curtin ranch.

Finally, he bedded down for the night in a draw above Fossil Springs and slept soundly until daylight brought a sun that crept over the rocks and shone upon his eyes. He was up, made a light breakfast of coffee and jerked beef, and then saddled up.

Wherever he went now, he could expect hostility. Doubt or downright suspicion would have developed as a result of Reed's accusation in Yellowjacket, and the country would know the U.S. marshal was looking for him.

Debating his best course, Matt Sabre headed west through the mountains. By nightfall the following day, he was camped in the ominous shadow of Turret Butte where only a few years before, Major Randall had ascended the peak in darkness to surprise a camp of Apaches.

Awakening at the break of dawn, Matt scouted the vicinity of Yellowjacket with care.

There was some movement in town—more than usual at that hour. He observed a long line of saddled horses at the hitch rails. He puzzled over this, studying it narrow-eyed from the crest of a ridge through his glasses. Marshal Collins could not yet have returned, hence this must be some other movement. That it was organized was obvious.

He was still watching when a man wearing a faded red shirt left the back door of a building near the saloon, went to a horse carefully hidden in the rear, and mounted. At this distance, there was no way of seeing who he was. The man rode strangely. Studying him through the glasses—a relic of Sabre's military years—Matt suddenly realized why the rider seemed strange. He was riding eastern fashion!

This was no westerner, slouched and lazy in the saddle, nor yet sitting upright as a cavalryman might. This man rode forward on his horse, a poor practice for the hard miles of desert or mountain riding. Yet it was his surreptitious manner rather than his riding style that intrigued Matt. It required but a few minutes for Matt to see that the route the rider was taking away from town would bring him by near the base of the promontory where he watched.

Reluctant as he was to give over watching the saddled horses, Sabre was sure this strange rider held some clue to his problems. Sliding back on his belly well into the brush, Matt got to his feet and descended the steep trail and took up his place among the boulders beside the trail.

It was very hot there out of the breeze, yet he had waited only a minute until he heard the sound of the approaching horse. He cleared his gun from its holster and moved to the very edge of the road. Then the rider appeared. It was Keys.

Matt's gun stopped him. "Where you ridin', Keys?" Matt asked quietly. "What's this all about?"

"I'm riding to intercept the marshal," Keys said sincerely. "McCarran and Reed plan to send out a posse of their own men to hunt you; then, under cover of capturing you, they intend to take the Pivotrock and hold it."

Sabre nodded. That would be it, of course, and he should have guessed it before. "What about the marshal? They'll run into him on the trail."

"No, they're going to swing south of his trail. They know how he's riding because Reed is guiding him."

"What's your stake in this? Why ride all the way out there to tell the marshal?"

"It's because of Jenny Curtin," he said frankly. "She's a fine girl, and Bill was a good boy. Both of them treated me fine, as their father did before them. It's little enough to do, and I know too much about the plotting of that devil McCarran."

"Then it is McCarran. Where does Reed stand in this?"

"He's stupid!" Keys said contemptuously. "Mc-Carran is using him, and he hasn't the wit to see it. He believes they are partners, but Prince will get rid of him like he does anyone who gets in his way. He'll be rid of Trumbull, too."

"And Sikes?"

"Perhaps. Sikes is a good tool, to a point."

Matt Sabre shoved his hat back on his head. "Keys," he said suddenly, "I want you to have a little faith in me. Believe me, I'm doing what I can to help Jenny Curtin. I did kill her husband, but he was a total stranger who was edgy and started a fight.

"I'd no way of knowing who or what he was, and the gun of a stranger kills as easy as the gun of a known man. But he trusted me. He asked me to come here, to bring his wife five thousand and to help her."

"Five thousand?" Keys stared. "Where did he get that amount of money?"

"I'd like to know," Sabre admitted. Another idea occurred to him. "Keys, you know more about what's going on in this town than anyone else. What do you know about the Sonoma Grant?"

Keys hesitated, then said slowly: "Sabre, I know very little about that. I think the only one who has the true facts is Prince McCarran. I think he gathered all the available papers on both grants and is sure that no matter what his claim, the grant cannot be substantiated. Nobody knows but McCarran."

"Then I'll go to McCarran," Sabre replied harshly. "I'm going to straighten this out if it's the last thing I do."

"You go to McCarran and it will be the last thing you do. The man's deadly. He's smooth-talking and treacherous. And then there's Sikes."

"Yes," Sabre admitted. "There's Sikes."

He studied the situation, then looked up. "Look, don't you bother the marshal. Leave him to me. Every man he's got with him is an enemy to Jenny Curtin, and they would never let you talk. You circle them and ride on to Pivotrock. You tell Camp Gordon what's happening. Tell him of this outfit that's saddled up. I'll do my job here, and then I'll start back."

Long after Keys had departed, Sabre watched. Evidently, the posse was awaiting some word from Reed. Would McCarran ride with them? He was too careful. He would wait in Yellowjacket. He would be, as always, an innocent bystander. . . .

Keys, riding up the trail some miles distant, drew up suddenly. He had forgotten to tell Sabre of Prince McCarran's plan to have Sid Trumbull cut him down when he tangled with Sikes. For a long moment, Keys sat his horse, staring worriedly and scowling. To go back now would lose time; moreover, there was small chance that Sabre would be there. Matt Sabre would have to take his own chances.

Regretfully, Keys pushed on into the rough country ahead. . . .

Tony Sikes found McCarran seated in the back room at the saloon. McCarran glanced up quickly as he came in, and then nodded.

"Glad to see you, Sikes. I want you close by. I think we'll have visitors today or tomorrow."

"Visitors?" Sikes searched McCarran's face.

"A visitor, I should say. I think we'll see Matt Sabre."

Tony Sikes considered that, turning it over in his mind. Yes, Prince was right. Sabre would not surrender. It would be like him to head for town, hunting Reed. Aside from three or four men, nobody knew of McCarran's connection with the Pivotrock affair. Reed or Trumbull was fronting for him.

Trumbull, Reed, Sikes, and Keys. Keys was a shrewd man. He might be a drunk and a piano player, but he had a head on his shoulders.

Sikes's mind leaped suddenly. Keys was not around. This was the first time in weeks that he had not encountered Keys in the bar.

Keys was gone.

Where would he go—to warn Jenny Curtin of the posse? So what? He had nothing against Jenny Curtin. He was a man who fought for hire. Maybe he was on the wrong side in this. Even as he thought of that, he remembered Matt Sabre. The man was sharp as a steel blade—trim, fast. Now that it had been recalled to his mind, he remembered all that he had heard of him as marshal of Mobeetie.

There was in Tony Sikes a drive that forbade him to admit any man was his fighting superior. Sabre's draw against Trumbull was still the talk of the town—talk that irked Sikes, for folks were beginning to compare the two of them. Many thought Sabre might be faster. That rankled.

He would meet Sabre first and then drift.

"Don't you think he'll get here?" McCarran asked, looking up at Tony.

Sikes nodded. "He'll get here, all right. He thinks too fast for Trumbull or Reed. Even for that marshal."

Sikes would have Sabre to himself. Sid Trumbull was out of town. Tony Sikes wanted to do his own killing.

* * *

MATT SABRE WATCHED the saddled horses. He had that quality of patience so long associated with the Indian. He knew how to wait and how to relax. He waited now, letting all his muscles rest. With all his old alertness for danger—his sixth sense that warned him of climaxes—he knew this situation had reached the explosion point.

The marshal would be returning. Reed and Trumbull would be sure that he did not encounter the posse. And that body of riders, most of whom were henchmen or cronies of Galusha Reed, would sweep down on the Pivotrock and capture it, killing all who were there under the pretense of searching for Matt Sabre.

Keys would warn them, and in time. Once they knew of the danger, Camp Gordon and the others would be wise enough to take the necessary precautions. The marshal was one tentacle, but there in Yellowjacket was the heart of the trouble.

If Prince McCarran and Tony Sikes were removed, the tentacles would shrivel and die. Despite the danger out at Pivotrock, high behind the Mogollon Rim, the decisive blow must be struck right here in Yellowjacket.

He rolled over on his stomach and lifted the glasses. Men were coming from the Yellowjacket Saloon and mounting up. Lying at his ease, he watched them go. There were at least thirty, possibly more. When they had gone, he got to his feet and brushed off his clothes. Then he walked slowly down to his horse and mounted.

He rode quietly, one hand lying on his thigh, his eyes alert, his brain relaxed and ready for impressions.

Marshal Rafe Collins was a just man. He was a frontiersman, a man who knew the West and the men it bred. He was no fool—shrewd and careful, rigid in his enforcement of the law, yet wise in the ways of men. Moreover, he was southern in the oldest of southern traditions, and being so, he understood what Matt Sabre meant when he said it was because he had killed her husband that he must protect Jenny Curtin.

Matt Sabre left his horse at the livery stable. Simpson looked up sharply when he saw him.

"You better watch yourself," he warned. "The whole country's after you, an' they are huntin' blood!"

"I know. What about Sikes? Is he in town?"

"Sure! He never leaves McCarran." Simpson searched his face. "Sikes is no man to tangle with, Sabre. He's chain lightnin'."

"I know." Sabre watched his horse led into a shadowed stall. Then he turned to Simpson. "You've been friendly, Simpson. I like that. After today, there's goin' to be a new order of things around here, but today I could use some help. What do you know about the Pivotrock deal?"

The man hesitated, chewing slowly. Finally, he

spat and looked up. "There was nobody to tell until now," he said, "but two things I know. That grant was Curtin's, all right, an' he wasn't killed by accident. He was murdered."

"Murdered?"

"Yeah." Simpson's expression was wry. "Like you he liked fancy drinkin' liquor when he could get it. McCarran was right friendly. He asked Curtin to have a drink with him that day, an' Curtin did.

"On'y a few minutes after that, he came in here an' got a team to drive back, leavin' his horse in here because it had gone lame. I watched him climb into that rig, an' he missed the step an' almost fell on his face. Then he finally managed to climb in."

"Drunk?" Sabre's eyes were alert and interested.

"Him?" Simpson snorted. "That old coot could stow away more liquor than a turkey could corn. He had only **one** drink, yet he could hardly walk."

"Doped, then?" Sabre nodded. That sounded like McCarran. "And then what?"

"When the team was brought back after they ran away with him, an' after Curtin was found dead, I found a bullet graze on the hip of one of those broncs."

So that was how it had been. A doped man, a skittish team of horses, and a bullet to burn the horse just enough to start it running. Prince McCarran was a thorough man.

"You said you knew that Curtin really owned that grant. How?"

Simpson shrugged. "Because he had that other claim investigated. He must have heard rumors of trouble. There'd been no talk of it that I heard, an' here a man hears everythin'!

"Anyway, he had all the papers with him when he started back to the ranch that day. He showed 'em to me earlier. All the proof."

"And he was murdered that day? Who found the body?"

"Sid Trumbull. He was ridin' that way, sort of accidental-like."

The proof Jenny needed was in the hands of Prince McCarran. By all means, he must call on Prince.

"Stand Up—and Die!"

Matt Sabre walked to the door and stood there, waiting a moment in the shadow before emerging into the sunlight.

The street was dusty and curiously empty. The rough-fronted gray buildings of unpainted lumber or sand-colored adobe faced him blankly from across and up the street. The hitch rail was deserted; the water trough overflowed a little, making a darkening stain under one end.

Somewhere up the street but behind the buildings, a hen began proclaiming her egg to the hemispheres. A single white cloud hung lazily in the blue sky. Matt stepped out. Hitching his gun belts a little, he looked up the street.

Sikes would be in the Yellowjacket. To see McCarran, he must see Sikes first. That was the way he wanted it. One thing at a time.

He was curiously quiet. He thought of other times when he had faced such situations—of Mobeetie, of that first day out on the plains hunting buffalo, of the first time he had killed a man, of a charge the Riffs made on a small desert patrol out of Taudeni long ago.

A faint breeze stirred an old sack that lay near the boardwalk, and farther up the street, near the water trough, a long gray rat slipped out from under a store and headed toward the drip of water from the trough. Matt Sabre started to walk, moving up the street.

It was not far, as distance goes, but there is no walk as long as the gunman's walk, no pause as long as the pause before gunfire. On this day, Sikes would know, instantly, what his presence here presaged. McCarran would know, too.

Prince McCarran was not a gambler. He would scarcely trust all to Tony Sikes no matter how confident he might be. It always paid to have something to back up a facing card. Trust Prince to keep his hole card well covered. But on this occasion, he would not be bluffing. He would have a hole card, but where? How? What? And when?

The last was not hard. When—the moment of the gun battle.

He had walked no more than thirty yards when a door creaked and a man stepped into the street. He did not look down toward Sabre but walked briskly to the center of the street, then faced about sharply like a man on a parade ground.

Tony Sikes.

He wore this day a faded blue shirt that stretched tight over his broad, bony shoulders and fell slack in front where his chest was hollow and his stomach flat. It was too far yet to see his eyes, but Matt Sabre knew what they looked like.

The thin, angular face, the mustache, the high cheekbones, and the long, restless fingers. The man's hips were narrow, and there was little enough to his body. Tony Sikes lifted his eyes and stared down the street. His lips were dry, but he felt ready. There was a curious lightness within him, but he liked it so, and he liked the setup. At that moment, he felt almost an affection for Sabre.

The man knew so well the rules of the game. He was coming as he should come, and there was something about him—an edged quality, a poised and alert strength.

No sound penetrated the clear globe of stillness. The warm air hung still, with even the wind poised, arrested by the drama in the street. Matt Sabre felt a slow trickle of sweat start from under his hatband. He walked carefully, putting each foot down with care and distinction of purpose. It was Tony Sikes who stopped first, some sixty yards away.

"Well, Matt, here it is. We both knew it was coming."

"Sure." Matt paused, too, feet wide apart, hands swinging wide. "You tied up with the wrong outfit, Sikes."

"We'd have met, anyway." Sikes looked along the street at the tall man standing there, looked and saw his bronzed face, hard and ready. It was not in Sikes to feel fear of a man with guns. Yet this was how he would die. It was in the cards. He smiled suddenly. Yes, he would die by the gun—but not now.

His hands stirred, and as if their movement was a signal to his muscles, they flashed in a draw. Before him, the dark, tall figure flashed suddenly. It was no more than that, a blur of movement and a lifted gun, a movement suddenly stilled, and the black sullen muzzle of a six-gun that steadied on him even as he cleared his gun from his open top holster.

He had been beaten—**beaten to the draw.**

The shock of it triggered Sikes's gun, and he knew even as the gun bucked in his hand that he had missed, and then suddenly, Matt Sabre was running! Running toward him, gun lifted, but not firing!

In a panic, Sikes saw the distance closing and he fired as fast as he could pull the trigger, three times in a thundering cascade of sound. And even as the hammer fell for the fourth shot, he heard another gun bellow.

But where? There had been no stab of flame from Sabre's gun. Sabre was running, a rapidly moving target, and Sikes had fired too fast, upset by the sudden rush, by the panic of realizing he had been beaten to the draw.

He lifted his right-hand gun, dropped the muzzle in a careful arc, and saw Sabre's skull over the barrel. Then Sabre skidded to a halt, and his gun hammered bullets.

Flame leaped from the muzzle, stabbing at Sikes, burning him along the side, making his body twitch and the bullet go wild. He switched guns, and then something slugged him in the wind, and the next he knew, he was on the ground.

Matt Sabre had heard that strange shot, but that was another thing. He could not wait now; he could not turn his attention. He saw Sikes go down, but only to his knees, and the gunman had five bullets and the range now was only fifteen yards.

Sikes's gun swung up, and Matt fired again. Sikes lunged to his feet, and then his features writhed with agony and breathlessness, and he went down, hard to the ground, twisting in the dust.

Then another bullet bellowed, and a shot kicked up dust at his feet. Matt swung his gun and blasted at an open window, then started for the saloon door. He stopped, hearing a loud cry behind him.

"**Matt!** Sabre?"

It was Sikes, his eyes flared wide. Sabre hesitated, glanced swiftly around, then dropped to his knees in the silent street.

"What is it, Tony? Anything I can do for you?"

"Behind—behind—the desk—you—you—" His faltering voice faded; then strength seemed to flood back, and he looked up. "Good man! Too—too fast!"

And then he was dead, gone just like that, and Matt Sabre was striding into the Yellowjacket.

The upstairs room was empty; the stairs were empty; there was no one in sight. Only Hobbs stood behind the bar when he came down. Hobbs, his face set and pale.

Sabre looked at him, eyes steady and cold. "Who came down those stairs?"

Hobbs licked his lips. He choked, then whispered hoarsely. "Nobody—but there's—there's a back stairs."

Sabre wheeled and walked back in quick strides, thumbing shells into his gun. The office door was open, and Prince McCarran looked up as he framed himself in the door.

He was writing, and the desk was rumpled with papers, the desk of a busy man. Nearby was a bottle and a full glass.

McCarran lay down his pen. "So? You beat him? I thought you might."

"Did you?" Sabre's gaze was cold. If this man had been running, as he must have run, he gave no evidence of it now. "You should hire them faster, Prince."

"Well"—McCarran shrugged—"he was fast enough until now. But this wasn't my job, anyway. He was workin' for Reed."

Sabre took a step inside the door, away from the wall, keeping his hands free. His eyes were on those of Prince McCarran, and Prince watched him, alert, interested.

"That won't ride with me," Matt said. "Reed's a stooge, a perfect stooge. He'll be lucky if he comes back alive from this trip. A lot of that posse you sent out won't come back, either."

McCarran's eyelids tightened at the mention of the posse. "Forget it." He waved his hand. "Sit down and have a drink. After all, we're not fools, Sabre. We're grown men, and we can talk. I never liked killing, anyway."

"Unless you do it or have it done." Sabre's hands remained where they were. "What's the matter, Prince? Yellow? Afraid to do your own killin'?"

McCarran's face was still, and his eyes were wide now. "You shouldn't have said that. You shouldn't have called me yellow."

"Then get on your feet. I hate to shoot a sittin' man."

"Have a drink and let's talk."

"Sure." Sabre was elaborately casual. "You have one, too." He reached his hand for the glass that had already been poured, but McCarran's eyes were steady. Sabre switched his hand and grasped the other glass, and then, like a striking snake, Prince McCarran grasped his right hand and jerked him forward, off balance.

At the same time, McCarran's left flashed back to

the holster high on his left side, butt forward, and the gun jerked up and free. Matt Sabre, instead of trying to jerk his right hand free, let his weight go forward, following and hurling himself against McCarran. The chair went over with a crash, and Prince tried to straighten, but Matt was riding him back. He crashed into the wall, and Sabre broke free.

Prince swung his gun up, and Sabre's left palm slapped down, knocking the gun aside and gripping the hand across the thumb. His right hand came up under the gun barrel, twisting it back over and out of McCarran's hands. Then he shoved him back and dropped the gun, slapping him across the mouth with his open palm.

It was a free swing, and it cracked like a pistol shot. McCarran's face went white from the blow, and he rushed, swinging, but Sabre brought up his knee in the charging man's groin. Then he smashed him in the face with his elbow, pushing him over and back. McCarran dove past him, blood streaming from his crushed nose, and grabbed wildly at the papers. His hand came up with a bulldog .41.

Matt saw the hand shoot for the papers, and even as the .41 appeared, his own gun was lifting. He fired first, three times, at a range of four feet.

Prince McCarran stiffened, lifted to his tiptoes, then plunged over on his face and lay still among the litter of papers and broken glass.

Sabre swayed drunkenly. He recalled what Sikes had said about the desk. He caught the edge and jerked it aside, swinging the desk away from the wall. Behind it was a small panel with a knob. It was locked, but a bullet smashed the lock. He jerked it open. A thick wad of bills, a small sack of gold coins, a sheaf of papers.

A glance sufficed. These were the papers Simpson had mentioned. The thick parchment of the original grant, the information on the conflicting Sonoma grant, and then . . . He glanced swiftly through them, then, at a pound of horses' hoofs, he stuffed them inside his shirt. He stopped, stared. His shirt was soaked with blood.

Fumbling, he got the papers into his pocket, then stared down at himself. Sikes had hit him. Funny, he had never felt it. Only a shock, a numbness. Now Reed was coming back.

Catching up a sawed-off express shotgun, he started for the door, weaving like a drunken man. He never even got to the door.

THE SOUND OF GALLOPING HORSES was all he could hear—galloping horses, and then a faint smell of something that reminded him of a time he had been wounded in North Africa. His eyes flickered open, and the first thing he saw was a room's wall with the picture of a man with muttonchop whiskers and spectacles.

He turned his head and saw Jenny Curtin watching him. "So? You've decided to wake up. You're getting lazy, Matt. Mr. Sabre. On the ranch you always were the first one up."

He stared at her. She had never looked half so charming, and that was bad. It was bad because it was time to be out of here and on a horse.

"How long have I been here?"

"Only about a day and a half. You lost a lot of blood."

"What happened at the ranch? Did Keys get there in time?"

"Yes, and I stayed. The others left right away."

"You **stayed**?"

"The others," she said quietly, "went down the road about two miles. There was Camp Gordon, Tom Judson, Pepito, and Keys. And Rado, of course. They went down the road while I stood out in the ranch yard and let them see me. The boys ambushed them."

"Was it much of a fight?"

"None at all. The surprise was so great that they broke and ran. Only three weren't able, and four were badly wounded."

"You found the papers? Including the one about McCarran sending the five thousand in marked bills to El Paso?"

"Yes," she said simply. "We found that. He planned on having Billy arrested and charged with theft. He planned that, and then if he got killed, so much the better. It was only you he didn't count on."

"No." Matt Sabre stared at his hands, strangely white now. "He didn't count on me."

So it was all over now. She had her ranch, she was a free woman, and people would leave her alone. There was only one thing left. He had to tell her. To tell her that he was the one who had killed her husband.

He turned his head on the pillow. "One thing more," he began. "I—"

"Not now. You need rest."

"Wait. I have to tell you this. It's about—about Billy."

"You mean that you—you were the one who—?"

"Yes, I—" He hesitated, reluctant at last to say it.

"I know. I know you did, Matt. I've known from the beginning, even without all the things you said."

"I talked when I was delirious?"

"A little. But I knew, Matt. Call it intuition, anything you like, but I knew. You see, you told me how his eyes were when he was drawing his gun. Who could have known that but the man who shot him?"

"I see." His face was white. "Then I'd better rest. I've got some traveling to do."

She was standing beside him. "Traveling? Do you have to go on, Matt? From all you said last night, I thought—I thought"—her face flushed—"maybe you—didn't want to travel any more. Stay with us, Matt, if you want to. We would like to have you, and Billy's been asking for you. He wants to know where his spurs are."

After a while, he admitted carefully, "Well, I guess I should stay and see that he gets them. A fellow should always make good on his promises to kids, I reckon."

"You'll stay then? You won't leave?"

Matt stared up at her. "I reckon," he said quietly, "I'll never leave unless you send me away."

She smiled and touched his hair. "Then you'll be here a long time, Mathurin Sabre—a very long time."

No Trouble for the Cactus Kid

Even the coyotes who prowled along the banks of the Rio Salado knew the Cactus Kid was in love. What else would cause him to sing to the moon so that even the coyotes were jealous?

The Cactus Kid was in love, and he was on his way to Aragon to buy his girl some calico, enough red and white calico to make a dress.

It was seventy miles to Aragon, and the dance was on Friday. This being Monday, he figured he had plenty of time.

Red and white calico for a girl with midnight in her hair and lovelight in her eyes. Although, reflected the Cactus Kid, there were times when that lovelight flickered into anger, as he had cause to know. She had made up her mind that he was the only man for her, and he agreed and was pleased at the knowledge, yet her anger could be uncomfortable, and the Cactus Kid liked his comfort.

The paint pony switched his tail agreeably as he cantered down the trail, the Kid lolling in the saddle. Only a little ride to Aragon, then back with the calico. It would take Bonita only a little while to make a dress, a dress that would be like a dream once she put it on.

Love, the Cactus Kid decided, was a good thing for him. Until he rode up to Coyote Springs and met Bonita, he had been homeless as a poker chip and ornery as a maverick mule.

Now look at him! He was riding for Bosque Bill Ryan's Four Staff outfit, and hadn't had a drink in two months!

Drinking, however, had never been one of his pet vices. By and large he had one vice, a knack for getting into trouble. Not that he went looking for trouble; it was simply that it had a way of happening where he was.

The Cactus Kid was five feet seven in his socks, and weighed an even one hundred and fifty pounds. His hair was sandy and his eyes were green, and while not a large man it was generally agreed by the survivors that he could hit like a man fifty pounds heavier. His fighting skill had been acquired by diligent application of the art.

On this ride he anticipated no trouble. Aragon was a peaceful town. Had it been Trechado, now, or even Deer Creek . . . but they were far away and long ago, and neither town had heard the rattling of his spurs since he met Bonita . . . nor would they.

It was spring. The sun was bright and just pleasantly warm. The birds were out, and even the rabbits seemed rather to wait and watch than run. His plan was to stop the night at Red Bluff Stage Station. Scotty Ellis, his friend, was majordomo at the station now, caring for the horses and changing teams when the stages arrived. It had been a month since he had visited with Scotty, and the old man was always pleased to have visitors.

The Cactus Kid was happy with the morning and pleased with his life. He was happy that Bosque Bill had let him have a week off to do as he pleased, work being slack at the moment. Next month it would be going full blast, and every hand working sixteen hours a day or more.

The Cactus Kid didn't mind work. He was, as Bosque Bill said, a "hand." He could ride anything that wore hair and used his eighty-foot California riata with masterly skill. He enjoyed doing things he did well, and he had found few things he couldn't do well.

The saw-toothed ridge of the Tularosa mountains combed the sky for clouds, and Spot, the sorrel-and-white paint, bobbed his head and cocked an ear at the Cactus Kid's singing. The miles fell easily behind and the Kid let the paint make his own pace.

They dropped into a deep canyon following a winding trail. At the bottom the two-foot-wide Agua Fria babbled along over the gravel. The Kid dropped from the saddle and let Spot take his own time in drinking. Then he lowered himself to his chest and drank. He was just getting up when the creek spat sand in his face, and the report of a rifle echoed down the canyon walls.

The Cactus Kid hit his feet running, and dove to shelter behind a boulder just as a bullet knocked chips from it.

Spot, in his three years of carrying the Kid, had become accustomed to the sounds of battle and rifle shots, and in two quick bounds was himself among the rocks and trees and out of sight.

The Kid had hit the dirt behind his boulder with his Colt in his fist. His hat off, he peered from alongside the rock to see who and why. A glance was enough to tell him his Colt wasn't going to be much help, so rolling over, he got into the rocks and scrambled back to the paint. Holstering the Colt, he slid his Winchester from its scabbard. Then he waited.

His position wasn't bad. It could be no more than an hour's ride to Red Bluff Station, and he had until Friday to return with the material. Well, until Thursday, anyway. How long did it take to make a dress?

No more shots were fired, but he waited. At first he was calm, then irritated. After all, if the dry-gulcher wanted a fight why didn't he get on with it?

No shots, no sounds. The Cactus Kid removed his hat again and eased it around the boulder on a stick. Nothing happened.

The Cactus Kid, rifle ready, stepped from behind his rocks. There was no shot, nothing but the chuckling of the stream over the gravel. Disgusted, he swung into the saddle and turned his horse upstream. In a few minutes he glimpsed a boot heel.

Rifle ready, he circled warily. It was not until he drew up beside him that he saw the man was dead. He was lying flat on his face and had been shot at least twice through the head and twice through the body. Kneeling beside him, the Cactus Kid studied the situation.

One shot, which wounded the dead man, had been fired sometime before. The wounded man had crawled here, seeking shelter. He had been followed and shot at least twice more while lying on the ground.

Whoever had done the killing had intended it to be just that, a killing. This was not merely a robbery.

The dead man's pockets were turned inside out, and an empty wallet lay on the ground. Empty of money, that is. There were several papers in the wallet, a couple of faded letters and a deed. A sweat stain ran diagonally across the papers.

Pocketing them, the Cactus Kid looked around thoughtfully. Seeing some bloodstains, he followed the track left by the wounded man back to the main trail. Here the story became simple.

The man had been riding along the trail toward the canyon when shot. He had fallen from his horse into the dust, had gotten to his feet, and had fired at his killer. Two empty cartridge cases lay on the ground.

Evidently the wounded man had ejected the two empty shells and reloaded, and then had been hit again and had tried to crawl to a hiding place or a better place from which to fight.

Scouting around and checking obvious ambush sites, the Kid found where the killer had waited, smoking a dozen or more cigarettes. There were marks in the dust where a saddle had rested.

A saddle, and no horse? Scouting still more, he found the horse. It was a rangy buckskin, and from the looks of it the horse had been literally run to death. Its hair was streaked with dried sweat and foam.

"Whoever he was," the Kid said aloud, "he was goin' someplace in a hurry, or gettin' away from something. He killed his horse, then holed up here until a rider came along, dry-gulched him, robbed the body, and rode off on his horse."

Returning, the Kid rolled the dead man's body over a small sandbank, then caved the sand over him and added rocks and brush.

Whoever had fired at him had been the killer, and he could not be far ahead. The hour was now getting close to sunset, and if the Kid wanted to join Scotty Ellis at supper he had best hurry.

The sun was over the horizon when he loped his horse down to the Red Bluff Station. Scotty came to the door shading his eyes against the last glare of sunlight.

"Kid! Sakes alive, Kid! I ain't seen you in a coon's

age! Some cowhand from over at the Four Star told me you was fixin' to get yourself hitched up."

"Got it in mind, Scotty. A man can't run maverick all his life." He led his horse to the corral and stripped the gear from his back, glancing around as he did so. No strange horses in the corral, no recent tracks except for the stage, a few hours back.

He followed Scotty into the station, listening with only half his attention to the old man's talk. It was the chatter of a man much alone, trying to get it all said in minutes.

As he dished up supper the Kid asked, "Any riders come through this afternoon?"

"Riders? Yep, two, three of them went by. One big feller headin' toward Coyote Springs, and a couple more pointin' toward Aragon."

"Two? Riding together?"

"Nope. They wasn't together. A big feller on a blood bay come through, and a few minutes later another feller, almost as big, ridin' a grulla mustang. Neither of them stopped. Folks are getting' so they don't even stop to pass the time o' day!"

Two men? He had seen only one, but if they arrived at about the same time then the other rider must have been within the sound of the rifle when the killer had fired at the Kid.

At daybreak he rolled out of his blankets, fed and watered his horse, then washed and dried his hands and face at the washbowl outside the door.

"Scotty," he asked, over his second cup of coffee, "did you get a good look at either of those riders?"

"Wal, don't recollect I did. Both big fellers. Feller on the bay hoss had him one of those ol' Mother Hubbard saddles."

Riding out for Aragon, the Kid reflected that none of it was his business. The thing to do was report what he'd found to the sheriff or his deputy in Aragon, then buy his calico and head for home.

He smiled at himself. A few weeks back, before he met Bonita, he would have been so sore at that gent who fired at him that he'd not have quit until he found him. Now he was older and wiser.

Aragon was a one-street town with a row of false-fronted buildings on one side, on the other a series of corrals. The buildings consisted of a general store, two saloons, a jail with the deputy sheriff's office in front, a boarded up Land Office and two stores.

As he rode along the street his eyes took in the horses at the hitching rail. One of them was a blood bay with a Hubbard saddle, the other a grulla. The horse with the Mother Hubbard saddle had a Henry rifle in the boot. The grulla's saddle scabbard carried an old Volcanic.

The deputy was not in his office. A cowhand sitting on the top rail of the corral called over that the deputy had ridden over to Horse Mesa. The Cactus Kid walked back along the street and entered the busiest saloon. One drink and he would be on his way. Picking up the calico would require but a few minutes.

Several men were loitering at the bar. One was a lean, wiry man with bowed legs, and a dry, saturnine expression. He glanced at the Cactus Kid and then looked away. There was another man, standing near him but obviously not with him, who was a large, bulky man with bulging blue eyes which stared at the Kid like a couple of aimed rifles.

Of course, even the Cactus Kid would have admitted that he was something to look at when not in his working clothes. He was, he cheerfully confessed, a dude. His sombrero was pure white, with a colored horsehair band. His shirt was forest green, and over it he wore a beautifully tanned buckskin vest heavily ornamented with Indian work in beads and porcupine quills. His crossed gun belts were of russet leather, the belt and holsters studded with silver. His trousers were of homespun, but striped, and his boots were highly polished, a rare thing on the frontier.

The larger of the two men eyed him disdainfully, then looked away. The Kid was used to that, for those who did not know him always assumed he was a tenderfoot, a mistake that had led to more than one bit of the trouble that seemed to await him at every corner.

The larger of the two men had several notches carved in his gun butt.

The Kid ordered his drink, but he decided he did not like the man with the bulging eyes. He had never liked anybody who carved notches in their gun butts, anyway. It was a tinhorn's trick.

The Kid looked at Joe Chance, the bartender, who was obviously uneasy, and had been so ever since the Kid walked into the saloon.

The Kid had promised Bonita not to get into trouble, but nonetheless what he had found had been a cold-blooded, ruthless murder and one of the two men had done it. Both had been riding, as was obvious from the trail dust they carried, and, from the attitudes of the others in the room, both were strangers.

"Chance," he said, "what would you think of a man who dry-gulched a passing rider, then walked up and shot into him a couple of times to make sure he was dead, then took his horse?"

Joe Chance knew the Cactus Kid. The mirror he now had behind the bar had caused the Kid to cough up three months wages to pay for it, and it had only been in place about sixty days.

Chance shifted his eyes warily and reached for a glass to polish. "Why, I'd think the man was a dirty murderer who deserved hangin'!"

After a pause, his own curiosity getting the best of him, he asked, "Who done such a thing?"

"Why, I don't rightly know at this minute, but I got an idea we'll find out. He came over the trail just ahead of me. He robbed the man he murdered, and he's in town right now!"

The bowlegged man lifted his eyes to meet those of the Kid. There was something mocking and dangerous in those eyes. The Kid knew he was looking into the eyes of a man who both could and would shoot. "I just rode in," the man said calmly.

"So did I." The big man put his glass down hard on the bar. "Are you aimin' that talk at us?"

"No," the Kid said mildly, "only at one of you. Only, the other man must have heard those shots, and I'm wondering why he didn't do anything."

"What did you do?" the bowlegged man asked.

"Nothing. The killer caught sight of me and tried to cut me down, too. Hadn't been for that I'd have ridden right on by and I'd never have seen the dead man.

"The man who was killed," he added, "went by the name of Wayne Parsons. He was from Silver City."

"Never heard of him." The bigger of the two men obviously shifted his gun. "I come from Tombstone." His eyes rested on the Cactus Kid, and their expression was anything but pleasant. "They call me the Black Bantam."

"Never heard of you," he lied. Bantam was a notorious outlaw who had been riding, it was said, with Curly Bill.

"There's plenty of people who has," Bantam said, "and if I was you, young feller, and I didn't want to get all them purty clothes bloody, I'd go herd my cows and leave my betters alone."

"I didn't come to town huntin' sheep," the Cactus Kid said calmly, "or I'd dig my hands in your wool. Nor did I come for cows. I came to get some calico for my girl's dress, which doesn't leave me much time to curry your wool, Bantam.

"All I've got to say is that one of you is riding a dead man's horse and carryin' stolen money."

Bantam's fury was obvious. He was facing the bar, but he turned slowly to face the Kid. Men backed off to corners of the room, and the bartender took a tentative step toward them, then changed his mind and backed off. "Now, see here—!" he started to say, when—

"Hold it, Bantam!"

All heads turned at the interruption. It was the bowlegged rider. "Nobody's asked me who I am, and I'm not plannin' to explain. If you need a handle for me just call me Texas.

"But, Bantam, it seems to me this is between us. He says one of us is guilty, so why don't we settle this between us? Just you and me?" Texas smiled. "Besides, I don't think you'd like takin' a whippin' from that youngster."

"Whuppin'? Why, I'd—!"

"No, you wouldn't, Bantam. I've known all about you for a long time, and you never did hunt trouble with anybody who'd have a chance. This dude youngster here is the Cactus Kid.

"Now it seems to me it is between us, so why don't we just empty our pockets on the table here so everybody can see what we're carrying.

"The Kid is handy at readin' sign, so maybe he will see something that will tell him which one of us is the killer." He moved closer, his eyes dancing with a taunting amusement. "How about it, Kid?"

The Kid's eyes shifted from one to the other, the one taunting and challenging, the other stubborn and angry.

"Why not?" Bantam thrust a big hand into his pocket and began putting the contents of his pockets on the table. The man who called himself Texas did likewise.

"There it is, Kid. Look it over!"

Joe Chance leaned over the bar to watch, as did Slim Reynolds and Art Vertrees, the only others present.

In the pile Texas made were a worn tobacco pouch, a jackknife, a plug of chewing tobacco, several coins, a small coil of rawhide string, and a small handful of gold coins wrapped in paper. There were two rifle bullets.

In Bantam's pile there was a wad of paper money, some sixty dollars worth, some small change, a Mexican silver peso, a jackknife, a plug of chewing tobacco, a stub pipe, a tight ball of paper, a comb, and some matches.

Thoughtfully, the Cactus Kid looked over the two piles. There was nothing that could be identified with any man. It was merely such stuff as could be found in the pockets of any cowhand. Except—he picked up the ball of tightly rolled paper and slowly unrolled it.

It unfolded into a plain sheet of writing paper that had been folded just once. There were also marks that made it appear the paper had been folded about something. The crinkling from being rolled up was obviously more recent that the soiled line of the old crease.

It was not the fold the Kid was noticing, nor the faint imprint of what might have been carried within that folded sheet but rather the diagonal line of the sweat stain that ran across the papers.

"That ain't mine!" Bantam protested. "I had no such paper in my pocket!" He was suddenly frightened and his lips worked nervously. "I tell you—!"

Texas had drawn back to one side, poised and ready.

The Cactus Kid drew the dead man's papers from his pocket and placed them beside the folded paper. The diagonal sweat stains matched perfectly.

"So?" Texas said. "It was you, Bantam! You killed him!"

"You're a liar!" Bantam said angrily. "I done no—!"

Texas's hand streaked for his gun, and Bantam grabbed at his own gun. The two shots sounded almost as one, but it was Bantam who fell.

Texas holstered his gun. "Had no idea he'd draw on me, but a man's got to watch those kind."

Nobody replied, and he gathered his things from the bar and went outside.

The Kid turned back to Joe Chance. "Better give me another shot of rye; then I'm picking up my calico and headin' for home. This town's too sudden for me."

Two of the bystanders took the big man's body out, and later Slim Reynolds came in. "He must have cached that stolen money somewhere because he surely didn't have it on him."

"Bantam's had it coming for a long time," Vertrees said, "and Texas was right. He never killed anybody in a fair fight."

"What about that grulla mustang of his?" Reynolds asked. "That's a mighty fine horse."

The Kid put his glass down on the bar. "Did Bantam ride the grulla? Are you sure?"

"Of course," Vertrees replied, surprised. "I was on the street when he rode in. He was only a little ahead of Texas, who was riding a bay."

The Cactus Kid turned and started for the door. He was in the saddle and started down the street when he thought of the calico.

Bonita wouldn't like this. He had promised her faithfully he'd return with that calico, and after all, hunting killers was the sheriff's job. Angrily, he turned the paint and trotted back to the store. "Got some red and white calico?" he asked.

"Sure haven't! I'm sorry, Kid, but a fellow just

came in and bought the whole bolt. Red and white it was, too."

"What kind of a fellow?" The Kid asked suspiciously.

"A pretty salty-lookin' fellow. He was bowlegged and had a Texas drawl."

"Why, that dirty, no-account—!" The Kid ran for his horse.

As he started out of town Reynolds flagged him down.

"Kid? What d' you make of this?" He indicated a place in the skirt of Bantam's saddle where the stitching had been slit. Obviously something had been hidden there. "Do you believe that Texas man stole that money?"

"No, he was the killer, himself!"

Why Texas had headed back along the trail down which they had come he could not guess, but that was exactly what he was doing.

It was a grueling chase. The paint pony liked to run, however, and although the bay was a long-legged brute they moved up on him. Occasionally, far ahead, he glimpsed dust. Then it dawned on him that Texas was not trying to escape. He was simply staying enough ahead to be safe for the time being.

That could mean he planned to trap him in the hills somewhere ahead. After all, Texas had dry-gulched that other man.

When they reached the hills, the Kid turned off

the trail. This was his old stomping grounds, and he had hunted strays all through these hills and knew their every turn and draw. He knew Mule Creek and the Maverick Mountains like it was his own dooryard.

Climbing the pony up the banks of the draw, the Kid skirted a cluster of red rocks and rode down through a narrow canyon where the ledges lay layer on layer like an enormous chocolate cake, and emerged on a cedared hillside.

He loped the paint through the cedars, weaving a purposely erratic path, so if observed he would not make an effective target, then he went down into the draw, crossed the Agua Fria, and circled back toward the trail, moving slowly with care. He was none too soon.

Texas was loping the bay and glancing from side to side of the trail. Almost opposite the Kid's hiding place, he reined in suddenly and swung down, headed for a bunch of rocks across the way.

The Kid stepped into the open. "It was a good idea, Texas," he said, "only I had it, too."

Startled, the man turned very slowly. "I knew you'd figure it out, Kid. I thought I'd just buy all that calico to make sure you followed me. I just don't want any witnesses left behind.

"Anyway, that girl of yours would still need a dress, and I could always say your dyin' words were that I should take it to her, and that I was to stay by an' care for her, like."

He let go of the reins of his horse. "I **would** like to know how you figured it out, though."

"It was the Henry rifle. When you rode off on the bay with the Henry in the scabbard I knew it had to be you. I found a shell from that rifle.

"Bantam was really surprised when he saw that paper. You'd slipped it into his pocket when you were standing close, then you called him a liar and killed him before he had a chance to talk. Then you went to his saddle and recovered the money."

"It was this way, Kid. I'd tailed Parsons to kill him for his money, but after I did, Bantam opened fire on me and run me off. He'd been trailing him, too. Then he went down to the body, got the money and lit out.

"Anyway," Texas added, "now you know how it was. When you came into sight, Bantam took a shot at you to warn you off until he could get out of sight.

"But I guess you got me, so it all went for nothing. I'm not sorry about Bantam, he was simply no good, but as for you—"

He would hang for what he had done, and both he and the Kid knew it, and the Kid, knowing his man, knew he would take a chance. Texas went for his gun and the Kid shot him.

Then he walked over to the bay, which showed no intention of running away, and recovered the bolt of calico, and then the money from Texas's body.

"Parsons will likely have some folks who can use this," he told himself, then rolled the body over the bank, tumbled rocks and sand over it and, gathering the reins of the bay he mounted the paint and headed for home.

When he cantered up to the gate Bonita came running, eyes sparkling with happiness. Having known other girls before, he was not sure whether it was for him or the calico, but contented himself with the conclusion it was probably a little of both.

"See?" she said. "When you just go into town and come right back there's never any trouble. It's easy to stay out of trouble if you just want to. Now this wasn't any trouble, was it?"

"No, honey, no trouble at all."

He glanced at the paint pony, who was looking at him with a skeptical eye. "You shut up!" he told the paint, and followed Bonita into the house.

The pony yawned and switched his tail at a fly.

Medicine Ground

The Cactus Kid was in a benevolent mood and the recent demise of Señor "Ace" Fernandez was far from his thoughts. Had the Kid's own guns blasted a trail down the slippery ladder to hell, he would have been wary, for he knew well the temper of the four brothers Fernandez.

He had not, however, done a personal gun job on Ace. He had merely acted for the moment as the finger of destiny, and but for a certain small action of his, the agile fingers of the elder Fernandez might still be fleecing all and sundry at the Cantina.

Nobody who knew him could question the Kid's sense of humor, and it extended as far as poker, which is very far indeed. The humor of Martin Jim (so called because he was the second of two Jim Martins to arrive in Aragon) was another story. Jim had a sense of humor all right, but it ended somewhere south of poker. Martin Jim was a big, muscular man who packed a pistol for use.

On the memorable afternoon of Ace's death, that

gentleman was sitting in a little game with Martin Jim, the Cactus Kid, Pat Gruen, and an itinerant miner known as Rawhide. The Kid, being the observant type, had taken note of the smooth efficiency of Señor Ace when he handled the cards. He also noted the results of a couple of subsequent hands. Thereafter the Kid was careful to drop out when Ace was doing the dealing. The others, being less knowing and more trustful, stayed in the game, and as a result the pile of poker chips in front of Ace Fernandez had grown to an immodest proportion.

Finally, when Pat Gruen and Rawhide were about broke, there came a hand from which all dropped away but Ace Fernandez and Martin Jim. With twelve hundred dollars of his hard-earned money (cowhands were making forty a month!) in the center of the table, Martin Jim's sense of humor had reached the vanishing point.

The Cactus Kid, idly watching the game, had seen the black sheep lead the burly lamb to the slaughter; he also chanced to glimpse the cards Ace Fernandez turned up. He held a pair of fours, a nine, ten, and a queen. A few minutes later his eyes shifted back to the hand Fernandez held and there was no nine, ten, or queen, but three aces were cuddling close to the original pair of fours.

Naturally, this phenomenon interested him no end, especially so as he had seen the way, an odd way, too, Ace held his arm.

* * *

WHEN THE SHOWDOWN CAME, Martin Jim laid down two pair, and Ace Fernandez, looking very smug, his full house.

Leaning forward as if to see the cards better, the Cactus Kid deftly pushed the cuff of Ace's white sleeve over the head of a nail that projected an inch or so from the edge of the table.

Smiling with commiseration, Ace Fernandez made his next-to-last gesture in a misspent life. He reached for the pot.

As his eager hands shot out there was a sharp, tearing sound, and the white sleeve of the elder Fernandez ripped loudly, and there snugly against his arm was what is known in the parlance of those aware of such things as a sleeve holdout. In it were several cards, among them the missing nine, ten, and queen.

For one utterly appalling instant Ace Fernandez froze, with what sinking of the heart you can imagine. Then he made the second of his last two gestures. He reached for his gun.

It was, of course, the only thing left to do. Nobody from the Gulf to the Colorado would have denied it. Martin Jim, as we have said, wore a six-gun for use, and moreover he had rather strict notions about the etiquette of such matters as poker.

He looked, he saw, he reached. By the manner of presentation, it must not be inferred that these were separate actions. They were one.

His gun came level just as that of Señor Ace Fernandez cleared his holster, and Martin Jim fired twice right across the tabletop.

Lead, received in those proportions and with that emphasis and range, is reliably reported to be indigestible.

The test of any theory is whether it works in practice, and science must record that theory as proved. They buried Señor Ace Fernandez with due ceremony, his full house pinned to his chest over the ugly blotch of blood, the torn sleeve and holdout still in evidence. If, in some distant age, his body is exhumed for scientific study, no poker player will look twice to ascertain the cause of death.

Now, as we have said, the Cactus Kid was giving no thought to the abrupt departure of Ace Fernandez, nor to the manner of his going. Nor did he think much about the fact that he might be considered a responsible party. The Kid was largely concerned with random thoughts anent the beauty and the grace of Bess O'Neal, the Irish and very pretty daughter of the ranching O'Neals, from beyond the Pecos.

It was the night of the big dance at Rock Creek School, and Bess had looked with favor on his suggestion that he meet her at the dance and ride home with her. What plans were projected for the ride home have no part in this story. It is enough to say the Kid was enjoying the anticipation.

Twice, the Kid had agreed to meet Bess, and twice events had intervened. Once he had inadvertently interrupted a stage holdup and in the resulting exchange of comments had picked up a bullet in the thigh. Not a serious wound, but a painful one, so painful that he missed the dance and almost missed the funerals of the two departed stage robbers.

On the second occasion, someone had jestingly dared the Kid to rope a mountain lion. The Cactus Kid had never roped a lion and was scientifically interested in the possibilities. Also, he never refused a dare. He got a line on the cat, but the cat reversed himself in midair, hit the ground on his feet, and left the ground in that same breathtaking instant, taking a leap that put him right in the middle of the Kid's horse.

It is a scientifically accepted fact that two bodies cannot occupy the same place at the same time, and the resulting altercation, carried on while the frightened horse headed for the brush at a dead run, left the Kid a bedraggled winner.

His shirt was gone and he was smeared head to foot with mingled lion and human blood. The Kid had handled the mountain lion with a razor-edged bowie knife, and regardless of their undoubted efficiency, they simply aren't neat.

Accordingly, Bess O'Neal, with Irish temper and considerable flashing of eyes and a couple of stamps of a dainty foot, had said he either must arrive on hand and in one piece or no more dates. Should he be in no condition to dance with her, he could go his way and she would go hers.

*   *   *

Hence, the Cactus Kid, wearing a black buckskin jacket heavily ornamented with silver, black-pearl in-laid gun belt and holsters, black creased trousers, highly polished boots and a black, silver-ornamented sombrero, was bound for Rock Creek School.

His gelding, a beautiful piebald with a dark nose and one blue eye, stepped daintily along doing his best to live up to his resplendent master as well as to the magnificent saddle and bridle he wore.

These last had been created to order for Don Pe-dro Bedoya, of the Sonora Bedoyas, and stolen from him by one Sam Mawson, known to the trade as "One Gun" Mawson.

Mawson decided they would look best on the Kid's horse, and attempted to effect an exchange by trading a bullet in the head for the horse. He failed to make allowances for an Irishman's skull, and the bullet merely creased the Kid, who came to just as Mawson completed the job of exchanging saddles and was about to mount. The Cactus Kid spoke, Mawson wheeled and drew . . . One Gun was not enough.

The outlaw's taste, the Kid decided, was better than his judgment. He departed the scene astride a one-thousand-dollar saddle.

With Rock Creek School a bare six miles away where Bess O'Neal would be looking her most lovely, the Cactus Kid, a gorgeous picture of what every young cowhand would wear if he had money enough, rode along with a cheerful heart and his voice lifted in song.

"Lobo" Fernandez was big, rough, and ugly. He had loved his brother Ace—but then, Lobo never played poker with him. With Miguel, a younger brother, he waited beside the road. Someone had noticed and commented on that deft movement of the Kid's fingers that foretold the demise of Ace, and then, Lobo had never liked the Kid, anyway.

Out in the West, where men are men and guns are understood, even the bravest of men stand quiet when an enemy has the drop. The Kid was a brave man, but Lobo and Miguel Fernandez, two men on opposite sides of the road, had the drop on him, and clearly the situation called for arbitration.

He reined in the piebald and for one heart-sinking, hopeless instant he realized this was the third and last chance given him by Bess O'Neal.

"Buenas noches, señores!" he said politely. "You go to the dance?"

"No!" Lobo was more emphatic than the occasion demanded. "We have wait for you. We have a leetle bet, Miguel and I, he bet the ants finish you before the buzzards. I say the buzzards weel do it first."

The Cactus Kid studied them warily. Neither gun wavered. If he moved he was going to take two big lead slugs through the brisket. "Let's forget it, shall we? The dance will be more fun. Besides, ants bother me."

There was no humor in the clan Fernandez. With hands bound behind him, and one Fernandez six feet on his left, another a dozen feet behind, the Cactus Kid rode away.

He knew what they planned, for the mention of ants was enough. It is a quaint old Yaqui custom to bind a victim to an anthill, and the Fernandez brothers had been suspected of just such action on at least two occasions. On one of these the Kid had helped to remove the body from the hill before the ants finished. It had been a thoroughly unpleasant and impressive sight.

The moon he had planned for Bess (by special arrangement) was undeniably gorgeous, the lonely ridges and stark boulders of the desert seemed a weird and fantastic landscape on some distant planet as the Cactus Kid rode down a dim trail guided by Lobo. Once, topping a rise, he glimpsed the distant lights of Rock Creek School, and even thought he heard strains of music.

The trail they followed dipped deep into the canyon of the Agua Prieta and skirted the dark waters of the stream. The Cactus Kid knew then where they were taking him—to the old medicine camp of the Yaquis. With the knowledge came an idea.

Suddenly Miguel sneezed, and when he did, his head bobbed to the left.

"Ah!" the Kid said. "Bad luck! Very bad luck!"

"What?" Miguel turned his head to stare at him.

"To sneeze to the left—it's the worst kind of luck," the Kid said.

Neither Fernandez replied, yet he had a hunch the comment on the old Yaqui superstition impressed them. He knew it had been a belief of many of the southwestern tribes that if the head bobbed left when one sneezed, it spelled disaster. He had a hunch both men knew the old belief.

"Tsk, tsk," he said softly.

MIGUEL SHIFTED UNCOMFORTABLY in the saddle. The high black cliffs of the canyon loomed above them. Both men, he knew, had been here before. Being part Yaqui, they would be impressed with the evil spirits reported to haunt the old medicine camp of the tribe.

He worked desperately with his cramped fingers, trying to get the rawhide thongs looser. A stone rattled somewhere, and he jumped.

"What was that?" he said, in a startled voice.

Lobo Fernandez looked up, glared at him, then glanced around uneasily. There was no moonlight here, and nothing could be seen. The Kid's gun belt hung over the pommel of Lobo's saddle, and with a free hand a lot might be done.

"Wait!" he said suddenly, sharply.

The brothers reined in, and he could almost feel their scowls. "Listen!" he said sharply. Their heads came up with his word, and he had a hunch. When one listens for something at night, there is invariably some sound, or seeming sound.

Somewhere, rocks slid, and the canyon seemed to sigh. Lobo shifted uneasily in his saddle, and spoke rapidly to Miguel in Spanish, and Miguel grunted uneasily.

"Ah?" the Cactus Kid said. "You die soon."

"Huh?" Lobo turned on him.

"You die soon," the Kid repeated. "The Old Gods don't like you bringing me here. I'm no Yaqui. This here is a Yaqui place. A place of the spirits."

Lobo Fernandez ignored him, but Miguel seemed uneasy. He glanced at his brother as if to speak, then shrugged. The Kid worked at the rawhide thongs. His wrists were growing sweaty from the warmth and the constant straining. If he could get rid of them for a while, or if he had a little more time—

Then suddenly the trail widened and he was in the flat place beside the stream, the place where the Yaquis came, long ago. Once before, chasing wild horses, the Kid had been through here. There was an old altar, Aztec, some said, at the far end in a sort of cave formed by the overhang. The Mexican rider he had been with had been fearful of the place and wanted very much to leave.

"Maybe you die here," the Kid said. "My spirit say you'll die soon."

Lobo snarled at him, and then they halted. About here, the Kid recalled, there was a big anthill. They had certainly brought him to the right place, for no one would ever come by to release him. This was a place never visited by anyone. Probably only two or three white men had ever descended to this point, and yet it was no more than fifteen miles at most from Rock Creek School.

Lobo swung down, and then walked over to the Kid and, reaching up with one big hand, dragged him from the horse. The Kid shoved off hard and let go with all his hundred and forty pounds.

It was unexpected, and Lobo staggered and fell, cursing. Miguel sprang around the horse, and the Kid kicked out viciously with both feet and knocked the younger Fernandez rolling. But the Kid's success was short-lived.

Lobo sprang to his feet and kicked the Kid viciously in the ribs, and then they dragged him, cursing him all the while, to the anthill. He felt the swell of it under his back. Then, as they bound his feet and Miguel began to drive stakes in the ground, Lobo drew his knife and leaned over him. He made two quick gashes, neither of them deep, in either side of the Kid's neck.

Then he drew the sharp edge of the knife across the Kid's stomach, making no effort to more than break the skin, and then on either of his ankles, after pulling off his boots. It was just something to draw enough blood to invite the ants. The rest they would accomplish in time, by themselves.

The two brothers drew off then, muttering between themselves. His talk of evil spirits had made them uneasy, he knew, and they kept casting glances toward the cave where the altar stood. Yet there seemed some other reason for their hesitation. They muttered between themselves, and then walked away, seeming to lose interest in him. Yet as they left he heard one word clearly above the others: **señorita.**

What señorita? He scowled, still struggling with the thongs that bound his ankles. They were growing slick from perspiration now, and perhaps some blood. The ants had not discovered him, and probably would not until morning brought them out.

He was lying across the anthill, lying on his side. Stakes driven into the ground on either side of his body, but some distance off, tied him in position so he could not roll away. The rawhide thongs binding him to the stakes were tight and strong. Other stakes had been driven into the ground above his head and below his feet. From the stake above his head a noose had been slipped under his jawbone and drawn tight, so his head was all but immovable. His ankles had been roped tight down to the stake below his feet.

It was with no happiness that the Cactus Kid contemplated his situation. Yet two factors aroused his curiosity; the señorita the brothers had talked about, and why they did not mount and leave the canyon.

Their work here had been done. Neither brother was immune from superstition, and in fact, both of them were ignorant men reared in all that strange tangle of fact and fancy that makes up Yaqui folklore.

This place had a history, a weird history that extended back to some dim period long before the coming of the red man, back to those pre-Indian days when other peoples roamed this land.

Artifacts had been found in the caves, and back there where the idol was, there were stone remains of some kind of crude temple built under an overhanging shelf. A professor who explored the canyon had once told the Kid that the base of the supposedly Aztec god had provided a base for some other figure before it, that it was another type of stone, and one not found nearby.

Yet there was nothing in all this to help him. What he had hoped for, he did not know, but any uncertainty on their part could act favorably for him, so when the idea came to him, he had played on their superstition and the natural feeling all men have when in a strange, lonely place during the dark and silent hours. It had come to nothing. He was strapped to an anthill, and when the sun awakened them to full vigor and they began their work, they would find the blood, and then they would swarm over him by the thousands.

Doggedly, bitterly, almost without hope, he worked at the rawhide that bound his wrists. Fearful of what he might do if they had been freed even for a moment, the brothers Fernandez had left his hands tied when they threw him on the ground and staked him out. Yet despite the blood and perspiration on his chafed and painful wrists, the rawhide seemed loosened but little. Nevertheless, he continued to work, struggling against time and against pain.

Then suddenly, in a bitter and clarifying moment, he realized what they had meant when they spoke of a señorita. They had been talking about Bess.

The instant the idea came to him he knew he was right.

Not over a week ago when he rode up to her home and swung down from the saddle, she had told him about Lobo Fernandez and his brother, the smooth, polished one, the one called Juan. They had stopped her in front of the store and tried to talk. Juan had caught at her arm. She had twisted away, and then Ernie Cable had come out of the general store and wanted to know what was going on, and they had laughed and walked away. But she had noticed them watching the house.

They had been talking about Bess O'Neal. But **what**? What had they said?

Where were the other brothers? Where were Juan and Pedro?

The low murmur of voices came to him, and as he lay on the low mound of the anthill, he could see the glow of their cigarettes. They were sitting on the ground not far from the image, smoking. And waiting.

Using all his strength, he tugged at his bonds. They were solid, and they cut into his wrists like steel wire. He relaxed, panting. He could feel sweat running down his body under his shirt. This was going to be hell. Even if he got free, he still must get his hands on a gun, and even then, there would be four of them.

Four? There were only two, now. Yet once the idea had come to him, he couldn't get it out of his mind. Juan Fernandez was no fool. It was such a good chance, they could kill two birds with one stone. Juan wanted Bess O'Neal. If the Cactus Kid and Bess vanished at the same time, everyone would shrug and laugh. They would believe they had eloped. No one would even think to question the opinion. It was so natural a thing for them to do.

Revenge for their brother's death, and the girl. They could take her to Sonora or back in the hills, and nobody would even think to look.

Then he heard the sound of horses on the trail. He tried to lift his head to listen, but it was tied too tight. He lay there, hating himself and miserable, listening to the horses. Desperately, his mind fought for a way out, an escape. Again he strained his muscles against the binding rawhide. He forced his wrists with all his might, but although he strained until his hands dug into the sand under him, he could do nothing, he found them tight as ever. The sweat and blood made his wrists slippery so they would turn, ever so little, under the rawhide, but that was all.

His fingers were touching something, something cool and flat. For an instant, listening again to the approaching horses, that something made no impression, it refused to identify itself. Then on a sudden it hit him, and his fingers felt desperately.

A small, flat surface, light in weight, triangular—an arrowhead!

There were many of them here, he knew. All over this ancient medicine ground of the Yaqui Indians, delicately shaped from flint.

He gripped it in his fingers and tried to reach it up to the rawhide that bound his wrists.

They had crossed his wrists, then bound them tightly, and had taken several turns of the rawhide around his forearms, binding them tightly together, but by twisting his fingers he could bring the rawhide thong and the edge of the flint arrowhead together. Straining in every muscle, he commenced to saw at the thong.

The horses were still coming. In the echoing stillness of the canyon, he knew he would hear them for a good half hour before they arrived. The steep path was narrow, and they must come slowly.

Minutes passed. The cutting pain in his wrists was a gnawing agony now, and the salt of perspiration had mingled with it to add to his discomfort. Yet he struggled on. It was desperately hard to get the edge of the flint against the rawhide now, but he could still manage it, and a little pressure.

A voice called out, then another. The horses came into the basin, and he heard a question in Spanish, then a laughing response. Then a light was struck,

and a fire blazed up. In the glow of the fire applied to
sticks gathered earlier, he could see the four brothers,
and Bess O'Neal.

She was standing with her back to him, her wrists
tied, and Juan gripped her arm. Lobo stared at her
greedily, and then Juan asked a question. Leading
the girl, they turned toward the anthill and the Cactus Kid.

Bess cried out when she saw him. "**You!** When
they told me you were here, I thought they lied. They
said you were hurt—that you— Then when I was
outside talking to them, I suddenly realized something was wrong, but when I tried to leave and go
hack inside to get someone else, they grabbed me,
tied me, and brought me to this place."

"Keep your nerve, honey," the Cactus Kid said
grimly. "This isn't over!"

Juan laughed and, leaning down, struck him
across the mouth. "Pig!" he snarled. "I should kill
you now. I should cut you to little pieces, only the
ants will do it better. And if you die, you would not
hear what happens to the señorita. It is better you
hear!"

He straightened up, and they trooped back to the
fire. The frightened, despairing look in the girl's eyes
gave him added incentive. He scraped and scratched
at the rawhide, staring hard toward the fire.

The brothers were in no hurry. They had the girl.
They had him. He was helpless, and no one sus-

pected them. Moreover, they were in a place where no one came. They could afford to take their time.

Suddenly he braced himself again and strained his muscles. He felt a sudden weakness in his bonds, and then his straining fingers found a loose end. He had cut through the rawhide!

Working with his swollen, clumsy fingers, he got the loose end looser, then managed to shake some of the other loops from his wrists. In a matter of minutes, his hands were free. He lay still then, panting and getting his wind, then he lifted his hands to the halter on his head and neck. A few minutes' work and that was freed, then the thongs that bound his wrists and ankles.

HE WAS OUTSIDE the glow of the fire, which was at least a hundred yards away. He chafed his swollen wrists and rubbed his hands together. Then he got several pieces of rawhide and stuck them into his pockets. One piece, about eighteen inches long, he kept.

The Cactus Kid got slowly to his feet, stretching himself, trying to get life into his muscles. In the vast, empty stillness of the black canyon the tiny fire glowed, and flamed red, and above it the soft voices, muted by distance and the enormity of the space around them, sounded almost like whispers.

Tiptoeing to the edge of the stream, he felt for the rock he wanted, two inches long and evenly balanced in weight. Taking the eighteen-inch rawhide, he knotted one end of it securely about the stone. Then he tried it in his hand.

Fading back into the shadows then, his boots still lying where Lobo had dropped them when they were jerked from his feet, the Kid melted into the almost solid blackness and began to cross the space between himself and the fire.

He didn't like killing, and he didn't like what he was going to have to do, yet he was not the one to underrate the fighting ability of the brothers Fernandez. They were cruel, vindictive men, lawless and given to murder. He knew what they would do to the girl, he knew the horror in which she would live for a few days or a few weeks, then murder. They dared not leave her alive, possibly to get back to Aragon.

To think that only a few miles away now, the dance was in progress! Only a few miles away old Buck Sorenson was calling dances and his sons were sawing their fiddles. There was help there, but it was too far. What was to be done, he must do himself.

Miguel knelt above the fire. He was cooking. Juan sat near the girl, and kept a hand on her. From time to time he made remarks to her in his sneering, irritating voice. Lobo sat across the fire, his eyes never leaving the girl's slim body or her face.

In the darkness, the Cactus Kid watched. His guns were there, he could see them lying on a blanket. They were too far away. There was no chance to get them.

He waited. It was a deadly, trying waiting. Minutes seemed like hours. Then Miguel straightened. "Pedro!" he snapped impatiently.

The Fernandez who dozed on the sand looked up.

"Get me some water from the spring, you lazy one!"

Pedro started to complain, then Juan looked up.

"Get it!" he snapped.

Grudgingly, Pedro picked up a canteen and started off into the darkness. The Cactus Kid came to his feet, moving like a ghost in his socked feet, moving after Pedro.

He waited, while the hulking Mexican held the canteen in the spring to fill it, and then as he straightened, the Kid moved in behind him, holding a loop of the rawhide in his left hand and gripping the stone in his fingers.

He threw the stone suddenly, and its weight swung the rawhide around the Mexican's neck. He had swung the stone from the right and with a quick, backhanded motion, and as it came around Pedro's neck the Kid caught it with his right. Then he jerked hard with both hands, cutting off the startled yell that started to rise in the man's throat, and gripping the rawhide hard, the Kid jerked his knee up into the small of Pedro's back and turned his knuckles hard against the back of Pedro's neck.

It was sudden, adroit, complete. For an instant the Kid held the man, then lowered him to the ground. Perhaps he was dead. Perhaps—there was no question now. Withdrawing the thong, the Kid searched him in vain for a gun, then slid away into darkness, and once more got close to the camp. He sighed regretfully. Pedro had been unarmed.

"Where is that fool, Pedro?" Miguel demanded impatiently. Then he yelled, "**Pedro!** Where are you?"

There was no answer.

The echo of Miguel's voice died, and for a minute the three brothers stared at each other. Lobo got to his feet, staring into the darkness. There was no sound out there but the falling water in the spring, and the rustle from the stream.

Lobo Fernandez shifted uneasily, staring around into the darkness. "I'll go see where is he," he said, finally.

Lying close, the Kid waited. What he wanted was a chance at those guns. Once the guns were in his hands, all would be well. Was he the Cactus Kid for nothing?

Lobo walked off into the darkness. Suddenly there was a startled yell from him.

"Juan!" Lobo screamed. "Come quickly! **Pedro is dead!**"

Juan Fernandez sprang to his feet and lunged toward Lobo's shouting voice. Miguel started up, his face ashen, and the Kid sprang, quickly, silently. Again the rawhide thong swung out, and again a man was jerked from his feet, but this time the Kid had no desire to kill.

"It is the spirits!" Lobo shouted. "The gringo told me they would be angry!"

Juan's shout broke in. "The Keed? He has done this! He has gotten away!"

The Cactus Kid heard them rushing toward the anthill where he had been tied, but he dropped the unconscious Miguel and sprang for the guns. He came up with the gun belt swinging in his hands and, with a quick movement, caught it and buckled the guns on. Then he sprang across the fire to the girl and dragged her into the darkness.

While she sobbed with relief he tore at the knots with frenzied, eager fingers.

"Where are the horses?" he said. "Get to them quickly! Get two and turn the others free. Then wait for me where the trail begins."

The girl asked no more questions, but slipped off into the darkness.

There was not a sound from the brothers. Miguel, his face blue, lay on the ground near the fire. He was not dead.

The Kid glided from behind the fire and, staring into the darkness, began to probe for the brothers Fernandez. Both were armed, as Pedro had not been. Both men were deadly with six-guns, and in any kind of a shoot-out they would be hard men to handle. Keeping his eyes away from the fire, he moved into the shadows, hoping to get near the horses, but out of line with the girl.

There was no sign from her. Then he heard a

horse stamp and blow. He waited. Then he heard a footfall, so soft he scarce could hear. He whirled, gun in hand, and in the darkness he saw the looming figure of Lobo, just the faint outline of his figure in the light from the fire.

Their guns came up at the same instant, and both blasted fire. The Kid felt a quick stab at his side, not of pain, but rather a jolt as though someone had jerked him violently. Then he fired again, and saw the big figure of Lobo wilting, saw the gun dribble from his fingers, and at the same instant there was a scream from near the horses.

Turning in his tracks, he charged toward the scream and came up running. There was a wild scuffling in the dark, then a muttered curse and the sound of a blow. He saw them, and holstering his gun, the Kid lunged close and caught Juan with one hand at his shirt collar and one at his belt.

With a tremendous jerk, he ripped the Mexican free and shoved him violently away. With a cry, Juan turned like a cat in midair and hit the ground in a sitting position. He must have drawn as he fell, for suddenly his gun belched fire and then the Kid fired.

Juan Fernandez rolled over and the Kid dropped to the ground. They lay there, only a few feet apart, each waiting for a move from the other. Somewhere off to the right the girl was also lying still. Back at the fire Miguel might be coming to. What was to be done must be done now.

He could hear the horses moving, so evidently

Bess had reached them safely again after he had pulled Juan away from her. All was quiet, and then he thought he detected a movement off to the right.

Picking up a small pebble, he tossed it into the water. It drew no fire, no reaction. Getting carefully to his feet, he tried to penetrate the darkness ahead of him. Circling, he headed toward where he believed Juan to be. Yet when he reached the spot, the outlaw was no longer there!

Glancing back toward the fire, he saw that Miguel, too, was gone.

Gun in hand, he started working toward the entrance to the trail where he had warned Bess to meet him.

The whereabouts of the brothers disturbed him. Their hatred over his responsibility, small as it had been, in the death of Ace, would be nothing at all now that he had escaped them, killed Pedro, and taken Bess O'Neal from them. Above all, once the two left this valley, the brothers Fernandez would know only too well their day around Aragon was over.

A movement near him, and he froze into a crouch, his gun lifted. Then he saw a dark shadow, and just as he lifted the gun and turned it toward the figure there came to his nostrils a faint, scarcely tangible breath of perfume!

A moment only he waited, then he took a chance. "Bess!" he hissed.

In a moment she was beside him. Her lips against his ear, she breathed softly, "Miguel is at the trail entrance! We cannot get away!"

"The horses?"

"I've yours and mine in the cutback under the shelf. Near that image!"

Taking her hand, he began to move on careful feet toward the place she mentioned. It was dark there, in the overhang of the cliff. He drew her to him and slipped his left arm around her waist. Freed from his bonds, with Bess O'Neal beside him, and his guns on his slim hips, the Cactus Kid was once more himself. Grimly, he waited.

Morning would come, and with it—well, the brothers Fernandez could run, or they could die, as they wished.

Dawn came, as dawns will, slipping in a gray mystery of beginning light along the far wall of the narrow canyon, then growing into light. The gray turned softer and lay down along the gravel bench. The ants, unaware of what they had missed, began to bestir themselves, and the Kid, seated against the wall with the head of Bess O'Neal on his shoulder, watched the light and was thankful.

No living thing beyond the ants appeared on the bench. He arose, and awakening the girl, they swung into the saddle and, walking their horses, started cautiously for the trail. When they rounded the cluster of boulders that concealed it from them, there was no one in sight. "Looks like they've gone!" he said.

"Not yet."

Juan Fernandez, sided by the younger Miguel, stepped from the boulders at their side. Juan's eyes were hot with hatred, and the gun in his hand spoke clearly of what was to come.

"We are going to kill you, señor."

"Looks like it," the Kid said calmly. "Can I smoke first?"

Juan shrugged. "Why not? If your tobacco and papers are in your breast pocket?"

Very carefully, the Cactus Kid reached for them and built a cigarette.

"Too bad," he said, "a few more minutes and we'd have been in the clear." He put the cigarette in his mouth, then struck the match on the saddle. Holding it in his fingers, he grinned at Juan. "No offense," he said, "but I should have killed you last night. Still, they'll get you, the bunch at Aragon. They'll figure this out." The match was burning slowly. Too slowly. "Somebody must have seen you kidnap Bess."

"Nobody saw us," Juan said, with satisfaction. "If you are going to smoke, you better light that cigarette."

"Nevertheless," the Kid protested, "I think—" Then the flame of the match burned down to his fingers, and at the twinge of pain, he yelled "Ouch," and jerked back his hand, dropping the match.

Only his hand never stopped moving. He palmed his gun, and his gun bellowed with that of Juan Fernandez. The bullet of Juan cut a furrow across the saddle fork in front of him, but his own bullet slammed Juan in the chest and he staggered and fell to the sand even as the Cactus Kid's gun spoke another time.

Miguel let go his gun and grabbed at his side with an expression of shocked surprise in his eyes. He fell from the saddle and sprawled on his face in the sun. Juan tried to rise, then fell back.

Two hours and some twelve miles farther away toward the ranch where Bess lived with her uncle, the Cactus Kid tilted his sombrero back on his head and looked at Bess. Her eyes were bright and shining with promises. "You were very brave!" she said.

The Kid lifted a deprecating shoulder. "Not very," he said. "It wasn't that, but luck." Then, recalling in the flush of his success the ancient arrowhead, he added, "It was luck, and the Yaqui gods. They were with me, with us."

"Give them all the credit you want!" she insisted. "I think you're wonderful!"

The Cactus Kid smiled benevolently and brushed his fingernails lightly against the front of his shirt, then glanced at them.

"Of course," he said, "you may be right. Who am I to argue with a lady?"

Love and the Cactus Kid

FLOWERS FOR JENNY

Jenny Simms, who was pocket-sized and lovely, lifted her determined chin. "If you loved me, you would! You know you would! It's just that you don't love me enough! Why, just look at what the knights used to do for their ladies! And you won't even get me some flowers!"

"Flowers?" The Cactus Kid stared at her gloomily. "Now it's flowers! Girls sure do beat me! Where in this country would a man find flowers?"

His wave at the surrounding country where their picnic lunch was spread was expressive and definite. "Look at it! Ain't been a drop of rainfall in four months, and you know it! Scarcely a blade of grass that's even part green! Worst drought in years, and you want flowers!"

"If you loved me you'd get them!" Her voice was positive and brooked no argument. "If a man really loves a girl he can do anything!"

Her blue eyes flashed at him, and their beauty shook him anew. "Nesselrode, if you love me . . . !"

"Sssh!" he pleaded, glancing panic-stricken around. "If anybody heard that name they'd hooraw me out of the country. Call me Clay, or Kid, or anything but Nesselrode!"

"It's your name, isn't it? Nesselrode Clay. I see nothing wrong with it, nothing at all! Furthermore"—she was not to be diverted—"if you love me you'll get me some flowers! I told the girls you were giving me flowers and they laughed at me! They did. They said there were no flowers closer than California, this time of year."

The Cactus Kid rolled a smoke and stared at it with dark disgust. Women! He snorted. What they could think of! Jenny could think of things nobody else would dream of. That came of reading so many books, all romances and the like. Made her look for a man on a white charger who would do great feats to win her love.

Not that he wouldn't. Why right now, instead of being on a picnic with Jenny, he ought to be out with the posse chasing the Herring boys. There were three of them, and all were gun-slick and tough. They had stopped the U.P. train on a grade about fifteen miles from here, killed the express messenger and the fireman. They had looted the safe of forty thousand dollars in gold and bills. There was a reward on them, a thousand apiece for Benny and Joe, and four thousand for Red.

With the money he could buy some cows and stock that little ranch he was planning on. He could set up a home for a girl like Jenny to be proud of, and with his know-how about cows they could soon be well off. But no, instead of hunting for the Herrings, she wanted him to go hunt flowers!

"It's little enough to do for me," she persisted. "All you think of is running around shooting people in the stomach! You ought to be ashamed, Nesselrode!"

He winced and started to speak, but his voice was lost in the storm of words.

"If you don't bring me some flowers for my birthday, Nesselrode, I'll never speak to you again! Never!"

"Aw, honey!" he protested. "Don't be like that! The sheriff asked me particular to go along and hunt for the Herrings. The boys'll think I'm scared!"

"Nesselrode Clay! You listen to me! If you don't get me those flowers, I never want to see you again! And don't you be shooting anybody, either! Every time you go to do something for me you get into trouble, shooting somebody in the stomach!"

Jenny Simms was five feet one inch of dark-haired loveliness and fire. Almost, sometimes, the Cactus Kid wished there were less of the fire. At other times, he welcomed it.

The fact that she was the prettiest girl in four counties, that her five feet one inch was firm, shapely, and trim as a two-year-old filly, all conspired to make the Kid cringe at the thought of losing her. He was, unfortunately, in love, and the male animal in love is an abject creature when faced by the tyranny of his beloved. At the time he should be firm, he is weak. At the time he should have been getting her accustomed to driving in harness he was so much in love that he was letting her get the bit in her teeth.

The Cactus Kid, five feet seven inches of solid muscle and bone, curly-haired and given to smiling with a charm all his own, was the most sought-after young man around. At the moment, nobody would have guessed. Nor would they have guessed that the black-holstered, walnut-stocked .44s hanging just now on his saddle were considered by some to be the fastest and deadliest guns in the Rocky Mountain country.

"All right," he said weakly, "I'll get your flowers. Come hell or high water, I'll get 'em!" He gave her his hands and helped her up from the flat rock where she was sitting.

AWAY FROM THE FLASHING BEAUTY of Jenny's eyes, he was no longer so confident. Flowers! There wasn't a water hole in fifteen miles that wasn't merely cracked earth and gray mud. The streams had stopped running two months ago. Cattle were dying, all that hadn't been hurriedly sold off, and the leaves on the trees had turned crisp and brown around the edges.

Flowers! He scowled thoughtfully. The Widow Finnegan had a garden, and usually there were flowers in bloom. Now maybe . . .

The piebald gelding with the pink nose and pink-rimmed eyes was a fast horse on the road, and it moved fast now, going through the hills toward the Slash Five and the Widow Finnegan's elm-shaded yard. Yet long before he reached it he could see that even the elms looked parched and bare.

The Widow Finnegan was five feet ten and one hundred and eighty pounds of Irishwoman and she met him at the gate.

"Not here!" She looked about as approachable as a bulldog with a fresh bone. "Not here you don't be gettin' no flowers, Kid!"

"Why, I . . ." His voice trailed away under the pale blue of her glaring eyes.

"There'll be no soft-soapin' me, nayther!" the Widow Finnegan said sharply. "I know the likes of you, Cactus Kid! Full of blarney an' honey-tongued as a thrush! But I know all about the flowers ye'll be wantin', an' there's few enough left, an' them withered!"

"You . . . heard of it?" he asked.

"Heard of it? An' hasn't that colleen o' yours been sayin' all aboot that ye were bringin' her flowers for her birthday! Flowers enough to decorate the rooms with? Flowers in this country where a body is that lucky to find a green blade of grass?"

He glanced thoughtfully at the fence around the small patch of flowers, most of them looking very sick from the hot winds and no rain. She caught his look, and flared.

"No, ye don't! I'm not to be fooled by the likes of

ye, Cactus Kid! Ye come back here at night an' every hand on the Slash Five will be digging rock salt out of your southern exposure! An' it's not just talkin' I am!"

A HALF-DOZEN MEN loafed in the High Card Saloon and they all looked up when he shouldered through the door.

"Rye!" he said.

"What's the matter?" Old Man Hawkins leered at him. "Ain't you after the Herrings? Or have they got you buffaloed, too?"

The Cactus Kid looked at him with an unfriendly eye. "Got to get some flowers for Jenny," he said lamely, "and she's fussing about me getting into shooting scrapes."

" 'S the way with women," the barkeep said philosophically. "Fall for a man, then set out to change him. Soon's they got him changed they don't like him no more. Never seen it to fail, Kid."

"Speakin' of flowers," Sumner suggested, "I hear tell there's a gent over to Escalante that orders 'em shipped in."

"Be all dried up," the barkeep objected. "Jenny'll want fresh flowers."

"Ain't goin' to find none!" Old Man Hawkins said cheerfully. "Might's well give up, Kid, an' hightail it after the Herrings. You would at least git some money if you got them . . . **if** you got 'em."

The Cactus Kid stared malevolently at his unoffending drink. Meanwhile he tried to arrange his thoughts into some sort of order. Now, flowers. Where would a man be apt to find flowers? Nowhere on the flatland, that was sure. The grass was dried up or the season wrong for any kind he knew of.

A man got up and walked to the bar and stopped beside the Kid. He was a big old man wearing a greasy buckskin shirt.

"I'm Ned Hayes," he said, "prospector. Heard you talkin' about flowers. You'll find plenty in the Blue Mountains. Ain't no drought up thataway. Country shore is green an' purty."

"Thanks." The Kid straightened up, suddenly filled with hope. Then he hesitated, remembering Jenny's admonition about fighting. "Ain't any trouble down thataway, is there? I sure aim to keep out of it this trip."

Hayes chuckled. "Why, man, you won't see a living soul! Nobody ever goes down there 'cept maybe a drifting Injun. Robber's Roost is some north, but they never git down so far. No, you won't see a soul, but you better pack extra grub. There's game, but you won't find no cattleman an' nary a sheep camp. I never seen nobody."

THE EIGHT PEAKS of the mountain group were black against the sky when the Cactus Kid's first day on the trail was ending. This was rough, wild, wind-worried and sun-scorched country, all new to him. Its wild and majestic beauty was lonely as a plateau on the moon, and water was scarce. He pushed on, remembering that Ned Hayes had said there was no drought in the Blues and not wanting to pitch dry camp out on the escarpment.

"Grassy on the east slopes, Kid," Hayes had added. "What yuh'll want to do is to cross the Divide. That is, go over the ridge to the west slope, and there you'll find the greenest forest you ever saw, rushing mountain streams, an' a passel of wildflowers of all kinds and shapes."

All day he had seen no track of horse or man, not even the unshod track of an Indian pony. It was eerie, lonely country and the Kid found himself glancing uneasily over his shoulder and staring in awed wonder at the eight peaks. The mountains were new to him, and they comprised a large section of country, all of sixteen miles long and about ten across.

The piebald was climbing now, and he bent to it with a will. The Kid had stumbled upon the semblance of a trail, an ancient Indian route, probably not used in centuries. It was marked at intervals by small piles of stones such as used to mark their trails in the deserts farther west.

The horse liked it. He could smell the rich, nutritious grass, and was ducking his head for an occasional mouthful. He had no idea where this strange master of his was taking him, but it looked like horse country. Grouse flew up from under his feet, and once a couple of black-tailed deer darted away from his movement, then stopped not a dozen yards away to study him.

Before him the hills showed a notch that seemed to offer a pass to the farther side, and the Cactus Kid swung his horse that way. Then he reined in sharply and stared at the ground.

Three hard-ridden horses had cut in sharply from the north, then swung toward the same cut in the hills that he was heading for. And the trail was fresh!

"What d' you know?" the Cactus Kid muttered. "Riders in this country! Well, nothing like company!"

Yet he rode more warily, for well he knew that riders in such an area might be on the dodge. North and west of here was a district in the canyons already becoming famous as Robber's Roost, and strange bands of horses or cattle occasionally drifted through the country, herded by hard-eyed riders who kept their own counsel and avoided trails.

CHAPTER II

A RED HERRING

Shadows were gathering into black pools in the canyons when he finally saw the notch in the hills deepen into a real opening. The piebald, weary as he was, walked now with his ears cocked forward, and once the Cactus Kid was quite sure he smelled dust in the air.

Despite the heat of the day, the evening grew chill and the night would be cold. The atmosphere was thin here, and the altitude high, yet he wanted to go over the pass before he bedded down. His eyes and ears were alert for sight or sound of the riders who preceded him, but he heard nothing, saw nothing.

At last he rode into the deep shadows of an aspen grove and, hearing water, pushed toward it. Here, on the banks of a small stream, he found a hollow. He built a fire, carefully shielded, and picketed his horse. After a brief supper and coffee, he rolled in his blanket and poncho and slept the night through.

He awoke to find his fire only the soft gray of wood ashes, the sky of the same shade and texture. Chilled, he threw off his blankets and built a fire of mountain mahogany, young pine, and branches broken from the dead lower limbs of the aspen. Soon the fire was crackling and he had water on.

The morning was still and cold. Below him the tops of trees were like islands in the mist rising from the forest, a thick fog like the smoke of leaf fires. The air was damp and the smoke held low, but the hungry tongues of the fire ate rapidly at the dry branches. In a matter of minutes there was the smell of coffee and of beef frying.

Several times he walked away from the task of preparing breakfast to look out through the woods beyond the hollow in which he was camped. Without any reason, he felt uneasy and his mind kept returning to the three riders. No honest men would be in this country unless they were passing through, and there were easier routes to the east and north. He thought of the Herrings but dismissed it at once. They were east of here and by now the posse probably had them.

His breakfast over, he led the piebald to water, but the horse refused to drink from the cold stream. Quickly he saddled up, then mounted. The black-and-white horse pitched a few times in a casual, disinterested way, more as a matter of form than of conviction. The Kid moved out.

Almost at once he saw the flowers. Many of them were sego lilies, faintly orchid in these mountains rather than pure white. There were other flowers, mostly of purple or violet colors, shading to white and some to blue. Lilac sunbonnet, forget-me-not, chia, and many other flowers seemed to be blooming here, most of which he knew but slightly or from the Indian use of some of them as remedies or food.

Sighting a particularly thick field of flowers, the Cactus Kid swung from his saddle and started into the field. He had stooped to pick flowers when a hard voice spoke behind him.

"Hold it right there, sprout," the voice said unpleasantly, "or you get a Winchester slug in your spine."

The Kid froze, startled but puzzled. "What's the matter?" he asked mildly. "I ain't troubling nobody."

"You ain't goin' to, neither." This was another voice. "What you doin' here?"

"Came after some flowers for my girl," the Kid said, realizing as he spoke that it sounded ridiculous.

A big man lumbered around in front of him, glancing at his face. "Yeah, you're right, Red. It's him. It's the Cactus Kid, all right. Shucks, I figured him quite a man from all I heard! This one's only a sprout."

"I don't like that word," the Kid said coldly. "Who are you, and what do you want with me?"

The big man chuckled. "Hear that, Red? He don't like being called sprout, an' he's only up here pickin' flowers! Now, ain't that sweet?"

The man guffawed, then sobered suddenly and struck the Kid a wicked, backhand blow that knocked him to the ground. The Kid, fury rising in him and throttling his good sense, grabbed for his guns. Instantly, a hawk-faced red-haired man confronted him and there was no arguing with the rifle in his hands.

"Drop it, Kid! We hear you're mighty fast on the draw, but you ain't that fast!"

Reluctantly, the Cactus Kid lifted his hands away from the guns and raised them shoulder-high.

"Keep that big lug off me, then," he protested, "or else take my guns and turn me loose! I'll tear down his meat house!"

"Why, you dumb sprout!" The big man started forward. "I got a notion to . . . !"

"Cut it out!" Red said angrily. "What's the matter, Joe? You lettin' him get your goat? Forget it." The red-haired man turned his cold gray eyes on the Kid. "Who's with you?"

"Nobody! I come up here alone, and like I said, I'm after **flowers**."

"Flowers!" Joe sneered. "He's after flowers! Now, wouldn't that kill you? The Cactus Kid, gunfighter and manhunter, after **flowers**!"

The Kid glared. "I'll peel your hide for this, you buttonheaded maverick!"

"Shut up!" Red spoke harshly. "Get along toward that dead fir. Right over there! Joe"—Red's voice was sharp—"bring that piebald. We can use a good horse."

"You aiming to set me afoot?" The Kid spoke more quietly. "Look, Red Whatever-your-name-is, I'm on the level about this flower business. My gal down to Helper, she's giving a party. You know how women are."

"How are they?" Red questioned. "I ain't talked to a woman in three months. You keep movin', an' watch your talk to Joe an' Benny. They get mighty touchy."

Joe and Benny . . . and Red.

The Herring brothers!

HE WAS SO STARTLED he almost missed his footing and fell, but caught himself in time. Of course! What had he been thinking of not to guess at once who they were? Joe and Benny Herring, killers both of them, wanted for bank and train holdups, but nothing at all to the deadly Red Herring, the gunman from the Gila. A cold-blooded and vicious killer with a flashing speed that had sent more than one marshal and sheriff to Boot Hill.

The Herrings . . . and they had him cold turkey. The boys who had forced a banker to open the bank safe, then escort them from town, and on the outskirts had coolly shot him dead.

And Jenny had warned him against getting into a fight. He groaned, and Red Herring prodded him with a rifle barrel.

"What's that for?" he demanded.

"Aw, Jenny . . . she's my girl. She warned me not to get in any fights."

Red chuckled without humor. "Don't worry, cowhand, you ain't in no fight, nor liable to be. You lost this one afore it started. Frankly, we'd as soon hang your hide on the cabin wall as rob a bank. We heard of you."

The Kid decided nothing was to be gained by conversation. He had no doubt Red meant just what he said. They might have had friends, if such men ever had friends, whom he had gunned down or helped send over the road to the pen. Anyway, in outlaw hangouts the killing of the Cactus Kid would be something to boast about.

Suddenly the earth broke sharply off in a thick

grove of aspen where a steep, rocky trail wound downward through the trees. It was a one-man-at-a-time trail, and when they reached the bottom they were in a nest of boulders mingled with ancient trees, huge white-limbed deadfalls, and the sound of running water.

Benny Herring was a thin, saturnine man with a scar on his chin. He looked up at them, staring at the Kid.

"He the one followed us?" He stared evilly at the Kid. "How'd you spot our trail? Who else knows about it?"

"He says he come up here huntin' flowers!" Joe sneered.

Benny eyed him without humor or interest. "What did you bring him back for? Why didn't you shoot him an' leave him lay?"

"Buzzards." Red's voice was casual. "Tie him up, Joe."

"Sure." Joe shambled up to him, grinning out of his narrow eyes. Then he smashed the Kid across the face, over and back, caught him before he fell, and shoved him against a stunted tree scarcely taller than the Kid himself.

The Cactus Kid felt blood trickling down his chin, and he glared at Joe, taking a deep breath. Joe tied him tightly and thoroughly. Then he stared at the Kid, who stared back at him. Setting himself, Joe hooked a right to his wind and the Kid felt his breath leave him with a gasp.

Without a backward glance, Joe Herring slouched to the fire and the three began eating, talking in a low-voiced, desultory fashion. Despite their questions about who else knew of their trail, they seemed unworried, so the Kid deduced they had actually seen him behind them on the previous day, and knew he was alone.

He was no fool. His situation was desperate. That they would not hesitate to leave him dead, he knew. All three of these men would hang if caught alive and they had proved too many times in the past that they had no hesitation about killing a helpless man. None of them was the sort to be troubled by qualms or conscience.

Red was obviously the leader, yet from his looks Benny was no fool. Joe was a hulking brute, physically powerful, but mentally his range was bare.

The Kid's chances looked nil, and they might kill him at any time. However, if they would leave him alone for a while . . . He had his own ideas about that, and his first ruse had worked.

Red had said they did not kill him because of buzzards. They were afraid attention might be drawn to the area by some chance rider seeing circling buzzards. That implied they were not ready to leave. For all he knew, this area might be a permanent hideout for them, and might explain why they had so often dropped from sight on previous occasions.

Tentatively, he tried his bonds. Having taken a deep breath and swelled his muscles before being tied, he now had a little slack. It was little enough, but he was thankful that he had not been hit in the wind before being tied, as that little slack might make all the difference in the world. His four inches of chest expansion had been a help before this, but never had he needed it so much.

His wrists, however, were tightly bound, although he knew he could move around the tree with some ease if left alone.

When they finished eating, Benny mounted a horse and drifted out of the hollow—to act as a lookout, the Kid guessed. Red smoked a cigarette and eyed the Kid irritably. Obviously, he was in the way, and wouldn't be kept around for long.

Red Herring was wise in not attracting attention to their hideout, for the Cactus Kid knew that searchers were not even coming this way, and as this country was seldom traveled, it was perfection itself for their purposes. There was small chance that anyone might see the circling buzzards, but at this time caution was the smart thing and Red Herring had the cunning of a wolf. At the same time, the Kid knew that it would serve no purpose to keep him alive. He was only an encumbrance, and the sooner they rid themselves of him the better off they were.

An idea came to the Kid suddenly, an idea that might keep him alive a little longer, and he desperately wanted to live.

"You got it mighty good here," he said. "Only that money won't do you much good in this hole."

"We don't aim to stay." Red threw a couple of dry sticks on the fire. "Just to let things quiet down."

"They'll be watching for you at Hanksville, Greenriver, and Dandy Crossing. At Helper and Henrieville, too."

Herring looked up, studying the Kid. "How'd you know that?"

"They wanted me in the posse. I wouldn't go because my girl wanted the flowers."

Red grunted. "You stickin' to that story? Why come way down here?"

"Figure it out for yourself. With this drought there ain't none anywhere around. Prospector told me about these flowers. Hombre name of Hayes."

Red nodded. "Know about him. So they got us bottled up, have they? Why tell us? Why not let us ride into a trap?"

The Kid grinned wryly. "Because I want to live. To get you killed after I'm dead doesn't help me, and the way I figure it, you don't aim to let me live that long."

"That's right. We'll kill you before the day's out. Drop you in a hole over west of here. Still, I don't see why you tell me."

"I said, because I want to live . . . and there's a way out of this country."

"Out of here? How?" The Kid was aware of Red's awakened interest. If he could keep him hooked . . .

"South of here, if you know the water holes. Otherwise, you can die out there."

"South?" Red studied the situation. "That's a mighty long ride. I heard a man couldn't make it through. You know the water holes?"

"Sure, I know 'em. And I know the trails like an Injun. You boys aren't known down thataway, either, are you?"

Red got to his feet and walked over, rolling a smoke. He stuck the cigarette in the Kid's lips and lit it.

"No, we ain't." He studied the Kid carefully. "You figure we'll let you go if you take us through?"

The Kid grinned. "No. I never heard of you doing anybody any favors, Red. But the longer I stay alive the better my chances are. You might decide to lay off, or I might get a chance to light a shuck."

Red chuckled but without humor. "Yeah, that's reasonable enough. You're buying time."

CHAPTER III
DESPERATE CHANCE

Nothing more was said and they waited the hours out. The men changed jobs from time to time, and there was much low-voiced discussion among them. As the night drew on, it became rapidly colder. At dusk Benny came in from watching and the three ate, talked longer, then rolled up in their blankets and went to sleep.

The Cactus Kid shivered in the cold, crisp air, his

body held immobile by his bonds. He tried tensing groups of muscles to keep his circulation alive and ward off the worst of the cold, and after a while he tried his bonds. The four inches of chest expansion had given him a little slack with which to work, and he could turn his body on the dead tree. Yet for all his straining he could do little with the rawhide thongs that bound his hands behind him.

Morning dawned cold and crisp and Benny walked over to him and untied him. "Set and eat," he said briefly.

For an hour they questioned him about the route south, and his answers evidently satisfied them. Much of this country was as strange to him as to them, but he did know that trail out, and he was sure that once they were traveling, his chance would come. Anyway, it was a reprieve, if only for a few days.

After having him collect more wood while watched by Joe with a rifle, they tied him again, and this time left him sitting on the ground. This time, too, he held his breath and bulged his muscles while straining for slack. And again he got it, although not so much as before.

Red was the first guard and he walked away from camp right away. Benny returned to the Kid and plied him with questions about the trail. He seemed disturbed by the trip, but why, the Cactus Kid could not gather.

Then, almost at noon, Red came in leading the horses. "We'll go," he said. "Nobody's coming. Far's a man can see, that trail's empty. We've lost 'em, but to go out thataway would be asking for trouble. The Kid can guide us over this south trail."

Although his weapons were carried by Joe Herring, the Cactus Kid was left unbound. At once, he headed off south through the mountains with Red beside him and the other Herrings immediately behind. Leaving the hills, they descended to Sage Plain, skirted Elk Ridge and the Bear's Ears, dropped into Cottonwood Wash and proceeded along it and then out into a fantastic world of eerie towers and spires like the images of cathedrals cast in stone.

At dark, he brought them up to a spring, a small trickle of water running from a fracture in the rock into a small basin, which overflowed in turn to be lost in the sand. Nearby were several windbreaks made by Indians from pine boughs or slabs of rock. There was no evidence of human life other than that, and no sign that anybody had been near in months.

Once, on the rim of a canyon, Red Herring drew up sharply.

"Thought you said there was nobody down this-away?"

"What do you see?" the Kid asked curiously.

"House, or building over yonder." Herring stood in his stirrups and squinted. "Sort of tower."

"Oh, that?" The Kid shrugged. "Injun ruins. Lots of them down here." He turned the piebald down a steep trail to the canyon bottom. Here, in this well-watered place, they rode into groves of fir, pine, and black balsam, while snowberry and manzanita grew thick along the canyon walls. There was grass, and yet here and there clumps of desert plants had invaded this richer, moister soil.

Late in the afternoon Red Herring suddenly snapped his rifle to his shoulder. Its report bellowed against the canyon walls and a mule deer plunged to its knees, tried to get up, then sprawled out.

"Nothing like fresh meat," Red said with satisfaction.

"Who skins it?" Joe demanded belligerently. "Why don't we make this sprout work?" He grinned at the Kid. "Let him earn his keep."

"Good idea," Red said, "you're cook from here on, Kid."

"Good!" the Cactus Kid said. "Now I can get some decent chuck for a while. That Joe cooks like he was fixing food for hogs."

Joe glared, and Benny chuckled. "Danged if it ain't the truth!" he said. "He had you there, Joe!"

Accepting the knife tossed to him, the Kid got busy over the deer, cutting out some fine steaks. As he worked, he was thinking swiftly. This might be the gamble he wanted, and in any event, it was worth taking a chance. As he gathered fuel for the fire and started his broiling of the steaks, he thought rapidly.

Back along the line there had been some desert brush, among them a plant he had recognized. It was a low-growing shrub, without leaves at this time of year, but with its stems dotted with odd, glandlike swellings. As he worked, the Kid kept his eyes busy and finally located the plant he sought, a relative of the rue known in many lands for medicinal effects. Carefully, from under the plant he gathered some of the dried leaves and, when making coffee, crushed a double handful and dropped them into the boiling water with the coffee. Finding more of the plants, he gathered a stack of the leaves while collecting wood and put them down not far from the fire.

Red bit into his first piece of steak, then looked up at the Kid. "You just got yourself a few more days, podner. This is **grub**!"

Even the surly Joe agreed that the Cactus Kid could cook, but when he tasted the coffee, he stared at it.

"Tastes funny," he said, scowling.

Red picked up his cup and tried it. "Tastes good to me," he said. "It's just that your taster has been ru-int by that alkali and coffee junk you put out for coffee."

The Kid added more fuel to the fire. Soon they would tie him, but how soon? He had to guess right and beat them to it. Whether his stunt would work, he did not know, but it was a gamble he had to take. The Utes had told him of the plant and its effects, that it was used by them as a sedative, and that leaves thrown on a fire provided undisturbed sleep.

He poured a liberal cup of coffee for himself, but he managed to see that his cup came only after they had been served, and from a second batch that contained none of the leaves. Getting up, the Kid threw some more brush on the fire, and with it the small mound of leaves he had gathered. They burned slowly, and the smoke grew thicker, but the aroma was not unpleasant.

Benny looked up suddenly. "Joe, you better tie him up. I'm getting sleepy."

"Me, too," Red agreed. "That was a long ride, and I ate more'n usual."

Joe Herring lumbered to his feet. Crossing to the Kid he jerked his wrists behind him and tied them together, his fingers clumsy with sleep. Then he tied the Kid's feet together and walked back to his bedroll.

Red was already asleep, his blanket pulled over him. At the fire, Benny dozed, and while the Cactus Kid watched hopefully, smoke drifted across his face and the man nodded. Finally, with a glance over at the Kid, Benny got up and went to his bedroll. And then, for a long time, there was silence.

THE KID WAS WORKING HARD. His breath coming hoarsely, he struggled with the poorly tied thongs on his wrists. Unable to do much with them, he hooked the toes of his boots under a log and carefully, with much struggling, succeeded in drawing his feet out of the boots. Then he backed around to them and managed to dig their toes down into the sand so that he could rub the rawhide on the rowels of his spurs. It took him more than an hour and then the thongs dropped free and he drew his wrists from behind him. They were chafed and bloody, but free!

Sitting perfectly still, he worked his fingers to restore circulation, then removed the thongs from around his boots and put them on. Crossing to the stack of guns, he picked up his own and belted them on, then put his rifle carefully to one side and considered the situation.

The Herrings were not doped. Not, at least, to the extent that they had passed out. From what he had heard, the qualities of the plant he had used were sufficient only to induce a sound sleep, which, added to their natural drowsiness from the long day in the saddle and warm food, had been sufficient. Yet he was sure that the slightest sound of a squabble and they would awaken.

Knowing them, he knew they would come awake fighting. They would gamble. Whether he could manage without awakening them he did not know, and his first instinct was for flight. Yet here they were, the men wanted so badly, and the reward would do a lot toward stocking a ranch as well as removing from circulation some badmen no better than mad dogs.

Red was sleeping with his guns on and his rifle beside him. Benny had been more careless, yet his weapons were close. Joe, who had been carrying the Kid's weapons, had left them all together.

Moving carefully out of camp, the Kid got the piebald and saddled him. When he was ready, in case of emergency, the Kid walked slowly back to camp.

Very gently, he slipped a loop over Joe's wrists and drew it as tight as he dared. The big man was sleeping with his knees drawn up, so the Kid bound his wrists down to his knees. He was just straightening up when, lifting his eyes, he looked into the startled, staring eyes of Ben Herring!

Instantly, Ben yelled, "Red! Look out! The Kid's loose!" And at the same instant he grabbed for his gun.

"Drop it!" The Cactus Kid's gun leaped into his hand. "Drop!"

Ben's finger whitened on the trigger and the Kid's gun bellowed. It was point-blank range and a fast shot. The bullet hit the cartridges in Ben's belt and glanced, smashing his elbow. The thin man dropped his gun and grabbed his arm, while on the ground Joe thrashed around, trying to free himself.

A gun bellowed from the brush and the Kid dove for shelter among some rocks. Red had not waited to draw iron, but had leaped instantly for shelter. Now he crouched there across the fire, and the Cactus Kid knew he was in for the fight of his life.

"Quiet down, Joe," the Kid called, "or I'll put a slug in you!"

Joe ceased struggling and Ben sat there by the fire, gripping his bloody arm. "I'm out of this! You crippled me!"

"See you stay out of it!" the Kid replied shortly. Then he faded back into the deeper darkness.

He was desperately worried. The night was intensely dark, and he knew from his own moving around that a man could move easily and make no sound. The trees were not too close together, and the clumps of brush could be avoided. And Red Herring was a killer, a man with every sense alert, knowing that if captured he would hang.

Moreover, the man would be filled with hatred now, and the Kid knew he had never faced a man more dangerous, more filled with concentrated evil and malice, than Red Herring.

CHAPTER IV
JENNY'S PARTY

The Cactus Kid lay still, well back from the fire. He knew that every second he was out of sight of the camp was a second fraught with even greater danger, for if they realized he was gone, Ben would free Joe and he would be facing two men and possibly a third.

There was no sound. The darkness lay thick and still around him. The stars were lost above a cushion of thick cloud; there was no wind. Somewhere a stone rattled, but it was far away. The Kid began to sweat. His stomach felt hollow and he stared, straining his eyes into the darkness, fighting down his desire to move, to get away from there. Yet to move might mean death, and his best plan was not to move, but to lie still, to force Red to come to him.

And he knew that Red Herring, outlaw and murderer, would do just that.

One of the horses stamped, and somewhere a grouse called into the night. The Cactus Kid shifted his gun and dried his sweaty palm on his shirt. Ever so carefully, the Kid moved, sliding his body along the ground, edging toward a clump of manzanita that would permit a view of the fire.

Ben was fighting to bind his arm, and Joe was cursing steadily, staring toward the outer circle of darkness. The Kid waited, and an hour went slowly by.

Suddenly, he stiffened with realization. While he waited, tense with watching for Red, who would be stalking him, the fire was dying!

With the fire dead, and the two men in the circle of its light freed from his watching eyes, he would lose control over the situation and at once he would become the hunted, not the hunter!

Yet he dared not call out to order them to build the fire. To speak would be to have his position riddled with bullets. Cold in the blackness, he fought for a solution, and then, suddenly, he had what seemed to be the answer.

The loot.

It lay almost halfway around the circle, on the edge of the firelight. Soon the place where it lay would be in darkness. Probably as soon as he could get to it. Lying there, forgotten in the face of more immediate problems, it could be the key to the whole show. If he could get the money, then get to his horse, he might at least save the loot. And he might succeed in drawing the Herrings into a trap. For if he had the money, they would follow him.

Slowly, inch by inch, he worked his way along the ground, circling the fire. At any instant he might come face to face with Red; at any instant they might shoot it out. And over there in the circle of trees, the fire was flickering only in a few spots now.

Then the sacks of loot were there, only a short distance from his hands. With infinite care, he reached out and lifted them one by one back into the brush. Fortunately, there was little gold, so the weight was nothing to worry about. With the sacks in his left hand he eased back and got to his feet.

He found the piebald by his white spots and moved to him. The horse sidestepped and instantly the area flamed with light! A gun bellowed and a shot plucked at his sleeve.

Red Herring, guessing he would come for the saddled horse, had waited beside a stack of dry brush covered with leaves!

The flare of the fire, the stab of the shot, and his own action were one. Flinging himself in a long dive, the Kid went, not for shelter or for the horse, but straight at the stabbing flame of the shot!

A gun roared again and he heard the slam of the shot past his ear and then he was in the brush. Red Herring sprang to his feet and triggered the gun at point-blank range, but the Kid was coming too hard, and as he fired, Herring tried to step back. A rock rolled under his foot and his shot missed, and then the Cactus Kid hit him with his pistol.

Herring staggered, then caught himself and swung wickedly with the barrel of his gun for the Kid's head, but, rolling over, the Cactus Kid smashed his body against Herring's legs and the cursing outlaw went down.

Both men came up without guns and the Cactus Kid, fighting with the madness of fear, realizing his time was short, slashed into the outlaw with both fists winging. His right caught Herring on the jaw and knocked him into a tree, and before Red could set himself, the Cactus Kid closed in, smashing left and right to the head, a smashing right to the body, and a wicked left that broke Herring's nose and showered him with blood. Herring swung, missed, and his chin blocked a wicked right with all the Kid's lean, muscular power behind it. Herring hit the sand flat on his face and the Kid dove for his gun even as Joe and Ben came plowing through the brush.

"Freeze!" The Kid's gun was on them. "Drop 'em, boys, or I'll plant all of you right here!" He had the drop . . . and they let go their guns.

IT WAS MIDAFTERNOON, four days later. The town was crowded with the Saturday flux of ranchers. Suddenly, there was a startled yell, and men poured into the streets.

Down the dusty main drag came four riders.

Three rode abreast, and all who saw them immediately recognized the three bloody Herrings. Joe, who rode on the right, had a huge armful of sego lilies, as did Ben, who rode on the left. Red, who rode in the middle, his horse carefully roped to the other two, carried a huge armful of western forget-me-nots and purple verbena mingled with a few bunches of lilac sunbonnets.

The town stared, then it cheered, and the Herrings glowered. Up the street they went, followed by the crowd, and halted before the Simms's home.

"Oh, Nesselrode! You're **wonderful**! You got my flowers!"

"Yeah." He dismounted stiffly and began taking the flowers from the arms of the three surly outlaws. Red's head was wrapped in a bloody bandage torn from a shirt. Ben's arm was in a sling.

"Got 'em. Better get 'em in water. They may be wilted some."

If Jenny noticed the Herrings it was not obvious. "Oh, Nesselrode! I knew you could do it! I just **knew** you could!"

Joe Herring glowered. "Huh! Nesselrode! Kotched by an hombre name of **Nesselrode**!"

The Cactus Kid turned and his eyes were deadly. "I never shot a man with his hands tied, but you mention that name again and you'll be the first!"

The sheriff came pounding up with two deputies and took the prisoners.

"Well, what do you know, Jenny!" he exclaimed. "This cowpuncher of yours caught the Herring boys!"

"The Herring boys?" She smiled prettily. "Oh, Sheriff, will you ask your wife to come over and help me decorate? I don't know whether that verbena would go better in the parlor or—"

The sheriff bit off a chew.

"You catch the three meanest outlaws west of the Rockies," he said to the Kid, "and she wants to know whether the verbena will look better in one room or t'other!" He spat. "Women! I never will get 'em figured out!"

The Cactus Kid grunted, and dug out the makings. He was unshaven and the desert dust was thick on his clothes. He was half dead from his long ride and lack of sleep.

Jenny appeared suddenly in the door. "Oh, Nesselrode? Will you help me a minute, please? Pretty please?"

The Kid looked at the sheriff, and the sheriff shrugged. "Yeah," the Kid said, low-voiced. Then he looked up. "Coming, honey!" he said.

The Cactus Kid
Pays a Debt

Four people, two women and two men, boarded the San Francisco boat in company with the Cactus Kid. Knight's Landing was a freight landing rather than a passenger stop, and the five had been drawn together while waiting on the dock.

Mr. Harper, pompous in black broadcloth, wore muttonchop whiskers and a prominent mustache. Ronald Starrett, younger and immaculate in dark suit and hat, looked with disdain at the Kid's wide white hat, neat gray suit and high-heeled boots.

The Kid carried a carpetbag that never left his hands, a fact duly noted by both men and one of the women. The Kid, more at home aboard the hurricane deck of a bronc than on a river steamer, had good reason for care. He was taking fifteen thousand dollars, the final payment on the Walking YY, from his boss, Jim Wise, to old MacIntosh.

"What time does this boat get in?" the Kid asked of Harper.

"Around midnight," Harper said. "If you haven't a hotel in mind, I'd suggest the Palace."

"If you go there," Starrett added, "stay out of the Cinch Room or you'll lose everything you have."

"Thanks," the Cactus Kid responded dryly.

Five feet seven inches in his sock feet, and a compact one hundred and fifty pounds, the Kid, with his shock of curly hair and a smile women thought charming, was usually taken to be younger and softer than he was.

On the Walking YY and in its vicinity the Kid was a living legend, and the only person in his home country who did not tremble at the Kid's step was Jenny Simms—or if she did, it was in another sense.

"It's a positive shame!" the older woman burst out. "A young man like you, so nice-looking and all, going to that awful town! You be careful of your company, young man!"

Nesselrode Clay, otherwise the Cactus Kid, flushed deeply. "I reckon I will, ma'am. I'll be in town only a few hours on business. I want to get back to the ranch."

Harper glanced thoughtfully at the carpetbag and Starrett's eyes followed. The younger woman, obviously a proud young lady, indulged in no idle conversation. Miss Lily Carfather was going to San Francisco with her aunt, somebody had said.

"It looks like a dull trip," Starrett's voice was casual. "Would anybody care for a quiet game of cards?"

Mr. Harper glanced up abruptly, taking in the

young man with a suspicious, measuring eye. "Never play with strangers," he replied brusquely.

"I think," Lily Carfather said icily, "gambling is abominable!"

"On the contrary," Starrett defended, "it is a perfectly honorable pastime when played by gentlemen, and we are gentlemen here."

He drew out a deck of cards, broke the seal and shuffled the cards without skill. The Cactus Kid considered Ronald Starrett more carefully.

Harper glanced at his watch. "Well," he mumbled, "there is a good bit of time. . . . A little poker, you said?" He glanced at the Kid, who shrugged and moved to the table.

"If," Starrett glanced at the women, "you'd care to join us? Please don't think me bold but—a friendly game? For small stakes?"

Lily Carfather dropped her eyes. "Well—" she hesitated.

"Lily!" The older woman was shocked. "You wouldn't."

"On the contrary"—her chin lifted defiantly—"I believe I shall!"

Ronald Starrett shuffled the cards and handed them to Harper for the cut. No limit was set, the Kid noticed, as play began. Picking up his cards the Kid found himself with a pair of jacks.

THE CACTUS KID HAD LOST his innocence where cards were concerned in Tascosa when he was sixteen, and as this game proceeded, he grew increasingly interested. He stayed even, while his observant eyes noted that the end of the middle finger on Starrett's left hand was missing. Also, Mr. Harper played a shrewd and careful game, while behind the seeming innocence of Lily Carfather was considerable card savvy.

Suddenly the Kid found himself holding three nines. He considered them, decided to stay and on the draw picked up a pair of jacks. He won a small pot. And he won the next two hands.

"You're lucky, Mr. Clay," Starrett suggested, smiling. "Well, maybe we'll get some of it back later."

The Kid drew nothing on the following hand and threw in, but on the next he won a fair-sized pot. He found himself feeling a little like a missionary being banqueted by cannibals. He lost a little, won some more and found himself almost a hundred dollars ahead. He was not surprised when Starrett dealt him four kings and a trey. He tossed in the trey, drew a queen and began to bet.

After two rounds of betting, Harper dropped out. Starrett had taken two cards as had Lily. On the next round, with both the Kid and Lily raising, Starrett dropped out. On the showdown Lily had four aces. She gathered in the pot, winning more than a hundred dollars from the Kid alone.

Harper dealt and the Kid lost again, then Lily dealt and the Kid glanced at his cards and tossed them into the discard. The fun was over now and he was slated for the axe. When it came his turn to deal, he shuffled and easily built up a bottom stock from selected discards, passed the cards to Lily for the cut, then picked up the deck and shifted the cut in a smoothly done movement and proceeded to deal swiftly, building his own hand from the bottom until he held the three he wanted.

Harper threw in his hand but Starrett and Lily stayed. The Kid gave Starrett three, Lily two, and himself—from the bottom—two. Picking up his hand he looked into the smug faces of a royal flush.

Lily glanced at her hand. "I want to raise it twenty dollars," she said sweetly.

"I'll see that and raise it ten," the Kid offered, "I feel lucky."

The pot built up until it contained almost four hundred dollars. Starrett called with a full house and Lily followed with a small straight. Coolly, the Kid placed his royal flush on the table and gathered in the pot.

Harper bit the end from his cigar and Lily's face grew pale, her eyes very bright. Starrett's face flushed dull red and his eyes grew angry. "You're very lucky!" he sneered.

It was Starrett's deal and the Kid knew it was coming right at him. And it came, starting with three aces. Coolly, he tossed in his hand and Starrett fumbled a card.

Lily smiled icily at the Kid. "What's the matter?" she asked, too sweetly. "Not lucky this time?"

"I'm a hunch player," the Kid lied, "and this isn't my hand."

Twice in the next hour the Cactus Kid realized they had him set for the kill, but he avoided it by throwing in a hand or making only an insignificant bet. Harper was a little ahead but Starrett was in the hole for more than six hundred and Lily had lost just as much. The Cactus Kid was over a thousand dollars a winner.

Suddenly, the Kid realized that Lily's aunt was no longer with them. Even as the thought came to him, she returned to the room. "I was worried," he said. "I was afraid you had taken my luck with you."

The aunt's eyes met Lily's and Lily glanced around the table. "Is anyone else thirsty?" she asked. "I am— very!"

"Let's call a waiter and have a few drinks," Starrett suggested.

The Kid nodded agreement, gathering up the discards. There had been an ace in those discards and Harper had held two kings. Now if— He palmed the ace and two kings and slipped them into a bottom stock. Riffling the cards he located another ace and king, adding them to the stock. Then with swift, practiced movements he worked up two good hands for Starrett and Harper. He won again.

Starrett's polish was gone now and when he looked at the Kid, there was hatred in his eyes. Harper said nothing at all, but glanced thoughtfully at Lily.

The drinks were brought in and as they were

placed on the table the Kid fumbled a chip, and in grabbing for it knocked over Lily's drink. The Kid sprang to his feet.

"Oh, I'm very sorry, Miss Carfather!" he exclaimed. "Here," he sat down and moved his own glass to her, "you're the thirsty one. Take mine."

Her eyes blazed with fury. "Keep your drink!" she flared. "I won't take anything from you!"

The Cactus Kid grinned suddenly. "No," he agreed, "none of you will."

Their eyes were on him, hard and implacable. "It was too easy," the Kid said cheerfully. "Starrett with that bobbed middle finger. It makes a bottom deal easier but it's a dead giveaway."

With his left hand he pulled the money toward him and began to pocket it. Their eyes, hot with greed, stared at the gold coins.

"I'll be damned if you take that money!" Harper's voice burst out low and hard.

The Cactus Kid smiled his charming, boyish smile. "Stop tryin' to work that derringer out of your pocket, Harper. I've got a Peacemaker in my hand under the table, an' if you feel like gamblin' on a .44 slug, start something."

Harper's gun was out, but he pointed it at Starrett. **"Don't!"** he barked. "Don't start anything, you fool! You want to get me killed?"

"He wouldn't care much, would he, Harper? They'd just have one less to split with."

*　*　*

WITH A SWIFT, catlike movement, the Cactus Kid was on his feet, his gun covering them all. "Put that derringer in your pocket, Harper. You might get hurt."

His face red, Harper shoved the gun into his pocket. "All right, you got our money. Why don't you get out of here?"

"One thing yet," the Cactus Kid smiled, "an' maybe I'll hate myself for this, but I did hear her say she was thirsty. Lily, you drink my drink."

"Why—why." She sprang to her feet. "I'll do nothing of—"

"Drink it," he insisted. "You ordered it for me. Try your own medicine."

"I won't! You'd never have the nerve to shoot a woman! You wouldn't dare!"

"You're right. I wouldn't want it on my conscience, and threatening to shoot one of your friends wouldn't help. I think you'd see them both die first. No, there's a better way. You drink it or I'll turn you over to the vigilantes. I hear there's some around again."

Her frightened eyes went to Starrett. "Drink it, Lily," Starrett said carefully. "We don't dare have them after us. You know that."

She stared at them with pure hatred, then picked up the glass. "I'll kill you for this!" she fairly hissed at the Kid. Then she downed the drink.

His eyes on them, the Kid stepped quickly back to the door, taking his carpetbag with him. Closing the door behind him he ran on tiptoes to the bow of the boat and down into the fo'c'sle. A tired and greasy sailor was tying his shoes.

"Look, mister," the seaman said, "this isn't—"

"I know it," the Kid produced a gold eagle, "I'll give you this for the use of your bunk until we dock and if you forget you saw me."

The seaman got up, grinning. "I'm due on watch, anyway. That's the easiest twenty I ever made!"

The Cactus Kid sat down to think. Obviously they had known he was carrying a large sum of money and had planned to get it away from him with the cards. He had outsmarted them and then spoiled their attempt to dope him. After what he had just done they would make a play not only for the money but for his life as well.

The Cactus Kid frowned. Four sharp operators had not chosen him by accident, but so far as he knew only Jim Wise and old MacIntosh knew what he was carrying. It was preposterous to think that either might be involved in this.

Easing out of the bunk, the Kid crept up the ladder and looked out on deck. He froze into stillness in the shadows. A burly, sweatered figure was standing near the bulwark a little aft of the companionway. As this man waited another came up and spoke to him. It was Harper!

So they had hired thugs on the boat. Feeling trapped, the Kid returned to the bunk to consider the matter. Opening the carpetbag he took out his other Colt, strapped the holster under his armpit, and tied it in place with piggin strings.

Finally he dozed, then slept. Awakening with a start he heard the sounds that told of coming alongside the dock and knew they were in San Francisco. Acting on a sudden inspiration, he worked swiftly with the contents of the carpetbag. When he was satisfied he walked boldly out on deck and headed for the gangway. Harper spotted him and spoke to the thug beside him.

None of the poorly lighted streets that led away from the dock looked inviting, but a four-horse carriage marked PALACE HOTEL stood waiting for prospective guests, and the Kid made for it. He was surprised to find Starrett in the carriage, for he had believed he was the first person down the gangway. The driver, a burly ruffian with a red mustache, glanced sharply at the Kid, then let his eyes move to Harper, who stood near a pile of packing cases. Harper nodded.

Other men crowded into the carriage, among them two huskies, and the Kid at once became alert.

The carriage swung into one of the dark streets, then turned into a cross street between high, unlighted buildings. One of the huskies reached up and took down the Palace Hotel sign. The other one looked at the Kid and grinned.

"Pull up!" Starrett ordered. "This is far enough!"

The Cactus Kid left his seat with a lunge, springing to neither right nor left as they probably expected, but straight ahead. He landed astride the nearest horse and with a wild Texas yell kicked with both heels. All four of the frightened animals lunged into their collars and took off down the cobbled street with men shouting and grabbing for holds behind them.

Slipping from the back of the horse to the tongue, the Kid worked his way forward to the lead team. The driver was trying to fight the horses to a stand, but the Kid reached and grabbed the reins. With a vicious jerk, he pulled them loose, and the driver, over-balanced, fell from his seat to the cobblestoned street. The horses picked up speed and ran wild, eyes rolling, jaws slavering.

The Cactus Kid heard the crack of a pistol and a shot went by his ear. Gripping the hip strap with his left hand, which also clutched the carpetbag, the Kid took a chance shot under his arm. Several of the riders had dropped from the rig but the others made a solid block that could scarcely be missed.

A YELP OF PAIN sounded behind him and several men sprang from the carriage. Shoving the pistol into his waistband, the Kid swung astride the off lead horse and hauled desperately on the reins. As the carriage slowed he slid from the animal's back to the street. He scrambled up and ducked into an alley.

Someone yelled from the carriage as it rattled by, and a dark figure loomed in the alley and shouted a reply, then started for him. The Cactus Kid palmed his six-shooter and fired. The charging man fell on his face and the Kid wheeled and ran.

He ducked in and out of alleys until he was winded. Then a door showed suddenly, and he tried the knob. Miraculously, it was not locked and he stepped in, closing and barring it behind him. Feeling his way up dark stairs he knew from the faint sounds of tinny music that he was in a building that housed some kind of resort.

On the second-floor landing he tried a door, but it was locked so he went on to the third floor. A door opened into a hallway with doors on either side. Swiftly, the Kid hurried down the hall to the head of another flight of stairs. A beefy man with a red face and a walrus mustache stood there.

"Hey!" he demanded roughly. "Who'd you come up with?"

"I came up the back stairs," the Cactus Kid replied, "and I'm going down the front stairs."

"Yeah?" His eyes traveled over the Kid from the broad hat to the carpetbag. "Yeah? Well, we'll talk to Bull Run first."

"Who's Bull Run?"

"Bull Run?" The thug was incredulous. "You ain't heard of Bull Run Allen?"

Something turned over inside the Cactus Kid. He had heard many cowhands and others talk of the BULL RUN, at the corner of Pacific Street and Sullivan Alley. It was one of the toughest and most criminal dives in a town that could boast of many of the worst in the world. He could not have found his way into a worse trap.

"No need to talk to him," he said. "All I want is to go through. Here"—he took a coin from his pocket—"say nothing to anybody. I had some trouble back in the street. Had to slug a gent."

The thug looked avariciously at the money. "Well, I guess it ain't none of my—" His voice broke and he gulped.

The Cactus Kid turned and found himself facing an elephant of a man in a snow-white, ruffled shirt with diamond studs. His big nose was a violent red, his huge hands glittered with gems.

"Who's this?" he demanded harshly. "What's goin' on?"

The thug swallowed. "It's this way, Bull Run," he began to explain. As he talked Allen nodded and studied the Kid. Finally he dropped a huge hand to the Kid's shoulder.

"Put away your money, son," he said genially, "and come wit' me. In trouble, are you? Couldn't have come to a better place. Law doesn't bother my place. I tell 'em you work for me an' it's all right. Let's go to my office."

Seating himself behind a huge desk, he grinned at the Kid. "Cattleman, hey? Used to figure I'd like that line my own self, but I got tied to this joint and couldn't get away. But I make plenty."

He bit the end from a black cigar and leaned forward, his smile fading. "All right, you got away with something good. Just split it down the middle and you can go—and you'll not be bothered."

"You've got me wrong, Allen," the Kid protested. "I've nothing of value. They fired me back on the ranch so I figured I'd come to town. Lost all I had, about fifteen bucks, to some gamblers on a boat. I slugged one of them an' got part of my money back, but they'd already divvied up."

Bull Run Allen scowled. "Describe the gamblers," he ordered.

At the Kid's description his eyes narrowed. "I know 'em. That gent who called himself Harper was Banker Barber, one of the slickest around here. Starrett—I can't figure that play. Starrett works society. He only plays for big money."

Suspicion was alive in his eyes as he studied the Kid. Seeing it, the Cactus Kid gambled. "Say, maybe that explains it! They were hunting somebody else an' got me by mistake! They seemed to think I had money, tried to get me to bet higher. Shucks," the Kid smiled innocently, "I've never had more'n a hundred and twenty dollars at one time!"

Bull Run Allen was not convinced. He wanted a look inside that carpetbag. On the other hand this youngster might be telling the truth and while they talked a rich prize might be getting away.

Bull Run stepped to the door and yelled to a man

to send up One-Ear Tim. The manager and bouncer was a burly character with one ear missing and a scarred face.

"Get hold o' the Banker," Bull Run ordered. "I want a talk with him." He grinned at the Kid as Tim walked away. "Now we'll find out about this here."

The Cactus Kid got to his feet. "Sorry I won't have time to wait," he said. "I'm heading for the Palace Hotel. You can see me there."

Allen gave vent to a fat chuckle of amusement. "Don't think I couldn't," he said, "but you sit still. We'll talk to the Banker first."

"No," the Kid replied quietly, "I can't wait." In his hand he held a .44 Colt. "You come with me, Bull Run. Only you go first."

Allen's eyes grew ugly. "You can't get away with this!" he sneered. "I ain't goin' nowheres, so go ahead an' shoot. No durned kid can—" he lunged, both hands spread wide.

The Cactus Kid was in his element. He struck down Allen's reaching left and smashed the barrel of his Colt over the big man's ear, and Allen hit the floor as if dropped from a roof. Quickly, the Kid stepped outside to the balcony. Still clutching the carpetbag with his left hand, his right hovering near the butt of his .44, he walked down the stairs to the brawling room below, crowded with gamblers and drinkers.

Almost at the door he ran into Tim. The bouncer stopped him. "Where you goin'? The boss wanted you to talk to the Banker."

"He wanted the Banker himself," the Kid said shortly. "Hurry it up, he's already sore."

Tim stared hard at him, but stepped aside, and the Kid walked out into the dark street. Turning left he walked swiftly for a dozen steps then crossed the street and ducked into a dark alley. A few minutes later he arrived at the Palace Hotel.

IT WAS BROAD DAY when he awakened. While he bathed and shaved, he thought about his situation. Whoever had tipped the Banker and Starrett to the fact that he carried money must have been close to MacIntosh.

Two attempts had been made to get the money from him and it was likely that two groups now searched for him, only now both groups not only wanted the money but to kill him as well. Allen would not take that pistol blow without retaliation. He dared not—not in this town.

In a town where a man could be murdered for a drink, where it was the proud boast of many that "anything goes," daylight would not end the search for him. Allen had not been boasting when he said his reach included the Palace. So, figure it this way: Bull Run Allen knew where he was. He would know within a matter of minutes of the time the Kid left the hotel. Even in such a fine place as the Palace was, men could be found who would give information for money.

The Kid's safest bet was to get word to MacIntosh

that he had the money, then make contact somewhere away from his business office, which might be watched. He checked his guns and returned them, fully loaded, to their places and walked into the hallway, carrying the bag.

A man in a brown suit sat at the end of the hall. He glanced up when the Kid stepped out, then, apparently unconcerned, went back to his paper and turned a page.

The Cactus Kid walked briskly along the hall. Around the corner, he sprinted to the far end and ducked down the back stairs, taking the first flight in about three jumps. Walking the rest of the way more slowly, he stepped out of the back door when the janitor's back was turned. Entering the back door of another building he walked on through to the street and boarded a horsecar.

A roughly dressed man loitered in front of the building where MacIntosh had his office, and when the Kid got down from the car the fellow turned and started down the street, almost at a run. The Kid grinned and walked into the building and down the hall to the office door. MacIntosh's name was on the door but he hesitated. If they were waiting for him elsewhere they might also have men planted here. Glancing around, he spotted a door marked **Private.** Taking a chance he opened it and stepped inside.

A big-shouldered man with a shock of white hair and a white, carefully trimmed beard looked up. He was about to speak when the outer door opened and a girl stepped in. Her eyes went wide when she saw the Kid and she stepped back hastily.

"Lily," he exclaimed, and started forward.

Before he could get halfway across the room that door opened again and Banker Barber stepped in. His jaw was hard and his eyes cold. He held a gun in his hand. He motioned toward the carpetbag. "I'll take that!" he said sharply. "Drop it on the floor and step back!"

The Kid knew from his eyes that the Banker would shoot. He also guessed he was more anxious to get the money than revenge and would not shoot in this building unless necessary. The Kid dropped the bag reluctantly and moved back. The Banker took a quick step forward and grasped the handle. Backing away, he unsnapped the top and thrust his hand inside. Keeping his eyes on the two men he drew out a thick sheaf and glancing quickly, his eyes came up, hard with triumph. Dropping the packet back into the bag he snapped it shut.

"Thanks!" he said grimly. "It was worth the trouble!"

"Be careful that Bull Run doesn't take that away from you," the Cactus Kid advised. "He has this place watched and he knew I came here."

"Don't worry!" the Banker replied grimly. "He won't get this! Nobody," he added, "gets this but me." He backed to the door and opened it. "I'd like to know who taught you to bottom deal. You're good!" He stepped back through the door. "And don't try to follow me or I'll kill you."

He jerked the door shut. There was a thud, a grunt, and something heavy slid along the door. Then there were running footsteps. Outside in the street there was a shout, a shot, then more running feet.

MacIntosh leaned back in his chair. "Well," he said testily, "I'm not taking the loss! The money was still in your possession! I'm sorry for Jim Wise, but he still owes me fifteen thousand dollars!"

With a cheerful smile the Cactus Kid went to the door and pulled it open. The body of Banker Barber fell into the room. His skull was bloody from the blow that had felled him, but he was still alive.

"Down in the street," the Kid said, "somebody was just shot. I'm betting it was Starrett. And in a few minutes Bull Run Allen will be cussing a blue streak!"

"He got the money," MacIntosh said sourly, "so why should he cuss?"

The Cactus Kid grinned broadly. From his inside coat pocket he drew an envelope and took from it a slip of paper. He handed it to MacIntosh. "A bank draft," the Kid said complacently, "for fifteen thousand dollars! This morning after I slipped away from them, I went to the Wells Fargo and deposited the money with them. Now make out the receipt and I'll make this right over to you."

Old MacIntosh chuckled. "Fooled 'em, did you? I

might have known anybody old Jim Wise would send with that much money would be smart enough to take care of it. What was in the bag?"

"Some packets of carefully trimmed green paper topped with one-dollar bills," he said, grinning. "It cost me a few bucks, but it was worth it."

MacIntosh chuckled, his eyes lively with humor. "I'd like to see Bull Run's face when he opens that carpetbag! He fancies himself a smart one!" Then he sobered. "You called that girl by name. You know her?"

"She was with them on the boat," the Kid explained. "She even got into the poker game when they tried to rook me. She's good, too," he added, "but she must have been the one who tipped them off. It had to be somebody who knew I'd be carrying money. Who is she?"

"She's been working for me!" MacIntosh said angrily. "Working until just now. I never did put no truck in womenfolks workin' around offices but she convinced me she could help me and she didn't cost me no more'n a third what a man cost!"

"With a woman," the Cactus Kid said, "it ain't the original cost. It's the upkeep!"

Battle at Burnt Camp

The Cactus Kid had crossed the Terlingua and was bearing right toward Black Ridge, when he saw the girl.

She was young and she was made up and she was pretty as a bay pony with three white stockings. She was standing beside the dim trail with her hands on her hips and her nose red from the sun.

The Kid drew up. "Howdy," he said gravely, "goin' far?"

"Without a horse?" Her eyes flashed. "Where could anybody go in this country without a horse? Where, I ask you?"

"Well," the Kid said seriously, "it depends on what you're lookin' for an' how far you need to go. Would you mind tellin' a feller what you're doin' out here afoot?"

"That's none of your business!" she flared. "Are you going to give me a ride, or not?"

The Kid looked at her sadly. "Ma'am, for one who's askin' favors you sure aren't very polite. Where were you raised, anyway?"

Her eyes narrowed. "Why, you—!" She stopped, flashing a sudden smile. "I'm sorry. It wasn't your fault at all. Please, would you give me a ride?"

"Get up behind," he said. "I'd sure not want to leave a lady out here in the desert with nobody to fuss at but rattlers. It wouldn't be civilized!"

Putting her foot in his stirrup, she swung up behind him, and then before he could even speak she shucked one of his guns from its holster and shoved the muzzle into his spine. "Get off," she said coldly. "Get off, an' see how it feels to be afoot!"

"Now, look—!" The Kid started to protest, but the gun peeled hide from his spine and he heard the hammer click back as she cocked it. "Get off!" she ordered. "One yelp out of you and I'll shoot your ears off!"

Carefully, the Kid swung down, and without a word she slapped spurs to his horse and started off. His lips parted in a smile, the Cactus Kid let her go, then suddenly he pinned his lips over his teeth and whistled shrilly. The horse stopped so sharply that the girl had no chance. She went right off over his head and fell hard. The horse trotted back toward him.

The Kid came up on the run, and before she could retrieve his gun, he grabbed it up. Then he caught her by the hands and twisted them behind her. With a piggin string from his belt he tied her wrists despite her struggles. He got to his feet and wiped the dust from his face and stared down at her. "There, now. That should hold you. Now, what's the idea?"

She glared furiously. "I'll kill you for this! I'll kill you!"

"No reason to get so wrought up." The Cactus Kid coolly began to build a smoke. "What's all the fuss? No need to steal my horse an' set me afoot just because you're mad at somebody. Tell me where you want to go an' I'll take you there."

"Untie my hands!" she demanded.

"Not a chance. You might try to steal my horse again."

"That was a nasty, vile trick!" she declared. "I skinned my nose!"

"That," he said, studying her nose critically, "won't do it any harm. I figure maybe it's a mite too long anyway."

She glared at him. "Let me up!" she demanded. "Turn my hands loose!"

"It's up to you. Be good and you get a ride to wherever you're goin'. Keep on fussin' an' I'll leave you right here to cook."

She stopped, still angry, but aware that he meant what he said. "All right," she said, "but you just wait!"

This time he took her on the saddle in front of him and that made it necessary for his arm to be around her waist, which was, he realized appreciatively, a small, firm, and very nice waist. Her reddish hair came against his cheek and her body pressed closely to him. This, too, he found agreeable.

She said nothing, but sat quietly. Finally, he asked, "Where do you want to go? Where's home?"

"I want to go to Burnt Camp, in the Solitario."

Now, the Cactus Kid, whose birth certificate might have said he was Nesselrode Clay, knew but little of the Big Bend of Texas. What he did know was that Burnt Camp in the Solitario was no place for a beautiful girl of eighteen or so. In fact, it was to just that place that the Kid himself was going, but for no friendly purpose. "That's no place for a girl," he said. "I'll take you to another place."

"You'll take me there, and when they find me with my hands tied, it will be a sad time for you! Just wait until I tell Kit Branch about this!"

"He your sweetheart?" The Kid wanted to know.

"Branch?" she scoffed. "He'd like to be, but he's not! I'm Kirby Brock!"

"Bully Brock's daughter?" The Kid was aghast. "Don't tell me that old blister sired a sweet little filly like you!"

"He's my uncle! And he's not an old blister! Although I'll tell him you said that and he'll wipe the floor with you, that's what he'll do!"

The Cactus Kid chuckled. He felt good this morning. He wore his tailored gray trousers, a bright red shirt, and a black handkerchief tight about his throat. His hat was black with a snake-hide band, and his boots hand-tooled. The Kid was five feet seven and weighed exactly one hundred and fifty pounds soaking wet. He consulted a large railroad watch that he kept in the pocket of his pants; it was ten forty-five in the morning.

Black Ridge was north of them now and they cut the trail leading to the Black Tinaja. Although the Cactus Kid had never visited the wild and lonely region called the Solitario, he knew well the route that led to it. Leaving the tinaja, they would turn due west and hit the canyon of the Lefthand Shutup, which would take them right into the region.

As they rode he puzzled over the situation. What had Kirby Brock been doing out in the desert without a horse? And how could such a girl be the niece of Bully Brock? For years now Bully had ranched in the wild region around the canyon west of Burnt Camp. It was an area frequented by smugglers from over the border and by rustlers. And that was why he was coming here now. He was looking for some men.

Several days before, in San Antonio, he had left the Variety Theatre one night, and had seen a man behind him. Later he had seen the same man, and knew he was being followed. And then there had been three men.

He had turned the corner near his hotel when they closed in on him, one coming toward him, one crossing the street, and the third had come from nowhere to grab his arms. He had been slugged, robbed, and left lying in the street.

After he recovered he devoted two days to making inquiries, only to discover finally that the men had left town. The three were known as Farbeson, Breeden, and Jewell. They were known thieves and rustlers, and they ran with Kit Branch.

At Del Rio, he heard about Branch and that he could be found in the Solitario, but that a man would be some kind of a fool to try to go in after him. The Cactus Kid was that kind of a fool. They had slugged him, which was bad enough, but they had taken seven hundred dollars from him. It was more money than he had ever had all at one time.

"How's it happen you're afoot?" he asked suddenly.

"My horse threw me," she replied sullenly.

At the Black Tinaja they stopped, watered the horse, and drank. The dun was feeling the double burden, so the Kid put him on some grass and sat down in the shade. He glanced at Kirby and smiled. "Might as well sit down," he said. "We'll have to let that horse rest a mite."

She was looking at the ground nearby. Glancing over curiously, he saw she was intently studying some tracks.

Suddenly she looked around at him. "Let me use that gun. I can get some horses for us." She spoke in a near whisper and appeared to tense.

"Nothing doing. You'd run off and leave me high and dry." He had untied her hands.

"Suit yourself," she said.

"So, Kit's bad medicine, is he? What about Jewell?"

She stiffened with surprise. "What do you know about him?"

"Not much. Not any more than I know about Breeden or Farbeson."

A slight sound made him turn, but there was no chance to draw. The man holding the shotgun was Jewell and he was no more than fifteen feet away. At that distance he would tear the Kid apart. His eyes widened when he saw the Kid. "You, is it? I figured you'd still be lyin' in the street. What you doin' here?"

"Huntin' you." The Kid spoke quietly. "Huntin' you an' those louse-bound partners of yours. I want my money."

The man laughed coarsely. "You'll git something, but it ain't gonna be what you're lookin' for!" he promised. Then: "Where'd you meet **her**?"

"Down the road a piece. Do you want to hand me over that money now or do I take it out of your hide?"

"My hide?" Jewell stared. "Who's holdin' this shotgun, anyway?" He did not move his eyes, but said, "Pick up his guns, Kirby. Go behind him."

He felt the girl move up behind him and felt his guns leave his holsters. His eyes narrowed slightly as he saw the evident relief in Jewell's eyes. Slowly, the shotgun lifted and he realized with a shock that the man was going to murder him.

"I wouldn't if I were you." Kirby Brock had the guns in her hands and was watching Jewell. "Bring up the horses and we'll ride in. Bully will want to see this gent."

Reluctantly, Jewell lowered the gun. When he led up the horses, the Cactus Kid was surprised to see that one of them was obviously the girl's horse. It carried a sidesaddle and the stirrup was just right for her. The Kid was ordered to mount and they turned west.

It was late afternoon when they reached the houses and old stone corral at Burnt Camp. The smoke from several fires was rising, and the Kid saw a man come out and shade his eyes at them. They rode on into the camp and the Kid watched the big man coming toward them. He was almost twice the size of the Kid, towering several inches above six feet and weighing well over two hundred pounds. He had a thick black beard.

He looked at the Kid, then turned his eyes to the girl. The Cactus Kid frowned uncertainly, for the big man seemed almost frightened when he recognized her.

Other men came forward. Farbeson was one of them. He was almost as large as Bully Brock and he grinned when he saw the Cactus Kid. Breeden, who was standing nearby said, "What do you think, Farb? This kid came up here to git his money?"

The others all laughed and then the crowd parted for a slender whiplash of a man with a narrow face and wide gash for a mouth. He came down the path and stood staring at Kirby with a slight smile. "Didn't get far, did you?" he said. "I told you we were meant for each other."

Breeden laughed and Farb joined in. The younger man made an inquiry about the Cactus Kid and was told the story of what had happened both in San Antonio and here. He listened, nodding slightly. "All right," he said, "we'll get this over with all at once."

He turned on Brock. "Bully," he said, "you're through here. We're taking over your ranch and all that goes with it. I"—he smiled unpleasantly—"will personally take over Kirby. We're going to show this country what we can do."

Brock stared back at him. "You're a fool, Kit. The Rangers never bothered us here because this was my place and they knew me. You know they can get in here an' they will, sure as you start anything."

"The Rangers ain't comin' now that we got Kirby back. Sendin' her was a dumb idea, Bully. You tipped your hand an' now we won't be needin' you any longer." Kit Branch turned his hand on a gun.

The Cactus Kid was still sitting his horse, as was Jewell. Now, suddenly, he slapped the spurs into the dun, and as the startled animal leaped, the Kid grabbed the shotgun from Jewell's hands as the dun lunged by. Straight into the center of the crowd he went, low over the horse's neck. Behind him a shot rang out, then another. The dun faltered, stumbled, and then fell all sprawled out. The Kid hit the ground rolling and came up with the shotgun at his shoulder. The first person he saw across the sights was Breeden. He squeezed the trigger and saw the big outlaw take the full charge in the stomach. The man gave a grunt and sat down hard and rolled over to his face.

The Kid lunged to his feet in a spatter of bullets and ran into the rocks. He made them, felt the tug at his shirt, and hit the ground sliding. Almost as soon as he hit it, he was up and ducking into a thick stand of greasewood. He froze in place. Behind him were shouts and yells, so he moved on quietly, circling toward the corral. The men had fanned out and were working toward him. Studying the terrain, he felt himself grow sick. No alternative awaited him. The basin was rockbound and to climb that wall would mean that he would be picked off before he had gone a dozen steps. Nor could he remain where he was, for they were moving in.

The shotgun was a single-barreled gun, a breech-loader. And he had no more shells.

The outlaws searching for him were not fooling. Obviously, they had decided to organize, take over Brock's ranch and saloon as a hangout, and raid the country. Kirby Brock seemed to have slipped away for help but then had lost her horse. She had probably taken him for another outlaw.

Still clutching the shotgun, the Kid rolled behind some rocks and wormed his way right back toward the stone corral and the houses. Several times he had to lie still to allow men to pass within a few feet of him. When he reached a nest of rocks to one side of the corral, he peered out.

Three men remained in the yard with Brock and the girl. Bully Brock had blood running down his face where he had been struck with a gun barrel, and his hands were tied behind him. The girl's hands were also tied, and Kit Branch stood nearby, with Farb and Jewell. The body of Breeden was nowhere to be seen.

Other men were scattered out, and from time to time he could hear shouts from them. He had succeeded in getting back through their line, but they would be doubling back at any time and he must at all costs find a place to hole up. As he had crawled an idea had come to him. There might yet be a chance to use the shotgun.

Beyond the stone corral, back from the scattered area of campfires and shelters, was an ancient stone wall that appeared to be the face of a dugout. Obviously unused, it was the place most likely to be overlooked in any search for him. Using the corral as shelter, the Kid worked his way along the far side, then ducked into the open door of the dugout.

It was about twenty feet long and the roof sagged dangerously. The remains of some crude bunks and a few pieces of broken bench were mingled with the litter on the floor. Working his way back into the dugout, the Cactus Kid found it was L-shaped, and around the bend of the L the roof was intact except at the very back, where a hole about three feet across opened into a pile of brush, boulders and cacti.

Crouching in the half-dark of the dugout, the Kid opened the breech of the shotgun. There had been no chance to dispense with the brass shell, for he had been moving too fast and had nothing to replace it, anyway. Now he got out his pocketknife and went to work. Taking several bullets from his cartridge belt, he opened them and extracted the powder. Outside, the search continued, but in the dugout sweat poured down the Kid's body as he worked. Several times he stopped to wipe his hands dry and then went on with his work. He cut several of the pistol bullets into three pieces and with a rock pounded off the rough edges of the lead and shaped the pieces into fairly round slugs. With utmost care he pried a primer out of one of the shells and fit it into the back of the shotgun cartridge. It was a bit loose but seemed like it would stay centered. He now had a heavy charge of powder and twelve slugs; using some bits of paper from an old letter in his pocket as wadding, he soon had a charge for his shotgun. When it was reloaded he felt much better. If they got him now, he was at least taking one man with him. At close range his contrived shotgun shell would tear a man wide open.

As he waited, his eyes accustomed to the dim light, he looked around the interior of the ruined dugout. The floor was a litter of old paper, sacks, bits of rawhide, old clothes, and odds and ends of broken bottles. Suddenly he had an unaccountable fit of depression. Unaccountable for him, for the Cactus Kid was wont to look upon life as his particular bailiwick, and he had spent most of his time trying to find the bright side of every situation.

This, he decided, was the limit of something or other. That he, the Cactus Kid, whose cheerful grin and ready sense of humor had carried him through the worst of times, should be hiding here in a ruined dugout in the last hours of a hot Texas day was absolutely unacceptable. The Cactus Kid made up his mind. Come what may, he was going out and he was going to leave his mark on this outfit—but good.

Dusk came at last and the fires were built up and soon he could smell coffee. With nothing to eat since daybreak, that added to the Kid's disgust. In all this time he had not dared look out, yet now, with the darkness bringing deep shadows around the dugout, he moved to the back and thrust his head and shoulders through the hole. He found himself looking out through a curtain of brush over the whole area of the hideout. To his left was the stone corral, part of it almost in front of him, and in the corral were the horses. Beyond it, on the slope and almost facing him, was the main house. There was an old stable, open-faced and now used by some of the outlaws, and there were four fires going. In all, he surmised there must be sixteen to twenty men at the hideout.

Slipping out of the hole, he crawled down to the corral wall. Flipping a loop over a horse's neck, he drew the animal to the wall and saddled it. A second horse snorted and leaped when the rope touched it and one of the men at the fires got up. "Somethin' botherin' the horses," he said.

"Aw! They're just fightin'!"

The outlaw stood looking toward the corral, but as all was quiet he soon subsided and returned to his seat. Swiftly, the Kid saddled the second horse and another. Then he tied the three horses and circled the corral.

Lying flat on his stomach, he looked past the corner at the group of outlaws. If he only had his guns! The one shot in his shotgun meant little; he could only take one man, two at best, and then they would have him.

Suddenly the girl and her uncle were led from the house and brought down to the nearest fire. With them were Kit Branch and Farbeson. Jewell was at the fire and he got up as they approached, grinning at Bully Brock. "Does me good to see this!" He sneered. "You been struttin' high-an'-mighty for a long time!"

Brock straightened his shoulders. "Branch, give Kirby a horse an' let her go. She's done nothin' to you. Let her go back home to San Antone."

"Not a chance! We've got her an' we'll keep her. We'll keep you, too, Brock, as long as you behave.

We've got an idea that maybe you can keep the Rangers off us."

"Don't be a fool!" Brock retorted. "The only reason the Rangers stayed away was because nobody from around here did anything but rustle a few head of cows once in a while. They knew I was mostly honest and they didn't want to come all the way out here for a few young fellers who they could never prove had done anything. You start somethin' an' they'll be down on you like a flock of wolves."

Branch smiled. "You expect me to believe that, Bully? You **know** folks. Come daylight we'll round up that kid. He won't get far without water or knowin' the country."

A big man sat with his back to the Kid and not over twenty yards away. The Kid could see the pistol in his belt. If he was going to start something, it would have to be soon. The horses might be discovered if he waited, and the sheer surprise might help, also; the girl and her uncle were close at hand now, but after they had eaten, they would probably be returned to the house.

They had just come to the fire. It would be twenty minutes, thirty at most, before they would be returned to the house. There was a chance. He drew back suddenly, straightened to his feet, and turned.

He stumbled straight into the very same outlaw who had been bothered by the horses acting up. The Kid's sudden rise from the ground had been a complete surprise and now he gaped foolishly at the Kid. Then his surprise faded and he began to grin. "Got you!" he said hoarsely. "I got you!"

"You got **me**?" The Kid jerked the shotgun. "What do you think this is?"

"You had one shell." The man was grinning, enjoying himself. "You killed Breeden with it . . . **uuhhh!**"

The Cactus Kid acted suddenly. He was gripping the shotgun with both hands and he simply jammed the end of the barrel in the man's solar plexus with wicked force. The outlaw grunted and hit the dirt on his knees. Instantly, the Kid smashed him on the back of the skull with the butt of the shotgun, then stripped the man's gun from his holster. Swinging the extra cartridge belt over his shoulder, the Kid quickly rounded the back corner of the corral toward the haystack. Dropping to his knees, he struck a match, then another and another.

Grabbing a pitchfork as the flames leaped up, he forked two quick bunches of flaming hay high into the greasewood surrounding the camp. Then he went over the corral rails with a leap, grabbed the bridle reins of the three horses, and swung into the saddle.

"**Fire!** The hay's afire!" Other voices took up the call and men charged toward the stack. The fire scattered in the greasewood, caught, and the resinous wood and leaves burst into a crackle of flame. Crouching low in the saddle, his shotgun ready, the

Kid rode for the corral gate and kicked the latch open. The balanced gate swung and instantly he was through.

A man saw him coming and the Kid yelled, "Get the horses! Save 'em!" With a shrill whoop he rode down on the fire where Bully Brock stood beside the girl. Her hands were free, but his were still bound and they had been making the girl feed him, fearing what he might attempt if he wasn't restrained.

Men were racing toward the flames, and the Kid's call made them realize the danger of the horses without noticing who it was that yelled. Racing up to the fire, the Kid called to Kirby. "Hit the saddle! Hit the saddle! Let's **go**!"

After one startled instant of hesitation Brock raced for the nearest horse and, without even waiting to have his hands untied, jumped for the saddle and got a foot in the stirrup. With his left hand, the Kid pulled the big man into the saddle while Kirby swung up. Behind them there were yells and he could hear Kit Branch shouting angrily. Turning in the saddle, the Cactus Kid saw a big man take three running steps and stop, whipping a Winchester to his shoulder. The Kid pulled the trigger on his shotgun and the gun boomed and slammed his shoulder. The big man staggered and the Kid wheeled, jumping his horse away as he threw the shotgun into the face of another man. And then they were off and running.

Behind them men raced wildly about, grabbing at the thrashing horses, the whole scene lighted by the whipping flames. The breeze was stiff and the flames had leaped across the greasewood until the whole hillside was a roaring flame. Kirby was leading the way due west and the three rode desperately, crouching low in their saddles to escape the hail of bullets.

Weaving among the boulders, Bully led west, then south, then doubled back to the north. At a stop to let the horses breathe, the Kid leaned over and cut Brock's hands free of the top loop of rope, and Brock did the rest himself. Slowing down, the Cactus Kid looked around and could see the loom of Solitario Peak off to the north and a little east. Kirby was riding west, following some vague sort of trail, weaving through some rough country. Dropping into Fresno Canyon, they turned north and kept a good pace until the peak of Solitario was behind them to the east. Then she led them out, going northeast. They stopped briefly at a tinaja; nearby was the dark outline of what had once been a frame of a mine scaffold and prospector's shack, now partially collapsed.

Bully chafed his wrists and grinned at the Cactus Kid. "You sure are hellfire when you cut loose, mister! We'd better hightail it northwest. Maybe we can make a settlement before they catch up to us. I'd at least like to have a gun!"

"You ride on." The Cactus Kid shoved his hat back on his head and began to build a smoke. "I'm going back."

"Back?" Kirby cried. "Are you crazy? You want to go back there and get shot?"

"No, ma'am, I sure don't. On the other hand, those hombres took seven hundred dollars of money off me. I want it."

"Why are you so interested in getting—!" Kirby was breathless. The moon was rising and he could see her face in the light.

"Here, now!" Brock said mildly. "Let him alone. If he wants to go back, he wants to go back and that's his affair. Although," he added, "I do think it a foolish thing."

"Nevertheless," the Kid insisted stubbornly, "I am going back." He turned his horse. "You two ride on. I've got business to attend to!"

Kirby stared at him, her anger fading. "Don't go back!" she pleaded. "They'll kill you! They will! I know they will!"

Brock held up his hand. "You won't have to go back," he said gravely. "I can hear 'em coming."

"How far off?" The Kid strained his ears to listen.

"Down the canyon. It could be a mile or more."

"Hit the saddle, then," the Kid said quietly. "I'll wait for 'em. I've got a Colt and plenty of ammunition. I'll stand 'em off."

"We'll wait," Kirby said. "Maybe we can get hold of some guns once the fighting starts."

"Then get out of the way," the Kid agreed, ". . . back near that mine. I'm going to wait right here by the tinaja for them."

It was well after midnight, but how late he was not sure. The Kid waited, occasionally drying his palms on his jeans. The riders were taking their time, evidently searching the rocks as they came along. Probably they were not sure which way the Brocks had gone with the Kid. When at last he heard them close by, there was a faint gray in the east. The outlaws—and he decided there were at least four of them—drew up in the blackness near the cliffs.

His horse concealed among the rocks, the Cactus Kid settled down for a wait. He could hear voices arguing, and then a rider started forward. When he was still some thirty yards off, the Kid spoke. "Better stay where you are. I'm heeled for trouble."

"If you hadn't butted into this"—it was Branch speaking—"everything would be all right. Suppose you mount up an' light a shuck? We want the Brocks, not you."

"Sorry. It'll cost you to get 'em. I got a gun now."

"Don't be a fool!" Branch said angrily. "You won't have a chance!"

The Cactus Kid settled himself for a wait. Without doubt most of the outlaws were awaiting daylight to hunt up their horses, and he had a hunch that Branch would wait for day also. Well, that suited him.

An hour passed, and the gray grew stronger. Another hour, and although the sun was not up, it was light. Behind the Kid was the canyon mouth where Bully and Kirby Brock had taken shelter; beside the Kid was the tinaja with its store of water. Before him the slope fell away to the bottom of a shallow canyon and somewhere across it were Branch and the others.

Once, the Kid thought he heard a stone rattle, then a footstep. He got to his feet and peered around but could see nothing—and then he saw Kirby, motioning violently.

"Hey!" she called. She held up a brown stick in her hands. "Blasting powder!"

Scrambling back over the rocks, he stopped beside her. "Uncle found it in the prospector's shanty. There's almost half a box, and some caps and fuses."

The Cactus Kid grinned suddenly. "Bring 'em down! This'll be good!"

A half hour later Branch called out. He was not over thirty yards away, probably less. "You comin' out or are we comin' after you?"

"Come and get us," the Kid said hopefully. "Come right on up." As they hesitated he lighted a short fuse. The giant powder was tied to a rock for better throwing, and as the fuse spattered, the Kid drew back his hand and threw, and Bully Brock, nearby, did the same.

He never saw the dynamite. The stick hit somewhere in front of him and blew up with a terrific concussion, scattering rocks and gravel. Brock's throw had been the stronger and it lit between two head-sized rocks atop a boulder. It blasted with even greater force and scattered rock in every direction.

Jewell came out of the rocks, running, and Farb with him. Both men had their hands up.

"Come on, Branch!" Brock yelled. "The next one's right in your lap!"

Kit Branch came out of the rocks. He came walking toward them, his hands swinging, and the Cactus Kid stepped out in the open. Branch stared vindictively. "Nobody gets the best of me, boy. You're gonna get yours and I'm gonna be the one givin' it to you."

The Kid's eyes never left those of the gunman. "Well, I'll be—!"

Branch's hand swept down for his gun. Triumph was on his face as the gun lifted and then something struck him a wicked blow just below the breastbone. He staggered, seeing the smoking gun in the Kid's hand, then fell over on his face.

The Cactus Kid walked over to Jewell. "All I want from you is my money," he said. "Dish it out."

Reluctantly, the two outlaws dug out the money and handed it back. When he counted it, the sum came to two hundred dollars more than he had lost. "For my trouble," he said calmly, and pocketed it. "That's all I want with you fellows. You can beat it."

"Oh, no, they can't!" Kirby Brock walked up to Jewell and Farb. "Push me around, will you?" She kicked Jewell right on the shins.

Farbeson bellowed with laughter, and coolly, she turned and kicked him in the same place. With both men howling with pain, Kirby turned and gathered up the reins of her horse. "Maybe," she said, glaring at the Cactus Kid, "that wasn't ladylike, but it sure was satisfying!"

The Cactus Kid gathered up their weapons.

Farbeson had been wearing the Kid's own guns. Gravely, he handed guns to both Brock and Kirby.

Mounting up, he studied Kirby. "You know, ma'am," he said, "if you get a husband who'll keep a tight rein on you, you'd make him a mighty good wife, but if you ever get the bit in your teeth, heaven help him!"

He turned his horse and headed off up the trail.

The Cactus Kid

Pausing at the head of the four steps that led to the floor of the dining room, the Cactus Kid surveyed the room with approval. In fact, he surveyed the world with approval. For the Cactus Kid, christened Nesselrode Clay, had but an hour before he closed a sale for one thousand head of beef cattle, and the check reposed in his pocket.

Moreover, the Kid was young, the Kid was debonair, and the Kid walked the earth with a light-hearted step and song on his lips. His suit was of tailored gray broadcloth, his hat of spotless white felt, his shirt was white, his tie black, and his black, perfectly polished hand-tooled boots were a miracle of Spanish leatherwork. Out of sight behind the black silk sash was a Smith & Wesson .44, one of the guns for whose skillful handling the Kid was renowned in places other than this.

He was handsome, he was immaculate, he was alive in this best of all possible worlds, and before him lay the expected pleasure of an excellent meal and a bottle of wine, and afterward a cigar. Surely, this was the life!

The wild grass ranges of Texas, Arizona, and Nevada were a dim memory, and lost with them was the smell of dust and cattle and singed hair and all the memories that attended the punching of cows.

Only one seat remained unoccupied, and the Cactus Kid descended to the main floor with the manner of a king entering his domain, and wove his way among the crowded tables, then paused briefly, his hand on the back of the empty chair. "You do not object, gentlemen?"

The two men who occupied the table lifted black, intent eyes and surveyed him with a cool and careful regard. Their faces were stern, their manners forbidding. "You are," one of them said, "the Americano?"

"As you can tell"—the Kid gestured with both hands—"I am most definitely an Americano."

"Be seated then, by all means."

Had they meant to emphasize that "the"? Or was it his imagination? The menu took his attention from such mundane matters, and he looked upon the gastronomic paradise suggested by the card with satisfaction. A far cry, this, from beef and beans cooked over an open fire with rain beating down on your back while you ate! As the waiter drew near, the Kid looked up, and found the two men regarding him intently.

He returned their attention with interest. Both men were prosperous, well-fed. The waiter spoke, and the Kid turned and in flawless Spanish he ordered his meal. He was conscious, as he did so, that he had the undivided attention of his companions.

When the waiter had gone they looked at him and one spoke. "You speak Spanish."

"As you see."

"It is unexpected, but fortunate, perhaps."

Something in their tone gave him the feeling they would have been more pleased had he not known their language.

"So"—it was the first man again—"I see you arrived all right."

There was no reason for argument on that score. Despite various difficulties he had succeeded in bringing his herd of cattle through, and he had, he decided, arrived all right. "Yes," he admitted.

"You are ready?"

A good question, the Kid decided. He decided, being in fine fettle, that he was undoubtedly ready. "Of course," he said carelessly. And then he added, "I am always ready."

"Good! The hour will be at six, in the morning."

Their meals came, giving the Kid time for thought. Now what the deuce had he run into, anyway?

"That's mighty early," he suggested.

They looked at him sternly. "Of course. It must be early. You will be waiting outside?"

Perhaps, if he agreed, more information would be forthcoming.

"Yes, I'll be waiting."

Instead, they finished their meals in silence and left him, and he stared after them wondering. Oh, well. It was an entertaining dinner, anyway, and that was that. Catch him getting up at six in the morning! This was the first time in months that he'd had a chance to sleep late.

He scowled. What was it all about? Obviously, they thought he was someone else. Who did they think he was? His boss had told him to go ahead and enjoy himself for a couple of days after the cattle were delivered, and the Cactus Kid meant to do just that. And one way he planned to enjoy himself was sleeping late.

He was sitting over a glass of wine and a cigar when the door opened and he saw a tall, fine-looking old man come in with a girl—a girl who took his breath away.

The Cactus Kid sat up a little straighter. She was Spanish, and beautiful. Her eyes swept the room and then came to rest on him. They left him, and they returned. The Kid smiled.

Abruptly her glance chilled. One eyebrow lifted slightly and she turned away from him. The Kid hunched his shoulders, feeling frostbitten around the edges of his ego. The two seated themselves not far away, and the Kid looked at the older man. His profile was what is called "aristocratic," his goatee and mustache were purest white. The waiters attended them with deference, and spoke to them in muted voices. Where one nonchalant waiter had drifted before, now a dozen of them rushed to and fro, covering the table with dishes, lavishing attention.

One waiter, and suddenly the Kid was aware that it was the same who had served him, was bending over the table talking to them in a low voice. As he talked, the girl looked toward the Cactus Kid, and after the waiter left, the older man turned and glanced toward him.

That he was an object of some interest to them was plain enough, but why? Could it have some connection with the two odd men he had just shared his meal with? In any event, the girl was undoubtedly the most beautiful he had ever seen—and quite aware of it.

Calling the waiter, he paid his bill, noting the man's surreptitious glances. "Anything wrong?" he asked, studying the waiter with a cold glance.

"No, no, señor! Only . . ." He paused delicately.

"Only what?" the Kid demanded.

"Only the señor is so young! Too young," he added, significantly, "to die so soon!"

Turning quickly, he threaded his way among the tables and was gone. The Cactus Kid stared after him, then walked to the dining-room steps and climbed them slowly. At the door he glanced back over his shoulder. The girl and the older man were watching him. As he caught their glance the girl made a little gesture with her hand and the Kid walked out of the room.

Whatever was happening here was too much for

him. Unfortunately, he knew nobody in this part of Mexico except the man to whom he had delivered the cattle, and that had been more miles to the south. Somehow he had become involved in a plot, some development of which he knew nothing at all.

An hour of fruitless speculation told him nothing. He searched back through the recent weeks to find a clue, but he found no hint. And then he remembered the mysterious appointment for six tomorrow morning.

"At six?" he asked himself. "Nothing doing!"

An old Mexican loitered at the gate that led from the patio into the street. Casually, the Kid drifted across the patio to him, and there he paused. Taking his time, he built a cigarette, then offered the makings to the old Mexican.

The man glanced up at him out of shrewd old eyes. "**Gracias,** señor," he said softly. He took the makings and rolled a cigarette, then returned the tobacco and papers to the Kid, who was about to strike a match. "No, señor," he whispered, "behind the wall. It is not safe."

The Cactus Kid scowled. "What isn't safe?" he asked. "I don't understand."

"You have not been told? The man has many friends; they might decide it is safer to kill you now. The señor," he added, "has a reputation."

"Who do you think I am?" the Kid asked.

"Ah?" The peón looked at him wisely. "Who am I

to know such a thing? It is enough that you are here. Enough that you will be here tomorrow."

The Kid studied it over while he smoked, taking his time. The oblique angle seemed best. "Who," he said, "was the beautiful señorita in the dining room?"

"What?" The old peón was incredulous. "You do not know? But that is she, señor! The Senorita Marguerita Ibanez." With that the old peón drifted off into the street and the Kid turned and walked back to the inn and climbed to his room. He opened the door and stepped inside, closing it carefully after him.

Then he struck a match and lighted the candle. "Señor?" It was a feminine voice, but he turned sharply around, cursing himself mentally for being so careless. He was wearing but one gun, in position for a right-hand draw, and the candle was in that hand.

Then he stared. Before him, a vision of loveliness, was the señorita from the dining room.

"I have come to tell you," she said hastily, "that you must not do this thing. You must go, go at once! Get your horse, slip out of the compound tonight, and ride! Ride like the wind for the border, for you will not be safe until you cross it."

THE CACTUS KID CHUCKLED suddenly. Puzzled as he was, he found himself enjoying it. And the girl was so beautiful. He put the candle down and motioned for her to be seated. "We've some talking to do," he said. "Some explanations are in order."

"Explanations?" She was plainly puzzled at the word. "I know of nothing to explain. I cannot stay, already my uncle will have missed me. But I had to warn you. I had not expected anyone so—so young! An older man—no, it cannot be. You must go! I will not have you killed because of me."

"Look, ma'am," he said politely, "there's something about this I don't understand. I think you've got the wrong man. You seem to believe I am somebody I am not."

"Oh!" She was impatient. "Do not be a fool, señor! It is all very well to conceal yourself, but you have no concealment. Everyone knows who you are."

He chuckled again and sat down on the bed. "Everyone but me," he said, "but whatever it is, it does not matter. No matter what happens I shall always be able to remember that I was visited once by the most beautiful girl in Mexico!"

"It is not time for gallantry," she protested. "You must go. You will be killed. Even now it may be too late!"

"What's this all about?" he protested. "Tell me!"

"Oh, don't be a fool!" She was at the door now and there was no mistaking her sincerity. Her face was unusually pale, her eyes enormous in the dim light from the candle. "If you kill him, they will kill you. If you do not kill him—then he will kill you." Turning quickly, she was gone.

"Well of all the fool . . ." He stopped speaking. What was happening, he could not guess, but somehow he was right in the middle of a lot of trouble, and trouble of which he knew nothing. Now the Cactus Kid was no stranger to trouble, nor to gunplay, but to go it blind and in somebody else's country, that was a fool's play. The girl was right. The only way was to get out. If he stayed he was trapped; to kill or be killed in a fight of which he understood nothing.

He hesitated, and then he looked suddenly toward his saddlebags and rifle. There was a back stairs—it would be simple to get to the stable . . . and he could be off and away. It wasn't as if he was running. It simply wasn't his fight. He had stumbled on a lot of trouble, and . . .

THERE WAS NO MOON and the trail was only a thin white streak. He walked his horse until he was a mile away from the town, and then he lifted into a canter. He glanced back just once. The señorita had been very lovely, and very frightened.

He frowned, remembering the man in the shadows. For he had not escaped without being seen. There had been a man standing near the wall, but who he had been, the Kid had no idea. There had been no challenge, and the Cactus Kid had ridden away without trouble.

STEADILY HE RODE NORTH, slowing at times to a walk. Remembering the trail on the way down, he recalled a village not far ahead, and he was preparing to run out and skirt around it when he heard a rider coming. He slowed and started to swing his horse, then the other horse whinnied.

The Cactus Kid shucked his six-gun. "Who is it?" he asked in Spanish.

"I ride to the inn with a message for Señorita Ibanez, have you been there?"

"You will find her," the Kid paused for a second, "but be careful, there is trouble."

The man sat on his horse, a dark shape against the stars. "Much trouble, yes? You speak like an American, I think."

"Yes, I am. Why?"

"At my house there is a wounded man, an American. He tries to tell me things I do not understand." He rode closer and peered at the Kid from under a wide sombrero. "He is dying. It is better, perhaps, that you talk to him, rather than a gentle lady."

They rode swiftly, but the distance was short. It was an isolated cabin of adobe off the main trail and among some huge boulders. Swinging down from their horses, the Mexican led the way into the house.

The man on the pallet was finished, anyone could see that. He was a big man, and his hard-drawn face was pale under what had been the deep brown of his skin. Nearby on a chair was a pair of matching Colts and the man's bloody clothing. Yet he was conscious and he turned his head when the Kid came in.

"I'm . . . I'm a lousy coyote if it ain't . . . ain't a Yank," he said hoarsely.

The Kid, with the usual rough frontier knowledge of treating wounds, bent over him. It required no expert skill to see these simple Mexican folk had done all that could be done. The amazing thing was that the man was alive at all. He had been shot at least six times.

"I'm Jim Chafee," he whispered. "I guess they got me this time."

The Cactus Kid stared at the dying man. Chafee! General in at least two Mexican revolts, almost dictator in one Central American country, and a veteran soldier of fortune. Even in his dying hours, the man looked ten years younger than he must have been.

"Hey!" Realization broke over the Kid. "I'll bet you're the guy they thought I was." Bending over the wounded man he talked swiftly, and Chafee nodded, amused despite his condition.

"He's bad," Chafee whispered. "I was dry-gulched . . . by her uncle and six gunmen."

"Her uncle?" The Kid was startled. "You mean . . . what do you mean?"

The Mexican interposed. "Bad for him to talk," he objected.

Chafee waved the man aside. "I'm through," he said. "I only wish I could get even with those devils and get that girl out of there!" He looked at the Kid. "Who're you?"

"They call me the Cactus Kid," he replied.

Chafee's eyes gleamed. "I've heard of you! You're that hell-on-wheels gunfighter from up Nevada way."

He sagged back on the pallet. "Kid," he whispered, "go back there an' help that girl. But don't trust nobody."

The Cactus Kid stared down at the wounded man. His face was relaxing slowly, yet his eyes were still bright. . . . "Knew her father," he whispered, "good man. That old devil . . . the uncle, he killed him . . . she don't know that."

While the Kid sat beside him, the dying man fumbled out the words of the story, but only a part of it, for he soon stopped talking and just lay there, breathing heavily.

Slowly, the Kid got to his feet. He had gone to his room at about nine o'clock. He had been riding north for almost three hours . . . if he started now and rode fast, he could be back in half that time. From his pocket he took a handful of silver pesos, more money than this peón would see in three months. "Take care of him," he told him, "keep him alive if you can, if not, see there is a priest. I will come by again, in a few weeks."

"He shall be my brother, señor," the Mexican said, "but take your money. No money is needed to buy care in the house of Juan Morales."

"Keep it," the Kid insisted. "It is my wish. Care for him. I'll be back."

With a leap he was in the saddle, and the horse was legging it south toward the town. As he rode, the Kid was suddenly happy again. "I never rode away from a fight before—nor a girl that pretty!" he added.

IT SEEMED he had been in bed no more than a few minutes when he was called. Yet actually he had crawled into bed at two o'clock and had all of four hours' sleep behind him. He dressed swiftly and went down the stairs. The Mexicans in the kitchen looked at him wide-eyed, and one huge woman poured him a brimming bowl of coffee, which he drank while eating a tortilla and beans. He was saddling up when the two men from the dinner table appeared.

"Ah, you are still here," one said. "Did you sleep well?"

"Oh, very well!" the Kid replied glibly. He turned to them grinning. "Now just who are you?"

"I am Pedro Sandoval! This man is Enrique Fernandez. We rode with the old general, and you must have heard of us. Surely, Señor Chafee—!"

They mounted up and rode around the inn and started out the road. Nothing was said for almost a mile, and he was puzzled. Both Sandoval and Fernandez seemed unusually quiet, yet he did not dare ask any questions.

Without warning the two men beside him swung their horses into the woods and he turned with them. On the edge of a clearing, they swung down. On the far side were several men, and now one of them came hurrying toward them.

"You are late!" he said impatiently. "We have been waiting. Señor DeCarte is most angry."

"It was unavoidable," Fernandez replied shortly. "Señor Chafee slept late."

"Slept?" The man stared at the Kid in astonishment. "That soundly?"

"Why not?" The Kid shrugged, and then glanced across the clearing. A big man on the far side had taken off his coat and was now selecting a pistol from a box.

The Cactus Kid stopped in his tracks . . . it was ridiculous . . . it couldn't be!

But it was. Fernandez was beside him. "Your jacket, señor?" he said. "You will remove it?"

The Kid slipped out of the jacket, then asked, "By the way, you know in the States we don't do this quite the same way. Would you mind telling me the rules?"

Fernandez bowed. "I am sorry. I thought this had been done. You will face each other at a distance of twenty paces. At the word, you will lift your pistols and fire. If neither scores a hit, you will advance one step closer and fire a second time."

Fernandez's eyes searched the Kid's anxiously. "I . . . hope you will win, señor. This is all very strange. Somehow you do not seem . . . if I did not know I would think . . . you will pardon me, of course, but . . ."

"You don't think I'm Jim Chafee?" The Kid chuckled. "You're right, amigo, I'm not." Before the startled man's words could come, the Kid said quickly, "Chafee was ambushed. He is either dead by now, or dying. I am taking his place, and you may be sure I'll shoot as straight.

"Now tell me: Who am I shooting, and what for?"

Fernandez stared. He gulped, and then suddenly, he laughed. "This is most unbelievable! Preposterous! And yet . . . amusing.

"This man is Colonel Arnold DeCarte. He is one of certain deadly enemies of General Francisco Ibanez, the father of Marguerita. In fact, he is believed to be their leader and one of those in a plot to dispossess the señorita of her estates.

"He challenged Ibanez and was to have fought him today but Ibanez was slain by assassins. Now you tell me that Jim Chafee, who took up the fight, has also been slain, or badly wounded, at least."

The Cactus Kid looked at the pistol in his hand. It would have to serve, but he would have preferred his own Smith & Wesson .44. DeCarte was advancing to position, but now he stopped, staring at the Cactus Kid.

The Frenchman turned abruptly. "What farce is this? This is not Señor Chafee . . . it is a child!"

As the others turned, the Kid stepped forward, interrupting the excited babble of their voices. "What's the matter, DeCarte? Afraid? Or do you prefer to shoot your men down from ambush, as General Ibanez and Chafee have been shot?"

DeCarte's face turned dark with angry blood. "You accuse me of that?" he roared. "By the—!"

"Control yourself, señor!" Fernandez said sternly. "The duel is arranged. If you wish to retire from the field, say so. This gentleman is taking the place of Señor Chafee."

DeCarte stared at the Kid angrily, yet as he looked, his expression changed. The Cactus Kid stood five feet seven in his socks, and weighed one hundred and fifty pounds. His hair waved back from his brow and his face looked soft. He was deceptively boyish-looking, a fact that had cost more than one man dearly. The Kid could almost see the thought in DeCarte's mind. This boy . . . I will shoot him down. . . .

"Take your place!" DeCarte snapped. "Let the duel commence!"

Coolly, the Cactus Kid walked to his place. This was different from the gun duels he was accustomed to where men met in the street or elsewhere and moved and shot as they wished. For this sort of thing there was a ritual, a ceremony, and he wished to conform. He glanced down at the heavy pistol. It was a good pistol, at that. It was a single-shot gun, and a second was thrust into his belt.

The third man stepped to his position. "One!" he barked.

The Cactus Kid stiffened and stood, his right side turned toward DeCarte. The man seemed very near. "Two!"

They lifted their pistols. The guns were heavy, but

the Kid's wrists were strong from the endless hours of roping, riding, and range work. He held it steady and looked along the barrel at DeCarte.

"Three!"

Flame stabbed at him and something brushed at his face. DeCarte stood very still, then turned slowly toward the Kid and fell flat on his face. He had been shot through the right eye.

The Kid put his hand to his cheek and brought it away bloody. He touched his cheek again. The bullet had burned him, so near he had been to death. Excited men gathered about DeCarte, and the Kid picked up his jacket and slipped into it. His own .44 was still behind the sash where he had carried it since his arrival in Mexico.

Fernandez came to him. "A splendid shot!" he said. "A remarkable shot! But we must go, at once! He has many friends. You must leave Mexico."

"Leave?" The Cactus Kid shook his head. "I can't do that," he said quietly. "I must stay. And I want to see the señorita."

"That is impossible." Sandoval had come up to them. "It is not to be considered. If you are not out of Mexico in a matter of hours, his friends will have you arrested."

"That I'll gamble on," the Kid said shortly. "I'm staying."

Sandoval's face stiffened slightly. "As you wish," he said, and turned abruptly.

As they swung into their saddles, Fernandez leaned closer to the Kid. "I will take you to her. We ride now to the hotel. Go at once to your room!"

They rode swiftly over the road back to town and then to the inn. The Kid stabled his horse and then checked his gun. Swiftly, he mounted the stairway. In his room he changed at once into range clothes and belted on both his guns. That there would be further trouble, he did not doubt. What lay behind all this he did not know, nor exactly who his enemies were. Chafee had warned him to trust no one, and had said that Marguerita's uncle was one of those trying to grab the vast estate of which he had heard only hints.

Waiting irritated him. He packed his few things into his saddlebags and the small carpetbag in which he carried his gray suit. From the window he looked down into the patio. There was nobody in sight, although it was well along toward midday. Nor was there any sound of anyone approaching his room.

Suddenly, through the gate came a half-dozen mounted soldiers and an officer. Four of the soldiers swung down and started for the entrance. The Kid wheeled to rush to the door, then heard a faint sound from without—the merest scrape of a foot!

He hesitated, picked up a chair in one hand, and laid the other on the doorknob, stepping back as far as he could while still retaining his grip. Then he swung the door wide and hurled a chair into the hall!

Yet as he jerked wide the door and swung the chair, a shotgun blasted and the heavy charge smashed into the chair bottom, some of the shot ricocheting from the doorjamb. Leaping out, gun in hand, he was just in time to see a man rushing down the hall. The Kid stepped out of the door and shot from the hip.

The running man seemed to stumble and then he sprawled headlong to the floor. From below there was a shout, and he heard the soldiers rushing toward the stair. Grabbing his saddlebags and carpetbag, he darted out of the door, slamming it after him, and turning down the hall, ran past the fallen man and through a door that waited beyond. It led down a narrow stair to the ground outside the inn.

He hit the bottom running and charged into the open, seeing a horse standing there. Instantly, he sprang into the saddle, swung the horse wide, and spurred it into the brush. In two jumps it was running all out. Behind him there were yells and running feet, but he was already out of sight.

Instantly, he drew up. No need to let them hear the running horse to know his direction. Turning at right angles to his original course, he swung around the town and headed into the chaparral. It was rough going and there was no trail, but he worked his way back through the brush, heading toward the mountains. It was scarcely noon now, and he had many daylight hours ahead of him. He paused a moment to fasten down his saddlebags. He patted the horse's flank.

What had become of Fernandez? And of Marguerita?

* * *

THE CACTUS KID SAVED his horse but worked, on a zigzag trail, back into the roughest kind of country, yet avoiding the canyons that led into the Sierra Madre. It would be his luck to ride into a box canyon and be trapped.

Several times he studied his back trail from the summits of ridges he crossed, taking precautions so as not to be seen. He saw no dust or evidence of pursuit.

Finding a faint cattle trail, he followed it, winding along the slope of the hills. The trail suddenly divided, and one path led higher up into the rugged mountains. He chose this way and dismounted to save his horse. It was not his own, but it would do, and was a powerful gray gelding with the deep chest and the fine legs of a runner and stayer.

At the crest of the range, with several miles of terrain exposed below him, he turned into the trees and stopped, slipping the bit from the gelding's mouth so it could feed properly. Then he picketed the horse and sat down on the slope.

Almost an hour had passed before he saw any sign of life, and then it was only a peón driving a goat. The man was coming up the trail and making a hard time of it. When almost to the Kid, the goat suddenly stopped and shied away. The peón straightened and looked at the trees. "It is all right, old one," the Kid said softly, "I am a friend."

He saw then that the man's face was bleeding from

a cut across the cheek. The peón did not come toward him but stood there, holding his hand against his face. "If you are he they seek," he said, "may you go with God. Those others—they are devils!"

"They struck you?"

"With a whip." The peón turned his head now and stared at the Kid, who was visible to him but out of sight of anyone below. "They asked me if I had seen a gringo. I told them no and they swore I lied. I had not seen you, señor. Then they struck me."

"Where are they now?"

"In the canyon below. They search for tracks."

The Kid nodded. They would find them, of course. Then they would be on his trail. He gathered up his picket rope and put the bit back in the gelding's mouth.

"Old one," he said, "do you know the hacienda of Ibanez? Is it near?"

"It is north," the old man said, "you are pointing for it now. It is thirty miles from east to west, and fifty miles from north to south. If you ride straight on, you can reach there for dinner. But they are there also, the devils."

"Ibanez was killed."

"Sí, we know this, but those who come in his place, ah!"

The Cactus Kid mounted. "They won't have it so good, old-timer," he said grimly. "I'm looking for some of them now."

* * *

THE WORST OF IT WAS, he reflected as he rode on, that he did not know whom he was looking for. What he intended to do was to find Marguerita and talk to her. She would put him straight, and he grinned at the thought; talking with her would cause him no pain. If one had to be trapped into defending or aiding a girl, it was pure luck that she turned out to be so beautiful.

The Ibanez hacienda was something to look at, and the Kid studied the place thoughtfully. The house was surrounded by a wall on three sides, the back of the house making up most of the fourth side. There were orchards and meadows, irrigation ditches and row crops. The fields were not small, but stretched on for acres and acres. On a far hill he could see cattle grazing; whiteface cattle such as they were now bringing into Texas.

Keeping to back trails, he rode for the house itself and finally stopped under some eucalyptus trees a hundred yards off. No pursuit was in sight, and he doubted if they would find him soon, for they would still be hunting him in the mountains. He was about to mount up when he saw a peón standing under the trees, watching him.

He was gambling on the dislike the peóns seemed to have for his own enemies, and he said, "I am a friend to the Señorita Marguerita. I have just killed in a duel an enemy of the old general. I need a fresh horse and to see the señorita. She is here?"

The man had a thin face and large, hot eyes. He

came forward quickly, showing beautiful teeth in a quick smile. "She is here, señor. She has come within the hour. And already the story is told that you . . . you must be the one . . . who killed DeCarte. We are happy, amigo!"

The Mexican came forward and took the horse. "I will prepare for you a fine horse, señor, who runs like the wind and never stops! And I will warn you if they come. Go down to the house . . . but be careful."

Taking nothing with him but what he wore, the Cactus Kid turned and walked swiftly toward the gate. Now he would find out what this was all about and there need be no more going it blind. That he was far from out of the woods, he knew. Whoever these enemies of the old general were, they seemed to have influence enough to employ the army, and they would certainly want him dead. Yet the Kid knew that he was relatively unimportant and what they feared was that he might try to aid the señorita.

He walked through the gate and across to the door of the house. When he stepped through he became immediately conscious of his dusty, disheveled appearance. His boots sounded loud on the worn stone floor and he walked on into the large room with dark panels on the walls.

The whisper of a footstep startled him and he turned. It was Marguerita, her magnificent eyes wide and frightened. "Señor! You must leave at once! They are searching for you everywhere. Here they will look, and we, my uncle and I, we are suspect."

"Your uncle?" His eyes searched her face. "He is here?"

"Yes, of course. He was so pleased when he heard of your victory. It was magnificent, señor. But," she hurried on, "you must not stay. DeCarte had powerful friends and they are searching for you. My uncle says you must not come here."

"He didn't see me come now?" the Kid asked hastily. "If he didn't, don't tell him."

"And why not?" The voice was cool. "You think me ungrateful, my young friend?"

The Cactus Kid half turned to face the tall, aristocratic man with the white goatee and mustache. Certainly, he had never seen a finer appearing man, and yet as the uncle drew nearer, the Kid could see the hard lines around his mouth, half concealed by the mustache, and the coldness in the man's eyes.

"I am Don Estaban," he said, "the master here. We are at your service."

"You own the ranch?" The Cactus Kid looked surprised. "It was my impression that it belonged to the señorita."

Don Estaban's lips tightened and his eyes flashed hard and cold. This man, the Kid reflected, had a mean temper. "So it does," Don Estaban said quietly. "I am but the manager, the master in function, if you will."

The Kid turned to Marguerita. "May I talk with you? There is much to say."

Before she could reply, Don Estaban interrupted.

"It is not the custom in Mexico," he said, "for young ladies to talk to gentlemen unchaperoned. I cannot permit it."

"Perhaps he would like to bathe and prepare for dinner, Uncle Estaban," Marguerita said quickly. "If you would show him to a room. Or I can call Juana."

Turning, she called out and a slender girl came quickly into the room, and the Kid followed her away. Behind him he heard low conversation.

Once in the room, he glanced suspiciously about. It was spacious, with a huge four-poster bed. Throwing his hat on a hook, he poured water into a basin and unfastened his neckerchief and started unbuttoning his shirt. Then the door opened quickly and the señorita stepped into the room. "Always I come to your room!" she whispered. "It is most improper!"

"I like it." The Kid looked at her appreciatively. "I like it very much. I wish you'd make a habit of it. Now tell me what this is all about, and quickly."

The story was simple enough, and she told it rapidly with no time wasted on details. The ranch was part of a grant that had been in the hands of her family since the Conquest, but of late it had become more and more valuable. During the reign of Maximilian—who had been shot only a short time before—it had been taken from their family and given to the DeCartes, who were adventurous followers of the French king.

When he was thrown out, the estate had been returned to its original owners, but by that time De-

Carte had married into an influential Mexican family and he had continued to claim the estate. There had been some furious words between the old general and DeCarte, and the resulting challenge. The fact that the general had been a renowned pistol shot might have had something to do with his assassination. Jim Chafee had been planning to take up the challenge when he himself had been shot, and the arrival of the Cactus Kid at the time Chafee was expected had led Fernandez and Sandoval to believe he was their man.

DeCarte was dead . . . the bullet had killed him instantly, but the trouble was only just begun.

"You must not stay here," Marguerita told him quickly. "It is not safe. You must return to your own country."

"What about you?" he asked. "How will you deal with your uncle?"

"My uncle?" She turned on him quickly. "What do you mean?"

"Your uncle is one of them, Marguerita. He is trying to get your estate for himself, to divide it with DeCarte and someone else."

Her face paled. "Oh, no! You don't mean that! You can't!"

Yet even as she spoke he could see the dawning of belief in her eyes. She turned on him. "Where did you get that idea? Who would suggest it?"

"Chafee told me it was he who killed your father. He said it was your uncle who had him ambushed."

She stood very still, and then suddenly she sat down on the chair near the table. "What am I to do? He was the only one . . . there is no one, nobody to help me."

"Why not me?" The Cactus Kid sat down on the bed and began to build a cigarette. "Marguerita," he said quietly, "I'm in this up to my ears. Even for my own safety, I would be better off staying here and licking it than trying to beat them to the border. Go on, we don't want you to get caught here . . . I'll see you at dinner."

IT WAS A LONG TALL ROOM but there were only three places set at the big table. As the Cactus Kid ate and talked, he also listened, his ears attuned to the slightest sound from without. Yet Don Estaban seemed not to be expecting anything. Later, as Marguerita played the piano, the Kid stood nearby, watching her.

How lovely she was! How fine was this life! How simple and easy! Good food, good wine, quiet hours in this wonderful old Spanish home, the stillness and coolness inside the house that seemed so far from the fevered air outside, or the work and struggle of the cattle trails to which he had been born. Yet beneath it all, there were the stirrings of evil, plotting men who wished to take all this from a slender, lovely girl, robbed of her father by the man who now sat in that high-backed chair, so certain everything would soon be his.

Don Estaban spoke suddenly. "You are an excel-

lent shot, señor. It was most unexpected, your victory."

"I think it surprised a lot of people."

"Do you always wear two guns?" queried his host.

"When I am expecting trouble."

"You expect trouble here? Now?" Don Estaban
permitted his voice to carry a note of surprise. "In
this house?"

The Cactus Kid turned his head slowly and
looked to the older man. "I sure do," he said quietly.
"I expect it everywhere. The hombres who killed the
general, who shot down Chafee, they expected me to
be killed by DeCarte. Now that I'm here they'll try to
kill me."

THE CACTUS KID OPENED his eyes and sat bolt upright in bed. It was dark and still. But outside in
the hall, there was a faint footfall. Like a cat he eased
into his trousers without a whisper of sound . . . he
got his guns belted around him . . . reached for his
boots . . . and then the door opened!

In the doorway stood Sandoval, and in his hands
was a shotgun, half lifted to point toward the empty
bed. Sandoval spoke softly, "Señor?"

"Hand that gun to me," the Kid said softly, "butt
first."

Sandoval hesitated, then took a gamble. Springing
back through the door, he swung the shotgun into
position and the Kid fired. It was a wild gamble, for

Sandoval's leap had carried him back out of range, but the Kid fired his shot through the wall.

Sandoval cried out and the shotgun fell with a clatter to the floor. Instantly, the Kid swung around into the doorway. Sandoval had backed up against the wall and was clutching his stomach with both hands.

Along the balcony on the other side of the great hall, there was a scuffle of sound and the Kid ran in his stocking feet toward it. He reached the turn that led to Marguerita's quarters and skidded to a halt. Two men stood at the door of the girl's room, rattling the latch. Beyond them was Don Estaban.

"Open up," Estaban called. "Open up, or we'll break the door!"

The Cactus Kid swung around the corner and instantly, the two men whirled and lifted their rifles to fire. They were slow . . . much too slow!

The Kid dropped to a half crouch and fired three rapping, thundering shots. The nearest man cried out and fell against the shoulder of Don Estaban, disturbing his aim. The Kid's second shot smashed the second rifleman, and his third was a clear miss. Don Estaban leaped forward and swung up his gun. In the close confines of the hall the Kid swung the barrel of his pistol. It thudded against the don's skull, and he wilted to the floor.

"Marguerita?" He stepped quickly to the door. "It's the Kid. Better come out."

She came quickly, her eyes wide at the carnage. Swiftly they ran down the hall to the Kid's room, where he got into his boots. He said, "Do the peóns like you?"

She nodded.

"Take me to the best one," he said. "We'll arm them and be ready for trouble. If somebody wants a fight, we'll give them one!"

HE WAS THE SAME young Mexican whom the Kid had seen on his arrival, the one who had promised him the horse that so far had not been needed. Briefly, Marguerita explained and he listened attentively. "I will have twenty men within the hour," he said then, "men who will die for the daughter of Ibanez!"

Swiftly they walked back through the trees, then stopped. A half-dozen riders were around the main gate, and there were as many empty saddles. More men had arrived. Suddenly a tall, slightly stooped man came through the gate and threw a cigarette into the dirt. He wore leather trousers, tight-fitting and flaring at the bottoms, and he wore two guns, tied down. His jacket was velvet and embroidered in red and gold, his sombrero was weighted with silver.

Only his chin was visible, a sharp-boned chin with a drooping mustache. Marguerita caught his arm. "It is Bisco!"

The Kid looked again, his skin tightening over his stomach, his scalp crawling. So . . . now it was Bisco!

Three times the man had been across the border to raid and kill; he was the most feared gunman in Mexico. Half Yaqui, he was utterly poisonous. "They've brought him here for me," he said quietly. "They know who I am."

"Who are you?" Marguerita turned toward him, her eyes wide.

"My right name is Clay. I'm nobody, Marguerita, but he's a man who is brought in to take care of trouble."

"You are modest, I think. Yes, you are too modest. I heard you sold cattle here for your employer. That he trusts you to do this. I think you are brave, good, and I think you are most handsome!"

He chuckled. "Well, now. After that I should be up to almost anything. Right now I've got an urge to go out there and brace that Bisco."

"No"—her face was white—"you must not! You must not be killed by him. Or by anybody."

He looked down into her wide eyes and something seemed to take away his voice, so he stood there, with the cool wind on his face, and then almost without their own volition, they were in each other's arms.

Then he stepped away, shaking his head. "You take a man's mind off his business," he said softly, "and if we expect to get out of this alive, we can't have that happening."

Behind them there was a light footfall. "No," said a voice, "we cannot!"

The Cactus Kid froze where he stood. The voice was that of Don Estaban.

The Kid felt his guns lifted from their holsters, and then Don Estaban said quietly, "Now walk straight ahead . . . to the gate."

Anger choked the Kid as they started forward, the girl beside him. The Kid saw Bisco turn and stare toward them, then come forward with long strides, grinning widely. "So! It is the Cactus Kid! I have long hoped we will one day meet, but—what is this? Perhaps I am not necessary."

"If I had a gun," the Kid replied, speaking Spanish, "you'd be necessary, all right! I'd take you right now!"

Bisco laughed.

The Kid looked past him and saw Fernandez standing in the gateway, his face puzzled. The young Mexican came forward swiftly. "Don Estaban! What does this mean? This man is our friend!"

The older man shook his head. "No, Enrique, he is not."

Enrique's face was stiff. Then he shrugged. **"Perdoneme,"** he said, "you know best." He turned and strolled indifferently away.

The Kid stared after him, his eyes blazing. Watch yourself and trust nobody! That was what Chafee advised, and he had certainly been right!

"We'll get this over at once!" Don Estaban turned to a man that stood near him. "Pedro, I want a firing squad of four **vaqueros**. We are going to execute this man—and then"—he smiled—"we will say he was plotting against the government, that he was executed formally."

"You're a white-livered thief." The Cactus Kid spoke without violence. "With the heart of a snake and the courage of a coyote."

Don Estaban's face whitened and his eyes glittered. "Speak what you will," he said contemptuously. "Soon you will be dead."

Four men came into the yard with rifles, and the Cactus Kid was immediately led to the wall. Unbelievingly, Marguerita stared, and then she whirled to her uncle. "You cannot do this thing!" she cried out. "It is murder!"

Don Estaban smiled. "Of course. And unless you obey me you shall join him. What do you think?" He turned on her suddenly. "Am I to turn all this over to you? A foolish girl? Why do you suppose your father died? What do you think that—?" He went on, his tirade growing louder. He was speaking in English, which only Bisco and the Kid could understand.

Suddenly, from behind the wall where he stood, the Kid heard a whisper:

"Amigo, if I make trouble, can you get over the wall?" It was Enrique Fernandez!

"Yes!"

"Your guns are here. Below the wall."

Don Estaban turned away from the girl. "Enough!"

he said. "Bisco, hold her. Now"—he turned to the man who had brought the riflemen—"tie his hands and shoot him."

"Wait!" All eyes swung toward the gate. It was Fernandez. "You must not do this thing!"

At the word "wait," the Kid spun on his heels and leaped at the wall. He had gauged it correctly and he caught both hands on the top. With a powerful jerk upward, he pushed himself belt-high to the top of the wall, and then swung his feet over.

Fernandez had succeeded even better than he expected, for the Kid was swinging over the wall before he was seen. A snap shot missed, and as he hit ground the Kid went to all fours. The guns were not three feet away, and he caught up the belt and swung it about him, buckling it hastily.

Inside there was a chorus of yells and a shot. The Kid raced around the corner of the wall to see Fernandez staggering back against the wall with a bullet through his shoulder, and then the riflemen poured from the gate.

They expected to find an unarmed man—instead they found a deadly gunfighter, and the range was less than twenty feet.

Four men came through the gate, and in the first burst of firing, three spilled over the ground. The last sprang back, and the Kid, turning abruptly, raced back the way he had come. There was a small wooden door in the far corner of the wall. He had noticed it earlier, and now he raced to it and jerked it open. Inside, a heavily constructed two-wheeled cart stood between him and the confusion in the courtyard. Bisco had let go of the girl who was standing near the door to the house. Don Estaban, gun in hand, was shouting orders to Bisco and the remaining guard, and the leader of the firing squad.

Suddenly, from outside there was a clatter of hoofs and wild shouts, "**Viva** Ibanez! **Viva** Ibanez!"

Don Estaban turned and started for the door, then stopped. "Bisco!" he said hoarsely.

The gunman turned at the word, then froze, his hands lifted and poised.

The Cactus Kid stood beside the wooden cart, facing them. His guns were in his holsters. "You can all give up," he said quietly, his eyes on Bisco, "if you want to. Those are Ibanez men out there."

"I never give up!" Bisco's eyes held eagerness and challenge. His hands dropped and grasped his gun butts, the guns lifted and the black muzzles opened their eyes at the Kid, and suddenly the Cactus Kid's guns bucked in his hands, and Bisco crumpled to the dust.

MUSIC SOUNDED SOFTLY from the patio, and Marguerita stood close beside him. "You are going then?" she asked him.

"I've got to," he said. "I've got to go back north to deliver that money. I wouldn't fit in here. This life is pleasant, but it's not for me."

"You won't miss me?"

Sure I will, he thought, but sometimes ropin' a girl was like ropin' a grizzly. There might be great sport in the catching but it was hard to figure out what to do with one once caught. Later, as he turned his horse into the road that led to the border he laughed. Once you'd had your fun puttin' a loop on a bear, the best thing to do was to shake loose and run.

About Louis L'Amour

**"I think of myself in the oral tradition—
as a troubadour, a village tale-teller, the man
in the shadows of the campfire. That's the way
I'd like to be remembered—as a storyteller.
A good storyteller."**

It is doubtful that any author could be as at home
in the world re-created in his novels as Louis
Dearborn L'Amour. Not only could he physically
fill the boots of the rugged characters he wrote about,
but he literally "walked the land my characters walk."
His personal experiences as well as his lifelong devo-
tion to historical research combined to give Mr.
L'Amour the unique knowledge and understanding
of people, events, and the challenge of the American
frontier that became the hallmarks of his popularity.

Of French-Irish descent, Mr. L'Amour could trace
his own family in North America back to the early
1600s and follow their steady progression westward,
"always on the frontier." As a boy growing up in
Jamestown, North Dakota, he absorbed all he could
about his family's frontier heritage, including the
story of his great-grandfather who was scalped by
Sioux warriors.

Spurred by an eager curiosity and desire to broaden

his horizons, Mr. L'Amour left home at the age of fifteen and enjoyed a wide variety of jobs, including seaman, lumberjack, elephant handler, skinner of dead cattle, miner, and an officer in the transportation corps during World War II. During his "yondering" days he also circled the world on a freighter, sailed a dhow on the Red Sea, was shipwrecked in the West Indies, and stranded in the Mojave Desert. He won fifty-one of fifty-nine fights as a professional boxer and worked as a journalist and lecturer. He was a voracious reader and collector of rare books. His personal library contained 17,000 volumes.

Mr. L'Amour "wanted to write almost from the time I could talk." After developing a widespread following for his many frontier and adventure stories written for fiction magazines, Mr. L'Amour published his first full-length novel, **Hondo,** in the United States in 1953. Every one of his more than 120 books is in print; there are more than 300 million copies of his books in print worldwide, making him one of the bestselling authors in modern literary history. His books have been translated into twenty languages, and more than forty-five of his novels and stories have been made into feature films and television movies.

His hardcover bestsellers include **The Lonesome Gods, The Walking Drum** (his twelfth-century historical novel), **Jubal Sackett, Last of the Breed,** and **The Haunted Mesa.** His memoir, **Education of a Wandering Man,** was a leading bestseller in

1989. Audio dramatizations and adaptations of many L'Amour stories are available on cassettes and CDs from Random House Audio publishing.

The recipient of many great honors and awards, in 1983 Mr. L'Amour became the first novelist ever to be awarded the Congressional Gold Medal by the United States Congress in honor of his life's work. In 1984 he was also awarded the Medal of Freedom by President Reagan.

Louis L'Amour died on June 10, 1988. His wife, Kathy, and their two children, Beau and Angelique, carry the L'Amour publishing tradition forward with new books written by the author during his lifetime to be published by Bantam.